ENGAGEMENT
OF CONVENIENCE

Georgie Lee

First published in Great Britain 2013
by Mills & Boon, an imprint of Harlequin (UK) Limited,
Large Print edition 2014
Eton House, 18-24 Paradise Road, Richmond, Surrey, TW9 1SR

© 2013 Georgie Reinstein

ISBN: 978 0 263 23951 5

Harlequin (UK) Limited's policy is to use papers that are natural,
renewable and recyclable products and made from wood grown in
sustainable forests. The logging and manufacturing processes conform
to the legal environmental regulations of the country of origin.

Printed and bound in Great Britain
by CPI Antony Rowe, Chippenham, Wiltshire

0556458

A dedicated history and film buff, **Georgie Lee** loves combining her passion for Hollywood, history and storytelling through romantic fiction. She began writing professionally at a small TV station in San Diego, before moving to Hollywood to work in the interesting but strange world of the entertainment industry. During her years in La-La Land she never lost her love for romance novels and decided to try writing one herself. To her surprise, a new career was born. When not crafting tales of love and happily-ever-after, Georgie enjoys reading non-fiction history and watching any movie with a costume and an accent. Please visit www.georgie-lee.com to learn more about Georgie and her books. She also loves to hear from readers, and you can e-mail her at georgie.lee@yahoo.com

This is Georgie Lee's fabulous debut novel for Mills & Boon® Historical Romance!

Enjoy the witty, playful attraction between Julia and Captain Covington. There will be more historical novels by Georgie Lee, coming soon…

A very special thank you
to Natashya Wilson for seeing the
potential in this story and for all her help.
Thanks also to my editor, Linda Fildew, my
agent, Ethan Ellenberg, and my friend Kristi
for sharing her knowledge of horses.

Also, thanks to my dear husband, Matt,
who always believes in me, even if
he wouldn't have believed it if someone
told him years ago he'd someday be
married to a romance writer.

Chapter One

October 31, 1805

Julia heard the shot from the top of the hill. It split the early morning still, sending a shock through her body and silencing the birds in the surrounding trees. Pulling hard on Manfred's reins, she brought the large black horse to a halt and examined the woods below the riding path for signs of the shooter. Brilliant shades of orange, red and yellow dominated the trees and a gentle breeze sent many of the leaves cascading to the ground. A flock of birds rose from the forest, indicating the shot's origin, but she saw nothing of the gunman. Uncle George often hunted here, but he was not expected back from London until later today.

How dare they, she fumed, nudging Manfred down the sloping hill and into the thick cluster of trees growing along the small valley floor. Only a guest of their neighbours, the Wilkinses, possessed the audacity to hunt uninvited on Knollwood land.

Low branches tugged at her hair, freeing it from the loose bun fastened at the nape of her neck. Pushing it back out of her face, she knew her sister-in-law Emily would object to such a display, but Julia didn't care. She wasn't about to allow the Wilkinses' good-for-nothing friends to poach in her woods.

As she urged Manfred deeper into the thicket, it didn't occur to her to fetch the gamekeeper until the horse stepped into a small clearing as the culprit let off another shot in the opposite direction. Julia flinched at the thunderous noise, but Manfred, true to his warhorse breeding, stood rock still. Only his twitching ears acknowledged the explosion.

'What do you think you are doing?' Julia demanded.

The stranger whirled to face her and she drew in a sharp breath. Here was no fat wastrel, but the most handsome rogue she'd ever seen. The low sunlight cutting through the trees highlighted the deep-red tones in his dark hair and sharpened the bones of his cheeks. The shadow of a beard marked the square line of his jaw, emphasising his straight nose and strong chin. Her pulse raced with an emotion far different from fear. She could not name it, but it emanated from deep within her body.

'I'm hunting,' he answered plainly. Leaning his gun against a tree, he straightened into a stance reminiscent of the one her brother Paul assumed when a superior officer commanded him to relax.

'You are poaching in my woods. Now remove yourself at once before I call the gamekeeper. He's only a short distance away,' Julia lied, hoping he believed it. The knowing smile tugging at the corner of his lips told her otherwise.

'I'd like to see your gamekeeper try to remove me.'

Julia scrutinised him, hard pressed to imagine any of the servants, except perhaps the blacksmith, taking on such a sturdy man. He was tall and slender but solid, his wide shoulders and strong chest radiating a strength his loose-fitting hunting clothes could not hide. Following the line of his long arms to his hands, she imagined them around her waist, lifting her down from Manfred and pressing her against his body. She bit her bottom lip in anticipation of him claiming her mouth, the warmth of it driving away the morning chill.

Swallowing hard, the danger of the situation

rushed back to her at the sight of the hunting knife dangling from his belt and she mustered her anger to counter the scandalous thoughts. His gun might be empty, but there was no way to know his skill with the blade. 'I demand you leave, at once.'

'I must say, I've never been addressed in this fashion before.' His blue eyes dipped down the length of her, then rose to her face. 'Especially not by such an attractive young lady.'

Julia grasped her riding crop tighter, ready to whip him if he threatened her, but he still did not approach. 'If I were trespassing on your land, I'd have the decency to be humble, but since you are trespassing on my land I may address you as I please.'

'You would have to travel a great distance to trespass on my land.' He laughed, much to Julia's chagrin.

'Then be off,' she ordered, 'for the sooner you leave, the sooner you may reach your land.' With all the grace of an accomplished horsewoman, she pulled Manfred around and cantered away.

James watched the woman disappear through the trees. Her horse, if one could call such a beast a horse, kicking up the soft earth, leaving behind clouds of dust to dance in the dappled sunlight.

Nothing came to mind except pure awe, like the first time he'd been at sea with no sight of land. Neither the dark maidens of the islands hardened by tavern life, nor the plantation owners' daughters with their languid speech, ever struck him as this woman had. No, she seemed too much of the world, yet strangely innocent of it. What would he give to slip her from her horse, lay her on the damp leaves and make her more knowledgeable?

His body stiffened at the delightful fantasy before the shifting sun piercing the trees nearly blinded him. Judging by its height, he knew it was time to go. Grabbing the haversack from the ground with his left hand, he felt pain tear through his shoulder and the bag fell from his weakened hand, landing on the ground with a thud.

'Hell.' He snatched it up with his right hand and flung it over his shoulder. The gun's recoil had irritated his wound more than he'd realised. Despite the stinging ache, he didn't intend to give up hunting. He'd already lost too much to sacrifice more.

Picking up the gun, he hurried through the woods along a small footpath leading up to the top of the hill. Climbing out of the shallow valley, the pain and all the emotions it brought with it taunted his every step.

Damn it, damn it all, James thought bitterly, striding off down the opposite side of the hill and up the next steeper one, scattering a small group of sheep grazing in the wet grass.

Up ahead, Creedon Abbey rose before him, its grey stone, small windows and numerous turrets and chimneys betraying its roots in the Middle Ages. James's old friend Captain George Russell had done well for himself, investing some of the fortune he'd gained in the Navy in this small estate. Only the broken and charred roof timbers and smoke-blackened stone ruined the idyllic scene. George had failed to extinguish an oil lamp one night two weeks ago and the resulting fire had gutted a large portion of the house. Scores of workmen now bustled about the front drive, unloading large blocks of stone from carts or carrying wood inside to begin the first day of repairs.

James shook his head at the damage, not sure whether to feel sorry for his friend or to laugh. Thirty years in the navy, fifteen as a captain and George had never once lost a ship. Within four years of resigning his commission, he'd nearly burned his house to the ground. For all George's bragging about how much he'd learned from his niece about running an estate, he'd failed to master the simple skill of not setting it on fire.

James's amusement faded as he walked. He'd seriously considered investing his money in an estate like this, but now he wasn't so sure. Whatever he decided to do, he needed to do it soon. With his wound sufficiently recovered, it was time to settle on something meaningful to occupy his days, instead of frittering them away.

He moved faster up the footpath following the drive, eager for activity, anything to shift the restless agitation dogging him this morning.

'What's the hurry?' a familiar voice called out from behind him. 'Run across a ghost in the woods?'

James turned to see George leading Percy, his large, cream-coloured stallion, up the drive. In his friend's wide, carefree smile, James caught traces of the bold captain he'd first met in the colonies ten years ago. At fifty, the lines of George's face were deeper now, while the quiet life of a country gentleman had lightened his once sun darkened skin and thickened his waist.

'I might have.' James fell in step with his friend. 'Describe your niece again.'

'Why?'

'Because I'm curious.'

George shrugged. 'Just what you'd expect from a girl of one and twenty. Clever, well formed, somewhat eccentric. Takes after me in that regard. Why?'

'I met her in the woods.' James remembered the striking young lady with her auburn hair falling in delicate waves about her face, her creamy skin flushed with excitement and a few headier emotions.

'Really?' A noticeable gleam danced in George's eyes. 'And?'

'Eccentric, well formed. Though from all your descriptions, I'd taken her for more of a dour governess and less of an Artemis.'

'When I described her she was still a girl.'

'She's no girl now.' James wondered if such a woman had ever truly been a girl or if she'd simply sprung from the foam of the sea.

'I'm glad to see you find her so interesting. Staying at Knollwood will give you a chance to get better acquainted. Who knows what you might discover?'

James shifted the haversack on his back, resisting the urge to run his fingers over the jagged scar on his left shoulder. 'Must we go to Knollwood?'

'Yes, it's all been arranged. Besides, by the end of the day it'll be more like a shipyard here than a house and, with the weather turning, you don't want the rain leaking on your head.'

'It wouldn't be the first time. I've lost track of the number of storms I've slept through at sea.'

'And my guess is you won't miss it. We wouldn't have stayed here last night if we hadn't dallied so long at Admiral Stuart's dinner, but I hated to disturb everyone at Knollwood so late at night.'

James laughed. 'I wasn't the one who insisted on opening another bottle of port.'

'It doesn't matter who caused the delay. I'll be happy to sleep in a comfortable room that doesn't smell like a cooking fire. And here I'd thought those bedrooms had escaped damage.'

'You've gone soft.'

George shrugged. 'You will, too, in time.'

James didn't respond, this revelation not improving his mood. He'd already lost too much since resigning his commission to contemplate losing something as simple as his hardiness. 'Why didn't you tell me before we left London that the house wasn't fit to live in?'

'I think I greatly underestimated the damage.' They stopped as two men carrying a large plank walked past them. 'Besides, the ladies are quite excited at the prospect of meeting a new gentleman.'

'You know I came here to escape such affairs.'

'Does any man ever truly escape them?'

'You seem to have avoided it.'

'And you wish to follow my lead?'

James scrutinised his old friend, suspecting more to all this than the extensive fire damage simply slipping his mind. 'What are you about, George?'

'Nothing.' George held up his hands innocently but only succeeded in looking guiltier. 'I want you to enjoy yourself while you're here. Now hurry and change. We're expected at Knollwood.'

George pulled Percy off to the stables and James headed around to the back of the house, his footsteps heavier than before. Reaching under the loose jacket, his fingers traced the raised scar on his left shoulder through the thin fabric of his hunting shirt. Unconsciously, he flexed his left hand, feeling the weakness and cursing it. He stomped on a large clump of mud, mashing it into the earth. This was exactly what he didn't want, the whole reason he'd allowed George to convince him to come to the country.

He cursed his luck and George's carelessness. If his friend had extinguished the lamp instead of leaving it to overheat, James could have spent the next two weeks here, not forced into Artemis's cave waiting to be ripped apart by her wild beasts. He'd experienced enough clawing and tearing in the ballrooms of London. He had no stomach for it here in the country. Give him a French fleet any day; it was preferable to a matron with a marriageable daughter.

A flash of movement on the opposite hill made him stop at the rear door. He watched the young woman ride at a full gallop over the green downs, the horse moving like a shadow, her amber hair a streak of sunlight through the dark clouds. The memory of the little Artemis astride the black beast, face flushed with anger, pert breasts rising and falling with each excited breath, filled his mind. His loins stirred with desire before he checked himself. It was one thing to idle away hours with the willing widowed sister of a provincial governor; it was quite another to dally with the niece of his best friend.

Besides, no spirited creature wants a broken man. He pushed away from the wall, angrily slapping the door jamb. The rough stone stung his palm, reminding him that any interest in Miss Howard could only be to learn from her estate management skills which, according to George, were considerable. If James decided to follow his friend into the life of a country gentleman, he'd need to know more about it than what little he'd learn from books.

Manfred reached the crest of the hill, breathing hard, his dark coat glistening with sweat. Julia eased him into a slow walk and they ambled down the bridle path tracing the top. A thin mist crept through the crevices of the valley while sheep grazed quietly in the green meadows. The three estates situated on the three high hills overlooking the rolling valley came into view. Creedon Abbey, the smallest, stood on the hill closest to Knollwood. Though some five miles off, the tips of the turrets were just visible above the surrounding trees. All the land here had once belonged to the old monastery before the Reformation and some debt-ridden descendant saw it sold off to create Knollwood and Cable Grange. There was little difference between Creedon land and Knollwood land, but drastic changes marked the boundary between Knollwood's lush, well-tended meadows and Cable Grange's weed-choked fields. Cable Grange stood on the third-highest hill in the area. Farther away than Creedon, she could just see it sitting on its hilltop perch, the distance obscuring its neglected state. Being so close to Knollwood, she knew Cable Grange could be one of the finest houses in the county.

If only it were mine. She didn't know who to curse more, her brother Charles for inheriting Knollwood or Mr Wilkins for ruining Cable Grange.

Adjusting her leg against the pommel, she wished she'd chosen her standard saddle instead of the side-saddle. It was still early and the rest of the house had yet to rise, making it unlikely Emily would catch her riding astride. Soothed by Manfred's gentle gait, she settled into the seat, her mind wandering back to the woods and the handsome stranger.

He called me attractive, she mulled, remembering the heady way his blue eyes raked her body, their heat warming her skin. Four years ago, standing against the wall during London balls, she'd seen gentlemen examine other young ladies with similar hot eyes, nudging each other knowingly. For all her London finery, not one gentleman had cast a single amorous glance in her direction. How strange to garner a lustful stare while dressed in her old riding habit.

If only he weren't one of the Wilkinses' good-for-nothing friends. She sighed, wondering what it would be like to feel his lips tease her neck while he whispered forbidden things in her ear. A strange thrill coursed through her before she forced the wicked daydream from her head. He was a scoundrel and not worth a second thought.

Digging her heel into Manfred's flanks, she drove him hard across the open ground, guiding him towards a hedge separating the fields. Pulling back on his reins, she sat forwards as he leapt and they easily cleared the bushes before landing on the other side.

'Well done, Manfred!'

She slowed him to a walk and, coming to another path, looked longingly east. A smooth mound stood out against the flatter fields, the ruins on top silhouetted by the rising sun. At a full gallop, they could reach the old fortress in a few minutes and she might spend a quiet hour picking through the high grass searching for relics. Her heel itched to tap Manfred, but she resisted, reluctantly directing him back to Knollwood. Emily expected her at breakfast. Why, she couldn't imagine. Neither Simon nor Annette, her stepcousins, had risen before noon since their arrival and when they were awake, they only complained about the country.

What could Uncle Edward possibly hope to ac-

complish by sending them here? she wondered, wishing he'd hurry up and recall them to London.

They trotted into the paddock, greeted by the fresh scent of hay and the sharper smell of horses.

'I see you've had another fine ride, Miss Howard,' John, the head groom, remarked, helping her down from the saddle. 'I've always said the two of you were made for each another.'

'That's because I believed in him when no one else did. Didn't I, Manfred?' Julia rubbed the horse's nose and he shook his head as if in agreement. 'John, please speak to the gamekeeper. I saw a poacher in the forest this morning.'

'A poacher?' He held Manfred's reins, disbelief deepening the lines of his forehead. 'We've never had such trouble before.'

'Well, I believe the man is a poacher, though it may have only been one of Mr Wilkins's guests.'

'Mr Wilkins has no guests, Miss Howard.'

Then who could he be? Julia tapped her riding crop against her palm, then handed it to John. 'No matter. Please ask the gamekeeper to take care of it.'

'Yes, Miss Howard.'

'Oh, and please don't mention it to Mother or Emily. They'll only worry and then Emily will lecture me if she discovers I went riding without you.' Emily had been married to her brother Charles for less than a year, but she'd prove his equal when it came to chastising Julia about proper behaviour.

'I won't say a word.' John laid a knowing finger against the side of his ruddy nose before leading Manfred inside.

Thank goodness for his loyalty, she thought, fastening up the long hem of her riding habit. Without him, she and Manfred might never be allowed to enjoy their solitary rides.

Walking up the path from the stables, she passed through a small grove of trees and into the large, open lawn. Crossing the wide space, she kicked the head off a dandelion, sprinkling her skirt with bits of grass and dew.

I must speak to Bill about bringing the sheep here to trim the grass, she reminded herself before passing through a gate in the low stone wall surrounding the garden on the other side.

Wandering down the gravel path through the semi-formal plant beds, she saw the house rise up in front of her, its many windows reflecting the morning sun. She removed her right glove and grazed the top of a large rosemary bush with her fingers before snapping off a sprig and inhaling the tangy scent. All the troubles she'd forgotten during her ride came rushing back, especially Charles's letter.

'His estate.' Julia threw the rosemary sprig on the ground, crushing it beneath her half-boot. 'What does he know of running Knollwood?'

She'd burned the hateful parchment after reading it, watching with delight as the neat script crumpled and charred in the flames. However, all the burned letters couldn't stop her brother from claiming his inheritance.

Pausing at the small pond in the centre of the garden, she stared into the dark water. Goldfish flitted beneath the glass surface, failing to disturb the reflection of the thick clouds passing overhead.

Why should he have Knollwood? Tears of frustration stung her eyes. *He's never taken an interest in it the way I have.*

Nor did he appreciate all her hard work to keep it prosperous. Only Father and Paul had ever recognised it, but with Paul serving with Admiral Nelson's fleet and Father—

No, she commanded herself, refusing to cry. Tears would not help her deal with Charles.

Heading up the garden path, she passed her mother's cherished rose garden, then hurried up the stairs of the column-lined stone portico lead-ing to the back sitting room.

'Good morning, Miss Howard,' Davies, the but-ler, greeted, pulling open the large French door.

'Good morning.' She handed him her gloves and he held out a small paper-covered parcel.

'This arrived from Mr Charles Howard.'

'My book.' She tore off the wrapper to reveal a leather-bound copy of *The Monk*. 'I can't believe Charles sent it. He's always so concerned about not disturbing my delicate female mind. It's for-tunate he doesn't know the half of what Paul tells me.'

'Yes, very fortunate indeed,' Davies solemnly concurred. He'd been Paul's valet when Paul still lived at Knollwood, making him well acquainted with her brother's nature and most of his esca-pades.

'Has Uncle George returned from London yet?'

'Captain Russell arrived a short while ago to collect Percy and speak with Mrs Emily How-ard. He's returned to Creedon Abbey to see to the repairs.'

'Uncle George was here and didn't wait for me?'

'No, miss, but it appears we are to expect an-other gentleman.'

'Who?'

'Mrs Howard did not say, but she instructed me to open Paul's room for him.'

Julia chafed at the news. 'When is he arriving?'

'This afternoon.'

'Thank you, Davies. Please tell Mrs Howard I won't be joining her for breakfast.'

'Yes, miss.'

Julia walked down the hall to the study, determined to avoid the breakfast room no matter how many lectures it might create. What right did Emily have to make decisions at Knollwood? The maids and footmen were stretched thin enough with Uncle George staying here and all her step-cousins' demands.

Crossing the study's large, woven rug, Julia sighed. Emily, as Charles's wife, had every right to invite whomever she pleased, even if it did mean additional work for Julia and the staff. For a moment she imagined herself mistress of her own home, free to make decisions and live without her brother's censure, then dismissed the thought. Once Charles took control, he'd soon realise the limitations of his estate management skills, or return to London for Parliament in the spring, leaving Knollwood in Julia's hands once again. Or so she hoped. Her brother had a habit of being very stubborn.

She sat down behind the large, mahogany desk situated at the far end of the study. High bookcases lined one wall while south-facing windows with a view of the garden dominated the other. A tall, wooden bookstand supporting a fine atlas stood guard near the window, flanked by two leather chairs. Her father had decorated the room, choosing every element down to each book. From here he conducted all family business, patiently bearing Charles's sermons about the proper education for Julia, dealing with one of Paul's many near scandals or teaching Julia to run Knollwood.

It'd happened by accident, after she'd fled here one day to avoid drawing lessons. Sitting with her father while he reviewed the figures, she'd asked questions and he'd answered them, noticing her interest. The next day, he'd invited her to join him again and it became their habit. In the afternoons, they'd ride the estate, speaking with the workers and learning their methods and the land. Then, one day, he told her to do the figures, allowed her to sit in the room while he met with the overseer and gave her correspondence to read and answer. No one in the family except Charles questioned her strange education and Father would laugh him off, saying he wasn't about to lose his best manager because she was a girl.

Julia smiled at the memory, then opened the large, leather-bound ledger. Settling herself over the accounts, she reviewed the figures, wrinkling her nose at the increased expenditures brought on by her stepcousins' visit. Closing the ledger, she gathered up the large bundle of letters resting on the corner of the desk. She read through the missives, the minute details of the dairy and reports from the tenant farmers helping her forget the excitement of the morning.

Chapter Two

The study door swung open, startling Julia, and her pencil slipped, leaving a dark mark across two rows of figures.

'Yes?' she answered testily as Davies entered the room.

'Captain Russell and his guest have arrived.'

Tossing down the pencil, she sat back in the chair, needing just a few more minutes to finish balancing the accounts. 'They're early.'

'I believe they are on time.'

She looked at the windows, finally noticing how the sun and shadows had shifted in the garden and the room. 'How long have I been working?'

'All morning, Miss Howard.'

'Then I'd better hurry and join them or I'll never know a moment's peace with Emily.' Closing the ledger, she stood and started for the door. 'Though

I know Uncle George won't mind my being late. He isn't one for formality.'

'Excuse me, Miss Howard…' Davies coughed '…perhaps a change of dress is advisable.'

She stopped, inspecting the riding habit skirt, her loose hair falling over her face. Bits of leaves stuck to the honey-coloured fabric, making the damp hem noticeable and emphasising the creases along with the habit's older style. She hardly ever wore this habit, but she'd soiled her better one yesterday by taking Manfred over a fence and through the mud on the other side. Had she seen the puddle, she wouldn't have jumped him.

'I'll never hear the end of it if Emily catches me greeting guests in such a state. Where are they?'

'The morning room.'

'Do you think I can sneak upstairs and change before she sees me?'

'It is quite possible, Miss Howard.'

'We shall see.'

She hurried from the study and down the corridor. Approaching the entrance hall, she crept over the stone floor to the stairs, listening to Uncle George's robust laughter followed by the deep tones of the other gentleman in the morning room. The stranger's voice sounded oddly familiar, but she didn't dare peek inside for fear of being seen.

Stealing past the open door, she turned the corner to slip upstairs, coming face to face with her sister-in-law.

'What are you doing in your riding habit?' Emily demanded in hushed tones, her delicate eyes darting nervously to the morning room. 'And your hair? You can't welcome your guests looking like a dairy maid.'

'My guests?'

'Never mind. We'll say you were out riding and then you can meet the captain now before Uncle George drags him off for who knows how long.' Emily pulled her in front of the gilded mirror beneath the stairs and out of sight of the door.

'Did you say Uncle George's guest is a captain?' Julia winced as Emily untangled a small twig from her hair.

'Yes, Captain Covington.'

'Uncle George's friend from Tortuga?' Julia twisted around to face Emily before her sister-in-law gently spun her back to the mirror, dividing her hair into three sections, then working them into a braid.

'Yes, I believe so.'

Julia forced down a frustrated sigh. Single gentlemen were a rarity at Knollwood and Julia could practically see Emily's matchmaking machinations. It was the only explanation for why she insisted on this hurried first meeting. Apparently, she didn't know as much about Uncle George's friend as Julia did or she wouldn't be so excited, or eager to make the introduction. 'Well, if Captain Covington is to stay with us, I'd better instruct Davies to lock up the brandy.'

'Captain Covington isn't that kind of gentleman.'

'Then I'd better lock up the maids.'

'Julia!' Emily stared at her in the mirror, her pale face alight with shock. 'Young ladies shouldn't know about such things.'

Thankfully Paul thinks I should. If Emily and Charles ever learned the full extent of what Paul had told her, they'd probably chaperon their every conversation.

Emily smoothed the sturdy wool of Julia's habit, picking off stray leaves, her hands fluttering while she worked.

'You received another letter from Charles, didn't you?' Julia asked. Emily's concern for propriety always increased after a letter from her husband.

Emily blushed, pink spreading from her cheeks to her light blonde hair. 'Am I so obvious?'

'I'm afraid so.'

'It's only because we want to see you well settled.'

'No, it's because Charles thinks I don't act like a proper lady and such behaviour will cause a scandal and hurt his career in Parliament.'

Emily laid a motherly hand on Julia's shoulder. 'Your brother loves you and only wants to see you happy.'

Despite the well-meaning remark, Julia wasn't ready to concede defeat. 'I'm happy as I am.'

Emily moved behind Julia, fastening the braid into a small bun at the nape of her neck. 'I know, but time doesn't stand still. Some day you may want more.'

'What about Simon and Annette? They aren't greeting Uncle George. Why not censure them?'

'It's not my place to comment on their conduct.' Emily frowned and pulled her lips tight. 'They are both indisposed and will be down later.'

Julia bit back a sharp retort about the two of them always being indisposed when another idea came to mind. 'Perhaps I can speak to Captain Covington about Paul's promotion. Maybe he knows someone in the Admiralty who can arrange for Paul to get his own ship. I can't believe he didn't receive a command. If I ever find the man who wrote his bad recommendation—'

'I'm sure your brother is capable of managing his own affairs,' her mother interrupted, descending the stairs. Her grey eyes took in Julia, neither approving nor disapproving of her attire. Under her arm Charlemagne, her King Charles spaniel, panted, his pink tongue dangling from his mouth. Mother swept into the morning room, her plain dress whispering about her legs, her dark hair flecked with grey pulled neatly into a twist at the back of her head. Julia envied Mother's refined presence and decorum, wondering how many difficulties she could have avoided if fate had given her even a small portion of Mother's poise.

Emily, eager to fulfil her duties as hostess and, Julia thought, to fling her in the captain's path, guided Julia to the morning room. 'Come along. We've kept our guest waiting long enough.'

Inside, Mother exchanged pleasantries with Uncle George and the captain, who stood with his back to Julia.

'Your lands are some of the best I've seen,' he complimented, the rich, familiar voice vibrating through Julia. She noticed the dark hair curling just above the collar of his uniform and the way the sunlight falling through the window high-lighted the deep-red tones.

The stranger! A sudden rush of excitement mixed with fear jolted her and she froze just over the threshold.

'Are you all right?' Emily whispered and Julia shook her head, taking a large step back.

'No, I think I should change.' He'd seen her riding without a groom. If he mentioned it to Emily, there'd be no end to the reprimands.

'It's too late now.' Emily gripped her arm tight to keep her from fleeing as she motioned to Uncle George.

'And here is the party responsible for Knollwood's prosperity.' Uncle George ushered the captain to them. 'Captain Covington, Miss Julia Howard.'

If she had thought him handsome in plain hunting clothes, he took her breath away in uniform. The dark coat with the gold epaulettes emphasised his wide shoulders and the powerful presence she had felt in the forest. Without the advantage of Manfred's height, she had to look up at him. Though not overly tall, he stood a good head above her. The fantasy of being swept into his arms filled her mind once again and she swallowed hard.

'A pleasure.' He bowed.

Her eyes travelled the length of him as he straightened. Well-muscled calves stretched his hose tight while slightly looser breeches could not hide his strong thighs and other unmentionable areas. Feeling her cheeks burn, Julia focused on his face as she held out her hand. 'Captain Covington, welcome to Knollwood.'

He wrapped his fingers lightly around hers, then swept his lips across the bare knuckles. Julia drew in a ragged breath, trying not to tremble. The white-trimmed collar of the coat framed his now clean-shaven face and she curled her fingers slightly around his to stop herself from tracing the smooth line of his jaw.

'Good morning, Artemis.' His breath tickled the back of her hand and her body tightened in shock. 'I assume I am no longer trespassing on your land?'

She leaned closer, inhaling the earthy smell of his lavender shaving soap. 'That remains to be seen.'

He squeezed her hand, then let go. Julia stepped back, very aware of Emily shifting from foot to foot behind him.

'Have you two met before?' Emily asked in a high voice.

'I had the privilege of encountering Miss Howard while she was riding in the forest this morning,' Captain Covington explained, oblivious to the trouble he'd just caused.

Julia braced herself for the coming scolding, wishing the captain had held his tongue.

'You were riding without the groom again?' Emily asked, the nervous quaver in her voice more irritating than a bur in a boot.

'No, the groom was with her,' James lied before Julia could answer. 'But I'm afraid I failed to properly introduce myself and she mistook me for a poacher.'

Julia gaped at him, surprised he'd lie for her after the way she'd addressed him in the woods.

'George left no detail untold regarding your management,' he continued. 'You have quite an estate. I'm very impressed.'

'Thank you,' she faltered, the compliment catching her off guard. Usually gentlemen scoffed at her unusual accomplishment. 'I'm quite protective of it, as you may have gathered.'

'Indeed. I've never met such a fearsome protector of woodland creatures in all my life.'

'I'm sure many innocent creatures need protection from Navy men.'

Emily inhaled sharply and Uncle George snorted

out a laugh while her mother continued to pet Charlemagne, barely noting the exchange.

The captain's lips tightened in an attempt to keep from laughing and suddenly Julia regretted her impudent tongue. With all she knew of him from Uncle George's stories, to fire off such forward remarks, no matter how innocent, might give him the wrong impression and it wasn't very gracious, especially after he'd lied to help her.

'Shall we sit down?' Emily interrupted, nervously studying Julia and the captain.

'Yes, thank you.' He allowed Emily to escort him to the sofa and chairs near the window, her mother following close behind.

Julia stayed by the door, hoping she could slip away without Emily noticing. Decorum dictated she stay and entertain the captain, but something about him unnerved her. It was one thing to speak so frankly to family, quite another with a stranger, no matter how well he knew Uncle George. Better to leave now than risk another slip.

'I see you hiding there.' Uncle George came up alongside her, thumbs hooked in his jacket lapel.

'I'm not hiding.'

'Then come and join us.'

Julia smiled half-heartedly, watching the captain as he answered one of Mother's questions, his smile steady as he spoke. Whatever the captain thought of her unconventional behaviour, he'd already forgotten it. Deep down, some part of her wanted him to notice her, the way he had in the woods. As if sensing her, he shifted in the chair, meeting her eyes, and she turned to Uncle George.

'No, I have business to attend to.'

'Leave it for later. I think you'll enjoy the captain. You two already have quite the rapport.' He tugged her ear playfully, the way he'd done since she was a child.

The friendly gesture usually made her smile. Today it increased the irritation chewing at her. 'My work can't wait.'

'If you insist. But you can't hide at Knollwood for ever. Eventually, you'll have to get out in the world and live.'

'I'm not hiding,' Julia protested.

'Of course not. Silly of me to say it.' He patted her arm. 'Go back to the study. I'll make your excuses.'

Julia left, pausing a moment to listen to the muffled voices, suddenly feeling very alone. Walking through the back sitting room, she took in the sturdy walls of Knollwood covered in hunting prints and old portraits of well-dressed ancestors. Here she felt safe and, when not entertaining guests, confident in herself. Anywhere else she felt awkward and unsettled. What would happen if Charles took this away from her?

She slipped out of the French doors and crossed the garden to the far corner where the tall box-wood hedges hid her from the house. At the centre of this private courtyard stood a fountain of a man and woman locked in a passionate kiss, a copy of some nameless Greek statue. It had been a gift to their father from Paul after his first visit to Greece. Having no use for the statue in the house, her father had it made into a fountain, scandalising Charles, who insisted on hiding it in this secluded corner.

Julia plunked down on the stone bench in front of the fountain, watching the water run over the naked marble bodies. The polished stone glistened in the noon sun, intensifying the urgency of the lovers' embrace. The man's fingers dug into the hard flesh of the woman's thigh, his hands entwined in her hair as she pressed her naked form against his. Her long, gracefully carved fingers rested against the taut muscles of the male's well-chiselled back. Studying the lovers' embrace, their bodies so close not even water could separate them, Julia felt her chest constrict. What would it be like to inspire such passion in a man?

Picking up a small stone, she flung it into the pool at the base of the fountain, sending a large splash up and over the side. Reaching down for another rock, she heard the pitter-patter of paws on gravel as Charlemagne barrelled down on her. The small dog threw his front paws up on her knees, his wagging tail shaking his whole body as Julia stroked his soft fur.

'I thought I'd find you here,' her mother said, scooping up Charlemagne and sitting down next to her.

'Did Emily send you here to chastise me for not being a perfect lady?'

'Emily is a sweet girl, good for Charles and I adore her,' her mother remarked, settling the wiggling dog on her lap. 'But I seldom listen to her advice or Charles's. I suggest you do the same.'

'I've tried, but it only makes them more persistent.'

'Yes, he takes after your grandfather in that regard.' Charlemagne refused to be still and Mother put him on the ground. 'You're worried about Charles taking over Knollwood, aren't you?'

Like Uncle George, Mother could be very direct and Julia found it both helpful and at times hindering. She watched Charlemagne sniff around the fountain, jumping back when an errant bead of water landed on his nose.

'When he does, what will I do?' Julia choked, digging the toe of her boot into the ground.

'I think you'll find something. You're much more resourceful than either Charles or Paul.'

'But what else could there possibly be for me?'

Her mother took Julia's face in her hands, pushing a strand of hair off of her cheek. 'That's up to you to discover.'

She kissed Julia's forehead, then rose, snapping her fingers at Charlemagne.

'Do I hide from the world here?' Julia asked before her mother could leave.

'Who put such an idea in your head?'

'Uncle George.'

The older woman laughed softly. 'Since when do you take my brother seriously?'

Julia shrugged. 'Emily and Charles are always saying it, in their own way.'

'I think only you know the answer.' She strolled out of the garden, Charlemagne close on her heels.

The quick click of a lady's perturbed step drew James to the morning-room door. Miss Howard strode into the entrance hall, moving like a tempest, oblivious to everything but her own energy. Fascinated, he wanted to draw her out, but hesitated. Better to let her go than risk the blunt blow of her dark mood. However, something in the troubled frown on her pretty face prompted him to speak.

'Miss Howard?'

The stomping girl vanished, replaced by an awkward young woman conscious of the world around her. 'Yes?'

She stood on the bottom stair, one small hand on the oak banister, poised like a doe to flee. He wondered what had happened to make such an exuberant creature so timid. 'I want to apologise for this morning. You took me quite by surprise.'

'Yes, I imagine I did.' She moved to leave, but he wasn't ready to let her go.

'I don't usually meet young ladies in the forest so early in the morning.'

'Why didn't you tell me who you were?' she demanded with startling directness.

'You didn't ask,' he laughed, his mirth evaporating under her stern glare. 'Allow me to apologise. I should have introduced myself.' He offered a humble bow, but it did not soften the small crease marring her smooth brow.

'I wish you had for it might have saved us both a great deal of trouble.'

'I shall endeavour to be more agreeable to you the next time we meet in a forest.' The image of them alone among the trees, her hair loose about her naked shoulders, their bodies entwined came to mind. His hand itched to reach up and trace the gentle curve of her cheek, slip his fingers behind her long neck and draw her close.

'There will be no next time,' she corrected, ending the pleasant fantasy.

'I think it quite possible,' he teased. 'Judging by this morning, I assume it is your habit to ride out alone in the mornings.'

'Shh.' She stepped closer, waving a silencing hand and filling the air between them with the faint scent of rosemary.

'Your mother doesn't approve of you riding alone?' he asked in a low voice.

'Mother doesn't care, but Emily does.' She stepped off the stair and stood in front of him, her face softening. 'Thank you for not telling her you saw me riding without a groom. You spared me a great deal of trouble.'

'It was my pleasure, and I'll gladly do it again if the need arises.'

'I hope it doesn't come to that.' She smiled, her face glowing with amusement.

'You're very pretty when you smile,' he offered

without thinking, amazed at how much her pleasure delighted him.

Her smile disappeared and she raised one disbelieving eyebrow. Something of the confident Artemis he'd seen this morning flashed in her hazel eyes, rousing his blood.

'I know the country is lacking in diversions, but do not think to amuse yourself with me.'

James straightened, forgetting his desire. He should have been insulted, but he could hardly blame her for saying what he'd momentarily imagined. 'You misunderstood my meaning. I have never, would never behave as you intimate.'

She fixed him with the same scrutinising look he once used on seamen when they told him a tall tale to cover their misdeeds. 'I am not naïve, Captain. My brother and uncle tell me everything, so I know what Navy men are about.'

'Do you?' He struggled to keep the laughter out of his voice, still unable to believe a young woman with her hair pulled back like a dour nun could be so forward. He leaned against the wooden banister, bringing their faces much closer than intended. She did not step back. 'I may have to change your opinion of Navy men.'

'I'm afraid you have only worked to confirm it.'

Her saucy eyes teased him. Were this Tortuga,

he would have covered her full mouth with his, allowed his fingers to free her hair from the bun as he pulled her close to kiss away the wry smile dancing about her lips. However, his good breeding, not to mention his status as George's guest, prevented such a blatant breach of etiquette.

'Julia!' Emily appeared at the morning-room door. Julia stepped back, her cheeks burning, awkwardness replacing her courage. Silently, she cursed her impetuous nature, wondering what it was about the captain that kept causing her to forget herself. A few minutes in the gentleman's presence and she was once again acting like a strumpet instead of a lady. How much had Emily heard? Hopefully nothing or she and Charles would feel vindicated in all their chastising.

Before anyone could say anything, baby Thomas's wail filled the upstairs hallway and the nurse appeared at the top of the stairs, carrying the infant. He was only two months old, but he'd been born early and Emily fretted over him like no other well-born mother in the county.

'Mrs Howard, it is time for his feeding,' the nurse called over the screaming baby.

Emily glanced from the captain to Julia to upstairs, weighing her desire to reprimand with the need to see to her child. Luckily, Thomas's cries grew louder, making the decision for her.

'If you'll excuse me, Captain, I must attend to my son.' Emily shot Julia a silent warning before hurrying up to escort the nurse to the nursery. For all of Charles's and Emily's priggishness, they were firm believers in Rousseau's ideas of breastfeeding. It was one of the few things Julia admired them for.

'Despite being born two months early, my nephew has a healthy appetite and powerful lungs,' Julia observed.

'His lungs will serve him well if he enters Parliament. Like his father, his opinions will always be heard,' Captain Covington teased.

Julia laughed, the captain's joke putting her at ease. She was about to respond when a small cough from the landing interrupted them.

'Good morning, Captain Covington.' Annette glided down the stairs, her blue eyes raking over him. Dressed in a fashionable walking dress of expensive yellow silk, she stepped in between Julia and the captain. Her haughty air irked Julia and she clasped her hands together to keep from smacking the chit on the back of her elegantly coiffed blonde head. Though they were the same age, they had nothing in common and had never been more than civil to each other since Annette's arrival.

'Miss Taylor, a pleasure to see you again.' The captain bowed over her extended hand, the relaxed Navy man from a moment before replaced by a proper gentleman.

Julia noted the change and her heart sank. Obviously, he respected the polished manners of a London lady to the questionable conduct of a country girl.

It doesn't matter, she told herself. *Neither of them will be here for ever.*

'How are your dear sister and mother?' Annette asked, her voice light and charming.

'My sister Charlotte is in Wiltshire with her husband. My mother is with them at the moment, though she returns to town next week. She prefers London to the country.'

'Who of us doesn't?' Simon yawned from the top of the stairs, his voice heavy with the Devonshire lisp so popular in town. Tall and lean, Simon wore a suit of the finest material cut tight to accentuate his slender body. He possessed the same sharp features as his sister, but the affected boredom of his dandified style softened them considerably.

Annette's face reddened at Simon's remark. 'You remember my brother?'

'Of course.' Both men nodded to one another, no affection lost on either side.

'We are going to the local town. Please join us for I'm eager for some society after such isolation.'

'Did I hear someone suggest a ride into Daringford?' Uncle George asked, coming up behind the captain.

'Yes. Care to join us?' Captain Covington invited.

While they made their plans, Julia started up the stairs, sure no one would notice her absence. They had each other; they did not need her. She froze when the captain called out to her.

'Miss Howard, would you like to join us?'

Surveying the waiting group, Julia wondered how much more of his company she could endure without gaining a reputation as a hoyden. Until she could learn to control her tongue in his presence, it was probably better to avoid him. She moved to make her excuses when Annette's condescending sweep of Julia's riding habit changed her mind. 'Yes, but allow me to change. I'll only be a moment.'

'Your dress is passable. Come and let's be off,' Uncle George impatiently called.

Julia reluctantly stepped off the stairs. Emily would have a fit if she knew Julia wore her old riding habit into town. Oh, well, what was one more reprimand? Besides, it was worth the rebuke to annoy Annette.

'Come, Captain Covington.' Annette motioned for his arm and like a true gentleman he offered it, leading her outside to the waiting carriage. Julia watched the way her stepcousin moved, the rich material and fine cut of her dress emphasising her willowy figure. A slight twinge of jealousy took hold and Julia wondered if things would be different if she made an effort to dress so well every day or demonstrate proper, genteel manners.

'My lady.' Uncle George offered her his arm with an exaggerated flourish.

'Why, thank you, sir,' she answered with equally false formality.

'What do you think of the captain?' he asked in a low voice as they strolled out to the waiting carriage.

'He strikes me as quite the man about town. He's already caught Annette's attention.'

'Any man with a pocketbook catches her fancy,' George huffed. 'You shouldn't let her have him.'

'I have no interest in a Navy man, especially one with a thin London polish.'

'He's no Simon, if that's what you're worried about. He's rich, too. Thanks, I might say, in part to many of my lucrative schemes.'

Julia suppressed a laugh, knowing how proud Uncle George was of the numerous profitable ventures he'd embarked on during his time in the Navy. 'Why did the captain resign?'

'George, stop gossiping and get in,' Captain Covington interrupted from beside the open carriage door. 'No need to give away all my secrets on the first day.'

'Not possible, Jim. You've got too many.' Uncle George chuckled.

'May I?' Captain Covington held out his hand, a playful smile lighting up his face. Julia reached for his upturned palm, hesitating a moment before pushing against the strength of it to step up into the carriage.

'Thank you.' She didn't dare meet his eyes, but slid across the squabs and settled in next to the far window, her hand still tingling from his touch. Uncle George sat beside her in an attempt to place some distance between her, Annette and Simon and she was grateful. The captain took a seat across from them, next to Annette, much to the chit's visible delight.

Simon paused to adjust his cravat, then carefully climbed into the carriage, moving like an old lady to avoid wrinkling his morning coat. The door closed behind him, but Simon wasn't fully seated when Uncle George rapped on the roof. The vehicle sprung into motion, throwing Simon into the seat next to his sister.

'I say,' Simon complained to George.

'Sorry about that.' George shrugged, unruffled by Simon's outburst.

'Men can be so silly, don't you agree, Captain Covington?' Annette laughed, reprimanding her brother with a look he pointedly ignored.

'Yes, they can be.' The captain allowed the conversation to drop, watching the countryside pass by outside the window, a strange melancholy clouding his face. Julia noted the way the afternoon sunlight spread over his features, highlighting a very small scar on his cheek and giving him a bit of mystery and depth she'd never seen in any London gentleman. Then his eyes darted to hers and she turned away, her heart fluttering, the heat in the carriage rising sharply.

What's wrong with me? she wondered, touching the warm skin of her neck. It wasn't like her to act so hen-witted in the company of a man, especially a Navy rake like the captain. Struggling to regain control, she concentrated on the river flowing in the gully below the road. No matter how much she focused on the clear water pouring over the rocks, the captain lingered on the edge of her vision. When she dared to look at him again, she found him still smiling at her.

'Captain Covington, were you at Lady Wellsingham's ball last month?' Annette asked.

'No, I'm afraid business kept me away,' he answered with a slight frown before covering it with a gracious smile.

Perhaps he's not so taken by London charms, Julia mused, sitting back to observe the conversation with a new interest.

'What a pity. You would have enjoyed it. All anyone could talk about was Lord Langston's comment on Napoleon. He said the Emperor's coat was too tight to suit a real gentleman, and if the Emperor had a better tailor, he might not be so fond of war.'

'I thought politics a taboo subject at balls?' Julia asked, more to annoy her stepcousin than out of any real interest.

'We were discussing Lord Langston's comment, not politics,' Annette arrogantly clarified. 'Surely you've heard of the earl, even here?'

Julia bit back a sharp retort, struggling through gritted teeth to remain cordial.

'Yes. Charles keeps me abreast of the latest London news, though I pay it no mind. I hardly feel the comments of a man who thinks only of clothes and dancing is worth the breath to spread it. Were he a man of actual accomplishments, such as Lord Nelson, I might take more interest in what he has to say.'

'Here, here, Julia.' George slapped his knee and Annette pursed her thin lips.

'Sounds like a rather American idea to me, Miss Howard,' Captain Covington asked.

'Have you been to America, Captain?' Julia asked.

'Yes, it's an interesting country.'

'I don't agree with the Americans. The French followed their example and all their patriotism and liberty turned out dreadful,' Annette interjected, but both Julia and Captain Covington ignored the remark.

'I'm a great admirer of Mr Jefferson. Are you familiar with his agricultural inventions?' Julia asked.

'Yes, I read one of his books while I was in London. I read quite a number of books while I was at home.' He paused, watching his left hand open and close before he looked up at her again. 'I don't recall the specific of Mr Jefferson's designs, but I remember them being quite innovative.'

'He devised a plough specifically for hills. It's proved most beneficial to Knollwood,' she volunteered, encouraged by his response. 'Like Mr Jefferson, I've discovered the best way to develop new techniques is to ask the workers. I regularly speak with mine to keep abreast of their progress and any potential problems.'

'How plebian to be so familiar with your servants,' Annette sneered.

Julia went silent, the conspicuous difference between her and her London cousin making her self-conscious.

'I agree, Miss Howard, servants are often aware of more than their employers realise,' the captain offered with a smile.

'Indeed, they know the land and conditions better than anyone else.'

Careful not to gloat over the obvious check to Annette's mocking remark, Julia continued her discussion of agriculture, encouraged by the captain's extensive knowledge. The bulk of it came from books, but he asked many questions about the practical application, eager to learn. While they spoke, Julia watched the way Annette hung on his every word, fluttering her eyelashes at him while praising his wit and intelligence. Each compliment brought a smile to his face and as much as Julia's opinion of him rose with their current discussion, his apparent infatuation with Annette lowered it. Perhaps the captain thought her cousin a better country amusement than Julia. After all, the way Annette fawned on him made her interest apparent. How typical of a man to fall prey to such a shallow woman.

The carriage rattled into town, coming to a stop near the centre of the High Street. James stepped out into the crisp autumn air and took a deep breath. Being confined for so long next to Miss Taylor reminded him of a tight gun deck on a humid day in the islands. Only Miss Howard's airy voice and sparkling eyes offered any respite from Miss Taylor's cloying company.

'What an exile,' Mr Taylor sighed, taking in Daringford's dusty streets lined with shops. 'I'll return shortly.'

'I thought you were going to stay with me?' Miss Taylor whined as James handed her out of the carriage.

Mr Taylor ignored her, strolling off towards the Sign of the Swan tavern, much to his sister's visible displeasure.

James turned back to the carriage to help Miss Howard out, only to see her alight from the other side before hurrying around to join them.

'I'm afraid I must leave you as well,' George announced. 'I have some business to attend to with my solicitor. Take good care of the ladies, Jim.' He went off in the opposite direction, leaving James alone with Miss Taylor and Miss Howard.

'Well, ladies, where shall we go?'

'The milliner's shop,' Miss Taylor decided. 'I must purchase some lace, though I doubt it will be of the same quality here as in London.'

'The milliner it is, unless Miss Howard has somewhere she wishes to go?'

Miss Howard shook her head. 'No, I'm simply here for the diversion.'

'One could hardly call this place a diversion.' Miss Taylor made for the row of shops lining the north side of the street, stepping gingerly around the dirt and mud.

'I suppose we must follow.' Miss Howard sighed.

'I suppose we must.'

Their progress across the square was slow, with Miss Howard stopping more than once to speak to some farmers' wives. He stood by while they conversed, noting how she addressed the women without arrogance or conceit. There were no signs of her former awkwardness and he thought it strange she should get along so well with these women, yet seem utterly out of place with people like the Taylors. It baffled him, but he enjoyed it, her friendly attitude a refreshing change from rigid London ways.

When they finally reached the milliner shop, James held open the door, then followed her inside. 'Do you come to the village often?'

'Yes, it seems I am always purchasing necessities for Knollwood.'

Miss Taylor ignored them in favour of the shopkeeper who hustled to help the London girl spend her blunt. Miss Howard did not shop, but loitered with him near the front window, as out of place here as Miss Taylor would be among estate labourers.

'You have no interest in lace?' James asked.

'I've come to town in my riding habit. I assure you, I have no interest in lace.'

He noted the older cut of the habit with its lower waist and fitted bodice. The style skimmed her flat stomach and accentuated her curved hips. He preferred the form-flattering shape to the high-waisted style dominating Rotten Row. 'I like your dress.'

'Do you?'

He heard disbelief in the question, but also a note of hope. 'I do.'

She played with a small piece of ribbon dangling off the table next to her, then nodded at Miss Taylor, who stood at the counter negotiating with the shopkeeper over the price. 'She certainly drives a hard bargain. I'm amazed she bothers to be so economical.'

'Perhaps her situation is not what it seems.'

Miss Howard's puzzled face indicated her ignorance of the London rumours regarding the Taylors. However, before she could respond, a round matron followed by a blonde young lady with similar full features entered the store.

'Miss Howard,' the older woman called out, crossing to where they stood. 'What a pleasure to see you in here. I didn't think you one for the milliner's shop.'

Miss Howard's lips drew tight and James's ire rose at the belittling way the matron's eyes swept over Miss Howard, making her flush with embarrassment.

'Mrs Johnson, may I introduce Captain Covington.' Miss Howard motioned to him. 'He is a friend of my uncle and staying with us. Captain Covington, this is Mrs Johnson and her daughter, Miss Caroline Johnson.'

The two ladies curtsied to James, sizing up his value as a potential husband.

He bowed, unwilling to remain here or give this woman another chance to insult Miss Howard. 'If you'll excuse us, we were just about to step outside and leave you *lovely* women to your shopping.'

He offered Miss Howard his arm. She slipped her hand in the crook of his elbow and flashed the disbelieving Mrs and Miss Johnson a wide smile as he escorted her out of the shop.

'I see some mamas are as rude here as they are in London,' James fumed once they were outside. 'What did she hope to gain by being condescending to you?'

'I don't know, but please pay it no mind. I'm quite used to it.' Miss Howard withdrew her hand and placed a respectable distance between them. He brushed his fingers over the spot where she'd held his arm, missing the soft weight of her touch.

'You should make a habit of responding to rude people,' James suggested.

'Why? Emily and Charles would only hear of it, then chastise me for being ill mannered. It seems

I must be civil to everyone while everyone may speak to me as they please.'

'There are many ways to appear courteous, yet still strike a cutting blow.'

'Then you must teach me some for I'm tired of putting up with such nonsense.' She laughed, the charming sound carrying over the noisy rattle of equipage in the street.

'It would be my pleasure. What sort of remark would you like to learn first?'

'James Covington,' the long-forgotten but familiar female voice called out from behind them, slicing through him like a sword and shattering his jovial mood. 'I can hardly believe it.'

He turned, watching Melinda Knight saunter up the street, a wicked smile decorating her full lips. A low-cut gown showed off her ample white bosom, much to the appreciation of the passing village men. Many paused to admire her, elbowing one another as their lecherous eyes enjoyed the well-displayed assets. They obviously deemed her a beauty, but James, who'd known her in his youth, saw the toll London indulgence had taken. Her dark-brown eyes seemed tired and dull while her once slender form had grown more stout, filling out her face and keeping away, for a few more years at least, the lines forming about her eyes and the corners of her lips.

'Miss Knight,' he greeted through clenched teeth.

'I'm Mrs Wilkins now, or have you forgotten?'

James's lip curled in loathing. 'So you married him?'

'Is that any way to greet an old friend?' Her seductive voice had once heated his blood; now it left him icy with disgust.

'I would hardly call us friends.'

She wedged herself between him and Miss Howard, her bosom brushing his chest. 'At one time you called me a great deal more.'

'That was a long time ago.' He stepped back, fighting the urge to push her away. The reaction unnerved him. He thought he'd forgotten her treachery years ago. Taking control of his surging emotions, he turned to Miss Howard, noting her stunned expression. 'May I introduce Miss Howard of Knollwood.'

Melinda faced Julia, taking her in and dismissing her all at once. 'We already know one another. My husband owns Cable Grange. My, what a pretty riding habit. Did you ride here?'

'No,' Miss Howard retorted, her dislike of Melinda palpable.

'Must be the new fashion. I find it so hard to keep up. You country girls have such different tastes.'

Melinda laid a gloved hand on James's arm and he pulled away, leaving her fingers hanging like talons before she lowered them. Far from being embarrassed, she seemed to take pleasure in his revulsion. 'You should come and visit us, James. I know Rowan would love to see you. Now, if you'll excuse me, I must be going.'

She swept off down the street, collecting more appreciative stares as she went.

'You know her?' Miss Howard gasped.

'I knew her once, a long time ago. It's of no importance.' He wondered how best to correct whatever false impression his acquaintance with Melinda left. He refused to be judged by a past mistake, but no proper explanation came to mind.

'Here comes George.' James motioned over her shoulder, thankful for the distraction.

George rushed along the road, the light of delicious news in his eyes.

'I can tell by the way he's hurrying, he's heard gossip,' Julia observed. 'He enjoys a story more than any old matron in Daringford.'

James laughed at the candid and accurate description. 'It is good to know some things haven't changed.'

'Julia, you won't believe what my solicitor told me,' George blurted out between winded pants when he reached them. 'Cable Grange is to be sold at auction in ten days if Mr Wilkins can't pay his London creditors.'

Chapter Three

Julia jumped from the carriage the instant it halted in front of Knollwood. Flying up the front stairs, she ran down the hall, throwing open her mother's sitting-room door, not caring what anyone thought of her very unladylike entrance.

'Cable Grange is to be sold by the bailiff in ten days. You must write to Charles and tell him to arrange for my inheritance at once.'

'Julia, do not stomp about the house,' her mother instructed without missing a stitch in her embroidery. Charlemagne watched from a basket at her mother's feet, his tail wagging lazily.

'Mother, did you hear what I said?' she demanded, chafing in the face of her apathy.

'You know he won't approve.' Her mother pulled a long, red thread through the fabric. 'He hardly approves of you running Knollwood in his absence.'

'That's why I need you to write him. Demand my inheritance, but don't tell him why. I can't have him buying Cable Grange out from under me.'

'I have little influence with Charles, especially in this matter.'

'But he has to give me the money,' Julia cried, pacing the room. 'This could be my only chance to secure an estate of my own.'

Her mother paused mid-stitch. 'Without a husband? He'd never allow it. You must be married first.'

'To whom? One of the many young men throwing themselves at my feet?'

'My dear, don't sound so despondent. Some day you will find a gentleman who loves you.'

'Not in time to purchase Cable Grange.' Julia sat down hard in the window seat.

'Perhaps George can supply the necessary funds?'

'Creedon Abbey is profitable, but not enough to finance another estate, especially not with the repairs from the fire.' She knew because she often helped Uncle George with his accounting.

'Then I'm afraid Cable Grange will go to another.'

Julia bit her thumbnail in frustration, feeling

like a rabbit caught in a snare. Though the money was hers, her father's will gave Charles control of it until she married or Charles died. At the moment, she wanted very much to kill her obstinate brother.

She picked at the gold thread on a pillow. 'Why did Father put Charles in charge of my inheritance? Why not Uncle George or even Paul? They wouldn't be so difficult.'

Her mother rose, sitting down next to Julia and taking her hands. 'It's what his solicitor advised. Your father intended to change it once George purchased Creedon Abbey, but his illness was so sudden—'

Silence heavy with grief settled between them. Outside, birds chirped in a nearby tree and Julia heard the distant bark of Uncle George's hunting dogs.

'It's not fair.'

'No, it isn't, but don't fret, my dear. Nothing is hopeless. Now, go and change for dinner.' Her mother kissed her gently on the forehead, then returned to her embroidery stand.

Julia wandered down the hall to her room, her mind working over the current dilemma. She had to have Cable Grange. She refused to be shoved aside at Knollwood by Charles or to let him control her life. Paul would never do such a thing if it were up to him.

Closing the door behind her, she wondered if Paul could arrange for the money. Knowing how freely he spent while in port, she doubted he possessed the means to buy an estate and his failure to gain command of his own ship hindered his ability to make his fortune. Even if he could help, there was no way to reach him before the auction.

Julia paced her room, her mind working to think of a solution. The only way to buy Cable Grange was to obtain her inheritance. The only way to get her inheritance was to marry. At present, she had no suitors. To be honest, she had never had suitors, not here or during her one Season in London.

Julia stopped pacing, her mind seizing on an idea. What if she was only engaged? If Charles thought she intended to marry, surely he'd give her the money in time to purchase Cable Grange. Even he could see the benefit of making Cable Grange part of the Howard lands. But what gentleman could she possibly convince to make her a false offer?

Through the window overlooking the garden, she spied Simon strolling among the roses. It wasn't like him to be awake at this time of day.

Usually, he napped in the late afternoon in anticipation of an even later evening. How a man could spend all night gambling was beyond her comprehension.

The idea hit her like a bolt of lightning. Simon. As a gambler, he must need money. They could make a deal, pretend to be engaged and once she had her inheritance and Cable Grange, she'd give him a few hundred pounds to jilt her.

She rushed to the door, eager to strike the bargain, when a terrifying thought froze her hand on the doorknob. If he accepted the deal, could she buy his silence at the end of the engagement? If not, it would create a scandal, then who knew how Charles or even Mother would react. Charles might force her to go through with a ruinous marriage to avoid disgrace.

Julia resumed her pacing, desperate for a solution. Simon was no different from other London peacocks. How hard could it be to use her money, or the future possibility of money, to snare him? Instead of entangling herself in a potentially shocking agreement, she'd flaunt her wealth, then allow his greed to lead him to her. Once she had her inheritance and Cable Grange she could easily dismiss him. Simon would suffer no more heartbreak than the other London pinks who proposed to every unmarried rich woman who entered a ballroom. Even if breaking the engagement labelled her a jilt, it wouldn't matter. She'd have her inheritance and Cable Grange and everything else could go to the devil.

Standing at the wardrobe, Julia tore through the dresses, selecting one of her better frocks. Slipping off the habit, she put on the light-blue dress, then sat at her dressing table to do her hair. The sight of herself in the mirror dampened her enthusiasm. Though the cloth of her frock was fine enough, the cut was unflattering and her hair, which was still fastened in the simple braided bun at the nape of her neck, did nothing to improve her features.

'If only I were pretty enough to catch Simon without my money.' She sighed and then dismissed the ridiculous notion. 'I might as well wish for gold to fall from the sky.'

Pulling out the bun, she brushed out her hair. A man like Simon couldn't resist the allure of money and she'd parade herself in front of him like a fat cow at market. Dignity be damned. She had to have Cable Grange for if she ended her days as a spinster aunt, she'd do it on her terms in her own house.

* * *

'I never thought I'd see Melinda again.' James smacked the cue stick hard against the white ball, sending it skipping over the slate, off the table and across the library's wood floor.

George picked it up, laying it back on the table. 'You aren't still chewing on that, are you? Let it go. No good can come of it.'

'Except an estate. I wasn't planning it—I couldn't have planned it—yet here it is, in my lap. I only have to wait for the bailiff to act, then I'll watch them go and be done with it.' Revenge coiled inside him with unnerving force. Even in the days after Melinda betrayed him, he hadn't felt this much hate, but things were different then. His naval career had stretched out before him to blunt the disappointment and at sea he'd been too focused on succeeding and surviving to dwell on lost love. Now, with his career a shattered heap, his whole life crushed and bruised with it, there seemed nothing to distract him from old wounds. He flexed his left hand, cursing the dull pain. How he hated it and the way it made him hate everything.

George shook his head. 'That's not the Jim I remember.'

'A lot of things changed last year.'

'No, you just think they have. Look to the future. Don't concern yourself with some past offence that no longer matters.'

'You think it doesn't matter?'

'I think Rowan did you a favour, showed you who she really was before she leg-shackled you.' George leaned across the table and took a shot, scoring another point. 'Of course it's your decision and Cable Grange will suit you, but you'll need something more or you'll be bored in a fortnight.'

'You thinking running an estate won't be enough?' He reached for his glass of brandy sitting on the edge of the table.

'Not for a man like you. You need adventure and what better adventure than marriage?' George announced.

James stopped drinking mid-sip. 'Marriage?'

'Yes, marriage.' George hooked his thumbs in his coat, quite pleased with himself.

'What new scheme are you planning?' He didn't trust George's happy manner.

'Scheme? I never scheme.'

'Never scheme?' James laughed. 'What was all that business with the rum in Jamaica?'

'Merely an investment.'

'And the plantation owner's wife in Barbados?'

'One could hardly fault me for such an escapade.'

'Except the escapade's husband.'

George shrugged, unrepentant. 'You're a man of your own mind. I never forced you to participate in the rum venture or follow me to the plantation.'

'I followed you to save your hide and keep her husband from running you through.'

'Perhaps.' George fingered his cue stick, then levelled it at James. 'But you went along with the other ventures because you wanted to, making a handsome profit on more than one occasion if I remember correctly.'

'Yes, I have a great deal of my current fortune to thank you for.'

'So why distrust me now?'

It wasn't George he distrusted. It was himself. He hadn't seen Miss Howard since returning from Daringford, but following George through Knollwood, he kept searching for her in every room, hoping she might appear. Her presence touched a place deep inside him he thought destroyed with his career and the feeling left him wary and unsettled. One woman had already preyed on the weakness of his youth. He couldn't allow another to take advantage of his ruined life.

George fixed him with a stern, superior officer's stare. 'Seriously, Jim, you had a bad run last year, but you can't live in the past. You're young, full of possibility. You need a good woman by your side.'

'I suppose you have someone in mind? Your little Artemis, perhaps?'

George leaned towards James, the glint of mischief in his eyes. James knew this expression all too well. How many times had he followed it into a tavern, or the heat of battle? 'Now that you mention it, perhaps Julia is just the kind of woman you need. Sizeable inheritance. Brother in Parliament. Adept at running an estate. She's a good match.'

James shook his head as he readied his cue stick. Is this what his life had come to? Discussing marriage over a billiard table? Country life must be very dull to lead an old salt like George to such a pastime. 'Interesting suggestion—however, it has two flaws.'

'And they are?'

'One, I have no desire to marry, which you well know.'

'At the moment, yes, but there's always the future.'

'And two, your Artemis doesn't like me.'

'Of course she likes you. She's just an awkward girl. Spent too much time in the country, odd relatives and all that.'

'Odd indeed.' James hit the cue ball and it sailed past the red ball. 'I see a great deal of Paul in his sister.'

'There you are with the past again. Forget it. Paul was young. You were young and both of you stupid.'

'I'd hardly say stupid.'

'Stubborn, then, if you like. You'd be surprised to see him now.'

'"Surprised" is not the word. Does your Artemis know I wrote to the Admiralty against Paul's promotion?'

'I didn't see the need to inform her and I suggest you don't either if you wish to have a pleasant visit. You don't want to be on the wrong end of my niece's temper.'

As if I needed the warning. 'You don't think she'll find out?'

'He's off at sea and you're here, not likely to meet.'

James had to admire George's devil-may-care attitude. Here was a man who always believed everything would work out swimmingly and somehow for him it always did. What James wouldn't give for even a small measure of George's optimism, but the last year had left him anything but optimistic. The long days of his recovery followed by the even longer days of stalking the Admiralty, asking, then begging for another commission, had taken their toll.

During the year of his recovery, younger, fitter men with more prestigious connections had passed him by, and not even his loyal years of service were enough to secure him another ship. He could almost smell the oil on the wood panels of Admiral Stuart's office the day he told James there would be no more commissions and encouraged—insisted, one might say—James enjoy his fortune while he still could.

In the end, despite his disappointment, he'd secretly been relieved. It shamed him to admit it, but he couldn't lie to himself. Death had passed over him. Ten years ago he'd have shrugged it off and raced to face the devil once more. This time he couldn't. He wanted to live free of violence and risks, to take care of his family and see his sister's future children grow up, but without his command he saw nothing, no meaning or activity, just an endless set of days stretching out before him.

James refilled his drink from the small decanter

of brandy on the table near the window. He hated this emptiness. It made him feel like a ship in a storm with a broken rudder at the mercy of driving winds and an unforgiving sea. He took a deep drink, careful not to enjoy too much the burning in the back of his throat. He'd seen other men come home and lose themselves in gin, women and cards, their energy wasted by a lack of duty and direction. He put the glass down, knowing his future wasn't at the bottom of a bottle, but was it really as close as Cable Grange? Perhaps an estate would give him a sense of purpose again, a chance to do something more than grieve for his past and the future he'd planned for himself.

James watched while George calculated his next shot. 'Why isn't your little Artemis already married?'

'Says she's not interested.'

'A woman not interested in marriage? Next you'll tell me you believe in mermaids.'

'I do. I saw one off the coast of Florida once. She's not interested in marriage. However, a man with an estate could change her mind. If you're determined to buy Cable Grange, she's the woman you need to run it.' George took his time lining up his shot, looking quite proud of himself for what he considered a brilliant idea.

James couldn't resist the opportunity to rib his old friend. 'So your niece is only interested in marrying a man for his estate?'

George whiffed the cue ball then straightened up, indignant. 'She's not that kind of young lady. She's clever, a real woman of substance, made running Knollwood her life, but the place isn't hers. Charles plans to assume control when he comes home at the end of the month. Where will she be then?'

'You could leave her Creedon Abbey.'

'I probably will…' George floundered. Clearly he hadn't thought of this and James enjoyed watching the older man work to recover himself. 'But I'm not at death's door yet. I plan to live at least another twenty years. Spend some time with her, get to know her, you'll see what I mean.'

James walked to the window, noticing the threatening clouds gathering overhead. Their darkness layered the hills with damp shadows, making the hour feel late. Somewhere across the hills and valleys sat Cable Grange. Watching the wind shake the tall hedges of the garden, he tried to picture himself as lord of the manor, spending his days in land management with all its hundreds of concerns, but he had trouble imagining it.

Reaching up under his jacket, he felt for the jagged, raised scar. Yes, he was lucky to be alive and sometimes it made him think he wanted a wife and a family. What would it be like to enjoy the kind of happiness he'd witnessed between his parents before his father died or the love he saw in his sister's eyes when she walked with her husband? He'd tried so many times while convalescing to imagine the future, but always it remained shrouded in a grey fog of uncertainty. The sudden end to his naval career made the years before him seem meaningless while old wounds and betrayals arose from the past to dominate his mind.

A bolt of lightning split the distant horizon and the image of Miss Howard atop that beast of a horse commanding him like a common seaman seared his mind. Tight desire coursed through him at the memory of her tongue tracing the line of her lips and the curious need illuminating her face. Her free spirit and courage reminded him of Caribbean ladies, bringing a smile to his face at the memory of warm afternoons and even warmer nights in the islands. Those days seemed like a lifetime ago yet today, in Miss Howard's presence, their carefree ease sparked deep inside him for the first time in over a year.

The feeling made him uneasy. He'd experienced

something like it once before, allowing it to guide him, and he'd come to regret it.

He downed the last of the brandy, forcing back the encroaching sadness. He wasn't ready for another life-altering change and certainly had no intention of courting Miss Howard.

As James examined the cut-crystal glass, an idea suddenly came to him, so simple yet brilliantly amusing. George was determined to meddle with yet another scheme. Why not catch him up in one of James's devising, give him a friendly taste of his own medicine?

'Perhaps you're right. I should give more thought to the idea of marriage,' James announced, strolling back to the table and scrutinising the position of the balls.

George's smile broadened. 'Indeed.'

'A man needs a woman to make a comfortable home for him.'

'One with a sense of how to run things properly.'

'The perfect mistress to complement him.'

'Exactly.'

'A woman like Miss Taylor.'

'Annette?' George sputtered. 'You must be joking.'

'I'm quite serious. She's well brought up and

pleasing to view.' James leaned over the table to take a shot, pretending not to notice George's stunned expression.

'But there's nothing there, no substance.'

'Good. It makes life less complicated.' James hit the cue ball, sending it bouncing off the side to hit the red ball. Straightening up, he worked to contain his laughter as George stared slack jawed at him.

'Annette?'

James smiled to himself, realising just how much fun this harmless revenge would be.

Chapter Four

The clock in the hallway chimed six times as Julia rushed across the marble floor, late for dinner again. Stopping outside the dining-room door, she ran her hands over her hair, tucking a loose tendril into her *coiffure*. Mary, her lady's maid, had been too busy with Annette to arrange Julia's hair so she'd done it herself, pulling it back into a more flattering bun and allowing a few curls to hang about her face. The *coiffure* was far from stylish, but it framed her features much better than Emily's plain creation. Pulling the bodice of the light-blue muslin dress lower, she hitched up the pink sash in an effort to make it appear more fashionable. The ribbon refused to co-operate, slipping back down to her waist. With a sigh of frustration, she gave up, knowing she'd dressed as well as could be expected for dinner at Knollwood, which was never a formal affair.

Until tonight. The instant Julia stepped into the dining room she remembered Emily's instructions to dress for their new guest. She'd been so distracted by planning her tactics with Simon, she'd completely forgotten.

'I'm so glad you could join us. I was afraid Knollwood business would keep you away.' Emily's high, nervous voice pulled Julia out of her momentary shock and she took in everyone's attire. Mother's deep-maroon mantua, though of an older style, suited her matronly frame while Emily and Annette's dresses were the height of London fashion. Simon wore a coat of the finest material and Uncle George and Captain Covington looked dashing in their uniforms. Plain muslin in the face of so much silk only emphasised her lack of fashion. For a moment, Julia contemplated making her excuses, feigning a headache or some other feminine nonsense, then changed her mind.

I've already made a fool of myself. No sense starving now. Throwing back her shoulders, she strode into the room.

'Yes, Knollwood business can be quite exacting, but I wouldn't dream of missing dinner.' She took her place next to Simon, across from Annette and Captain Covington.

'You look very lovely this evening,' the captain offered across the table.

'Thank you.' Was he teasing her? It was difficult to tell. His beguiling smile reminded her of the one Paul always used to flatter pretty ladies at the assembly hall.

'The affairs of Knollwood must be very demanding to make you lose track of time,' Annette mocked.

'No, I was quite aware of the time,' Julia replied coolly, annoyed by her stepcousin's condescending tone.

'Perhaps you could learn a thing or two about managing your affairs, Annette,' Simon suggested, dabbing the corners of his mouth with his napkin.

'Now you prefer bluestockings?' Annette frowned. 'I thought you felt education was wasted on women?'

'I do. It leads a woman to interfere too much in a man's business.' He fixed an icy stare on his sister, who coloured under the remark, but said nothing.

Julia sensed more to this conversation than a simple debate of female education, but having no interest in the intricacies of the Taylors' personal business, she concentrated on enjoying her meal.

'Julia, Jim was telling us the latest news from London regarding Napoleon,' Uncle George announced. 'It appears Admiral Nelson will face him before the month is out?'

The food turned to dirt in her mouth. 'Do you think so?'

'It's a very real possibility,' the captain answered with measured words, fingering the spoon next to his plate.

'Paul's ship, *HMS Pickle*, is with Admiral Nelson's fleet. He could be injured, or worse.' Her voice quavered with worry and she didn't care who heard it or what they thought.

'Even if there is a battle, *HMS Pickle* is a small ship used to send messages or fetch supplies. She won't see much action.'

'But there's still a chance Paul will be involved in the fighting?'

'There is, but let's hope if Admiral Nelson and your brother face him, the battle is quick and decisive in Britain's favour.'

His sympathetic eyes touched her and she wished they were alone so she could pour out all her worries to him. He would understand, perhaps even take her in his sturdy arms and, with tender, reassuring words, drive away all her fears for Paul.

'Admiral Nelson will lose more than a battle if he continues his indiscretion with Mrs Hamilton,' Annette added, indifferent to Julia's concerns. 'Don't you agree, Captain Covington?'

'I'm afraid I don't follow town gossip,' he answered, but Annette refused to relinquish his attention or the table's.

'Don't you find his indiscretion scandalous?'

Julia noticed the way his fingers tightened on the stem of his wine glass. 'Great men are always granted some leeway.'

'If society shunned him, then who would lead the Navy against France?' Julia demanded, irritated by Annette's prattle. 'Or would you prefer the French on our shores? Perhaps they would be more delightful in the drawing room.'

'How droll to discuss politics at dinner,' Annette sniffed. 'Captain Covington, you must tell me all about your sister's wedding.'

With a twinge of regret, Julia left the captain to Annette and focused on the dandy beside her. How could she possibly capture his interest? She couldn't simply announce the size of her inheritance and hope he took the bait. Conversation seemed the key, but since his arrival they'd barely exchanged ten words. Now she had to captivate him with witty repartee? It seemed a Herculean feat, but one she had to accomplish.

'Simon, do you ride?' she asked in her most pleasing voice. The young man turned his pointed chin over his starched cravat, staring at her as though she possessed three heads.

'Of course,' he sneered.

Julia clamped her hands together in her lap, screwing the smile on her face. 'I suppose no country ride could compare to the fashionable hour in Rotten Row?'

'On at least that point you are correct,' he lisped, returning to his meal.

Her cheeks burned with the strain of holding her smile. For a moment, the game felt like more trouble than it was worth, but the thought of having her own estate urged her on. 'You must be an excellent horseman.'

Simon's knife and fork clanked against the plate. 'I prefer the elegance of a phaeton—surely you've heard of them, even here in the country.'

She resisted the urge to empty her plate in his lap, continuing to remain charming as though nothing was amiss. 'Oh, yes. When I receive my inheritance I plan to purchase one. Perhaps you can help me select the best?'

'Your inheritance?' His bored eyes almost sparkled at the mention of money. She leaned towards him, dropping her voice.

'Yes, I receive it as soon as I'm married. Tell me about your phaeton. I imagine it is one of the finest in London.'

Just as she suspected, flattery worked. Simon puffed up at the opportunity to discuss himself. 'It's second only to the prince's.'

Despite the loss of her appetite, Julia soldiered on. 'Oh, you know the prince? How wonderful.'

'He complimented me on my rig.' Simon's voice dripped with pride.

'Please, tell me all about it.'

What followed was the most boring and tortuous hour of Julia's life as Simon described, in minute detail, his phaeton. From the corner of her eye she noticed Uncle George and Emily exchanging baffled looks. Even Captain Covington threw her a sideways glance and for a brief moment she felt ashamed of her plan. Only her mother seemed indifferent, slipping bits of food to Charlemagne, who sat on the floor next to her chair.

'The squabs are far more comfortable than the average phaeton. I had the leather dyed dark green,' Simon continued and Julia gazed up at him through her lashes, mimicking the way Annette flattered the captain. If only her dress were cut as deeply as Annette's. However, such a ploy might make her scheme too obvious.

After what felt like an eternity, Emily rose, ending dinner. 'Shall the ladies retire to the drawing room?'

Julia forced herself not to jump up and run into the adjoining room. Instead she smiled coyly at Simon as she rose. 'Perhaps we can discuss it more later?'

'Perhaps.' He didn't seem enthusiastic at the prospect.

Massaging her aching cheeks, Julia followed the other women into the drawing room. Taking *The Monk* out of her dress pocket, she situated herself on the sofa to read, hoping the others would leave her in peace. Her hope was short lived when Emily walked over to the card table near the window and shuffled the deck. 'Ladies, would you care for a game of piquet?'

'I'd love to play,' Annette announced, choosing her place at the table and taking the deck from Emily. 'I'll deal.'

Julia buried her nose in her book, pretending not to hear the invitation, even when Emily cleared her throat to gain her attention.

'Come play, Julia,' her mother gently ordered.

With a sigh, Julia put down her book and joined the others at the table.

'We're always playing in London and the stakes are often very high. Sometimes gentlemen lose a great deal at the tables,' Annette explained, dealing the cards.

'Perhaps the men of London are not very sensible, for it takes only a tiny amount of sense to know one should not bet what one cannot afford to lose.' Julia laid down a card, then chose another.

'No gentleman worth his salt would dare refuse a wager.'

'Then there must be many poor fools about the London ballrooms.'

'Do you consider Captain Covington a fool?'

Julia shrugged, trying to imagine the captain dancing, but she could only picture him gambling in some tropical den of iniquity. She fought back a laugh, struggling to keep her face a bland mask of uninterest. 'I haven't known the captain long enough to comment on the merits of his wit—however, if he lives in London, the odds are against him not being a fool.'

'I assure you, Captain Covington is no fool,' her mother interjected. 'He has proven himself a hero on more than one occasion.'

Julia didn't respond, wondering what her mother

would think if she knew about the captain's involvement with the Governor of Bermuda's widowed sister. She'd overheard Uncle George telling Paul about it once. It was quite shocking.

'How long has George known Captain Covington?' Annette asked.

'Ten years,' Mother answered. 'Captain Covington was a lieutenant on George's ship in the war against France during the First Coalition. His service was so distinguished he was given command of his own ship. He's very well travelled, Julia.'

'Is he now?' Julia barely heard her. She was too busy concentrating on which card to play next so she could lose and end the game.

'George tells me Captain Covington is a very sensible man when it comes to money, much like you, Julia,' her mother remarked, attempting to draw Julia into the conversation.

'Interesting,' Julia mumbled, disappointed by her excellent hand for it made losing very difficult.

'Captain Covington and I spoke a great deal this afternoon and it was as if we've known each other for years. We have a great deal in common for we both adore cheese,' Annette continued.

Julia selected another card and scowled for it

was a good one. 'Most men in London adore food. That's why there's so much gout in town.'

Emily coughed disapprovingly.

'London is a gourmand's paradise,' Annette insisted. 'I advised Captain Covington to hire a French chef. All the best houses have them. He's a very affable man. I'm surprised he's not married for he'd do well with a wife.'

'A man of thirty with a sensible head is a rarity these days,' Emily said more to Julia than to Annette.

'He's very handsome,' Annette added.

'Yes, he is, don't you agree, Julia?' Mother entreated.

Julia took another card and smiled to find it a bad one before she noticed the three women waiting for her response. 'Pardon me?'

Emily scowled at Julia's inability to follow the conversation. 'Captain Covington is very handsome, don't you agree?'

Yes, she did, but she was not about to admit it. 'I hadn't thought on the matter.' She rearranged her cards, needing only another bad one to lose.

'I'm told he's a very accomplished horseman,' Emily added. 'Perhaps, Julia, you could accompany Captain Covington on a ride tomorrow?'

Julia watched the rain hit the window, streaking down the panes. Without his afternoon ride, Manfred would need a good gallop. She did not relish the idea of trying to control him in a gentle trot alongside Captain Covington's mount. Hopefully the weather would clear by morning and she could take Manfred out before duty intruded on the day.

'I'm sure Uncle George will escort him if he wishes to ride.' Julia continued to study her cards, avoiding Emily's chastising scowl. 'He's better company for the captain than I am.'

'Of course nothing can compare to Rotten Row at the fashionable hour. Captain Covington promised to join me there when we return to London,' Annette said, drawing another card. Julia judged from the smile on her narrow face that Annette had a good hand. It was only a matter of moments before Julia could lose the game and put an end to this tiring conversation.

'I won. I won,' Annette announced much to Julia's great relief, though she pretended, like Emily and Mother, to be disappointed. They slid their sovereigns across the table and Annette swept the coins into her palm, making Julia wonder how someone from London with a carriage and four could covet a few crowns.

'Shall we play again?' Annette shuffled the

deck and the entrance of the men saved Julia the trouble of declining.

'Ladies, we're here to amuse you,' Uncle George announced, making his way to the card table. Simon didn't come in with the men and Julia wasn't the only one who noticed his absence.

'Where's Simon?' Annette asked, dealing the cards.

'It appears he had some pressing business in Daringford,' Uncle George explained with obvious disdain, taking Julia's place at the table.

Julia stood behind Uncle George, drumming her fingers on the back of the wooden chair, watching him arrange his hand. She felt disappointed, but also relieved at being spared another hour of Simon's pompous chatter. Unable to charm a missing man, she decided to learn more about gambling, thinking it might be the only real way to capture her stepcousin's very small heart.

James stepped into the room, his eyes seeking out Miss Howard. She didn't acknowledge him, but stood over George's shoulder watching the play. He resisted the urge to join her and initiate the intelligent conversation he now craved after a dinner spent listening to Miss Taylor's vapid gossip. However, showing Miss Howard too much attention would only make George more determined in his matchmaking efforts. Instead he walked to the sofa and picked up the small book lying open on the cushions.

James examined the cover of *The Monk*, then held it up. 'Miss Taylor, I believe you left your novel here.'

'That is mine.' Miss Howard crossed the room, gesturing for the book.

'I wouldn't have guessed you one for Gothic novels,' he quipped. He expected her to read dry tracts on crops, not notorious novels. What other passions lay hidden beneath her quiet exterior?

'You think a woman who manages an estate can't enjoy novels?'

She took the offered tome and her fingers brushed his, sending a shock through him. She must have felt it, too, for he noticed the slight hint of a blush under the scattering of freckles across the bridge of her nose.

'Not at all. What other books have you enjoyed?'

She sat down on the sofa, looking as though she wasn't sure if she should tell him. A single ringlet teased the soft sweep of her jaw and the flickering candlelight caressed the fine line of her cheeks. 'I recently finished Edward Ive's *A Voyage from England to India*.'

He sat on the sofa across from her, leaning against the padded back. 'An excellent book.'

Her face brightened. 'You've read it?'

'You think a man in the Navy can't enjoy books about travel?' he teased, delighted by the easy smile it brought to her lips.

'Not at all.'

He sat forwards, his elbows on his knees. 'I read a great deal last year. Have you travelled?'

'Only as far as Portsmouth. But with the way Mr Ives describes India, I know one day I will have to see it.'

Her face lit up at the prospect of visiting India, the passionate response striking his core. She might dress like a stern governess, but he'd seen too much of the woodland nymph to be fooled. What would it be like to make her blaze with more sensuous emotions, his fingers stoking the heat simmering beneath her compliant exterior? He shifted on the sofa to cover the sudden fullness in his loins. What a powerful effect this curious young woman had on him. 'Then why not set out for Bombay?'

She laid the book on her lap with a sigh. 'A woman does not have the freedom of a man to travel.'

'Perhaps you need an adventurous husband.'

She raised one disbelieving eyebrow. 'No such creature exists.'

'Then you'll have to go alone.' He couldn't resist teasing her, delighting in the honest reaction it provoked. 'Someone of your pluck would prove quite the explorer.'

She glanced at the card table and, satisfied the others were too busy playing to notice, leaned forwards, bringing them much closer than decency allowed. He smelled the crisp scent of rosewater, noticed the slight curl of her long lashes. He chanced a brief peek at her breasts. Though well hidden by the dress's high bodice, they pressed against the blue fabric, offering a hint of the creamy skin beneath. The heaviness in his manhood increased and he dug his fingers into his thigh to keep from leaning forwards to claim her full, teasing lips.

'Do you assume because my accomplishments are unusual that I have a flagrant disregard for convention?' Her mischievous eyes dared him to respond.

He leaned closer, dropping his voice, eager to meet her challenge. 'I very much admire your accomplishments. And your disregard for convention.'

'You like unconventional women?'

'Indeed. It gives them a certain mystery.'

'Really?' She leaned closer, her heady voice and smouldering eyes tightening the desire coursing through him. 'I suppose you've met many mysterious women.'

'I've known a few.'

'Yes, your time in the Navy must have acquainted you with many ladies in many ports.'

'Julia!' Emily exclaimed.

They both turned to see everyone staring at them. He'd forgotten about the others and obviously she had, too. He expected the rebuke to make her retreat back into a compliant, self-conscious miss. Instead, she rose with all the composure of a lady of the first water.

'It was a pleasure debating with you, Captain.' Ignoring her sister-in-law's stunned face, she dipped a slow, graceful curtsy, then strode from the room. He watched her leave, captivated and impressed. Here was no Artemis, but Venus waiting for the right man to draw her out.

'She's a real spitfire, Jim.' George laughed.

'A bit too forward, if you ask me,' Miss Taylor remarked and George snorted.

'No one did, Annette.'

* * *

Julia closed her bedroom door, leaning against the smooth wood to catch her breath. Her fingers felt beneath the doorknob for the brass key and, turning it in the lock, a sense of relief accompanied the click.

What had just transpired? She didn't know, but it thrilled her as much as riding Manfred at a full gallop across the hills. What had she seen in the captain's eyes? Desire, excitement and a few more dangerous emotions she felt along the back of her spine.

She hurried to the window seat, her hands shaking as if she'd almost been caught rifling through Charles's private papers. Leaning her forehead against the cool glass, she watched the rain falling in sheets, running down the window and blurring the view of the garden. If Paul were home, she could tell him about the captain and the taunting riot of emotions tightening her stomach. He'd put a name to them, help her understand why the captain ignited her senses.

Fingering the books strewn about the upholstered window seat, she pushed aside a pamphlet on crop rotation to reveal a large book on India. Flipping through it, she examined the coloured plates of Indian gods and goddesses and the dark ladies with their almond eyes, veils and jewels. Pictures of the Mughal emperors riding their elephants, accompanied by exotic animals and splendidly dressed courtiers, decorated the pages.

The women in the paintings of the palace stretched their arms out towards the men, their breasts taut against crimson saris, their round hips hugged by the delicate fabric. The image of Captain Covington's sharp eyes, the rich tones of his voice and the heat of his fingertips brushing against hers filled her mind. There'd been a moment during their discussion when she thought he meant to kiss her.

No, I must have imagined it. The captain couldn't possibly possess an interest in her and if he did it was an entirely dishonourable one. The idea should have scandalised her, but deep down she felt flattered.

As she turned the pages, thoughts of the captain continued to dominate her mind. She imagined him sitting atop an elephant, inspecting the fields of an exotic plantation as the monsoons overtook the land, the heat and spices all coming together in his skin, hair and eyes. She pictured herself beside him, standing on a veranda overlooking the jungle. With steam rising from the hot earth, she'd run her hands up over his chest, push the jacket off his shoulders, then follow the line of his back to his waist and hips. She'd tug the white shirt from his breeches, trace the hard flesh and muscles of his stomach with her fingers, then dip lower to more sinful places.

Abandoning the book, she hurried to the wardrobe and pulled the doors open. Dropping to her knees, she felt around the bottom, behind shoes and old quilts, to a plain box near the back. She took off the lid and removed a shimmering red-and-gold silk sari, a present from Paul many years ago after his first trip to India. Slipping off her frock and the cotton chemise, she wrapped the shiny silk around her naked body. It felt glorious next to her skin and she could almost smell the curry in its deep-red sheen. She imagined the cool feel of the silk to be the monsoons washing over her, rinsing away the dust and heat of Bombay.

A flash of lightning caught her eye. She turned to see her reflection in the window as the thunder rolled overhead. She pulled her hair out of its bun and it fell over her shoulders, their creamy white colour further whitened by the dazzling sari. The way the fabric traced the curve of her thighs, hugging her breasts and hips like the alluring women in the pictures, delighted her.

Is this what the captain meant by mysterious?

Her skin tingled to discover his meaning and she wondered if the weight of him on top of her would feel as heavenly as the silk? Perhaps he'd run his hands over the firm, round line of her hips? Cup her breast like the men in another, more wicked book she'd once seen.

Suddenly the other book came to mind, the one she'd found a few years ago hidden in Paul's wardrobe. Those pages held the same almond eyes, voluptuous women and robust men, only the pictures were more intimate, sensual and forbidden. What would it be like to delight in some of those illicit poses with the captain?

She shuddered, simultaneously excited and embarrassed. What would Charles or Emily think if they knew she had such wicked thoughts or acted like a Cyprian in private?

Unwinding the sari from her body, she folded the fabric, then returned it to the box and the back of the wardrobe. She slipped on her shift, blew out the candle and settled into bed. Staring up at the dark ceiling, she wondered if she should have set her cap at the captain instead of Simon. Lightning flashed, branding the twisted shadow of the oak tree outside across the ceiling before the room went black. Like the shadow, the idea of pursuing the captain gave her a small shock of fear. He acted on her nerves like no man had ever done before, the effect both thrilling and terrifying. If she played her game with him, could she jilt him? Would he let her?

Sitting up, she bunched the flatness out of her pillow. Of course he'd let her jilt him. Hadn't he spent the entire meal entranced with Annette, making his preference for her stepcousin clear? He'd only showed an interest in her when she'd acted like a strumpet. In the future, she must behave like a perfect lady in his presence.

She rolled over, pulling the blanket up under her chin and nestling into the warm mattress. Another bolt of lightning illuminated the room, followed by a deep roll of thunder. The steady plunk of rain hitting the window lulled her to sleep, weaving into her dream about monsoons falling on thick jungles, swelling the river roaring past the grassy bank where she stood, Captain Covington at her side.

Chapter Five

'Thoughts of a certain someone keep you up last night?' George nudged James as they made their way down to the stables. The clouds had cleared overnight and though everything was wet, there was no hint of rain in the brisk morning air.

James laughed, pulling on his riding gloves. 'I never thought you for a romantic.'

'We all have our secrets.'

'What secrets are you hiding?'

'Never mind.' George adjusted his white cravat. 'What exactly were you two so intently discussing?'

'Travel.'

'Who knew it was such an engrossing subject.'

'Very.' James didn't elaborate, for once not wanting to discuss a lady with George. His tête-à-tête with Miss Howard had disturbed him far more than he wanted to admit. He'd seen her surprise when she realised she wasn't properly dressed for dinner and had expected her to flee the room. When she'd determinedly crossed the threshold, he'd silently applauded her decision to stay. Then, during their exchange, the low cadence of her voice and her irrepressible enthusiasm made him feel again like a carefree young naval officer.

James slapped the riding crop against his tall boot. What was he now? A crippled man fit only to languish in the country, the past hounding the unfilled hours, the future torturing him with its emptiness. He'd come so far since his first days in the Navy, the prospect of advancing to commodore discussed more than once with the Admiralty. Not until the bullet struck him had he realised how fast fate could crush a man.

Near the stables they came upon Mr Taylor. Dark circles hung under his red eyes and his clothes, normally as fine as five pence, were ruffled as if he had spent the night in them.

'Simon, fancy a morning ride?' George asked, much to James's surprise. He planned to inspect the Cable Grange land and didn't want any additional company. But sensing George's eagerness to give his stepnephew a difficult time, James didn't object to the invitation.

'I have no interest in a ride,' Simon sneered, trying to slink past them, but George refused to be put off.

'Come, some fresh air will do you good.' He threw his large arm around Simon's slight shoulders, directing him back to the stables, much to Simon's visible displeasure.

The stables occupied a flat parcel of land hidden from view of the house by a small grove of trees. Crossing the paddock, George led them inside where the groom sat polishing a saddle.

'John, please help Simon find a suitable mount,' George instructed, pushing Simon at the man.

'Yes, Captain Russell,' John answered. 'If you'll follow me, Mr. Taylor, I have just the animal for you.'

'Happy to see me, Percy?' George stood at the first stall, running a hand over his horse's chestnut mane. 'Choose any you like, Jim. They're all some of the finest horseflesh in the county. Another of Julia's accomplishments.'

'Yes, an impressive collection.' James walked down the line of horses, trying to decide which to ride. All the stallions impressed him, but none so much as the black one in the last stall. Here was the darkest, largest, most sinister horse he'd ever seen. He recognised it as the animal Miss

Howard had ridden when she'd surprised him in the woods.

'That's Manfred. Miss Howard's horse,' John offered with pride. 'She jumps him when she has a mind, too.'

James moved to rub the horse's massive neck, but it backed up, its eyes wide and wild. 'If I hadn't seen her riding him myself, I'd say he's too much animal for such a young lady.'

'If he's truly too much animal, Captain Covington,' a soft female voice sang from behind him, 'I'm sure we can find an even-tempered gelding for you.'

James turned to see Miss Howard watching him, a challenging smile decorating the corners of her full lips. She wore a stylish dark-blue riding habit, well tailored to her petite figure. The same saucy air she'd captivated him with last night made her cheeks glow, igniting his blood. The image of her beneath him on a fresh mound of hay, the golden morning sun illuminating the pink tones of her flesh while his fingers undid the long row of buttons on the back of her habit, teased his already aching body.

'I'm sorry if I've given offence, Miss Howard. It's not my intention,' he apologised, letting the image of the soft velvet sliding from her shoulders linger for just a moment longer before forcing it away. 'I'm merely surprised such a beast is suitable for a lady.'

She walked past him, rubbing the horse lovingly on the nose, taming the fire in the creature's eyes.

'Or do you think the lady is unsuitable for the horse?' she challenged with a sly grin, the playful curve of her lips exciting him more than he cared to admit. 'Would you like to ride him?'

James examined the beast, hesitant. One throw might undo the last year of recovery. However, something in the way the little Artemis challenged him made the risk irresistible.

'May I?'

'If you think you can handle him. He'll need a firm rider since he didn't have his afternoon exercise yesterday.'

James flexed his left hand, feeling the loss of strength more keenly than ever before. He shouldn't ride. He should admit he couldn't handle the beast and decline like a reasonable man, but this morning he didn't feel like being reasonable. 'I've handled a ship in a storm. I can handle a horse.'

'If you like.' She stepped back, motioning for John to take control of Manfred.

'Good luck to you, sir. Thrown off everyone

who's tried to ride him, 'cept Miss Julia and Mr Paul Howard,' John remarked, leading Manfred out of the stall. The horse strained against the harness with pent-up energy and James balled his left hand.

'Shall we?' James waved towards the paddock.

Following Miss Howard outside, he admired the gentle sway of her hips as she strode into the sunlight, realising there was more to her than exuberant youth. She possessed a firm determination he admired, even if others in society did not.

John led an agitated and now saddled Manfred into the yard, ending all of James's pleasant thoughts. George, sitting astride Percy, shot him a questioning look, but James brushed it aside, his attention firmly focused on the beast. He'd never shrunk from a challenge, but if the horse proved too difficult to manage, the idea of being thrown in front of such an audience held no appeal. Unconsciously, he touched his shoulder.

'You aren't afraid, Captain? Are you?' Miss Howard teased, her capricious smile steeling James's resolve.

'What's to fear? He's only a horse and I've certainly faced worse.' James took the reins and Manfred shook his head, pawing at the packed dirt. 'Easy, boy.'

He stroked the horse's neck, cautious of the animal's dark, wild eyes. Manfred settled down long enough for James to step into the saddle. Ignoring the throbbing in his left shoulder, he gripped the reins with both hands in an effort to hide his weakness. Once comfortably astride, James shot Julia a surefire grin.

'I told you I could handle him.'

No sooner were the words out of his mouth than Manfred, contemptuous of a foreign rider, bucked. James clamped his thighs tight against the animal, determined to stay in the saddle. Manfred landed hard on all fours, then bolted, shooting out of the paddock. The countryside flew by, the wind more cutting than the pebbles and mud kicked up by Manfred's hooves. James sat back in the saddle, choked up on the reins and pulled hard, but the beast fought him. Gritting his teeth at the searing pain tearing through his shoulder, James seesawed the reins until Manfred, tired from his exertion, had no choice but to relent. Slowing down, Manfred trotted in a circle, breathing fast and snorting before finally coming to a halt.

James bent over in the saddle and closed his eyes, the pain in his shoulder making him dizzy. His right hand shook from fatigue and his thighs burned when he eased his hold on the beast's flanks. With a deep breath, he straightened and allowed his body to relax. The throbbing in his shoulder subsided to a dull ache and he opened his eyes, amazed by how much ground they'd covered.

'Well done, Manfred!' James shouted, his excitement echoing off the nearby hills. He laughed hard for a long time, the thrill of the ride charging him like St Elmo's fire. He'd experienced the same feeling once before during a hurricane off Barbados when he'd manned the helm after the rigging broke loose and knocked out the helmsman.

'Now I see why your mistress enjoys riding you. Perhaps there is some excitement in the country after all.' Still laughing, he slapped Manfred on the neck. 'Come, let's return to your lady. I think she'll be surprised.'

The horse's ears twitched and the animal settled into a challenging but manageable trot. They returned to the paddock, greeted by the cheers and shouts of the gathered crowd. Word of his daring ride must have spread among the servants for there were double the number of grooms and stable hands than before and James noticed a fair bit of blunt changing hands. Even George caught a coin flipped up from John. It wasn't the first time

James had found himself the subject of a wager, but today it held a certain triumph intensified by Miss Howard's impressed eyes.

She stood away from the others in the shade of the stable, clapping her gloved hands in congratulations.

He manoeuvred Manfred next to her, clucking him to a stop. 'An enjoyable beast, Artemis. No trouble at all.'

With an impish smile, she tapped his right hand with her riding crop. 'Then perhaps you should loosen your grip.'

Releasing his tight hold, he knew she'd caught him out, but he didn't mind. Having controlled the horse and proven his mettle made the experience worth the agony he'd surly endure tonight.

Manfred snorted, stepping back and forth. 'Whoa,' James soothed, calming him with a quick tug of the reins.

'Jim, if you're done playing with Manfred, then let's be off,' George joked, guiding Percy towards the bridle path. Simon's gelding fell into step behind Percy, much to its rider's visible displeasure.

James nodded at Miss Howard, who curtsied in return, her upturned face and playful smile calling to him. He wanted to pull her up behind him, dash off across the countryside with her clinging to his back, the two of them alone together. Unfortunately, such daydreams were better left to poetry and he kicked Manfred into a walk, directing him next to Percy.

'Never thought I'd see the day when anyone but Julia or Paul took Manfred's reins,' George said, impressed.

'I still can't believe the woman rides this beast.' Manfred tensed as if intending to rear, forcing James to concentrate on the animal beneath him. This would be no leisure ride for the horse would throw him if James ever let his control wane. No, he had to keep working Manfred to make him behave.

'I'm surprised to see you taking such a risk.'

'So am I,' James admitted, feeling something more than pain, bitterness and anger for the first time in months. He was careful not to revel too much in the feeling, knowing it might not last.

George led them along a path circling the woods, past newly planted fields and pastures full of grazing sheep. A wide valley stretched out around them. Beyond it, woods surrounded by neat rows of well-ploughed fields extended up into the hills. Labourers worked while the overseers stood nearby giving directions.

'They rotate the four fields to get a better crop.

Julia introduced the idea after reading about it.'
George turned in his saddle to face Simon, who'd
fallen behind. 'You could learn a lot from Julia,
Simon.'

'I doubt it.' Simon hunched over in the saddle,
shielding his eyes from the morning sun. 'I have
no interest in riding further.' He turned his horse
around and cantered off to the stables.

George moved to recall him, but James stopped
him. 'Let him go. Looks like he's been in his cups
all night.'

'You don't know the half of it.'

'Why not put a stop to it, or speak to your
brother about ending it?'

'If Simon wants to ruin himself, so be it.'

'What about Miss Taylor? Shame to let him drag
her down.'

'She has a small inheritance from her mother
and will probably catch some poor fool with a
sizeable income.'

'I hardly call myself a fool.' James puffed up
with mock indignation.

'You aren't for her.' George scowled.

They rode for some time, George relaying London gossip as they crossed meadows, streams and
fields. James listened to George's tales with half
an ear, enjoying the crisp air and the steady gait

of the horse. A few wispy clouds hung in the sky, which shone a rich shade of blue like many he'd seen during still days at sea. The chill of autumn filled the air, but it wasn't sharp or biting, and James hoped the winter cold would come late this year. After spending so much time in the dirty air of London, he craved more days like this.

'We're on Cable Grange land now,' George announced after they'd ridden a good distance.

James took in the sudden change in the landscape. The topography was the same, but the meadows showed the lack of the prosperity so evident at Knollwood. Thin, ragged sheep grazed in the meadows while the fields, many of which should have been well ploughed, stood fallow and full of weeds.

They moved from the small path to a wide country lane. The road split, one branch winding down the hill, the other sloping up to the iron gates of Cable Grange. Stopping at the fork afforded them a view of the rutted and muddy drive leading up to the main house. Even from this distance the neglect was evident in the dingy grey capstones, dirty windows and ivy-choked walls.

'Quite a difference,' James remarked.

'No revenge you could have exacted would have done what they've done to themselves.'

James didn't answer. He'd expected to find satisfaction in seeing Melinda's ruined estate. Instead he felt a certain pity for her, the emotion taking him by surprise. Maybe George was right. Perhaps the past didn't matter now.

'Let's go before someone sees us.' George turned Percy around and James followed. They had started down the road when a curricle came over the hill, slowing as it approached. James's stomach tightened at the sight of the driver and his female companion.

'Well, well, well, now of all times James Covington gets on his high horse to pay me a visit,' Wilkins sneered from his seat, taking in James and Manfred. Rowan still possessed the greasy features of a scoundrel and his dark hair, cut short, failed to enhance his thin face or hide the hard lines under his red eyes. As with his wife, London living had taken its toll. 'Here to kick me while I'm down?'

'You brought this on yourself, Wilkins.'

'Still the moralist. You'd think killing all those foreign soldiers might have taken it out of you. But I suppose you didn't come to see me.'

'No, he's not so hard-hearted, Rowan, though

he's not above bragging,' Melinda answered with a sweet smile that turned James's stomach. 'He's come to flash his blunt at the auction, show me what I missed out on all those years ago.'

'Shut up, you. We're not going anywhere,' Rowan spat.

'Of course we aren't.' Melinda laughed, then blew James a kiss. 'Have a lovely ride.'

Rowan flicked the reins, setting the curricle into motion. It tore down the drive, pitching when the wheel caught a rut before righting itself.

'Now you've seen it, do you still want it?' George asked.

'Yes.' Memories of a summer in Portsmouth twelve years ago when he'd loved a woman and she'd thrown him over for lack of a fortune taunted him. He'd been a fool to lose his heart to someone like her. Studying the crumbling stone walls and overgrown fields, he knew her decaying life should vindicate him, but he wasn't cruel enough to delight in her misery, only his own.

'It won't suit you,' George said.

'What won't?'

'The peace of the country. It'll do for a time, but eventually you'll need more adventure than just what crops to plant and when.'

'I'm done with adventure.'

'Says the man riding Manfred.' George laughed, turning Percy around.

The desire to return to sea hit him with the force of a hurricane. He craved the peace of the ocean, the gentle roll and pitch of the ship, his only concerns their position and the strength of the wind. Feeling under his jacket for the scar, bitter bile rose up in his throat, choking out everything except the throbbing in his shoulder before he forced it down. He would not let anger and longing torment him. No, he would command his feelings like he'd commanded his crew, setting a course and not allowing the fickle winds of emotion to drive him about. The sea was no longer his life and there was no use pining for it.

The small china clock on the mantel chimed the noon hour. Julia sat at her dressing table, knowing there was no way to avoid nuncheon today. Mary stood behind her, arranging her hair into a simple style. Out of the bedroom window, Julia watched Uncle George and Captain Covington ride across the meadow towards the stables.

'Are you all right, miss?' Mary asked, hearing Julia sigh.

'Yes, thank you.' *I'm having my hair done while*

the captain is riding Manfred. This would be her permanent lot if Charles and Emily had their way.

Mary hummed a soft tune while she worked and Julia's mind drifted back to the stables and Captain Covington. She hated to admit it, but he was dashing atop Manfred. She'd almost taken John's wager that the captain would be thrown, but the captain's tenacious eyes matched with the steady, fluid way he pulled himself into the saddle made her hold on to her coin. His daring reminded her of Paul, but he possessed a seriousness and maturity her brother lacked. Unlike Charles's self-imposed austerity, the captain's seemed more contemplative, as if something weighed on him. It only appeared in small flashes when he thought no one was looking, but she'd seen it more than once. Whatever it was, it failed to dampen his deep humour. She enjoyed his wit, even if she was jealous of his ability to act and display his talents without fear of rebuke. How often was she able to display hers?

'What do you think, miss?' Mary asked.

Julia examined herself in the mirror. The hairstyle was simple, but not fashionable, and the white muslin dress with the pink check obscured all hint of her figure. Even with the promise of money, dressing like a frump would not help

Simon imagine her decorating his arm at a London ball. She might not want to marry him, but she had to make him believe her suitable for society or he'd never make an offer.

'Mary, please bring down my London dresses from the attic,' Julia instructed. The gowns were no longer the height of fashion, but they'd suit her better than her current attire.

Mary's stunned eyes met Julia's in the mirror before the older servant caught herself and dipped a quick curtsy. 'Yes, Miss Howard.'

James watched Miss Howard enter the dining room, Miss Taylor's idle chatter fading away into the background. She glowed like a white sand beach on a sunny island, the sight of her as welcome as land after a long voyage. She took in the room, briefly meeting his eyes. Her face lit up, making the breath catch in his chest. He leaned forwards in his chair, ready to rise, cross the room and feel her hand on his arm while he led her to her seat. He didn't care who saw them or what they said. Let George rib him; it would be worth the teasing to enjoy the sound of her light voice.

The image shattered when her eager eyes went to Mr Taylor and she took her place next to him. James picked up his ale glass and took a long sip to cover his near move, all the while watching Miss Howard over the rim.

'Simon, did you enjoy your morning ride?' she asked.

'It was far from pleasant.' He picked at the food on his plate, his lips turned up in exaggerated disgust.

Her smile faltered before she bolstered it, but her irritated eyes betrayed her true feelings. James wondered what she was about and why she worked so hard to appeal to the dandy. Perhaps Mrs Howard desired their better acquaintance, though from everything he'd witnessed Miss Howard rarely complied with her sister-in-law's requests.

'Captain Covington,' Miss Taylor interrupted his thoughts. 'I would be happy to paint your portrait.'

'Thank you.' He continued to watch Miss Howard, feeling Miss Taylor's irritation. He tossed her a charming smile, exhausted by the constant effort involved in foiling George's matchmaking plans.

Miss Taylor started to say something and James put down his glass, leaning towards Miss Howard. 'Thank you for allowing me to ride Manfred.'

Miss Howard paused in a comment to Mr Taylor. 'You're welcome.'

'I'd like to ride him again if you don't mind.'

'Of course,' she replied off-handedly, turning back to the fop.

'Tomorrow, perhaps?'

Her perturbed eyes snapped to his. 'Any time you wish.' She returned to Mr Taylor, but James refused to let her go.

'Tell me, how did you come by such a beast?'

'Ah, now there's a story.' George laughed from the end of the table.

Miss Howard forgot her irritation, flashing what James sensed was her first genuine smile of the meal, Mr Taylor forgotten. 'It's Uncle George's fault. He bought Manfred in London.'

'I had a mind to breed warhorses when I first left the Navy,' George added between bits of meat. 'He's a Friesland and who knows what else, but steady as a rock around gunshot.'

'Certainly explains his colour and height,' James remarked. 'But how did you end up with him, Miss Howard?'

'Manfred may be steady as a rock, but he has a temper.'

'Horse dealer failed to mention it,' George admitted.

'The price alone should have made you wary,' she chided.

'Horse dealer did seem awfully eager to be rid

of him, but it's my own fault. What do I know about horses? I'm a Navy man.'

'And not one to think through any scheme.' James laughed.

'Perhaps there's some truth to it.' George clapped his hands together. 'Well, none of my men could control him, and after a fortnight I had a mind to put him out to pasture.'

'But this time, he asked my opinion first. I observed Manfred with the grooms and something about him just called to me. Uncle George's men were trying to make him behave, but they were going about it all wrong. Manfred needed a patient hand and a gentle but strong voice.'

'And you possessed both,' James complimented.

'I suppose I did, but I prefer to think it was because I believed in him when no one else did and he thanked me for it.'

'You may be right.'

Miss Howard smiled and he delighted in the dimples at the corner of her lips. For a moment, there was only the two of them in the room. Her amber eyes met his and he felt their heat deep in his body, but the moment was short lived.

'How wonderful you're such an amazing horse-woman,' Miss Taylor interrupted. 'Are you also a skilled painter?'

'I'm adept at no art except running an estate,' Miss Howard admitted with confidence and James silently cheered her for standing up to the ridiculous criticism.

'Yes, I forgot. I plan to draw in the garden this afternoon. I've asked the captain to accompany me. He even volunteered to carry my easel for it can be such a cumbersome thing.' She smiled at James, who shifted in his seat, having forgotten about his offer and wondering how he could extricate himself from it without being rude.

'I think some time outside would do us all a world of good,' Emily announced, trapping James in this bland game.

Half an hour later found everyone in the garden enjoying the unusually warm autumn weather. Even Mr Taylor deigned to drag himself outside, much to Miss Howard's visible delight.

James listened in disbelief when she complimented Mr Taylor on his excellent description of his last evening at White's.

What is she after? he wondered. Was she playing him for his money? Surely she knew he had nothing more than the ready extended by his London creditors. James shifted restlessly, hating the way she nodded, enraptured by the pretentious pink's description of a card game. He refused to admit his anger was jealousy, but there it sat, gnawing at him.

Swallowing it back, he watched Miss Taylor arrange Emily and George into a formal pose on the opposite side of the fish pond. Was this really his life now? Garden parties and flattering London chits? He kept glancing at Miss Howard. Here was a woman who would keep life interesting— if only he could tear her away from the damned coxcomb.

'Should I pull my arm in my sleeve?' George joked once Miss Taylor returned to her canvas. 'I may not be as handsome or slender, but I think I might make a good Nelson.'

Everyone laughed except Miss Taylor, who sketched with her charcoal, and Mr Taylor, who took a pinch of snuff from his silver snuffbox with an affected flourish.

'Rather shameful, the Admiral continuing in such a ruined state,' Mr Taylor lisped. 'Hardly speaks well of Britain to have such a specimen leading our Navy.'

James almost leaned over and punched the idiot in his pursed mouth. If they'd been at White's he'd have called him out, but for the ladies' sake he allowed the comment to drop.

Miss Howard, despite her newfound infatuation, refused to let it stand. 'I think it very fitting he continue. It shows weakness in a man not to carry on after an injury, if he can.'

The remark hit James like a cudgel to the chest. 'Do you extend that opinion to all Navy men, or just Admiral Nelson?'

'All Navy men. If every sailor with a cut or scrape retired we'd have no hope of winning any war.' There was no malice in the statement, just a simple declaration. He wondered if George had told her about his wound.

'What of duty to one's family? Is an only son to die at sea for no other reason than to prove he's not a coward, leaving the future of his family to the cruel whims of fate?'

'A man who chooses the Navy knows the dangers. If his family truly faces ruin then perhaps he should apprentice himself and enter a safe trade, such as tailor.'

'What if he comes home wounded to find responsibility for his mother and sister upon his shoulders?' James flexed his left hand, the memory increasing the pain in his shoulder.

'I cannot speak for every man's situation, but if Admiral Nelson soldiers on then so can other brave men.'

'I think you speak a great deal about something you know nothing about,' he chastised, but she refused to back down. He had to admire the girl's courage, despite her infuriating views.

'And I think you, like most men, dislike opinionated women.' She didn't wait for his response, but turned on her heel and strode off.

'Julia, where are you going?' George said, but she didn't stop.

'I have some urgent business to attend to,' she answered over her shoulder, then disappeared inside.

Mr Taylor coughed as he took another pinch of snuff. 'As I said before, bluestockings always get in a man's business.'

James turned a hard eye on the dandy, who wilted under the harsh gaze. He had a mind to thrash the man, but even with his weak arm it wouldn't be a fair fight. Instead, he decided to enjoy the fine afternoon and have his portrait done as a Christmas present for his sister. He leaned over Miss Taylor's shoulder to admire her sketch, but, unable to keep still, he began pacing, chewing over Miss Howard's remark.

Had she just called him a coward? Did she even know about his injury? Maybe George hadn't told her. Despite George's love of gossip, he had an annoying habit of conveying worthless stories while forgetting to relay critical information, such as Melinda living next door or just how close Miss Howard was to Paul. It was a wonder George had thought to tell him about Cable Grange before the actual sale took place.

'What do you think, Captain?' Miss Taylor asked.

He paused long enough to watch her apply the first colour to the sketch. 'Excellent portrait.'

Why did he care so much about Miss Howard's opinion? It was only the assumption of an ignorant country girl with no real understanding of the world. Let her think him a coward. Once he returned to London, he'd never be troubled with her again.

'Jim, what's wrong? You're acting like a nervous hen,' George called and James finally noticed everyone's curious eyes.

'I just remembered a matter I must attend to.'

'But your portrait,' Miss Taylor protested.

'Another time, perhaps. Please, excuse me.' He bowed, then headed into the house.

Julia scratched out the last line of figures, marring the ledger page with yet another mistake. Outside, Uncle George laughed and her temper flared. Throwing down her pencil, she leaned back in the chair, watching the others laugh and pose for Annette and noticing Captain Covington wasn't with them. After this morning, she'd thought him a different type of man. Just now, he'd proven himself exactly like all other men, dismissing her opinion, then getting angry when she refused to defer to his better judgement. Of all people, he should have supported the logic of the argument, not defended a London fool.

Outside, Simon sat on the garden bench swatting at a fly.

To think my future lies in the hands of such a pathetic specimen. Reluctantly, she closed the ledger and rose. She'd allowed Captain Covington to interfere with capturing the dandy's affection. If she wanted Cable Grange, she had to continue her pursuit and secure a proposal before the auction.

The door clicked open and Captain Covington stepped into the room.

'If you mean to bait me further, please refrain. I'm in no mood for arguments,' she snapped, tense at the idea of facing him so soon after their disagreement.

'I have no intention of baiting you. I thought I might read. George said you have an excellent book on crop rotation.'

'Crop rotation?' She eyed him suspiciously, doubting his interest in the subject.

'Yes.' He fingered a small wooden figurine on the table near the door.

'It's there, on top.' She pointed to a stack of books on the table next to a large leather chair, then sat back down. Opening the ledger, she expected the captain to thank her and leave, but instead he lingered.

'Do you mind if I browse your other books?'

Julia waved her hand at the bookshelves without looking up from the ledger. 'You're more than welcome to anything in my collection.'

'Thank you.'

He walked along the row of bookshelves, examining the spines, his tension evident by the way he kept tapping the crop book against his hand. Julia tried to ignore him, shaking her head at a miscalculated line of figures. He stopped at the large, coloured atlas on the bookstand, flipping through the pages before marching to stand in front of the desk.

'Do you really think a man is a coward for retiring after being wounded?' He stood before her the way a superior officer stands in front of a line of sailors.

She fixed him with a hard stare, refusing to be cowed. 'I told you I won't be baited.'

'Surely you don't believe it applies to all men?' He walked back and forth across the carpet as though on the deck of a ship, hands behind his back, every inch the Navy officer. 'What if your brother was wounded and forced to resign his commission. Would you call him a coward?'

Julia opened her mouth to answer, but the captain raised his hand, stopping her. Irritation flared, but she forced it back. Shouting at a guest, no matter how rude he might be, was definitely a breach of etiquette.

'What if the man's father died a few years ago and the investments he left to support his wife and daughter failed, leaving his son responsible for his sister's dowry and his widowed mother's affairs?'

The strange conviction in his eyes warned her off meeting the challenge. 'I respectfully decline to answer. We obviously have a difference of opinion so I see no reason to continue the debate.'

'Then you'd insist he return?'

Julia stayed silent, the lingering sadness in his piercing eyes hinting at the truth. Had he been wounded? Is that why he'd resigned? No, it wasn't possible. Running her eyes up the length of him, admiring his trim waist, flat stomach and wide chest, he was too strong to be injured. Surely if he were, Uncle George would have said something. Perhaps he'd lost friends or maybe his father had died in debt? Whatever drove him, it emanated from somewhere deep inside and she knew to tread carefully.

'Each man must decide what is best for him,' she answered in an even voice. 'It's not up to me to make such decisions.'

The tightness in the captain's jaw eased while the feverish hunger to debate faded from his eyes. 'This is quite a room for a young lady,' he remarked, his voice softer, but no less strained than before.

'A great many people have said so,' she agreed, relieved at the fading tension. 'It was my father's. He did his business here. I saw no reason to change it.'

'Do you think your father would approve of you hiding yourself away from the world in here?'

The anger rushed back and she jumped to her feet. 'And where do you hide, Captain?'

'I don't hide.'

'Then why are you here in the country?'

He turned to the window, staring past the garden with a sense of loss she could feel. 'London wearies me.'

'Ghosts have a way of haunting a person to exhaustion,' she observed, more to herself than to Captain Covington. Why else was she so desperate to stay at Knollwood if not to hide? Who outside its walls had ever accepted her or her talents? If she lost Knollwood, she lost her life's meaning for she could see no other. Unless she secured Cable Grange.

'You think I'm haunted?'

'I can't pretend to know the full measure of your mind. I only know everyone has fears.'

'We must face our fears to overcome them.'

'Then neither of us is hiding, are we?' No longer interested in his company or conversation, she made for the door. There was work to do outside, the prospect of which suddenly tired her.

James watched her leave, stunned, the full impact of her accusation striking him. He walked to the large atlas near the window and turned the coloured pages until he came upon the familiar maps of the Atlantic and the Caribbean. With his finger he traced the shipping routes, the miles of ocean once so familiar to him. England to Africa, Africa to Jamaica, Jamaica to America, America to the coast of Spain.

He slammed the book shut. He'd faced pirates,

angry colonists, hostile natives and the French. He did not hide from his problems.

'There's one.' James pointed at a duck flying up out of the tall grass along the edge of the lake.

George took aim and fired, but the bird continued its ascent and flew off. 'Missed another one. I think I'd do better with a cannon and grapeshot today.'

'Perhaps,' James concurred, finding little humour in the joke. He'd joined George in the hopes the fine afternoon would take his mind off his shoulder and his irritation. After more than an hour of walking through tall grass or watching the sun reflect off the lake, he still felt tense and plagued by pain.

George handed the empty gun to a waiting footman and took a new one. 'Are you sure you won't shoot?'

'Not after this morning's exertion.' He rolled his shoulder, trying to ease the ache, but it didn't help. No doubt he'd strained it by showing off this morning and it nagged at him as much as Miss Howard's comments in the study.

They picked through the mud and damp of the marshy bank before George aimed at another bird rising from the reeds and fired. The duck crumpled in midair, falling with a splash into the lake. A dog bounded past them, flinging itself into the water and swimming excitedly towards the carcass.

'Excellent shot,' James muttered, unable to rouse much enthusiasm.

'What's got you so glum?'

'Nothing.' James stomped off, his boots sinking in the soft dirt, George close on his heels.

'If you say so.'

'Did you tell Julia about my injuries?'

'No.'

'Why not?'

'It's not my place to choose who to tell. That's your decision.'

So she didn't know. It explained her strong opinion, but not her remark about him hiding. 'Would you say I hide from problems?'

'I've never known you to back down from a challenge.'

'But do I hide from them?'

George thought for a moment. 'Other people's or your own?'

'My own, of course.' He didn't like the sound of this last question. 'Miss Howard is under the impression I hide from problems.'

'Do you?'

'Of course not.' George's inability to directly answer led him to believe Miss Howard might be right. 'Though I suppose it depends on the problem.'

George laid his gun over his shoulder and stared at the ground, thinking while he walked. 'Jim, a man goes to sea for a number of reasons. I was a second son, I had to make my way and the Navy appealed to me. You joined to avoid a career in law.'

'You know I had no interest in it.'

'But your mother did.'

'She thought I'd make an excellent barrister. There was quite a row the night I informed her I'd purchased a commission. Mother is very formidable once she sets her mind to something.'

'Yes, I know.' George chuckled.

'How do you know?'

'From everything you've told me, of course,' George stammered, tugging on the sleeves of his coat. 'So you escaped the law.'

'You could say that.'

'And you accepted my invitation to the country to escape London.'

'I wouldn't say "escape".' James ran his hand over the back of his neck, seeing George's point all too clearly. 'But two instances hardly make me a coward.'

'You're no coward. I've seen you in enough battles to know. But what man doesn't sidestep a problem now and then? I've been known to turn tail a few times myself. Why do you think I never married? But seriously, there's a lot of unpleasant business in life. We deal with it as we can. You and I have seen enough of it in all corners of the world. Julia, she's seen her share here and in London. A brave man faces what he can, but no one has the strength to face it all. You're no coward, but, like all men, you have your weaknesses.'

James flexed his hand, admiring the peaceful green hills of Knollwood rising in the distance. 'Is my weakness so obvious?'

'I wouldn't call it a weakness and I'm amazed Julia mentioned it, though of all people she'd be the first to recognise it.' A suggestive twinkle replaced the pondering thoughtfulness in George's eyes. 'Why do you care what my niece thinks? I thought you had no interest in her?'

The urge to escape suddenly gripped James. 'I don't. I only wondered at what she said, nothing more.'

'Then it's settled. You're no coward and you

have no interest in my niece. Now, let's head back. I have business to take care of before dinner.'

James followed George through the high grass to where the horses stood tethered to an old post, his mind far from clear. Why did he care so much about Miss Howard's opinion if he wasn't interested in her? He couldn't lie to himself. She intrigued him with her disregard for convention and her bold, adventurous spirit. However, her interest in Mr Taylor, combined with her disdain for wounded naval officers, infuriated him.

Would she change her opinion if she knew about his shoulder? He flexed his left hand. It was useless to ponder. She had no interest in him and there was no point pursuing such a woman. Besides, Miss Taylor now expected his attention and, despite her annoying simpering, he couldn't be rude.

He mounted Hector, the stallion he'd chosen to ride, and gritted his teeth with the effort of pulling himself into the saddle. Once astride the brown horse, he settled into the seat, his grip light on the reins. The animal was so well trained, it took little but a tap of his foot or pressure from his legs to control it. With such an easy horse beneath him, he couldn't resist the solitude and freedom of wide open fields.

'You go back to the house. I'm going for a ride.'

'I think a storm is coming in.' George pointed at the dark clouds hovering on the horizon.

'It doesn't matter.' James dug his heels into the stallion's sides and the animal tore off over the grassy field.

Julia hurried across the paddock, the wind playing with the bottom of her habit and scattering leaves across the path. She'd made absolutely no progress with Simon. The minute she'd returned to the garden, he'd pleaded a headache and went to his room to lie down. Emily then cornered her with an impromptu drawing lesson from Annette. It resulted in nothing but a mangled green blob meant to resemble a tree and the urge to dump the paints in her sister-in-law's lap.

Thankfully, baby Thomas's nurse appeared with the crying infant, freeing Julia from Emily's attempts at female education. Pleading the same headache as Simon, Julia fled to the quiet of her room to read. However, with the weather holding and the daylight fading, she knew this would be her only chance for a ride before dinner.

'Good afternoon, Miss Howard,' John greeted, brushing down one of the horses.

'Saddle Manfred,' Julia called out, hurrying

past him down the line of stalls. 'Use the standard one.'

'Yes, Miss Howard.'

While John went to work, Julia slipped into the small closet at the back of the stable. Pushing the lid off the large chest on the floor, she pulled out the horse blankets to reveal an oilcloth-wrapped bundle. Untying it, she lifted out the special riding habit crafted of dark-blue wool. Removing her regular habit, she donned the other garment. When walking it hung like a skirt, but the excess fabric hid the trouser-like design sewn into the dress. Julia had paid John's wife to sew it and for a tidy profit she also kept it laundered and mended.

Once dressed, she grabbed *The Monk* from the regular habit's pocket and hurried to where John stood holding Manfred.

'Watch the clouds,' John advised, helping her up into the saddle. 'You don't want to be caught out in a storm.'

'I'll be careful.' Julia kicked Manfred into a steady gallop, directing him east.

They followed the valley down to a small brook and across a crude wooden bridge constructed to herd sheep back from pasture. The land on the other side flattened out, leading to another higher hill visible in the distance. Julia pointed Manfred at it and horse and rider moved seamlessly past a large lake, another small forest, and through a herd of sheep scurrying to make way for them.

During afternoon rides, Julia and Manfred usually ambled so she could take in the condition of the sheep, the walls, the fences, the height of the river, all the things so important to running the estate. Today she had no interest in business, only the desire to be alone.

They approached the next hill and she slowed Manfred to a walk, guiding him up the rocky path to the stone keep commanding the top. It was a Norman relic, abandoned ages ago by men who no longer mattered. She loved coming here for its lichen-covered stone walls offered a solitude she sometimes failed to find at Knollwood. Guiding Manfred alongside a large stone wedged into the ground, she slid off his back, her boots gripping the coarse surface. Pulling *The Monk* from her pocket, she tossed the reins up over his back, leaving him free to graze on the sweet grass covering the ancient site. He never wandered far and she was safe to steal an hour alone among the ruins.

Inside the old tower, she picked her way up the narrow stone staircase, her left hand clutching the book, her right hand tracing the wall as it rose up towards the battlements. At the top, she stepped out on to the last of the rampart, taking in the view of Knollwood and some of Creedon Abbey. Thick, menacing clouds covered the horizon while birds criss-crossed her view, arching and rolling as they chased each other.

A small alcove in the stones sheltered her from the wind and she settled in with her book, tucking the length of the riding habit about her legs for warmth. She opened *The Monk* and began to read, the sound of Manfred's whinny mingling with the warble of birds and the whistles of the wind through the grass. She devoured the descriptions of far-off places she'd probably never see, and frustration plagued her, subtly at first, but growing stronger with each new line. She snapped the book shut and tilted her head back to look at the sky, breathing in the heavy smell of rain and noting the dark clouds floating overhead. Today, her future seemed dim and bleak, the chances of obtaining her inheritance in time to purchase Cable Grange an impossible feat. What future could she hope for without her own estate? Perhaps she could live with Paul and keep house for him? Even then she wouldn't be free, but tethered to the whims and demands of Navy life and open to the gossip of vicious people who would wonder why she wasn't married.

Why is everyone so concerned with what I do? she thought, picking a piece of moss off the wall. She'd never crossed the lines of propriety and in public she always acted like a proper young lady, even if she did occasionally wear her riding habit to town. Yes, she preferred riding to the pianoforte, but Father had always encouraged the exercise and besides, every unconventional thing she did was always done among family who understood her. Or did they? Obviously Charles and Emily didn't. No, in their minds she was a veritable Jezebel for riding without a groom or preferring the business of an estate to the latest fashions. They were more concerned with the opinion of the few local families who laughed at Julia's strange habits, but dismissed them as nothing more than eccentricities. After all, her father and mother were, in their own ways, eccentric. Why should Julia be any different?

A hawk screeched and she watched the bird float on the up draught, searching the field for prey. If only she could be more conventional and refined like the other young ladies in the county. How many times had she tried and failed? After all, she couldn't spend days painting screens when the entire fortune of an estate rested on her shoulders.

The hoofbeats of an approaching horse echoed through the keep.

Am I never to have a moment's peace? she fumed, peering over the battlement and spying Captain Covington approaching. Ducking down behind the stone, she cursed her luck. Of all the people to happen upon her, did it have to be him?

'Manfred? Where's Miss Howard?' he asked in an anxious voice.

She thought of staying hidden, but she didn't want him to worry. Gripping the rough wall, she pulled herself into view. 'I'm here.'

He looked up at her, his dark hair falling back off of his forehead. Her heart skipped a beat at the sight of him atop the chestnut stallion. Dressed in the same hunting clothes he'd worn in the forest, their brown tones warmed his face and softened the line of his jaw. For a brief moment she wished she could draw so she could capture the way the greying light caressed his features.

'What a relief. When I saw him alone, I thought something had happened.' He rose up in the saddle to dismount.

'Stop there,' Julia demanded. 'If you're as contentious as you were at nuncheon, then leave now. I've had enough of irritable people for one day.'

Instead of sitting, he swung his leg over the

horse and dropped to the ground. 'You're a very direct young lady.'

'And quite serious.' She crossed her arms over her chest.

'I promise to be pleasant and cheerful.' He placed his hand on his heart, bowing deferentially, then snapping up into a formal military stance. 'Permission to come aboard.'

The stories she'd heard about him demanded a refusal, but they also fuelled her curiosity. If nothing else, here was her chance to discover the truth behind Uncle George's tales. Emily would faint if she discovered them alone, but if the captain kept this meeting a secret, then what was the harm in conversing? 'Granted. Tie Hector to the post.' She pointed at the ruins of an old fence near the keep's entrance.

He wrapped the horse's reins around the mouldering wood, then made his way inside, taking the stairs two at a time before stepping out on to the rampart. Julia admired the steady, sure way he crossed the ledge.

'I'm surprised to find you here,' he remarked.

'I often come here to be alone.'

'Then I apologise for intruding on your solitude.'

'It does not matter.' Julia leaned against the

short wall, admiring the view and struggling to appear indifferent despite the strange nervousness creeping through her. The captain leaned next to her, resting his elbows on the stones, the nearness of him making her jittery excitement worse.

'This is an impressive place.' His eyes scanned the landscape and for the first time she noticed the small lines about his mouth.

'Indeed.' She moved closer into his circle of warmth and for a brief moment considered slipping into the crook of his body, out of the wind and damp air.

'Are all Uncle George's stories true?' she asked, eager to break the awkward silence and distract herself from Captain Covington's warm body.

'What do you know?'

'I know about his liaison with the plantation owner's wife, the rum running and your dalliance with the governor's sister.'

Captain Covington threw back his head and laughed. 'Yes, it's all true and then some, for I doubt he told you everything.'

'He told me enough. You have quite a reputation, Captain.'

'Me? No, I take no responsibility. It was all George's doing.'

'Including the governor's sister?'

The corners of his lips pulled up. 'I assure you, the story was exaggerated.'

'Why didn't you marry her?'

He sobered, but not enough to remove the wicked smile. 'We were not suited for marriage. Nor was the lady inclined. It seemed she'd had enough of husbands and very much liked her freedom.'

For a moment Julia envied the woman, especially her intimacy with the captain. What she wouldn't give to have such control over her life and enjoy someone like him without censure. 'What of your other adventures with Uncle George?' she asked, trying to distract her wandering mind.

'Some were true. I leave it to you to discover which ones.'

'Then you admit you went along.'

'Only to keep a very good friend out of trouble.'

'And to make a bit of profit.'

'In that regard I am guilty.'

'I envy your grand adventures.'

'Do not envy them. They weren't all grand.' He straightened, rubbing his left shoulder, a scowl darkening his features.

A gust of wind hit the keep, pulling a strand of Julia's hair loose. Tucking it behind her ear, she noticed the thickening clouds moving faster across the sky. It was time to ride back, but she wasn't ready to leave. Emily would scold her if they got caught in the rain, but she no longer cared. What did any of it matter—propriety, etiquette—if one were always confined to this small corner of the world? Julia sighed and the captain turned a curious eye on her.

'Something troubles you?'

She shook her head, wondering how much to confide in him. In many ways he reminded her of Uncle George or Paul, of someone who would listen without judgement. But for all his resemblances, he was still a stranger. 'I wish I could be more like Annette,' she admitted, throwing convention to the wind.

'Do not envy her. She has nothing you don't possess.'

'Except perfect manners.'

'Your manners are not so very imperfect.'

'But they're not polished enough for my brother or Emily or most of the countryside.' She picked a small stone off the ledge and hurled it over the edge. It arched in the air before dropping to the grass with a soft thud. 'I don't shun propriety, Captain. I do my best to follow Emily's suggestions, only—'

'—they're always at odds with your nature.'

Yes, he was very much like Paul and Uncle George. 'It was different when Father was alive. He didn't mind if I wore the wrong dress or went riding alone in the mornings.'

'And your mother?'

'She's quite content with her roses and Charlemagne. She loves me, but doesn't fret like Charles and Emily. They don't realise how much I try to behave. They think I'm like Paul and being contrary for the sake of being contrary. Charles believes because it's so easy for him to be proper that it's easy for everyone. He's turned into a dreadful, puritan bore.'

'I wouldn't call Charles a puritan,' the captain snorted.

'What do you mean?' What did he know about Charles that she didn't?

'Nothing. I was only thinking of your brother Paul. I'm sorry if I confused the two.'

'Oh, yes, well, Paul certainly doesn't follow convention. But he's a man and allowed to do as he pleases.' She turned back to the view, her world suddenly feeling small. 'Paul is out there having adventures and Charles is in London, making great speeches and deciding my future.'

'No one decides your future unless you let them.'

'Those are the words of a man who can make his own choices and live as he pleases.' She reached back, tucking the waving strand of hair into the loose bun.

'Men don't always live as they please. Sometimes they live as they must,' he responded with some resignation.

'Even then you have choices,' she encouraged, willing him to be strong. If a man like him gave in to fate, what chance did she have?

He moved to object before his lips spread into a smile. 'You don't strike me as a young lady resigned to someone else deciding her future.'

She picked at the stone wall. 'Perhaps, but for the moment, here I am.'

James watched her work loose a pebble, her face bereft of a smile. No, she was not a woman to give up, no matter what she might say. She would continue to strive, to struggle, to fight for what she wanted. 'Where would you be if you could be somewhere else?'

'India. Paul gave me a book about it once. It seems so magical. Have you been to India?'

'Once, a long time ago.'

'Was it magical?'

He turned to her, admiring the excitement of

youth and innocence reflected in her eyes. While he pined for what he'd lost, she waited to hear about what she might never experience. Suddenly his sadness seemed self-indulgent, giving him a new appreciation for his past. 'Yes, it was. Blazing white palaces crowded with men and women in dazzling colours. The air so thick with curry and moisture, you feel as though you could slice it with a sword.'

'Paul brought me curry powder once. I gave it to cook and she didn't know what to do with it. She put it in the chicken and the house reeked of it for days. It's like nothing I've smelled or tasted before. Would you go there again?'

He watched a pair of deer race through the high grass before disappearing into a thick clump of trees. Would he go back? There was nothing to stop him. He could go there and a hundred other places he longed to see. He thought of Paris, Vienna and Venice and for a moment pictured himself walking through the ancient city, Miss Howard by his side. The image startled him though it wasn't an entirely unpleasant idea. 'Yes, I would.'

'I wish I could go.' The wind pulled a small curl across her cheek.

'Perhaps some day you will.' He tucked the

strand of hair behind her ear, allowing his fingers to linger at the nape of her neck. She didn't pull away. Instead her eyes held his with nervous anticipation. He stepped closer and her head tilted up invitingly. He felt her rapid pulse through the warm skin beneath his fingertips and was close to claiming her soft, parted lips when a loud clap of thunder broke overhead.

A sudden gust of wind pungent with rain swept past them, ruffling the skirt of her habit.

She stepped away from him, an awkward blush colouring her cheeks. 'We'd better get back before it rains.'

He didn't want to leave, but he couldn't object. Staying alone together here was dangerous and he possessed no desire to expose her to vicious gossip or her sister-in-law's criticism. To compromise her in such a way would only confirm Julia's previous suspicions about him and he very much wanted her good opinion.

Julia followed the captain down the stone steps, watching his broad shoulders lead the way through the tower's deep shadows. He'd almost kissed her. She'd almost allowed him to kiss her. She stopped in the middle of the staircase, fear gripping her. How could she have been so weak? It was unlike her to lose her head over a gentleman, especially one with questionable intentions.

At the bottom he hopped off the last step, turning to help her down. 'Is something wrong?'

'No, not at all.' She hurried down the stairs, taking his offered hand and allowing him to help her. She delighted once again in the feel of it, the strength and warmth. Their eyes met as a bolt of lightning cracked overhead followed by a deep roll of thunder.

'We'd better hurry.' He pulled her towards the horses.

Julia grabbed Manfred's reins and led him next to the large stone. She saw the captain's surprise when she threw her leg over Manfred's back, revealing the trousers in the riding habit.

'Very clever.'

'Please don't tell Emily.'

'Your secret is safe with me.' He winked, then swung into the saddle, pain flashing across his face before he settled his feet in the stirrups.

She was about to ask if he felt well when another heavy blast of wind hit them, flattening the tall grass and scattering bits of earth and leaves.

'Do you think we can outrun the storm?' he called over the gust.

'I think we should try.' Digging her heels into

Manfred's flanks, she shot off down the hill. In seconds the captain was next to her, leaning over Hector's neck, spurring him on. Remembering the way he'd ridden this morning, she pushed them hard, guiding them around trees and boulders and over the crest of hills. She avoided the hedges, not knowing the captain's capacity for jumping, but she couldn't resist leaping the small gully. Though Hector was no match for Manfred, the captain never let up or veered off course. He urged the stallion up and over the rushing water, meeting her on the other side, his wide smile revealing his excitement. Her heart skipped a beat at the sight of his exuberant face and she kicked Manfred back into a gallop. The captain followed, his body matching Hector's gait with satyr-like fluidity.

The horses were fast, but the storm moved faster. She could have ridden for ever with the captain, but the icy rain fell hard, pouring down her hair and soaking her back. With visibility declining, she guided them on to a wide country lane. Racing around a bend in the road, the horse's hooves kicked up mud from the deep puddles, the rain matting their manes against their necks. The captain's speed did not waver as he kept pace with her. Water dripped from his chin and his keen eyes watched the road, at intervals meeting hers with an intensity as highly charged as the lightning.

The glowing windows of Knollwood came into view through the deluge and the captain followed Julia down away from the house to the stables. She pulled Manfred to a halt in the yard, the captain drawing Hector up alongside them. She breathed hard, every inch of her wet, her fingers aching with cold, but she didn't care. The exhilarating ride warmed her, as did the captain's blazing eyes. Large drops of water dripped off the wet hair matted against his forehead, sliding down his cheeks, tracing the fine sinew of his neck before disappearing beneath his collar. His charging pulse beat against the exposed skin, echoing the steady rhythm in her chest. She wrapped the reins around her fingers as he leaned hard on one hand, tilting towards her and she leaned closer, noticing the small beads of water sticking to his eyelashes. He was exactly as she'd imagined him in her dream about the monsoon, his chest rising and falling with each deep breath.

The wind cut a sharp line through them and Julia shivered.

'We'd better get inside,' the captain yelled over the pounding rain. Julia nodded, water running into her eyes as she walked Manfred into the warmth of the stable.

'I'm glad to see you back. I was getting worried.' John rushed to take Manfred's reins and help her down.

'I'll only be a moment,' she called to the captain, then slipped into the small room. Stripping off her soaked riding habit, she hung it on a hook, knowing John's wife would see to its cleaning like she always did. She wrung out the bottom of her chemise then pulled the dry habit over her damp stays and hurried out of the room to where Captain Covington waited by the open stable door. Water dripped from his coat, pooling on the hard-packed dirt.

'Should we wait it out?' he asked, pushing the wet hair off his face. The rain fell in thick sheets on the paddock with no sign of letting up.

'No. Wet or dry, I'm sure to receive a tongue lashing for this.'

'Then we'd better hurry. The sooner it begins the sooner it may end. After you.'

She ran past him into the downpour and in two large strides he was next to her. They rushed up the small hill, but she stumbled, her boot sticking in the mud. He grabbed her by the elbow, pulling her free and into the grove of trees. Lightning split the sky and the air crackled with electricity, the deep roll of thunder vibrating in Julia's chest.

'Perhaps we should go back to the stable until it passes,' the captain suggested, pulling her closer, his hand protectively on her arm.

Julia gauged the distance between the house and the stable, seeing no safe, clear path in either direction. 'No, we're halfway there. We might as well keep going.'

'Come along, then. I have no desire to be struck by lightning.' He slipped his hand in hers and pulled her out of the trees. She hung on tight, his strength soothing some of her fear during their mad dash over the gravel path and up the back portico.

Another lightning bolt cracked overhead as the captain closed the French door behind them. He followed Julia laughing and dripping into the hall at the front of the house, wet footprints trailing them across the stone floor.

'Maybe we should have stayed in the stable.' Julia smiled, shaking the water off her skirt.

'No. I enjoyed our adventure, even if I won't dry out for a week,' he laughed, wiping his hands on his soaked trousers.

'Julia, Captain Covington.' Emily's voice echoed off the walls. Julia whirled around to see her standing at the top of the stairs, her delicate face red and her pale eyes dark. 'What is the meaning of this?'

'We were caught in the rain.' Julia shifted from foot to foot, her stockings squishing in her half-boots.

'Forgive me, Mrs Howard. It was my fault. I allowed Miss Howard to dally on our ride and the storm came upon us faster than we anticipated.'

'And was the groom with you? No, he wasn't because John came to the house looking for Julia after it started to rain,' Emily answered before he could. 'He was worried about her—we all were.'

Emily flew down the stairs, her stern face fixed on the captain. 'Such behaviour from Julia does not surprise me. She is young and not well versed in the ways of the world, but not from you, Captain. If you wish to remain in my house, I insist you behave like a gentleman.'

'My apologies, Mrs Howard. It was not my intention to offend you or place your sister-in-law's reputation at risk.'

'I certainly hope not. Now come along, Julia.'

Julia resisted the urge to unleash a torrent of words as Emily hustled her up the stairs and into her room. Inside, her mother sat on the small sofa by the window, petting Charlemagne, a slight smile raising the corners of her mouth.

'How dare you speak to the captain like that, or me? How dare you make such accusations?' Julia said sharply.

'Don't you see how compromising such behaviour is? To be out alone with a man who knows where doing who knows what.'

'Out riding and doing nothing. Why do you and Charles always believe the worst of me? What have I done to make you think I might do anything compromising?'

Emily twisted her hands in front of her, some of her anger fading. 'Even a young woman of solid character may slip and cause herself a great deal of grief.' From the adjoining dressing room, baby Thomas let out a wail, nearly drowning out the nurse's soothing coos. 'Besides, your mother was worried about you.'

Her mother stopped petting Charlemagne, shocked to find herself pulled into the conversation. 'No, my dear, I was not worried for this is not the first time you've been caught out in the rain.'

Emily stared at her mother-in-law in frustration. 'She was alone with a gentleman.'

Mother rose, tucking Charlemagne under her

arm. 'As I said, I was not concerned.' She left, closing the door behind her.

'See, it is only your own fear playing on you.'

Emily placed her hands on Julia's shoulders, her face softer than before. 'I am only trying to help. Others will speak badly of you if they witness such behaviour.'

'You're the only one talking now.'

'But think of the Taylors. What would they say?'

'I don't care what they think and I'm tired of enduring Annette's foolishness.'

'Please try to be more cordial to her. There are things concerning the Taylors of which you are not aware and they may have a direct impact on Annette's current mood. She can be a very sweet young lady.'

Julia crossed her arms with a disbelieving huff. 'Annette constantly derides me, points out my faults to all and yet you describe her as sweet. I do nothing and you treat me like the whore of Daringford.'

Emily pinched the bridge of her nose, the dark circles under her eyes made deeper by the candlelight. Julia knew Emily was tired from nursing Thomas through the night in keeping with Rousseau's ideals and Charles's instructions, but at the moment she had no sympathy for her sister-in-law. 'You must learn to get along with people. Life is not all deferential servants and friendly tenant farmers.'

'Of this you and the Taylors have made me very aware,' Julia fumed through clenched teeth, barely able to stand still with the anger coursing through her.

'Forgive me. I was not clear.'

'No, I understand perfectly,' she seethed, balling her fists at her sides. 'Despite everything I've done and can do, you two are ashamed of me. I'll have no peace until I become a simpering wet goose or marry and leave. Why not simply send me to Paul, then you might never be bothered with such an embarrassing sister?'

'Julia, please...'

'No, I've heard quite enough for one day.' She left, afraid of what she might say if she stayed longer.

Once in her room, her hands shook so hard with anger she could not undo the buttons on her habit without Mary's help.

'You are soaked through, miss,' the maid giggled, dropping the soggy garment in a large china bowl along with her wet hose and gloves.

'I'm quite aware of my current state of wetness.' Julia bristled, then instantly regretted it. 'I'm sorry, Mary. I don't mean to be cross.'

'It's all right, miss.' Mary smiled, lacing the dry stays, then helping Julia into an afternoon dress. 'An exciting run with a man like the captain would be enough to send any woman into a state.'

'I wish it was the captain who'd put me in such a state,' she let slip, then caught herself as Mary shot her a knowing glance. Snatching the towel from the washstand, Julia rubbed her soaking hair, eager to do anything to relieve her agitation. 'That will be all, Mary.'

Mary curtsied, then left. Julia threw down the towel and braided her hair, fastening it with a ribbon at the base of her neck.

How could Emily say such a thing to me and the captain? She flipped the braid over her shoulder and, determined to put the incident from her mind, headed for the study, craving the solace.

Once inside, she took a deep breath, hoping to gain some measure of calm from the familiar surroundings, but for once not even this comfortable place made her feel better. The fire had been allowed to burn out, taking with it all remaining warmth and leaving only the ashen tones of the rain-drenched light from outside. It made the room cold, the books heartless, the large mahogany desk uncaring. Despite the chill, she loved it all, but it wasn't hers, as Emily had made abundantly clear.

'Her house,' Julia snorted. Emily might be Charles's wife, but since her arrival she'd never lifted a finger to do more than arrange dinners or fuss over Thomas. The urge to march upstairs and hand the accounts to Emily was overwhelming. Let her manage the estate if she was so quick to call it her own. Instead Julia sat down at the desk and took the pencil in her shaking fingers. If nothing else, she still loved Knollwood and owed it to Father to keep it prosperous.

Lightning lit the room and a hard wind drove the rain against the window. Julia watched the heavy drops bounce off the stone patio. Her thoughts wandered back to the captain and their mad dash across the garden. Was this the kind of life he offered? Turning a rainstorm into an adventure, a ride into an energetic race? Chewing the end of the pencil, she remembered his face when he'd leaned close to her at the keep, the way his fingers brushed her neck sending chills of excitement racing along her skin. She'd wanted him to kiss her, to taste him, to give in to the urges swirling inside her. It might be worth compromising herself to live in such a daring way.

No, a man like the captain might make her forget herself, but he'd also make her regret it.

Tapping the pencil against the desk, she debated calling a footman to relight the fire, then decided against it. She didn't feel like being alone. On rainy days when he was with them, Uncle George usually played billiards in the library with a warm fire and a glass of port. She hesitated, knowing Captain Covington would be with him. The thought of his company appealed to her as did the desire to spite Emily, though it would hardly be spite with Uncle George playing the chaperon.

'I wondered when you'd join us,' Uncle George greeted when she stepped into the library, the crackling fire and friendly faces a welcome contrast to the lonely study. 'Will you play?'

She caught the captain's eye. He offered an apologetic smile before disappearing into a glass of port.

Julia shook her head. 'No, finish your game. I'll join the next one.'

'She's quite the player, Jim. Takes after me.' George leaned over the table, taking aim at the red ball and striking it with the cue ball.

'She also has your spirit of adventure.' The captain strolled to the scoreboard standing near the fireplace behind her. 'I'm sorry to have caused you trouble,' he whispered, sliding a tally along the line.

She ran her fingers over the smooth-wooded side of the billiard table. 'It's not your fault. Emily has a great concern for propriety.'

'Which is surprising considering,' Uncle George commented, sipping his port as James took his shot.

'Considering what?' Julia asked.

George turned a strange shade of pink, then pulled on the sleeves of his jacket. 'Nothing.'

'Tell me. You know you can't keep a secret.'

'Of course I can keep a secret.'

'No, you can't.'

'Name one secret I've failed to keep.' Uncle George leaned over the table, practising before he took his turn.

'Only one?'

'One will do, thank you.'

Julia thought a moment, studying the wood-beam ceiling, debating whether to reveal a certain scandalous and unladylike bit of knowledge. With Emily's rebuke still ringing in her ears, she decided to be bold. 'The woman you visit in London.'

Uncle George whiffed the cue ball and jerked

up straight. 'You know better than to distract a man when he's taking a shot. You'll ruin his game. Besides, how do you know about her?'

'Paul, of course.'

'Did he tell you who she is?'

Julia sighed in frustration. 'No.'

'You see—' he pointed his cue stick at her '—I can keep a secret.'

'I'm sure it's the only one.'

'Who is she, George?' the captain joined in. 'Miss Howard is right, you know. You can't keep a secret.'

'Don't think the two of you will get me to reveal it.' He was about to say more when Davies stepped into the room.

'Captain Russell, the foreman from Creedon Abbey is here to discuss the progress of the repairs.'

'Excellent.' George straightened, his smile wider than Julia would have liked. 'If you'll both excuse me.'

'You can bring him in here if you'd like,' Julia offered, uneasy about being left with the captain.

'No, I'll return shortly and tell you all the details. In the meantime, please continue my game.' Uncle George handed her his cue stick, then left, the proud way he carried himself making her suspect there was no foreman for him to meet.

She gripped the cue tightly, worry creeping through her. Despite her previous desire to spite her sister-in-law, the very real threat of Emily catching her alone in a room with a gentleman worried her.

'So, who is this woman George is seeing in London?' the captain asked, the mischief in his eyes dissolving some of her concerns.

'I don't know. I wasn't even sure she existed until just now.'

'Clever.'

Julia swelled her chest with mock pride. 'Paul taught me well.'

The captain leaned far over the table to execute a difficult stroke and Julia admired the way his breeches pulled over his backside. She wanted to run her hands from his hair, over the length of his back to the snug breeches, feeling every contour of his body.

A small medallion slid out from beneath his shirt, glinting in the candlelight and stopping her mind from wandering too far.

'What's that?'

'A reminder.' He fingered the pendant, his voice more measured than before. Distant thunder rolled outside, the storm moving off deeper into the countryside. 'I had it on the last time I was aboard ship. We were off the coast of Spain when we came across a French frigate and it opened fire.'

He unclasped the chain from around his neck and handed it to her. She examined the bronze surface, running her thumb over the dent with its worn and nearly illegible letters.

'It stopped the bullet?'

'Yes, but there were two.' He took the medal back, fastening the chain around his neck and tucking it into his shirt.

'And the other?'

He hit the cue ball with such force it rolled around the table, bouncing off the sides and missing the red ball. 'It struck me in the left shoulder.'

Their eyes met and she realised why he'd reacted so vehemently to her comments about Admiral Nelson. No wonder he'd been so intent on challenging her reasoning. What must he think of her? Would she never learn to control her tongue? Embarrassment overwhelmed her accompanied by the urge to make her excuses and flee. 'Is that why you resigned?'

'Mostly.' He picked at the end of his cue stick. 'But I had other responsibilities. My father died four years ago, while I was at sea. He left a large share in a shipping company to maintain my mother and sister, but the company faltered after losing a number of ships to storms. My mother tried to manage as best she could, but neither she nor my sister possess your business acumen. I discovered the troubles a few weeks into my recuperation when a bailiff appeared to collect the debts. I instructed my solicitor to pay them and once I was sufficiently recovered, took over Mother's affairs and saw to my sister's dowry.'

'Once everything was settled and you were well, couldn't you have gone back to sea?'

'I wanted to, but it seems the Navy is quick to forget a man once he's away from active service.'

'Didn't they know you were recuperating?'

'They did, but there are always younger, eager men craving ships and, unlike me, those men have not been badly wounded.'

'But Admiral Nelson was wounded and he commands the fleet.'

'As Admiral Stuart was kind enough to point out, I am no Nelson.'

She gasped. 'How could he be so cruel?'

'He wasn't cruel. He was honest. Admiral Stuart and I have known each other a long time and, despite a mutual respect, we both know the way of things. I just needed someone to state it plain enough for me to acknowledge it.' He laid the cue stick on the table and traced the polished wood with one finger. 'The Navy isn't an easy life. George is one of my oldest friends, but I've lost too many others to sickness or French bullets. Most men pursuing commands need to face those hardships to make a living. I'd made a handsome fortune and the Admiralty knew it. Thanks to Admiral Stuart's honesty, I have the chance to enjoy my rewards instead of suffering who knows what fate.' He touched his shoulder, a far-off sadness filling his eyes before he jerked his hand to his side and turned to face her. 'It wasn't easy resigning my commission and it still troubles me, as much as my shoulder.'

Julia stepped back, rolling the cue ball, wishing lightning had struck her on their run, allowing her to avoid this embarrassment. 'I'm sorry for what I said about wounded men. I shouldn't have been so callous or spoken so freely.'

He slid his hand along the table's edge, allowing it to rest very close to hers. 'Don't berate yourself for your views. It's a brave person who does not bend under pressure to others' opinions.'

His fingers brushed the tops of hers, sending a shiver through her body. All of this was inappropriate, his touch, the seclusion but she couldn't bring herself to leave. He stepped closer, his expression more tender than she deserved. She met his soft eyes, anxious, wanting, eager to follow him down whatever road he led her.

The clock on the mantel chimed, the tinkling bells bringing her back to reality.

Cursed interruptions. It was almost time for dinner. If she wished to avoid her *faux pas* from the night before, she needed time to prepare. 'Please excuse me. I must dress for dinner.' Sliding her hand out from beneath his, she noticed his fleeting disappointment as she hurried from the room.

Chapter Six

'Are these all of them?' Julia stared at the dresses draped over every surface, her room resembling the inside of a milliner's shop.

'No, miss. I left the three formal dresses in their trunks.' Mary laid an assortment of gloves on the writing desk. 'Should I bring those down, too?'

'Yes, for heaven knows I may have use for them yet.' Julia fingered the hem of a pink-silk pelisse.

'Which dress would you like to wear tonight?' Mary asked, arranging a few fans on the bedside table.

Julia circled the room, examining each one, trying to remember which one had looked the best on her. She barely remembered the ensembles, having banished them to the attic the instant they'd returned from her horrible Season in London. She'd have gladly given it all to Mary, but her mother had stopped her, insisting she might one day need it. Tonight, Mother would discover how right she'd been. 'Which do you suggest?'

'The green one, it was so pretty on you in town.'

Julia nodded, allowing Mary to help her out of the simple afternoon frock and into the fancy, green-silk creation. The dress highlighted her amber eyes and showed off her curves to their best advantage. However, the low-cut bodice made her feel exposed and very self-conscious. Examining herself in the mirror, she felt all of her London awkwardness come rushing back.

Her embarrassment increased when, half an hour later, after patiently bearing Mary's many attempts at a fashionable *coiffure*, Julia curtly dismissed her. As she stared at the lopsided style in the mirror, tears of frustration stung her eyes. How could she possibly hope to capture Captain Covington's interest with dishevelled hair?

Not his interest. Simon's, she corrected herself, furiously combing out the style, then tossing the brush down on the table where it rattled against a small vase with a lone rose. *Obviously my money isn't enough to attract him. The stupid peacock.*

Despair crept along the edges of her irritation, but she shook it from her head with the last of the hairpins. She couldn't afford to lose hope now.

I will catch Simon's eye. I have to. With renewed determination, she twisted her hair up the way Mother did, fastening it with a tortoiseshell comb while leaving the front curls, Mary's sole accomplishment, to fall about her face.

James trailed his fingers on the marble mantel, wincing at another of Miss Howard's hollow laughs. Twice today he'd nearly kissed her. Twice he'd allowed the wanting in her eyes to overcome his better sense, yet there she sat on the sofa next to Mr Taylor, seemingly enthralled by the twit. What game was she playing in her London finery, her white, round breasts well displayed by the curving neckline of the green dress? What hold did Mr Taylor have over her? He wondered if she knew about his affair with the dowager baroness or the wager at White's as to whether or not they would elope to Gretna Green? Surely she must know, having previously claimed a broad knowledge of London gossip.

Flexing his left hand, he leaned his elbow on the mantel, pretending to study a small horse figurine. He'd watched her throughout dinner, noticing the way her eyes lost their sparkle whenever Mr Taylor turned away. This was not the same woman who'd dared him to keep up with her on the downs or challenged him in the library.

He thought of asking George what his niece was about, but it would only make his feelings obvious. What where his feelings? He'd struggled against them ever since they'd met, yet this afternoon at the keep he could no longer lie to himself. She enchanted him, amused him. She was an original in every way, fresh and free spirited, tethered by a prudish brother and an indifferent mother. How she'd blossom if she ever cut herself loose from Knollwood. Yet she clung to it like a man clings to a sinking ship, praying against all odds it might still save him.

Miss Taylor's voice accompanied by the tinkling notes of the pianoforte drifted to him from the far corner of the room. She flirted with him from across the instrument's polished surface, dropping her head coquettishly, her eyes betraying her true intention. James knew he could not go back to such women. However, it was a fool's errand to chase after a young lady who held no real interest in him. Melinda had taught him that lesson years ago. He must find some way to draw Miss Howard out and drive thoughts of Mr Taylor from her mind.

* * *

While Simon spoke of his London house at length, Julia stole a number of glances at the captain. He stood by the fire, watching the flames consume the log with a sense of distant wondering. He wore his blue uniform, the high collar framing his strong chin. The firelight danced in his dark hair and blue eyes. For a moment she pictured him on the deck of a ship as it sailed into Bombay, watching the far-off coconut trees on the rolling hills sway in the warm breeze, just as Mr Ivers described in his book. Only the strange sadness surrounding him interrupted the lovely dream. Seeing the way it darkened his eyes, she wanted to take him in her arms and caress it away, but with so many people around them, she couldn't even entreat him to tell her what troubled him.

'It is such a bother to turn one's own music,' Annette remarked from her place at the pianoforte. 'Captain, will you turn the pages for me?'

'Simon can turn the pages for you,' George responded.

Simon stopped his chattering long enough to heave a small sigh. 'She knows the tune by heart and can play without the sheet music.'

Annette's face went pale before she fixed a

charming smile back on her lips. 'How silly you are, Simon, to make such a joke. You know very well I do not know this piece.'

Julia caught Uncle George's eye. He glanced from her to Simon, scrunching his brow with a silent question. Julia flicked her hand in his direction, waving the question away, but she could tell he wasn't deterred. Panic stole through her. Uncle George didn't believe her sudden interest in Simon and suspected something. Had he guessed her scheme? She hoped not. She didn't need any more obstacles.

'Mr Johnson told me Mr Wilkins is hosting a game at the Sign of the Swan tonight,' Uncle George announced with a sly grin.

Drat, Julia thought, wishing they were still at dinner so she could kick him under the table. She didn't need him working against her, but she also wasn't ready to let him in on her plan.

'A game, you say?' Simon asked, taking his gold chronometer out of his pocket and checking the time.

'Quite a large one from the sound of it. A man could make a lot of money. It seems Mr Wilkins is very keen to win back some of the blunt he lost last night. Though I doubt he'll succeed. He's a terrible player.'

'Simon, tell me more about your horses,' Julia implored in a feeble attempt to outmanoeuvre Uncle George, but it failed. Simon rose and sauntered over to the card table, quite forgetting their conversation.

'You've played the man?' he asked.

'Once or twice. He has no face for the game. Reveals his hand—hardly a challenge.' George laid a card on the table and drew another.

'Where's the fun in an opponent who gives away the game? A real gentleman wants a challenge, a chance to truly flaunt his talent,' Annette chided Simon, who, for the first time since their arrival, didn't respond to his sister's rebuke. Instead he stood, fingering the button on his coat, appearing to weigh Uncle George's announcement with Annette's comment before the gambler in him won the debate.

'If you'll excuse me, I believe I'll retire for the evening.'

'But it's only nine. Stay,' Annette pleaded. 'I'm sure George can make room for you at the table.'

'The country has tired me. Goodnight, ladies.' He bowed to Mother and Emily, then made his way out of the room. He didn't fool anyone with his excuse and Julia knew it would only be a matter of minutes before they heard him sneak out of the front door.

Annette's hands lingered over the keys and she looked torn between following him and returning to her pursuit of Captain Covington. It took only a moment for her to reach a decision and she resumed her pretty playing.

Julia sat on the sofa, clutching her hands in her lap in frustration. Beyond a few dinner conversations, she hadn't made any progress with the dandy.

'Captain Covington, would you mind turning the music for me?' Annette sang to him.

'Would you care to accompany me across the room?' The captain stood in front of Julia, his hands behind his back. She had no desire to watch Annette fawn over him, but with no Simon or interest in cards, annoying her stepcousin seemed the only thing left to do.

'It would be my pleasure.'

'Perhaps Miss Howard and I may play a duet,' Annette suggested with false gaiety when they approached.

'You are quite aware I don't play.' She was in no mood for another discussion of her accomplishments.

'You don't play. And you don't draw.' Annette's

fingers paused, giving her astonishment the most effect before she resumed her piece. 'How do you expect to find a husband without such accomplishments?'

Julia restrained her urge to slam the keyboard cover on Annette's pale fingers and wipe the pompous look off her face.

'I think many gentlemen would be pleased to have a wife skilled in running an estate for he would never have to agonise over his purse or hers,' Captain Covington offered, coming to her defence against Annette again.

'Even without a gentleman, it's a comfort to handle one's own affairs instead of trusting them to men who only gamble them away,' Julia added, staring down her nose at Annette.

Annette struck a sour note, then stood, turning hard eyes on Julia. 'Do not be so proud. A lady's fortune is always in the hands of her male relations, no matter what her accomplishments.'

Her words rang more of sad bitterness than malice and Julia's spirits fell, the realisation striking deeper than any other comment Annette had ever made about her. For the first time, Julia felt sorry for her stepcousin, thinking they had more in common than she knew.

'If you will excuse me.' Annette pushed past them towards the door, disappearing upstairs.

'If I had an estate, I would wish for a wife like you to run it,' Captain Covington offered and Julia responded with a weak smile, unwilling to accept his pity.

'But you have no estate. And neither do I.'

'Perhaps in time that will change for both of us.'

'Yes, you will buy an estate and I—well, I'll wait for my brother to return and then I can be the spinster aunt.' She meant the comment to sound like a joke, but it fell flat. Desperate for something to occupy her hands, she sat down at the despised instrument and began picking out the tune in front of her. She tried to concentrate on the black notes in their cosy lines and not the captain standing close behind her.

'No, you will not be a spinster. Do not listen to the likes of Miss Taylor. There are many gentlemen who want a lady with a head for business.'

'Then they must all be married for I've never met such a gentleman.'

She came to the end of the stanza and he reached over her shoulder to change the page, his cheek tantalisingly close to hers. She closed her eyes, listening to the sheet music rustle, hearing his heavy breath in her ear. She only had to turn her head to sweep her lips across his skin, bury her face in the warm crease of his neck while reaching up to lace her fingers in his dark hair.

'I am not married,' he whispered, his breath teasing her neck.

Her hands dropped to the keyboard, the clanging notes snapping her out of her daydream. Going back over the stanza, she tried to make her awkward fingers behave, but they kept tripping over the keys. She glanced at the card table, noting the way Emily watched them before Uncle George distracted her with some comment. She also felt the captain's eyes lingering on her. Why did he insist on staring? Julia hit another wrong note, increasing her agitation until she could no longer bear it.

'If you'll excuse me, Captain, I'm tired.' She stood, closed the keyboard, then fled for the door.

George leaned back in his chair. 'Retiring so early, Julia?'

'Yes, goodnight.'

She hurried from the room before Uncle George could compel her to stay. Reaching the top of the dimly lit stairs, she heard a faint noise, like someone crying. She followed the sound, tiptoeing over the carpet, expecting to see a maid in one of the small chairs situated near the window. Moving past the cushioned retreat with a view of the garden, she found it empty. Down the hall, light slipped out from beneath Annette's door. Cautiously approaching it, Julia heard her step-cousin's muffled sobs. She felt sorry for the girl and raised a hand to knock, then thought better of it. If Annette was rude downstairs, Julia could only imagine her fury if she interrupted her now.

Once in her own room, Julia sat in the window seat, snatching up the agricultural report in an attempt to lose herself in the dry pages. She read the first two lines, then tossed it aside, too frustrated to concentrate. Leaning her forehead against the cool glass, she watched a few stars peep out through a break in the moving clouds.

What did the captain mean by suggesting gentlemen wanted women with a head for business? Did he mean he wanted such a lady? No, he was not interested in a sensible wife, only a country fling, no matter how much tender sincerity filled his eyes. Paul had warned her about a man's ability to charm a woman for purely dishonourable reasons. She could not let herself fall into the captain's trap, no matter how easily her body reacted when he stood so close.

The idea that she might be too weak to resist him scared her as deeply now as it had at the keep and in the library. Pulling her knees up under her chin, she wrapped her arms around them in an effort to ward off the sudden cold. Everything felt so uncertain, as if the captain's arrival had changed more than just the place settings for dinner. Not even Knollwood or her own conviction to buy Cable Grange seemed steady any more.

If only Paul was here. He'd know what to do about the captain, the Taylors and Cable Grange. However, he was at sea and about to face unimaginable dangers. Even if she could get a letter to him, it wasn't right to burden him with her concerns at a time like this. She would have to solve these problems herself.

James lay in bed, staring at the white plaster ceiling, his aching shoulder preventing any chance of sleep. He'd gritted his teeth more than once during the ride back to Knollwood, but the pain seemed a worthy price to pay for the excitement he experienced racing Miss Howard. Outside, the wind rattled the window, knocking a tree branch against the house. Thoughts of Miss Howard continued to torment him despite all attempts to drive them from his mind. He could not care for her. He would not. What did he have to offer her but a weak body and a meaningless life?

As he pulled the medallion back and forth across

its chain, those old familiar protests sounded hollow tonight. Over the last few days, he'd felt freer than he had since being wounded and dreams of the future crept into the long hours of the night. Perhaps he'd travel to Rome, inspect the ruins, then carry on to Greece or Constantinople. He might even return to India and explore more than the port cities. Miss Howard's eyes would flash at the sight of the palaces and market places.

James twisted the chain tight around his finger until the metal bit into his flesh. How many times had he lain here, distracting himself from his painful shoulder with dreams of her young, supple body? He'd almost groaned when she'd appeared in the dining room tonight, her low-cut gown displaying the delicate curves of her body. He wanted nothing more than to slip his hands beneath the green silk, to feel the soft flesh of her thighs, taste the sweet hollow of her neck while his hands caressed her stomach. Did she know how she teased him and made him ache with need? She wanted him as much as he wanted her. He'd seen it in her eyes at the keep, felt it in the way she'd held his hand when they'd run through the rain. Yet still she went back to the dandy.

Smacking his fist against the sheets, he tried to ignore the subtle throbbing in his member as it overcame the sting of his shoulder. He'd placed his happiness in the hands of a woman once before, only to be cruelly disappointed. What did Melinda matter now? George was right; she was in the past where she belonged. Thinking about her did nothing but weaken his spirit. No, there were other, more pleasant things to consider, such as the taste of Miss Howard's lips. He'd been tantalisingly close so many times today, yet she continued to elude him.

Shifting on the bed, he searched for a more comfortable position. Guilt filled his mind. He couldn't ruin George's niece, not for simple need, nor could he ask for her hand. Or could he? A woman with her talents would be an asset and he could well imagine her accompanying him to India or on any other whim. But were these reasons good enough to tie him to a woman for life? Miss Howard would certainly keep things interesting, assuming she'd have him. He remembered George's suggestion that a man with an estate could capture her heart. He'd wanted Cable Grange for revenge; now he had another, sweeter reason. For once the idea of marriage didn't seem distasteful, but was he ready to spring the parson's mousetrap? If so, he'd need a tempting bit of cheese to catch this mouse.

Chapter Seven

Julia ambled back from the stables, the cold, early morning air chafing her cheeks. Stifling a yawn with the back of her hand, she tried to blame last night's restlessness on Annette or the problem of Simon, but it was Captain Covington who'd kept her up until almost sunrise. With the auction date drawing closer, it was time to put such foolishness aside and be serious about her pursuit. She calculated again the ready locked in the desk drawer, wondering how much it would take to buy Simon and his silence. Father had always kept the money at hand, mostly to send to Paul when one of his frequent letters arrived asking for more. She'd left it there out of habit; now she could use it to her advantage. She'd corner Simon once he finally awoke and came down to eat, assuming he'd even returned from his rousing night at the Sign of the Swan.

A flash of pink caught Julia's eye and she noticed her mother, parasol in hand, inspecting her roses. Charlemagne trotted beside her, his tail wagging in happy excitement. The rose garden was her mother's domain, the one area of Knollwood off limits to both Father's and Julia's management, and she coaxed from it flowers of amazing beauty. Watching her with her precious bushes, her hem wet, feet encased in sturdy shoes instead of slippers, she knew her mother played a small part in her own love of the land.

In no mood to risk a serious discussion, Julia slunk past the garden, hoping her mother wouldn't turn around. She was nearly to the house when Charlemagne let out an excited yip.

'Come here, dear,' her mother called in a voice Julia could not ignore.

She wondered if Emily had told her about their conversation yesterday. It wasn't in her mother's nature to scold, but she was not above the occasional reprimand. 'Yes, Mother?'

'Do you have feelings for Simon?' She turned over a leaf, searching for signs of disease.

Julia hesitated, hating the blunt questions. It made evading it difficult. 'He's an affable gentleman.'

Her mother stared hard at her. 'The truth, please.'

'No, certainly not,' Julia admitted, knowing it was better to level with her mother than continue the charade.

'Then why show him so much preference?'

'I thought if I could make him ask for my hand, then an engagement would be enough for Charles to give me my inheritance in time to purchase Cable Grange.'

'I suspected as much.' Her mother plucked off a wilted bloom and tossed it over the wall. 'Even if he did propose, Charles wouldn't allow it. Simon has too much of a reputation in town.'

'Must my entire life be governed by what Charles does and does not like?'

'I thought you didn't care for Simon?'

'I don't, but I hate Charles's high-handed meddling.'

'Be kind, dear. He does love you and only wants your happiness.'

Julia didn't agree, but held her tongue. Arguing with her mother would get her nowhere and with the plan to entice Simon unravelling, she needed her help. 'What am I going to do?'

'Have you considered Captain Covington?'

Julia fingered a stem, snapping off a thorn with

her thumb. During the long hours without sleep she'd considered the captain many times, in many different ways, none of which was suitable to discuss with her mother. 'I chose Simon because I thought the promise of a fortune would be enough to attract him. I won't have the same influence with the captain. Besides, he's infatuated with Annette.'

'I don't believe he is. I've watched him and I think he tolerates her simply to be courteous.'

Julia knew she was right. At certain unguarded moments, the captain did appear bored or annoyed with Annette.

'I'd have to tell him directly of my scheme and what if he told others?' She knew he wouldn't, but she felt the need to make some kind of protest. If she agreed too speedily to the idea, her mother might suspect something more, something Julia didn't even want to admit to herself.

'I don't think he'll reveal your secret. He's honourable, possesses a good reputation and George can vouch for him. Charles is more likely to accept him. And think of Paul. A friendship with the captain may help his career. He must know people in the Admiralty and he might be in a position to bend their ears.'

Despite her mother's reasoning, Julia hesitated.

Such a game with the captain would prove far more dangerous than with Simon. Could she trust herself to spend enough time with him to give the appearance of genuine affection without compromising herself? Of course she could. Couldn't she? 'I'll think about it.'

'If nothing else, imagine how it will annoy Annette,' her mother suggested with a wry smile.

Julia gasped. 'I never knew you were so wicked.'

'I'm your uncle's sister, am I not?'

'Indeed.'

'Now come along, for I believe George has a surprise for us about nuncheon.'

Uncle George's nuncheon plans did come as a surprise. Somehow, without Julia discovering it, he'd arranged for an outdoor picnic on a grassy hill near Knollwood. He'd ordered a number of oilcloths spread on the still-wet grass and brought over from Creedon Abbey a large canopy acquired during a visit to India. From their high vantage point, they could see Cable Grange perched on a distant hill and one turret of Creedon Abbey peeking above a far-off line of trees.

Julia sipped her tea, studying the captain and Annette over the rim of her cup. Annette served him a slice of cake while leaning over to reveal the tops of her breasts pushed up by her low-cut bodice. Uncle George had advised them to wear clothing appropriate for the cool autumn weather but she'd ignored his advice, dressing instead for husband hunting.

'Annette will catch her death of cold pursuing the captain,' Julia whispered to Emily, noticing the chit's goose bumps from across the oilcloth.

'You shouldn't laugh at people,' Emily chided, popping a small sandwich into her mouth to cover an agreeing smile.

Julia focused on the captain, noting how often he turned away from Annette's charms to take in the view. After a moment, his eyes met hers and she concentrated on her tea cup, sipping the tepid liquid with as much ease of manner as she could muster. The idea of revealing her scheme to him and asking for his help terrified, yet intrigued her. Would he go along? If she kept the mood light, made him understand it was all a game, why wouldn't he? After all, he'd participated in many of Uncle George's schemes.

If it all seemed so simple, then why was she afraid of asking him? She'd almost risked her reputation on a dandy. Why did a man like Captain Covington frighten her?

Deep in her heart she knew the reason. His

dashing features and the easy way they laughed together would make it difficult to jilt him and jilt him she must. As a single woman, Cable Grange would be hers completely. Married, the property would belong to him, leaving her in a position no better than her current one with Charles. Though she doubted Captain Covington would act like her brother, it was still risky to gamble her future on a man she barely knew.

She turned towards Cable Grange, watching the sunlight dance off the dirty sandstone, trying to imagine it clean, the sheep well fed and bred, the fields high with wheat and barley. The thought of such a beautiful estate left to moulder broke her heart. No matter what her fears, she had to face them and get Cable Grange.

Julia put down her tea cup and stood, smoothing her dress with her gloved hands. 'I think I'll go for a walk.'

Catching the captain's eyes, she nodded in the direction of the woods. He met it with a questioning frown before comprehension dawned on his face, bringing with it a roguish smile. Julia, confident he understood, turned and walked off down the hill. What exactly he understood she wasn't sure. He certainly wouldn't expect her proposal, but he couldn't anticipate a sordid rendezvous, not with everyone sitting only a few hundred feet away.

'More tea, Captain Covington?' Miss Taylor asked, forcing James to stifle a smile. He'd seen the signal, the same one George used to use when they needed to escape a room and discuss their next move. What did Miss Howard wish to tell him that the others could not hear?

'Annette, leave the captain alone. He'll float away if you ply him with much more tea,' George chided.

'I'm sure Captain Covington is quite capable of knowing when he has and has not had enough tea,' she snapped and James seized the chance to leave.

'I think I'll join Miss Howard.' He hurried after her before Miss Taylor or anyone else could offer to join him.

The hill quickened his pace and his feet fell hard on the firm dirt. Miss Howard watched him approach from where she sat on the twisted trunk of a fallen tree, standing once he reached her. A strange sort of nervous anticipation decorated her face and he wondered what serious secret made her so eager to speak with him in private.

'You've set their tongues wagging by following me.' She walked deeper into the woods and he followed, leaves crackling beneath his boots.

'George's tongue is already wagging.'

'What do you mean?'

'He's playing the matchmaker and would like very much to see us married.'

She stopped and her fingers flew to her lips in fearful surprise. 'Really?'

'You didn't know?'

'No.' She resumed her languid pace, her face more tightly drawn than before.

'As much as I enjoy teasing him, if I have to spend one more minute eating out of Miss Taylor's hands just to see the stunned expression on his face, I may expire from fatigue,' James admitted with a smile.

'Thank heavens,' she breathed, sounding more nervous than amused. 'I was afraid you'd succumbed to her fake charm.'

'I might say the same of you and your present infatuation with Mr Taylor,' he countered, eager to get at the truth of her relationship with the dandy.

'You can't believe I'm interested in him.' She picked up a stick and smacked a brown leaf off an overhanging branch. 'He's weak and useless and no woman wants such a man. Like you, I was merely pretending.'

James flexed his left hand, resisting the urge to feel under his shirt. 'Why would you feign interest in a man? You aren't after a husband, are you?'

She stopped abruptly and turned to him. 'No, I'm in search of a fiancé, or, more correctly, someone like you who can pretend.' The words came out in such a winded rush he almost missed their meaning. He stared at her, waiting for a laugh, smile or some other indication of a joke, but she only watched him with the same nervous fear as before.

'You're serious?'

'It's my intention to purchase Cable Grange with my inheritance, but I don't receive it until I'm married. However, if Charles believes I'm engaged—'

'—he'll give you the money.'

'Yes. Once I've purchased the estate, I'll cry off the engagement and you'll be a free man.' She broke the stick in half and tossed it aside.

James stepped back, unsure how to respond. An engagement for Cable Grange? It seemed impossible, yet exactly like something a girl of her pluck would suggest.

'I'd hoped to entice Simon into an engagement,' she continued when he didn't answer, 'but the gentleman is thicker than mud and, according to Mother, quite unsuitable. Charles isn't likely to approve of the match. But as an old friend of Uncle George's you're—'

'—perfect.'

'Well, I wouldn't say "perfect", but you'll do.'

'Will I now?'

'You have a fondness for schemes.'

'So it seems.' James leaned back against a large oak, crossing his arms over his chest in amusement. The woman was unbelievable.

'Please. It's the only way. I have to have Cable Grange.' The desperation in her voice and the dejected way she drew the pelisse's satin ribbon through her fingers touched him. He wanted to take her sad face in his hands and kiss away the small line between her brows. The idea was doomed to fail. He knew something of Charles. Her brother was exacting and wouldn't simply give her the money on a promise. If James agreed to the scheme, it could only end in either their marriage or her ruin. He might have contemplated marriage in the middle of the night, but in the light of the day, under such dubious circumstance, it was quite a different prospect.

She bit her bottom lip in anticipation of his answer. Did she care for him? Sometimes, when he caught her observing him, he suspected some interest. However, she was a determined girl and she'd set her mind on Cable Grange. She'd never admit any feelings for him if they interfered with her plans.

'What will you tell your brother when you end the engagement?'

'I don't think Charles likes Navy men, so I doubt he'll be too put off by the idea.'

'Or he might insist.'

'You're a free man—refuse him.'

'It's that important to you?'

'It's the only future I have.'

If this were any other woman, he'd think she was trying to trap him, but the way she admitted her situation with such raw agony told him she had no designs. Like him, the realities of life frustrated her and she did her best to overcome them. It took courage to reveal her situation and propose the plan and he respected her bravery. An engagement would force them together, giving him a chance to know her better, perhaps convince her not to jilt him if his feelings and hers proved true. If he was wrong and there was no interest, they'd break the engagement. It all seemed so uncomplicated, but he knew it wasn't. Was he ready to agree to her arrangement and risk the very real possibility of marriage?

'You have George's talent for schemes,' he said.

'So it seems,' she agreed.

'You know about most of the plots I was entangled in?'

She nodded.

'Then I'll have to tell you the rest during our engagement.'

'You'll do it?'

'I followed George. It seems only fitting I follow his niece.'

'Thank you, Captain, thank you.' She threw her arms around his neck, hugging him close. He breathed in the clean scent of her soft hair, felt the warmth of her neck so close to his lips. He moved to wrap his arms around her, put his hand on the small of her back and draw her deeper into the arc of his body. His member eagerly responded to the sudden rush of desire, but knowing his breeches wouldn't hide it and in no mood to embarrass himself, he removed her arms from around his neck. Her eager eyes met his and he saw more in her happy expression than a scheme. He released her wrists, afraid of what might happen if he held her for too long.

'We must play the role of courting couple,' she explained matter of factly, covering the lingering tension. 'Give ourselves time to develop an attachment and for the others to see it. Charles must believe it is real. When would you like to begin?'

'Now, my little Artemis, before we change our minds.' He offered her his arm and she took it, allowing him to walk her back through the woods.

Was it his pulse or hers she felt racing beneath her fingers? Pausing for him to hold back a branch, she moved forwards, barely able to keep her body from trembling. Up ahead, the trees began to thin, the green hill just visible beyond the forest's deep shadows. Once they stepped out together, the game was on and would not end until she either had Cable Grange or—or what?

She stopped, nervousness making her whole body vibrate. 'You could turn back now,' she offered, more to herself than the captain.

'I wouldn't dream of it.' He took a step forwards, but she didn't move. 'You aren't afraid, are you?'

'Of course not.' *I'm terrified*, she thought, but didn't say it. Having her scheme turn real in so short a time was overwhelming.

'Good.'

He pulled her forwards, out of the trees and she blinked against the sunlight. He kept a tight grip on her arm, escorting her up the hill. Julia could almost feel the shock rippling through the group at the sight of them in such an intimate attitude. Annette's jaw dropped, Uncle George choked on a biscuit, Simon inspected them through his quizzing glass and Emily's eyes went large. Only her mother appeared not to notice, doting on Charlemagne in an attempt to hide a knowing smile.

'I think we've made an impression,' Julia whispered, her fear fading in the face of this small triumph.

'I believe we have.'

They sat down together on the oilcloth, a short distance from the others who continued to watch them in silence. Not even Uncle George had recovered enough to ask questions or do anything more than stare. Julia acted like nothing was amiss and for the first time in days felt hope for her future. Neither Annette's sour face nor Emily's dumbfounded expression could ruin the feeling.

'Tea?' Captain Covington offered, holding up the small teapot.

'Yes, please.' She held out her cup. When it was full she exchanged it for a small plate of tarts. 'Would you like one?'

'Thank you.' He reached for a delicacy, but Julia pulled it away, then held it out for him to taste.

'Subtlety,' he whispered, taking the treat from her fingers and breaking off a small bite.

'Why?' Julia whispered back. 'If I'm going to do this, I'm going to do it well.'

'George, you've outdone yourself with surprises today,' James congratulated when they returned from the picnic to find a game of battledore and shuttlecock arranged on the lawn.

'I'm not the only one,' George remarked as James took two battledores from the footman and handed Miss Howard one with all the tender flourish of a smitten suitor.

'What do you mean?'

George scowled in answer, then turned to Miss Taylor. 'Annette, you should play.'

Miss Taylor's pinched eyebrows drew closer together. 'I have no intention of remaining outside. My shoes are already soaked through.'

Holding up the wet hem of her thin gown, she marched inside.

'I believe I'll join her,' Mr Taylor added and no one tried to stop him.

James and Miss Howard began their game while the others fell into furious whispering. He noticed the volley of looks thrown their way, but the ping of the shuttlecock hitting Miss Howard's battledore forced him to focus on the game.

He ran for the wispy target, smacking it back to her and sending her running. She whacked it inches from the ground and it sailed through the air towards him. Lunging for it, he ignored his stinging shoulder, enjoying the lively play. With a quick swing, he shot the shuttlecock over her head and into the tall grass.

'You're an excellent player, Miss Howard.'

'You're trying to flatter me.' She laughed, retrieving the shuttlecock and preparing to serve.

'I never offer a compliment I don't mean.'

Their vigorous game continued, Miss Howard chasing the shuttlecock, her face flushed with excitement, hair slightly dishevelled and eyes vivid from the exertion. It reminded him of the moment they'd first met in the forest. What would it be like to drive her to such a state by the play of his fingers along her skin? Hopefully, he'd get the chance to discover it, but for now vigorous exercise must suffice.

James played with equal enthusiasm, chasing the shuttlecock all over the field. Then, in the middle of one challenging set, something over Miss Howard's shoulder made him pause. He let the shuttlecock drop to the ground, watching the stable boy run up the lawn towards them.

'What's wrong?' She turned and at the sight of the boy, threw down her battledore and rushed to meet him. 'Samuel, what is it? What's happened?'

'There's been trouble, Miss Howard.'

James hurried to her side and the flustered stable boy, breathing hard from his run, warily took them in.

'What? Tell me,' she demanded.

He hesitated, visibly torn between telling his mistress and getting in trouble.

James knew whatever he'd come to report had happened under suspicious circumstances.

'Tell her what happened,' James commanded, ignoring the disapproving glance Miss Howard tossed his way.

'There was a fight in the clearing near the lower pasture,' he explained, James's order loosening his tongue. 'Mr Wilkins's man was knocked out and Bill's bleeding badly.'

'I must put a stop to this at once. Come along, Samuel.'

'Can I stay here, miss?' the boy stuttered.

'Whatever for?'

'I believe the lad is afraid of losing face,' James offered, sensing the boy's predicament. He'd seen it many times aboard ship. 'Whatever's going on is a secret and the others might hold it against him if they learn he told you.'

'All right, Samuel, you may stay. But when I return I'd better find you working, not dallying or daydreaming.'

'Yes, miss.' He dashed off in the direction of the stables.

Miss Howard turned to the others, who watched from their place along the edge of the court. 'Mother, send John to fetch the medicine chest. Emily, have Davies send two men and a stretcher to the clearing near the pasture.'

'Where are you going?' Emily asked in a heavy, warning tone.

'To deal with this incident.' Miss Howard turned, striding off.

'I insist you let the farm manager deal with it,' Emily called after her to no effect. Miss Howard kept walking, pretending not to hear her sister-in-law.

'I'll go with her.' James knew the hot tempers of fighting men. He couldn't imagine the diminutive Miss Howard facing them alone.

'Me, too,' George offered.

Despite her quick clip, James easily caught up to her, his long legs giving him an advantage. Behind them, George huffed and puffed, struggling to keep pace with their steady strides. 'What will you do when you find them?'

Miss Howard didn't slow, but kept on down the rutted path. 'I don't know.'

'Do you think this is wise?'

'Is it wise to allow workers to neglect their duties?'

'Perhaps there is a better way to handle the situation.'

'How? By letting you command them? Perhaps you would like to oversee their wages as well or direct them where to plough?'

'The boy talked, didn't he?'

'That's not the point.'

'Then what is?'

'I have no wish to discuss it at this time.'

They walked a fair distance from the house, across one large field and down a rolling slope to where the land flattened again. Sheep watched them march by until they reached another clearing.

'What's going on here?' Miss Howard took the lead, her voice carrying across the grass to the circle of men. They turned, guilt washing over their faces. James stifled a laugh as the gruff field hands dropped their heads like a bunch of schoolboys caught cheating. He recognised a number of men from Julia's staff. The others appeared to be Mr Wilkins's men for they leered at Miss Howard, making James very glad he'd decided to come.

An unconscious man lay on the ground. Another, larger man sat next to him, holding his bloody arm. The two fighters were naked from the waist up, but Miss Howard seemed not to notice as she strode into the thick of things.

'I said, what's going on here?' she demanded again upon reaching the circle, her hands balled against her hips. All the men had strapping builds from years of labour and towered over their employer. James might fear for her safety, but he had to admire her spirit. She reminded him of a certain well-known tavern owner in Tortuga who didn't tolerate fighting in her establishment.

When no one answered, she turned to the bleeding man on the ground. 'Bill, tell me what happened.'

He blinked against the sun, his face long with shame. 'It was a friendly wager, Miss Howard. Tim said I could beat Mr Wilkins's man, and you know I can. But he had a knife. Cut me before I laid him out.'

'You lie,' one of the greasier men challenged,

his lascivious eyes raking Miss Howard, making James's blood boil.

'It's the truth,' Bill challenged, sparking a round of heated accusations.

'Bloody liar—'

'He cheated—'

'Can't trust a Wilkins servant—'

'That's enough!' Miss Howard shouted, her voice lost in a swirl of angry shouts and jabbing fingers. The jabbing rapidly escalated to shoving with Miss Howard caught in the middle. James pulled her from the centre as the first punch swung close to her head. Pushing her towards George, he summoned all his years as a commander and addressed the tangled rabble.

'Attention!' The men with military experience straightened up while the others stopped arguing long enough for him to take control of the situation. 'I want silence this instance. You men there, get back to Cable Grange.'

'And who are you to be ordering us around?' the greasy one sneered.

James stepped toe to toe with the man. 'What's your name?'

'Mark.' He spat on the ground at James's feet.

James fixed him with an insolent-wilting glare.

'Then get back to Cable Grange, Mark, and take your companion with you.'

The men slowly crept across the pasture towards Cable Grange. Mark and another man pulled up their groggy friend and with his arms over their shoulders dragged him off through the high grass.

'The rest of you listen to Miss Howard or you'll have me to answer to.' He stepped aside, waving his hand at the workers. 'Your men are ready.'

Her angry eyes flashed at him before she stepped forwards to face her servants.

'You know I don't condone fighting. I should dismiss every one of you for what you've done.' Alarm swept through the men, but they did not answer back. Watching her walk up and down the line of servants, she reminded him of a petite captain. It was strange to see a lady in such a position, but it boded well for a woman who, depending on how their scheme played out, might accompany him throughout the world under who knew what circumstances.

'I know you men all have families and you're all good, hard workers, so I'll forgive you today,' she continued. 'But if I ever catch any of you doing something like this again, you'll be instantly dismissed. Now, return to your duties at once, except you, Bill. We must see to your arm.'

The men filed past, thanking her profusely. She nodded sternly at each and when they were gone, turned to Bill. Behind her, John and two other servants appeared with the stretcher and a small wooden medicine chest.

'Well, Bill?' Miss Howard asked, standing over the injured man.

'Am I to be dismissed?' he asked, shamefaced.

'No, I think you've been punished enough for today.' She knelt down beside him. 'I want to see your arm.'

She motioned for it, but he held it fast, drops of blood seeping out from between his fingers.

'It's no sight for a lady.'

'Let me see it,' she insisted.

He removed his hand, revealing a gaping cut. It was small but deep and bleeding heavily. She didn't blanch, but examined it with care, then motioned for the chest.

'You need the surgeon.' She pulled off one glove and removed a bandage roll from the medical box, winding it tightly around Bill's wound. 'John, please fetch the surgeon. You two, help Bill back to the stable. Uncle George, can you accompany them?'

'Yes, but I want James to escort you back to the house.'

'I can find my own way.' She started to rise and George took her by the elbow, helping her to her feet.

'I insist he see you back.'

'Very well.'

George joined the servants making their way back to the house, leaving James alone with Miss Howard.

'That was very brave of you. I don't know another lady with such command of her staff and quite the strong stomach.' He kicked loose dirt over the small puddle of blood on the ground. 'I think you'd be very good in any crisis. You have a way with authority.'

'And you, Captain, have a way of interfering when you shouldn't. Kindly remember you are a guest at Knollwood, not its owner.'

Julia pushed past him, making for the path to the house. She heard the heavy fall of his boots on the ground as he caught up to her and she quickened her pace, nearly breaking into a run.

'Julia, wait.'

She whirled to face him, closing the short distance between them. 'How dare you address me in such an intimate manner?'

'I think it only fitting since we're engaged.' There it was again, his knowing smile, the one she found so infuriating. What was it about this man who annoyed her with such charm?

'Yes, engaged, and not even that, yet you already act like a husband.'

The comment wiped the smile from his face. 'Is this my thanks for helping you?'

'You weren't helping. You were undermining my authority, giving orders and interfering with my management of Knollwood.'

'If I hadn't undermined your authority, some servant would have pummelled you.'

'I do not wish to discuss it.' She continued on up the path, too worked up by the fight, the wound and the captain to stand still. A small pang of guilt needled her for being so cross. Yes, if he hadn't stepped in she might well have been injured, or worse. But she couldn't bring herself to thank him. She suddenly wished she were at Cable Grange with all of this ridiculous business behind her.

'Julia, please stop.'

The tender request held more power than any of his commands, bringing her to a halt. He walked around to stand in front of her, but she refused to meet his face. She kept her head down, studying his boots, noting the mud stuck to the sides and a small scuff on the toe.

'Whatever you think of my interfering, I only meant to help and whether our engagement is real or fake doesn't matter. I had no desire to see you hurt.'

She pulled on her glove, fumbling to fasten the small button at her wrist, unsure how to continue. He was right. She shouldn't be angry and she had insulted him again without good reason. Would she never learn? 'Perhaps we shouldn't play this game.'

He took her hand, his fingers slipping the ivory button through its hole.

'I very much enjoy this game, my little Artemis.' His thumb stroked the inside of her palm, firm and warm through her glove. Her heart raced and she worked to breathe evenly.

'Don't call me that.'

'But it suits you.'

Her anger, the fighting men and all her troubles faded away and she was aware of nothing but his hand on hers. 'I'm sorry if I seem ungrateful. I shouldn't be, especially after everything you've agreed to do for me. I do thank you for your help.'

'We all need help sometimes.'

'I'm not accustomed to asking for it.'

'You didn't ask. I offered.' He swept her into his arms, covering her lips with his. All the stories Paul had told her about Navy men urged her to pull away, but she didn't. Instead she went soft in his arms, falling into him as he pulled her close. His warm, firm lips drove everything from her mind: Cable Grange, the fighting servants, Charles. A thrill coursed through her, like riding Manfred over the hills on a sunny day. Her heart raced, her mind spun and then suddenly it was over. He stepped back, and she smiled as she stared at him, resisting the urge to throw herself into his arms and demand he continue.

'I think we should return to the house,' she stammered. What else did one say after allowing a gentleman to take liberties?

'Indeed.' He offered her his arm and she took it.

She hadn't been able to command one coherent thought on the walk back. So much had happened so fast she couldn't make sense out of any of it. Only when they entered the garden to find her mother and Emily waiting on the stone patio did her head finally clear. Emily's lips were drawn tight with worry, but her mother only raised a curious eyebrow at the sight of them walking so close together. Julia's grip on the captain's arm tightened.

'What's wrong?'

'I'm going to hear a great deal from Emily about being so rash. I don't suppose you wish to help me again?'

'If only I could.' The captain laughed. 'But I'm afraid you must handle this matter alone.'

Chapter Eight

Emily's clipped steps carried her across the morning-room rug, crossing back and forth in front of Julia, who stood by the fireplace, tapping her foot in irritation. Every day Emily sounded more and more like Charles and the constant lectures were proving quite tiresome. Cable Grange could not be hers soon enough.

'First you go out riding with the captain, alone,' Emily said.

'We didn't go out riding. He happened upon me at the keep.'

'Then you put yourself in danger by involving yourself with the servants in front of him.'

'You'd rather they fight instead of work?' Julia silently pleaded with her mother, wishing for once she'd intervene, but she did nothing except adjust Charlemagne's collar.

'Come, Emily, don't be so hard on Julia.' Uncle

George stepped in, refilling his glass of port from the decanter near the window. 'Girl has responsibilities.'

'Don't you understand the way this behaviour appears? Whether innocent or not, it is compromising.'

'In James's eyes, never.' Uncle George laughed. 'He isn't such an old biddy to get fired up over a ride or an incident with the field hands.'

'I believe you are both failing to see the point.'

'Excuse me, Mrs Howard.' Captain Covington entered the room, respectfully deferential. 'I believe I have some information to put your mind at ease.'

'Information?' Emily asked.

Julia shook her head, but he ignored her, reserving his gracious smile for Emily.

'This afternoon in the forest I asked Miss Howard to marry me and she accepted.'

The room went silent.

'Is it true?' Emily demanded.

Julia wasn't sure how to answer. She hadn't expected him to announce their engagement so soon, but now it was done and she had to play along. 'Of course it's true.'

'But—you hardly know one another.'

'In the short amount of time we've spent together we've discovered a great deal in common. It's as though we've known each other for years.' Captain Covington took Julia's hand and gazed lovingly into her eyes. Her heart fluttered with excitement before she reined in her runaway emotions. Reminding herself it was all a ruse, she returned the loving smile with one of her own, careful not to exaggerate it too much.

Emily twisted her hands in front of her. 'What will Charles say?'

'I have already spoken to Mother and Uncle George,' Julia lied, hoping they would play along, too.

'She did?' Emily asked her mother-in-law, who nodded.

'We discussed it this morning.'

'And you?' Emily turned to Uncle George.

'Jim mentioned it during our ride,' he mumbled, tossing back the last of his port.

Julia let out her breath. Uncle George would demand an explanation, but he could always be counted on to go along.

'Please excuse us, Captain.' Emily grabbed Julia by the arm, pulling her into the hall and closing the morning-room door behind them. 'What's going on?'

'I thought you'd be pleased. You and Charles are always telling me to marry.'

'Yes, but—?'

'But what? Isn't Captain Covington a respectable man?'

'To be sure, but—'

'But what? Uncle George has known him for years, he has a sizeable fortune, and he's amiable and well spoken of. What objection could you possibly have?'

'Marriage isn't something to be entered into lightly.'

'Why shouldn't I be as happy with him as any other gentleman?'

Emily took her by the shoulders, examining her with an older sister's overprotective concern. 'Is there something else to this I should know? You haven't engaged in any compromising behaviour?'

The captain's kiss suddenly came to mind, but her rising anger pushed the memory away. 'Beyond the list you've accused me of?'

'Please, be serious.'

Julia threw up her hands in exasperation. 'Of course not—how could you even make such a suggestion?'

'Because this is all so sudden. Do you love him?'

Julia looked out one of the tall windows flanking the front door where two turtle doves walked in the shade of the portico. Watching them coo to each other, Julia wondered at the question. Love. How would it feel to truly be in love? The fountain in the garden came to mind. Could she find such passion with the captain? No, he'd only prove as meddlesome as he had with the labourers.

'Well?' Emily demanded, breaking the long silence.

'Of course,' Julia lied. She was pretending to be engaged; why not pretend to be in love, too? 'He's the most interesting, well-travelled man I've ever met and quite handsome. You remarked on those exact qualities yourself the other night at cards.'

'Yes, but you seemed so uninterested.'

'I did not know him well then.'

Emily tapped her fingers on her chin, examining Julia, struggling to comprehend the strange turn of events. 'Do you think you'll be happy with him?'

'Yes. I'll have my own home to run. How could I not be happy?' This certainly wasn't a lie and it helped put Emily's mind at ease.

'Then I am glad for you.' She hugged Julia with all the affection of a sister before her smile tensed at the corners. 'Of course, Captain Covington should have asked Charles's permission first—

he is your guardian—but I don't think he'll object. I'll write to him about it at once.'

Julia didn't share Emily's worry. No doubt she'd already written to him about Julia's behaviour. If so, she knew Charles would jump to give his consent, if only to see her settled and out of Knollwood. For once, the idea didn't trouble her. 'I'll write him, too. I want him to know of my good fortune.'

They walked back to the morning room, a slight smile tugging at the edges of her lips. Cable Grange and freedom were in her grasp.

Inside, Uncle George pumped Captain Covington's hand, the port in his glass sloshing high along the rim. 'Congratulations, Jim. You don't know how glad I am to hear it. Julia, you couldn't have asked for a better man.'

Julia felt a slight twinge of guilt. If he was this excited by their engagement, how disappointed would he be when it all came to an end?

'Now I have some news to add to yours,' Uncle George announced. 'I've secured invitations to the Johnsons' ball Wednesday night. You two can announce the engagement to everyone.'

'I can't go. I have no dress and I can't have one made in such a short time.' She hadn't planned on making a public announcement. If no one outside the family knew, she could easily break it off with very few consequences.

'One of your London gowns will do,' her mother said and Julia blanched. Her mother knew the engagement wasn't real. Why would she encourage the ball? It must only be to convince Charles of its validity. What other reason could she have? She was almost afraid to imagine it. 'We'll choose a dress today, in case it needs any alterations.'

'Yes, of course.' Julia tried to sound excited, but with no desire to attend the ball it was difficult.

'Do you mind if I have a private word with your groom-to-be?' Uncle George asked and Julia had a good idea what he wished to discuss. At least it meant another person on her side against Charles, one who would speak up for her far more than her mother.

'Not at all. I must write to Charles and I believe Mother wishes to discuss dresses.'

Once the ladies were gone, George turned a suspicious eye on James. 'Out with it. What are you two up to?'

'You don't believe in true love?'

'Until today you've done nothing but tickle Annette's fancy—now suddenly you and Julia are engaged? Did something happen out on your ride?'

'I assure you, it's nothing like that.'

'Then what?'

'Cable Grange.'

George frowned. 'I thought you were over all that.'

'I am—apparently your niece is not. She thinks an engagement might force her brother's hand.'

'It may just force yours. Charles isn't like Paul and Julia. He may make you go through with it.'

James walked to the window, watching the shadow of clouds pass over the gravel drive. 'Perhaps by the end of it I may not mind.'

'You want to marry her?' George stammered.

'I suppose by the auction, we'll see.' He'd taken a chance announcing the engagement and wasn't sure what would happen by the time Cable Grange came up for sale.

'James…' George joined him at the window, dropping his voice, one eye on the morning-room door '…I've known you a long time and we've been through a lot together, but where Julia is concerned I'll side with her if things go badly. I hope it doesn't come to that, but if it does, you'll find me and Charles standing against you.'

James flexed his left hand, keeping his eyes fixed on a tree in the distance. 'I have no intention of allowing things to go badly. I will do the honourable thing where your niece is concerned, but she may not have me in the end.'

'What do you mean?'

James explained her plan to George, who nodded gravely, taking it all in with a large sip of port.

'I see what you mean.' George rubbed his chin with his hand. 'I knew she wanted the place, but I didn't think she'd go this far to get it.'

'I will do all I can to protect her and her reputation. But as you yourself said, she's spirited.'

'Yes, but better you than the fop.' He slapped James on the back, then headed for the port. 'If nothing else, it will be interesting.'

James laughed, joining his friend in a drink. Yes, it would be interesting.

'Well done,' her mother congratulated when Julia entered the sitting room after giving Davies the letter to Charles to post. She'd written it a few days ago in an effort to phrase her case without distraction or emotion, then simply rewritten it, replacing Simon's name with the captain's.

'Emily did not react well.' Emily had yet to join them and Julia knew she was busy writing her own letter. She could only imagine its contents and hoped Charles's business in London kept him from coming home to see the situation for himself. 'I thought she would be pleased.'

'She'll be less pleased if you jilt the captain.'

'When I jilt the captain,' Julia corrected, sitting at the small table across from her. 'You won't tell her, will you?'

'No, though at some point you'll have to tell Charles. That alone may stop you from breaking the engagement.'

'Surely you don't want me to marry the captain?'

Mother offered Charlemagne a titbit from the plate next to her. Julia picked at the lace tablecloth, the silence punctuated by the dog's chewing. It wasn't unusual for Mother not to answer, but this time something about it made Julia uneasy.

'I must also find a way to avoid the ball,' Julia added. 'I can't have the whole countryside knowing of my engagement. It will create a scandal when I break it.'

'You'll have a stronger case if it's public knowledge.'

At least Julia had been correct about her mother's motives. 'Yes, but if everyone knows, I'll be the talk of every country party this winter. I'd rather not subject myself to such gossip.'

'My dear, you must learn not to care so much about what people think.'

If only it were so easy, Julia thought, Emily's entrance ending their private conversation.

What followed was a boring hour of flipping through pattern books and discussing trimmings. They invited Annette to join them, but she declined, stating she had no need to rework a dress as those she had brought from London were adequate for a country ball. Very soon Emily and Mrs Howard were debating the merits of their different dresses and doing their best to engage Julia.

'See the way they've used the ribbon here. Wouldn't that be lovely on my white-silk gown?' Emily asked.

'Yes, lovely.' Julia listlessly flipped through a pattern book, eager to be free of all this idle chatter and return to plans for Cable Grange. She still couldn't believe Captain Covington had agreed to go along with her scheme and wondered why.

Julia touched her lips, the memory of his kiss searing the flesh. With all the excitement of the engagement, she hadn't had time to think about it. Now it came rushing back, followed by an unsettling feeling deep in her stomach. Why had he kissed her? Could he have feelings for her? Had she finally turned a man's head? No, of course not. He had no interest in her beyond their amusing game and she only wanted him in order to secure Cable Grange. As for the kiss, what did she expect? She'd acted like a strumpet more than once, so of course he treated her like one. She would have to be more careful in the future.

'I think your blue-silk dress will do very well,' her mother said.

'What blue dress?'

'The one you wore at Almack's.'

Julia shuddered at the memory.

'Oh, yes.' Emily clapped. 'It was so beautiful on you. Fetch it and we'll see if it needs any alterations.'

Julia reluctantly rose and went to her room. Cable Grange couldn't be hers soon enough for she was tired of all this ordering about.

Inside her room, she stood before her wardrobe, wondering which gown Emily meant. She remembered many things about her dreadful night at Almack's, but what she'd worn was not one of them. Too distracted to care, she snatched the first blue dress she saw. Walking back to her mother's room, a ribbon fell off, fluttering to the floor. Julia stooped to pick it up, then stopped at the sound of heated voices from Annette's room.

The door stood slightly ajar and Julia slowly approached, peering through the small crack. It wasn't her habit to stare in keyholes, but the angry tones made her more curious than cautious.

Inside, Annette sat crying on the small padded bench. Simon stood over her, his face red with anger.

'What I do is none of your concern.' For the first time there was emotion in his voice and no hint of his affected dandy lisp.

'Of course it's my concern. You'll ruin us both with your foolery.' Her tears came faster, but they did not soften Simon's hard expression.

'I'm not entirely to blame, dear sister. I've seen your milliner's bill.'

'What choice do I have? I must find a husband before you gamble away my dowry.'

'If you're pursuing Captain Covington, you're wasting your time. I heard him announce to Emily his engagement to Julia. You might as well set your cap at George for all the good it'll do you.'

'I'd rather marry a rich oaf than be sent to the workhouse by you.'

'Don't be so theatrical. You'll always have Mama and Edward to live with.'

'As a spinster if you spend everything. What man wants a penniless woman?'

Julia waited for Simon's response, but all she heard was the muffled sound of Annette's crying.

'If you're finished,' Simon sneered, 'I've hired a coach to take me back to London tomorrow.'

'But Mama and Edward said we must stay until he sorts out your debts with the creditors.'

'I don't care what Edward or Mama say. Stay if you wish, but I'm leaving.'

Simon headed for the door and Julia hurried down the hallway and around a corner. She watched from her hiding place as he emerged stiff-rumped and made his way down the stairs.

In his haste to be rid of his sister, he'd left the door wide open. There was no way to return to her mother's room without walking past Annette's. Releasing her tight hold on the dress, Julia crept down the runner, hoping to sneak by without being seen. Annette still sat on the bench, her face buried in a handkerchief, her shoulders racked with sobs. Despite everything Annette had done and said, Julia felt for the girl. Though she called Charles a great many things in private, he was not quite so hard-hearted as Simon.

Julia took a step and the floor squeaked. Annette's head jerked up in alarm. Caught, Julia hesitated, debating whether or not to comfort the broken-hearted girl. Embarrassment and shame marred Annette's features and Julia knew now was no time for reassuring words. She fled down the hall, hearing the door slam shut behind her.

'What's wrong?' Emily asked when Julia hurried into the room.

'I've just learned the most horrible thing.'

'Is it news from Paul?' Her mother clutched Charlemagne to her chest.

'Heavens, no. It's about Annette and Simon.'

'Oh.' Emily exchanged a knowing look with her mother-in-law. 'So you've found out?'

'Is this what you meant by her situation?'

'Yes, it's the reason they're here.'

'Our brother,' her mother interrupted, for she always referred to her elder brother Edward as 'our brother'. When Edward had married the much younger widow Mrs Taylor, it had sent Uncle George and her mother into fits. 'Thought it wise to remove them from London for a while in the hopes of curbing Simon's expenses.'

'You mean his gambling.'

The older woman nodded.

'Why doesn't his mother stop him? Or Uncle Edward?'

'The inheritance is entailed to Simon. Though he does pay Annette's bills, his debts have taken the vast majority of the money. If he does not stop gambling, he will be bankrupt by year's end.'

'Poor Annette. It certainly explains her peevish behaviour.' Julia sat on the sofa next to her mother.

'She does have a small inheritance of her own, but she regularly spends beyond her income. Our brother hoped you might make friends with her, teach her economy. He failed to take into account her difficult nature.'

'I'd be happy to help if only she weren't so disagreeable.'

She expected Emily to chastise her for the remark, but instead Emily leaned forwards, placing a hand on her arm. 'You must not speak of this to anyone outside the family.'

'Why would I?'

'No, I don't suppose you would, despite how nasty Annette has been to you.'

At least she has a high opinion of me in this regard, Julia thought, but held her tongue.

Chapter Nine

'What a beautiful day for riding, Artemis,' Captain Covington sang out from behind her. At first his nickname had irked her, but the more he used it, the more she liked it.

'I'd ride every day if only the weather would allow it.'

'So you should for that beast should never be cooped up.'

Manfred's ears twitched and Julia laughed, petting his strong neck. 'Ignore him, Manfred. You are no beast.'

Captain Covington laughed. 'Just a poor misunderstood creature.'

'I think we are all misunderstood in our own way, wouldn't you say, Captain?' Julia caught Annette's eyes over the captain's shoulder, but Annette turned away, fiddling with her gelding's reins.

The good weather had held strong overnight and

Julia, Captain Covington and Uncle George decided on a ride after nuncheon. Emily encouraged Annette to join them and, for the first time since arriving at Knollwood, she did. Julia suspected it had something to do with what Julia had discovered yesterday afternoon. Throughout the ride, Annette regarded her with caution, as if waiting for Julia to use her new knowledge in retaliation for everything she'd done. Julia might harmlessly annoy the chit from time to time, but it wasn't in her nature to be deliberately mean or spiteful and she had no intention of taunting Annette about her unfortunate circumstances.

They crested the hill along the boundary between Knollwood and Cable Grange, happening on a bit of excitement in a field on the other side. Two men raced questionable mounts across the field, turning around a moss-covered tree stump at the far end before galloping back to the starting point. The drunken group cheered, their own horses grazing in the grass and waiting for the chance to race. Julia recognised a few riders as the less savoury men of Daringford, more apt to be outside the Sign of the Swan and worse for their experiences inside, than bent over an honest day's labour. The rest of the men were strangers, probably travellers on their way north from London with more hope than brains.

Mr Wilkins sat atop his prize racehorse, Chester, watching the proceedings with a cool eye. Mark stood next to him managing the wagers and collecting a fair amount of blunt at the end of the race. A short distance away, a large barrel balanced on an old stump. Next to it, another of Mr Wilkins's servants dispensed generous tankards of ale to the gathered riff-raff who cheered Wilkins's health with each gulp.

Captain Covington stopped Hector next to Manfred. 'Is this a regular hobby of his?'

'Only when he's lost too much money. How no one has discovered his scam and warned those silly fools, I don't know.'

'Scam?'

'Mr Wilkins doesn't ride Chester into Daringford. Instead he rides Chester's father, Darby, a spry but older horse with markings almost identical to Chester's, but he's not nearly as fast. Inside the tavern, he befriends a few gullible travellers from London then convinces them to race. Once the men agree, Mr Wilkins rides home and exchanges Darby for Chester. These men, sodden with drink, don't realise they're racing one of the finest bits of blood in the county.'

'Don't the country men warn the town men?'

'No, they bet against them and win a few shillings, only to lose them again at the tavern.'

'How do you know so much about it?'

'I heard rumours from the servants after Tom, one of the new ones, lost some money to Wilkins. I wanted to know what he was up to, so I sent Tom back with a few coins and a horse.'

'You spy on your neighbour?'

'Of course. Doesn't everyone? I think it ungentlemanly of Mr Wilkins to wager against unsuspecting travellers. I know they're just as much to blame for trying to win money instead of earning it, but he's sorely mistaken if he thinks he can save Cable Grange off these poor souls.'

'I wouldn't be so sure. A small amount of blunt may be enough to stave off the bailiff.'

'No, he can't.' She watched another set of horses and riders take off across the meadow, noticing the money changing hands with Mark. She'd come too far to let Cable Grange slip from her fingers now. 'We must stop this, if for no other reason than to save those silly men from themselves.'

'For no other reason.' The captain winked. 'What do you propose?'

'It would be wonderful to give Mr Wilkins a taste of his own medicine.'

'So we shall,' Captain Covington replied, mischief igniting his eyes. 'Manfred against Chester—it's a fitting match.'

'I'd love to race Manfred and reveal Mr Wilkins for the scoundrel he really is.'

'It is unladylike for a woman to race, especially against men.' Annette manoeuvred her horse next to Manfred, the warning in her voice clear. 'Even here in the country.'

Julia wondered at the advice, unsure if it was meant to be friendly or yet another insult. Either way, she couldn't ignore the truth of it. Then the idea came to her.

'Captain Covington, we can change saddles and you can ride Manfred.'

'Won't Mr Wilkins recognise the beast?'

'Tell him he's a different horse. He can't risk challenging you and having his secret revealed. Offer him an appealing amount. I'm sure his greed will overcome any hesitation.'

'You don't fear for my safety?'

'Manfred will take care of you just as he's always taken care of me.'

Uncle George leaned forwards in his saddle to peer around Annette at Captain Covington. 'Has a lot of me in her, wouldn't you say?'

'Yes. Sounds very much like something you would have concocted.'

'Then you'll do it?' Julia asked.

'Of course.' The captain threw his leg over the saddle and slid off Hector. He walked around to Manfred and reached up to help Julia down. 'Lean against my right shoulder so I don't drop you.'

'You won't drop me.'

Julia slid from the saddle into the captain's waiting arms, careful to place her weight on his right shoulder. She wound her arm around his neck, allowing her fingertips to brush the smooth skin between the collar and his hair. He lowered her to the ground, the tart smell of his warm skin filling her senses. Their eyes met and for a moment the sound of the cheering men and snorting horses faded into the distance and there was nothing but his body so close to hers.

'I knew you wouldn't drop me.'

'Thank you.' He raised her gloved hand to his lips.

'James, I believe you have a race to attend to.' Uncle George coughed behind them, clearly enjoying what he saw.

She withdrew her hand, her face warm with a blush before she recovered herself. 'Uncle George is right. We must hurry.'

* * *

They set to work unbuckling the saddles on their respective horses. When they were free, James placed his saddle on Manfred while George worked to fasten Julia's side-saddle on Hector. When they were done, James helped her mount, then swung atop Manfred. The horse took a couple of agitated steps at the extra weight, but seemed to recognise him and relaxed and James knew Julia's faith in the beast was well placed.

Out of the corner of his eye, James saw Julia start Hector down the hill and he reached out, taking hold of the stallion's bridle.

'What are you doing?' she protested.

'I'm no stickler for convention, but Miss Taylor is right. It isn't proper for a young lady to be seen in such company. Watch from up here.'

She scowled, but didn't argue. 'If I'm to stay here, then you'd better give me a show worth watching.'

'Don't worry. I'll exact your revenge just as you instructed. Come, George, we have work to do.'

George guided Percy into step beside Manfred and the horses picked their way down the small hill. James kept the reins light, surprised by Manfred's docile turn. The horse, unlike before, didn't fight him, but responded fast and quick to the smallest tap of James's foot or the pressure of his legs, answering to these subtle commands as though the two of them had been riding together for years. James smiled, thinking Julia's acceptance of him had in some way secured Manfred's acceptance, too.

They approached the gathering as a race ended and the men exchanged money while enjoying more ale.

'Good morning, Rowan,' George called out. Rowan nodded coolly at George, his sly eyes fixed on James.

'What do you want?' Rowan sneered.

'To race, of course.'

Rowan's lips curled at the sight of the ladies watching from the top of the hill. 'This is a private race.'

'Nonsense,' George insisted. 'It wouldn't be November if you weren't racing and the captain has a mind to wager some blunt.'

'My poor old Darby is no match for Manfred.' Rowan shrugged apologetically, but James was not about to be put off, especially with everyone now listening intently to their conversation.

'This isn't Manfred—this is Whizzer.' James patted Manfred's flank, trying not to laugh.

'He looks exactly like Manfred.'

'Manfred was a bit lame this morning. Didn't see fit to bring him out. Whizzer here is an older horse and I think a suitable match for Darby.' With a look, James dared Rowan to challenge him and reveal the truth, making it clear he knew Rowan's game.

Rowan hesitated. Julia was right; he would not risk exposing James for fear of exposing himself, but James could tell he was forming another excuse and knew it was time to make his move. 'I'll wager five hundred pounds Whizzer can best Darby.'

Interest replaced the distrust on Rowan's face. 'You seem very confident in Whizzer.'

'He's the fastest old horse in the county. What do you say?'

Greed flickered in Rowan's eyes and James knew he had him.

'I accept your wager,' he answered loudly so the others could hear. 'Five hundred pounds says Darby can beat Whizzer.'

Sharp whistles and drunken shouts went up from the crowd and they rushed at Mark to place their bets.

'Shall we?' Rowan gestured to the starting line and James brought Manfred into place.

* * *

A horse whinnied from behind them and Julia turned to see Mrs Wilkins ride up next to her. She wore a tight-fitting habit of deep red. It highlighted her pale skin and emphasised her painted lips. 'Miss Howard, I see you're enjoying the races.'

Julia stuck her chin in the air, determined not to let this strumpet act like her better. 'Any excitement is always welcome in the country.'

Mrs Wilkins squinted at the riders. 'Is James about to race Rowan?'

'Yes, and he will win.'

'How sweet of you to root for him. One would almost think you cared for him.'

'She and the captain are engaged,' Annette volunteered.

Julia went stiff in the saddle, not sure how to react.

'Engaged?' Mrs Wilkins exclaimed in mock amazement, her wicked smile growing wider. 'Oh, you poor dear. I was engaged to Captain Covington once, a long time ago, in Portsmouth. Marry him fast, Miss Howard. He isn't the type of man to follow through on a promise.' She clicked her horse into motion, guiding it down the hill to join the spectators.

Julia watched Mrs Wilkins go, her head spinning, her stomach tight. The captain and Mrs Wilkins? It couldn't be true, could it?

'Why did you tell her?' She turned on Annette. 'I had no intention of sharing such personal information with that woman.'

'Better to tell someone like her yourself than let her hear it from others,' Annette answered, the advice almost friendly. Was she trying to help her? It didn't seem possible.

'You know her?'

Annette shook her head. 'I know of her. She has a terrible reputation in London. According to the *on dit*, a French count paid her bills when her husband couldn't. No one in good society will have anything to do with her.'

Surely a woman with such a scandalous reputation was capable of lying about the past. The hostile meeting in Daringford came to mind, adding a sickening validity to Mrs Wilkins's revelation. He had said he'd known her a long time ago. Could they have been set to marry? It scared her to think he might not honour the engagement, though she didn't know why since she had no intention of marrying either. She thought of his kiss and the way he'd helped her down from Manfred. Had he held Mrs Wilkins like that once?

No, it doesn't matter, she told herself, stamping down the jealousy. With the race about to begin, there were more important things to think about.

James held Manfred at the starting line, the beast tense and ready to run. He noticed Melinda on her horse making her way down from where Julia and Miss Taylor watched. Anger filled him and he took a deep breath, forcing himself to calm down and focus on winning. He would not lose in front of Melinda.

'I can't wait to give you a beating and knock down some of that chit's pride,' Rowan spat, his horse pawing at the ground.

James tightened his grip on the reins. 'I hope you have the five hundred pounds to make good on your wager.'

'Gentlemen, are ya ready?' Mark stood between the horses, arms raised.

'Don't fail me, Manfred. Your mistress is counting on us both,' he whispered and the horse's ears twitched in response.

Mark dropped his arms and James dug his heels into Manfred's sides. They shot out over the meadow, James crouched low over Manfred's neck, the wind stinging his eyes. He didn't try to control Manfred, but concentrated on moving with the horse, letting the animal guide them to a win. In a flash of brown, Rowan and Chester raced up beside them, the horses' heavy breaths and pounding hooves drowning out the cheering men. Rowan nearly slammed Chester against Manfred, trying to drive them off course, but Manfred proved the more dominant animal. He bumped Chester's flank, knocking James's legs into Rowan's with a thud.

'Hell,' Rowan cursed as Chester relented, falling behind enough for James to manoeuvre Manfred around the stump first and place a bit of distance between the racers. Under the crook of his arm, James watched Rowan slap Chester's flanks with his crop, urging him faster and faster, but the gap was too wide and Manfred dashed across the finish line.

'Well done!' Julia shouted, her kidskin gloves muffling her exuberant claps.

The captain rose up in his saddle, saluting her before the men crowded around, cheering as money changed hands.

'That'll show the Wilkinses,' Julia laughed, her excitement fading at the sight of Mrs Wilkins riding up next to the captain. They exchanged a few words, then James pulled Manfred's reins to the right, trotting over to where Uncle George and Percy stood.

Watching them, Mrs Wilkins's revelation sat like a dark shadow over Julia, dampening her enthusiasm. How could he have ever been involved with such a woman or had she once been respectable?

'Do you know anything about Mrs Wilkins's past?' Julia asked and Annette shook her head.

'No. I only know the rumours.'

Had Mrs Wilkins fallen from good society because of her involvement with the captain? Did the same fate await her?

'We shouldn't be here. It isn't proper.' Julia ignored the way Annette's eyebrows rose in disbelief. Without waiting for an answer, Julia turned Hector around and galloped back to Knollwood. She wanted to be alone, to think and settle the trouble gripping her heart. Surely there was another explanation. The captain didn't seem like the sort of man who ruined women and Uncle George would never have such a friend. Whatever the truth, she must make certain they played at nothing more than the pretend engagement. Her reputation would suffer enough when she jilted him. She did not need the additional scandal of being a fallen woman.

* * *

James walked with George back from the stables, a sense of unease nagging at him. Melinda's sudden appearance combined with her happy salutations for their engagement made him suspicious. He knew from her malicious smile she'd told Julia of their engagement, probably portraying their relationship in the worst possible light. Who knew what lies she'd attached to it? He had to find Julia and undo any damage the vile woman had done.

Davies met them at the back door with a letter. 'This arrived for you, Captain Covington.'

James took the note, not recognising the hand until he broke the seal and scanned the contents. Crumpling the letter, he stuffed it inside his coat pocket.

'What's wrong?' George asked.

'She wants to see me.'

'Julia?'

'Melinda. She wishes to discuss Rowan's debt and the sale of Cable Grange.'

'So you do still want it. Julia won't take kindly to you purchasing it out from under her.'

James laced his fingers behind his back. 'With Rowan in my debt, perhaps I can convince him to sell it to her. It's more reliable than an auction.

Please tell everyone I had business to attend to in Daringford. I'll return as soon as I can.'

'Let me come with you. I don't trust Melinda or you with her.'

'You think I'm so weak?'

'I think you're too angry. I thought you'd let go of the past, but I can see by your reaction to that letter that you haven't. My guess is, neither has she.'

The past still stung, but it no longer dominated his mind. Nor did the future seem so vague or purposeless thanks to Julia. Her spirited laugh, hopeful eyes and honest manner helped him imagine a life filled with travel, family and friends, all of it with her by his side. He loved her and he wanted to capture her heart, make it burn for him as powerfully as it did for her beloved Knollwood. He could no longer deny it was the real reason he'd agreed to the engagement.

Fear tinged the revelation. He'd been deceived by a woman once before, but he couldn't imagine Julia ever betraying him. She loved as strongly as she lived and would give herself completely to the man who captured her heart. He hoped by the end of next week he could make her his. If securing Cable Grange meant winning her, then he would buy it. 'The past is done. It's time to see to my future.'

* * *

James knocked on the heavy oak door of Cable Grange and waited, drawing his coat tight around his face to ward off the frosty night air. The sun had slipped below the horizon and although light still filled the western sky, the night's first stars sparkled overhead. The scrape of wood across stone and the squeak of rusty hinges split the silence as Mark pulled open the door. The single candle in his brass holder flickered in the draught, shadowing his bloodshot eyes.

'She's waiting for you upstairs,' he snarled.

James stepped inside, the dingy entrance hall no warmer than outside. Larger and more spacious than Knollwood's, it echoed like an old cavern, the chandelier overhead thick with cobwebs. 'Then lead the way.'

Without ceremony, Mark started up the staircase, the smoking tallow candle not doing much more than threatening to burn out. James peered down through the wavering shadows, trying to get a sense of the place. Dust covers sagged over the few scattered pieces of furniture and glaring clean spots on the dirty walls betrayed the paintings long since sold to pay bills.

At the top Mark turned, leading James down

the dank hallway. The carpets were missing here, too, along with the furniture.

'She's in here.' Mark stopped at the last door at the end of the hall. 'You can find your own way out when she's through with ya.'

'I trust I can.'

Mark walked off, taking the light with him.

Without knocking, James pushed open the door, blinking against the sudden light. The house might be decaying around them, but no expense was spared to make Melinda comfortable. The room resembled a Cyprian's palace with gilded chandeliers filled with candles. A grand four-poster bed hung with sumptuous draperies sat in the far corner of the room. At the other end a large fireplace blazed with a well-laid fire. Melinda reclined on a chaise before its heat, dressed in a mantua of red silk. A bottle of wine sat on the table in front of her, along with a small box of sweets. James could see half the contents of both had already been consumed.

'I didn't think you'd come.' She ran her fingers across the back of a velvet pillow.

'I almost didn't. What do you want?'

'Please sit down.' She motioned to the sofa across from her. In the low light there was something of the woman he'd once loved, the faint echo of her girlish beauty, the tempting smile and inviting eyes that had captivated him in his youth. Back then he hadn't recognised the worldliness in their shallow gleam, but it stood out now, repulsing him.

'You said you had news.' He sat on the edge of the cushion, eyeing the minx with caution. The elaborate scene felt like a gilded wire waiting to ensnare him.

'I do. Wine?'

He shook his head. 'Let's have it out. I can't stay here all night.'

'Why?' She leaned over the table to refill her glass, her mantua gaping open to reveal her breasts almost to the nipples. 'You have no wife to go home to.'

'But you have a husband.'

Disgust crossed her face before she hid it behind the wine glass, taking a long sip. 'He's in town trying to win enough money from your friend Mr Taylor to ward off the bailiff and you. I suspect Mr Taylor is as destitute as we are.' She chuckled callously, lying back on the *chaise* like an Egyptian queen. 'So you're to be married to the Howard girl? She's not woman enough for a man like you.'

'What do you know of me?' he demanded and she rose, sauntering forwards, the firelight silhouetting her round hips and curving body.

She sat down next to him, her eyes heavy, the sickeningly sweet smell of her perfume mixing with wine in the air between them. 'You loved me once.'

'I was too young to know the difference between love and lust.' He leaned back against the arm of the sofa. 'And if I remember correctly, I didn't have enough money to suit your tastes.'

She shrugged off the accusation. 'But you're here now.'

'Only to discuss the sale of Cable Grange.'

She smiled out of the corner of her hard eyes. 'You plan to give it to your fiancée.'

'How do you know?'

'Everyone knows she wants it. Her father offered to buy it before he died. He hoped to leave it to her. I convinced Rowan not to do it. As much as I hate this tomb, I'd rather see the bailiff sell it than let that bitch have it.'

He was on his feet in an instant, staring down at her with a rage he fought hard to control. 'We have nothing further to discuss.' He stormed to the door, determined to leave her in the past once and for all.

'I have an offer to make,' Melinda called after him.

He stopped, his hand on the doorknob, but didn't turn around. 'I'm listening.'

She slid up to him, wrapping her hands around his shoulders and laying her head on his back. Her fingers played with the skin of his neck, working their way under his collar and down to his chest. He resisted the urge to flinch. 'I'll talk Rowan into selling you this crumbling pile of bricks if you spend the night with me.'

He whirled around, grabbing her wrists and pulling them from around his neck. 'You over-value any feelings I ever had for you.'

Her wine-heavy eyes flared and she snatched her arms from his grasp. 'When did you ever care for me? You indulged your whim, then abandoned me?'

The accusation struck his sense of honour, increasing his anger. 'You gave yourself with wild enthusiasm, then trampled over me to get to Rowan and his money.'

'If you'd truly loved me, you'd have won me

back, not left me to that drunkard. My life is a shambles, ruined, and it's your fault.'

'You have no one to blame but yourself.' He reached for the doorknob, but she threw herself between him and the door.

'If you go, I'll tell the trollop you were here to-night.'

He leaned in close, waving a menacing finger inches from her nose. 'You say anything and I'll tell your husband you tried to seduce me.'

Fear flashed in her eyes. 'He wouldn't believe you.'

'I have your letter. If he finds out I was here, he'll toss you in the gutter where you belong.'

'You wouldn't dare,' she whimpered like a spoiled child.

'Not as long as you keep your mouth shut.'

He pushed her aside and strode into the hallway, his eyes struggling to adjust to the darkness. At the top of the stairs, his hand found the banister and followed the dusty wood down into the empty hall. He pulled open the front door, wincing at the sharp scrape of wood on stone.

Not until he was free of the house and galloping back to Knollwood did he dare reflect on what had happened. Why had he answered her letter? He should have known it was all a ruse, but once again he'd allowed himself to be fooled by her. Now there was a new fear. She might twist tonight's events to her own advantage and throw them in Julia's face. What would Julia think of him then? Only the worst and all hope with her would be lost. No, there was little chance she and Melinda would meet and even if they did, Melinda had no proof of their meeting.

James brought Hector to a stop at the turn to Knollwood. If he continued straight, he'd reach the road to London and it was little over two hours' steady riding to town. Melinda might hate Cable Grange, but Rowan had proved obstinate about selling it. Now, with his debt to James hanging over him, Rowan might be more desperate and willing to part with the estate. James could instruct his solicitor to make enquiries and to keep his identity secret since he doubted the Wilkinses would sell to him, no matter what their circumstances. It might all come to nothing. For all he knew, Rowan's luck had changed and he'd won enough to halt the auctions. However, if the deed to Cable Grange meant securing Miss Howard's affection, he was willing to try.

Julia lay in bed, turning over on her back for what seemed like the hundredth time since she'd blown out the candle. Captain Covington hadn't come to dinner. Uncle George said he'd gone to town, but by nine o'clock he still hadn't returned. She'd waited up for him in the study, hoping to discuss Mrs Wilkins and put some of her fears to rest, but by eleven o'clock she could no longer endure the silent waiting so she went to bed.

She rolled on her side, pulling her cool pillow close. The moon had set at least an hour ago, casting the room into darkness. Closing her eyes, she tried to sleep, but the memory of his lips, warm and tender, parting hers, kept her awake. She bit her lip, trying to banish the strange yearning coursing through her. Tracing a crease in the sheets, she remembered the feel of his neck beneath her fingers when he'd helped her off Manfred, his hands around her waist, his eyes riveted on hers. She imagined him laying her down in the soft grass, his body covering hers, his mouth doing things to her she could almost feel.

Julia sat up, smacking her pillow in frustration. She's never given a fig for any gentleman, yet the captain filled her with all sorts of sinful thoughts. They brought to mind another curiosity: Paul's book, the secret one she'd discovered hidden in the back of his wardrobe a few years ago. She wondered if it was still there and if she could get it without being seen. Everyone else was in bed and she had not heard anything to indicate the captain was back from Daringford. She could sneak in and out of his room without anyone ever knowing.

Rising, she threw on her wrapper, then cracked open the door and peered down the hallway. Small candles flickered in the sconces and a sliver of light showed under the door of Emily's room, but her mother's room was dark. Thankfully, she was a sound sleeper and Julia didn't expect her to rise. She listened for evidence of servants walking about, but only baby Thomas's muffled cries broke the sleeping silence. She sighed with relief, knowing his wails would cover any sound and keep Emily from leaving her room.

The hardwood floors alternating with the soft plush of the rugs teased her bare feet as she stole down the hallway. Stopping at the captain's room, she peeked through the keyhole to make sure he hadn't returned unnoticed. Orange coals glowed in the grate, throwing some light on the flat bed with its unwrinkled coverlet. Twisting the doorknob, she froze when it squeaked, her heart pounding against her chest while she listened for any evidence of discovery. The only sound was the continued cry of baby Thomas.

She pushed open the door and slipped inside,

swiftly closing it behind her. The faint light from the fireplace barely illuminated the room, but Julia knew it well. It was just as Paul had left it with a large wardrobe on the right, a four-poster bed between the two windows and a washstand and chair against the far wall.

Julia hurried to the wardrobe, pulled open the double doors and began feeling for the book. Her hands ran over the scratchy wool of Paul's old uniforms, slid under the folded trousers and bumped a pair of worn Hessians. She caught them before they hit the floor and, with a relieved breath, put them back. Reaching in deeper, she thought maybe he'd moved the book but then her fingers brushed against the leather tome.

She eased it out, careful not to disturb the folded garments or boots. Once it was free, she stood, clutching it to her breast. She traced the gold-edged pages, eager to open them and explore the forbidden content. The possibility of being discovered in a single gentleman's room added a certain thrill to the anticipation, but having no wish to be discovered in such a compromising situation, she moved to close the wardrobe doors. Only then did she hear the heavy fall of a man's boots in the hallway. She froze, her heart almost drowning out the sound. The footsteps drew closer, followed by the flickering light of a candle visible beneath the door. Julia searched for an escape, but there was no way out. As the doorknob turned, splitting the silence with its metallic squeak, she stepped inside the wardrobe and pulled the door closed behind her.

The wardrobe door hadn't fully closed, allowing Julia to see through the slight opening. Crouching low, her knees on the scratchy wool uniform, she watched the captain enter and place his candle on the washstand before closing the door. He removed his blue-wool coat and she clutched the book tight, afraid he might hang it in the wardrobe. She let out a long, silent breath when he threw it over the chair next to the bed. He poured some water from the pitcher into the basin, then splashed it on his face. Large drops dripped from his chin while he examined his face in the mirror, a dark scowl marring his features. Whatever he'd done that evening must not have been pleasant.

He walked around the bed, sitting down hard, facing the wardrobe. Julia rocked back away from the crack, her legs crying out from the impossible position. She hoped he went to bed quickly for she had no desire to stay in such a cramped situation all night. He removed his boots, tossing them off to the side, then reached over his head and pulled off his shirt. Julia's breath caught, but this time it was for quite a different reason. Through the crack, she examined his solid chest, the tight muscles of his stomach and his slim waist. In the candlelight his smooth skin glowed, soft and strong at the same time. She noticed at the base of his left collarbone the puckered skin of a scar. He stood and turned away from her, revealing a similar scar on his back. If only she could slip up behind him, run her fingers over his wide shoulders, trace the line of his spine to where it tapered down to his trousers and explore what lay covered by the fabric. He walked back to the washstand and she gripped the book, leaning further forwards to take him in. As he examined his scar in the mirror, his hands flew to his neck and he jerked up straight.

'Damn.' He tore through the fabric of his discarded shirt and jacket, then tossed them back on the chair in frustration. He dropped to his hands and knees, feeling under the bed. Whatever he searched for remained missing for he sat back on his heels, balling his fists on the edge of the bed, his anger changing to sad resignation.

He must have lost his medal. He said he always wore it, but she hadn't seen it when he'd taken off his shirt. She felt for him, knowing it must hurt to lose something so personal.

Her sympathy vanished when he stood, his fingers working the buttons of his trousers. She moved closer to the crack, a delicious sort of anticipation filling her. He hooked his thumbs in the waistband of his trousers and she leaned forwards, placing her hands on the wardrobe door, waiting, eager, hungry to see all he was about to reveal. Suddenly the door swung open and she tumbled out, her knee hitting the floor hard, the book landing with a thud in front of her.

'Artemis?' The captain buttoned his trousers with one hand while the other took her by the arm and pulled her to her feet. 'What are you doing in the wardrobe?'

What she wouldn't give for a good answer, but she had none. Instead she continued to stare at him, too embarrassed, shocked and bruised to answer.

'Well?' he demanded, his face inches from hers, his voice low and gruff.

'You weren't here and I wanted one of my brother's books.'

'From the wardrobe?'

'It's special.' Her eyes darted to where the book had fallen, relieved to see it lay closed. Then the captain reached for it.

'No, I'll get it.' She lunged for it, but he was faster, snatching it up and away from her.

'I know this book.' He turned it over in his hands, then to her horror flipped it open. He thumbed through the pages, his eyes widening, then his mouth settled into an amused grin. 'Special indeed.'

She wished the floor would open up and swallow her. It was bad enough to be caught in his room, but worse with him half-naked and with that kind of book. She followed the small line of dark hair leading down from his bare stomach into his trousers. His chest rose and fell much quicker than before while he examined the illustrations.

'May I have my book back?' She put out her hand, determined to reclaim as much of her dignity as possible.

He closed the book, then held it out, struggling to remain serious.

She took it, clutching it to her chest like a plate of armour. Her mind kept telling her to turn and leave before she compromised herself even further, but she found her feet rooted to the floor, her eyes riveted to his.

'I should be going,' she whispered.

He nodded, stepping closer. 'Yes, you should.'

She didn't move, but continued to stare until he bent his face down to hers. She closed her eyes, feeling his soft lips envelop hers. The heat of it spread through her body and her mouth responded, parting to accept his tongue. It caressed the line of her lips, sending a shiver through her body.

The book fell, landing with a thud on the carpet as he pulled her close, pressing every inch of him against her, his deep kisses making her forget about the noise and consequences. Only the captain mattered. As she leaned into his chest, her shift and wrapper did little to separate their bodies or hide his hard anticipation pressing against her stomach.

She slid her arms around his waist and ran her hands up his back, her fingers brushing his scar before curling over the roll of his shoulders. She'd imagined being this close to him, but never realised how delicious it would feel or the way it made her whole being come alive. Suddenly, she understood something about those pictures in Paul's book, but none of them captured the desire she felt in the captain's arms.

She inhaled the faint scent of smoke and wine in his hair as he traced the line of her jaw with his lips. Where had he been? She didn't know or care as his teeth grazed her earlobe, his breath hot on her neck. Julia closed her eyes, his touch increasing the need coiling within her.

'Captain?' she whispered, unable to tell him what she wanted, but eager to follow him wherever his caresses led.

'Artemis.' His husky voice tickled her ear before his lips found hers again.

He guided her to the bed and pressed her down on the thick coverlet. His body covered hers, firm and strong, as his hands caressed her arms, then trailed the side of her stomach. A shock went through her when he cupped her breast and his thumb stroked the nipple, bringing it to a tender point. Closing her eyes, she realised now how a man could make a woman forget herself.

He slipped the shift from her shoulder, exposing her breast, and the cool air tickled her heated skin. She gasped, her fingers digging into his arm when he took her nipple in his mouth, flicking it with his tongue. Pleasure curled deep in her body and she moaned, wanting everything the captain offered. His deft hand traced the line of her leg, skimming the smooth flesh of her hip and sliding the shift up around her waist. While his tongue circled her breast his fingers brushed the top of her thigh until they found her aching centre.

Clinging to him, she thought she would die when he caressed the delicate skin. No pictures in any book could have prepared her for this. She moved against him, her body tightening, craving, hungry, and soon she was without reason, her breath fast, her body bending towards something she couldn't name, but it was there, in his fingers, his mouth, the smell of him. She arched her back, his mouth covering hers to muffle the cries as waves of pleasure tore through her body.

He withdrew his fingers and she lay against the pillows, weak and trembling like a newborn foal, but at the same time eager and anxious.

'Again,' she whispered, kissing his neck, his need evident against her leg. She ran her hand over the firm muscles of his chest, following the ripples of his stomach down to his breeches, knowing there was more and wanting to experience it all.

He took her hand and she opened her eyes, studying his face in the dim light. It burned with passion and wanting and something very much like guilt.

'We can't do this.' He pulled her shift down over her legs, then stood.

She sat up, confused and in some way wounded. 'Why?'

'Because it's not right. And there might be consequences.'

What she wouldn't risk to feel such pleasure again, but his sober face drained away her passion, replacing it with shame. 'You don't want me?'

'I want you very much.' He traced her jaw with his finger, brushing the hair back off her shoulder. 'But I can't dishonour you like this.'

'No, of course not.' He didn't want her. No man did and the hurt cut deep. She pulled her shift tighter, her embarrassment more powerful than her sense of caution as she fled the room, struggling to hold back tears.

In her haste, Julia failed to notice Emily standing in her darkened room, her door ajar. Baby Thomas had finally settled to sleep and she'd heard a loud thump. She never expected to see her sister-in-law emerging from Captain Covington's room.

Chapter Ten

Julia pulled back the bow, aiming for the centre of the target. Opening her fingers, the arrow flew, hitting the large white area outside the target. She nocked her next arrow with a huff, convinced nothing was meant to go her way this week. Even riding Manfred this morning hadn't cleared her mind. Luckily the captain had accompanied Uncle George to Creedon to help make some decisions concerning the repairs, sparing her the embarrassment of sitting across from him at breakfast.

Memories of last night tortured her. She let another arrow fly, watching it sail over the target to land in the grassy field. He was right—what they'd done was wrong—but the lingering sensation in the deepest parts of her and the delicious way he'd brought her to pleasure replaced the shame and increased her yearning. Only the thought of his quick dismissal made her blush with embarrassment.

She pulled back the bowstring, struggling against her shaking hands to aim. How did one face a gentleman after such an encounter? How would he react to her? He would be discreet and she'd never tell anyone, but she feared when they were together with other people, the pleasure of their brief encounter would be written all over her face for everyone to see.

She released the arrow and this time it hit closer to the centre.

'Excellent shot, Artemis,' Captain Covington congratulated from behind her.

She whirled to face him, her chest tight with fear. A meeting was inevitable, but she hadn't expected it so soon.

A smile graced his features, but it fell when Julia pinned him with a hard glare. He stood near the equipment table arranging the arrows, his tousled hair falling over his forehead. She longed to run her fingers through the dark strands, then caress the smooth skin of his face. Plucking the bowstring, she willed the urge away and forced herself to remain calm. This constant craving for him made her feel like a runaway carriage no one could stop and she hated it.

'There is a slight wind, otherwise I would have hit the mark.' She tried to sound nonchalant, but it came out more irritable than intended.

'I see.' He held up the fletched end of the arrow, but not one feather moved. 'I think the wind has died down. Perhaps you should try again.'

She snatched it from his outstretched hand, then stormed back to her mark. Knocking the bow, she aimed and fired. The arrow missed the bullseye again but stuck in one of the centre rings.

'Yes, I see the wind has increased,' the captain observed dryly, his meaning all too clear. She realised this probably wasn't his first awkward morning encounter with a lady. If only she were as well schooled in after-pleasure etiquette.

Julia stepped aside, sweeping her arm in the direction of the range. 'Please, take a shot. Being a sailor, you must know a great deal about how the wind blows.'

'I do, though I'm not always correct.' He nocked his arrow, pulled back the bow and let it fly. The arrow stuck in the outer ring of the target. Lowering the bow, he grimaced in pain before recovering himself. Despite her anger, she moved to comfort him before catching herself, feeling a little guilty at goading him once again into straining his wounded shoulder.

'It appears you judged wrong this time.' Julia clapped, the sound hollow in the quiet between them. Selecting an arrow, she stepped forwards, aimed and hit the target dead centre.

'You seem to have a much better grasp of how it blows—perhaps you can advise me?'

'A gentleman of your experience hardly needs my advice.'

'My experience is not quite as developed as you believe.'

Julia moved to choose another arrow but Captain Covington stepped in front of her, his eyes pointed. She smiled up at him, refusing to betray the fluttering in the pit of her stomach at his commanding presence. Despite her anger and embarrassment, having him so close only made her think of his hands on her bare skin, the strength and weight of his chest, the hot feel of his lips and tongue playing with hers. She turned away, laying the bow on the table and fingering the leather strap of her armguard. She did not want to have feelings for a man who only feigned interest in her or who might abandon her as he had another.

'Let us be frank with one another. I apologise for my inappropriate behaviour. It will not happen again. Can you forgive me?'

Something in the sincerity colouring his blue

eyes while he searched her face for a response made her want to forgive him, to throw herself in his arms and reveal—reveal what? How could she express feelings she barely understood herself? If she told him, he would laugh and she couldn't face more humiliation.

'Perhaps we should end our sham engagement now.' She worked the leather knot of her arm-guard, refusing to meet his face. If they ended the game, they wouldn't be forced into each other's presence and she could collect her thoughts and return everything back to normal. There was still time to find another way to get Cable Grange.

'If that's what you wish.' He took her elbow and untied the leather strap. His eyes told her the truth but the way he held her arm said more and it scared her. If she asked him to end this, he would. She only needed to speak, but she didn't possess the words or strength to end the pleading in his eyes.

'Please know this is no longer a game for me. I am quite serious and I believe you are, too.' He moved nearer and she closed her eyes, his breath warm on her cheek before he kissed her. In his lips she felt a need and hope echoed in her own heart. She added her silent questions to his, unsure of the answers. No, this was no longer a game. It was something much deeper.

Someone cleared his throat and they jumped apart. Davies stood a short distance away, his calm demeanour betraying nothing. 'Miss Howard, your presence and the captain's is requested in the study.'

'Requested? By who?'

'Captain Russell.'

Julia almost reprimanded Davies for interrupting them, then realised she should thank him. Once again she'd been weak in the captain's presence. Davies might be the most discreet of servants, but what if someone less reliable had seen them?

'Shall we?' Captain Covington offered Julia his arm and she took it.

The tangle of emotions continued to plague her until she wanted to scream with frustration. What did he mean it was no longer a game? She knew, though she refused to admit it. Why couldn't people leave her alone so she could think? Instead here was yet another demand and from Uncle George of all people. Usually, he was the one person at Knollwood who didn't order her about. Perhaps there was news from London or of Paul? A new fear filled her and her hand tightened on the captain's arm.

'Is something wrong?' the captain asked, squeezing her hand.

She shook her head. 'Davies, is it news of Paul?'

'No, Miss Howard.'

Her grip relaxed and they followed Davies up the stone steps and through the back sitting room. The instant they entered the study, everything became clear.

'What are you doing here?' Julia demanded.

Charles turned around, his grey eyes growing darker at the sight of her hand on the captain's arm. Her mother sat quietly in the window seat, her lips drawn tight, and Julia knew she'd been forced to endure another of his long-winded tirades.

'I received Emily's letter.' He held up the wrinkled paper as though Julia needed reminding. How typical of Charles to be so dramatic.

'I was told Uncle George wanted to see me,' Julia answered.

'I'm the one who summoned you. I knew you wouldn't come if Davies said it was me.'

'I thought as much.' Julia crossed her arms, already tired of Charles. 'Did you bring my inheritance?'

He stepped closer, but she did not step back. Try as he might, he didn't scare her for she knew he was more bluster than any real threat. To his credit and her relief, the captain remained by her side. 'I'm here to find out what you're up to and save you from who knows what scandal.'

'What scandal?' *If only he knew.* Julia dug her nails into her palm to keep from laughing. For once Charles was correct, but she'd deny it to the grave before she let him know.

'Riding alone with a gentleman, confronting a mob of angry men…' Charles ticked off on his fingers '…visiting a gentleman in the middle of the night.'

He knows! Someone must have seen her leaving the captain's room. It didn't matter for she had no intention of admitting anything. 'I don't know what you're talking about.'

'Don't dare deny it. Emily saw you last night.'

Over Charles's shoulder, Emily sat, shamefaced, the tips of her pale ears red. Julia's heart pounded in her chest and she tried to think of some explanation or way to redeem herself. No, despite his proof, she would give him nothing. If she let him bully her now, she'd never be free of his heavy hand. She drew herself up to face him, but the captain spoke first.

'Mr Howard, I assure you nothing inappropriate took place. She was retrieving one of your brother's books while I was gone. Unfortunately, I came back early.'

'Thank you, sir, for your explanation, but you have a great deal to answer to in regards to my sister's honour.'

'Charles,' her mother chided, 'you of all people should not give such lectures.'

Charles's face went red and his mouth fell open, his stunned expression matched by Emily's. Julia threw her mother a silent question, but received no response before Charles recovered himself.

'Captain Covington, please excuse us for a moment. I wish to have a private word with my sister before you and I speak.'

'Of course.'

James closed the door behind him, taking a deep breath in the cool dark of the hallway. Through the heavy oak he heard Julia and Charles arguing at the top of their voices.

'I don't know what you're up to with this rash engagement, but after last night you will marry him,' Charles insisted.

'I will do no such thing.'

'Be reasonable.'

'Reasonable, from the man who is the most un-reasonable.'

'It's only a matter of time before the story is known.'

'Why? Do you and Emily intend to spread it?'

James had not confessed his feelings to her. He'd been on the verge when they were interrupted. Now everything stood in the balance. Charles knew about their encounter last night, but Julia's stubborn nature worried him more than Charles's. Despite her true feelings, of which he had a good sense, she would never marry him if her brother insisted.

The door opened and Mrs Howard marched up to him.

'Captain Covington, if you have any interest in my daughter, now is the time to make it known, especially to her.' She walked off down the hall, her spaniel trotting behind her.

Inside the study, the sibling argument rose three octaves.

'If you had no intention of marrying him, why did you become engaged?' Charles demanded.

'You wouldn't understand.'

'Then Emily's suspicions were right.'

'You'd like nothing better than for all your suspicions to be right. Perhaps if you suspected good in me, you'd be less disappointed.'

'Please lower your voice.'

'Stop ordering me about.'

'Julia, be reasonable.'

If he didn't intervene now, he might lose all chance with her. The more her brother insisted, the more she'd resist, no matter what was in her heart. And what was in her heart? He'd seen it in her eyes outside: passion, longing and the faint traces of love. But there was trepidation there, too, of loving without return, broken trust and betrayal. He knew the power of those emotions, but, striding into the study, he refused to succumb to either her fears or his own.

Charles sat at the desk, his head in his hands. Julia stood on the other side, her back to James, her palms flat on the smooth wood surface. Did she know how formidable she was? He doubted it, for with men like Charles always underestimating her, she greatly underestimated herself.

'Excuse me.' James cleared his throat.

Brother and sister looked at him.

'Tell him nothing happened for he obviously doesn't trust me,' Julia insisted, her eyes pleading with him to help.

'If I may,' James addressed Charles. 'I believe

I have a solution to the current dilemma. But I must speak to Miss Howard, alone.'

Charles studied the two of them, his frustration reflected in his nervous, wide-eyed wife, who sat by the window. 'As you like. But I only wish to entertain one resolution.'

'On this we are both in agreement.'

Charles nodded. 'Come, Emily. Let's leave them alone.'

Emily took Charles's hand and together they left, closing the door behind them. Once they were alone, Julia turned fiery eyes on James.

'There is nothing you can say to solve the situation. I suggest you return to London at once so we may avoid any more of these awkward situations.'

'I have another, more practical solution.'

'Which is?'

'For us to marry.'

'Marry?' Her eyes widened with surprise and, unless he was mistaken, flattered hope, before narrowing in suspicion. 'Whatever for?'

'Mutual enjoyment and benefit.' At this moment with her temper high, he doubted she'd believe him if he told her the truth behind his very sincere proposal. Once he had her, there would be time to reveal his heart. 'I know you don't relish the idea of marriage, but do you really wish to stay here at Knollwood with your brother, for the rest of your life?'

'Of course not. I want Cable Grange.'

'What if I offered you more than Cable Grange?'

'More?'

He cocked one suggestive eyebrow. 'Much more.'

She crossed her arms over her chest. 'And when the thrill of much more fades?'

'There is a great deal more than that.' He drew her to the atlas, the delicious scent of rosewater filling his senses. He longed to touch her face, caress her cheek with his hand, but he had to proceed slowly or she would spook and all would be lost. 'The Caribbean, perhaps, or Venice, even India.'

His fingers traced the illustrated countries and seas and her eyes followed the routes with interest. 'But what about Cable Grange?'

'You may still have it, and this—' he tapped the gilded pages '—but unmarried, you'll have neither.'

She shook her head. 'And when there is a parcel of children dragging at my heels, will I really have this?'

He leaned in with a wicked smile. 'I'm a Navy man. I know a great deal about a great many things, including avoiding a parcel of children.'

'You didn't last night.'

'I was unprepared by your sudden appearance. In the future I'll be more ready for such situations.'

Her eyes widened in shock. 'Really?'

'Yes, my little Artemis. Though I may insist on one or two children.'

'Well, that's not unreasonable.' She turned back to the atlas, eyebrows knitted while she pondered his suggestion. 'Why me? Why not Annette or some other woman?'

'Because you have a courageous nature well suited to adventure.'

'And the rest?' The word lingered between them.

'In time, it will come.' He brushed her lips with his own, feeling her excitement and anticipation.

Gently, his mind cautioned. He stepped back, her sultry eyes stealing the wind from his chest, yet he found the breath to whisper, 'Marry me?'

Chapter Eleven

With a single word, Julia found herself at the centre of a frenzy of activity. For two days she was tugged in a hundred directions while Emily and her mother rushed to plan the wedding. The captain was spared the madness. Shortly after his proposal, he received word from his solicitor in London and departed to take care of business. He also planned to buy their wedding rings and make arrangements for a short honeymoon while in town. He was set to return this evening, in time for the ball, and there they would make their engagement public.

She shivered at the thought.

'Are you all right, miss?' The seamstress looked up at Julia from where she knelt, pinning the hem of the London dress they'd chosen for the wedding.

'Yes, thank you.'

'You'll need a proper shift, perhaps more than one,' Emily said from the sofa, reviewing the ever-growing trousseau list.

'Whatever you think is best,' Julia agreed, her mind still whirling. What had she done?

'I don't believe you'll need linens,' Emily mused and her mother nodded.

'She can have my mother's set.'

Julia did her best not to roll her eyes in frustration at this inane conversation. Here she was, prepared to lash herself to a man she barely knew, and all Emily could think about was linens and lace. Though the captain's long friendship with Uncle George gave her some measure of confidence in her current and what would very soon be her future situation, she still worried. A gentleman was apt to act differently with other gentlemen than he was with ladies, especially a wife.

The seamstress motioned for her to turn and she complied, her mind lingering on the memory of the captain when he'd asked—no, bargained with her to marry him. His eyes had held a pleasant mix of hope and—dare she believe it—love? No, it wasn't possible. But if it wasn't, then why would he insist she marry him? He had nothing to gain by the union. And what had he meant at the archery range by the game meaning more?

'My man of affairs secured the special licence and I spoke to the vicar. The ceremony is set for tomorrow at three,' Charles announced, stepping into the room. A wave of dread hit Julia, but she couldn't move for fear of being stuck by one of the many pins in her dress. Besides, she wasn't about to let Charles know she harboured any doubts about her decision.

'I can't possibly arrange everything by then,' Emily complained, tapping her list. 'And what about Captain Covington's family? He isn't expected back from London until this evening and with his mother and sister in Wiltshire, how can he possibly arrange for them to be here by tomorrow?'

'I'm sorry they'll miss it, but if Julia wants her inheritance and Cable Grange, she will marry tomorrow.'

'Or, instead of being so high handed, you could simply allow me to purchase the estate. Then the captain and I can marry at our leisure,' Julia suggested, her brother more irritating than the pins in her dress.

'No, I don't want any reason for you to decline. I've sent instructions for my solicitor to arrange the money for Saturday's auction. Once you and Captain Covington are married, I will bid for

Cable Grange on your behalf, then establish it in trust for you.'

Baby Thomas let out a small cry. Charles picked him up from where he lay in the rocker at the nurse's feet. He held the baby in his arms, his hard expression softening as he carried the infant to the window, laying a kiss on his little head. Emily rose and joined them, moving aside the blanket so they could see more of the baby's smiling face. For the first time in her life, Julia envied Charles and Emily. They both annoyed her, but they loved each other and always did what they thought best for everyone in the family.

Julia's stomach tightened. What if she never found such love and happiness with the captain?

'Enough wool-gathering,' her mother interrupted, picking up Emily's list and examining it. 'There is still much to do.'

Julia slipped out into the garden, eager to escape all the talk of both her wedding and the ball and be alone so she could think. She pulled the neck of her pelisse close, trying to warm her cheeks in the high collar. The fine weather had turned and, though the sky was clear, the air was sharp and cold. As she ambled over the gravel, the confidence she'd felt a few days ago while sitting here with her mother felt like a distant memory. Her future at Cable Grange had seemed so secure then; now she could see nothing but the unknown dotted with the chance of adventure and travel. What would life hold for Mrs James Covington? Would it really be like he promised or did she run the risk of becoming Mrs Wilkins? Wandering into the hedged garden, she sat down in front of the fountain, listening to the gentle plunk of water dripping into the pool from the clinging bodies.

Captain Covington offered many things in his proposal, but not love. He said it would come in time, but there was no guarantee. If he never grew to love her did it matter? Cable Grange would be hers and she could live the way she'd always dreamed of, but with the freedom of a married woman. The thought should have comforted her, but it didn't. Instead it only added to her loneliness and confusion. Turning back to the fountain, she felt her heart catch. Love was not part of their deal. It never had been.

The sound of someone walking on the gravel caught her attention and a moment later, Annette came around the corner, her heavy dress and pelisse more appropriate for the chilly day.

'Good afternoon, Julia,' she greeted with a light voice.

'Good afternoon,' Julia mumbled, in no mood for her stepcousin.

To Julia's surprise, Annette sat down next to her, drawing her pelisse tight. Julia watched her with caution, wondering what she wanted. It wasn't like her to be so cordial and her sudden nearness felt awkward. In no mood to entertain the chit and knowing she did not possess the patience to be polite, Julia moved to make her excuses and leave, but Annette stood first. 'Would you please take a turn with me around the garden?'

Julia almost declined, but something in Annette's manner, less arrogant than before, made her curious. She didn't like the idea of spending time alone with Annette, but with nervous fretting over the wedding being the only thing waiting for her inside, walking seemed very appealing. 'Of course.'

She rose and led Annette away from the hedges and down the main garden path. Small birds, searching the stones for food, hopped out of their way, then flew up into the surrounding bushes, chirping in protest at being disturbed.

Annette further surprised Julia by taking her arm in a casual, sociable manner. Julia didn't pull away but braced herself for an insult, knowing all this friendliness had something to do with Julia discovering the girl's secret.

'You are aware of the situation concerning my brother and myself?' Annette asked, confirming Julia's suspicion.

'I inadvertently learned of it.' There was no reason to lie since they both knew what Julia had seen.

'I realise our relationship has not been the best these past few weeks.'

It has never been good, Julia thought, but remained silent, wondering where all this was leading.

'I know I have no right to ask for your confidences or your discretion, but I implore you to keep what you know a secret.'

'I have no intention or reason to tell anyone.' And she didn't. Besides, Julia guessed from previous comments by both the captain and Emily that everyone already knew their situation.

'Why wouldn't you tell?' Annette demanded. 'It would be perfect revenge for my less-than-courteous behaviour.'

'Yes, but I'm not interested in revenge.' Julia sympathised with Annette, knowing she lived in a world where people tore each other to pieces without hesitation or remorse. The same pity she'd felt for her a few days ago came back along with Uncle Edward's hope that Julia could advise Annette on her finances. Helping Annette would prove a welcome distraction from Cable Grange, Charles, Emily, Captain Covington and everything else determined to plague her this week. 'I might be able to help you, if you wish.'

She snatched her hand from Julia's arm. 'I don't need your charity.'

'I don't mean charity,' Julia continued in an even tone, 'but advice on how to arrange your finances. Emily told me about your small inheritance. Perhaps we can devise a budget to relieve some of your debts and your worries.'

Annette's eyes softened, then narrowed as if contemplating many things at once, all of which seemed somewhat incomprehensible. 'I didn't think, especially after how mean I've been, that you'd be so generous. Why?'

'Because I know what it's like to have one's future influenced by a less-than-understanding brother.'

'At least Charles genuinely cares for your happiness.'

'Does he?'

'He's gone to a great deal of trouble to maintain your reputation and assure himself of the captain's suitability. Simon would never do the same for me.'

Julia resumed her languid pace, Annette staying by her side. She didn't want to admit it, but Charles did have her best interest at heart. If he wasn't so domineering, she might appreciate it more.

'I'll have to examine your finances to decide the best course of action,' Julia hazarded, the opportunity to review figures irresistible. 'You'll need to make a list of everything you owe, your expenses and your income.'

Annette fingered the lace of her pelisse, contemplating Julia's offer. 'Why do you want to help me?'

'Because it's the proper thing to do.'

'You're right—London is ridiculous,' Annette admitted with a laugh. They'd spent the last two hours reviewing her debts and income. She owed a great deal to a milliner and other London merchants, but her situation was not beyond hope.

'I never thought I'd hear you say it.' *Or be so friendly*, Julia thought, enjoying the new warmth between them.

'I don't think I'd admit it to anyone else. The silly things I have to do to try to secure my future.' She waved her hand over the scraps of paper littered with figures. 'And still nothing is settled.'

'Since you live with Uncle Edward and your mother, you can save a great deal, but you'll have to economise. No more lace and no more dresses.'

Annette sat back with a sigh. 'It won't be easy, but I suppose I must.'

'Just until you find a rich husband,' Julia teased, putting the finishing touches on Annette's plan to pay her debts and invest her inheritance, then passing it to her for inspection. 'I think this will do very well.'

'Yes, it will.' She laid the paper aside. 'I'm truly sorry for being nasty to you, only I've been so worried lately, what with Simon's gambling and Mama no help. I thought Captain Covington might be an answer. I never thought of taking matters into my own hands. You're lucky to have a man like the captain. He'll make a good husband and you two will be quite the talk of the ball tonight.'

Julia twisted the pencil in her hands, apprehension replacing her former calm. 'I don't particularly care for balls.'

'Why? You can dance, can't you?'

'Yes, it's one of the few social graces I mastered while in London.' Charles had hired a dancing instructor for that purpose and Julia had proven a quick study. If only everything else about London society had come so easily.

'And you can converse with people.'

'Of course.'

'Then why are you afraid?'

'Because everyone sneers at me for running Knollwood instead of painting screens. They seem to have nothing else to occupy their simple minds except how I choose to spend my time.'

'Well, I can't stop them from thinking that running an estate is strange, but I can teach you not to care.'

Julia shook her head. 'It's not possible?'

'Of course it is. All London women do it. Do you know how many girls would cry in the halls of Almack's if they didn't pretend not to care?'

'No, I've seen the women in London. They possess more confidence in society than I could ever master.'

Annette stared her straight in the eye. 'Come now, Julia. I've seen you stand up to Mrs Wilkins and your brother. I know you aren't lacking in courage. You helped me—now allow me to help you.'

'How?'

Annette stood, taking Julia's hand and pulling

her to her feet. She spun Julia around, studying her with a practised eye. 'First, to play the part, you must dress the part.'

An hour later, Julia stood before the mirror, admiring her transformation into a diamond of the first water. She wore her finest London gown of white silk with thin, shimmering gold stripes running through the fabric and a gold ribbon around the waist. At the gentle swell of her bosom, Annette fixed one of Emily's diamond brooches and loaned her a pair of teardrop-pearl earrings. Annette then instructed Mary on how to style Julia's hair in the Roman fashion with a gold ribbon threaded through the *coiffure*.

'Anyone who saw you would instantly think you're a member of the *ton*.' Annette stepped back, inspecting her handiwork.

Julia gazed at her reflection, turning from one side to the other to view her dress and hair. For the first time in a long while, she felt beautiful, but there was more to commanding a ballroom than a pretty gown. 'I may dress the part, but I don't feel it.'

'It's an easy one to play. Come, I'll show you.' Annette led Julia to the far side of the room. 'When you walk, keep your head up, your shoulders back. Meet everyone with confidence and don't forget to smile.'

Annette demonstrated the walk, then motioned for Julia to try it. Julia felt silly, but she'd come too far to stop now. Pulling back her shoulders, she put her chin in the air and crossed the room.

'Very good, but this time smile, acknowledge everyone and remember to hold their gaze a moment before moving on.'

Julia repeated the walk with more purpose, smiling and nodding to the imaginary guests.

Annette clapped at the performance. 'If the captain wasn't already in love with you, then he'd lose his heart tonight.'

Julia stopped, stunned by Annette's announcement. 'The captain doesn't love me.'

'Of course he does. It is as plain as the sun.'

Julia opened and closed the ivory fan dangling from her wrist. 'Now you're teasing me.'

'Do not think so little of yourself, Julia. He loves you as much as you love him.'

Julia opened the fan, studying the painted roses twining together along a vine. Yes, she loved him. She'd spent days denying it, but hearing Annette state it so plainly she could no longer pretend it wasn't true.

But did he love her?

She examined herself in the mirror and for the first time saw not Julia, the awkward girl of Knollwood, but a sophisticated lady engaged to the handsome captain. It seemed too unbelievable to be real. Deep down, she feared everything would come crashing down and she'd wake tomorrow to find it was all just a dream. Unless, as Annette thought, he really loved her. If not, the humiliation would be more than she could bear. It seemed there was only one thing to do. Tonight she would have to find out.

Chapter Twelve

Julia stepped out of the carriage, the biting night air cutting through the delicate material of her gown. Young people, accompanied by matrons and older men, wound through the crush of carriages to the Johnsons' wide front door. Julia followed her mother and Annette, admiring the tall, white columns lining the façade, thinking similar details would make Cable Grange stately. She tried to take in more of the house's architecture, but the crowd pressing into the entrance hall made it difficult. They were supposed to arrive earlier, but baby Thomas had taken ill, causing a delay when Emily and Charles decided to stay behind. She'd noticed Uncle George's carriage outside and knew he and the captain were already here. The captain had returned from London in the early evening, but Annette refused to let him see her and insisted he and Uncle George ride on ahead to the ball. She wanted Julia to make an entrance and surprise the captain.

Once inside, Julia looked for him, eager for him to see her. However, nothing except the tall ostrich feather in the hair of the lady in front of her was visible in the crush.

They stepped into the receiving line, moving forwards to where Mr and Mrs Johnson and the eldest Miss Johnson stood and Julia's stomach tightened. Despite Annette's lessons, she didn't relish the idea of facing the scrutiny of the other country families. Picking up the short train of her dress, she knew she had no choice but to carry on.

'Mrs Howard, how lovely to see you,' Mrs Johnson addressed Julia's mother, who curtsied with her usual grace. She turned to Julia, her beady eyes wide with astonishment. 'And, Miss Howard, your gown is beautiful.'

'The colour makes you glow,' the eldest Miss Johnson offered. Taller and less buxom than her younger sisters, she'd always been kinder than either they or their mama.

'Thank you.' Julia curtsied, enjoying Miss Johnson's compliment and taking pride in showing Mrs Johnson she could dress as fine as any other lady.

Her mother led her off to the left and through

the hall leading to the ballroom. Numerous gentlemen and ladies filled the space, chatting and enjoying aperitifs and ices. Julia paused at the threshold, taking in the crowd before Annette linked her arm in hers.

'Remember what I told you. Everyone will be watching us for I am new and you are unexpected. There'll be lots of stares and whispers, but walk like you know, but don't care.'

They stepped together into the thick of the revellers and a hundred glances and whispers were thrown their way. The mothers and young ladies who'd always ignored Julia now stared, taking in the fine style of Julia's dress and the graceful figure she cut. She did her best to emulate Annette, smiling at Miss Diana Johnson, who sat surrounded by her usual set of admirers. Miss Diana spied Julia, her jaw dropping before she fell to whispers with the young bucks, but Julia never let her smile falter. For once Julia enjoyed being the subject of so many conversations.

The soft strains of Handel greeted them at the entrance to the ballroom. Sweeping the room, her eyes immediately set upon the captain. His blue uniform highlighted by a crisp white shirt, brass buttons and gold epaulettes made him stand out in the sea of men in sober black evening attire. The

unmarried young ladies and their mothers covet-
ously examined the captain while Miss Caroline
Johnson claimed the envious position of chatting
with him. Her fan fluttered in front of her face
while they spoke, but Julia could tell he wasn't
listening for his eyes roamed everywhere but over
the silly goose's round, exuberant face.

He's looking for me. Her heart jumped with excitement and she started forwards, eager to join
him, but Annette held her elbow tight.

'Wait. Make him come to you.'

She could barely stand still, waiting for him to
notice her. As if sensing her presence, he turned,
starting at the sight of her. His blue eyes swept her
before an impressed smile spread over his face.
Making his excuses to Miss Johnson, he started
across the room. Many ladies dipped behind their
fans to comment on the handsome stranger striding towards Julia. She didn't care what they said
or thought—only the captain mattered. She hadn't
seen him since the proposal and until this moment
didn't realise how much she'd missed him.

'You're gorgeous, Artemis,' he breathed, standing over her and taking in the transformation.

Julia arched one saucy eyebrow, enjoying the
confidence created by his admiration. 'Are you
trying to flatter me?'

'No flattery of mine could do you justice.' The musicians began an allemande and the captain offered her his elbow. 'May I have this dance?'

She hesitated. It had been a long time since she'd danced and, with her confidence soaring, she didn't want to trip over her feet and bring herself crashing back down to the ground.

'Come now. A woman who faces fighting men isn't afraid of a dance?' he teased.

Julia laid her hand on his arm. 'I'm not afraid.'

'Good. I'm glad to hear it.'

The captain swept her through the steps of the dance, the heat of his body radiating between them during the turns and acting like wine on her senses. The image of him shirtless above her filled her mind and she nearly stumbled, but his strong presence kept her steady and with even steps they moved in time with the others over the polished floor.

Whispers swirled around them from all those who knew her and her family and for the first time Julia didn't care. Instead of wanting to escape, to run back to Knollwood and the comfort of the study, she grasped the captain's hand tighter and raised her head higher. She enjoyed exceeding these people's expectations, for most of them believed spinsterhood to be her fate. It felt wonderful to prove them wrong and be more than they, and perhaps even Charles, ever thought she'd be.

All too soon the dance ended and the captain escorted her to where Annette stood.

'Well done, Julia,' she congratulated. 'You've set the room ablaze and are to be commended.'

'Do you really think so?'

'Most definitely.' Annette strolled off to rejoin Mrs Howard as Miss Diana Johnson hurried up to them, her eyes raking over the captain.

'Miss Howard, we did not expect to see you here tonight. I didn't think you liked balls,' Diana said, her voice innocuous, but the cutting remark clear.

'Whatever gave you such an idea?' Julia asked.

Diana's smile faltered, leaving her at a loss for an answer. Not wishing to prolong the awkward moment, Julia turned to the captain. 'Allow me to introduce my fiancé, Captain James Covington.'

'Fiancé?' Diana dipped a wobbly curtsy, her small eyes wide with surprise.

'Yes, I asked Miss Howard to be my wife and she accepted me.' The captain patted Julia's hand proudly.

'Best wishes to you both. If you'll excuse me.' She hurried off across the room to rejoin a group of young ladies Julia recognised, but didn't know well. They bowed together in a furious mingling of waving fans and gasps while Diana conveyed the news.

'The whole room will know in a matter of minutes,' Julia remarked.

'Good.' Behind them the musicians started the next dance. 'Shall we?'

'Of course.'

The hour slipped by in a blur of music and the captain's touch. She revelled in the feel of him next to her while they moved through two more dances, oblivious to everything but each other. She could dance with him for ever if only one fear didn't continue to plague her. She was no closer to knowing the truth of his heart, but she was reluctant to break the ball's beautiful spell with an awkward discussion or some horrible revelation. Tomorrow she'd discover the truth. Tonight she'd enjoy herself.

At the end of the Scottish reel, he led her to the edge of the room. She waved her fan, the heat of the crowd and the rousing dance making her flush.

'Would you like some punch?' the captain asked, his hair damp at the temples from the exhilaration of the reel.

'Yes, thank you.'

He made his way to the refreshment room, leaving Julia near a large painting of some Johnson ancestor. She wrinkled her nose at the round face staring out from the canvas, thinking it very unfortunate such a feature should be so dominant in the family.

'Good evening, Miss Howard.'

Startled, she turned to see Mrs Wilkins standing behind her. She wore a deep-green dress of velvet cut too low, her modesty saved only by a wide gold necklace.

'Mrs Wilkins,' Julia greeted icily, making it clear she had no wish to speak to the woman, but Mrs Wilkins seemed indifferent to the rebuke.

'Had I not seen it for myself, I never would have believed it. You strike me as too dour for a man like James.'

'The captain likes his women refined.' Julia's heart pounded in her ears. She'd never been confronted like this and she wasn't about to let the woman get the better of her.

'You needn't be so high and mighty with me, Miss Howard,' Mrs Wilkins snapped. 'Do you really think he'll marry you?'

'I believe you're bitter because he didn't marry you.'

'I could have had him if I'd wanted him, but I'm

not one to pine for the past. Perhaps this time he'll actually go through with the marriage.'

'Come to the church tomorrow at three o'clock and you'll see for yourself.'

'I think not. Please give him this. He left it in my room when he came to see me the other night.'

Mrs Wilkins held out James's dented medal and it dangled between them, glittering tauntingly in the candlelight. Julia held out her hand, struggling to control the shaking while Mrs Wilkins coiled the gold chain in her upturned palm. 'Oh, and please tell him we sold Cable Grange yesterday.'

'You sold it,' Julia choked.

'Yes. A solicitor in London purchased it for his employer. Rowan and I just returned from London this afternoon to see to our things as the new owner wishes to take possession at once. Frankly, I'm glad to be rid of the place. I never did enjoy the country. I always found the society a bit too small.' Mrs Wilkins sauntered off across the room.

Anger, hurt, betrayal, disappointment and sorrow all slammed together, making it impossible to think or make any sense of the emotions crushing her. Julia gripped the medal tight, her heart shattering along with her dreams. After everything she'd done, Cable Grange was gone and with it Captain Covington. She forced herself to remain composed, refusing to fall apart in front of everyone who'd seen her so happy only a moment before. She needed somewhere to go, a place to hide, but the crowded room offered no sanctuary.

Before Julia had a chance to think or clear her mind, the captain appeared at her side. 'What did she want?'

'To offer her congratulations,' Julia replied through clenched teeth.

'What's wrong?'

She laid open her palm, revealing the medallion. He turned to where Mrs Wilkins disappeared in the crowd, his eyes narrow with seething hate. 'That miserable woman. Whatever she told you, it is a lie.'

'Were you with her the other night?'

'Yes, but allow me to explain.'

She shook her head, the room around her threatening to whirl. If Mrs Wilkins had the audacity to confront her tonight, it wouldn't be long before she told everyone the story of James's indiscretion. Moments ago she'd been the belle of the ball; now she'd end the evening the subject of vicious gossip. They'd laugh and say she wasn't ladylike enough to keep her intended. They'd watch her with a mixture of pity and condescension all because she'd trusted him and allowed herself to believe he loved her. How could she have been so foolish? He'd dallied with Annette in jest, then turned to her when it suited his lust only she'd been too blind to see the truth.

'Please, let's go outside and discuss this?' the captain said, taking her elbow.

'Why?' she retorted. 'So you may tarnish my reputation further?'

Before he could answer, a loud gong reverberated through the room. Everyone turned to watch Mr Johnson, accompanied by a servant carrying the gong, step up on the dais in front of the musicians.

'Everyone, please may I have your attention?' The music trailed off, bringing the dancers to a halt. Whispers swept the room, everyone speculating on what announcement was important enough to interrupt a ball. 'News has just reached us from London. The British Navy met Napoleon's fleet at Trafalgar and won a stunning victory.'

The room erupted in cheers, applause and whistles, but Mr Johnson rang the gong three more times, cutting the excitement short. 'Britain has also suffered a great loss. Though we won the battle, Admiral Nelson was killed.'

Men gasped and women burst into tears, the hero's death touching everyone.

Uncle George appeared next to Julia. 'There is other news from London.'

Fear turned her cold. 'Paul?'

'Yes, we must return to Knollwood at once. Your mother and Annette have already left. We'll take my carriage.'

Uncle George led them through the sober crowd and out of the large front doors to the waiting carriage. Inside, James sat next to her as Uncle George climbed into the seat across from them. He rapped on the roof, setting the carriage in motion.

'Do you know anything?' Julia asked, barely able to get the words out, her throat dry with dread.

'Only that Charles received a letter concerning Paul. I don't know the contents. Jim, did you hear anything in town about the battle?'

He shook his head. 'No, I was too busy this morning and I didn't see any of the papers before I left London.'

They fell into worried silence, the jangling equipage grating on her strained nerves. Anticipating the awful news waiting for her at Knollwood made her body shake. Was Paul dead or just badly wounded? What would she do without him, especially now?

The captain slipped his hand in hers and squeezed it, but she snatched it away, in no mood for his sympathy. She felt him watching her, the weight of his concern adding unwanted tension to her already tormented mind. She scanned the darkness outside the carriage for any landmark indicating their distance from home, but only the vague silhouettes of trees stood out in the dim light of the rising moon. The carriage drove for what felt like an eternity before the bright windows of Knollwood came into view. The moment the carriage stopped, she threw open the door and rushed inside, James and Uncle George close on her heels.

She hurried into the morning room, taking in Mother, who sat next to Emily, her face a white mask of controlled pain. Annette stood behind them, sombre.

'Is Paul all right?' Julia asked.

Mother held out her arms and Julia rushed into them, doing her best to hold back tears of worry.

'He's alive, but wounded and missing,' Mother answered and Julia sat back.

'What do you mean?'

'Lieutenant Lapenotiere, his commander, sent us a letter. *HMS Pickle* arrived in Falmouth on Monday. They came home because Lieutenant

Lapenotiere was charged with telling the Admiralty about the battle and Admiral Nelson. Paul, because of his wound, rode with Lieutenant Lapenotiere to London to see Dr Childers.'

'Excellent fellow,' Charles muttered.

Mother scowled at Charles, then continued her story. 'They arrived very early this morning and Lieutenant Lapenotiere, after finishing his duties at the Admiralty, paid a call to Dr Childers to make sure Paul was all right. According to Dr Childers, Paul never arrived and now no one knows where he is.'

'Perhaps the wound is worse than he realised and Paul's in some hospital, alone,' Julia said worriedly.

'Lieutenant. Lapenotiere doesn't know and, because of his official duties, he can't search for Paul. It's why he sent us an urgent letter suggesting someone from the family come to London at once to find Paul.'

Julia turned to Charles. 'When are you leaving?'

Charles looked aghast. 'I'm not leaving. I've written a few letters and will send them tomorrow.'

'Letters? You're sending letters?'

'What else would you have me do?'

'Go to London and search every hospital until you find him.'

'Search the hells and coffee houses, you mean,' Charles scoffed from his place by the fire, tapping the mantel. 'No doubt instead of going straight to Dr Childers, Paul decided to visit his mistress, or some hell to run up more debts.'

'How can you say such a thing?' Julia demanded, her voice high and tight. Only the firm squeeze of her mother's hand prevented her from hurling more words at Charles.

'I can say it because I've spent more time than I care to admit dealing with our brother's creditors. Now, through his foolishness, he's gone and got himself in another mess.'

'He's wounded. He may be ill and in need of our help. Now is no time to preach about his responsibilities.'

'Why not? He's a grown man and it's time he took them seriously.' Charles snatched up the poker and jabbed at the logs. 'Besides, Paul has a talent for surviving and for trouble. He's sure to turn up soon.'

Julia stood, balling her fists at her sides to keep from pounding them against Charles's unfeeling chest. 'London and all your airs have made you hard.'

'You don't understand the ways of the world,' he replied with marked condescension, returning the poker to the stand.

'I quite agree with Julia.' Her mother rose, pinning Charles with angry eyes. 'You have become too hard for my liking.'

'Mother, please, you misunderstood my meaning,' Charles began, but his mother raised a silencing hand, then swept out of the room.

Charles chased after her, his weak protests trailing them both down the hall.

Julia dropped into a chair, biting her thumb. Across the room, Uncle George and Captain Covington stood by the fireplace, each contemplating the evening's news. Her eyes briefly met the captain's, their blue depths filled with a need she would not answer.

Paul wasn't dead, but wounded, and Charles had no intention of helping him. She knew the condition of hospitals and how a healthy man could easily succumb to illness while a wounded one stood almost no chance of recovering. Paul must be found and brought back to Knollwood to be cared for properly, not left to die in who knew what squalor.

'Charles will find him. Everything will be all right—you'll see,' Emily offered, patting Julia's shoulder. Reaching into her dressing-gown pocket, she produced a letter and handed it to Julia.

'What's this?' She recognised Paul's large handwriting.

'It arrived after you left for the ball. He must have sent it some time ago.'

Julia sat on the edge of her seat, fingering the letter, afraid to open it for fear it might be the last she ever received from him.

Emily made her way out of the room, followed by Annette, who offered a comforting smile.

Julia tore open the letter.

Dear Julia,

Forgive my brevity. We are in port taking on supplies for the fleet and I wanted to send word since it may be my last opportunity to write for some time. I hope everyone at Knollwood is doing well. Uncle George wrote to inform me of his plan to bring Captain Covington to stay at Creedon Abbey in November, and to meet you all. I was shocked by his announcement, given our history, of which Uncle George has surely informed you. Perhaps it means the captain has finally forgiven me and will rescind his poor recommendation and I shall have my ship after all. If he hasn't forgiven me, I depend upon you to do nothing but speak of my great character and change his mind for you can be quite persuasive when you want something.

I must go now, but I'll write more when I can. Give my love to Mother.

Your devoted brother,
Paul

Without thinking, she marched up to the captain, the paper fluttering in her shaking hands. 'It was all about revenge, wasn't it?'

He stared at her, stunned. 'I don't understand.'

'You wrote Paul's poor recommendation. You stopped him from getting his own ship.'

'I did.'

'Why?'

The captain ran his hand through his hair. 'Your brother served with me many years ago in Portsmouth. During that time he failed to demonstrate qualities necessary to command a ship. There were questions about whether or not he could be trusted to follow orders or do the honourable thing.'

'It was more complicated than that,' Uncle George added.

'You knew about this and didn't tell me?' She

gaped at Uncle George, who tugged on the sleeves of his jacket. She felt lied to and betrayed by both of them and, combined with her worry for Paul, it was more than she could bear.

'Julia, please.' Captain Covington moved forwards, but she stepped away.

'How dare you speak of honour when you have none. For years you've had a grudge against Paul and when you couldn't strike at him you decided to take advantage of me.'

'That's not it at all. Please allow me to explain.' He took her by the arms, but she shook off his grasp.

'Explain what? How instead of receiving his own ship and perhaps being hundreds of miles from danger, he's now missing? How you went to Mrs Wilkins, exposing me to the humiliation of the entire countryside because you made me think you cared?'

'I do care. Don't you see?'

'No, I won't have any more of your lies.' She ran from the room and up the stairs, not daring to breathe until she crumpled to her knees in the privacy of her room, large tears rolling down her face.

'I was a fool to go or at the least I should have taken you along,' James lamented, remembering his brief time in Melinda's room. He should have known she'd strike at him like this. Once again he'd underestimated her. He thought of her letter in the drawer upstairs. He could make good on his promise and send it to Rowan, but what difference would it make now?

'What I don't understand is how she got your medal.' George paced back and forth across the room with slow, heavy steps.

'I remember Melinda putting her arms around my neck. She must have taken it then.'

'Sounds more like a cutpurse than a lady.'

'From everything I heard of her while in London, I wouldn't be surprised if she's turned to thievery to keep herself from ruin.'

George paused near the card table, fingering the deck, his face long. 'I should have been honest with Julia, told her about you and Paul. I hate to think I've hurt her.'

'She loves you too much not to forgive you and once everything is settled, she'll understand why you did it. She might even thank you for it,' James offered, trying to bolster his friend's spirits. He'd only seen George this upset once before when a young officer they both admired was killed in a skirmish off Martinique. Despite winning the skirmish and taking a grand prize, the entire crew had been affected by the officer's death, much like tonight's news had touched everyone at Knollwood.

'I hope you're right. She means the world to me.' George took a deep breath, flipping over a card and laying it face up on the table. 'I only kept it a secret because I wanted her to give you a chance.'

'Then why did you write Paul about it?'

'Because I didn't think he'd write to her about it. Apparently, I was wrong.' He flipped over another card and laid it beside the other. 'But enough about my troubles. What'll you do?'

James shook his head. 'Tonight, nothing. In the morning I'll make her listen to me—whatever it takes to get her to the altar.'

Julia leaned against her bedroom wall, wrung out and tired. The evening had started out so glorious, and now it was gone, all of it: the captain, Cable Grange, her future. Fresh tears rolled down her face at the thought of enduring the wagging tongues of the countryside and Charles's endless sermons. She scowled, hating her brother very much at this moment.

Across the room, she noticed her books and agricultural tracts stacked in a neat pile on a table next to the window. On top sat the book Paul had given her on India. Where was he? Why wouldn't Charles search for him? She would if she could.

She sat up, drying her cheeks with the back of her hand as the plan began to form in her mind. Paul. She could find him, nurse him back to health if need be and live with him, away from Charles, Knollwood and the captain.

It was dangerous and if she went through with it, there would be no going back, not that it mattered now. Even if Julia told Charles the truth about Captain Covington, he would still insist on a wedding. No, she wouldn't be bound to a man who didn't love her or who wouldn't be faithful. Life with Paul was the only option, if she could find him, if he was still alive.

Rising, Julia cracked open the door and peered into the empty hallway, listening to the muffled voices of the captain and Uncle George from downstairs. Hurrying along the hall, she slipped inside Paul's room, careful to lock the door behind her. Pulling open the wardrobe, she grabbed one of Paul's old uniform jackets, a shirt, a pair of breeches, the Hessians, a hat and haversack. Stuffing the clothes in the haversack, she felt around, hoping to find a pistol or even a sword, but there was nothing else except a few old blankets. Closing the wardrobe, she carefully opened the bedroom door. Charles's whining tone carried from their mother's room, his pleas fading down the empty hallway.

A few candles flickered in their holders, the flames dancing as Julia stole by. At the bottom of the stairs she stopped, listening for the captain and Uncle George. The clink of a crystal stopper followed by a slight cough punctuated the low cadence of their voices. The bottom stair creaked and she froze. The men's muffled conversation didn't falter and she slipped unnoticed past the door and to the study.

Inside, she didn't dare light a candle. Pulling the key from its hiding place in the ink blotter's handle, she unlocked the top desk drawer and drew out the money pouch. It jingled loudly and she clutched it tight, silencing the coins. Slipping it into the haversack, she locked the drawer, returned the key to its hiding place, then fled the room, making her way out of the house through the back.

Her feet flew over the gravel walkway as she ran down the hill to the stables, gripping the haversack with one hand while her other one held up the hem of her dress. The frosty night air bit at her exposed skin while the satin slippers failed to protect her feet from every stone embedded in the path.

Pushing open the stable door, the horses whinnied, then shifted back and forth in their stalls. They watched her run to the small room at the back where she stripped off the white-and-gold dress and hung it on a peg. It sagged there like an old skin, taunting her with what might have been. Why had she tried to be anything other than who she was? And who was she? Not Mrs James Covington, nor a polished London lady, only the fallen, spinster sister of a lieutenant in his Majesty's Navy. She forced the bitter sadness from her mind, knowing she'd never accomplish anything tonight with such heartache weighing on her. Paul needed her and he was all that mattered.

She slipped on the jacket, the rough wool scratching through the simple linen shirt, but giving welcome relief from the cold stable. She pulled on the trousers and then the Hessians, which fit surprisingly well for being two sizes too large. Walking in a tight circle, she admired the easy way the outfit allowed her to move. Removing the pins and ribbon from her hair, she arranged her locks into a ponytail, securing it with the ribbon and tucking it up under the hat. It was a poor disguise, but with luck it would be enough to keep anyone with a mind for trouble from picking her out. Tossing the haversack over her shoulder, she pulled open the door, letting out a yelp when she came face to face with John.

'Miss Howard,' he gasped, holding a pitchfork tight. 'I thought you were a thief. What are you doing here at this time of night and dressed like that?'

She pushed past him, grabbing Manfred's saddle. 'I'm going to London, to find Paul. He's been wounded and he's missing.'

'You can't.' John took hold of the heavy saddle, but she didn't let go. 'Not without Mr Howard or Captain Russell. If anyone found out, you'd be ruined.'

'I have to find him.'

'But think of your mother and brother.'

'Charles doesn't care about anything but his propriety.' Julia tugged on the saddle, but John held it tight.

'Miss Howard, I can't let you do this.'

The concern in his face touched her. He'd kept so many secrets for her in the past. Now she needed him to keep one more.

'Please, I must. Paul needs me. He's wounded and might die if I don't find him.' She hated sounding so desperate, but she couldn't keep the fear out of her words.

John shook his head, relaxing his grip on the leather. 'You know I can't refuse you.' He took the saddle into Manfred's stall and threw it over the horse's back.

Julia joined him, helping with the buckles. 'Thank you, John.'

When they were done, John led Manfred out to the paddock, then helped her up.

'Please be careful. Your family needs you. Knollwood needs you.'

Regret hit her with surprising strength and for a moment she considered returning to the house and finding some other way to help Paul. No, there was no other way and no life except the one she could create with him in some distant port. For all his silly faults, at least he would understand and not judge her. He was her future now, not Knollwood, Cable Grange or Captain Covington.

'I'll be careful.' She kicked Manfred and horse and rider cantered out into the night.

James leaned against the mantel, watching a smouldering log collapse. Admiral Nelson was dead. He'd been wounded so many times, survived so many battles and now, on the brink of perhaps his greatest victory, he'd been killed. A shiver ran through James—he might have shared the same fate a year ago, or perhaps even today if he hadn't resigned his commission. He'd wasted so much time lamenting the past, mourning everything he'd lost instead of living. And what had he lost? He wouldn't know until morning when he could speak to Julia, explain what had happened at Cable Grange and confess his love. He berated himself for not telling her sooner.

'Excuse me, sir.' John stood in the doorway, his hair dishevelled and his lined face stricken.

'What's wrong?' George asked.

'Miss Howard—she's taken Manfred and left for London.'

'What?' James couldn't believe it.

'She's gone to find Mr Paul Howard. Found one of his old uniforms and rode off dressed like a sailor.'

'Why did you let her go? Don't you know how dangerous it is for a woman to travel the roads alone at night?'

The groom shrunk back. 'I couldn't stop her.'

It seemed too far-fetched to be real, but knowing Julia's impetuous nature it sounded exactly like something she would do. 'Saddle up Hector. I'm going after her.'

'Thank you, sir.' John left to prepare the horse.

'I'll go with you,' George said.

'No, I need you to stay and tell Julia's mother what's happened, but not until morning and not unless we haven't returned.'

'What about Charles?'

'Wait as long as you can to tell him. I don't want him following us. He'll only make things worse. I'm sure I can catch up to her and convince her to come back.'

'And if you can't?'

James opened and closed his left hand. 'Then on to London to find Paul. I'll send word when I can.'

George clapped him on the back. 'I hate to miss this adventure. Good luck, Jim.'

James ran upstairs to change into his older uniform, buckling his sabre to his waist before he left the room. Outside, he hurried down the hill to the stable where John waited in the paddock with Hector. The lanterns from the stable shone off the stallion's dark coat but did little to pierce the darkness beyond the building.

'When did she leave?' he asked, pulling himself into the saddle, ignoring the sting to his shoulder.

'Right before I came to get you. She's sure to take the main road, but if you go through the woods, there's a path that leads west. It's not hard to find and comes out further down the road. If you hurry, you can cut her off. She's not likely to run Manfred in the dark and risk injuring him.'

'Thank you.' James turned the horse for the woods, riding as fast as he could without risking Hector. Despite the high half-moon, heavy clouds kept passing in front of it, plunging the country-side into periods of darkness.

He rode a good distance without finding a break in the trees or anywhere where the bald path di-verged. He thought of doubling back, fearing he'd missed the fork when the trail split, veering off into the dense copse. He slowed the stallion, nudg-ing him to the right and the trees closed in around them, blocking out all but the faintest slivers of moonlight. James's eyes strained against the dark-ness to see the hard-packed earth in the dim light.

A low, sharp branch caught his neck and he reached up, feeling warm blood. Wiping it away, he laughed, remembering the last time he'd rid-den hell-bent towards a town in the middle of the night. It was in Bermuda and he never thought he'd be doing it in England or chasing after a headstrong girl to aid a man he disliked. Life would never be this exciting without her and, if helping her find Paul meant winning her, he'd ride the length and breadth of the country.

* * *

An owl screeched, dipping down over the road in front of Julia and Manfred before flying off over the trees. Julia sat up straight, startled, her skin crawling with goose bumps. She might be dressed like a man, but any thieves in search of easy prey would discover the truth the moment they pounced. Then what would she do? She didn't have so much as a riding crop to defend herself with.

Somewhere in the distance a dog barked and Julia hunched over in the saddle, pulling the coat closer around her face. The ball, Mrs Wilkins and the captain's betrayal all mingled with the night to press down on her and dampen her spirit and resolve. What seemed a rational idea in the midst of a disappointing evening now felt like a mistake. Even if she made it to London, she had not the first idea where to begin her search. She should go home. It would be easy to slip into the house without anyone being the wiser, but then what would she do? Charles was too stubborn to help and even Uncle George had sided with the captain against Paul. If only the captain hadn't been such a scoundrel. He would have helped her.

Fresh tears threatened to fall and she bit her lip to keep from crying. She'd been so forward with her silly engagement scheme. No wonder he took advantage of her and thought nothing of exposing her to the censure and ridicule of the entire countryside. Though if he only sought to amuse himself with her innocence, why had he stopped the night he found her in his room and why had he suggested they marry? She smacked the saddle as she remembered the momentary weakness and the easy way he'd cast her aside. It must have all been a cruel joke because he obviously preferred the charms of a Cyprian like Mrs Wilkins to a silly girl like her. Wiping her eyes, she wondered if she'd ever be able to love again and her heart tightened with loss.

Rustling in the bushes up ahead put her on edge. Manfred's dark ears, tipped with moonlight, turned towards the noise and he raised his head higher, sensing something in the trees lining the road. She squinted, trying to see the source of the sound, but a heavy cloud passed over the moon and everything darkened. Branches cracked and her body tensed, her feet ready to kick Manfred into a gallop.

She heard the unmistakable thud of hooves on packed earth before the horse and rider sprang from the trees. The strange rider positioned himself in the middle of the road in an attempt to block her, but she moved fast, digging her heels into Manfred's side.

'Yah!' Manfred bolted past the rider, his hooves pounding the road. The stranger launched into pursuit, his horse matching Manfred's steady gait, but not his speed. Fear gripped Julia. She couldn't take Manfred into the forest without risking a broken leg. All she could do was rely on him to outrun the danger.

'Come on, Manfred,' she urged before the faint strain of a familiar voice reached her ears.

'Julia, wait.'

The stranger called out twice more before she recognised the captain's voice. Pulling Manfred to a halt, she watched the captain bring Hector to a stop a few feet away.

'What are you doing here?' she demanded, hoping the horses' heavy breathing covered the sound of her thundering heart.

'I've come to stop you from making a mistake.'

'I've already made many mistakes.' The sky briefly cleared and the moon's soft light caressed his face. Sadness hit her more powerfully than the fear she'd experienced only a moment before. They'd never be together with the same love and desire as before. She turned Manfred around and started him down the road and Captain Covington brought his stallion alongside hers.

'Why are you doing this?'

Julia didn't answer, unwilling to tell him the truth and be vulnerable to him again.

'Julia, please?' He manoeuvred Hector in front of Manfred, bringing them both to a stop. 'Tell me what's wrong and how I can help.'

'Why? You don't care. Go back to Knollwood and Mrs Wilkins. Leave me be.'

'Whatever she told you was a lie.'

'She said you were at Cable Grange. Is that a lie?'

He drew in a ragged breath. 'I was. But not for the reasons you think. I received a note from her regarding Rowan's debt. I'd hoped to use the money he owed me from the race as leverage to purchase Cable Grange. When I arrived she was alone and threw herself at me. I refused her, which is why she did what she did at the ball.'

'You wanted to buy Cable Grange? Why?'

'For you.'

Hope flared in Julia's heart, but she stamped it down. 'I don't believe you.'

'Would I be here on a lonely road in the middle of the night following a woman dressed as a naval officer if I was lying?'

Was it possible? Did he really want her with all of her silly habits and unconventional traits? Her heart wanted to believe him, but her mind couldn't. The image of Mrs Wilkins smiling in victory crushed her hope. No, she could not trust the captain in matters of love.

'Go back to Knollwood.' She manoeuvred Manfred around him, but he refused to be put off.

'I'm coming with you to London.'

'You needn't bother. I don't need your help.'

'I'm still coming.'

'Why?'

'Because you must have an accomplice in this adventure, especially someone who knows his way around town and can help you.'

'Adventure?' Until this moment she hadn't thought of it in such terms, but now the idea, despite her hurt and anger, appealed to her.

'What else would you call it?'

He was right, though she didn't want him to be right. She didn't want him to be anything but a distant memory. However, now that he was here and determined to stay, he could prove useful.

'Do as you like. But as soon as we find Paul, I never want to see you again.'

'Let's get to London first. We'll worry about the rest later.'

He started Hector down the road and Julia followed, the darkness not as frightening or lonely as before. Despite her decision to remain wary and angry with him, she felt a genuine thrill to be on an adventure like all the ones Paul and Uncle George had described. Her excitement was tempered by the heartache spurring her on. Despite his betrayal, deep down she knew he was honourable enough to protect her if they met any unsavoury characters. This offered some measure of comfort and she settled into the saddle for the long journey.

The time passed slowly, the moon falling towards the horizon before disappearing behind dark clouds. Early on he tried to talk to her, but she cut him short, unwilling to hear any more of his lies or to speak for fear her voice would reveal too much of her true emotions. Eventually, he gave up and they rode for miles in silence. Fatigue crept into her muscles and soon the gentle bob of Manfred's gait made her sleepy. She nodded off before a sturdy hand roused her.

'Don't fall asleep.'

Her head jerked up. 'I wasn't sleeping.'

A distant flash of lightning streaked across the horizon. 'The storm will be upon us soon. Is there an inn near here or a house, anywhere we can take shelter until it passes?'

Julia examined their surroundings, trying to get her bearings. Another distant lightning flash silhouetted a large, twisted oak tree near a bend in the road, a familiar marker she knew well.

'There's a coaching inn not far from here, but it isn't the most reputable establishment.'

The captain laughed. 'Two lone travellers, one a single woman dressed like a man. Sounds like a perfect place for us.'

The first heavy drops started to fall when they reached the inn and the quiet stable next to it.

'Stay here while I see to the horses,' James ordered. Julia didn't argue, but waited near the stable entrance while James spoke to the groom. The weather kept the rest of the patrons indoors, leaving only the groom and one stable boy who ignored them while he mucked out a stall. James paid the groom well to see to the horses then, taking Julia by the arm, led her across the muddy yard to the inn's front door.

'What are you doing?' she demanded, stepping through a large puddle.

'Shhh.' He pulled her under the eaves where two large drops slipped off the wood overhang and dripped down his neck. 'Once inside, say nothing. Your voice will give you away.'

'Do not order me about.'

He held up a warning finger. 'You have no experience in these matters. As we are both dressed in our uniforms...' he shook his head at the absurdity of the situation '...take direction from me as any junior officer would.'

'But—'

'No disobedience. Follow me or I'll throw you over Manfred and drag you back to Knollwood.'

'Yes, sir.' Julia saluted.

'That's more like it.' He pulled open the door. 'Come along, Julius.'

'Julius?'

'A suitable name for a boy of your temperament.'

They stepped inside, the overpowering stench of dirty travellers, tobacco and meat assaulting them. He expected Julia to blanch, but she stared through the smoky room, fascinated by the men hiding in dark corners and the barmaids plying their trade.

'What do you think?' he asked, enjoying her reaction.

'It's exactly like Paul described.' Her eyes followed a voluptuous blonde who walked by with two tankards and a surprising amount of uncovered flesh. 'Is she a—?'

'Yes. Come along, Columbus. Let's get something to eat.' He took her arm and pulled her through the benches of drinking, carousing men to a small, isolated table near the stairs. From a shadowed corner across the room, a man leaned against the wall, chewing on the end of a pipe. James noticed the way he watched them from under a dirty tricorn hat pulled low over his face. Something about him seemed familiar, but the stranger tilted down his head, obscuring his features.

'Wait here. I'll see to our room.' He pushed her into a chair with her back to the wall and a good view of the patrons.

'Shouldn't we stay here, in public?' she whispered with unmistakable worry.

Being alone with him seemed to frighten her more than a lonely road or a common room full of thieves, drunks and whores. He cursed himself for allowing the distance between them to widen, determined by the end of today to fill her eyes with wanting and love, not suspicion and worry.

'Privacy is safer in a place like this.' He was about to walk away when a woman with wild red hair and large breasts teetering precariously along the top edge of her dirty dress perched herself on the table.

'Fancy something special, Captain?'

'No, nothing, thank you.' James smiled, eager to send the woman on her way without any trouble.

The trollop's hooded eyes swept Julia. 'Then perhaps something for the lad?'

'He's fine, I assure you.'

'Seems kind of green to me. Perhaps he needs just a taste.' She leaned across the table and slid her hand between Julia's legs. The woman's eyes met hers in stunned shock, but before either of them could say anything James took the harlot's hand, slipping two sovereigns into her palm and placing it against his chest.

'I know you can understand such a delicate situation and as a true lady will maintain your discretion.'

Her fingers closed on the coins, a sly smile spreading over her pocked features. 'Whatever you like, love, makes no difference to me.'

'I knew you'd understand. And I know you'll do anything to help us.' He held up two more sovereigns in front of her face. 'We need a room, the best you have, and your continued discretion regarding the lad.'

'Anything you say, Captain.' She took the coins, then walked off, her large hips swaying.

He sat down next to Julia, noticing the wary mistrust in her eyes. 'You seem quite practised in the art of charming women.'

'Better a woman is your friend than your enemy.'

'What am I?'

'Much more than a friend.' He reached for her hand under the table, but she pulled it away.

'Don't.' She leaned back in the chair, watching the room from under her hat. James missed her easy trust and wondered how he could regain it. He wanted to reveal his true feelings, but this was no place for such an intimate conversation.

Very soon the harlot hustled back to them. 'Your room is ready, milord.' She dangled a key in one dirty hand while the other held a candle in a pewter holder.

'Not milord, just Captain.'

'Is that what she calls you?' She threw back her large head of red hair and laughed, the gravelly sound barely carrying over the din. James nodded for Julia to rise and they followed the wench up the stairs and down a pokey hallway to the back of the inn. The stench of unwashed bodies and stale beer increased, as did the heat, laughter and other assorted sounds from all the people packed into the small space under the eaves.

'Here ya are. The best we have.' The harlot threw open the door and James held up another coin.

'Your help is very much appreciated.'

'My pleasure,' she purred, taking the coin from his hand and sliding it over the flesh of her breasts and down the front of her dress. 'Ya wouldn't be needin' me to help you and the lad, would ya?'

From beside the harlot, James saw Julia's jaw fall open. 'Thank you, but we couldn't possibly intrude on your hospitality any longer.'

'Well, ya know where to find me if you change your mind.' She handed James the candle, then sauntered off down the hall.

'Did she just ask if...?' Julia gasped.

'Yes, she did.' James nudged her into the room, not wanting to linger in the hallway or explain any more about the proposal than Julia had already grasped.

He closed the door, placing the candle and key next to the chipped china bowl on the battered washstand near the door. Julia approached the narrow bed situated against the wall and pulled back the thin blanket with her thumb and forefinger to inspect the sheets.

'Does it meet with your approval?'

She jumped back, almost knocking over the rickety chair under the window. The room was tight, with little space for two people to walk around. He stood over her, keenly aware of her warm body so close to his.

'Yes, I suppose it will do.'

'What do you think of your adventure now?' The tightness in his voice caught him off guard and he realised he'd only been alone with her like this once before. The memory of it made his body ache with need and he busied himself removing his gloves.

'It keeps getting stranger.' She took in the small, dingy space, her hat shadowing her nervous eyes. 'Where are you going to sleep?'

'The floor.'

'The floor?'

'It's only appropriate.' Disappointment flashed across her face before she sat down to pull off her boots. 'Leave your clothes on and keep your coat and boots nearby in case we need to make a hasty retreat.'

Her eyes lit up. 'Really?'

'Yes, now get some sleep.' James slid the coat off his shoulders and a bolt of pain shot through him. He sucked in a quick breath, waiting for it to pass.

'What's wrong?'

'Nothing. I overworked the arm perhaps.' He grimaced, working to slide off the coat without making the pain worse.

'Let me help you.' She reached up to assist him, but he pulled away.

'I can manage.'

'Please, I insist.' She took the coat by the collar and gently pulled it down his arms. Once it was off, she draped it over the back of the chair. The tender move touched him and he knew, despite everything that had happened tonight, she still cared for him.

'Thank you.' He started to rub his sore shoulder, but she pushed his hand away, massaging his aching flesh with her slender fingers. The nearness of her teased his senses and clouded his mind.

'If it bothers you too much, I can sleep on the floor and you can have the bed,' she offered.

'I'm not weak enough to kick a lady out of her bed.' He laughed, but it came out choked. He stood, removing her hands from his shoulder to keep from losing all self-control. Did she know how she affected him? He wasn't sure, but he couldn't take advantage of her innocence, no matter how much hesitant yearning filled her eyes. He'd never win her back if he gave in to the desire raging through him. 'I can leave if you prefer and try to find another room.'

Her hand clasped his tighter. 'No, I don't want to stay here without you.'

He glanced at her chest, the linen shirt barely hiding the gentle curve of her full breasts rising and falling with each fast breath. He stepped closer, a desire deeper than lust driving him forwards. He wanted to smash all the obstacles between them and feel her in his soul. Did she want the same thing? 'Are you sure?'

'Yes.'

Pulling her to him, he covered her lips with his.

Julia slipped her hands around the captain's neck, heady with the heat of his body so close to hers. She knew she should stop, but she couldn't. She'd already abandoned good society tonight. Now she wanted to give in to her desire and curiosity and experience everything she'd been denied the night he'd first touched her in Paul's room. In the morning she could regret again.

His free hand slid up under the shirt, cupping her breast and she moaned softly as his thumb made her nipple hard. With his other hand, he pushed the linen from her shoulders and she pressed against him, dizzy with need. He kissed her neck, then lowered to take one pert nipple in his mouth. Her legs went weak when his tongue traced wet circles around the tender point, his breath on her damp skin making her sigh. Scooping her up, he laid her on the bed, then stood over her, removing his breeches and revealing his desire. A twinge of fear filled her for she knew something of what came next, but wanting drove all other thoughts from her mind.

He pulled his shirt off over his head, dropping it on the floor before settling down next to her in bed. Perched on one elbow, he admired her body, the hot desire in his eyes making her shiver. She reached for the sheet to cover her nakedness, but he stopped her.

'Don't.' His hand traced the curve of her stomach, heightening the need coiling within her. She grasped his arm when his fingers slid into her moist depths, his gentle caress bringing her closer and closer to her passion. Then he stopped, withdrawing his touch.

'No,' she pleaded, wanting him to fill the emptiness and lead her to the same ecstasy she'd experienced the other night.

'We shouldn't,' he whispered, but she was beyond reason or caring about anything except being close to him.

'Yes. Please.'

His knees nudged open her legs and he settled his hips between them. The heat of his manhood touched her thigh and she trembled in anticipation. He covered her mouth with his, his member probing her depths, sliding, stretching her until she opened to take him in. She gasped at the pain, but it quickly disappeared, replaced by a sensation of fullness as he rocked within her.

His thrusts were slow at first, caressing, teasing, but grew more frenzied as she tightened around him. Clinging to his back, she moved her hips to match his pace, thrilling at the sound of his heavy breath in her ear while he continued to push into her, deeper, harder until the spasms of her pleasure exploded through her. Inside she felt his body quiver before he collapsed on top of her, panting with his own release.

Julia stroked his back, their heavy breathing subsiding as they clung to one another. The thump of someone stumbling down the hallway accompanied by a wench's throaty laugh reminded Julia of where she was and why.

'James?' she ventured, wanting to know what this all meant to him and them. Did he love her?

Did he care for her or did he think her no better than the harlot who'd showed them to their room?

He withdrew, kissing her forehead, then cradling her against him. 'Tomorrow, everything will be clear,' he whispered as if sensing her questions. 'Tonight we need sleep.'

Julia closed her eyes, his damp skin on her cheek, his beating heart soothing her worried mind. Yes, tomorrow they'd deal with everything and one way or another it would seem right. Or would it? She didn't know. Snuggling into the crook of his arm, she closed her eyes, fatigue pulling her into a deep sleep.

Julia awoke with a start, struggling through thick sleep to recognise her surroundings. The dirty walls and rough sheets on her bare body brought the events of the night before rushing back. Emotions collided: betrayal, love, pleasure, heartache—all plagued her as powerfully as the exhaustion pulling at her muscles. Wrapping the sheet tighter around her neck, she sank back into the bed, snuggling close to James, eager for more sleep, but it eluded her. His steady breathing reminded her just how far she was from Knollwood and good society, and she had no idea what would happen when he awoke. For a brief moment he'd made her forget his unfaithfulness and the reason she'd first set out for London. Paul.

Her eyes flew open. Outside the window, the orange glow of the inn's lantern mixed with the grey morning light. Muffled snoring punctuated the silence, the other patrons deep in either their travel-weary or ale-laden sleep. She gazed at James and the way the dim light outlined his features. Reaching up to stroke his cheek, she stopped, afraid to wake him. She'd trusted him with her body, savouring the pleasure and hope in his touch, but she couldn't trust him with her heart. Under different circumstances, perhaps they could be happy together, but not with his infidelity hanging over them. There was no use continuing the journey with him or torturing her mind with what could never be. If she left now, she'd have the beautiful memory of their lovemaking instead of the awkward scene of facing him and listening to his lies and explanations. He'd surely follow her, but with a head start, he'd never be able to find her in the crowds of London.

She slid from the bed, careful not to disturb him. Gathering up her clothes from the pile on the floor, she dressed, anxious he might awake, but his breathing remained steady. Tying back her hair, she tucked it up under her hat. She grabbed the boots, unlocked the door and slipped into the hallway, closing it behind her. She didn't pull on her boots until she reached the top of the stairs, then she descended into the common room, noting the few people asleep at the tables or stretched out on the wooden benches. One man remained awake. He sat in the corner, a tricorn hat pulled down low over his eyes. She sensed something familiar in the cut of his jaw, but she could not see his features clearly through the heavy shadow covering his face. Having no desire to be recognised dressed as a man in a coaching inn during the early hours of dawn, she didn't linger, but hurried across the room and out of the door.

A few stars still twinkled in the grey sky, but the horizon glowed lighter with the approaching sunrise. The stable was empty except for the horses and, walking along the stalls, she found Manfred, who greeted her with a nervous toss of his head.

'Steady, boy. It's only me.' She reached up to caress his nose, but he pulled back, his dark eyes wide. Only then did she hear the sound of boots crunching the hay on the floor behind her. Turning around, she expected to see the groom or James and let out a scream when the man with the tricorn hat flew at her.

He grabbed her by the throat, pinning her up against the wall, his hands cutting off her scream. His hat toppled off and she recognised Wilkins's man, the one who'd challenged her about the fight.

'I thought it 'twas you. How lucky for us to meet when I'm on me way back from London,' he sneered, pressing his body against hers. 'Not so high and mighty now, are ya?'

'Get away from me,' she choked, scratching at his hand, but his grip on her neck remained tight.

'Oh, no, me minx, now you've shown yer true colours, old Mark's going to have a reward. I sees you and I thinks to myself, what would a proper lady like yourself pay to keep me from spreading this around the whole county?'

'You'll get nothing from me,' she spat, her throat burning with the effort to breathe.

'Oh, I think I shall have something.' He leaned closer, his ale-laden breath stinging her face.

A large shadow rose up behind him, pulling him back. The fingers around her throat released and she dropped to the ground, gasping for air. James slammed Mark against the opposite wall, his sword pointed at the scoundrel's throat.

'Please, governor, I meant no harm,' he pleaded,

his eyes wide with terror. 'I only wanted to help the lady, her being a good neighbour and all.'

'You have a strange way of helping,' James growled.

'Please, sir, I was helping. I can prove it. I know about her brother, the one in London.'

Julia was next to James in an instant. 'What do you know?'

'I know where he is.'

'How? Where?' Julia's heart leapt with hope.

Mark hesitated and James brought the edge of his sword up against Mark's neck.

'Answer her.'

The servant started to shake. 'Giltspur Street Compter.'

'Debtors' prison?' Julia cried.

'You're lying.' James pressed the sword deeper against Mark's flesh. A small drop of blood slipped out from beneath the blade and Mark's eyes widened, his fingers clawing at James's hand.

'No, I helped put him there. Mrs Wilkins told me to do it. She saw him when we was in London. Mrs Wilkins knows one of his creditors, so she sent me to fetch the man and he had me fetch the bailiff. It's why I'm back from London so late.'

'Why would she have Paul arrested?' Julia asked, trying to make sense of it all.

'To spite you both for wanting Cable Grange and for putting Mr Wilkins in debt to Captain Covington at the race.'

'But Paul had nothing to do with it.'

'The loathsome woman doesn't care. If she can strike a blow, she'll do it, no matter who it hurts.' James released Mark, who slumped to the ground, clutching his bruised neck. 'Mrs Wilkins paid you well for this?'

'Yes, sir.'

'I'll pay you better for your silence.' James tossed a few sovereigns at Mark's feet. Forgetting his sore throat, Mark snatched up the coins. He stretched to reach the last one, but James stopped him with his sword, resting the shiny blade against his cheek. 'I hear one whisper of either Paul's story or Miss Howard's and you'll regret it. I know a press-gang boss who'd gladly take a man like you for a ship. Do I make myself clear?'

'Yes, sir.' He cowered back, clutching the money to his chest.

James hauled Mark to his feet, shoving him at the stable door. 'Now get out of my sight.'

The servant stumbled before running off into the morning.

James sheathed his sword, fixing Julia with hard eyes. 'Why did you run off?'

She turned away from him, her shaking hands fumbling with Manfred's saddle. 'I don't owe you any explanations.'

He stepped up behind her, his body vibrating with anger. 'Do you know what could have happened if I hadn't found you?'

She knew exactly what she'd have suffered if he hadn't followed her. Having come so close to danger, she wanted to cry from fear, throw herself into his arms and let him comfort her, but she didn't have the courage to face him.

'Don't ever scare me like that again.' He walked to his own horse, throwing the saddle over its back in a noisy clank of stirrups and buckles. Tears burned at the corners of her eyes, but she refused to let them fall, determined not to cry in front of him.

Chapter Thirteen

The sun crested the horizon, glinting off the tightly packed roofs and wet streets of London. Smoke rose from the thousands of chimneys, joining the voices of ballad singers, fishwives and hawkers beginning their day. Despite the growing tightness in her stomach, Julia followed James into the sprawl of farmers, dyers and the like crouched outside the city proper and spreading into the surrounding countryside. The stench of rot and filth grew stronger the closer they got to town, the smell instantly taking her back to her Season in London and conjuring up the feelings of loneliness and inadequacy she'd suffered then. She wondered at the odd circumstances bringing her back here today. Was this her future, the rank air of London instead of the clean air of Cable Grange?

James sat rigid atop his horse. They'd barely

spoken since leaving the inn and if he didn't want her before, she felt sure he couldn't wait to be rid of her now. How tired he must be of chasing after a hoyden with a knack for getting in trouble. He'd probably leave her the moment they found Paul.

She buried her nose in the wool sleeve of her jacket, noting how James seemed impervious to the odours. 'How can you stand the smell?' she asked, unnerved by his continued silence and eager to reclaim the easy familiarity between them.

'Compared to a few months at sea with filthy men, bilge water and dead rats, this smells positively charming.' He sounded almost jovial and her shoulders relaxed, glad to see he'd lost some of his irritation. The feeling disappeared when his eyes went stern. 'Here, just as in the inn, do as I say.'

Julia nodded, rubbing her sore throat.

They manoeuvred their horses down the wide streets, dodging carriages, carts and various workers going about their morning business.

'How do you know where it is?' she asked.

'This isn't the first time I've had to bail a fellow officer out of debtors' prison. Though I never thought I'd be doing it for Paul Howard.'

'I find it hard to believe you dislike one another. You're so much alike.'

'No need to insult me,' James laughed.

'I meant it as a compliment,' she teased, happy to see the light return to his eyes.

They approached the old stone prison, the morning sun just beginning to rise over the tops of buildings. Giltspur Street Compter seemed strangely situated next to shops, its uninspiring façade dotted with rows of windows. A parade of women and children wandered in and out of the iron gates. The more fashionable ladies buried their faces in white handkerchieves, crying over the loss of a dowry or their only source of income while the common women carried large baskets of food or dragged crying children into the prison.

James signalled for them to dismount, then handed her his reins. 'Stay here while I speak with the guards.'

'I want to come with you.'

'No. We can't leave the horses unattended or some desperate person might steal them. Don't worry. It isn't as bad as you think.' He cuffed her under the chin, then hurried across the street to talk to the guards lounging on either side of the main door. She watched them perk up when he slipped them a few coins before they ushered him inside.

She stood with the horses, cautious of the people walking the streets. Shady characters eyed the horses with appraising interest and she wondered how many of them would gladly slit her throat to steal the animals. Clutching the reins, she worried as she waited, imagining Paul lying in some dank cell, his wounds uncared for and at risk of infection. Once James had freed him, she'd take him straight to the London town house and call for Dr Childers. Hopefully, she was not too late. She didn't know what she would do if she lost him to gaol fever or gangrene.

Finally, James emerged from the jail and if it weren't for the horses, she'd have rushed across the street to meet him. Instead she waited, her fears receding some when he came to stand next to her.

'I spoke with the warden. He'll summon your brother's creditors, then I'll settle the debt.'

'I brought money.'

He held up his hand to silence her. 'Allow me, please. I've dealt with these matters before and will not be cheated.'

She nodded, embarrassed once again at how unprepared she was for London. At Knollwood she was master of her realm; here she found herself at the mercy of others. 'Can I see Paul? I want to make sure he's all right.'

'Yes, I've made arrangements.'

He paid a guard to attend to the horses, then escorted Julia inside. The stench of unwashed bodies and damp stone rivalled the smell outside and Julia covered her nose with her hand.

He led her into a small office off the main entrance. Inside a large man wearing a dirty wig sat behind an old desk, poring over paperwork. Julia took a deep breath, the dusty smell of the office preferable to the noxious odours outside.

The gruff man ignored Julia in favour of James and what he knew to be a large and generous purse. 'You want to see him?'

'The lad wishes to see him, older brother and all. Mother wants to make sure he's being treated right.'

'A visitation will cost ya,' the warden finally acknowledged her, his wig slipping off to one side of his bald head.

'Cost?' Julia's voice came out high and she covered it with a cough. 'Cost?' she repeated, trying to deepen her voice.

'You'll have to excuse him—he's young.' James

fixed her with a reprimanding glare, then slid two coins across the desk. 'He doesn't understand things the way we do.'

'Young officer needs to learn this is a business. A man has to make a living.' The warden stuck two fat fingers on the coins and drew them to him. He dropped them in his dirty pocket, then nodded to the man standing behind Julia. 'Harvey there will take you back. Captain stays here to discuss the financial arrangements.'

'But—' Julia started, but James waved her off.

'Not to worry, Julius. The warden here is a sensible man. He knows the value in making sure no harm comes to you.'

The warden raised a greedy eyebrow, grasping James's meaning. 'Of course. Harvey will see nothing happens to the lad.'

'Yes, sir.' Harvey opened the door, hustling Julia into the hallway. 'This way.'

Julia followed him deeper into the prison, worry helping her ignore the eye-watering smell. At every cell they passed, a man's hand jutted out between the bars, his hoarse voice begging for money to buy food, his own cell or freedom. They reached the day rooms where children of various ages ran circles around men and their wives, who sat nursing babies.

'There are families here?' she asked, astonished.

Harvey grunted at her ignorance. 'Them that can afford it lives in the Rules of the Compter.'

'Rules?'

'Three miles 'round the Compter. Them that can't stay here.'

Taking in the wretched conditions, Julia fell silent, afraid of what she'd find when they reached Paul. He might already be sick, lying in squalor at death's door with no one to even bring him water.

Finally they reached a small row of cells near the back of the jail. The accommodations here weren't nearly so dirty, but Julia wouldn't call them 'clean'. A rat scurried across their path and she jumped back with a high squeal.

Harvey laughed, the key ring in his hand jingling. 'You wouldn't make it long on a ship.'

'How is my brother?' Julia adjusted her coat, following him to the last wood-and-iron door.

'Doing as well as ya can imagine. Here ya are.' He slid a large, black-iron key into the lock. The grating sound of metal against metal filled the hall before he threw open the door. ''ave a visitor for ya, Lieutenant.'

Julia stepped forwards, steeling herself for the worst and caught off guard by what she saw inside. The room, by no means palatial, was tidy and better appointed than the one she'd slept in last night. A wooden bed with white linens took up one wall while a well-built writing desk occupied the other. In the centre of the room, in a cushioned chair, Paul sat with a book in his lap, reminding her very much of a pirate captain surrounded in a cave by his sumptuous loot. Only the angry red cut on his forehead kept her from laughing.

He started at the strange sight in front of him, then rose, taking in the uniform with a lopsided grin.

'Well, fancy this. I didn't expect you of all people to rescue me, especially not like this.'

'Rescue you—' Julia balked, looking around at the cell '—I should have known you'd arrange the best accommodations, even in gaol.'

'Right crafty, this one,' Harvey mumbled. 'Wouldn't mind if we had more like him.'

Despite the humour, the emotions of the last day combined with the exhaustion of the night and her relief to find Paul overcame her. She threw herself into his arms, hugging him tight, quite forgetting herself and her disguise.

'Now then, lad, I know the ship has missed me, but really.' Paul patted her back, attempting to maintain the charade.

A deep, raspy laugh rolled out of Harvey. 'No point pretending. She ain't the first to come here dressed like that.'

'She's my sister,' Paul protested and Harvey laughed harder.

'Ain't the first to say that, too.'

Paul hugged Julia close while she cried into his dirty coat. It smelled of smoke and gunpowder and the scratchy wool reminded her of James. 'Now then, what's all this? You've never been this excited to see me.'

'I was so worried. They said you were injured.' She reached up to touch his head and he caught her hand. 'What happened?'

Julia and Paul sat down on the bed and Harvey stepped out of the cell and closed the door, giving them a little privacy.

'After the battle, we were rescuing French seamen. We should have left the scoundrels to drown. They were so thankful, they tried to take over *HMS Pickle*. We beat them back, but not before one of the French dogs got hold of a sword and rushed at Lieutenant Lapenotiere. I stepped between them, running him through just as he brought down his sword. He caught me here.' He touched his wound and winced. 'I was out for a while and bled like a stuck pig. Lieutenant Lapenotiere thought I might die, but the surgeon patched me up. Said all I needed was rest and I'd be back to fighting form in no time, though I'll have a scar to show for it. Lieutenant Lapenotiere was so grateful, he invited me to accompany him back to London.'

'Thank heavens.' She hugged him again, but he leaned back.

'Now, what are you doing here and dressed like that?'

'You have no idea what's happened this last week.'

'Then tell me all about it.'

She described at length the events of the last week, telling him everything except her very intimate encounter with the captain last night. Paul might listen without judgement, but she knew even he had limits where her honour was concerned. A few moments after she finished her story, Harvey pulled open the door.

'Come on. It's time for you two to go.'

They followed Harvey out of the cell and back down the halls.

'Paul, Dr Childers said you never arrived at his office. What happened?'

Paul rubbed his neck, a shamefaced smile

spreading across his face. 'I'm afraid I didn't go straight to Dr Childers, though I wish I had.'

'Yes, it would have saved us all a great deal of trouble and worry,' Julia chided. 'Where did you go?'

'I was on my way to Dr Childers when I ran into an old friend and he invited me to a card party.'

'Paul, how could you?' She wasn't sure who she was more angry with: Paul for being so silly or Charles for being right. 'You were supposed to rest.'

'I spent the last two weeks of our voyage back to England resting. I needed a little fun. I saw the Wilkinses there. Mr Wilkins was bragging about selling Cable Grange for more than it's worth. I'm sorry you weren't able to get it. You'd have really made something out of it.'

She offered him a half-hearted smile, not wanting to think about it.

Harvey stopped at a small sitting room across from the main office. 'You can wait here while the captain finishes settlin' your accounts. It's the warden's private room.'

'Thank you, good man. We'll have cake with our tea,' Paul ribbed.

'I've changed my mind. I'm glad to be done with ya,' Harvey grumbled, closing the door.

Paul walked leisurely about the shabby room, fingering the chipped porcelain knick-knacks probably left behind by some long-ago tenant. 'Now that Cable Grange is gone, what will you do?'

'I'll stay with you.'

He leaned against the thick windowsill, crossing his arms over his chest. 'You can't stay with me.'

'What other options do I have? I can't go back to Knollwood, not under these circumstances.'

'You could marry Captain Covington.'

'Haven't you heard anything I've told you?' Julia threw up her hands, for the first time in her life frustrated with Paul.

'I heard it all, which is why I think you should simply admit you're in love with him and put all this business behind you.'

'I don't love him.' Julia threw herself into a nearby chair, a puff of dust escaping from the threadbare fabric. New tears fell down her cheeks, leaving small watermarks on the dingy chintz. 'I did love him, but not any more.'

Paul sat on the chair's matching ottoman, taking Julia's hands in his. 'I think you still love him very much. Do you know how I know?'

She shook her head, wiping her eyes with the back of her hand.

'Because I've never seen you cry.'

'Of course I cry.'

'Not like this.' He pulled a stained handkerchief from his pocket and handed it to her.

'Well, what do you expect? I'm not a statue.' She wondered if she shouldn't have taken Charles's advice and left Paul in London.

'Come now. Why the tears?'

'Because he doesn't love me.'

'What makes you think he doesn't love you?'

'Mrs Wilkins.'

'He explained why he was there.'

'He was lying, like all Navy men.'

'Captain Covington may be a Navy man, but he's no liar. He's also not a man of whims. If he didn't love you, he wouldn't have come to London to help you, especially not to help me. I think he loves you just as much as you love him. He just needs to get around to telling you so you'll finally believe him.'

Julia twisted the handkerchief, unable to deny his logic. The captain had followed her to London, saved her from Wilkins's servant and helped her find Paul, but she'd continued to doubt him because of her own fears and because he hadn't said the words. Could the answer be so simple?

Her head ached from trying to figure it all out. 'What about your recommendation?'

'I understand why he wrote it. At the end of my first year, we were in Portsmouth waiting for our orders. It was rather dull there and I got into some trouble with a parson's daughter.'

'Paul, you didn't.'

'Unlike your captain, I am a typical Navy man. But I wasn't the first officer she'd taken long walks with in the woods. I just had more money than the last bloke. The next thing I know she tells her father I ruined her and the parson complains to my superior officer.'

'Captain Covington.'

'Of course. Well, it's his first ship so he's a real stickler for rules and orders me to marry her.'

'But you refused.'

'I wasn't about to introduce a girl like her to Mother, or Charles for that matter. Luckily, before Captain Covington could bring me up on charges, her fiancé comes in to port. His ship took a frigate off the coast of Africa, so now he has money and they run off to Gretna Green.'

Julia clapped her hand over her mouth to cover a laugh. This was just the kind of trouble and escape Paul always managed to find. 'Once the truth came out didn't Captain Covington understand?'

'He did, but I'd still disobeyed a direct order. Caused him quite a bit of embarrassment.'

'So now, all these years later, he writes a poor recommendation. Seems rather petty.'

'I don't blame him. Besides, he's more than made up for it now.'

He patted her hands, then the door opened and James entered the room.

James took in brother and sister. She clutched an old handkerchief, watching him with large, red eyes glistening with tears. He could only imagine what she'd told her brother and wondered how his old crewmate would react. He didn't relish the idea of a duel.

To his amazement, Paul crossed the room, holding out his hand in greeting. 'Captain Covington, thank you for getting me out of this pinch.'

'You have Miss Howard to thank.' James hesitantly took his outstretched hand and Paul pumped it heartily.

'Don't be so modest. I know you played a part in it. My sister told me all about your exciting journey last night.'

'Did she?' James tightened his grip and Paul matched the hold with a smile. *The man is as arrogant as ever*, James thought, determined to make Paul relent first, despite the numbness in his fingers.

'Come now, Jim.' Paul leaned forwards, dropping his voice. 'We both love the little lady, so why not put the past behind us?'

James released Paul's hand, flexing his fingers to bring the blood back. What had she told him?

'Now, if you'll both excuse me.' Paul moved towards the door. 'I have some private business with the warden and you two have a great deal to discuss.'

'Paul, wait.' Julia jumped to her feet, but Paul didn't stop, winking at her before slipping out of the door.

A small porcelain clock on the mantel ticked off the long seconds of silence. James stood unmoving, his eyes watching her with honest longing. Could Paul be right? Did he really love her? She searched for the words to ask, the right phrase to confirm everything in her heart and cross the chasm of uncertainty dividing them, but words were unnecessary. He marched across the room, swept her into his arms and kissed her.

All the worry about her actions and future disappeared. Pressing close, she surrendered more now than she had in the late hours of the night, giving him her heart, soul and life, knowing he would guard them as faithfully as he'd guarded her through this entire journey, binding their hearts together so nothing could ever separate them again.

Their lips finally parted and she felt the rough stubble of his cheek against hers. 'I love you,' he whispered.

'I love you, too.' She buried her face in his jacket, revelling in the peace and comfort of his beating heart. She'd never felt this happy or content and it filled her with a new energy and the eager anticipation to begin their life together.

'There's plenty of time to make it to Gretna Green,' she suggested, tracing a brass button with her finger.

'Nonsense. If I know George, he's convinced your brother not to cancel the wedding.'

'I'm surprised Charles hasn't hurried after us with a vicar already.'

'Then I know the wedding will still take place. We just have to get there on time.'

The clock chimed eight o'clock.

'Then we'd better hurry or we'll never make it.'

Outside the jail, Paul waited with the horses, winking at a young woman sauntering past.

'I'm glad to see you've resolved your differences.' He laughed as Julia and James approached.

'I suppose it's my turn to thank you,' James said.

'You'll have plenty of time to thank me once you're married. But first, we need to eat. I know a place not far from here where we can get some food and a horse.'

'You mean I'll have to hire a horse for you since you have no blunt,' Julia corrected.

'How kind of you to offer, sister, though I have plenty of blunt, just not here in London—'

'If you don't mind,' James interrupted, 'I have a much better suggestion.'

Chapter Fourteen

'I thought you said your suggestion was better?' Julia hissed, taking in the dark-wood entrance hall of the well-appointed town house, her stomach tight with worry.

The captain put his arm around her shoulders and offered an encouraging squeeze. 'Have faith, Artemis.'

Her worried eyes met Paul's, not sure what to expect. The butler had left them to fetch the mistress of the house, which belonged to none other than James's mother.

'Perhaps we should go to Charles's town house,' Julia pleaded, stepping back towards the door.

'No, I want to introduce you to my mother.'

'Like this?' She waved her hand over the uniform, not wanting to meet her future mother-in-law in such scandalous attire.

'She'll understand.'

A stout woman in her early fifties appeared at the top of the stairs, her plump frame draped in a silk morning wrapper. A linen cap covered her dark hair and she had the pinched groggy expression of someone who'd just been roused from bed. 'What are you doing here?'

'Good morning, Mother.' He met her at the bottom of the stairs with a respectful hug. 'I see you're safely returned from Charlotte's.'

'And very, very late last night thanks to the miserable roads, which is why you'd better have a good reason for disturbing me so early this morning.'

'Who's in a spot of trouble now?' Paul chuckled in Julia's ear and she elbowed him silent.

Mrs Covington stepped back from her son, taking in the motley, unwashed group dressed in dirty uniforms, her forehead wrinkled in confusion. 'I thought you were in the country?'

'I was but I had business in town, some of which might interest you.'

'I doubt it, but get on with it so I can return to bed.'

He took Julia's hand and pulled her forwards. 'I want to introduce you to my fiancée.'

'What kind of joke is this?' she sputtered, grasping her robe tight around her neck. 'I will not stand for this kind of tomfoolery so early in the day.'

'I assure you, this is no joke. I'd like you to meet Miss Julia Howard.'

He pulled off her hat and Julia's long braid tumbled down her back. She squared her shoulders, put her chin in the air and stepped forwards with as much grace as she could muster in a pair of men's Hessians.

'Mrs Covington, I'm delighted to meet you.' Julia curtsied, using everything Annette had taught her about behaving in society to stay poised, but Mrs Covington's eyes remained stony.

'And the gentleman?' she asked, nodding at Paul.

'My brother, Lieutenant Paul Howard.'

'A pleasure, madam.' He swept into a low bow, more to cover his smile than to show his respect.

'Am I to assume the three of you have stopped here on your way to Gretna Green?'

'Of course not,' James said. 'We have an appointment at the church near Miss Howard's estate today at three. Miss Howard is George Russell's niece.'

Mrs Covington's stony eyes warmed. 'The one who runs the estate?'

'The very young lady.'

'Well, why didn't you say so sooner?' She rushed at Julia with arms outstretched, enveloping her in a big hug. 'My dear, I'm so pleased to have you here.'

'Thank you.' The sudden change in emotion caught her off guard, but she preferred it to the rebuke she'd imagined.

Mrs Covington stepped back, clasping her hands together in excitement, the lace at her sleeves fluttering. 'Your uncle told me a great deal about you, but of course my son doesn't write to tell me he's getting married and to George's niece of all people.'

'It all happened very fast and you were travelling. The letter wouldn't have reached you.'

'That's no excuse for showing up like a vagabond and announcing it.' She wagged a reprimanding finger at Paul. 'I hope you have more respect for your mother.'

'Of course.' Paul nodded solemnly but Julia noticed the laughter in his eyes.

'Mother, we must borrow the chaise if we're to make it back to Knollwood in time,' James informed her, attempting to regain control of the situation, but Julia could tell Mrs Covington had no intention of relinquishing it.

'Borrow—oh, no, I'm going with you. But first,

we must get Miss Howard some suitable travelling attire.'

'There isn't time.'

'Then we'll be quick because if you think I'm going to have my future daughter-in-law traipsing about the countryside dressed like a man, you're quite mistaken.' She examined Julia's dust-covered uniform, tutting under her breath. 'You're about Charlotte's size. My daughter always leaves a couple of dresses here. One is sure to fit. Come along and we'll find one. And, James, arrange to have breakfast sent up to your sister's room. You probably haven't even fed the poor girl. You two can have breakfast in the morning room.' Mrs Covington took Julia's arm and escorted her up the stairs.

Julia wasn't sure which moved faster, their chaise or Mrs Covington's conversation. The woman talked without breathing or pausing, jumping from one topic to the next as they sped past the mile posts. Paul had left town shortly after breakfast, riding ahead on James's London stallion to inform Knollwood of their impending arrival and to arrange their meeting at the church. Manfred and Hector were stabled in James's mews, enjoying a well-deserved rest.

James, Julia and his mother had not started for Knollwood until nearly eleven. Business had delayed them in London, something to do with the Admiralty, though James never said what. Now, if they hoped to make it to Knollwood by three, they had to hurry. Mrs Covington's post-boy was an excellent driver and they made good time, despite one stop to change the horses.

They'd maintained a sensible pace until the turn to Daringford, then Mrs Covington insisted on speed. Despite the post-boy's skill, Julia found the fast pace unsettling. She might have developed her brother's taste for adventure, but an overturned carriage did not figure into any of her plans.

'Perhaps we should slow down? If the vicar was convinced to hold the ceremony today, he'll be just as easily persuaded to hold it tomorrow,' Julia suggested while Mrs Covington paused to take a breath. The woman shook her head, grasping the windowsill when the carriage took a sharp corner, forcing James to hold the strap to keep from leaning into Julia.

'Heavens, no, my dear. You two have a date at the altar and I intend for you to keep it. Do you know how many years I've waited for James to marry? I have no intention of putting it off any longer. Besides…' she leaned forwards, patting

Julia's hand and smiling '…I like you and I have no intention of letting you get away from him.'

'Or perhaps you have no intention of letting George get away from you,' James suggested.

'I have no idea what you mean.' Mrs Covington flapped her handkerchief in front of her face.

The captain offered Julia a conspiratorial wink. 'Perhaps we can make it a double wedding.'

'Oh heavens, who said anything about marriage?' Mrs Covington hid a wicked smile behind the coloured silk.

Julia's mouth fell open. 'You mean she and Uncle George?'

'Exactly.'

'How long have you known?' Julia asked, still trying to take it in.

'I've suspected it for a while, but she only just confirmed it.'

'Oh, you think you are so clever,' Mrs Covington huffed.

'I don't know if I approve of my mother conducting herself in such a fashion,' James playfully chastised and Mrs Covington pointed one stern finger at her son.

'In your present circumstances, you have no right to criticise.'

Julia didn't know what to say after the stunning

revelation, but then Daringford appeared in the distance, ending the discussion.

Hesitant anticipation filled her at the sight of the familiar rolling hills and river-etched valley. Though very eager to reach the altar, she had no idea what waited for them at the church. Mother and Uncle George would take the events of the last day with their usual detached demeanour. It was what Charles might say which worried her. Would he object to the marriage, afraid to entrust his sister and her inheritance to a man he might now view as a scoundrel? Or would he drag her up the aisle as fast as possible in an attempt to keep her and the family's reputation intact? Either way, he was sure to cause a scene she had no stomach for.

'What's wrong?' James asked. 'Not having second thoughts, are you?'

'I'm dreading another of Charles's lectures.'

'He has no cause to lecture anyone.'

'What do you mean?'

'Haven't you guessed about your nephew?'

The truth she'd somehow missed before hit her like a ton of stones. 'Thomas wasn't early. Charles and Emily, they—I mean, well, you know, it must have happened before they were married.'

'According to George it did,' James confirmed.

'It explains why they were so quick to marry last February. I can't believe I never realised it before.' Julia sat back, shaking her head in indignant disbelief. 'All this time Charles chastised me for my behaviour when he'd done so much more.'

'The fallen ones are always the most puritanical.' Mrs Covington sniffed. 'You must stand up to him, my dear, for you will have to stand up to James. He can be very stubborn at times.'

'Good, for if he weren't I might not be so happy.'

'We might not be so happy,' he corrected, kissing the back of her hand. The gentle tickle of his lips raised a shiver of delight along her spine. She saw the wanting in his eyes, felt their heat spreading through her and lowered her head so Mrs Covington wouldn't notice the burning exchange.

The carriage entered Daringford, slowing its mad pace and clattering through the narrow streets to the church situated on the other side. Her heart leapt with the excitement of being so close to home, but it was tempered by a new feeling. Though the familiar stone buildings were comforting, everything now seemed old and small. This place would never be far from her heart, but she couldn't wait to leave it and embark with the captain on the next journey and adventure.

The carriage jostled to a stop in front of the

church, the long shadow of the steeple falling
the churchyard. James stepped out, then hand
her down. She was not two steps from the carriage
when the church's large oak doors flew open and
her family rushed to greet them.

'You made it.' Emily threw her arms around
Julia. 'We were so worried about you. I brought
your dress. You can change in the vestibule.'

'Where are Charles and Paul?'

'Inside, speaking with the vicar.'

'Jim, I brought your other uniform, thought you
might need it,' George said before running his
hand over the chaise's high mudguard. 'I recognise this coach.'

'I thought perhaps you might.' Julia laughed.

'Hello, Captain Russell.' Mrs Covington sat forwards at the door, meeting Uncle George with
teasing eyes.

'I see you've finally learned her name,' he whispered to Julia.

'You never could keep a secret.'

'Hello, Mrs Covington.' Uncle George held out
a steadying hand and she took it, descending from
the carriage, her eyes never leaving his. He tucked
her hand in the crook of his arm, then led her to
Julia's mother, Emily and Annette. 'Everyone,
may I introduce Jim's mother, Mrs Covington.'

Emily and Annette stood dumbfounded at the announcement. Only Julia's mother maintained her usual grace and confidence, moving around the others to welcome her.

'It is a pleasure to meet you. We are so delighted you could be here.'

'I wouldn't have missed it. I've waited a long time for this day.'

'We all have.' Her mother winked at George, who tugged on his cravat.

'You made it.' Paul bounded out of the church, washed and cleaned and wearing a fresh uniform. 'The vicar is ready. And who is this?'

He bowed to Annette, who stood away from the group, doing her best not to be seen. A slight blush spread over her cheeks at Paul's sudden attentiveness and Julia stepped forwards to rescue her. 'This is Miss Annette Taylor, Uncle Edward's stepdaughter.'

'I've heard a great deal about you.' Paul motioned for Annette's hand, which she offered with her usual measure of grace.

'Hopefully not too much.'

Julia noticed Annette's lack of affected London airs, thinking the natural reaction suited her very well. Obviously Paul thought so, too, for he lingered over her hand.

Emily chuckled, breaking the spell. 'Come along, Julia. The vicar will not wait for ever.'

Julia followed Emily and Mother into the church and up the dim side aisle to the vicar's small room behind the nave. The musty smell of cold stone and smoke hung heavy in the air. Charles paced in front of the door, stopping at the sight of her. She cautiously approached, expecting anger but his eyes were soft, almost sheepish.

'I'm glad to see you returned unharmed. We were worried about you.'

'Were you?' Julia ventured, noticing the tender concern in his eyes. She'd only seen it once before, when he'd comforted her after Father's death.

'Of course. I know you believe I think little of you, but I don't. I'm only trying to help and protect you. Perhaps I've been going about it the wrong way. Mother told me about your bargain with the captain. I also spoke to Emily, who gave me quite a tongue-lashing for being so unsympathetic about Paul. I think some of your nature has rubbed off on her for she was quite forceful.'

'She'll need a strong hand to run Knollwood.'

He took her hands. 'You don't have to marry him if you don't want to.'

'I do.'

'Do you?'

Julia nodded.

'Will you be happy with him?'

'I love him and he loves me. Besides, I have a fondness for Navy men.'

He pulled her into a hug. 'Then I'm very happy for you. You couldn't have chosen a better, more deserving man.'

'Thank you.' She rose up and kissed him on the cheek, then slipped into the vicar's room. Her mother helped her exchange the borrowed gown for the London one altered for the wedding. Emily instructed Mary on how to arrange Julia's hair, then they stepped back to admire their work.

'You're beautiful.' Emily smiled and Julia's mother nodded.

'I think the captain will be very pleased.'

Minutes later, Julia stood at the back of the church on Paul's arm. The organist began a hymn, the church doors opened and the guests stood. Some faces she knew well, others were less familiar and she imagined a number of villagers and country folk had come to see for themselves the maid of Knollwood finally married.

Of all the eyes watching, she sought only James's. He stood near the altar with Uncle George, his smile taking her breath away.

'Are you ready?' Paul whispered.

'Yes.'

He escorted her down the aisle, offering her hand to James at the vicar's instruction. The rest of the ceremony passed in a blur and she was conscious of nothing but the vicar's even voice and James standing beside her. She thought of the fountain at Knollwood and her old longings. Standing beside a man who loved her and who she loved with all her heart, those days seemed liked a lifetime ago.

'You may now kiss the bride,' the vicar announced and James leaned over, placing his warm lips on hers. She met his kiss with all the passion in her heart, forgetting the guests and even where they stood.

'Patience,' Uncle George whispered, interrupting them and they broke into happy laughter, hurrying back up the aisle and into the soft evening light.

Outside the church, they received everyone's congratulations, enjoying the festive atmosphere.

Paul approached, twirling her in a large hug. 'I'm so happy for you, Sister. And you, too, Captain Covington. Congratulations.' He held out his hand to the captain, who took it without hesitation.

'Congratulations to you as well.'

'Pardon?'

'I paid a quick visit to Admiral Stuart while we were in London.' The captain reached into his coat pocket and presented Paul with a letter sealed with red wax. 'I rescinded my previous recommendation. Congratulations on your new posting, Lieutenant-Commander Howard.'

For the first time ever, Paul stood at a loss for words. He took the letter and opened it, a wide smile spreading across his face as he devoured the contents.

'My own ship. I can't believe it.'

'It's a sad vessel, barely fit for duty, but if you make something of her, you'll earn a name for yourself.'

'I will. Thank you. You won't regret this.'

'No, I don't believe I will.'

Paul hurried off to show his mother his new orders and Julia threw herself into James's arms.

'Thank you. Though you didn't have to do it.'

'Of course I did. If it hadn't been for Paul, you may never have come to your senses.'

More congratulation accompanied them to the Howard family carriage. Stepping up into it, she noticed, over the heads of the revellers, Uncle George escorting Mrs Covington to his carriage.

It seemed she wasn't the only one destined to find love this November.

The carriage set off and with a sigh of relief, Julia settled against the captain's chest, enjoying the feel of his arms around her.

'I have a present for you.' He reached into his coat pocket.

She ran her hand up his thigh, eager for all the wedding events to be over so they could be alone. 'I think you shall have much more before the night is out.'

'Saucy wench.' He pinched her cheek, then held out a slim leather wallet. 'This is for you.'

She took the worn leather and untied the straps. Her heart leapt when she unfolded it and read the old paper. 'The deed for Cable Grange!'

'It is.'

'But how did you manage it? Mrs Wilkins said it was sold to a London gentleman.'

'I told you not to believe her. I had my London solicitor arrange the purchase anonymously. It seems Mr Wilkins owed more to creditors than even his wife knew. He was very eager to part with the estate for the sum I offered. I've since learned their debts were so crushing they fled to France right after the ball. Not even the amount I paid for Cable Grange was enough to save them from ruin.'

'Thank you. Thank you.' She gave him an enthusiastic kiss, teasing his tongue with hers before sitting back. 'But what about Venice and India? You promised to show me the world.'

'So I shall, but we need somewhere to live between travels,' the captain whispered, nibbling at her neck, his breath heavy. 'Do you still have that book of your brother's, my sweet Artemis?'

'I think I can remember enough of it,' she breathed, pushing his jacket off his shoulders.

He kissed the exposed skin above the bodice of her dress, his tongue making sweet circles on her sensitive breasts. 'Don't you wish to wait?'

'No.' He was hers now without shame or censure and she wanted to feel him deep inside her again.

His jacket fell to the carriage floor and she pulled his shirt from his breeches, then slipped her hands beneath the linen to trace the taut muscles of his stomach. Answering her invitation, he settled her on his lap, his hands firm on her waist, anchoring her body to his. In his strong grip, she felt the security of their future while his tender lips filled her with the excitement of today.

She wrapped her arm around his shoulders, revelling in the feel of him so close to her. With her tongue, she imitated the wet circles on his neck, breathing on the moist skin and smiling when he groaned.

She had little time to delight in her newfound wickedness before his other hand slid beneath her dress, teasing the skin along the line of her calf and thigh. She gasped when he found her centre, unable to think of anything except the pleasure building inside her.

'No,' she protested when he withdrew his hand.

'Yes,' he answered, heavy desire igniting his eyes and making her shiver.

He helped her shift astride him, holding her hips to keep her steady as she worked open the buttons of his breeches. She pulled the material down about his thighs and, taking his desire in her hands, stroked the firm shaft.

'You do remember the book,' he rasped.

'I can't wait to try the positions.'

'First let's begin with just one.'

Pushing up her skirts, he settled her on to the heat of his manhood. She gripped the squabs behind him as he filled her, biting back a cry of delight.

She drew in deep breaths as he moved within her, his fingers digging into the flesh of her thighs.

She closed her eyes, bringing her cheek next to his as the rocking carriage made each thrust more fierce. His breath in her ear matched by her own quickened as she tightened around him until they cried out together, clasping each other in quivering excitement.

She laid her head on his shoulder as everything around them came back to her.

'I think we shall have quite an adventure, my beautiful Venus,' he breathed and she looked up, her face close to his.

With one finger, she traced the curve of his smile, feeling his joy deep in her own heart. 'Yes, I think we shall.'

* * * * *

Discover more romance at

www.millsandboon.co.uk

❤ WIN great prizes in our exclusive
   competitions

❤ BUY new titles before they hit the shops

❤ BROWSE new books and REVIEW
   your favourites

❤ SAVE on new books with the
   Mills & Boon® Bookclub™

❤ DISCOVER new authors

PLUS, to chat about your favourite reads,
get the latest news and find special offers:

f Find us on facebook.com/millsandboon
🐦 Follow us on twitter.com/millsandboonuk
❤ Sign up to our newsletter at millsandboon.co.uk

HANDBOOK ON THE EXPERIENCE ECONOMY

Handbook on the Experience Economy

Edited by

Jon Sundbo

Professor of Innovation and Business Administration, Department of Communication, Business and Information Technologies, Roskilde University, Denmark

Flemming Sørensen

Associate Professor of Management and Innovation, Department of Communication, Business and Information Technologies, Roskilde University, Denmark

Edward Elgar
Cheltenham, UK • Northampton, MA, USA

Published by
Edward Elgar Publishing Limited
The Lypiatts
15 Lansdown Road
Cheltenham
Glos GL50 2JA
UK

Edward Elgar Publishing, Inc.
William Pratt House
9 Dewey Court
Northampton
Massachusetts 01060
USA

A catalogue record for this book
is available from the British Library

Library of Congress Control Number: 2013935039

This book is available electronically in the ElgarOnline.com
Business Subject Collection, E-ISBN 978 1 78100 422 7

ISBN 978 1 78100 421 0

Typeset by Servis Filmsetting Ltd, Stockport, Cheshire
Printed and bound in Great Britain by T.J. International Ltd, Padstow

Contents

Contributors

Åke E. Andersson, Professor, Jönköping International Business School, Sweden.

David Emanuel Andersson, Lecturer, University of Nottingham, UK and Ningbo, China.

Jørgen Ole Bærenholdt, Head of Department and Professor of Human Geography (Dr Scient. Soc., PhD), Department of Environmental, Social and Spatial Change, Roskilde University, Denmark.

Albert Boswijk, Founder and Director of the European Centre for the Experience and Transformation Economy, Amsterdam, the Netherlands.

Laurence Chalip, Brightbill-Sapora Professor, University of Illinois at Urbana-Champaign, USA, where he also serves as Head of the Department of Recreation, Sport and Tourism.

Philip Cooke, Professor, Centre for Advanced Studies, Cardiff University, UK.

Britt E. Dale, Professor in Human Geography, Department of Geography, Norwegian University of Science and Technology (NTNU), Trondheim, Norway.

Marlene Dixon, Associate Professor and Fellow in the T.L. Long Professorship for Education, University of Texas, Austin, USA.

Dorthe Eide, Associate Professor in Organizing and Management, Bodø Graduate School of Business, Nordland University, Norway.

Lars Fuglsang, Professor, Lillehammer University College, Norway and Associate Professor, Roskilde University, Denmark.

James H. Gilmore, Co-founder, Strategic Horizons LLP and Adjunct Lecturer, Graduate School of Business Administration, University of Virginia, USA.

B. Christine Green, Associate Professor and Coordinator of the Sport Management Program, Department of Kinesiology and Health Education, University of Texas, Austin, USA.

Sune Gudiksen, PhD Fellow, Aalborg University, Department of Communication and Psychology, Aalborg, Denmark.

Michael Haldrup, Associate Professor (PhD), Research Unit on Space, Place, Mobility and Urban Studies (MOSPUS), Department of Environmental, Social and Spatial Change, Roskilde University, Denmark.

Gry Worre Hallberg, Associate of Performance Design, Roskilde University, Denmark and Co-founder, House of Futures, Fiction Pimps, Sisters Hope, Club de la Faye and Staging Transitions.

Ann H. Hansen, PhD Fellow in Tourism, Bodø Graduate School of Business, University of Nordland, Norway.

Olav Harsløf, Professor of Performance Design, Roskilde University, Denmark.

Fabian Holt, Associate Professor, Department of Communication, Business and Information Technologies, Roskilde University, Denmark.

Jan K. Jacobsen, Adjunct Professor, Department of Communication, Business and Information Technologies, Roskilde University, Denmark.

Christian Jantzen, Professor of Experience Design, Department of Communication and Psychology, Aalborg University, Denmark.

Jens F. Jensen, Professor of Interactive Multimedia, Department of Culture and Global Studies, Aalborg University, Denmark.

Francesco Lapenta, Associate Professor, Department of Communication, Business and Information Technologies, Roskilde University, Denmark.

Jonas Larsen, Associate Professor (PhD), Head of Research Unit on Space, Place, Mobility and Urban Studies (MOSPUS), Department of Environmental, Social and Spatial Change, Roskilde University, Denmark.

Yen-Chun Lin, PhD Fellow, Department of Kinesiology and Health Education, University of Texas, Austin, USA.

Anne Lorentzen, Professor in Geography, Department of Development and Planning, Aalborg University, Denmark.

Lena Mossberg, Professor, Marketing Group, School of Business, Economics and Law, University of Gothenburg, Sweden and Visiting Professor, Bodø Graduate School of Business, University of Nordland, Bodø, Norway.

Berit T. Nilsen, PhD Fellow, Department of Geography, Norwegian University of Science and Technology, Norway.

B. Joseph Pine II, Co-founder, Strategic Horizons LLP and Visiting Scholar, MIT Design Lab, USA.

Gerhard Schulze, Professor of Sociology, Faculty for Social and Economical Sciences, University of Bamberg, Germany.

Anna Snel, PhD, Academy for Information and Management, Amsterdam, the Netherlands.

Flemming Sørensen, Associate Professor of Management and Innovation, Department of Communication, Business and Information Technologies, Roskilde University, Denmark.

Donna Sundbo, Postdoc Fellow, Department of Communication, Business and Information Technologies, Roskilde University, Denmark.

Jon Sundbo, Professor of Innovation and Business Administration, Department of Communication, Business and Information Technologies, Roskilde University, Denmark.

Connie Svabo, Assistant Professor (PhD), Research Unit on Space, Place, Mobility and Urban Studies (MOSPUS), Department of Environmental, Social and Spatial Change, Roskilde University, Denmark.

Ted Tschang, Associate Professor of Strategic Management, Lee Kong Chian School of Business, Singapore Management University, Singapore.

Jan Vang, Associate Professor, Center for Industrial Production, Department for Business and Management, Aalborg University, Denmark.

1.   Introduction to the experience economy
Jon Sundbo and Flemming Sørensen

1.1   THE EXPERIENCE ECONOMY AND EXPERIENCE ECONOMY STUDIES

This book deals with the experience economy, which is a name for a scientific and management approach that deals with business and economic activities related to peoples' experiences. No authorized definition of the experience economy exists, but in this handbook we emphasize that the experience economy concerns activities carried out in the public and private sectors that focus on fulfilling peoples' need for experiences. It also focuses on how the users or receivers react to, and use, experiential elements. The experience economy encompasses more than the creative industries and cultural economy (cf. Caves, 2000; Du Gay and Pryke, 2002); it also includes the way in which the use and consumption of goods and services can be experiential. The experience economy is a topic that has attracted increased attention in the last decade, particularly in Northern Europe, but also to some degree in the USA and Canada, Asia, Australia and South America. An increasing number of books and articles have been published on the subject (for example, Pine and Gilmore, 1999, 2011; Department for Culture, Media and Sport, 2001; Mossberg, 2003, 2007; O'Dell and Billing, 2005; Bærenholdt and Sundbo, 2007; Boswijk et al., 2007; Caru and Cova, 2007; Sundbo and Darmer, 2008; Horn and Jensen, 2011; Lorentzen and Hansen, 2012). The topic has been a basis for business development in firms, for industrial policy (Department for Culture, Media and Sport, 2001; KK Stiftelsen, 2003; Erhvervs- og byggestyrelsen and Center for kultur- og oplevelsesøkonomi, 2011) and for national, regional and local development initiatives (Sørensen et al., 2010; Erhvervs- og byggestyrelsen and Center for kultur- og oplevelsesøkonomi, 2011; Freire-Gibb, 2011; Lorentzen and Hansen, 2012). Certain theoretical assumptions, research questions and analytical traditions have emerged and point to the experience economy being a scientific paradigm with its own discussion and explanatory agenda. One may generally term this emerging scientific paradigm 'experience economy studies'. This handbook collects together most of these issues to present a state-of-the-art of experience economy studies and new findings and theoretical contributions.

The handbook thus presents how far the scientific field of experience economy studies has come. It presents general knowledge – something in between textbooks and scientific articles. The chapters are research based; however, they present a general perspective. Some are more empirical, but presented in a generalized and theoretical perspective, others are more theoretical.

The perspective of the book is on business and economic (including planning and innovation) processes. However, other aspects are also included. Psychological and sociological aspects are treated because these are necessary for explaining how and why people as customers or citizens actually experience. However, it is not a handbook on psychology just as it is not a handbook on leisure, aesthetics or content analysis

1

of culture and experiences in the humanistic way (such as critics of films, concerts or novels) – even though these aspects may be included in some of the chapters to explain experience economic behaviour. The economic approach is not a classic micro-economic one, but relies on a broader institutional and business economic approach. The economy and business are also explained from psychological, sociological and technological perspectives. Thus, the book is of an interdisciplinary nature.

This introduction develops definitions of the key concept (experiences and experience economy). It discusses the experience economy as a societal phenomenon and it presents different theoretical understandings of the experience economy and its sectoral delimitation. Finally, an outline of the book is presented.

1.2   KEY CONCEPTS

1.2.1   Experience

To give a thorough explanation of what the experience economy is we need first of all to establish an understanding of what experience is, what the economic aspect of the topic is and why we emphasize the combination of the two.

The term experience has recently been used in a number of books and articles without any particular definition and no authoritative definition exists (however, see Pine and Gilmore, 1999; Sundbo, 2009). We therefore begin this book by attempting to define the experience economy. We begin by stating that experience is a mental phenomenon. It does not concern physical needs (such as goods do) or solving material or intellectual problems (such as services do). An experience cannot be stored in the same way that a good can and it does not necessarily solve any problems. An experience is something that happens in peoples' minds, it is determined by external stimuli and elaborated via the mental awareness that people have from earlier experiences, mental needs (such as self-realization, un-stressing, avoiding everyday life through escapism) and personal strategies (cf. Giddens, 1991). Experience can be released by stimuli that affect all the senses. Some authors suggest that internal mental processes even have a physiological basis – that an experience can be (or maybe always is) a result of physiological reactions to external stimuli (Jantzen and Vetner, 2007). To what extent this implies that experience may be an unconscious process, and what the relation is between the physiological automatic reactions (such as Pavlov's (1960) dog experiments show) and conscious, intellectual reflections, is an ongoing debate.

An attempt to define the notion of experience somewhat more precisely is found in the concept of flow developed by the psychologist Csikszentmihalyi (2002). Flow is the feeling one gets when one carries out a certain activity (for example, climbing a mountain or reading Dostojevsky's collected works), when one is fully absorbed by an activity, when one succeeds and when nothing else matters. Csikszentmihalyi argues that such flow gives optimal experience. However, it can be argued that the concept of experience includes more than that. The passive non-intended observation of an unknown town-space (a square with special buildings or a special tower block) or a special series of events during the daily trip on the train can provoke an experience.

The definition of experience is also problematic because of a linguistic subtlety. In

English the word experience covers two different phenomena that in other languages are referred to by two different words (Snel, 2011). German, for example, has the word *Erlebniss*, which has connotations of amusement, escapism and the like (cf. Schulze's (1992) conceptualization of the experience society as *Erlebnissgesellschaft*) and the word *Erfahrung*, which has connotations with learning. These two different meanings characterize two phenomena that are seen as quite different and would never in German (or other Germanic languages) be confused. *Erlebniss* is the notion that would be used to characterize expressive, immediately consumed experiences (such as a concert). *Erfahrung* would be used to characterize more instrumental and long-term learning activities. One has to be aware of this linguistic subtlety to understand some of the theoretical discussions about the experience economy. It leaves us with an open question of whether the *Erfahrung* – 'learning' – aspects should be included in discussions of the experience economy. From a strict theoretical point of view one may argue that it should not because then one has to include education, practical craftsmanship and so on in the experience economy and that may water down the whole theory. The most correct solution is probably to agree that learning or *Erfahrung* (including education) is not part of experience and the experience economy per se. However, *Erlebniss*, or 'pure experience' (expressive, short-time consumed) may include an *Erfahrung*, or learning, aspect (cf. also Pine and Gilmore's (1999) notion of learning experiences). Thus, functions that carry out activities that produce 'pure experience' (*Erlebniss*) should be included in the experience economy but 'pure learning' (*Erfahrung*) functions should not.

Another discussion concerns whether an experience should be authentic to be an experience (for example, Cederholm and Hultman, 2005; Steiner and Reisinger, 2005; Gilmore and Pine, 2007; Bærenholdt et al., 2008). This discussion has a long tradition in tourism research (MacCannel, 1973; Pearce and Moscardo, 1986) but has also recently emerged as a criticism of commercials and their – in some people's view – artificial world that only have the aim of selling products that are perhaps not even needed. However, the authenticity discussion is very complex. One question is whether stimuli need to be authentic to provoke an experience. One may suggest that experiences are only provoked by authentic stimuli (as Gilmore and Pine, 2007, do). However, such a theory still has to be empirically investigated. The next question is what authentic stimuli really are. Some discussions (Cederholm, 2007) have emphasized how arguments that stimuli need to be authentic to provoke experiences easily lead to nostalgia and romanticism. Do local people need to wear outdated national costumes to give tourists an experience? Many would say no. Authenticity can be of many kinds and mean different things to different people who in different situations may have different preference levels for authenticity (Hughes, 1995). One author (Mossberg, 2003) suggests that people can get, and accept, an experience they get from fake stimuli as far as they know it is a fake or story. The post-modern tourist, for example, knows that he or she is a tourist and that tourism is 'a series of games' set up for the tourists and not an 'authentic experience' (Urry, 2002). Likewise, shopping malls may be considered fake milieus with fake facades and sales promotion camouflaged as the real 'wild west' or Mediterranean milieus. However, the users know that much is fake, but being in shopping malls may still be authentic to them: shopping malls have to be built as fake millieus otherwise they would not be authentic shopping malls.

Based on the above discussion, the following definition is suggested as a guideline for the readers of the book: Experience, in the context of the experience economy, could be defined as the mental impact felt and remembered by an individual caused by the personal perception of external stimuli. The impact might be entertaining or learning, but does not need to be so; the stimuli may be authentic, but does not have to be; and the combination of stimuli and personal perception may invoke flow but the definition includes more than optimal flow experiences. The definition does, however, imply that experiences are something extraordinary. This is in line with Pine and Gilmore's (1999) notion that experiences are memorable events, thus the events or signs that could provoke an experience are extraordinary. They must be outside daily routine to leave a memory.

The definition implies that experiences can be of many kinds. We do not only talk about entertaining experiences. Experiences can be learning and thus intellectual. They can also be active such as when one does sport. Pine and Gilmore (1999), for example, define four different types of experiences: escapistic, entertaining, educational and aesthetic. People can be active in seeking out experience provoking stimuli (such as when one goes to a concert or a football match) and people can passively and even unintendently receive stimuli that can give them an experience (such as when a TV commercial you coincidentally watch is surprisingly unconventional or when a series of events outside your daily routine happens at your job). Experiences can be what normally is considered positive, for example, when people get amused or get in a state of flow, but they can also be what normally is considered negative. Most people when asked whether a funeral can be considered an experience will answer that it can.

The definition leaves a problem concerning which routine activities – if any – might be classified as experiences for statistical purposes. We can mention watching TV on a daily basis (every person on average uses several hours per day watching TV), which often does not appear to us to be something special and does not leave any memories, but it may produce a feeling of pleasure. In that case it should probably be defined as leisure and not as experience but this creates problems in the statistical categories: when is watching TV experience and when not? Statistical consistency may be maintained by emphasizing that the definition of experience is not seen from the receiver's perspective, but from the provider's. The crucial issue is whether the provider's intention is to provoke an experience in the receiver, not whether he succeeds in doing so. Such a delimitation will include TV programmes in the experience economy. Several of the chapters in this book will return to these questions in more detail.

Irrespective of how we may draw the line between experiences and non-experiences, experiences happen inside peoples' minds and are provoked by external stimuli as stated above. The same stimulus does not provoke an experience in all people and not even in the same person in different situations. Whether an experience is provoked depends on the state of the individual's mental readiness in general and the specific situation. The definition also implies that, for example, firms do not deliver experiences. Firms can only deliver elements that function as external stimuli, thus receivers (for example, in their role as customers or audience) get an experience. However, the sender of the stimuli cannot be sure that all receivers will get an experience, and if they do, that they get the same experience. That depends on the momentary condition of their experience readiness.

Even though this approach recognizes that experiences are not produced by suppliers alone but come into being only in the minds of people, firms and industries may nevertheless throughout the book be characterized as 'experience firms' and 'experience industries'. Constantly expressing the above understanding of experience production will be too complex and will result in a very hard read. The understanding presented in this section is thus implied. Further, the handbook is written by different authors and, as always within social sciences, authors do not need to agree. It might be that not all authors agree about the appropriateness of the above approach. This, however, will be discussed more extensively in several chapters.

1.2.2 The Experience Economy

Though experiences happen in the minds of people, the experience economy is about business activities. This understanding was very much introduced by Pine and Gilmore's book *The Experience Economy* (1999) that saw the experience economy as a new business movement, which after the agriculture, manufacturing and service economies emerged as an area with strong possibilities for sales and profit. Peoples' physical, and maybe even intellectual, needs have been fulfilled and they look for new content in their lives. Experience can give such content. Experience thus has great value to people who demand it and are willing to pay a high price for experience-stimulating business activities. Experience-stimulating activities also take place in the public sector. This was not a field that Pine and Gilmore thought of in their book, which was more inspired by marketing, which naturally is market oriented. However, much activity that provokes experiences is carried out in the public sector (for example, culture, festivals, architecture and so forth) and whereas relevant activities in some countries are market based they are public in other countries. This is an argument for including public activities in the experience economy. Such activities are paid, however, via another economic system, namely by taxes.

We define the experience sector and experience industries as sub-sectors as follows: formal economic activities that have the aim to deliver elements that can provoke experiences in people who pay directly or indirectly for them. Those people can be defined as customers or citizens, depending on whether the delivery is market or public based. The scientific study of these activities can be called experience economy studies.

The elements may be of many kinds – physical or immaterial – thus many different types of private businesses and public organizations may be part of this economy. The definition leaves us with a problem of those activities in the informal economic sector (unpaid social activities) that also function as experience-provoking stimuli. The informal sector has, for example, in leisure studies been emphasized in line with private and public providers as a crucial provider of leisure experiences (Roberts, 2004). The voluntary sector is particularly important in countries with long traditions of non-profit organizational activities that are based on volunteers' free workforce, for example, in relation to sports activities, youth camps and so on. In many cases such activities are mixed up with the formal experience-provoking activities. For example, many festivals are a mixture of commercial business, publicly organized and voluntary activities. Consequently, the voluntary aspects of the experience economy must be taken into consideration when we try to understand and analyse activities in the experience economy.

Finally, people can of course get experiences from just being together with other people or from carrying out activities in solitude, without any public, private or voluntary providers being directly involved. Examples are running in the forest, hiking, picnicking or different home-based social activities. Such phenomena must be seen as experiences in line with the ones provoked by paid activities. These activities are interesting also from the economic point of view, because large industries provide means and accessories (clothes, tents, bicycles, GPS watches, specialized foods and magazines and so on) whose function often is to make better experiences out of such independently carried out activities. These providers form some of the largest commodity markets in the economy (Bryman, 2004).

The informal economy, which cannot be measured in economic terms, is important, but excluded from most definitions of the experience economy. The emerging tradition, or paradigm, of experience economy studies looks at the formal economic activities related to experiences and how they can be managed and developed. Other traditions or paradigmatic approaches emphasize activities outside the formal economic sector that might provoke, or have the aim of provoking experiences. Such approaches may be termed culture studies or sociological or anthropological disciplines of different kinds. These are also important complementary fields to the experience economy. However, to not create a total, and confused, social science, we need to have a kind of division of labour and specialize our explanations and paradigms. Experience economy studies is such a specialization. While many of the other fields have existed for a long time, the experience economy study approach – where experience stimuli are seen as business or planned public activities – is new and not much theory building and research exist. That is the reason why the experience economy study approach is emphasized in this handbook. Thus, the approach here is to let the formal economic perspective be the guiding one in explaining and understanding what goes on.

Even though we use the expression 'experience economy' as outlined above, the research field of experience economy studies is cross-disciplinary. It includes economic perspectives, business and management approaches, psychological and even physiological aspects. Furthermore, sociological and anthropological perspectives are also included. People do not experience in isolation (at least not always). Often they experience in interactions with other people, either as part of an audience or because they discuss the experience with their friends. Which experience-provoking elements people seek and how people experience are signals about one's social status (Gamson, 1994; Warde et al., 1999; Kurzman et al., 2007; Senft, 2008), thus experience is also used socially. Much experience is technology based. Experience on the Internet, via smart phones and other information and communications technology (ICT) platforms is perhaps the fastest growing experience area. Thus technological research, on hardware, software and content, is also an important part of the scientific experience economy field. One may even argue that different experiences and experience fields are substitutable to people. The most important is that your life is filled with interesting activities and that one experiences. One can do that by watching TV, going to a concert, playing computer games or taking a tourist trip. Thus, experience industries compete to fill out our time, which implies that market competition occurs across experience industries that all at some level compete with each other. Thus, knowledge about different experience fields and industries must be included equally in experience economy studies. This cross-disciplinary and cross-industrial approach is reflected in the book's chapters.

1.3   ABOUT EXPERIENCE AS A SOCIETAL PHENOMENON

1.3.1   Experience is an Old Phenomenon

Experience has always existed. Some of the oldest things left behind illustrating this are cave paintings that are 14000 years old. Thus, the phenomenon is not new. Also science has for a long time been interested in experiences and the experience notion has been used back in time (Holbrook and Hirschman, 1982; Valberg, 1992; Snel, 2011), but mostly as an aspect of other phenomena, for example, art (Dewey, 1934), tourism (Cohen, 1979), consumer behaviour (Holbrook and Hirschman, 1982) and service marketing (for example, Schmitt, 1999; Pullman and Gross, 2004; Kwortnik and Thompson, 2009; Verhoef et al., 2009). The latter assumes that customers get an experience from the service delivery and that experience is crucial for the customer's assessment of the service and his inclination to buy a service again.

Peoples' experience behaviour and habits have been studied for a long time within sociology, anthropology and cultural studies. The German sociologist Gerhard Schultze (1992) in a study of peoples' behaviour in the German city Nürnberg launched his results as an introduction of the concept of the experience society. Culture has been studied extensively and cultural economy studies is also an old scientific discipline (for example, Du Gay and Pryke, 2002; Andersson and Andersson, 2006). However, although culture is included in the experience economy, culture and the culture economy are narrower than the experience economy and experience economy studies emphasize the business aspects more than the culture economy normally does. The experience economy is related to more than culture, for example, nature, goods, sports activities and marketing.

Experience-provoking elements have also always been built in into goods, for example, as industrial design and services as marketing elements (cf. above). These phenomena have also been scientifically studied. However, experience economy studies as a scientific discipline has introduced and intensified the focus on experience-provoking elements in a cross-sectoral perspective: industrial design, for example, has common elements with the production of computer games and tourism in that they all attempt to provoke some experience in the receiver (or customer). Construction of these elements may thus have common principles across sectors, industries and different sorts of production. Innovation of experience may, for example, be scientifically understood generally across different industries and modes of production.

It is only since 2000 that the experience economy has been considered as an independent societal phenomenon. Experience economy studies has become an independent research field (for example, Boswijk et al., 2007, 2012; Pine and Gilmore, 2011) and the size and economic impact of the experience economy has been measured (Department for Culture, Media and Sport, 2001; KK stiftelsen, 2003; EU, 2010, Erhvervs- og byggestyrelsen and Center for kultur- og oplevelsesøkonomi, 2011). The experience itself has now become a research field and it is today a core phenomenon in tourism studies (Larsen, 2006; Mossberg, 2007; Ek et al., 2008), as a psychological and neurophysiological field (Jantzen and Vetner, 2007), as an aim of designing performances and events (Harsløf and Hannah, 2007) and as a factor in explaining the impression of physical landscapes (experiencescapes, O'Dell and Billing, 2005). The construction of experience-creating elements has become a research topic (Sundbo and Darmer, 2008); entrepreneurship in the experience economy is studied (Hjorth and Kostera, 2007); innovation in experience firms has become a special field within innovation research (Sundbo, 2009; Fuglsang et al., 2011); and experience has become a new element in the study of regional and local development processes (Florida, 2002; Sørensen et al., 2010; Freire-Gibb, 2011).

1.3.2   Why has Experience Recently Attracted Increased Awareness?

If experiences have existed for thousands of years, why has an interest in them suddenly emerged within the last decade? We can suggest at least two societal explanations of this.

One explanation stems from a combination of a psychological and production system logic. Pine and Gilmore (1999) see the experience economy as a new wave of economic activities after agriculture/fishing/mining, which satisfies our basic needs for survival, manufacturing, which satisfies our advanced physical needs, and service, which solves our most advanced physical problems and our intellectual needs (via knowledge services). This development has been characterized by using Maslow's (1954) theory of a pyramid of needs. This theory sees the most basic physical needs as the bottom of a pyramid. The layers above in the pyramid consist of more intellectual, emotional, experiential and personal life-fulfilling needs (such as self-realization). Because our most basic needs (the physical ones) can be satisfied by the societal production and market system, we seek to fulfil the needs in the upper layers of the need pyramid. We have now reached a stage where it is the feeling, sensational and self-realization needs that can be fulfilled via experiences. We are therefore focused on procuring elements that can give us experiences and are willing to pay a high price for them. The old goods and services that fulfil needs further down the pyramid are today taken for granted in most Western societies. They are 'need to have', but not 'nice to have'. As a consequence we are not interested in paying a high price for them. This development of waves of need-fulfillment and production systems (cf. Toffler, 1981) is one societal explanation of the increasing importance of and focus on the experience economy over the last decade.

Another but related explanation is more economic. It has been suggested that the experience economy and the focus on it emerged around the beginning of the new millennium because the societies (at least Western ones) have become richer. This may be one true element in explaining the emerging experience economy, but it cannot stand alone. Wealth cannot per se explain why an increase in demand for experiences emerges – theoretically the increased wealth could have been spent on other (potential) economic offerings. This economic explanation must be combined with the psychological and production system wave one. The psychological factor can explain the basic need for experiences. The production system wave approach can explain why we at the end of the twentieth century had developed a production system that could satisfy the need for experiences. The increased wealth in the societies can explain why people at the time could afford to buy the – often expensive – experience elements.

The economic explanation draws attention to which fundamental development of the experience economy we see just now. One may argue, parallel to what happened with the industrial society and later to the service economy, that when a market field becomes interesting and products and activities demanded, industrialization sets in. This is in line with Pine and Gilmore's (1999) suggestion that economic progress is about 'charging a fee for what was once free' (p. 67). When exploitation of the field, business-like as well as political, becomes important, competition and the focus on productivity increases. This may happen to the experience economy (cf. Sundbo, 2007) and what we witness with the contemporary focus on the experience economy is the industrialization (standardization and large-scaling) of the experience economy. Thus, the reason why the experience economy currently is interesting is not the experience phenomenon per se, but that we are witnessing a large-scale industrialization of the experience economy. This includes, for example, the growth of global TV entertainment and film producers and distributors, Internet content producers, producers of smart phones and applications and it involves the standardization and modulization of the production and delivery of experience-provoking elements (Pine, 1993; Sundbo, 1994). Suppliers become global corporations, renewal becomes more based on industrial innovation organizations and so forth. At the same time, however, the increased demand for experiences also sustains small-scale localized entrepreneurial business development (for example, in the arts and in tourism). Both types of experience activities may be supposed to grow and be important. While the small-scale activities may not dominate economic statistics, they are of importance locally and they may be the necessary basis for developing industrial experience products, just as research is a necessary basis for developing high-tech goods.

1.4 THEORETICAL APPROACHES TO THE EXPERIENCE ECONOMY AND ITS SECTORAL DELIMITATION

The theories of the experience economy have become differentiated and different understandings of the experience economy have developed that has also led to various understandings of the experience economy from a sectoral perspective. In some analyses, the experience economy is considered a statistical sector delimited from other economic sectors (such as agriculture, manufacturing and service). It is a group of industries that produce experiences (or, more precisely, according to what we have defined here, experience-provoking elements) (for example, Department for Culture, Media and Sport, 2001; KK stiftelsen, 2003; Erhvervs- og byggestyrelsen and Center for kultur- og oplevelsesøkonomi, 2008; EU, 2010; Fuglsang et al., 2011). Nevertheless, there is no international generally accepted convention of what should be included in this statistical sector, but different empirical analyses have made their own delimitations (for example, Department for Culture, Media and Sport, 2001; KK stiftelsen, 2003; Erhvervs- og byggestyrelsen and and Center for kultur- og oplevelsesøkonomi, 2008). Even though there may be some variation, the analyses agree on the main sectors and businesses to include and from such an approach the experience sector typically includes those listed in Table 1.1.

Some, or even the main part, of these industries are often called creative industries (Caves, 2000; Department for Culture, Media and Sport, 2001 and others) based on an assumption that they are dominated by artistic people or people who are creative in ways that are inspired by artists. There may also be variations in how creative industries are defined, but generally creative industries are more narrowly defined than the experience sector. The sectoral delimitations of the experience sector also include more business-like industries such as software (selling ICT-based experiences), activity-based industries such as sport (that is, people exercising, for example, in fitness centres or sports clubs) or

Table 1.1   Statistical sector of the experience economy

Sector	Businesses included (examples)
Tourism	• hotels • restaurants • travel agencies • marinas
Art and culture	• TV companies • music producers • theatres • cinemas
Entertainment and leisure	• amusement parks • museums • sport clubs
Lotteries and gambling	• national lotteries • casinos
Design, image and branding	• architects • photographers
ICT-based experiences	• internet-dating firms • computer game producers • producers of smart phones and applications

tourism sectors of which some can hardly be portrayed as more creative than many of the more traditional industrial sectors.

In other analyses the experience economy is considered a generic activity that is carried out in all industries and all types of firms. Experience can be an add-on to goods and services besides being a product of itself. Adding experience elements is done because experiences have high value for customers and thus can be the basis for more sales and higher prices. Experiences can be add-ons to goods or services such as the design of a car or furniture, a bank branch that organizes author cafés or TV in a train.

Experience has also been considered part of the marketing activities. It can increase attention to the products and increase customer loyalty. This is how Pine and Gilmore (1999) argued for the experience economy. Experience thus becomes a general product add-on and a general marketing approach. This understanding of the experience economy thrives in marketing research (for example, Arnould and Price, 1993; Schmitt, 1999; Mossberg, 2003; Pullman and Gross, 2004; Kwortnik and Thompson, 2009; Verhoef et al., 2009), which also focuses on the character of products and services because the character is crucial for the customers' assessment of the product or service and thus is a central competition parameter. One may further argue that public authorities such as municipalities and regions market themselves via experiences to attract tourists, inhabitants, companies and market products from the area (Sørensen et al., 2010; Lorentzen and Hansen, 2012). As a marketing theory, experience economy theory is a general explanation and prescriptive theory and experiences are supposed to replace older marketing elements, for example, mass announcement or the personal customer relation marketing that the service marketing theories have launched in the last decades (Gummesson, 1994; Grönroos, 2000). The customer relation service marketing theories have already used the notion experience (Kwortnik and Thompson, 2009; Verhoef et al., 2009) as a characteristic of customers' assessment of a service. Generally, however, these service marketing theories are concerned with how services can be sold and how experience is a means to create satisfied and loyal customers to goods and services. One may say that experience within the management and marketing framework is used instrumentally (to use an expression from sociology, Parsons, 1951). People use experiences to be aware of services that can solve their problems or goods that can fulfil their physical need. In the emerging experience economy marketing tradition, experiences are seen as expressive, that is, people seek experiences for their own sake; to experience is the only goal of the purchase. Thus, the marketing-oriented experience economy theories that we are talking about here go further than the service marketing theories in considering the experience of the final goal of a purchase (for example, Schmitt, 1999; Verhoef et al., 2009). One may say that experience marketing theory is one step further than the service marketing theory, but this one step can be considered the one that finally changes the view of experiences' role in goods and service delivery from instrumental (experience is a means to sell goods and services) to expressive (the experience is the primary goal of the purchase). Further, the experience economy approach emphasizes that sale and purchase of experiences (or experience-provoking elements) is an activity in itself in line with raw materials (such as metal or basic food), goods and services. Thus, to produce and deliver experiences becomes a new field, as Pine and Gilmore (1999) argue.

The other side of the experience economy, the demand side, has also been considered a general field where people seek experiences across industries and sectors, market segments and the formal-informal economy segregation. The psychological nature of peoples' experience has been investigated (Csikszentmihalyi, 2002; Mossberg, 2003; Jantzen and Vetner, 2007). Analyses have also investigated how people experience activities and consumption is socially determined. Thus, different social classes and status groups display different patterns of experience (Schultze, 1992; Kurzman et al., 2007).

If we return to the first understanding of the experience economy, the sectoral one, we may also draw some consequences of the second generic marketing understanding discussed above. The sectoral understanding assumes that the experience economy is about a business (and public) sector that has as its main aim to provide experiences. This sector includes firms (and public institutions) within culture, tourism, Internet-entertainment, sports, gastronomy and so forth. However, the experience marketing understanding implies that experiences are (or at least can or should be) produced in all industries including manufacturing and services. We may therefore suggest an understanding of the experience industries being divided in overall sectors, the primary and the secondary experience economy (inspired by Porat's (1977) analysis of the information economy), which reflects the combination of sectoral and marketing-generic understandings. The primary sector consists of industries – or firms and institutions – whose primary aim is to provide experiences. This sector includes the industries mentioned earlier (for example, TV, computer games, tourism, culture). The secondary experience sector consists of firms and institutions with another primary aim (for example, to provide goods or services) but which also provides experience-provoking elements.

Experience production is an add-on activity in the secondary experience sector. Only some functions and job positions in this sector are dedicated to producing experiences, for example, certain marketing functions, designers and software developers.

The experience economy may be measured statistically by counting all the primary experience sector functions (jobs or production value) adding the experience-oriented functions (jobs or production value) in the secondary experience sector (as done in a Danish statistical study, Erhvervs- og byggestyrelsen, 2008). There might be practical-statistical problems in doing this, but theoretically it is possible. However, more importantly, the division in a primary and secondary sector provides an approach to investigating the experience economy theoretically and analytically that embraces the variety of experience-producing firms and functions and their societal importance. This is reflected in the variety of approaches presented in the chapters of this book.

1.5   CONTENTS AND STRUCTURE OF THE BOOK

This handbook presents a varied collection of contributions that discuss different issues of crucial importance for our understanding of the experience economy. Some chapters of the handbook discuss in depth several of the issues that have been raised here in the introduction while other chapters raise new issues. Some chapters are mainly theoretical while others present new empirical research results. Some chapters present already known theoretical approaches to the experience economy while others present new theoretical developments. Some take a generic stance while others focus on different sub-sectors of the experience economy, such as the video games or theatre sectors. Furthermore, the different chapters represent different scientific approaches ranging from management approaches to, for example, mainstream economics and sociology. In this way the chapters provide an overview of different issues, approaches to and understandings of the experience economy. The handbook provides an entrance point for new experience economy readers but also presents a collection of new and innovative insights for those who already know the field well.

   The book is divided into three parts. In Part I different fundamental discussions about the nature and importance of the experience economy are presented. Part II presents more specific topics relevant to the experience economy, for example, innovation, networks and the design of experiences. Part III presents chapters that deal with experience economy issues that are more specifically relevant to, or illustrated in relation to, different sub-sectors of the experience industries.

1.5.1   Part I: Experience Fundamentals

In the opening chapter of Part I, Chapter 2, Pine and Gilmore introduce their view on the experience economy, its origin, present status and future development. The nature of the experience economy and its implications for business strategies, now as well as in the future, are discussed. The authors also discuss some of the criticisms that have been raised against their influential approach to the experience economy published in their now famous book *The Experience Economy* (Pine and Gilmore, 1999).

   Some of the remaining chapters of the handbook further develop some of the discussions introduced by Pine and Gilmore in Chapter 2. However, most of the chapters discuss other and new issues that are of relevance for a broader understanding of the experience economy, its dynamics, importance, present status, future development and implications.

In Chapter 3 Lorentzen outlines the similarities and differences between the experience economy and other closely related notions that in the public and professional discourse are often confused with the experience economy, namely the cultural and the creative economy. The author argues that the three notions provide different insights, have different origins, and also imply different strategic and practical conclusions.

The definition and categorization of the experience industries is the focus of Chapter 4. In this chapter Nilsen and Dale discuss various challenges concerning defining and categorizing the experience industries. The discussion is related to the older debate regarding how to define and categorize service industries. The chapter questions whether experiences should be seen as part of the service industries or if they may be considered a separate economic sector.

Andersson and Andersson focus on different dimensions of the experience economy in Chapter 5. They argue that all consumer goods and services are to some extent experience goods and that experiences can be conceptualized as a multi-dimensional range of characteristics. Five such experience-related characteristics are emphasized: learning by consuming, uniqueness, location and context dependence, interdependence and non-storability. The authors explain these dimensions and show how an increase in their value makes goods have greater 'experience content'.

Schulze in Chapter 6 explains, from a sociological point of view, the way in which the experience market is subject to a particular rationality. The author argues, among other things, how the rationality of the experience market can be explained by a distinction between outwardly and inwardly oriented consumption. The experience market's progression can only be explained inadequately with the increase of free time and financial possibilities. It is also important to understand the rationality of suppliers and demanders.

In Chapter 7 Snel discusses understandings of how experiences are produced. Three different approaches are emphasized: the 'environment-centred', the 'effect-centred' and the 'encounter-centred' approaches. Snel argues that each of these approaches has biases and limitations in explaining how experiences can be successfully created by organizations. The author suggests how experience-producing organizations may overcome these biases by taking a broader perspective on experiences.

Jantzen in Chapter 8 presents a psychological framework outlining the complexity of experiences. Based on a semantic discussion of the word 'experience', Jantzen discusses the paradox that experiences are both everyday and extraordinary phenomena and he emphasizes how experiences imply a tension between immediate experiencing, past and future experiences. The psychological framework discussed in the chapter has a number of important implications for both entrepreneurs and designers in the experience economy.

In the brief closing chapter of Part II, Chapter 9, Boswijk takes a look into the future. The author suggests that we find ourselves in a transitional stage from a service economy towards an economy of experiences and meanings in which meaningful experiences become central. The transition is discussed from the consumer and businesses points of view and it is suggested that the transition will result in a powerful change of the way the economy works.

1.5.2   Part II: Topics

In the first chapter of Part II, Chapter 10, Jensen focuses on information technology and experience. The chapter discusses and develops key concepts related to experience in connection with information technology, such as user experience, experience design and user experience design. A number of new understandings and a number of new and more precise definitions of the key concepts are presented. Furthermore, several conceptual paradoxes related to the key concepts are presented and solved in the chapter.

In Chapter 11 Hansen and Mossberg emphasize how immersion is a central aspect of experiences. The authors discuss definitions of immersion and show how immersion is related to other concepts like extraordinary experience, peak experience, peak performance and flow. They argue that underlying foundations for immersion can be found in the spatio-temporal dimensions of experiences and that immersion is facilitated by consumers' interactions within experiencescapes.

In Chapter 12 Sundbo, Sørensen and Fuglsang present a discussion and survey-based investigation of innovation in experience industries. The chapter shows that innovation is a common phenomenon in the experience industries. The characteristics of experience innovations and of innovative firms are similar to those found in services (and to a large degree in manufacturing). However, some important exceptions exist, for example, because of the creative basis that characterizes many experience industries, the importance of ICT and the multi-dimensionality of experiences.

In Chapter 13 Eide and Mossberg address how we should understand and conceptualize innovation types in the experience economy. The authors suggest an approach that focuses on customer interactions. They emphasize especially two types of interactions – between customers and between customers and personnel. The chapter illustrates how thinking in terms of these (and other) interaction types can help to conceptualize experience innovation and identify needs and restrictions for different types of innovations.

The role of entrepreneurship in the experience economy is emphasized in Chapter 14. In the chapter Fuglsang and Sørensen discuss how entrepreneurship in the experience economy in particular can face difficulties because it can be described as an open process that may come into conflict with different cultural barriers. However, the authors also show how entrepreneurs can succeed in spite of the existence of such cultural barriers.

In Chapter 15 Eide and Fuglsang discuss and illustrate the importance and dynamic nature of networks in the experience economy. They argue that the development and outcome of networks depend on network support structures termed 'scaffolding structures'. In particular, focusing the attention of the network, mobilizing its actors and creating activities and infrastructures around them is concluded to be important for networks' development potentials. This is illustrated in two case studies of regional innovative networks.

In Chapter 16 Svabo, Larsen, Haldrup and Bærenholdt discuss how spatial designs provide experiences and how visitors in practice experience them. The authors argue that experiences of a particular place emerge through engagement with other designs and with the specific social group that one is part of while experiencing. While designs are powerful in framing experiences, they do not determine how experiences emerge and take place.

The role that the sense of belonging to a community, particularly in sports, plays in experiences is the subject of Chapter 17. In this chapter Chalip, Lin, Green and Dixon discuss how the community surrounding consumption affects experience and they show how the sense of belonging to such a community can be supported. The issue is illustrated in a study of a community-based competitive swimming league for children and adolescents.

The role of communities is also the focus of the closing chapter of Part II, Chapter 18, but more specifically on what motivates volunteers to be part of communities of experiences. Gudiksen in this chapter also discusses the organizational structures and characteristics of experience organizations depending on the work of volunteers. The issues are discussed and illustrated in relation to both physical and online communities.

1.5.3   Part III: Application Fields

In the first chapter of Part III, Chapter 19, Holt and Lapenta discuss different approaches to the experience of cultural events. The chapter offers a grounded understanding of experiences in the study of contemporary cultural events. Different approaches to the study of such events are outlined drawing from diverse fields such as event management, media studies and marketing theory. Further, the authors suggest and detail two new contexts for contemporary cultural events: the post-industrial city and its cultural economy, on the one hand, and new media practices, on the other.

In Chapter 20 Cooke illustrates how a production site for experiences, in this case TV production, can lead to the development of other experience sectors and a creative cluster. The chapter describes how an experience setting developed out of a broadcasting context in Cardiff, Wales, responsible for, among others, the *Dr Who* TV series. It analyses how the impact of the on-location scenery of Cardiff helped a tourism industry develop and how many other creative companies today form an innovative cluster in the area.

In Chapter 21 Vang and Tschang discuss the determinants behind the spatial organization of the video games industry. Based on an analysis of the US video games industry the authors suggest that dominant research on the spatial organization of experience industries – focusing on clustering processes in larger urban contexts – needs to be extended. For example, reliance on in-house capabilities, other highly localized factors and collaboration in distant networks has consequences for the spatial organization of experience industries.

Sundbo, Sundbo and Jacobsen in Chapter 22 focus on food experiences, in particular New Nordic Cuisine. By understanding New Nordic Cuisine as a meaning-creating experience, the authors discuss if it can form the basis for a social movement. On this foundation they consider the success and diffusion of New Nordic Cuisine as a concept innovation. They conclude that the notion 'experience concept' can contribute analytically to explain fundamental dynamic social and economic phenomena.

Chapter 23 takes its departure in the world of theatre and peformance. Rooted in critical theory and a phenomenological understanding of experience, Hallberg and Harsløf discuss the need for spaces allowing for an aesthetic and sensuous mode of being in everyday life. This creates a new type of theatrical experience space that the authors describe as live and relational, fictional parallel universes in which participants are co-creators who live out the logics of the particular universe.

In the last chapter of the handbook, Chapter 24, Boswijk focuses on the secondary experience sector by presenting a short descriptive study of a hospital that has used experience as a way to improve the patients' stay at the hospital. The hospital's approach breaks with hospitals' traditional medical-centred approach to dealing with patients. The study shows how the experience economy is also of relevance in sectors where it may not at first be obvious.

BIBLIOGRAPHY

Andersson, Å. and D. Andersson (2006), *The Economics of Experiences, the Arts and Entertainment*, Cheltenham, UK and Northampton, MA, USA: Edward Elgar.

Arnould, E. and L. Price (1993), 'River magic: extraordinary experience and the extended service encounter', *Journal of Consumer Research*, **20** (1), 24–45.

Bærenholdt, J.O. and J. Sundbo (eds) (2007), *Oplevelsesøkonomi. Produktion, forbrug og kultur* (*Experience Economy. Production, Consumption, Culture*), Copenhagen: Samfundslitteratur.

Bærenholdt, J.O., M. Haldrup and J. Larsen (2008), 'Performing cultural attractions', in J. Sundbo and P. Darmer (eds), *Creating Experiences in the Experience Economy*, Cheltenham, UK and Northamton, MA, USA: Edward Elgar, pp. 176–202.

Boswijk, A., T. Thijssen and E. Peelen (2007), *The Experience Economy: A New Perspective*, Amsterdam: Pearson.

Boswijk, A., E. Peelen and S. Olthof (2012), *Economy of Experiences*, Amsterdam: European Centre for the Experience and Transformation Economy.

Bryman, A. (2004), *The Disneyization of Society*, London: Sage.

Caru, A. and B. Cova (eds) (2007), *Consuming Experience*, London: Routledge.

Caves, R. (2000), *Creative Industries*, Cambridge, MA: Harvard University Press.

Cederholm, E.A. (2007), 'At bare "være" – ægthed, relationer og intimitet i oplevelsesindustrien' ('Just to "be" – relations and intimacy in the experience industry'), in J.O. Bærenholdt and J. Sundbo (eds), *Oplevelsesøkonomi. Produktion, forbrug og kultur* (*Experience Economy. Production, Consumption, Culture*), Copenhagen: Samfundslitteratur, pp. 277–99.

Cederholm, E.A. and J. Hultman (2005), 'Tourists and global environmental change', in M. Hall and S. Gössling (eds), *Tourism and Global Environmental Change*, London: Routledge, pp. 293–304.

Cohen, E. (1979), 'A phenomenology of tourist experiences', *Sociology*, **13** (2), 179–201.

Csikszentmihalyi, M. (2002), *Flow*, London: Rider.

Department for Culture, Media and Sport (2001), *Creative Industries 2001 – Mapping Document*, London: Department for Culture, Media and Sport.

Dewey, J. (1934), *Art as Experience*, New York: Capricorne.

Du Gay, P. and M. Pryke (eds) (2002), *Cultural Economy*, London: Sage.

Ek, R., J. Larsen, S. Hornskov and O. Mansfeldt (2008), 'A dynamic framework of tourist experiences: space-time and performances in the experience economy', *Scandinavian Journal of Hospitality and Tourism*, **8** (2), 122–40.

Erhvervs- og byggestyrelsen (Danish Enterprise and Construction Authority) (2008), *Vækst via oplevelser* (*Growth via Experiences*), Copenhagen: Erhvervs- og byggestyrelsen.

Erhvervs- og byggestyrelsen and Center for kultur- og oplevelsesøkonomi (Danish Enterprise and Construction Authority and Centre for Culture and Experience Economy) (2011), *Vækst via oplevelser 2011* (*Growth via Experiences* 2011), Copenhagen: Erhvervs- og byggestyrelsen.

EU (2010), *Unlocking the Potential of Cultural and Creative Industries*, Green Paper, COM(2010) 183, Brussels: European Commission.

Florida, R. (2002), *The Rise of the Creative Class*, New York: Basic Books.

Freire-Gibb, L.C. (2011), 'The rise and fall of the concept of the experience economy in the local economic development of Denmark', *European Planning Studies*, **19** (10), 1839–53.

Fuglsang, L., J. Sundbo and F. Sørensen (2011), 'Dynamics of experience service innovation: innovation as a guided activity – results from a Danish survey', *The Service Industries Journal*, **31** (5), 661–77.

Gamson, J. (1994), *Claims to Fame: Celebrity in Contemporary America*, Berkeley, CA: University of California Press.

Giddens, A. (1991), *Modernity and Self-identity*, Cambridge: Polity.

Gilmore, J.H. and B.J. Pine (2007), *Authenticity: What Consumers Really Want*, Boston, MA: Harvard Business School Press.

Grönroos, C. (2000), *Service Management and Marketing*, Chichester: Wiley.

Gummesson, E. (1994), 'Making relationship marketing operational', *International Journal of Service Industry Management*, **5** (5), 5–20.

Harsløf, O. and D. Hannah (eds) (2007), *Perfomance Design*, Copenhagen: Museum Tusculum Press.
Hjorth, D. and M. Kostera (2007), *Entrepreneurship and the Experience Economy*, Copenhagen: Copenhagen Business School Press.
Holbrook, M.B. and E.C. Hirschman (1982), 'The experiential aspects of consumption: consumer fantasies, feelings, and fun', *Journal of Consumer Research*, **9** (2), 132–40.
Horn, P. and J.F. Jensen (eds) (2011), *Experience Leadership in Practice*, Roskilde: MOL Publishers.
Hughes, G. (1995), 'Authenticity in tourism', *Annals of Tourism Research*, **22** (4), 781–803.
Jantzen, C. and M. Vetner (2007), 'Oplevelsens psykologiske nature' ('The psychological nature of the experience'), in J.O. Bærenholdt and J. Sundbo (eds), *Oplevelsesøkonomi. Produktion, forbrug og kultur* (*Experience Economy. Production, Consumption, Culture*), Copenhagen: Samfundslitteratur, pp. 27–49.
KK Stiftelsen (2003), *Upplevelsesindustrin 2003* (*The Experience Industry 2003*), Stockholm: KK Stiftelsen.
Kurzman, C., C. Anderson, C. Key et al. (2007), 'Celebrity status', *Sociological Theory*, **25** (4), 347–67.
Kwortnik, R. and G. Thompson (2009), 'Unifying service marketing and operations with service experience management', *Journal of Service Research*, **11** (4), 389–406.
Larsen, J. (2006), 'Picturing Bornholm: producing and consuming a tourist place through picturing practice', *Space and Culture*, **6** (2), 75–94.
Lorentzen, A. and C. Hansen (eds) (2012), *The City in the Experience Economy*, London: Routledge.
Maslow, A. (1954), *Motivation and Personality*, New York: Harper.
MacCannell, D. (1973), 'Staged authenticity: arrangements of social space in tourist settings', *American Journal of Sociology*, **79** (3), 589–603.
Mossberg, L. (2003), *Att skapa upplevelser* (*To Create Experiences*), Lund: Studentlitteratur.
Mossberg, L. (2007), 'A marketing approach to the tourist experience', *Scandinavian Journal of Hospitality and Tourism*, **7** (1), 59–74.
O'Dell, T. and P. Billing (eds) (2005), *Experiencescapes*, Copenhagen: Copenhagen Business School Press.
Parsons, T. (1951), *The Social System*, New York: Free Press.
Pavlov, I.P. (1960), *Conditioned Reflexes*, New York: Dover Publications.
Pearce, P.L. and G.M. Moscardo (1986), 'The concept of authenticity in tourist experiences', *Australian and New Zealand Journal of Sociology*, **22**, 121–32.
Pine, B.J. (1993), *Mass Customization*, Boston, MA: Harvard Business School Press.
Pine, B.J. and J.H. Gilmore (1999), *The Experience Economy*, Boston, MA: Harvard Business School Press.
Pine, B.J. and J.H. Gilmore (2011), *The Experience Economy, Updated Edition*, Boston, MA: Harvard Business School Press.
Porat, M.U. (1977), *The Information Economy*, Washington, DC: US Department of Commerce.
Pullman, M.E. and M.A. Gross (2004), 'Ability of experience design elements to elicit emotions and loyalty behaviors', *Decision Sciences*, **35** (3), 551–78.
Roberts, K. (2004), *The Leisure Industries*, Basingstoke: Palgrave.
Schmitt, B. (1999), 'Experiential marketing', *Journal of Marketing Management*, **15** (1–3), 53–67.
Schulze, G. (1992), *Die Erlebnis-Gesellschaft* (*The Experience Society*), Frankfurt: Campus.
Senft, T. (2008), *Camgirls: Celebrity and Community in the Age of Social Networks*, New York: Lang.
Snel, A. (2011), 'For the love of experience: changing the experience economy discourse', PhD thesis, University of Amsterdam, Amsterdam.
Sørensen, F., L. Fuglsang and J. Sundbo (2010), 'Experience economy, creative class and business development in small Danish towns', *Urban Research and Practice*, **3** (2), 177–137.
Steiner, C.J. and Y. Reisinger (2005), 'Understanding existential authenticity', *Annals of Tourism Research*, **33** (2), 299–318.
Sundbo, J. (1994), 'Modulization of service production', *Scandinavian Journal of Management*, **10** (3), 245–66.
Sundbo, J. (2007), 'Pris på varm luft? Oplevelsesøkonomiens kerne' ('Price on warm air? The core of the experience economy'), *Økonomi og Politik*, **80** (2), 45–58.
Sundbo, J. (2009), 'Innovation in the experience economy. A taxonomy of innovation organisations', *The Service Industries Journal*, **29** (4), 431–55.
Sundbo, J. and P. Darmer (eds) (2008), *Creating Experiences in the Experience Economy*, Cheltenham, UK and Northampton, MA, USA: Edward Elgar.
Toffler, A. (1981), *The Third Wave*, London: Pan Books.
Urry, J. (2002), *The Tourist Gaze*, London: Sage.
Valberg, J. (1992), *The Puzzle of Experience*, Oxford: Clarendon Press.
Verhoef, P., K. Lemon, A. Parasuraman, A. Roggeveen, M. Tsiros and L. Schlesinger (2009), 'Customer experience creation: determinants, dynamics and management strategies', *Journal of Retailing*, **85** (1), 31–41.
Warde, A., L. Martens and W. Olsen (1999), 'Consumption and the problem of variety: cultural omnivorousness, social distinction and dining out', *Sociology*, **33** (1), 105–27.

PART I

EXPERIENCE
FUNDAMENTALS

2.   The experience economy: past, present and future
B. Joseph Pine II and James H. Gilmore

2.1   INTRODUCTION

It has been almost 20 years since we first described the next emerging wave of economic history as an experience economy. At the time, no one spoke of "experiential marketing" (its precursor was "marketing aesthetics"). The term "customer experience" had yet to be coined (all the talk concerned delivering excellent "customer service"). While a few technologists may have occasionally referred to the "user experience," the term had not taken hold to anywhere near the extent that it warranted an acronym; today no one in the digital world need explain what is meant by "UX." The word "experience" exploded in its usage with product names, marketing taglines, destination venues and digital media. Why the change in terminology? And why to language based on this word "experience"? Clearly, the notion of experiences resonated in the market place of ideas and the world of commerce.

Many factors contributed to the widespread acceptance of this lens through which to view the economic landscape. First of all, people were more than ready to embrace a new way of thinking about their offerings, as evidenced by the call to "exceed expectations" and other similarly wanting business buzzwords and mantras. Experience thinking provided a welcome new platform for pursuing new value-creating activity. Second, the very idea that consumers valued experiences more than goods and services was affirmed by personal experience. Regardless of their industry or vocation, individuals knew they cherished the experiences in their lives more than physical things, and certainly more than the mundane services that surrounded everyday life. But perhaps most importantly, executives and managers in various enterprises – for-profit businesses, non-profit charities, tourism bureaus, ad agencies, healthcare systems, colleges and universities, political campaigns, and even churches – saw experiences as an untapped means to differentiate.

As a result, certain research methods and innovation methodologies – ethnography, design thinking, improvisation skills – that had been largely neglected for decades suddenly found a groundswell of interest. Daniel Pink declared "the MFA is the new MBA." Strategy consulting work started to flow to the IDEOs (design firms; IDEO, n.d.) of the world, not just the McKinsey's. Howard Schultz discovered European café culture and latched onto Ray Oldenburg's concept of "a third place" (Oldenburg, 1997). Everywhere in the world Starbucks went was abuzz about experiences and being filled with new experiences.

In the mid 1990s, when we wrote the popular "How to profit from experiences" in *The Wall Street Journal* (Pine and Gilmore, 1997) and the more scholarly "Beyond goods and services" for *Strategy and Leadership* (Gilmore and Pine, 1997), we scrambled to find exemplars we could cite that would illustrate the various experience design principles we espoused. (We obviously recognized Disney as ahead of the pack, and have been wrongly accused by some ever since of wanting to "disneyfy" every place.) Today, however, we simply cannot keep up with the myriad experience innovations that continue to fill the world, from A (app after experiential app) to Z (zorbing).

The world has indeed become more intentionally experiential. Yet one point needs to be repeatedly emphasized: this all represents a fundamental shift in the very fabric of the global economy. Focusing on goods and services alone leads down the road of economic austerity. Experiences are a distinct form of economic output, and as such hold the key to promoting economic prosperity. The fact that so many still long for the return of hard industries, fantasize about restoring manufacturing jobs and cling to an industrial mass production mindset limits further progress. Today, around the world, goods and services must give way to experiences as the predominant form of new economic output, the foundation of growth in gross domestic product (GDP) and the source of new job creation.

The down economies around the planet, spawned by the desperate financial attempts to prop up a world of goods, now makes the perfect time to take a closer look at the still untapped upside to experience-based innovation and economic expansion. This chapter, therefore, looks at the past of the experience economy – how it was discovered and where it came from, with many never-before published details; at the present of the experience economy – our current understanding of it, plus the implications and issues that arise from it; and finally at the future of the experience economy – where it must head in the years and decades to come.

2.2   THE ORIGIN

It was back in late 1993 or early 1994. Joe Pine was teaching a class on Mass Customization to a number of staff in the IBM Consulting Group at the IBM Advanced Business Institute in Palisades, New York (where he had worked full time less than a year before).

As he often did, Joe talked about how mass customizing a good – making an individually customized physical product with low costs, high volume, efficient operations – automatically turned it into a service. He pointed out how economists make some classic distinctions to differentiate the two: goods are standardized while services are customized – done on behalf of an individual customer; goods are inventoried after production while services are delivered on demand – when the customer says this is exactly what he wants; and goods are tangible, whereas services are intangible. And part and parcel of mass customization is the intangible service of helping customers figure out exactly what they want. So mass customizing a good involves the business of defining, making and delivering an exact item that fits each individual customer's needs at a particular moment in time – and that's a service!

So one of the IBM consultants in the back of the room shoots up his hand and says, "You talk about mass customizing services too. What does it turn a service into?" And Joe shot back: "Mass customization automatically turns a service into an *experience*." Then he said to himself, "Whoa. That sounds good!" He stopped the class to write it down, just to make sure he wouldn't forget it. He needn't have, for the notion consumed his idle thoughts for months: delivering exactly the right service – precisely what an individual needs over a duration of time – can't help but make them go "Wow!" and turn it into a memorable event, an experience! And if that were true, then experiences were a distinct economic offering, as distinct from services as services were from goods. And that suggested that the developed world would shift into an experience economy, supplanting the service economy just as that had superseded the industrial economy in the latter half of the twentieth century, which in turn had unseated the agrarian economy a century before.

Late one night, a month or so later, Joe had made enough progress in his thinking to get out a piece of paper and write down all of the distinctions he could think of between each of the four economic offerings at the core of the four economies – commodities, goods, services and experiences – plus a fifth (and as it turns out, final) economic offering, transformations. (For into what does mass customizing an experience turn the offering? If you design an experience so appropriate for a particular person – precisely what he needs to be fundamentally affected by it over time – then it can't help but become a life-transforming experience that changes the customer in some way.)

Joe knew he really had something – something that would change how executives saw the world of business. So the next morning he typed it all up into a table, and flying off to see his favorite client – Jim Gilmore, then head of CSC Consulting's process innovation practice – faxed it to him in advance with special instructions to Jim's assistant not to open it until the two met. And together in Cleveland they mulled over the not-quite-complete and still-unrefined table (Figure 2.1), growing in their mutual appreciation for how the recognition of these two newly identified economic offerings could help executives think differently about how they created economic value for their customers. They soon knew they would have to write about it – culminating in the 1999 book *The Experience Economy: Work is Theatre and Every Business a Stage* (Pine and Gilmore, 1999) – and later decided to join together to found Strategic Horizons LLP, a thinking studio dedicated to helping companies conceive and design new ways of adding value to their economic offerings.

And the rest, as they say, is history. But history must also do justice to a number of thinkers and authors who were amazingly prescient in identifying this same trend – although not as strongly as we saw it as (we emphasize) *a fundamental shift in the very fabric of the economy* – some long before us and all unbeknownst to us until we started researching the then-embryonic experience economy. Way back in 1970 futurist Alvin Toffler included a chapter in *Future Shock* titled "The experience makers" where he asked, "Where does the economy go next? After the services, what?" and answered with "the growth of a strange new sector based on what can only be called the 'experience industries'" (Toffler, 1970, p. 221). But of course we can see now that experiences are not just a single sector of the economy; there are in fact many sectors (movies, sporting events, music festivals, art galleries, video games, corporate briefing centers, trade shows, tourist attractions, hotel resorts, membership clubs, and on and on the list goes) that together comprise the experience economy.

Even before Toffler, in 1959, sociologist Erving Goffman, in *The Presentation of Self in Everyday Life*, applied the principles of theatre to work and social situations as we too have applied it to work: not as a metaphor, but as a model (Goffman, 1959). Jay Ogilvy, co-founder of the Global Business Network, wrote *The Experience Industry*, a 1985 report for SRI International, demonstrating that demand for "vivid experiences" already drove marginal growth in the US economy – a factor that has only accelerated in the

Economies of Man: Past, Present, and Future

Economy	Agrarian	Industrial	Service	Experience	Transformation
Primary Economic Offering	Commodities	Products	Services	Experiences	Transformations
Economic Function	Extracted	Manufactured	Delivered	Created	Enabled
Nature of Offering	Fungible	Tangible	Intangible	Memorable	Incorporeal
Extent of Use	Subsumed in products	Permanence beyond production	Consumed at delivery	Experienced over a duration	Enduring
Character	Natural	Standardized	Customized	Individualized	Actualized
Development Method	Discover/ Planted/ Cultivated	Developed?	Fashioned ?		Formed?
Production Method	Extracting/ Harvesting	Batches	Co-production?	Co-experienced?	Symbiosis? Induced?
Delivery Method	Bulk Stored	Inventoried	Created at delivery	Participated in at creation	Subsumed in transformation
Marketed Attributes	Characteristics	Features	Benefits	Sensations	Realization/ Consummation
Basis of Purchase	Price	Transaction	Relationship/ Desire?	Content?	Aspiration/ Hope/Dream?
Observability	Detectable	Tactile	Perceivable	Sensorial	Sensible
Primary Flows	Physical	Financial	Informational	Social	Individual
Information Content Level[1]	Noise	Data	Information	Knowledge	Wisdom

Economic Relationships
- 'Commodities are only material components of the products in which they are comprised'
- '[Goods] are only physical embodiments for the services thet deliver'[2]
- 'Services are only temporal activities for the experiences they create'
- 'Experiences are only memorable events for the transformations they enable'
- 'Transformations are only the earthly possibilities for the perfection God can one day instill'

---

[1] Based on Haeckel's Hierarchy of Stephan H. Haeckel of the IBM Advanced Business Institute, as published in Vincent P. Barabha and Gerald Zaltman, *Hearing the Voice of the Market: Competitive Advantage through Creative Use of Market Information* (Boston: Harvard Business School Press, 1991), pp. 45–46.
[2] James Brian Quinn, *Intelligent Enterprise: A Knowledge and Service Based Paradigm for Industry* (New York: The Free Press, 1992), p.7.

Figure 2.1   Original table detailing experience and transformation offerings

past quarter century (Ogilvy, 1985). In 1992 Gerhard Schulze wrote of the "experience society" in *Die Erlebnisgesellschaft: Kultursoziologie der Gegenwart* (which we still hope someone someday translates into English) (Schulze, 1992). And at about the same time *The Experience Economy* came out in 1999, Rolf Jensen of The Copenhagen Institute for Future Studies published *The Dream Society* (Jensen, 1999). Like Toffler, but taking a more societal than economic vantage point, Jensen asked, "What comes after the Information Society?" and answered with "the Dream Society. It's a new society in which businesses, communities, and people as individuals will thrive on the basis of their stories, not just on data and information" (Jensen, 1999, p. 1). While these are the most important antecedents we have discovered, surely there are others whom we should be mentioning, and we hope that they all receive due recognition for their parts in predicting and describing the rise of today's experience economy.

2.3   SO WHAT IS THE EXPERIENCE ECONOMY?

Every economy is defined by its predominant economic offering: what a buyer obtains from a seller in exchange for money. In the agrarian economy, when the vast majority of the population lived and worked on farms, the predominant economic offering was of course agrarian commodities, bought and sold in the physical, open-air markets in the middle of every town of any size in the world. Commodities are distinguished by being undifferentiated. They are what they are, fungible offerings interchangeable with other commodities of the same kind (although the process of refining may create different classes of a particular commodity, such as separating apples by quality, rocks by size or oil by purity), and therefore purchased primarily on the basis of price.

Goods – physical, tangible offerings such as tools, equipment, clothing, furniture and so forth – were of course around during the agrarian economy, but they traded at a fraction of the total value of commodities when many lived at a subsistence level, and their manufacture employed far fewer people. Hundreds of years ago most people made their own tools, fashioned their own equipment, sewed their own clothes, finished their own furniture and so forth. But thanks to the Industrial Revolution, factories could produce each of these categories of goods and hundreds, thousands, millions more as well, much more cheaply than could individuals on their own. David Ricardo's Law of Comparative Advantage applies to households and communities as well as to nations, and so people moved off farms and into factories to produce more and more goods, using the money earned to purchase commodities (and other goods) on the open market. As goods became the predominant economic offering in the late nineteenth and early twentieth centuries, we shifted full-bore into the industrial economy, named for that collection of manufacturing enterprises, industry.

Services – intangible activities performed on behalf of another individual, such as cooking meals, distributing and merchandising goods, repairing tools or equipment, cleaning clothes, cutting hair, performing legal and accounting activities and so forth – were also around during the industrial and agrarian economies, but comprised a relatively small part of each. In fact, it wasn't until the late 1800s, we believe, that services were even recognized as a distinct economic offering. Adam Smith called service activity "unproductive labour" (Smith, 1776 [1994], p. 361) because services cannot be physically inventoried and therefore create no tangible testament that work had been done. But both consumers and companies increasingly found services of great value, enhancing their lives and their businesses, respectively, and so purchased them more and more frequently. The Law of Comparative Advantage applied once again, as people increasingly ceased doing certain service activities themselves and instead paid someone else who could do them more efficiently, more effectively and with higher quality. So people left factories to move into restaurants, retail stores, hotels, logistics facilities, call centers, hair salons, offices and so forth. By the latter half of the twentieth century more people were employed in services than in goods as the former comprised a greater portion of GDP than the latter. We had moved into a service economy.[1]

One effect of this shift was that people, despite what Adam Smith said, valued services more highly than goods, and so more and more treated goods as if they were commodities – undifferentiated "stuff" purchased primarily on price – so they could save their hard-earned money to spend on services instead. To combat increasing commoditization, manufacturers increasingly moved into services themselves via repair programs, contract warranties, service leases and other value-added activities.

That same effect of commoditization has long been a factor in services as well. Think of fast-food restaurants with all of their value prices, retail stores plastered with "SALE!" signs, mobile phone plans sold primarily on price and so forth. The Internet is the greatest force of commoditization ever invented, and while it initially attacked the price of goods it is now commoditizing such services as hotels, airlines, banks, telecommunications and brokers of all stripes. So now people increasingly buy services on price and thus are able to spend their hard-earned money – and harder-earned time – on economic offerings of even greater value. They increasingly purchase experiences.

Experiences – memorable events that engage each individual in an inherently personal way, such as going to a musical concert, theatrical play or athletic event; visiting a museum, art gallery or far-off destination; playing a game or sport; sipping coffee with friends in a cafe; having a birthday party; and on and on again the list could go – have also always been around. They are not a new economic offering – think of traveling troubadours, Greek plays, Roman competitions, *commedia dell'arte* performances – just a newly identified one. Intriguingly, when undervaluing services Smith singled out the experience stagers of his day ("players, buffoons, musicians, opera-singers, opera-dancers, &c."), concluding that "the work of all of them perishes in the very instant of its production" (Smith, 1776 [1994], p. 361). How true! But although the work of the experience stager perishes with its performance (precisely the right word), the value of the experience lingers in the memory of any individual who was engaged by the event.

Although experiences themselves lack tangibility, people greatly desire them because the value of experiences lies within them, where again it remains long afterward. That's why the studies performed by Cornell psychology professors Travis Carter and Thomas Gilovich concluded that buying experiences makes people happier, with a greater sense of well-being, than purchasing mere goods (Carter and Gilovich, 2010; see also Van Boven and Gilovich, 2003). Similarly, *The Economist* summarized economic research into happiness as "'experiences' over commodities, pastimes over knick-knacks, doing over having" (*The Economist*, 2006).

We have now entered an experience economy, where experiences supplant services as the predominant economic offering in terms of GDP, employment and especially actual value (Pine and Gilmore, 2011, pp. 19–21). This Progression of Economic Value, as we call it, can be seen in Figure 2.2 and outlines how the locus of economic activity – what is bought and sold in the marketplace – has changed over the centuries.

2.4   IMPLICATIONS OF THE EXPERIENCE ECONOMY

Concomitant with this new economy are a number of implications, of which the following are the most pertinent.

2.4.1   Mass Customization is the Route

Figure 2.2 also shows the effect of customization from the discussion about the origins of the experience economy. Customization (serving customers uniquely) is basically the

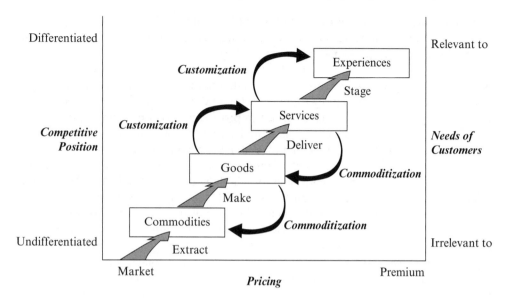

Source: Pine and Gilmore (2011, p. 111).

Figure 2.2   *The progression of economic value*

antidote to commoditization. (This effect does not occur for true commodities, which, being fungible, cannot be materially changed, much less customized.) Where commoditization drags down offerings (and the companies that offer them) year after year like the force of gravity, customization enables offerings (and the companies that offer them) to differentiate themselves, for if it is customized to an individual, it cannot be like every other offering. As a result, companies create offerings more relevant to the wants and needs of individual buyers, differentiate their goods and services from the sea of look-alike competitors and thereby increase the value provided, and thus the price charged, to users and clients.

Note that while commodities, goods and services all exist outside the individual buyer, experiences happen inside them. The experience stager effectively reaches inside customers with the sensations, impressions and performances they orchestrate together in order to engage each guest and create a memory. That's why customization is so important to experience staging. When a company customizes to an individual, it engages that person in the creation of an offering produced just for him, and can easily become a memorable event. With individuals at the heart of each and every experience, customization is critical, while mass customization (efficiently serving customers uniquely) lowers the cost of engagement.

Consider Progressive Insurance of Cleveland, which lowered the costs of automobile claims adjustment by outfitting claims adjusters in vans, called Immediate Response Vehicles (or IRVs), equipped with a personal computer, satellite uplink and everything else they may need to efficiently resolve a claim from the very site of an accident. While the other party may wait days or weeks for his insurance company's adjuster to fit him into the schedule and go through the rest of the standardized process, the Progressive claimant finds his particular needs handled right then and there. On a laptop computer, with wireless uplink to a mainframe computer, Progressive's claims adjuster knows everything about this particular person, his policy, his vehicle and where it can be fixed, and in the vast majority of cases hands him a check on the spot. The claimant receives not only a check but a cup of coffee as well and, if need be, a few minutes to calm down in the van and reassure his family (or arrange for a ride) over the adjuster's (free) cellular phone, going beyond the expected service to provide an experience appropriate to the physical and emotional needs of the claimant. Moreover, it actually costs Progressive less to run claims adjustment like this than the old, mass-produced way.

The key to such low-cost, efficient, high-volume customization – mass customization – is to break apart a company's offerings into modules that then can be brought together in different ways for different customers like LEGO building bricks. What can you build with LEGOs? The answer, of course, is anything you want. This is because of the many different sizes, shapes and colors of bricks as well as the simple, elegant system of tabs and holes that enables them to be easily snapped together. These two basic elements – a set of modules and a linkage system that dynamically connects them – define the modular architecture that equips a company to mass customize. This architecture determines the universe of benefits that a company intends to provide for customers and, within that universe, the specific combinations of modules it will deliver at this time, to this particular customer (Pine, 1993; Gilmore and Pine, 2000).

2.4.2   Work is Theatre

If your economic offering is an experience, then for you work *is* theatre. Again, as with Goffman, we do not mean this as a metaphor – work *as* theatre (Goffman, 1959). Rather, we recognize it as a model – work IS theatre! Whenever workers perform in front of the watching eyes of customers, they are acting – whether they know it or not, whether they do it well or not, they are acting. They must act in a way, therefore, that engages each guest with each and every interaction.

As renowned English stage director Peter Brook declared in the very first line of his book *The Empty Space*: "I can take any empty space and call it a bare stage. A man walks across this empty space whilst someone else is watching him, and this is all that is needed for an act of theatre to be engaged" (Brook, 1968, p. 9). The simplest definition of acting, in other words, is that one person watches as another person works. Anyone working in front of customers must therefore act in a way that draws them into the experience.

Consider the Geek Squad, a computer support task force selling to both consumers and businesses. Instead of interviewing prospective employees the company auditions them. Then it costumes them with white shirts, thin black ties – always clip-on ties, just in case they get caught in the printer – and black pants with devices hanging off the belt. Black shoes and white socks complete the costume, with shoes that have the Geek Squad logo emblazoned backwards on the soles in order to leave a distinct impression whenever the walking surface allows. Company cars – called Geekmobiles – are VW beetles painted as black-and-white squad cars. And each Special Agent uses particular performance routines to engage every customer. For example, when arriving at a customer's premises, one might pull out his identification badge and say something like, "Good morning! I'm Special Agent 384 from the Geek Squad. Slowly step away from your computer, ma'am . . . ." Then he charms his host with the unique blend of street theatre that is the Geek Squad experience while demonstrating his expertise in fixing any and all personal computer issues. Since the largest computer retailer in the world, Best Buy, bought the company from entrepreneur Robert Stephens in 2002, it has grown from a few score of Agents to now over 20 000.

2.4.3 Authenticity is the New Consumer Sensibility

In a world increasingly filled with deliberately and sensationally staged paid-for experiences, people increasingly see the world in terms of real and fake, and want to buy the real from the genuine, not the fake from some phony. They now decide where and when to spend their money as much if not more than they deliberate on what and how to buy. But in a world of experiences – an increasingly unreal world – consumers choose to buy or not buy based on how real they perceive an offering to be.

In other words, authenticity has become the new consumer sensibility. While authenticity has long been the center of attention in the arts, the rise of the experience economy means companies too must understand, manage and excel at rendering authenticity. Indeed, "rendering authenticity" will one day roll as trippingly off the tongue among executives and managers as "controlling costs" and "improving quality," for rendering is precisely the right term for what's involved. To be blunt: business offerings must get real. When consumers want what's real, the management of the customer perception of authenticity becomes the primary new source of competitive advantage – the new business imperative (Gilmore and Pine, 2007).

So what exactly is authenticity, in business terms? It's purchasing on the basis of conformance to self-image. Economic offerings that correspond in both depiction and perception to one's self-image are perceived as authentic. Those that do not match to a sufficient enough degree to generate a "sympathetic vibration" between the offering and the buyer are viewed as inauthentic. So consumers now purchase offerings based on how well they conform to their own self-image, both who they are and who they aspire to be – with lightning-quick judgments of "real" or "fake" hanging in the balance.

To render such authenticity within customers, companies must work from these two key standards:

1. Is the offering true to itself?
2. Is the offering what it says it is?

The first standard pertains to the offering itself, encompassing the self-directed nature of how well it maintains an internal consistency while matching the company that offers it. Every company desiring to contend with authenticity as a consumer sensibility should seek to understand its own identity, what it is, by asking itself such questions as: What is the self to which we and our offerings must be true? What is the essence from which all our values flow, and how have our values evolved – for better or worse – over the course of our history? What are the defining characteristics that set us apart from every other company, not just in our industry, but in the world? How would we delineate this identity for our enterprise?

The second standard concerns how the company represents the offering, involving the other-focused nature of how well it maintains an external consistency with customers' perceptions of the offering (and by extension the company that offers it and the places in which it is offered). Here companies should embrace what exactly they say (in any form) about their business and its offerings, and understand how and whether that matches the reality people encounter. They should ask themselves: What exactly does our business say about itself? What do we lead others to believe? How do we reveal ourselves through our words and deeds and how they represent our business and its offerings?

2.4.4   The Experience is the Marketing

No matter the business, today every company competes with every other company in the world for the time, attention and money of potential customers – the currencies of the experience economy. Attention is increasingly scarce as advertisers the world over bombard people with messages. But if one company grabs someone's attention, that attention is not being paid to any other business. Time similarly is limited; there's only so much time anyone can spend experiencing anything. But if someone spends time with one company, they're not spending it with any other business. Finally, money is consumable, meaning if a customer purchases some economic offering (whether a commodity, good, service or experience) from one company, then that's money they're not spending with any other business.

What every company – no matter its offerings – needs to do, then, is create an experience that first gains potential customers' attention, then gets them to spend time experiencing their offerings and finally causes them to spend their money by buying those offerings. The experience is the marketing, so companies must stage marketing experiences, experiences that do the job of marketing by generating demand for their core offerings. That's why so many manufacturers now stage experiences (a short list of such top-tier marketers includes LEGO, Volkswagen, Case Construction, Heineken and Apple), and why service providers, too, increasingly wrap a marketing experience around their offerings (such as ING Direct Cafés and Best Buy with its Geek Squad offering). Even commodity traders have gotten into the act, such as the wonderful theatre surrounding the Pike Place Fish Market in Seattle, the activities, contests and events within the Agrodome in Rotorua, New Zealand, and the countless farms in the USA profiting from hay rides, corn mazes, pick-your-own produce and birthday parties (Gilmore and Pine, 2007, pp. 147–77).

2.4.5   Charging Admission is the Economic Key

While many marketers give away the experience to better sell their existing offerings, eventually companies must align what they charge for with what their customers truly value. And for economic experiences that require charging for the time customers spend with the company, such as charging an admission fee. The history of all economic progress consists of charging a fee for what was once free. In the experience economy, instead of relying purely on our own wherewithal to experience the new and wondrous – as has been done for ages – we increasingly pay companies to stage experiences for us, just as we pay companies for services we once delivered ourselves, goods we once made ourselves and commodities we once extracted ourselves. We find ourselves paying to spend more and more time in various places or events.

This economic history can be recapitulated in the four-stage evolution of the birthday cake. As a vestige of the agrarian economy, mothers made birthday cakes from scratch, mixing farm commodities (flour, sugar, butter and eggs) that together cost mere dimes. As the goods-based industrial economy advanced, moms paid a dollar or two for brands such as Betty Crocker for pre-mixed ingredients from which they baked. Later, when the service economy took hold, busy parents ordered already-baked cakes from the bakery or grocery store, which, at US$10 or $20, cost ten times as much as the packaged ingredients. In today's experience economy, parents less and less make the birthday cake – or even throw the birthday party. Instead, they pay an admission fee of $100 or more to "outsource" the entire event to a Chuck E Cheese's, McDonald's, museum, farm or some other business that stages a memorable event for the kids – and often throws in the cake for free.

Economically, you are what you charge for. A company that charges for undifferentiated stuff is in the commodities business. One that charges for tangible things is in the goods business. One that charges for the intangible activities its people execute is in the service business. But if it charges for the time its customers spend with it, then economically it is in the experience business.

2.5   ISSUES SURROUNDING THE EXPERIENCE ECONOMY

A number of objections have been raised over the years since we first published *The Experience Economy* in 1999.

Some object to the word stage to describe the primary work activity, or economic function, of experiences. One could substitute an alternative verb – orchestrate and choreograph come to mind – but only at the risk of diluting our emphasis on the importance of stagecraft in, well, staging engaging experiences. Stagecraft it is, and frankly, more businesses besides show business need to embrace theatre as their model for directing work.

We also wish others who agree that an economic shift is indeed underway would stop trying to advance alternative terms for this wave of economic history, pushing such terms as the "information economy," "knowledge economy" or "attention economy" (for example, Davenport and Beck, 2002). Economic eras have always been named based on the corresponding nature of output (service economy for services) or dominant domain of work (agrarian economy for commodities, industrial economy for goods), so the only legitimate alternative to the experience economy would rightfully be the "theatrical economy" – which seems far less practical, especially given the aforementioned theatre misconception. Yet others simply need to be more precise with their terminology. We have no objection to referencing the "dream society" or "creative class," gladly recognizing and embracing these terms as properly identifying trends emerging alongside the experience economy (Jensen, 1999; Florida, 2002). But it does not help if others then make reference to a "dream economy" or a "creative economy." Having dreams and being creative have fueled innovation in previous economic eras (but so much more so in today's era that they may indeed give rise to a new social class); what is new about this new economy is that experiences represent the basis of economic activity.

Beyond these language issues, others have misread our intentions (perhaps reading in their own apprehensions as our aspirations). Some viewed experiences only as entertainment. Any basic reading of Chapter 2 of *The Experience Economy* should dissuade readers from this mistaken notion (Pine and Gilmore, 2011, pp. 41–64). Indeed, we see the "four Es" – entertainment plus the educational, escapist and aesthetic realms of experience – as a means to avoid amusing ourselves to death. Showing full-length movies in the classroom, putting up PowerPoint screens in church sanctuaries and showing non-sports-related video clips on ballpark scoreboards do not indicate thoughtful application of experience-staging excellence for teaching students, preaching to disciples or connecting with fans, respectively.

Another mistaken interpretation: assuming that all experiences must necessarily trend toward the inauthentic or the virtual. In fact, the experience economy allows for a vast array of alternative offerings, ranging from the more or less natural/artificial, original/imitative, genuine/disingenuous, real/fake, self-centered/other-focused – across all dimensions of time, space and matter. Contrary to yet another objection – that we seek to turn "all of life" into "a paid-for experience" (Rifkin, 2000) – we certainly recognize non-economic spheres of social and personal experience. As undeniably more of life becomes commodified, we should all carefully examine our lives as citizens, donors, students and worshippers – not to mention as parents and lovers – in terms of what we choose to buy and not buy, to sell and not sell, to experience and not experience. Yet for developed economies to remain prosperous, a shift to experiences must occur: goods and services are no longer enough to employ the masses. We would hope that concern about the possible deleterious impact of certain experiences would prompt critics to enter the economic arena and offer more virtuous forms of these economic offerings.

Four particular criticisms of *The Experience Economy* provide a very useful perspective, especially as they serve to propel further study into the nature of engaging experiences. First, as discussed in the Introduction to this *Handbook on the Experience Economy*, where the English word "experience" is quite broad, many European languages encapsulate the concept with two distinct words: *belevenis* and *ervaring* in Dutch; *opplevelser* and *erfaring* in Norwegian; *upplevelse* and *erfarenhet* in Swedish; *oplevelse* and *erfaring* in Danish; and *Erlebnis* and *Erfahrung* in German. (Finnish also has *elämys* and *kokemus*, although it has no etymological connection with the other languages.) The first word in each case relates to the word for "life" and implies things experienced in the moment, while the second is about those experiences that matter more over time, that are cause for reflection, that integrate into a person's life over time – that are, in short, meaningful experiences (Snel, 2011; Boswijk et al., 2012).

While readers can certainly infer that in *The Experience Economy* we talk primarily about *Erlebnis* experiences (particularly since every official translation uses the first term of the pairs in the title), we by no means exclude *Erfahrung* experiences, and in fact discuss many experiences that could only be of this second kind (particularly when discussing the four Es model mentioned above). Not as much as we should have, apparently, to make it abundantly clear that the experience economy covers all manners of experiences, from *Erlebnis* to *Erfahrung* – and beyond. The last two chapters of the book discuss that fifth and final economic offering we also discovered and delineated in the mid 1990s, transformations, where experiences are used to guide customers to change (Figure 2.3 for the full picture of the Progression of Economic Value). Transformations

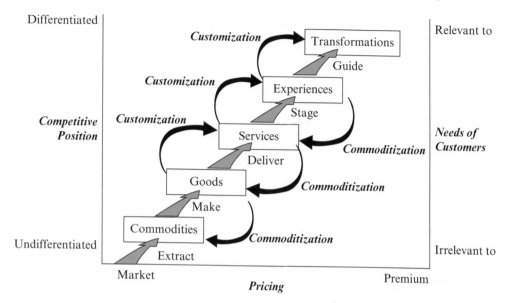

Source: Pine and Gilmore (2011, p. 245).

Figure 2.3   The progression of economic value in full

take *Erfahrung* experiences and so integrate them into a customer's life such that they change that customer – not just in degree but in kind – in some appreciable way. With transformations, and therefore *Erfahrung* experiences, an integral part of our formulation from the very beginning, we could say that in some ways the first eight chapters of *The Experience Economy* are a "Trojan horse" for the last two chapters and epilogue (Pine and Gilmore, 2011, pp. 241–95).

A second criticism is that we take a business/company viewpoint and therefore leave out the individual. We plead guilty to the first part – we are business capitalists who seek to help companies create greater economic value for their customers – but not to the second, for we firmly believe the way to create greater economic value for customers is to understand 'individual customers' (a term we fervently hope gets recognized for the redundancy that it is). Business success and individual well-being should not be seen as an either/or trade-off. As related above, the entire concept comes out of our original work on mass customization, which continues to permeate everything we write and talk about. In fact, the megatrend that incorporates both mass customization and the experience economy is best summed up as 'individualization' – creating more and more value for individuals by getting closer and closer to what each individual truly wants and needs, culminating in the individual-changing offerings of transformations. But yes, still, we primarily do so from an economic/business/capitalist/company viewpoint, from the supply side – not getting much into a psychological/behavioral/political/customer viewpoint concerning the formation of tastes and preferences, from the demand side. It is true, as one PhD dissertation put it, that "[t]o balance the experience economy discourse one should also take into account the individual's perspective" (Snel, 2011, p. 29), and we applaud those who do so as it enriches the topic and provides greater understanding for how companies can create greater value via individualization, which means that people gain that greater value in their lives, as human beings.[2] And we encourage non-business enterprises of all kinds – those that sell no offering, for any price – to challenge individuals to consider why they buy what they buy and how they consume what they consume. We value the discussion of values.

Extending from both these first two, a third criticism emphasizes the role of co-creation in the formation of experiences – and viewing our work as lacking sufficient appreciation for the role of customers/guests in creating their own experiences (stemming in part from our insistence on "stage" as the proper economic function of experiences)[3] (Prahalad and Rasmaswamy, 2004). The view is also understandable because of, again, our primary focus on the supply side of experiences. Our primary goal has been to encourage the creation of new experiences, so once again we focus much more on the stager of experiences. We do, however, fully recognize the power of co-creation, and have from the very beginning. Note, for example, in the original table of the Economies of Man shown in Figure 2.1 that "Co-production" is listed as the method of production and "Participated in at creation" as the Method of Delivery. That naturally flows from Joe's recognition of co-creation in *Mass Customization* back in 1993 where he discussed the "dynamic extended enterprise," writing that "Mass Customization can be achieved only through the committed involvement of employees, of suppliers, of distributors and retailers, *and* through the involvement of end customers themselves both in the identification and fulfillment of their wants and needs" (Pine, 1993, pp. 109–10, emphasis in original). And we call one of the four approaches to customization, that outlined in *The Experience Economy*, "Collaborative Customization," in which the "nature of value" is "mutually determined"; and a second approach, called "Adaptive Customization," where the "nature of [the] offering" is "customizable," inferring customer involvement in the final configuration of output (Pine and Gilmore, 2011, p. 142). All experiences are co-created, as we've always believed, because once again they happen inside the individual person in reaction to what is staged outside that person.

That said, we agree that a supply of new experiences indeed prompts many guests to want a more participatory role, a view we came to appreciate from Albert Boswijk and his co-authored book, *Economy of Experiences* (Boswijk et al., 2012). Moreover, this desire spills over to the relationships between clients and providers of services, and between users and manufacturers of goods as well. Alvin Toffler nailed it when he anticipated the rise of "prosumers" (Toffler, 1980, pp. 265–88). No one approach, however, should be rigidly imposed on experience design. It would be a mistake to suppose that all consumers want to be fully involved in the design and staging of wholly co-created offerings in every circumstance and in every category of good, service and experience. (Transformations in free societies are by their very nature fully co-created, with the company only guiding what customers, in the end, must themselves undergo; to treat transformation otherwise is tyranny.) What should be considered is the degree of control afforded in any given situation. Even at Walt Disney World and all the other Disney theme parks – places with a high degree of producer-staging and, we should point out, tens of millions of enthralled guests every year – guests themselves exert a great deal of consumer control over where and when they roam between rides. And one of us (OK, it's Jim) takes particular delight in being just a little too enthusiastic in shows like Country Bear Jamboree, with his over-the-top hooting and hollering effectively co-ruining the experience for others. At issue in terms of co-creation is the intentionality of the stager and the adaptability for the guest. We would welcome greater excellence in both dimensions.

The final valid concern we have seen contends that we place too much emphasis on experiences as memorable events. Let us share our twofold perspective. First, in envisioning engaging experiences, you can and should consider a multiplicity of dimensions. These include the multisensory nature of experiences, their level of personal meaningfulness, the way the experience is shared with others (if at all), the intensity and duration of various experiential elements, complexity (or simplicity), plus untold other characteristics of how people spend time. Cultural considerations and national and local sensitivities, as well as the prior life experiences of guests, all impact how people perceive experiences. Our belief is that no matter how viewed, any dimension of enjoyment usually translates into the experience being more memorable – even if few or no details can be recollected.

This takes us to a second aspect of the matter: recognizing the distinction between the memory of an experience and the enjoyment of the experience in the moment (apart from how memorable it later proves). Even here, people at least remember that they enjoyed the experience, even if they cannot recall or explain why. Of critical importance is how the experience concludes. Here, one new framework added to the updated edition of *The Experience Economy*, the nineteenth-century model of dramatic action devised by Gustav Freytag, explains the structure of compelling dramas and offers considerable insight (Freytag, 1898; Pine and Gilmore, 2011, pp. 160–62). In a nutshell, failure to adequately establish proper context, interweave building action or allow for falling action and a dénouement adversely diminishes the audience's memory of even the most climactic highs of an enjoyable experience (and even more adversely magnifies the memory of an unpleasant one). Bottom line: no, a strong memory is not required for every experience, but the greater the (positive) memory created and the longer it lasts, the more value created.

2.6   THE PRESENT STATE OF THE EXPERIENCE ECONOMY

Joe once gave a boardroom talk in Milan, Italy, to a number of executives from different companies. One was the vice president of a global coffee manufacturer, who said something amazing: "There's been no innovation in the coffee industry in fifteen years." Joe's response: "Have you never heard of *Starbucks?*" This gentleman could only conceive of innovation in physical goods, not in experiences, and therefore totally missed the shift in consumption from ground coffee to the coffee-drinking experience that Starbucks innovated by creating a place in which people wanted to spend time. (A particularly ironic circumstance given the interaction took place in one of the foremost coffee meccas of the world, the very city that inspired Howard Schultz to create that Starbucks coffee-drinking experience.)

That is what we desperately need in business today: experience innovation. For goods and services are no longer enough. That is the clear conclusion of the shift into the experience economy. But despite the recent economic crisis we are all still living through, that thesis has not sufficiently penetrated the minds of enough business leaders (and policymakers) to give full bloom to a truly new – and desperately needed – economic order.

Relying on the manufacturing of goods and the delivery of services remains the mindset of too many executives (and politicians), prohibiting the shift to more vibrant enterprises offering experiences (and thus more robust national economies). So let us here be most clear: goods and services are no longer enough to foster economic growth, create new jobs and maintain economic prosperity. To realize revenue growth and increased employment, the staging of experiences must be pursued as a distinct form of economic output. In a world saturated with largely undifferentiated goods and services, the greatest opportunity for value creation resides in staging experiences.

The actions of individual entrepreneurs prove the point. Contrast the success of leading experience innovators over the past 15 years with the failure of rival companies (and whole industries, for that matter) that either missed or ignored our economic message. Take retail. Countless chains have met their demise in this timeframe as they insisted on merely merchandising finished goods. Walmart and online sellers ate their lunch. Yet experiences such as Build-A-Bear Workshop flourished. In 1999, founder Maxine Clark, told by conventional retail experts that launching such an enterprise was foolhardy, drew inspiration from our July/August 1998 *Harvard Business Review* article, "Welcome to the experience economy" (Pine and Gilmore, 1998). Today, Build-A-Bear profitably operates more than 300 experience outlets in the USA alone, and almost 500 worldwide – all venues where consumers mass customize their own plush toy animals within an engaging retail factory experience.

Similarly, Pleasant Rowland opened her first American Girl Place in Chicago in late 1998. From the outset she conceived her American Girl dolls – each themed to a specific period of American history – as only a prop for broader book-reading and character-building experiences. With yet additional American Girl Places (as well as Boutique & Bistros) in place today, American Girl thrives inside Mattel, which otherwise struggles to revive Barbie and other toys (seen as mere goods by most American girls and boys today). And what store is now the envy of every mall owner and developer? Apple. Why? Customers clearly flock there for not only the goods but also the store experience, with the number one sales per square foot in the world by far, over an order of magnitude greater than those of the typical retailer.

Interestingly enough, Apple studied the hospitality experiences at both Ritz-Carlton and various boutique hotels for design inspiration in creating its revolutionary new retail format. (Gateway had previously attempted selling direct via retail stores, as had Dell with kiosks, but both lacked a rich appreciation for experience design, opting instead to retain typical merchandising footprints.) Thus, experiencing the wares at an Apple store feels uncannily like bellying up to the bar at a hotel lounge. Apple's in-store Genius Bars, iPod Studios and classroom amphitheatres bear a remarkable resemblance to the registration areas, concierge desks and meeting space experiences of better boutique hotels.

Moreover, these "design" hotels played a role in changing the competitive landscape in their own industry. Thanks to Bill Kimpton, Ian Shrager, Chip Conley and other boutique hoteliers, no hotel chain can today afford to merely provide basic service activities and ignore its guests' experiences. From furnishing sociable lobby spaces to providing beds that promise better sleep experiences (credit Shrager for kick-starting innovation in the former, and Westin's "Heavenly Bed" for the latter), the hospitality industry now clearly creates new value on the basis of experiences. As Schrager himself says, "We're in an experience economy. People pay a premium for it" (Schrager, 2012).

Consider again the Geek Squad. The thematic costuming integral to the Geek Squad being the Geek Squad (and readily and naively dismissed by other service providers) demonstrates the tangible value – to customers, to employees and to shareholders – companies create by boldly treating services as the stage and goods as the props for staging engaging experiences. Think of the number of fragmented service industries – car washes, home decorators, landscapers, laundromats and educational tutors, to name a few – that would benefit from an enterprise emulating the Geek Squad's experience mindset.

The economic doldrums in which much of the advanced world found itself after the 2008 economic crisis resulted from a failure to experientially innovate like each of these companies. The industrial economy has had its day. The invention and production of new goods once fueled the world's advanced economies. It is today very difficult to invent – and therefore rare to encounter – a truly new good; most differentiation of goods now involves the enhancement or modification of items within existing product categories and not the creation of wholly new categories. (Consumer electronics and medical technology represent two notable exceptions; but consider that when buying these items, customers most value not the goods themselves but the experiences and transformations they enable.[4]) Even when someone invents a truly new good, manufacturers instinctively seek to automate the work required to make it and scale up as soon as possible. Although revenue growth may follow, these manufacturers do not add jobs to the world commensurate with the revenue.

The service economy, too, has justifiably faltered. Any growth we saw in true services – government statistics still embed experiences (and transformations) within the service sector – largely came from financial services, and most of that from artificially propping up a world of goods (beginning with automobiles and housing and extending to mall development and other commercial ventures) with increasingly desperate attempts to devise financial instruments that more highly leverage old wealth (in the form of protected classes of assets). All this incessant financing created precious little tangible value. And so, as with the dot-com craze and crash that came before, eventually the bubble burst. What does the world need instead? New wealth generated from the formation of new experience-based enterprises.

2.7   THE FUTURE OF THE EXPERIENCE ECONOMY

Toward this end, five value-creating opportunities stand out that should drive further progress in the evolving experience economy. First, concerning goods, more offerings should be mass customized: what is needed is not more production of physical goods but more innovative methods for making those goods. Most manufacturers have ignored the pleas by us (and others) to shift from mass production to mass customization methods, to replace supply chains with demand chains, to convert raw materials into goods not as speculative inventory but only in response to actual demand. Mass customizing is not about being everything to everybody – a surefire way to increase costs. Rather, it means producing only and exactly what individual customers want. Despite being implemented decades ago by such companies as Lutron Electronics and Dell and named over 25 years ago by Stan Davis (Davis, 1987), to this day one cannot, for example, name a single US-made model of automobile that is truly mass customized to consumers. It's shameful.

It's why scores of dealerships have closed, with consumers awaiting new build-a-car experiences.

In effecting mass customization as a means of creating new value, perhaps the most ignored – and yet arguably the most powerful – concept is the notion of reducing or eliminating 'customer sacrifice.' Customer sacrifice is the gap between what individual customers settle for (in buying mass-produced goods and services) and what each wants exactly. Every business would benefit from asking itself: What one dimension of sacrifice, if eliminated, would create the greatest value for our customers? Once a business identifies that dimension, it should pursue solutions to help customers experience less sacrifice (Pine and Gilmore, 2000; Pine and Gilmore, 2011, pp. 120–43).

Second, concerning services, more companies should direct their employees to act. Organizations that have a service mindset focus solely on what tasks employees do; those with an experience mindset also consider how those tasks are performed and thereby embrace theatre as a model for performance. By and large, despite decades of management literature proffering customer service advice, consumers still endure many miserable encounters. Consider a typical "day in the life" of consumer service interactions – talking to call centers, waiting at convenience store counters, trying to be heard in drive-through lanes, waiting in line at bank-teller windows, getting rental cars, riding shuttle buses, enduring air travel, checking out groceries, visiting the mall, paying for gasoline and so forth. As a result, customers understandably hesitate to pay any premium. Profitability therefore suffers, wages stagnate and workers disengage – creating a downward spiral to yet more miserable service.

A huge first step in staging more engaging experiences needs to be taken. As the Geek Squad again exemplifies, companies must recognize that their employees are on stage and therefore need to act in a way that engages their customers. So managers need to give employees roles to play, help them characterize those roles and especially invest time in rehearsing before placing them on the business stage. When a business is treated as a mere service, hourly workers spend almost no offstage time preparing onstage behaviors. Actors prepare. Better human performances – focusing on the how and not only the what – turn mundane interactions into engaging encounters. So businesses should ask: What acts of theatre would turn our workers' functional activities into memorable events? Wise business leaders champion this new paradigm in their organizations; custodians of the old order fail to see the upside in investing in better workplace acting and seek only to cut headcount at every turn.

Third, concerning experiences, more offerings should find ways to explicitly charge for time. Time again is the primary currency of experiences. Today, some experiential marketing events require an admission fee; some experiential operations contribute to charging a premium for the supported goods and services; and some experiences are accessible only on a subscription basis. It is vital that more experiences in the future be available only by admission, for such holds the key to a long-lasting experience economy. Requiring customers to explicitly pay for the time they spend in places or events not only makes an experience a distinct economic offering but provides new sources of revenue growth. Many businesses languish today because they still have not asked themselves this fundamental question: What would we do differently if we charged admission? Addressing this question is most critical; identifying answers, most imperative.

Consider one particular pricing model ripe for such admission-fee innovation: time sharing, such as practiced by Netflix. It's no movie rental service, charging for each lent film. Rather, the company charges a monthly fee and subsumes the rental service in a movie-viewing subscription. The same sort of access-based experiences have emerged with corporate jets, recreational vehicles, snow removal equipment, housing and even women's designer handbags. Automobile ride-sharing programs have also met with some success, but real progress will come only when consumers can access a greater portfolio of vehicles for an assortment of driving needs. Almost any industry would benefit from seeking to differentiate based on for-fee experiences.

Fourth, whatever the genre of output, more companies need to wisely leverage digital technology in order to better fuse the real with the virtual. For more and more people are bringing their technological devices – iPods, iPhones, iPads and so on – with them wherever they go, with the diverting of their time, attention and money always just a glance away, a warm glowing trance away from remaining in the experience. This is not to say that companies should abandon Reality, for it will now and forevermore provide the richest of experiences, but with a migration going on to Virtuality, many experiences will increasingly need to fuse the two together to create new digitally infused experiences never before envisioned, engendered nor encountered (Pine and Korn, 2011).In some cases, this may require greater integration of the digital into the physical; but in other cases, it may mean removing digital devices that merely intrude on the face-to-face experience.

Finally – and most notably in thinking about the future of the experience economy – more experiences should yield transformations. While experiences are less transient than services, the individual partaking in the experience often wants something more lasting than a memory, something beyond what any good, service or experience alone can offer. People who buy memberships in a fitness center do not pay for the pain but for ongoing exercise regimens that will increase their physical well-being, helping them go from flabby to fit. Likewise, people return to psychiatrists as long as they see improvements in their mental or emotional well-being. People head for business school because they want to affect their professional and financial well-being. Exercise routines, counseling sessions, learning courses and also religious excursions are actually means of eliciting something that is more desirable, and more valued, than the experience itself.

As economic activity shifts further and further away from goods and services, those companies that stage experiences alone – without considering the effect these experiences will have on the participants and without designing the experiences in such a way as to create a desired change – will eventually see their experiences become commoditized. The second time you experience something, it will be marginally less enjoyable than the first time, the third time less enjoyable than that and so on until you finally notice the experience doesn't engage you nearly as much as it once did. Welcome to the commoditization of experiences, best exemplified by the increasingly voiced phrase, "Been there, done that."

Companies can escape this commoditization trap by the same route that all other offerings can take: customization. When you customize an experience to make it just right for an individual – providing exactly what he needs right now – you cannot help changing that individual. When you customize an experience, you automatically turn it into a transformation, which companies create on top of experiences (recall that phrase:

"a life-transforming experience"), just as they create experiences on top of services and so forth.

By staging a series of experiences, companies are better able to achieve a lasting effect on the buyer than through an isolated event. It is the revisiting of a recurring theme, experienced through distinct and yet unified events, that transforms. As multiple experiences emerge and compete for guests, companies staging these events will begin to realize that any experience can become the basis for a new offering that elicits a transformation.

As with experiences, some observers will surely argue that what we are calling transformations is really only a subclass of services. But there is just too much disparity between, say, eating at a McDonald's and firming up at a fitness center, between providing information reports and partnering in business outcomes and between cleaning a suit and cleansing a soul, to classify them all as a single economic offering.

With transformations, the economic offering of a company business is the change in the individual person or company changed as a result of what the offering company business does. With transformations, the customer is the product! The individual buyer of the transformation essentially says, "Change me." The company's economic offering is neither the materials it uses nor the physical things it makes. It's neither the processes it executes nor the encounters it orchestrates. When a company guides transformations, the offering is the individual.

Such transformations should therefore themselves command a fee in the form of explicitly charging for the demonstrated outcomes that result from the underlying experiences. In other words, companies enabling transformations should charge not merely for time but for the change resulting from that time. They should charge for the ends and not only the means of life-changing (or company-altering) experiences – and especially so in those industries that focus on making people healthy, wealthy and wise.

Truly market-based approaches in the healthcare industry would free parties to charge for demonstrated outcomes and not mere attempts to gain such noteworthy ends. Endless debate over health insurance would shift to actual innovation in healthcare, in which people would be charged only for the ongoing ensurance of wellness. Unsuccessful treatments that fail to remedy ailments would not be compensated fully (just as one doesn't pay a plumber who fails to fix a leaky sink), and new financial instruments tied to actual performance – perhaps securitizing future earnings streams of successfully treated patients – would necessarily emerge. Similarly, the reward systems in financial institutions would reflect the true results of investment decisions – and then move away from an exclusive spotlight on investments to granting wise counsel on life decisions concerning how best to spend and gift wealth. And colleges and universities, which in the US graduate barely half those who enroll in them (would we ever tolerate such dismal performance from any other industry?), should focus on the actual educational, personal and societal outcomes achieved, collecting all or part of the tuition only when those outcomes become clear at graduation and beyond. To do otherwise, in each of these fields, does a disservice to all.

Do not take this admonition for greater experience and transformation innovation to mean that there has not been great progress toward offering new experiences. Much has indeed emerged. But much more needs to follow. The experience economy is a long-term underlying shift in the very structure of advanced economies and the forces of creative destruction take time. New forms of economic output do not come automatically. They require individual people and individual enterprises to take action, to abandon old industrial and service economy paradigms in order to introduce new experiences and transformations, eventually resulting in the passing of the experience economy into the transformation economy.

2.8 SUMMARY

The world's economy is currently in a state of great flux, in times as turbulent as any non-wartime circumstances before it. Much of the difficulty stems from a failure to recognize and respond to the fundamental shift in the nature of economic offerings being sold by companies and purchased by consumers and businesses. This shift arises from both sides of the supply/demand equation. Companies seek out differentiation as their past offerings increasingly become commoditized while their customers seek out greater value for themselves as their wealth grows, desiring to spend their hard-earned money, their harder-earned time and their hardest-earned selves on offerings that provide them with more worth, more significance and more meaning than mere commodities, goods and services ever could.

While all five (and five only) economic offerings have always been around, until recently the final two – experiences and transformations – comprised just a small portion of employment, GDP and the purchase pie. The notion of the experience economy is not something we (or others who have described the same phenomenon from differing perspectives) invented; rather, it is something we all discovered. We discovered that up-and-coming companies – the true innovators – more and more were experientializing their goods, surrounding their services with engaging events, creating new and wondrous experiences, and eliciting transformations within those who seek help in achieving their aspirations.

The shift into today's experience economy – where experiences have become the predominant economic offering, the primary source of job creation and economic growth – comes with a number of implications that companies should keep in mind as they make the shift from commodity trading, manufacturing and service providing (or innovate wholly new businesses birthed in experiences). First, understand that mass customization is the route up the Progression of Economic Value, as customizing a good turns it into a service, customizing a service turns it into an experience and customizing an experience turns it into a transformation. Companies should focus on reaching inside of the individual, living, breathing customer, making their offerings as personal and as individual as the customer (whether a consumer or business) desiring that offering.

Second, understand that work is theatre. As the nature of economic output changes, so must the efforts that go into it. The word drama derives from the Greek *drao*, meaning simply "to do." In all companies, whether or not managers recognize it, the workers are playing not in some game but in what should be a well-conceived, correctly cast and convincingly portrayed real-life drama of doing. Business enterprises would gain an invaluable perspective simply by declaring their work to be theatre. For when a business calls its workplace a bare stage, it opens up opportunities to distinguish itself from the myriad humdrum makers of goods and providers of services that perform work without recognizing the true nature of their acts. With theatre furnishing the operating model, even the most mundane of tasks can engage customers in a memorable way.

Third, authenticity is the new consumer sensibility. Concomitant with the shift into the experience economy is a shift in the primary criterion by which people choose what to buy and from whom to buy. No matter the offering – commodity, good, service, experience or transformation – customers will judge it based on whether or not they view it as authentic, whether or not it conforms to their own self-image. While this criterion is primary, it will not trump quality that does not meet customer standards, costs that do not fit the budget nor a lack of availability in time or place to meet customers' needs. But companies better get good at managing the customer perception of the authenticity of their offerings, their places and their company, lest they invalidate themselves in the minds of customers as fake, contrived, disingenuous, phony, inauthentic.

Fourth, the experience is the marketing. Perhaps the worst offender when it comes to authenticity is advertising, as it has become a phoniness-generating machine. Companies should stop advertising and put their marketing money into experience places, where people can directly experience who they are. The best way to generate demand for any offering in today's experience economy is with an experience so engaging that customers can't help put pay attention and buy that offering. Marketing therefore needs to become placemaking, where companies create a portfolio of places, both real and virtual, to simultaneously render authenticity and generate demand.

The final insight to achieving success via the state-of-the-art in experience staging that we have discussed in this chapter is recognizing that charging admission is the economic key. Whenever there is such a shift in the underlying nature of the economy, companies always give away the next level of value in order to better sell what they have today. So back in the latter half of the twentieth century, as their goods began to be commoditized, manufacturers started giving away services – installation, repair, integration and so forth – to create preference for their goods. It worked, but eventually they realized that customers valued the services, and often more so than the goods, and so they started charging for them. Many manufacturers – think of IBM, for example – now make more money from their "ancillary" services than their "core" goods. In the same way, service companies (retailer, hotelier and so forth) gave away experience elements in order to better sell their offerings. Eventually, they must align what they charge for with what their customers value, and that means charging for time. An offering is only an experience, economically speaking, when customers pay for the time they spend with the company.

We do believe that pursuing these five fronts will greatly advance the vitality of the experience economy, now and into the future. Most significant is the final point regarding going beyond the experience to transformations. It may very well be that the world is not ready for the shift to this economic pursuit, for many people are still getting used to experiences and perhaps fear the sheer individuality of being so open about one's self as to ask for assistance from an outside enterprise in changing it. And in paying for it; it may be paying for demonstrated outcomes that would bother people the most if they thought about it

But that day will come. We can remember the early days of writing and speaking on the experience economy, where almost inevitably someone or some few would object to the very thought of it. Some did not think experiences were a distinct offering, some did not like the idea of paying for them, some did not like what kind of experiences were likely to surface, some did not like what would be left behind. We rarely if ever encounter such responses now, almost 20 years after we discovered the concept and 15 years after we first wrote of it. We do, however, still encounter similar objections when we talk about transformations.

But ready or not, we say again, that day will come, thanks to companies continuing to seek out new ways of differentiation, thanks to people seeking out better ways to spend their money and create value within them – and thanks to academics and students who continue to study what is going on in the world of business, and help the rest of the world understand it. It will come, but only if we act on it.

NOTES

1. It is interesting to note that the agrarian and industrial economies were names long after their economic offerings became predominant, the service economy as services took over from goods and the experience economy before it supplanted its predecessors.
2. It is not really true, however, that the dissertation "For the love of experience" (Snel, 2011, p. 30) "offset[s] the current bias in the experience economy discourse" by taking "the individual's perspective." Rather, the experience economy offsets the long-held individual bias by, for the first time, providing a business perspective! One can read marvelous books stretching back a century or more on the individual's perspective of experiences, but only in the past few decades have we been able to identify experiences as a distinct economic offering for which a business perspective becomes necessary.
3. Note that most discussions of co-creating experiences primarily revolve around the "customer experience" of designing and then making or delivering goods and services, respectively, versus experiences as a distinct economic offering.
4. Economist Stanley Lebergott (1993, p. 3) makes the point: "Consumers buy bazaars full of goods, but only to create the diversified experience they ultimately seek" and goes on to show with a wealth of data that those goods (and services, for that matter) that enable consumer experiences have seen tremendous growth in the twentieth century; that will continue to happen in the twenty-first century in concert with those that enable consumer transformations.

BIBLIOGRAPHY

Boswijk, A., E. Peelen and S. Olthof (2012), *Economy of Experiences*, 3rd edn, Amsterdam: The European Centre for the Experience and Transformation Economy BV.

Brook, P. (1968), *The Empty Space*, New York: Touchstone.

Carter, T.J. and T. Gilovich (2010), 'The relative relativity of material and experiential purchases', *Journal of Personality and Social Psychology*, **98** (1), 146–59.

Davenport, T.H. and J.C. Beck (2002), *The Attention Economy: Understanding the New Currency of Business*, Boston, MA: Harvard Business School Press.

Davis, S. (1987), *Future Perfect*, Reading, MA: Addison-Wesley.

Florida, R. (2002), *The Rise of the Creative Class*, New York: Basic Books.

Freytag, G. (1898), *Technique of the Drama*, 2nd edn, Chicago, IL: Scott, Foresman.

Gilmore, J.H. and B.J. Pine II (1997), 'Beyond goods and services', *Strategy and Leadership*, **25** (3), 10–18.

Gilmore, J.H. and B.J. Pine II (eds) (2000), *Markets of One: Creating Customer-unique Value through Mass Customization*, Boston, MA: Harvard Business School Press.

Gilmore, J.H. and B.J. Pine II (2007), *Authenticity: What Consumers Really Want*, Boston, MA: Harvard Business School Press.

Goffman, E. (1959), *The Presentation of Self in Everyday Life*, New York: Anchor Books.

IDEO (n.d.), http://www.ideo.com/.

Jensen, R. (1999), *The Dream Society*, New York: McGraw-Hill.

Lebergott, S. (1993), *Pursuing Happiness: American Consumers in the Twentieth Century*, Princeton, NJ: Princeton University Press.

Ogilvy, J. (1985), 'The Experience Industry: A Leading Edge Report from the Values and Lifestyles Program', report 724, Menlo Park, CA: SRI International Business Intelligence.

Oldenburg, R. (1997), *The Great Good Place: Cafés, Coffee Shops, Community Centers, Beauty Parlors, General Stores, Bars, Hangouts and How They Get You through the Day*, New York: Marlowe and Company.

Pine II, B.J. (1993), *Mass Customization: The New Frontier in Business Competition*, Boston, MA: Harvard Business School Press.

Pine II, B.J. and J.H. Gilmore (1997), 'How to profit from experience', *Wall Street Journal*, 4 August.

Pine II, B.J. and J.H. Gilmore (1998), 'Welcome to the experience economy', *Harvard Business Review*, **76** (4), 97–105.

Pine II, B.J. and J.H. Gilmore (1999), *The Experience Economy: Work is Theatre and Every Business a Stage*, Boston, MA: Harvard Business School Press.

Pine II, B.J. and J.H. Gilmore (2000), 'Satisfaction, sacrifice, surprise: three small steps create one giant leap into the experience economy', *Strategy and Leadership*, **28** (1), 18–23.

Pine II, B.J. and J.H. Gilmore (2011), *The Experience Economy, Updated Edition*, Boston, MA: Harvard Business Review Press.

Pine II, B.J. and K.C. Korn (2011), *Infinite Possibility: Creating Customer Value on the Digital Frontier*, San Francisco, CA: Berrett-Koehler.

Prahalad, C.K. and V. Rasmaswamy (2004), *The Future of Competition: Co-creating Unique Value with Customers*, Boston, MA: Harvard Business School Press.

Rifkin, J. (2000), *The Age of Access: The New Culture of Hypercapitalism, Where all of Life is a Paid-for Experience*, New York: Jeremy P. Tarcher and Putnam.

'Schrager's new design for living' (2012), *CMW*, 12 February, available at http://www.c-mw.net/featuredetails/114/schrager-s-new-design-for-living (accessed 30 October 2012).

Schulze, G. (1992), *Die Erlebnisgesellschaft: Kultursoziologie der Gegenwart* (*The Experience Society: Cultural Sociology of the Present Time*), Frankfurt am Main: Campus Verlag.

Smith, A. (1776), *An Inquiry into the Nature and Causes of the Wealth of Nations*, reprinted 1994, Modern Library edn, New York: Random House.

Snel, A. (2011), 'For the love of experience: changing the experience economy discourse', PhD dissertation, University of Amsterdam, Amsterdam.

The Economist (2006), 'Economics discovers its feelings', 23 December, p. 34.

Toffler, A. (1970), *Future Shock*, New York: Bantam Books.

Toffler, A. (1980), *The Third Wave*, New York: Bantam Books.

Van Boven, L. and T. Gilovich (2003), 'To do or to have? That is the question', *Journal of Personality and Social Psychology*, **85** (6), 1193–202.

3. Post-industrial growth: experience, culture or creative economies?
Anne Lorentzen

3.1 INTRODUCTION

With the decline of manufacturing employment, the expansion of the service sector, the development of still more efficient information and transportation technologies and globalization, people, businesses and governments face new challenges as well as opportunities. What these are more precisely have been the object of theorizing over approximately the last two decades. Different concepts have been developed to grasp post-industrialism, most prominently the knowledge economy and the new economy. One subgroup of notions relate to the increased importance of the symbolic content of production and consumption. Notions like the culture economy, the creative economy and the experience economy have been developed in order to describe and understand the new megatrend, often with the intention to deliver new strategic tools for businesses and governments.

The three notions, the experience economy, the culture economy and the creative economy, have reached such fame that they have become part of the daily language of journalists, politicians and planners. Often they are used interchangeably, even in research. This is a pity, as the three notions provide different insights, have different origins and also imply different strategic or practical conclusions. A distinction between culture and creative economy is helpful, as culture economy focuses on final culture products and producers, while creative economy focuses on creative processes preceding innovation and production. Compared to the creative and the culture economies, which entail a more traditional productionist perspective, the experience economy concept enables a view from the consumption side, placing the consumers together with the producers in a stage from which valuable (from a market perspective) experiences may emerge in complex innovation processes. It is argued that the notion of experience economy offers an innovative and integrative perspective for research and theory building, on the one hand and for policy, on the other hand.

This chapter presents the basic ideas related to the experience, the culture and the creative economies. This is followed by an analysis and discussion of the differences between the three approaches. It is shown that they are quite different in their focus, statements and contributions and weaknesses, and that this has implications for their locational perspectives and for their implications for policy. The conclusion points at the experience economy approach as the most innovative, holistic and integrated approach with a great potential for research and policy in local and regional development.

3.2   THE EXPERIENCE ECONOMY

The specific term 'the experience economy' was first introduced in 1998 in a short article by Pine and Gilmore (1998). The article was followed by their book *The Experience Economy* (Pine and Gilmore, 1999). The article and the book introduce experiences as a new and very promising source of economic value. The basic idea is that when a customer buys an experience, extra value is generated because 'he pays to spend time enjoying a series of memorable events that a company stages – as in a theatrical play – to engage him in a personal way' (Pine and Gilmore, 1998, p. 98). Basically what Pine and Gilmore do is to address the emotional dimension of consumption as a new source of value creation. Experiences as such are not new on the market, as they represent the core of, for example, different kinds of entertainment. The staging of experiences can thus be seen most outspokenly in theme parks such as Disneyland, which was established in 1955 as a place where people could meet the famous movie characters and enjoy a day with the family.[1] However, the point that Pine and Gilmore make is that today an increasing number of service providers stage their approach to customers in a theatrical way. The experience economy is thus a term describing an emerging marketing strategy, which can be detected mainly among service producers. The strategy has the potential to become even more pervasive as most final producers may enhance their market value by staging experiences for the customers in order to differentiate them from competing products. One gets the impression that the experience economy is a description of a whole new economic age (Pine and Gilmore, 1999, pp. 6, 13, 14, 22). The new age is characterized by new growth patterns of employment and changing price structures, arising from the new modes of value generation. Value is generated by charging for what was once free (Pine and Gilmore, 1999, p. 67) in a progressing social division of labour (Smith, 1776 [2001]). The book is rich with examples of how the purchase and consumption of mundane products, mostly service products, can be staged in effective ways. Apart from theming the experience (Pine and Gilmore, 1999, p. 46) engagement of the five senses is an effective way to make the experience more valuable (Pine and Gilmore, 1999, p. 59). The work of Pine and Gilmore has become very popular, in particular in Scandinavia, and the original book from 1999 has appeared in a new edition in 2011 (Pine and Gilmore, 2011).

3.2.1   Experiences in Consumer Studies

Even if Pine and Gilmore are not very explicit about their theoretical predecessors, they follow a reasoning, which is well known in consumer behaviour theories. Holbrook has made a useful overview of the history of the concept of the experience economy (Holbrook, 2006). The basic concepts of experience consumption go back to classic economists like Adam Smith and have been developed through the 1950s and 1960s by Abbott (1955) among others. The study of consumer behaviour was at that time questioning the rational information processing perspective, because it ignored more playful phenomena such as sensory pleasure, aesthetic enjoyment and emotional responses. An alternative 'experiential view' emerged, which regards consumption as primarily a subjective state of consciousness. According to this view, consumption has a variety of symbolic meanings, aesthetic criteria and hedonic significance (Holbrook and Hirschman, 1982, p. 132). Consumption thus seeks fun, amusement, fantasy, arousal and sensory stimulation (p.135), summarized as the three Fs: fantasy, feelings and fun. In this experiential view the multisensory psychophysical relationships in consumer behaviour is of particular relevance (p.134). Further, it was suggested that in particular creative and sensation seeking personalities seek experiential consumption (p.136). Later Lebergott (1993) suggested that economic activity aims not for output, but for experience via consumption. Schmitt, in 1999 published his book *Experiential Marketing: How to Get Customers to Sense, Feel, Think, Act and Relate to Your Company and Brands* (Schmitt, 1999 quoted in Holbrook, 2000). The theoretical development continued in consumption studies, for instance, with a handbook on experience and brand management (Schmitt and Rogers, 2006). Two decades later the experiential view was extended to the so-called four Es, in marketing and consumer research, namely experience (related to escapism, emotions, enjoyment), entertainment (related to aesthetics, excitement, ecstasy), exhibitionism (related to enthuse, express, expose) and evangelizing (related to educate, evince, endorse) (Holbrook, 2000). Then, in 2006 Holbrook expanded on the notion of customer value, which he defined as 'an interactive relativistic preference experience' (Holbrook, 2006, p. 715). The customer values of a product are economic, social, hedonistic or altruistic. These values can be categorized as self-oriented (for my own sake) and other oriented (for the sake of others), and both values can be either extrinsic (instrumental) or intrinsic (for its own sake). In sum, it can be argued based on consumer studies that interaction and non-economic values such as experience is, and has always been, a part of every relationship between the customer and the product. The question is thus not whether experience is part of the offering or not, but rather how this experience differs between products and customers.

With this background the ideas of Pine and Gilmore from 1998 and 1999 do not represent new academic insights. What they have to say is a reflection, however partial, of established insights. Their influence in Europe after 2000 is probably due to the way they communicate their points by plenty of illustrations, an energetic style of writing (Holbrook, 2000, pp.179–81) and not least a great deal of marketing.

3.2.2   Experiences in Sociology and Geography

Other related contributions deal with overall changes in the economy and the society. In 1970 Alvin Toffler in his book *Future Shock* (Toffler, 1970) suggested radical changes in the economic structure of the advanced economies. Under more affluent conditions the economy will deal with a new level of human needs. It will become geared to the provision of 'psychic gratification' and to the 'quality of life'. An experience industry would emerge as a response to the experience demand, and together they would develop into a provision system of experiences.

Along the same line, Schulze in 1992 launched the idea of the experience society (Schulze, 1992 [2005]). He described the aestheticization of everyday life, characterized by an increasing importance of the non-material aspects of products, of human relationships and of human habits. People's lives had turned into experience projects, and the society into an experience society. In Denmark Lund et al. (2005) similarly argued, focusing on the role of feelings, or customer experiences, in consumption. Rolf Jensen wrote in the *Dream Society* from 1999 and later revised (Jensen, 2006) that today people ask for stories and dreams, not only for products, and therefore emotions will be of increasing importance in the market place. The tangible products will become bi-products, and the most successful firms on the market place are those that have developed the best narratives.

In relation to economic development, economic geographers have discussed the importance of experience-based activities to employment and local and regional development (Smidt-Jensen et al., 2009; Lorentzen, 2011, 2012b; Hansen and Winther, 2012). Tourism researchers have discussed experience tourism as the innovative follower of mass tourism (Stamboulis and Skayannis, 2003), and in planning, the experiential development of places has been discussed (Smidt-Jensen, 2012).

3.3   THE CULTURE ECONOMY

The notion of the culture economy has also become popular in research and policy. It is, however, understood and defined in different ways in different contexts. First, it can be understood narrowly as a growth of so-called cultural products and services in the economy (Landes, 1969; UNESCO, 2003; Leriche and Daviet, 2010), and of groups of industries, which have been considered powerful engines of the present phase of capitalism (Pratt, 1997; Scott, 2000). Second, it can be understood in a more encompassing way as the growing importance of culture, meaning or 'signs' (Lash and Urry, 1994) in modern capitalism. Third, a particular strand of thought is occupied with culture as a view or discourse of economics and of economic geography (de Gay and Pryke, 2002 [2006]). 'The cultural turn' thus implies the consideration of meaning, representation and relationships in the economy. In the present context two particular subgroups of contributions are discussed. These are, on the one hand, contributions dealing with cultural industries as a subsector of modern capitalism, and, on the other hand, contributions dealing with the culture economy as a particular dynamic system within capitalism.

3.3.1   The Development of the Culture Economy Concept

Social scientists have responded to the changes happening in the advanced economies since the 1970s by identifying new dynamics and suggesting new terms such as 'post Fordism' (Hollingsworth and Boyer, 1997), 'the new economy' (Audretsch and Thurik, 2001), 'the knowledge economy' (Drucker, 1992) or the 'cognitive cultural economy' (Scott, 2007). A common denominator for these contributions is that they identify a movement away from standardized mass production and mass consumption towards mosaics of niche producers addressing segmented markets with products and services representing varying, but increasing degrees of symbolic, aesthetic or cultural value.

In a seminal paper Scott (1997) explains how capitalism of today has moved into a phase in which cultural forms and meanings become commodified as part of the production strategy of profit seeking economic actors (private firms). The result is the emergence of a very heterogeneous supply of cultural products, both goods and services, on the market. Cultural products are products with aesthetic or semiotic attributes (Scott, 1997, p. 323). Common for these products is that their utilitarian purpose is less important than their psychic gratification to the consumer. The culture economic sectors are, according to Scott, the most dynamic in capitalism today, and the background for this extreme dynamism is the expansion of disposable consumer incomes (p. 324). The ideas represented by, for example, Scott have been preceded by contributions such as Urry (1995), Zukin (1995), Bordieu (1984) and Harvey (1990).

The empirical delimitation of the culture economy represents a challenge. The sectorial approach is occupied with a description of the composition and weight of the cultural industries in the overall economy (Pratt, 1997, 2004, pp. 33–4; Scott, 2001, p. 12, 2008, p. 307). The list of culture economy sectors seems to grow (entertainment, fine arts, architecture, gastronomy, events) and there is an inconclusiveness regarding the delimitation of culture goods and services. A functional division is suggested by Leriche and Daviet (2010, p. 808). A concentric pattern made of core activities (music), intermediary activities (publishing) and peripheral activities (advertising) can be detected. They supplement this categorization with a value chain perspective according to which the extraction of intellectual creativity is the first phase, and its transformation in to cultural products and services such as films is the second phase (Leriche and Daviet, 2010, p. 808). The value chain perspective is also found in Howkins (2001 [2002]). Finally, Markusen (2010) suggests employment of culture workers as the most feasible way to assess the weight of the culture economy because jobs in the cultural industries are not synonymous with jobs in cultural occupations. Assessing the importance of the culture economy would therefore, according to Markusen, require careful analysis of cultural employment. As a whole, the contributions are quite descriptive, and the research results consist in empirical documentation of emerging industrial patterns, trends and differences in and between regions and countries.

3.4   THE CREATIVE ECONOMY

The conceptual forerunners of theories of the creative economy can be seen as the notions of the knowledge economy and learning, and the culture economy. For example, *Creative Industries: Contracts Between Art and Commerce* by Richard Caves in 2000 discussed the organization of art as business. Politically an interest in creative industries emerged early, in particular in Great Britain, where the Department for Culture, Media and Sport (DCMS) initiated a mapping and strategy of the creative industries in the late 1990s (for an overview see Newbegin, 2010). The list of DCMS has been influential as other countries and international organizations have copied it, for example, the United Nations Conference on Trade and development (UNCTAD, 2010), the World Intellectual Property Organization (WIPO)[2] and the United Nations Educational, Scientific and Cultural Organization (UNESCO).[3]

Today, the creative economy is a concept with considerable influence in research and policy. Two different strands of thought contribute to the development of this notion. One deals with the emergence and development of a particular sector in the economy, the creative industries (Howkins, 2001 [2002]). Another deals with the economy as a whole with a particular view on urban and regional development in the 'creative age' (Florida, 2004).

3.4.1   The Creative Industries

According to Howkins, creative industries are those industries that provide creative products with a market value (Howkins, 2002, p. 85). Most often creative products include intellectual property (patents, copyrights, designs and trademarks). Creativity is the ability to create something new and creativity enters the economy when it becomes tradable. A creative product is thus an economic good or service that results from creativity and that also has economic value (Howkins, 2002, pp. x–xi). According to Howkins, creativity is present at all levels of business, reaching from the management of a company to the development, branding and shaping of products (Howkins, 2002, p. xi). The core creative industries are, according to Howkins, advertising, architechture, art, crafts, design, fashion, film, music, performing arts, publishing, research and development (R&D) software, toys and games, TV and radio and video games (Howkins, 2002, p. 116). These industries all compete on ideas, but differ on other points such as technology, market and industrial structure. They exert a general influence on innovation and competitiveness of the whole economy because they provide a creative input to other industries. Creative management is needed to exploit the creative capital (Howkins, 2002, pp. 199, 211). This entails the employment of creative people (employees), creative entrepreneurs and the use of temporary organizational forms, networks and teamwork (Howkins, 2002, pp. 124 ff.).

3.4.2   The Creative Economy and the Creative Class

Another strand of thought considers creativity as a pervasive characteristic of the contemporary economy and of successful regions. Richard Florida, the protagonist of this paradigmatic approach, thus suggests that creativity is the main driver of economic growth today (Florida, 2004, p. xxix). The idea of 'the knowledge economy' was that globalization has shifted the comparative advantage of high cost locations to knowledge-based activities, and in particular search activities (Audretsch and Thurik, 2001, p. 306). Florida's argument is that not only knowledge but its creative development and application are the key to development in advanced economies. Florida's conception of creativity is threefold: (1) technological creativity; (2) economic creativity (entrepreneurship); and (3) artistic and cultural creativity (Florida, 2004, p. 33). The creative processes flourish in places where a broad ecosystem can be found to nurture and support them. The economic result is innovation and new firm formation (Florida, 2004, p. xxii).

At the heart of the creative economy and the creative ecosystem is the creative class. The creative class is defined economically as people in specific occupations (regardless of education and industrial affiliation), where they are paid to define and solve problems. The creative class consists of two groups, the creative core and the creative professionals. The creative core consists of scientists, engineers, university professors, poets and novelists, artist, entertainers, actors, designers and architects and trendsetters, non-fiction writers, editors, cultural figures, think tank researchers, analysts and other opinion-makers. The creative professionals work in a wide range of knowledge-intensive industries such as high tech, financial services, legal services, health care and business management.

Based on International Labour Organization (ILO) statistics, the size of the creative class in the 39 most advanced countries has been estimated. The USA accounts for the greatest absolute number of creative class workers, and the world's greatest share (Florida, 2007, pp. 135–6). The relative share of the creative class was greater, however, in Ireland, Belgium, Australia, the Netherlands, New Zealand, Estonia, the UK, Canada, Finland and Iceland, supposedly providing these countries with a considerable creative dynamic and competitive strength.

3.5   COMPARISON AND DISCUSSION OF THE THREE APPROACHES

The experience economy, the culture economy and the creative economy have thus developed in the same period of time as a response to the industrial challenges of the advanced economies. They share the search for competitiveness and growth triggers in the post-industrial transition, but have quite different theoretical roots, statements and perspectives. It is therefore useful to compare the three approaches more closely.

3.5.1   Focus and Aim of the Three Approaches

The three groups of theories share the intention of being useful and applicable to policy and management. They differ, however, a great deal in relation to their strategic foci, which are customer relationships, industries and sectors, and regional and urban dynamics based on particular creative labour groups. Also the levels of analysis differ (micro, meso and macro levels).

In the experience economy the development of the micro-level relationships between producers and consumers is the focus. The level of analysis is mainly the micro level, and the focus is on particular activities and investments that can be related to the achievement of consumer satisfaction. The consumer is seen as king in a staging system. The aim of the contributions is most often strategic and prescriptive, and deal with ways to enhance competitiveness of products, services or places through experience marketing, design, planning or innovation (see Boswijk et al., 2007). Schulze (1992 [2005]), on the other hand, represents a critique of the post-modern society.

The culture economy theories include a critical stance towards the increasing capitalization on culture. However, most of the work is quite descriptive, dealing with (changing) industrial and employment patterns on the national and regional levels. Based on the assumption of a huge growth potential the work on the culture economy and culture industries feeds into industrial policy at regional and national levels.

The creative economy addresses business, industry and regional development. While Howkins (2001 [2002]) is interested in the management issues and firm-level enablers of creativity, he simultaneously takes an industrial approach. Florida (2004) focuses on the regional and urban levels, and on how creative labour can be retained and attracted to cities and regions. The aim of the creative economy approaches has from the outset been to deliver the basis for business strategies and regional development policies.

3.5.2   The Key Factors Suggested by the Three Theories

The three groups of theories thus see three completely different factors as crucial, namely customer relationship, commodification and creativity.

In the experience economy approaches the key factor and focus of interest is a relationship, namely the relationship between provider and consumer. This relationship can be manipulated through the staging of experiences, resulting in customer loyalty, increased sales and profit. According to Pine and Gilmore there is no such thing as an artificial experience, as all experiences are real (Pine and Gilmore, 1999, p. 36). This point has served as a point of departure for a whole book on authenticity (Gilmore and Pine, 2007).

In the culture economy the key factor causing the expansion of cultural production is 'commodification' (Harvey, 1990, 2002). Commodification means the commercial exploitation of artistic, aesthetic and semiotic creativity (Leriche and Daviet, 2010, p. 808). Commodification is changing society. It drives the expansion of industries or firms producing and marketing cultural goods and services (Leriche and Daviet, 2010, p. 808). It changes the role and status of artists, who become culture workers instead of free thinkers or explorers of new ways of thinking (Leriche and Daviet, 2010, p. 808). Finally, it moves cultural output from the civic, religious or public sphere into the market sphere, where it appears as products, and must compete innovatively.

In the creative economy the creation of something new in a business context is the key factor that drives the success of businesses as well as regions. For Howkins, creativity is present in every business but concentrated mainly in a particular group of businesses, the so-called core creative industries. Creativity has a universal character as a basic element of life, and it is connected to talent and to particular personal traits (Howkins, 2002, pp. 10–15). This resonates with Florida (2004, pp. 21ff.) who identifies human creativity as an economic force of still increasing importance in the economy.

3.5.3   The Key Processes Identified by the Three Theories

The three theories are dynamic in the sense that they identify important processes leading to competitiveness and growth on different levels. These processes are experiential engagement, the clustering of cultural production and creativity.

In the experience economy the key process is the engagement of the individual/customer (Leriche and Daviet, 2010, p. 808). To engage the customer is more than to entertain him or her. This is illustrated in the idea of the four experience realms (Pine and Gilmore, 1999). The four realms illustrate different types of involvement and participation. The participation of the customer can be active or passive, and the customer can be absorbed or immersed in the experience show. Through engagement the provider obtains customer satisfaction and loyalty. Passive participation is typical of symphony goers, whereas active participation characterizes skiers or hikers. Absorption happens when the experience comes into the mind of the customer, while immersion happens when the customer becomes part of the experience as, for example, as a festival guest. In each case the potential for engaging customers increases with new technology such as interactive games, 3D movies, virtual reality and motion-based attractions, as already mentioned in 1998 (Pine and Gilmore, 1998, p. 99). Combined with the ideas of Schmitt (1999) this engagement process happens through the stimulation of senses, arousal of feelings, direction of thoughts and incentives to purchase and consume. This process takes place on the micro level.

In the culture economy the key process is 'clustering' (Scott, 2010a). Scott argues that culture producing firms tend to cluster due to two reasons. One is the high level of uncertainty that firms producing cultural products face as they depend on intensive transactions in networks of other producers. The other reason is that once established, the cluster functions as a polar axis of dense labour markets (Scott, 2010a, p.117). Also the meandering roads of artists during their careers presuppose proximity between the different providers of cultural jobs (Markusen, 2010). The clustering process is not different from the general observation in economic geography that proximity is related to high levels of uncertainty connected with innovation (Rutten, 2003) and to the need to share a pool of common knowledge (Corolleur and Courlet, 2003). This process takes place on the societal level.

In the creative economy the key process is creativity (as different from creativity as a resource). It is a business process leading to innovation and competitiveness (Howkins, 2001 [2002]) and a social process leading to prosperity (Florida, 2004). As a social process, creativity consists of entrepreneurship, technological R&D and artistic creativity (Florida, 2004, p.33). The creative class represents the creative potential of the economy, and its presence is suggested as critical to the three processes and to the subsequent virtuous circle of regional development. This process also takes place on the societal level.

3.5.4   The Contributions of the Three Approaches

The three approaches all contribute to fill the theoretical and strategic vacuum that emerged with the industrial transition in the advanced countries. The contribution of the experience economy approach is to draw attention to the potentials for business development in the consumer-provider relationship. Of great importance is the argument that market value is based on much more than functional features, and that this value can be enhanced and innovated through careful staging.

The contribution of the culture economy research is to identify and document new industrial patterns and growth potentials based on artistic and symbolic contents. The culture economy also represents an illustrative case of the basic mechanism of capitalism, namely commodification and clustering.

The creative economy as an approach is complex and less coherent than the other two approaches. The key contribution is the insistence on the role of creativity in the knowledge economy, personified in the notion of the creative class, and inserted together with institutions in a creative ecosystem. Creativity is not emotional and symbolic as it deals with technical creativity and entrepreneurship. The soft aspects appear in artistic creativity and other quality of place factors valued by the highly skilled.

The culture economy approach is the most traditional of the approaches as it is basically a productionist approach, repeating known insights in new empirical fields. The creative economy approach is more innovative as it integrates the role of labour and quality of life factors to the development of regions and industries in the knowledge economy. The experience economy is the most innovative as it turns things upside down by focusing on consumers and consumer values. The concept of valuation, and in particular of staging, are important contributions that may serve as a point of departure for further theoretical development, as a lens for empirical research and as an inspiration for policy.

3.5.5 The Economic Geographic Implications of the Three Approaches

The three approaches describe or predict industrial change of more or less encompassing kinds, described as a new age (Florida, 2004, pp. 21ff.), a new stage in the economy (Pine and Gilmore, 1999, p. 22) or just as new clusters and agglomerations of industries (Scott, 2008, p. 312). The socio-spatial implications of these industrial patterns of change are of great importance to the destiny of cities and regions.

The classic text on the experience economy does not deal with spatiality, but a great number of later contributions do. Experience-based innovation is in principle possible in all sorts of businesses, and is thus spatially neutral. Place is, however, important as a resource in the creation of experience value (Smidt-Jensen and Lorentzen, 2011). Certain places may represent flagship locations for marketing and sales of experience products and services. Places may also enhance the experience value of products or services by providing them with a narrative of the place, as in the case of Swiss watches (Kebir and Crevoisier, 2008) or regional food. Places as such, both urban and rural, may also represent an experientially valuable landscape for guests and citizens. Experiential value can, for example, be created in places such as old industrial buildings, harbour fronts, gravel pits or old farmhouses that are leftovers from earlier economic paradigms.

Experience-based industries are industries in which the experience content of the good or service is particularly strong, such as tourism. They tend to concentrate in big cities and traditional tourism areas. This is true for attendance-based experience offerings (Smidt-Jensen et al., 2009), but even more so in the footloose experience industries such as film production (Scott, 2002).

With the title 'The cultural economy of cities' Scott (1997) indicated the locational implications of the culture economy. Cities, and in particular big cities like Los Angeles and Paris, play a privileged role (Scott, 1997, p. 324). The role of cities in the culture economy is, on the one hand, an implication of localized cluster dynamics. Analysing data from 66 metropolitan areas (including both highly urbanized and less urbanized areas) in the USA, Scott finds a location quotient of 1.75 or more of cultural industries (Scott, 2010a, p. 116).

On the other hand, the location pattern of the culture economy has got something to do with the cultural assets and competences connected with place. Cultural producers, such as the film industry in Hollywood, draw on a complex web of local cultural assets, which provide the cultural products with distinctiveness. The products in turn create images of the city, on which future rounds of production may draw in a virtuous circle of development, leading to highly profiled phenomena. Place, culture and economy are therefore highly symbiotic, and a number of cities in this way enjoy 'monopoly powers of place' (Scott, 1997, p. 325).

In the creative economy the city is also the turning point. Florida's work deals with cities, most outspokenly in titles like *Who's Your City* (Florida, 2008) and *Cities and the Creative Class* (Florida, 2005). The creative class cluster in large cities and regions offer not only a variety of economic opportunities but also a stimulating environment and amenities for a diversity of lifestyles (Florida, 2004, p. 11). The notion of creative cities has been the focus of much research lately, and most prominently represented in the Handbook of Creative Cities (Andersson et al., 2011). From a historic perspective, Peter Hall shows how not just all cities but in particular the unstable ones have been highly creative through history (Hall, 2000). The linkage between instability and creativity is also dealt with by Hospers (2003). Other works deal more narrowly with the clustering patterns of the cultural and creative industries in big cities in different countries (Cooke and Lazzeretti, 2008).

The spatial perspectives of the three economies, the experience, the culture and the creative economy, are evident. They share the preference for cities but for different reasons. Experience-based innovation is in theory spatially neutral but empirically it concentrates in cities and other places with strong narratives and where the demand for experiences is high. The culture economy is highly urban, due to cluster dynamics and the fame of places. Finally, the creative economy is urban due to preferences of the creative labour force and the importance of diversity.

3.5.6 Policy Implication of the Three Approaches

Politicians looking for new sources of jobs and urban regeneration have to a large extent found their inspiration in the three approaches, the experience, the culture and the creative economies. The notions are used interchangeably, and policies have been equally blurred as shown in the case of Scandinavia by Bille (2012). A more careful analysis of the policy implication would potentially render the policies more effective.

3.5.6.1 Policy implications of the experience economy approach

In the experience economy approach the key factor is the consumer relationship and the key process is the engagement of the consumers as loyal customers by the staging of experiences. The approach thus implies a policy focus on consumption, and the ways in which consumption can be staged effectively. Particular experience industries (media, gastronomy) and places (tourist destinations) are also potential objects of policy. As already at the outset many actors, fields of expertise and facilities can be seen to contribute to the staging of experiences, the experiential perspective calls for integrated approaches and cross-sectorial collaboration (Lorentzen, 2009, 2011).To governments 'the experience discourse became for many a way of summarizing that planning for regional advantage was much more about lifestyle concerns as it was about traditional planning concerns such as efficient housing or adequate housing' (Power, 2009, p.448). This again calls for new alliances and forms of governance in urban development (Albrechts et al., 2003; Brenner, 2004; Healey, 2007).

Power shows how the experience discourse in Sweden became a way to turn the usual focus of planning on infrastructure and adequate housing towards consumer and lifestyle concerns (Power, 2009, p.448). In Denmark the wave of experience-related policies started with the report, *Denmark in the Culture and Experience Economy* (Regeringen, 2003), which defined a broad group of industries as promising growth industries, namely cultural and creative industries plus a few experience industries such as sports and tourism. This report followed a traditional productionist approach, and did not really apply the innovative relational perspective of the experience economy approach. Consumption and lifestyle approaches have instead developed on the local and regional levels. In Denmark a large part of the new municipalities established in 2007 have formulated local development policies informed by experiential approaches (Caspersen, 2009; Krogh and Lorentzen, 2011). They deal with culture offerings, housing quality, leisure and recreation facilities, tourism, environmental protection and so on in a more integrated way. They involve a multiplicity of governance forms, and a great deal of participation from the voluntary sector.

3.5.6.2   Policy implications of the culture economy approach

The commodification, clustering and growth pattern related to the culture economy inspires post-industrial growth policy. The commodification of still more cultural areas, stronger clusters and better promotion of culture products are the inherent strategic focal points of the culture economy approach. The culture economy has had appeal to international, European, national and subnational organizations and governments, as illustrated below.

The OECD published a report in 2005 on the role of culture in local development (OECD, 2005). The recommendations add up to a cluster policy for lagging regions: to develop educations and institution building in the field of culture; to stimulate production and consumption of cultural goods within the territory; to develop entrepreneurship in the field and to forge partnerships between artistic and non-artistic sectors. In a later report on competitive cities culture is discussed as a factor of competitiveness in large cities (OECD, 2006).

The European Commission has also given high priority to culture in the new millennium. The European Commission regards 'the cultural and creative sectors as significant drivers of growth and jobs in Europe, a key source of creativity and innovation, and contributing significantly to social cohesion and wellbeing'.[4] Since 2007 the European Commission has encouraged cultural policies in the member states by different measures. Culture policy is thus seen as one of the ways to enhance the international competitiveness of European regions. Skills and labour mobility, creativity and innovation, and regional development are focal points. The actions taken include a culture programme 2007–13, a European capital of culture programme, European Union culture prizes, artist mobility and so on. In a report from 2008, *The Economy of Culture in Europe* (European Commission, 2008), it is further recommended to implement new digital technologies in the sector and to foster creative educations and creative territories' position in the global competition for talent and investment.

As an example of national-level policies, the Danish strategy *Denmark in the Culture and Experience Economy* is an industrial or cluster policy consisting of three elements: (1) innovation and entrepreneurship; (2) new education and alliances between businesses and culture institutions; and (3) the expansion of commercial culture production (Regeringen, 2003, p.14). Further, the Danish government in 2007 initiated a programme of voluntary four-year culture agreements between groups of municipalities and the ministry.[5] These culture agreements have increasingly been formulated as local development strategies rather than culture strategies in their own right.

The culture economy has spread as a basic idea in the post-industrial policies on all levels of government. The application resonates with the theoretical statements of the culture economy approach (commodification, clustering and growth) except on one important point, namely in relation to place. Strangely enough, policies see the culture economy as a solution to growth problems in lagging regions, a strategy that is not supported by research.

3.5.6.3   Implications for policy of the creative economy approach

Creativity, and factors supposed to stimulate creativity, is the focus of the creative economy, mostly in terms of creative ecosystem, creative class and quality of place. Two lines of policy can be derived from the creative economy theories. One is to stimulate creative industries directly with institutions like incubator houses, education policy or incentives for innovation or export. The other is to focus on the quality of place dimensions with the intention of attracting talented people as labour and creative entrepreneurs to particular regions or cities. National governments and international organizations have followed the first track, while many cities have followed the second track. The UK was pioneering the first track to stimulate institutionally the creative industries with Tony Blair's campaign 'Cool Britannia' in the 1990s (Oakley, 2004). Lately 'Cool Japan' has emerged as a strategy to boost and launch Japanese creative industries internationally (Ministry of Economy, Trade and Industry, 2012). Creative industries were also part of the Danish globalization strategy from 2003 (Regeringen, 2003). In Finland the creative industry focus was on design (Power, 2009, p. 449).

International organizations also formulate policies on creative industries. The European Union has recently launched a support programme for Europe's cultural and creative sectors from 2014. 'Europe needs to invest more in its cultural and creative sectors, because they significantly contribute to economic growth, employment, innovation, and social cohesion.'[6] The new progamme ascribes a key role to cultural creativity in future development. The United Nations system has seen the creative industries as a development tool in the development of developing nations. At the launch of *The Creative Economy Report* (2011) Rebeca Grynspan, the Associate Administrator of the United Nations Development Programme (UNDP), thus told the reporters that 'The report shows that well-nurtured, along with the traditional sectors, the creative economy can be a source of growth, job creation, innovation and trade, at the same time contributing to social inclusion, cultural diversity and sustainable human development.'[7]

Many cities have followed the second track. Cities were reported to compete, to brand themselves, to redevelop run-down urban centres and to develop cultural and entertainment quarters in earlier wharfs and factories in the 1980s (Bianchini, 1993). Studying the examples of Austin, Barcelona and the Scandinavian Ørestad Hospers shows how policy-makers play a part by providing the underlying framework conditions for urban creativity (Hospers, 2003). Today, more cities try to develop themselves as 'cool cities' by using cultural urban planning to introduce positive experiential dimensions in urban space (Markusen and Metris, 2010). The struggle to attract members of the creative class has been extended to small provincial cities, as, for example, in Denmark, where local governments invest in expensive cultural amenities to make them attractive (Lorentzen, 2012a).

Summing up, the three approaches have different foci, namely consumer relationships, commodification and clustering and creative talent and industries, and therefore the strategic implementations are also different. The implications reach from the more holistic staging of the experience economy, over the cluster policy of the culture economy, to the development of urban amenities of the creative economy. Each of the approaches also call for industrial policy directed towards the more narrowly defined experience, culture and creative industries, which are surely not identical, but which overlap statistically.

It has been illustrated how national and international institutions tend to focus on the growth and clustering of industries in the culture and creative economies, while cities and local governments tend to apply holistic experience economy staging and quality of place approaches. In spite of the urban bias of the three approaches, policies too optimistically tend to apply them in lagging regions and small cities as the main driver of industrial transition.

3.5.7 Recent Developments

The three approaches have served as a point of departure for much research, often spurred by strategic governmental research programmes.

The experience economy approach is still being developed and applied in new fields. This is evident in Scandinavia, where research inspired by notions of the experience economy has evolved within different disciplines such as development and planning (Lorentzen, 2009), urban planning (Andersson, 2009), innovation (Sundbo and Darmer, 2008) and design (Jantzen and Vetner, 2007). Not surprisingly, tourism planning and tourism and hospitality research have taken up the concept of the experience economy (Andersson, 2007; Oh et al., 2007). Also retail management has developed research on the retail customer experience (Grewal et al., 2009; Puccinelli et al., 2009; Verhoef et al., 2009). In the field of planning the focus on the experiential qualities of small cities and rural areas is on the rise (Lorentzen, 2012a).

In the culture economy a recent study by Scott (2010b) breaks with the idea that the culture economy is urban, industrial and highly clustered. The formation of distinctive culture economies takes place in peripheral regions as well (Scott, 2010b, p. 1568). The English Lake District as a landscape of consumption is the focus of his recent work (Scott, 2010b). Here the local units of primarily tourist service providers are related in a loose system of interdependency, which Scott labels 'a diffuse cluster' (Scott, 2010b, p. 1573), through which the landscape is transformed into an object of consumption (Scott, 2010b, p. 1576) and of gentrification. Actually, 15.3 million people visited the region in 2008 (Scott, 2010b, p. 1576). This is not the result of new policies. The construction of this region as a landscape of consumption has taken place over almost two centuries.

Recent creative economy research broadens the empirical scope and questions some of the assumptions connected to the creative class thesis. A major new development in the creative economy research is the study of creativity in small cities (Waitt, 2006; Waitt and Gibson, 2009; Lorentzen and van Heur, 2012) and suburbs (ongoing work by Dr Alison Bain). The location preferences of the creative class is discussed, and the creative class is found in rural areas (Nuur and Laestedius, 2009; Scott, 2010b) and peri-urban places (Asheim and Hansen, 2009). The new work thus questions and modifies the role of big cities in the creative economy.

New research therefore expands the scholarly application of the experience economy approach less critically, while research on the culture and creative economies modifies the spatial determinism of the classic contributions.

3.5.8 Problems and Critiques of the Three Approaches

As interesting as they are, the three approaches have their flaws, and to inspire future research and theorizing it is important to consider some of them. The following points of critique may serve as a point of departure.

In the experience economy the focus is on the customer relationships and, in a wider perspective, the potential of increasing hedonistic demand for the economy. The production side is left out, and everything is a matter of staging, and of demand, which invites a Keynesian approach to economic growth. Against this view, Storper and Scott (2009) hold that investment in new jobs is the only road to (regional) growth. Pine and Gilmore's (1999) book is a textbook for managers, and basic assumptions, key concepts and causal relationships need clarification. Further, the contextual factors of the experience economy should be critically assessed. Can any of the observations of successful examples of experience offerings or staging be generalized or are they specific to certain places and conjunctures of high and increasing demand? Finally, if experience value is of general relevance, then how can we explain the success of discount supermarket chains and low cost airlines?

Compared to the experience economy approach the culture economy approach is rather simple and productionist, and it seems to be lacking the insights into consumption and lifestyle factors of the economy provided by the experience and the creative economy approaches. The most evident problem is the empirical definition of what belongs to the culture economy. The broad range of industries suggested implies that few general characteristics can be found in relation to market, technology, labour and so on, and this again makes it less fruitful as a point of departure for theoretical development and policy. Further, it is questionable if the prevailing industrial or sectorial focus is fully able to grasp the economic structure and dynamics of the actual culture production and employment (Markusen, 2010).

The creative economy approach is maybe the most contested of the three. First of all, it is not clear what creativity is, and what aspects of creativity are particularly important for the economy. Creativity is in most cases treated as a 'black box'. In terms of definition of creative industries and creative labour, the boundaries are more than blurred, and it is a question whether most work functions today are connected with creativity, as Taylorized mass production is on the retreat.

Economic geographers have challenged the causal relationship of Florida's creative class thesis (Peck, 2005; Storper and Scott, 2009). Can a localized supply of creative labour spur regional and urban development? And can an attractive urban environment attract creative labour in the first place? Or is it the other way around that productive investment spurs development as Storper and Scott (2009) suggest with an enhancement of place as a pleasant outcome?

3.6 SUMMARY AND CONCLUSION

The three concepts, the experience, culture and creative economies, represent new ways to think about economic opportunities in the post-industrial age. Table 3.1 summarizes and compares the points made throughout the chapter. Each of the approaches provides

Table 3.1   The cultural, the creative and the experience economies compared

	Cultural economy	Creative economy	Experience economy
Focus	Industrial production	Creative industries, creative people	Customer satisfaction
Level of analysis	Macro level, the economy	Meso level, the industry, the economic class	Micro level, the firm, the consumer
Aim	Descriptive	Strategic	Strategic
Key factor	Commodification	Creativity	Customer relationship
Key process	Clustering	Creation/innovation	Experience engagement
Contribution	New industrial pattern	New economic driver, lifestyle and the power of place	Customer relationships, consumption focus, integrated approach
Location	Big cities	Big cities	Spatially neutral
Policy	Cluster policy	Creative class, quality of place, creative industry	Consumer focus, intregrated planning
New development	Rural regions, consumption	Small cities, rural places	Tourism, retail, small cities
Problem	No clear focus	What is creativity?, causal relationship unsolved	Not really new, overoptimistic

interpretations of the paradigmatic shifts of the economy from industrial mass production to something different, combining high income levels with a demand for symbolic
and experiential content. Each of the three approaches also contributes to supplement
the mechanic and rationalistic approaches to innovation, economy and economic development by suggesting that market value is much more than a question of function and
economic optimization.

It has been argued in the chapter that the culture economy is the most traditional of
the approaches, with its focus on industrial production in particular sectors and clusters. The creative economy includes more innovatively the role of labour and the role
of diverse urban places from a consumption perspective, to economic growth in the
globalized knowledge economy. Finally, the experience economy represents the most
innovative approach with its focus on the dynamic development of consumer-provider
relationships and its integrating concept of the staging of consumer experiences. These
ideas have potential and relevance as a strategic frame for innovation for businesses and
local and regional development, and can be taken as a general reminder not to get lost
in biased and overspecialized approaches. This is of course to extend the original micro-
level experience economy ideas quite considerably but, as shown in this chapter, this has
been done already by numerous local governments and by a number of researchers.

This does not mean that the three approaches are without flaws, as shown, but the
major problem is maybe that they have been overoptimistically recommended as development strategies in less favoured regions, where neither a sufficient demand nor the
critical mass of producers is likely to exist. This is not to say that inspiration from the

three approaches cannot be used in less favoured regions, but more basic needs for infrastructure and jobs should not be overlooked.

Regards future research, it does not seem fruitful to continue discussing what the culture industry includes, but it is useful to remember and consider how the capitalist market economy involves the continued commodification of hitherto non-economic fields such as culture. The consumer perspective of place of the creative economy approach enables a holistic approach to place development but also the question of who place development is made for? The creative class is not all there is, and even this class is not well defined. The experiential approach entails a richness of research inspiration from the micro level to the macro level, such as, for example, experience design, communication and branding, organization and cooperation in relation to experience staging, trends in consumer preferences and behaviour, and consumers as co-producers and resources for innovation. Turning the focus to the experiential consumption process has the potential for triggering new insights in a broad range of fields.

NOTES

1. http://da.wikipedia.org/wiki/Disneyland_Park_Californien (accessed 12 November 2012).
2. http://www.wipo.int/ip-development/en/creative_industry/bibliography.html (accessed 22 April 2013).
3. UNESCO has creative and cultural industries as a focal point, see http://portal.unesco.org/culture/en/ev.php-URL_ID=35024&URL_DO=DO_TOPIC&URL_SECTION=201.html, http://www.unesco.org/new/en/culture/resources/ and http://www.unesco.org/new/?id=47779 (accessed 22 April 2013).
4. European Commission, http://ec.europa.eu/culture/our-policy-development/eurostat-essnet-culture_en.htm (accessed 29 May 2012).
5. 'Bekendtgørelse af lov om Kulturministeriets kulturaftaler med kommuner m.v. om regioners opgaver på kulturområde', https://www.retsinformation.dk/forms/r0710.aspx?id=12061 (accessed 22 April 2013).
6. European Commission, *Creative Europe: Support Programme for Europe's Cultural and Creative Sectors from 2014*, http://ec.europa.eu/culture/creative-europe/ (accessed June 2012).
7. UN News Center, http://www.un.org/apps/news/story.asp?NewsID=37948&Cr=economic&Cr1=development (accessed 1 June 2012).

BIBLIOGRAPHY

Abbott, L. (1955), *Quality and competition*, New York: Columbia University Press.
Albrechts, L., P. Healey and K. Kunzmann (2003), 'Strategic spatial planning and regional governance in Europe', *Journal of the American Planning Association*, **69** (2), 113–29.
Andersson, D.E., Å.E. Andersson and C. Mellander (eds) (2011), *Handbook of Creative Cities*, Cheltenham, UK and Northampton, MA, USA: Edward Elgar.
Andersson, L. (2009), *Byen og de kreative iværksættere (The City and the Creative Entrepreneurs)*, Aalborg: Institut for Arkitektur og Design, Aalborg Universitet.
Andersson, T.D. (2007), 'The tourist in the experience economy', *Scandinavian Journal of Hospitality and Tourism*, 7 (1), 46–58.
Asheim, B. and H.K. Hansen (2009), 'Knowledge bases, talents and contexts: on the usefulness of the creative class approach in Sweden', *Economic Geography*, **85** (4), 425–42.
Audretsch, D.B. and A.R. Thurik (2001), 'What is new about the new economy? Sources of growth in the managed and entrepreneurial economics', *Industrial and Corporate Change*, **10** (1), 267–315.
Bianchini, F. (1993), 'Remaking European cities: the role of cultural policies', in F. Bianchini and M. Parkinson (eds), *Culture Policy and Urban Regeneration*, Manchester: Manchester University Press, pp. 1–20.
Bille, T. (2012), 'The Scandinavian approach to the experience economy – does it make sense?', *International Journal of Culture Policy*, **18** (1), 93–110.

Boswijk, A., E. Peelen and T. Thijssen (2007), *The Experience Economy: A New Perspective*, Amsterdam: Pearson Education Benelux.

Bourdieu, P. (1984), 'The market of symbolic goods', in P. Bourdieu (ed.), *The Field of Cultural Production: Essays on Art and Literature*, New York: Columbia University Press, pp. 1–34.

Brenner, N. (2004), 'Urban governance and the production of new state spaces in Western Europe 1960–2000', *Review of International Political Economy*, **11** (3), 447–88.

Caspersen, O.H. (2009), 'Evaluering af kommuneplanstrategier Notat 2: Screening af planstrategier' ('Evaluation of municipal strategies: memorandum 2'), Københavns Universitet, Frederiksberg.

Caves, R.E. (2000), *Creative Industries: Contracts between Art and Commerce*, Boston, MA: Harvard University Press.

Cooke, P. and L. Lazzeretti (eds) (2008), *Creative Cities, Cultural Clusters and Local Economic Development*, Cheltenham, UK and Northampton, MA, USA: Edward Elgar.

Corolleur, F. and C. Courlet (2003), 'The Marshallian industrial district, an organizational and institutional answer to uncertainty', *Entrepreneurship and Regional Development*, **15** (4), 299–307.

De Gay, P. and M. Pryke (2002), *Cultural Economy*, London, Thousand Oaks, CA and New Delhi: Sage, 2nd edition 2006.

Drucker, P.F. (1992), *The Age of Discontinuity*, Princeton, NJ: Transaction Publishers.

European Commission (2008), *The Economy of Culture in Europe*, European Commission, available at http://ec.europa.eu/culture/key-documents/doc873_en.htm (accessed 9 August 2012).

Florida, R. (2002), *The Rise of the Creative Class*, New York: Basic Books.

Florida, R. (2004), *The Rise of the Creative Class*, Paperback edition, New York: Basic Books.

Florida, R. (2005), *Cities and the Creative Class*, New York and Abingdon, UK: Routledge.

Florida, R. (2007), *The Flight of the Creative Class*, New York: Collins.

Florida, R. (2008), *Who's Your City?*, New York: Basic Books.

Gibson, C. and L. Kong (2005), 'Cultural economy: a critical review', *Progress in Human Geography*, **29** (1), 541–61.

Gilmore, J.H. and J.B. Pine (2007), *Authenticity: What Consumers Really Want*, Boston, MA: Harvard Business School Press.

Grewal, D., M. Levy and V. Kumar (2009), 'Customer experience management in retailing: an organization framework', *Journal of Retailing*, **85** (1), 1–14.

Hall, P. (2000), 'Creative cities and economic development', *Urban Studies*, **37** (4), 639–49.

Hansen, H.K. and L. Winther (2012), 'On a road to nowhere: a comment on amenities and urban and regional development', in A. Lorentzen and B. van Heur (eds), *Cultural Political Economy of Small Cities*, New York and Abingdon, UK: Routledge, pp. 31–43.

Harvey, D. (1990), *The Conditions of Postmodernity: An Enquiry into the Origins of Cultural Change*, Cambridge, MA and Oxford: Blackwell.

Harvey, D. (2002), 'The art of rent: globalisation, monopoly and the commodification of culture', *The Socialist Register*, **3**, 93–110, available at http://socialistregister.com/index.php/srv/issue/view/439 (accessed 9 August 2012).

Healey, P. (2007), *Urban Complexity and Spatial Strategies*, Abingdon, UK and New York: Routledge.

Holbrook, M.B. (2000), 'The millenial consumer in the texts of our times: experience and entertainment', *Journal of Macromarketing*, **20** (2), 178–92.

Holbrook, M.B. (2006), 'Consumption experience, customer value, and subjective personal introspection: an illustrative photography essay', *Journal of Business Research*, **59** (6), 714–25.

Holbrook, M.B. and E.C. Hirschman (1982), 'The experiential aspects of consumption: consumer fantasies, feelings and fun', *Journal of Consumer Research*, **9** (2), 132–40.

Hollingsworth, R.J. and R. Boyer (1997), *Contemporary Capitalism: The Embeddedness of Institutions*, Cambridge and New York: Cambridge University Press.

Hospers, G.J. (2003), 'Creative cities: breeding places in the knowledge economy', *Knowledge, Technology and Policy*, **16** (3), 143–62.

Howkins, J. (2001), *The Creative Economy: How People Make Money from Ideas*, London: Penguin Group, reprinted in 2002, London: Penguin Press.

Jantzen, C. and M. Vetner (2007), 'Design for en affectiv økonomi' ('Design for an affective economy'), in C. Jantzen and T. Rasmussen (eds), *Oplevelsesøkonomi: Vinkler på forbrug (Experience Economy: Perspectives on Consumption)*, Aalborg: Aalborg Universitetsforlag, pp. 201–18.

Jensen, R. (1999), *Dream Society*, Columbus, OH: McGraw-Hill, reprinted in 2006, København: Børsens Forlag.

Kebir, L. and O. Crevoisier (2008), 'Cultural resources and regional development: the case of the cultural legacy of watch making', *European Planning Studies*, **16** (9), 1189–205.

Krogh, R. and A. Lorentzen (2011), 'De nye kommuner og oplevelsesøkonomien' ('The new municipalities and the experience economy'), in A. Lorentzen and S. Smidt-Jensen (eds), *Planlægning i oplevelsessamfundet (Planning in the Experience Society)*, Aarhus: Aarhus Universitetsforlag, pp. 165–90.

Landes, D.S. (1969), *Unbound Prometheus: Technological Change and Industrial Development in Western Europe from 1750 to the Present*, London: Cambridge University Press.

Lash, S. and J. Urry (1994), *Economies of Signs and Space*, London: Sage.

Lebergott, S. (1993), *Pursuing Happiness: American Consumers in the Twentieth Century*, Princeton, NJ and Chichester, UK: Princeton University Press.

Leriche, F. and S. Daviet (2010), 'Cultural economy: an opportunity to boost employment and regional development?', *Regional Studies*, **44** (7), 807–11.

Lorentzen, A. (2009), 'Cities in the experience economy', *European Planning Studies*, **17** (2), 829–45.

Lorentzen, A. (2011), 'Lokaludvikling i oplevelsessamfundet (Local development in the experience society)', in A. Lorentzen and S. Smidt-Jensen (eds), *Planlægning i oplevelsessamfundet (Planning in the experience society)*, Aarhus: Aarhus Universitetsforlag, pp. 35–62.

Lorentzen, A. (2012a), 'Sustaining small cities through leisure, culture and the experience economy', in A. Lorentzen and B. van Heur (eds), *Cultural Political Economy of Small Cities*, Abingdon, UK and New York: Routledge, pp. 65–79.

Lorentzen, A. (2012b), 'The development of the periphery in the experience economy', in M. Danson and P. de Souza (eds), *Peripherality, Marginality and Border Issues in Northern Europe*, Abingdon, UK and New York: Routledge, pp. 16–29.

Lorentzen, A. and H. Jeannerat (2013), 'Urban and regional studies in the experience economy: what kind of turn?', *European Urban and Regional Studies*, forthcoming.

Lorentzen, A. and B. van Heur (eds) (2012), *Cultural Political Economy of Small Cities*, Abingdon, UK and New York: Routledge.

Lund, J.M., A.P. Nielsen, L. Goldschmidt and T. Martinsen (2005), *Følelsesfabrikken: Oplevelsesøkonomi på Dansk (The Emotions Factory: Experience Economy in Danish)*, København: Børsens Forlag.

Markusen, A. (2010), 'Organizational complexity in the regional cultural economy', *Regional Studies*, **44** (7), 813–28.

Markusen, A. and A.G. Metris (2010), 'Arts and culture in urban and regional planning: a review and a research agenda', *Journal of Planning Education and Research*, **29** (9), 379–91.

Ministry of Economy, Trade and Industry (2012), *Cool Japan Strategy*, Tokyo: Creative Industries Division. Ministry of Economy, Trade and Industry, available at http://www.meti.go.jp/english/policy/mono_info_service/creative_industries/pdf/120116_01a.pdf (accessed 9 August 2012).

Newbegin, J. (2010), *The Creative Economy: An Introductory Guide*, London: British Council, Creative and Cultural Economy series 1, available at http://creativeconomy.britishcouncil.org/media/uploads/resources/GuideToolkit_30_withCover_LR.pdf (accessed 9 August 2012).

Nuur, C. and S. Laestedius (2009), 'Is the creative class necessarily urban? Putting the creativity thesis in the context of non-urbanised regions in industrialised nations', *European Journal of Spatial Development*, June, 1–12.

Oakley, K. (2004), 'Not so cool Britannia: the role of the creative industries in economic development', *International Journal of Cultural Studies*, **7** (1), 67–77.

OECD (2005), *Culture and Local Development*, Paris: OECD.

OECD (2006), *OECD Territorial Reviews: Competitive Cities in the Global Economy*, Paris: OECD, available at http://www.oecd.org/gov/oecdterritorialreviewscompetitivecitiesintheglobaleconomy.htm (accessed 10 December 2012).

Oh, H., A.M. Fiore and M. Jeoung (2007), 'Measuring experience economy concepts: tourist applications', *Journal of Travel Research*, **46** (2), 119–32.

Peck, J. (2005), 'Struggling with the creative class', *International Journal of Urban and Regional Research*, **29** (4), 740–70.

Pine II, J.B. and J.H. Gilmore (1998), 'Welcome to the experience economy', *Harvard Business Review*, July–August, 97–103.

Pine II, J.B. and J.H. Gilmore (1999), *The Experience Economy*, Boston, MA: Harvard Business School Press.

Pine II, J.B. and J.H. Gilmore (2011), *The Experience Economy*, Boston, MA: Harvard Business School Press.

Power, D. (2009), 'Culture, creativity and experience in Nordic and Scandinavian cultural policy', *International Journal of Cultural Policy*, **15** (4), 445–60.

Pratt, A.C. (1997), 'The cultural industries' production system: a case study of employment change in Britain 1984–91', *Environment and Planning A*, **29** (11), 1953–74.

Pratt, A.C. (2004), 'Mapping the cultural industries', in D. Power and A.J. Scott (eds), *Cultural Industries and the Production of Culture*, Abingdon, UK: Routledge, pp. 19–36.

Puccinelli, N.M., R.C. Goodstein, D. Grewal, R. Price, P. Raghubir and D. Stewart (2009), 'Customer experience management in retailing: understanding the buying process', *Journal of Retailing*, **85** (1) 15–30.

Regeringen (2003), *Danmark i kultur og oplevelsesøkonomien – 5 nye skridt på vejen. Vækst med vilje (Denmark in the Culture and Experience Economy: 5 New Steps Forward)*, Regeringen.

Rutten, R. (2003), *Knowledge and Innovation in Regional Industries*, Abingdon, UK and New York: Routledge.

Schmitt, B. (2003), *Customer Experience Management*, New York: Free Press.
Schmitt, B.H. (1999), *Experiential Marketing: How to Get Customers to Sense, Feel, Think, Act and Relate to Your Company and Brands*, New York: Free Press.
Schmitt, B.H. and D.L. Rogers (2006), *Handbook of Brand and Experience Management*, Cheltenham, UK and Northampton, MA, USA: Edward Elgar.
Schulze, G. (1992), *Die Erlebnisgesellschaft* (*The Experience Society*), Frankfurt am Main: Campus Verlag, 2nd edition 2005.
Scott, A.J. (1997), 'The cultural economy of cities', *International Journal of Urban and Regional Research*, **21** (2), 323–39.
Scott, A.J. (2000), *The Cultural Economy of Cities: Essays on the Geography of Image-producing Industries*, London: Sage.
Scott, A.J. (2001), 'Capitalism, cities and the production of symbolic forms', *Transactions of the Institute of British Geographers*, **26** (1), 11–23.
Scott, A.J. (2002), 'A new map of Hollywood: the production and distribution of American motion pictures', *Regional Studies*, **36** (9), 957–75.
Scott, A.J. (2007), 'Capitalism and urbanism in a new key? The cognitive-cultural dimension', *Social Forces*, **85** (4), 1465–82.
Scott, A.J. (2008), 'Cultural economy: retrospect and prospect', in H. Anheier and Y.R. Isaar (eds), *The Cultural Economy*, London: Sage, pp. 307–23.
Scott, A.J. (2010a), 'Cultural economy and the creative field of the city', *Geografiska Annaler: Series B, Human Geography*, **92** (2), 115–30.
Scott, A.J. (2010b), 'The cultural economy of landscape and prospects for peripheral development in the twenty first century: the case of the English Lake District', *European Planning Studies*, **18** (10), 1567–89.
Smidt-Jensen, S. (2012), 'Making a micropole: the experiensation of Vejle', in A. Lorentzen and B. van Heur (eds), *Cultural Political Economy of Small Cities*, Abingdon, UK and New York: Routledge, pp. 113–27.
Smidt-Jensen, S. and A. Lorentzen (2011), 'Planlægning i oplevelsessamfundet: Indledning' ('Planning in the experience society: introduction'), in A. Lorentzen and S. Smidt-Jensen (eds), *Planlægning i oplevelsessamfundet* (*Planning in the Experience Society*), Aarhus: Aarhus Universitetsforlag, pp. 7–31.
Smidt-Jensen, S., C.B. Skytt and L. Winther (2009), 'The geography of the experience economy in Denmark: employment change and location dynamics in attendance-based experience industries', *European Planning Studies*, **17** (6), 847–62.
Smith, A. (1776), *An Enquiry into the Nature and Causes of the Wealth of Nations*, London: Printed for W. Strahan and T. Cadell in the Strand, MDCCLXXVI, available at http://books.google.dk/books?id=lYNaAAAAY AAJ&printsec=frontcover&dq=adam+smith+wealth+of+nations+1776&hl=da&sa=X&ei=DkV1Ub-oBoi5O_jSgVA&ved=0CDYQuwUwATgK#v=onepage&q&f=false, reprinted in 2001, *Wealth of Nations* London: The Electric Book Company, available at http://site.ebrary.com/lib/aalboruniv/docDetail. action?docID=2001574 (accessed 22 April 2013).
Stamboulis, Y. and P. Skayannis (2003), 'Innovation strategies and technology for experience-based tourism', *Tourism Management*, **24** (1), 35–43.
Storper, M. and A.J. Scott (2009), 'Rethinking human capital, creativity and urban growth', *Journal of Economic Geography*, **9** (2), 147–67.
Sundbo, J. and P. Darmer (2008), *Creating Experiences in the Experience Economy*, Cheltenham, UK and Northampton, MA, USA: Edward Elgar.
Toffler, A. (1970), *Future Shock*, New York: Bantam Books.
UNCTAD (2010), *Creative Economy Report 2010*, available at http://unctad.org/en/docs/ditctab20103_en.pdf (accessed 10 August 2012).
UNESCO (2003), *Culture, Trade, Globalization*, available at http://unesdoc.unesco.org/images/0012/001213/121360e.pdf (accessed 10 August 2012).
Urry, J. (1995), *Consuming Places*, London: Routledge.
Verhoef, P.C., K.N. Lemon, A. Parasuraman, A. Roggeveen, M. Tsiros and L.A. Schlesinger (2009), 'Customer experience creation: determinants, dynamics and management strategies', *Journal of Retailing*, **85** (1), 31–41.
Waitt, G. (2006), 'Creative small cities: cityscapes, power and the arts', in D. Bell and M. Jayne (eds), *Small Cities: Urban Experience Beyond the Metropolis*, Abingdon, UK: Routledge, pp. 169–83.
Waitt, G. and C. Gibson (2009), 'Creative small cities: rethinking the creative economy in place', *Urban Studies*, **46** (5–6), 1223–46.
Zukin, S. (1995), *The Cultures of Cities*, Cambridge, MA: Blackwell

4. Defining and categorizing experience industries
Berit T. Nilsen and Britt E. Dale

4.1 INTRODUCTION

This chapter discusses various challenges concerning the definition and categorization of experience industries. To shed light on the various challenges regarding different aspects of this classification, the discussion is seen in the light of a long-standing debate regarding how to define and categorize service industries. We also ask whether experiences should be seen as a subclass of the services or whether they have sufficiently strong characteristics to justifying treatment of them as a separate economic sector.

Although a new and not yet clearly demarcated interdisciplinary field of research, the concept of 'experience industries' has drawn much attention in the last 10–15 years. Although theories relating to experience industries have not been fully developed, for many Scandinavian politicians such industries are at the centre of attention with regard to regional and rural development (Bille and Lorenzen, 2008; Lorentzen, 2009; Lorentzen and Hansen, 2009; Smidt-Jensen et al., 2009; Freire-Gibb, 2011; Bille, 2012) and clearly related to contemporary consumer trends (Lorentzen and Hansen, 2009). Lund et al. (2005, pp. 25–7) identify as many as eight prominent perspectives on the experience economy in the Danish context. Especially in Denmark the concept of the experience economy has become highly influential in local economic development policy and among academics, although recently more critical voices have been heard (Freire-Gibb, 2011; Bille, 2012). In order to gain a better understanding of the characteristics, possibilities and challenges of experience industries, it is necessary to develop a better definition and categorization of them than exists at present.

In our view a necessary starting point is to separate the 'experience economy' and 'experience industries' – two concepts that are often conflated in the literature. The experience economy should be seen as a broad general process in the economy, where integration of experiences can create increased value to all kinds of goods and services in what could be labelled the secondary experience sector. By contrast, experience industries should be delimited to economic activities where experience is the main product, that is, the 'primary experience sector' (Sundbo and Sørensen, Chapter 1, this volume). This is also in accordance with Nielsen's (2004, p. 8) claim: 'the term "experience economy" refers to society in general, while "experience industry" covers a limited number of industries'. In this chapter, we use the word 'experiences' to refer to experiences as economic activities or industries. This is parallel to the concept of 'services' used as shorthand for service industries. We consider the term 'experience sector' to be a common denominator for experience industries, even though it is open to debate whether it is possible to delimit such a sector.

Currently, experience industries are barely represented as a separate category in the Nomenclature statistique des Activités économiques dans la Communauté Européenne (NACE) system (discussed further in Section 4.4), which is a classification system used by both the European Union (EU) and member countries of the Schengen Area. This makes it difficult to comment on the scope and development of the industries. Also, within academia there is lack of agreement on the definition and categorization of experience industries. Commonly, references are made to how experience industries are not clearly demarcated, but at the same time without anyone really attempting to go thoroughly enough into the matter. To define and categorize experience industries requires knowledge of not only the industries themselves but also classification and hence an understanding of the principles of typology and taxonomy, or what can be termed 'definition' and 'categorization', respectively. As stressed by Salamon and Anheier (1997, p. 81), classification is not always prioritized in research:

> Classification efforts . . . often get short shrift in the development of new bodies of knowledge. It is, after all, somewhat dry work, lacking the drama of new empirical discoveries. Yet the importance of such work to our understanding cannot be overemphasized. Classification is the crucial prerequisite for scientific progress in any field of study.

The discussion of how to classify experience industries has strong parallels with the discussion of the definition of art and culture, an issue that has been long debated (Bille, 2012). Also, it has clear parallels to the discussion of how to define and categorize service industries, which reached a peak in the 1980s and 1990s and is drawn on in this chapter. One outcome of that discussion has been that the distinction between goods and services is becoming increasingly blurred. We demonstrate that this is also the case for the distinction between services and experiences. Thus, we strongly disagree with Pine and Gilmore's (1998, p. 97) statement: 'Economists have typically lumped experiences in with services, but experiences are a distinctive economic offering, as different from services as services are from goods.' Instead, we believe that, in common with services and goods, experiences and services have commonalities and therefore defining and categorizing experience industries is not a straightforward task.

The chapter is organized as follows. After a section discussing the principles of classification, we discuss the various definitions of service industries and experience industries and then compare the two types of industries. Thereafter, we discuss various options with regards to experience industries, namely avoiding the use of the concept, making do with existing statistics or attempting to classify the industries. We conclude the chapter with a summary of our discussions.

4.2   CLASSIFICATION: TYPOLOGY (DEFINITION) AND TAXONOMY (CATEGORIZATION)

Societies are constantly changing, and at all times scholars have tried to denote and describe society, as well as label its most readily apparent and dominant traits. However, it is not an easy task to tidy up the usually 'messy' reality with which we surround ourselves. In politics and research, classification is used extensively to group elements with common traits, as well as to distinguish between elements considered to differ in one or more central aspects (Bowker and Star, 1999). However, classification can be a matter of dispute, as expressed by Bowker and Star (1999, p. 6):

Assigning things, people, or their actions to categories is a ubiquitous part of work in the modern, bureaucratic state. Categories in this sense arise from work and from other kinds of organized activity, including the conflicts over meaning that occur when multiple groups fight over the nature of a classification system and its categories.

Although it may be extreme to talk of groups 'fighting' to categorize and define experience industries, there is nonetheless a lack of consensus regarding the issue. Economic activities that are to be presented in the form of statistics require systematic classification (Salamon and Anheier, 1997; Statistics Norway, 2008) and at some point consensus ought to be reached in this regard. Although classification is a foundation of all research, including the social sciences, the principles of classification are seldom discussed, perhaps because of their embeddedness in research practices (Bailey, 1994). Classification is essential but at the same time difficult, as no system of classification will fit all purposes (Salamon and Anheier, 1997). Classifying experience industries undoubtedly faces many of the same challenges or problems as the classification of other industries, albeit with different ones as well.

Bailey (1994, pp. 12–16) lists both the advantages and disadvantages of classification, some of which are highly relevant with regard to experience industries. One advantage is the mere descriptive qualities that classification can provide. Currently, there is no general agreement on the scope of experience industries. A second advantage is the reduction in complexity, as one of the central aspects of classification is that of presenting a disordered reality in an orderly manner. Third, identifying both similarities and differences in relation to other sectors and industries can be a useful aspect of classification. Bailey's critique of classification points out that classification is either descriptive, pre-explanatory or non-explanatory, where the latter two can be potentially problematic in a research context. In addition, Bailey mentions reification as a potential challenge if theoretical constructs that do not exist empirically are treated as real empirical entities. Further, the fact that classification is static rather than dynamic can be an objection to classification efforts.

Industrial classification concerns identifying systematic differences among the various businesses in a demarcated sector and grouping them in a sensible manner (Salamon and Anheier, 1997). In general, classification can be divided into two types of approaches: typology and taxonomy (Bailey, 1994). Typology deals with conceptual matters, or what we have termed 'definition', and taxonomy deals with empirical matters, or what we have termed 'categorization'. In the case of defining and categorizing experience industries, it is clear that both need to be considered as there is a need for both an operational definition and operational units categorized in a sensible manner.

4.2.1 Principles of Definition

It hardly feels like a choice *if* we ought to argue for a common definition of the experience industries or not. Agreeing on the content of central concepts is essential in science. Salamon and Anheier (1992, p. 127) very clearly articulate the central position of analytical concepts: 'The existence of analytical concepts is thus not a matter of choice: it is the *sine qua non* of all understanding.' Hence, by discussing how to define experience industries we are engaging in an ongoing debate in the research field. According to

Smidt-Jensen et al. (2009) most academic literature on the subject of experience industries revolves around conceptualizations of the term. Some of the debates are referred to in this chapter, but first we discuss concepts more generally.

Bal (2002) sees a concept as different from a word in that a concept can be seen as a miniature theory able to serve as a tool in an analysis. According to her, concepts are not objective representations and their intersubjective understandings ought always to be thoroughly defined. However, the process of defining is not a simple task because concepts are not fixed and stable entities but flexible and usually related to many disciplinary traditions, as in the case of experience industries. Bailey (1994) reminds us of the point of locating the fundamental or defining characteristics of a phenomenon in order to be able to conceptualize it. A further elaboration of the importance of definition is presented by Markusen (2003), who discusses what she calls 'fuzzy concepts'. She defines a fuzzy concept as: 'one which posits an entity, phenomenon or process which possesses two or more alternative meanings and thus cannot be reliably identified or applied by different readers or scholars' (Markusen, 2003, p. 702). She demonstrates that in literature framed by fuzzy concepts researchers may believe they are addressing the same phenomena but may actually be targeting quite different ones.

Although Bal (2002) points out that concepts are debatable and that these debates also can be very fruitful, she seems to agree with Markusen's (2003) claim that to have a constructive discussion; there must be agreement on the meaning of central concepts to some extent, both with regards to how the concepts are used and what they contain. Bal (2002) further claims that if a concept is to be used as a methodological tool, it is vital that the concept and the object being examined are confronted with each other and re-examined, as both are likely to change. First, it is necessary to clarify what is meant by a concept, before examining its relationship to what it is supposed to explain or represent, before the concept then is re-examined. Bal also points out that, in addition to merely developing, concepts also travel. They travel in time and space, between and within disciplines, and in the case of a given concept various contexts and authors will add or subtract value and content (Bal, 2002).

4.2.2   Principles of Categorization

According to Bailey (1994, p. 6), taxonomies are often both hierarchical and evolutionary, and like 'classification', 'the term taxonomy can refer to both the process and the end result'. There are standards for categorizing economic activities on several levels worldwide. NACE is a standard for classifying economic activity. It is common to all European countries and renders statistics comparable between European countries on all levels (Statistics Norway, 2008). The USA, Canada and Mexico use a six-digit classification code called North American Industry Classification System (NAICS) (Walker and Murphy, 2001), where the two top levels are comparable between the different systems used worldwide. However, high-level categories are heterogeneous and to locate more homogeneous categories one must look to the lower hierarchical levels (Illeris, 2007).

Perhaps the most important reason to classify the world is to simplify it. Very often, we operate with mutually exclusive categories, which imply that no element can belong to more than one category at a time. Also, a general principle is that of 'exhaustive categories', which means that each entity in an entire population under study will fall into at least one category (Bailey, 1994; Statistics Norway, 2008). Furthermore, the use of categories encourages us to concentrate on the similarities within a category – as well as the differences between the categories: 'By maximizing both within-group homogeneity and between-group heterogeneity, we make groups that are as distinct (non-overlapping) as possible, with all members within a group being as alike as possible' (Bailey, 1994, p. 1). Despite this, the fact that such tidy categories are supposed to represent chaotic realities is perhaps not sufficiently reflected upon.

Research on social categories has shown that shortly after a category becomes generally accepted and applied it will appear to be 'natural' and at some point we will stop questioning its construction (for example, Butler, 2001). But at the moment of creation, a new category's man-made origin will be blatant and trigger an urge to question its objectivity and 'naturalness'.

4.3 DEFINING AND COMPARING SERVICE AND EXPERIENCE INDUSTRIES

As mentioned in the introduction to this chapter, Pine and Gilmore (1998) make a sharp distinction between goods, services and experiences, seeing them as separate categories of economic offering based on separate and clear-cut definitions. In the following, we first give a brief review of how services have been defined and discuss the distinction between goods and services. We emphasize consumer services, that is, services directed towards individuals and households, not producer services (directed towards firms and other organizations), because only the former is relevant regarding experience industries. Second, we present a review of experiences, followed by a discussion of experiences compared to services. We show that it is not easy to find a general and satisfactory definition of either services or experience industries that does not include overlapping characteristics.

4.3.1 What Characterizes Services?

The conventional definition of services has evolved through practice and custom over the course of several hundred years (Marshall and Wood, 1995) and is based on a view of farming, mining and manufacturing as the basic economic activities. Originally, services were seen as 'residual', as the kind of economic activities that do not produce or modify material goods. This definition is still applied in public statistics, for example, NACE. As the service sector covers 70–80 per cent of all economic activity today, such a negative definition – focusing on what the services are not – is unsatisfactory.

Most suggestions of positive service definitions emphasize that a typical service consists of a relation between service producers and consumers and demands the simultaneous presence of producer and consumer, as services are often produced and consumed simultaneously. Services often require active participation by the consumer if they are to have an effect, as in the case of education. Furthermore, a service is non-material and cannot be stored. Traditionally it has therefore been assumed that a typical service has only use value, not exchange value (Illeris, 1989) and hence the service sector was perceived as unproductive and 'parasitic'. This is no longer the predominant view.

Most traditional definitions of services separate them from goods and in this sense they are in accordance with Pine and Gilmore's (1998) statement of a fundamental distinction between goods and services. However, it has become increasingly clear that the traditional characteristics of services have many exceptions, making them less and less separable from goods. Much of the service provision that formerly demanded face-to-face contact has become space-time independent due to new technology (for example, e-banking, Internet trade, distance education and various kinds of Internet-based information and entertainment services). In all cases, service has become materialized as a good (for example, PCs, tablet computers and DVDs), in other words, the good has become a service carrier (Selstad and Hagen, 1991). Thus, service has become both less intangible and ephemeral; it can be repeated and seen or heard as often as we want to. This blurring of the categories goods and services has been observed in the service literature since the late 1970s, and even Pine and Gilmore (1999, p. 8) mention that 'the line between goods and services can be blurry'. However, in contrast to most contemporary service researchers, they see the blurred cases as only minor exceptions.

Further, the difference between goods and services has become less distinct due to the increased tendency for products to consist of a good as well as a service; they are 'joint products' (Walker, 1985). Although some service input has always been needed to produce goods and vice versa, in recent decades the amount of service input in the production of goods has increased (for example, research and development (R&D), information and communications technology (ICT) solutions and marketing) and today it typically represents 70–80 per cent of total costs (Illeris, 2007). Conversely, material products are very often an integrated part of service products. Services support goods production and vice versa – they are complementary. Hence, the current economy should be seen as a complex and interdependent system of the production of goods and services (and experiences), a perspective that stands in sharp contrast to the view expressed by Pine and Gilmore (1998) quoted above.

Due to the scope, heterogeneity and blurriness of the service sector, it is challenging to find a satisfactory and generally accepted definition of services (Dale, 1994; Marshall and Wood, 1995; Illeris, 1996, 2007) and there is a huge body of research stating that service is typically a chaotic conception (Sayer, 1992) or fuzzy concept (Markusen, 2003) with diverse and multifaceted content. There have been innumerable attempts to provide a more up-to-date definition of services, but even the best-recognized attempts have produced either very complicated or too wide definitions that are difficult to apply (Illeris, 2007). An example of a wide definition has been made by Miles (1993, p. 656), who states that services are 'those industries which effect transformations in the state of material goods, people themselves, or symbolic (information)'. As we show in the next section, this definition can be seen as also covering experiences.

4.3.2   What Characterize Experiences?

When discussing experience industries – a term introduced by Toffler (1970) – we emphasize that it differs from the concept of the experience economy, which is Pine and Gilmore's (1998, p. 97) main concern. As mentioned above, experience industries can be understood as including only primary experience providers (Sundbo and Sørensen, Chapter 1, this volume) and therefore it ought to be possible to demarcate and categorize such industries. By contrast, the experience economy is rather referring to a megatrend that is indicative of a general societal development (Nielsen, 2004; Sundbo and Bærenholdt, 2007). The distinction between the two concepts is therefore crucial.

Most definitions of experience industries include a statement to the effect that they are industries where the actual experience is the main product. However, such definitions are not very productive because they do not contextualize or specify the nature of either an experience or an industry. In order to find a productive and functioning definition of experience industries, it is necessary on some level either to agree on what Bailey (1994) refers to as 'the fundamental characteristics' or to choose a path that Thomsen (2012) suggests of 'thinking in difference' rather than looking for the underlying essence. Thomsen's thoughts are rooted in post-structuralist thinking, where no such essence is thought to exist. We choose to gain inspiration from the idea, without pursuing the post-structuralist thinking any further.

Finding a general definition of a commercial experience is challenging, as it is not readily apparent why one product is an experience product and another is not. Where should we draw the line concerning what to label an experience product and what can be regarded as not having some sort of experience value for the consumer? Can a good in itself represent an experience, or only immaterial and ephemeral products? With regard to the latter, we face exactly the same problem as mentioned in our discussion on services versus goods, demonstrating that the boundary between experiences and goods can also be unclear. In the same way as with services, experiences can be materialized into a good, such as video game consoles and smart phones. The 'footloose' experience products (Lorentzen, 2009), that is, the kind of experience products that are sent to the market over long distances, are heavily dependent on such material 'experience carriers'. However, place-bound experience products such as festivals, wilderness tourism and theme parks are also facilitated by a range of material goods.

A possible starting point for localizing the essence of experience industries could be to accept that an anticipated experience is the reason for a purchase. Although the facilitation of a 'product' usually involves material components, in this context it is important to emphasize that the experience *is* the product, however non-material and ephemeral. As already mentioned, the focus of this chapter is on experiences as an economic activity or industry, and here we are talking about out-of-the-ordinary, paid for commercialized experiences. Consuming an experience is about creating a state of internal pleasure or well-being, either through an increase or decrease in stimuli or, as Lund et al. (2005) formulate it, through the production of emotions. The production can take many different forms, corresponding to a great variety of demands. While some groups find the experience they seek through being challenged (for example, Weber, 2001; Costa and Chalip, 2005; Page et al., 2006) others prefer experiences that in some ways are reassuring and create feelings of comfort and safety (Jantzen and Vetner, 2007) and well-being (for example, Sointu, 2005; Klepp, 2009; Voigt et al., 2010; Huijbens, 2011). Alternatively, the customer may seek meaning when purchasing experiences (Boswijk et al., 2007). The products corresponding to very varied experiences can range from, for example, rafting and parachuting to receiving a massage or being 'healed'. It is beyond our competence to examine further the psychological theories of needs and motives in relation to experiences, but Schulze (1992), Csikszentmihalyi (1990), Jantzen and Vetner (2007) and Jantzen (Chapter 8, this volume) all provide in-depth explanations of central aspects regarding the experience itself in experience industries.

For something to be defined as experience consumption, it requires (as with services) some form of participation or attendance by the consumer. Also, it is usually characterized by a relation between producer and consumer, where the consumer can also be a co-producer, or a 'prosumer' in Toffler's words (1981). In addition, the experience must be facilitated where this facilitation demands some sort of material or non-material staging of the product. A further characteristic of the purchase of a commercial experience is that it is not about fulfilling any basic needs, but rather about leisure or luxury consumption. Experience consumption is typically individual, although many individuals may have comparable experiences (Lorentzen, 2009). Experience products are closely linked to innovation (Sundbo, 2009), as an element of surprise is often demanded by the customer. However, this does not mean that an experience needs to be unique, as some experiences often are repeated (Lorentzen, 2009). In short, an experience can be defined as 'a sense or feeling; the act of encountering or undergoing something' (Boswijk et al., 2007, p. 11). This definition can easily be interpreted as included in the 'people themselves' part of the above-mentioned definition that Miles (1993) formulated for services (see Subsection 4.3.1). However, compared with most services, experiences can be said to cover something more, as successful experiences involve feelings and/or emotions. Furthermore, experiences are to some extent mind-altering and represent something out of the ordinary.

In the next subsection we take a closer look at what separates experience and service products to see whether this can help to enlighten our understanding of the two concepts. The best way to move forward may be to look at both similarities within a category as well as differences between categories, as done in classification theory. At this point, it is important to be mindful of the fact that a number of characteristics regarding services and experiences will only be apparent in contextual applications of the concept through empirical work. The task of defining therefore ought not to turn completely into a theoretical exercise.

4.3.3   Comparing Services and Experiences

As we have shown, there are both similarities and differences between how services and experiences as commercial products can be defined. We consider it clearly apparent that services and experiences have very much in common. As shown in the sections above, they are typically non-material, although usually in demand of some form of material facilitation. Further, they both often require simultaneous presence from both producer and consumer, where the 'product' is simultaneously produced and consumed.

A couple of characteristics are more debated. One such characteristic is 'supply domination', which is mentioned by Sundbo (2009) as more characteristic of the experience production process than the service production process. This might be true in many cases, as supply domination is a basic characteristic of art and entertainment, where the creators define the content and the customer quite passively may either accept or reject it (for example, attend an event or stay at home, or watch or turn off their screen). By contrast, Lyck (2008) mentions supply domination as one of the common traits of both experience and service industries. For example, the customer has little influence over the organizing of bank or insurance services or public transportation, but there are also many examples of the opposite case both within the experience sector and the service sector.

Technology is mentioned as an aspect that is more characteristic of experience production than service production (Sundbo, 2009), as exemplified by TV, computer games, experiences on websites and mobile phones as well as the fact that experiences can be stored on DVDs and shared via ICT networks. Even though the service industries are older than the experience industries, we should not fall into the trap of thinking that the service industries are not developing. Today even 'old' services such as banking and insurance services are heavily based on ICT systems. This applies also to retailing and education. Not only can experiences be stored on media such as DVDs and ICT networks, but also, for example, practical manuals, user instructions, dictionaries and educational programmes. Hence, technology is not an exclusive characteristic of experiences.

All of the above-mentioned characteristics have exceptions, but nonetheless they can be seen as general and shared characteristics of both service and experience industries. Despite this, it is also feasible to detect some dissimilarity in what can be considered the 'essence' of services and experiences, respectively. For the purpose of discussing the potential for categorizing experience industries, it may be worth taking a closer look at the differences between service and experience industries. We discuss whether these differences stand up to scrutiny, and whether the extensive similarities rather blur the distinction between the two types of industry.

The consumer's participation will always influence the quality of a 'product' in experience industries. As Sundbo (2009, p. 433) points out, 'users must be more engaged than in services because the experience takes place in their minds'. Whereas services usually require some form of participation, experiences always do, as they occur within the consumer. Without the user's participation or engagement, there would not be an experience product. This does not apply to all services; for example, it is possible to have your car repaired and even a haircut while asleep. In many respects, experience industries favour whatever is unique and reject standardization (Lyck, 2008), and the individual aspect is more outspoken in experience industries than in services. The staging or facilitation may be individually customized, or the same staging of an experience may be perceived differently by various people, and hence become different products. Although this may be more characteristic of experience industries than of a typical service, it is not hard to find exceptions. For example, the performance of a teacher, a shop assistant or a hairdresser may be experienced differently by different individuals, and the 'products' of such service workers (a lecture, a purchase and a haircut) may differ each time they are provided. Further, experience industries are more closely linked to and more dependent upon innovation processes, as many of their products require more or less constant reinvention: 'New experiences must continuously be presented to maintain the growth rate' (Sundbo, 2009, p, 436). By contrast, service industries more often benefit from standardization.

While traditionally services have had to be located relatively close to their customers in order to be the preferred service provider, several of the experience industries require their customers to travel some distance to reach the experience provider. For example, in the case of certain forms of tourism, customers have to travel to be able to experience place-specific attractions. It is less common to find services which are that unique that someone will be willing to travel far in order to purchase them. Even though willingness to travel does not apply to all experience production (for example, on TV, DVD and computer games), it can still be said to characterize the experience industries rather than the service industries. This point can be linked to another aspect separating the two industries, namely that it is typical of service industries to 'solve the customers' problems' (Sundbo, 2009, p. 432), or fulfil a need of some kind, very often a practical one, whereas an experience cannot be deemed a necessary purchase in the same way and is rather linked to leisure or luxury consumption aimed at providing a mental journey for the customer. Thus, the demand for experiences is flighty and capricious, as it is rooted in desires for luxury rather than basic needs. In other words, experiences can mainly be linked to the sphere of recreation and leisure, whereas services are required in connection with the more mundane necessities of everyday life (for example, shopping, travelling to work and paying bills). This finding correlates with Pine and Gilmore's (1999, p. 2) claim:

> [W]hen a person buys a service, he purchases a set of intangible activities carried out on his behalf. But when he buys an experience, he pays to spend time enjoying a series of memorable events that a company stages – as in a theatrical play – to engage him in a personal way.

Sundbo (2009, pp. 435–6) also mentions another aspect that could be defined as a unique characteristic of experience industries as distinct from service industries. He argues that the increasing demand for experiences is determined by factors such as seeking social status and more meaning and less boredom in life, along with psychological self-realization, all of which are issues that can be linked to 'identity narration'. Even though experiences can be very short-lived, they have another and perhaps even more valuable function as they can be used to signal our emotions, attitudes and values relating to our surroundings (Lund et al., 2005). Although identity narration is an expanding topic within consumption in general, it is arguably particularly relevant in the case of purchasing experiences (for example, De Bres and Davis, 2001; Hannam and Halewood, 2006; Boswijk et al., 2007).

Sundbo (2009, pp. 433–4) concludes his discussion of the differences between services and experiences by stating that 'even though experience production is in many respects similar to service production, there are differences'. One reason why arguing for a statistical categorization of experience industries is challenging is that both experience industries and services are extremely heterogeneous but also partly overlapping, as Sundbo (2009, p. 433) also argues: 'experiences, like goods and services, is a very diverse category'. These points are listed in Figure 4.1, and summarize the characteristics of service industries and experience industries as well as their substantial overlap.

Thus far, we have looked at both similarities and what we consider to be essential differences between services and experiences. In addition, we have pointed out why the boundaries between the two industries are blurred and overlapping. The fact that experiences are used to increase the value of services or goods (Pine and Gilmore, 1999; Lorentzen, 2009) is one example of a typical 'blur' between goods, services and experiences.

We disagree with Pine and Gilmore's claim of the distinction being obvious, and think their view complicates and obscures our understanding of service and experience industries. As we see it, services and experiences as commercial products have some clear links and similarities, but at the same time they are sufficiently different to justify being categorized separately.

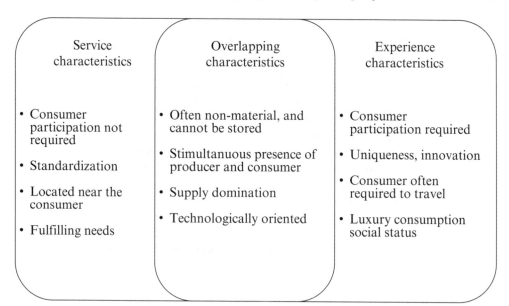

Service characteristics	Overlapping characteristics	Experience characteristics
• Consumer participation not required • Standardization • Located near the consumer • Fulfilling needs	• Often non-material, and cannot be stored • Stimultanuous presence of producer and consumer • Supply domination • Technologically oriented	• Consumer participation required • Uniqueness, innovation • Consumer often required to travel • Luxury consumption social status

Figure 4.1   Service and experience

4.4   CATEGORIZING EXPERIENCE INDUSTRIES

In Norway, the current status of the direct representation of experience industries in the official Norwegian statistics is described in subcategory 93.291: 'Experience activities. This category contains: the organizing and sale of own products, for example rafting, mountain climbing, sleigh riding, and beaver safaris (including the hiring out of equipment for these activities)' (Statistics Norway, 2008, p. 175, our translation). The subcategory is grouped under the main category 'R', which covers cultural activity, entertainment and leisure activities, and subcategory '93', which covers sports and leisure activities and managing amusement establishments, under the heading '93.29 Other leisure activities' (Statistics Norway, 2008, p. 175, our translation). Category 93.291 clearly covers parts of experience industries, but represents a rather narrow understanding of them. The choice of a wide or narrow understanding of the industries of course has a huge impact on what will be considered to be the size of experience industries, a topic already discussed at length in the research community. Some of the views from this discussion are presented below.

4.4.1   A Wide or Narrow Understanding?

Depending on what is being discussed, a wide or narrow understanding of experience industries can both be constructive. As in the case of Pine and Gilmore's (1999) discussion of a general trend in marketing, and a 'general and qualitatively new characteristic of advanced capitalism' (Smidt-Jensen et al., 2009, p. 849), there is no point in having a narrow definition. The reason is that virtually anything can be sold as an experience, and as Bille (2012, p. 101) aptly points out: 'we do not capture the whole experience economy by focusing on the industries that produce (and sell) pure experiences'.

A Danish governmental report categorizes experience industries as consisting of 'advertising, architecture, broadcasting, media, content production, cultural institutions, design, edutainment, events, fashion, film/video, music, performing arts, play tools and theme parks, publishing, sport, tourism and visual arts' (Regjeringen, 2003 cited in Bille, 2012, p. 94). The 'political' definition of the experience economy can therefore be based on a sector perspective with a very broad scope. However, a more recent Danish report (Erhvervs- og Byggestyrelsen and Center for Kultur- og Oplevelsesøkonomi, 2011) presents a view that is more in line with current research findings, namely that there are different 'categories' within the overarching label 'experience industries'.

In our case (discussing a possible entry for statistically measuring experience industries), a very broad angle such as the one Pine and Gilmore promote would be meaningless, and our focus would rather be on agreeing on certain primary and perhaps mainly place-bound industries that capture the essence of the industries (although including more than the current statistical category). Lorentzen (2009) also argues for a narrower definition, as she sees experience industries as based on a relationship between producer and customer: 'The focus . . . is on the consumer, on his/her expectations and involvement with the product, and sometimes even as co-producer' (Lorentzen, 2009, p. 833). Theme restaurants, theme parks, spectacular museums of arts, performances and events are mentioned as examples of place-bound and pure experience products, whereas she defines, for example, tourism, fashion, visual arts, film and video, advertising, television, computer games and cultural institutions as creative branches, and emphasizes that 'the creativity, innovativeness and culture "content" of the products does not make them experience products' (Lorentzen, 2009, p. 833). Lorentzen further divides place-bound experience products into three different categories: events (for example, festivals and sporting events); activities (for example, shopping, hiking, handicraft and art production); and 'services' (for example, theme restaurants, wellness services, exhibitions and galleries, theatres and cinemas). Even this narrow understanding and demarcation has a substantially broader angle than the current statistical category.

Bal's (2002) 'miniature theory' understanding of a concept makes a valid point here. If, for instance, the concept 'experience industries' is discussed without making it clear whether it is the primary or secondary part, or place-bound or footloose experiences that are being discussed, we can see how the same concept can imply different theories. This uncertainty can lead to a somewhat frustrated atmosphere, where some go as far as to suggest that 'it does not really make sense to try to measure the size of the experience economy . . . Depending on how many or few activities and industries are included, the experience economy becomes larger or smaller: you can add to it or subtract from it as you will' (Bille, 2012, p. 101), and conclude that 'TEE [the experience economy] is a concept that can hardly be measured or evaluated' (Freire-Gibb, 2011, p. 1851). Rather than agreeing with the two last quotes, and giving up on the attempt to measure or demarcate the experience industries we instead discuss what options exist and how different understandings of the concept 'experience industries' can be fruitful in relation to categorizing the industries. In the next subsection, we start with an example of what the outcome of simply avoiding the concept of the experience industry would be, before moving on to discuss two other options that are more constructive, namely using existing statistics or categorizing experience industries more accurately.

4.4.2 Avoiding the Concept 'Experience Industries'

One publication that ought to expand our knowledge of experience industries in Norway is the report *Kartlegging av kulturnæringene i Norge* (*Mapping Cultural Industries in Norway*) (Haraldsen et al., 2004, our translation). Its authors investigate on behalf of the Ministry of Commerce the role that experience industries, culturally based and creative industries play in the Norwegian economy. The report has a central position in the Norwegian debate surrounding the experience industries, even though the concept 'experience industries' is quickly rejected on the grounds that 'without further specification of the product than it being "an experience" it is, however, difficult to operationalize this definition' (Haraldsen et al., 2004, p. 17, our translation). This report is the closest we come to mapping the role of experience industries in Norway. It mentions the concept experience industries, but primarily debates whether to use the term cultural or creative, and decides in favour of the former. The three concepts culture, creative and experience are discussed as though they are interchangeable, thereby implying that they cover the same area or, to apply Bal's (2002) terminology, they represent the same mini-theory.

The argument used in Haraldsen et al.'s report is that the concept 'cultural industry' is more fruitful than the concept 'creative industries' because 'creativity exists more or less in all industries' (Haraldsen et al., 2004, p. 17, our translation). From our point of view, this problem regarding the concept of creative industries is no more significant than the challenges associated with applying the term 'cultural industries'. Despite Haraldsen et al.'s definition, culture can by no means be regarded as an unambiguous or unproblematic concept; rather, it is a concept specifically regarded as problematic (Bal, 2002). We would be the first to admit that none of the concepts (culture, creative and experience) are unproblematic. Still, clarifying the distinction between them would benefit all three concepts. This raises the question of what the 'mini-theories' ought to contain or explain. In our opinion, using the three concepts as though they are interchangeable is an approach that does not reveal any of their content (see Lorentzen, Chapter 3, this volume for more on this subject). However, even though the term 'culture-based business' is preferred to the term 'experience economy/industry', in Haraldsen et al.'s policy report it includes almost the same industries as in the Danish political definition (Bille, 2012, p. 95).

In 2007, Haraldsen and Hagen (2007, p. 243) state: 'during the last decade, we have seen an increased interest in the cultural industries. Mapping the industries both in Norway and internationally shows that they are important contributors to employment and value creation' (our translation). However, the report published by Haraldsen et al. three years earlier concludes with the following remark: 'These industries' part in both employment and GNP has been relatively stable since 1996 (c. 3.5%)' (Haraldsen et al. 2004, p. 61, our translation). Why, then, are we even discussing what to call this 'change' or 'development' if nothing has changed? Could the problem rather be a lack of sufficient debate around definition and categorization of the various industries? Is the result that change and development is hidden rather than illuminated and explained?

In the following subsection we present what we find to be a more constructive approach of how to perform a study of the scope and development of experience industries, based on existing statistics.

4.4.3   Categorization Based on Existing Statistics

The above-mentioned standards (NACE and NAICS), regarding classification followed by all countries that we would naturally compare Norway with, do not allow for a detailed statistical overview of the experience sector as a whole. Regardless, Smidt-Jensen et al. (2009) attempt to give an account of the situation in Denmark using the existing NACE categories. They ask what sectors and industries can be characterized as the experience economy and end up with a broad definition of experience products and services, including, for example, entertainment, amusement parks, hotels and restaurants: 'to make a comprehensive analysis on the basis of the data that are available to us, it has been necessary to use the relatively high level of industry aggregation to make an analysis on the level of municipalities' (Smidt-Jensen et al., 2009, p. 851).

Smidt-Jensen et al. (2009) are among the few researchers that have attempted to provide an operational definition of the experience economy. Like us, they start by making a distinction between the definition proposed by Pine and Gilmore (1998, 1999) and a definition that refers to specific industries. The latter definition is based on the industries where the experience content is especially strong. This means that the experience industries overlap with what often is alternatively defined as 'the cultural industries', 'the creative industries', 'the entertainment industries' and 'tourism' (Smidt-Jensen et al., 2009). Furthermore, Smidt-Jensen et al. (2009), like Sundbo and Sørensen (Chapter 1, this volume), make a division between the 'primary' experience sector, consisting of firms and institutions where the production of experiences is the main objective, and the 'secondary' experience sector, where experiences are add-ons to goods or services. The primary experience sector can also be said to deal with pure experience products (Lorentzen, 2009, p. 833), which are products with high experience values. Similar to Lorentzen's use of 'footloose' versus 'place-bound', Smidt-Jensen et al. (2009) further divide the primary experience sector into producers of detachable experience products and services (DEPS) and attendance-based products and services (AEPS). While DEPS can be sent to receivers all over the world as artefacts or electronic and digital impulses (for example, music CDs, books and television programmes), AEPS requires in situ attendance by the consumers (for example, festivals, restaurants and cinemas).

Smidt-Jensen et al. (2009) end up with a broad demarcation of experience industries, consisting of 'NACE 55 Hotels and Restaurants' and 'NACE 92 Entertainment, Culture and Sport', and estimate that approximately 80–85 per cent of the industries within these two categories are AEPS. Despite imperfect data, they still find enough to suggest that the growth of AEPS has been strong since the 1990s, especially in the large municipalities, while in the small municipalities, the growth has been more modest. Smidt-Jensen et al. also find that growth is unevenly distributed among various branches, and conclude that growth is more likely in traditional tourist places with natural, cultural or entertainment amenities. They conclude: 'However, for a majority of cities and municipalities, AEPS as a way to future prosperity may turn out to be a very fragile growth strategy, at least in terms of jobs and job creation' (Smidt-Jensen et al., 2009, p. 858).

In relation to national and international classification, as in the NACE system, there can be no competing 'truths'. Therefore, before experience industries could be more thoroughly represented in that classification system, it would be preferable to conduct a consensus among the users of the concept 'experience industries'. Even so, it is doubtful whether we will ever see the experience industries assembled in a higher-order NACE category of their own. However, it is possible to make use of the existing lower and 'scattered' categories, as Smidt-Jensen et al. (2009) demonstrate. To have comparable data between countries, such as the Scandinavian countries, would probably require formal cooperation and specifically ordered reports from the various countries' statistical bureaus.

4.5   CATEGORIZING EXPERIENCES VERSUS SERVICES

In this section we move the discussion up a level and instead of discussing characteristics within the service and experience industries, we look at the relationship between the two sectors. Should experience industries be seen as a part of the service sector or as an economic sector in its own right?

As pointed out by Bell (1974), all economic phases have had an extensive amount of service activities, although of differing character; from the private servants of the pre-industrial society through the intermediate support services of the industrial society to the dominance of welfare services and professional services of the post-industrial 'service society'. The service sector is clearly characterized as being extremely heterogeneous. One solution to solving challenges with a very large and heterogeneous category would be to define a fourth sector at the highest level of classification, as an addition to the traditional division into the primary, secondary and tertiary sectors. Such an attempt was made by Gottmann (1961), who suggested a 'quaternary' sector where sophisticated, highly qualified services are separated from the tertiary sector. Abler and Adams (1977) developed this categorization further, defining all services dealing with material objects as belonging to the tertiary sector, whereas services dealing with routine information were classified as quaternary. In addition, they suggested a fifth main sector, the 'quinternary' sector, consisting of all advanced, non-routine information processing and decision-making. A similar solution was suggested by Porat (1977), who tried to distinguish an 'information' sector, consisting of service activities dealing with information.

All of the above-mentioned attempts were faced with data problems, as they had to cut across even low-level statistical categories (Illeris, 2007). However, several of the ideas were followed up in later suggestions for classification, such as the one by Selstad and Sjøholt (1990) who, building on Miles's definition of services (mentioned in Subsection 4.3.1), suggest a division into 'goods handling services, person-related services, information services and knowledge services'. This division is also cross-classified with the dimension 'producer services – mixed services – consumer services'. Such classification schemes can be useful for some analytical purposes but not for others. As Illeris (2007, p. 21) claims, 'a number of subclassifications of services compete, and none of them has been accepted to cover all purposes'.

The idea of a quaternary sector is in many ways parallel to the arguments of Pine and Gilmore for a fourth sector, which they label 'the experience sector/economy'. The increased focus on experiences could then be seen as a new characteristic of contemporary good and service production, a response to new demands and a way to survive and prosper in today's market and economic reality. An alternative to creating a fourth sector would be to 'extend' the current praxis by continuing to see experience industries as a subclass of the service sector, although with a more prominent place than they have at present.

When creating such subclasses or categories, a revisit to the pros and cons of categorization would be recommendable. The critique that categories are descriptive is not necessarily a problem, as to problematize and discuss can happen elsewhere in a research process. Some would say that reification is the case with the experience industries; that what we are theorizing and discussing is a created phenomenon and not a 'real' industry. Hence, there is still a need for further research. Also, the fact that classification is static rather than dynamic may be a valid objection as the world it is supposed to represent is never static. This point may be even more relevant for the experience industries than many other industries as innovation, and thereby change, is of central importance in experience industries (Sundbo, 2009).

When categorizing according to the principles mentioned in Subsection 4.2.2, it is clear that car sales, regardless of the value of the experience gained from purchases, should be categorized according to the physical product that is sold, that is, the car, rather than the experience accompanying the purchase. By contrast, parachuting would fit better in an experience category than under sport, particularly in cases where a novice is strapped to an experienced parachutist and does not need any form of skills themself.

4.6   CONCLUSION

One point of departure for our discussion in this chapter was the claim by Pine and Gilmore (1998) that experiences are as different from services as services are from goods. As we have demonstrated, this is far from the case. The blurred distinction between goods and services has been acknowledged among service researchers for several decades, and the same kind of arguments also apply to the relationship between experiences and goods. Even if services or experiences are basically non-material 'products', in many cases both have been materialized into goods.

Despite a range of similarities between service and experience industries, we have also pointed out their differences. A shared, consistent and operational definition of experiences requires a base in the unique and fundamental characteristics of the primary or pure experience industries, instead of trying to cover the whole of the 'experience economy'. As experience industries and services are very heterogeneous groups, it is a challenging task to develop such a definition. Our discussion of characteristics (summarized in Figure 4.1) can nonetheless be seen as a contribution in that direction. As a starting point, experience industries can be defined as industries where experiences are the main product, that is, a product that gives the customer a unique, personal, out-of-the-ordinary and memorable event. In order to develop such a definition further, it would have to be tested and evaluated in empirical contexts.

Even though it is challenging and perhaps impossible to arrive at a consistent definition that can be applied to all experience industries, working towards a definition still seems to be the only way forward in order to assess the scope, growth, economic importance, regional distribution, possibilities and challenges of this group of industries. Another option would be to study one experience industry or branch at a time. In any case, a necessary next step would be to discuss in detail which industries or branches would fit such a definition. One place to start could be the existing lists of what can possibly be regarded as experience industries, such as those mentioned in the Danish reports.

In this chapter, we have also discussed some of the consequences of using a narrow versus a broad definition of experience industries, arguing that in the case of Norway, the present statistical category labelled 'experience activities' in official Norwegian statistics is far too narrow. On the other hand, some of the Danish studies and reports are operating with categorizations that are too broad in our opinion, and include all kinds of creative and cultural industries. That does not mean that we approve of the opposite standpoint or choice of avoiding the concept 'experience industries' by 'hiding' the industries under the cultural or creative label. Rather, we have tried to demonstrate that it is possible to do good research based on existing statistics, even with imperfect data.

Another point of departure for the discussion in this chapter was the question of whether experiences should be seen as a subclass of the services or whether their unique characteristics are sufficiently strong to justify categorizing them in separate economic sectors. The modest size of pure experience industries and their many similarities with services have led us to conclude that ideally they should be seen as a subclass of services, although allocated to a separate and distinct subcategory in order to ensure that they have a more clearly identified position than they have today.

Due to the complex and heterogeneous nature of experience industries, we consider it unlikely that they will be included as a separate category of any size in NACE in the near future. Moreover, their inclusion would also be dependent on similarities between the various member countries of the EU and Schengen Area that may not exist. Furthermore, the dynamic nature of experience industries indicates that categorizations and definitions will be challenged, as in many regards the industries represent trends, and therefore will continually change. As illustrated by our discussion regarding the problems of categorizing services and also very well illustrated by the discussions regarding the concepts 'cultural industries' and 'creative industries', these traits are by no means unique to the experience industries. Even so, the NACE system is impressively updated, and the experience industries may not be any more problematic to demarcate functionally in public statistics than any other industry.

REFERENCES

Abler, R. and J.S. Adams (1977), 'The industrial and occupational structure of the American labor force', *Papers in Geography*, No. 15, Pennsylvania State University, Pennsylvania.

Bailey, K.D. (1994), *Typologies and Taxonomies: An Introduction to Classification Techniques*, Vol. 102, London: Sage.

Bal, M. (2002), *Travelling Concepts in the Humanities: A Rough Guide*, London: Green College Lectures.

Bell, D. (1974), *The Coming of Post-industrial Society*, London: Heinemann.

Bille, T. (2012), 'The Scandinavian approach to the experience economy – does it make sense?', *International Journal of Cultural Policy*, **18** (1), 93–110.

Bille, T. and M. Lorenzen (2008), *Den danske opplevelsesøkonomi – avgrænsning, økonomisk betydning og vækstmuligheder* (*The Danish Experience Economy – Delimitation, Economic Importance and Growth Potential*), Frederiksberg: Imagine . . . and Samfundslitteratur.

Boswijk, A., T. Thijssen, E. Peelen and T.S.B. Johnston (2007), *The Experience Economy: A New Perspective*, Amsterdam: Pearson Education.

Bowker, G.C. and S.L. Star (1999), *Sorting Things Out*, Cambridge, MA: MIT Press.

Butler, J. (2001), 'Gender trouble: from parody to politics', in S. Malpas (ed.), *Postmodern Debate*, Basingstoke: Palgrave, pp. 136–44.

Costa, C.A. and L. Chalip (2005), 'Adventure sport tourism in rural revitalisation – an ethnographic evaluation', *European Sport Management Quarterly*, **5** (3), 257–79.

Csikszentmihalyi, M. (1990), *Flow: The Psychology of Optimal Experience*, New York: Harper and Son.

Dale, B.E. (1994), 'Service og samfunn i endring: Utviklingstrekk i tjenestesektoren belyst i et regionalt og forbrukerorientert perspektiv' (Service and society in change: development trends in the service sector seen in a regional and consumer oriented perspective'), PhD thesis, Department of Geography, University of Trondheim (now NTNU), Trondheim.

De Bres, K. and J. Davis (2001), 'Celebrating group and place identity: a case study of a new regional festival', *Tourism Geographies*, **3** (3), 326–37.

Erhvervs- og Byggestyrelsen and Center for Kultur- og Oplevelsesøkonomi (2011), *Vækst via oplevelser 2011 – en analyse af Danmark i oplevelsesøkonomien* (*Growth via Experiences 2011 – An Analysis of Denmark in the Experience Economy*), Albertslund, Denmark.

Freire-Gibb, L.C. (2011), 'The rise and fall of the concept of the experience economy in the local economic development of Denmark', *European Planning Studies*, **19** (10), 1839–53.

Gottmann, J. (1961), *Megalopolis: The Urbanized Northeastern Seaboard of the United States*, New York: Twentieth Century Fund.

Hannam, K. and C. Halewood (2006), 'European Viking themed festivals: an expression of identity', *Journal of Heritage Tourism*, **1** (1), 17–31.

Haraldsen, T. and S.E. Hagen (2007), 'Kulturnæringene – sysselsetting, lokalisering og innovasjon' ('The cultural industries – employment, localization and innovation'), in A. Isaksen, A. Karlsen and B. Sæther (eds), *Innovasjoner i norske næringer* (*Innovations in Norwegian Industries*), Bergen: Fagbokforlaget, pp. 243–65.

Haraldsen, T., S.K. Flygind, K. Overvåg and D. Power (2004), *Kartlegging av kulturnæringene i Norge*, ØF Rapport 10/2004, Lillehammer: Østlandsforskning.

Huijbens, E. (2011), 'Developing wellness in Iceland: theming wellness destinations the Nordic way', *Scandinavian Journal of Hospitality and Tourism*, **11** (1), 20–41.

Illeris, S. (1989), *Services and Regions in Europe*, Aldershot, UK: Avebury.

Illeris, S. (1996), *The Service Economy: A Geographical Approach*, Chichester, UK: John Wiley.

Illeris, S. (2007), 'The nature of services', in J.R. Bryson and P.W. Daniels (eds), *The Handbook of Service Industries*, Cheltenham, UK and Northampton, MA, USA: Edward Elgar, pp. 19–34.

Jantzen, C. and M. Vetner (2007), 'Oplevelsens psykologiske struktur' ('The psychological structure of experience'), in J.O. Bærenholdt and J. Sundbo (eds), *Oplevelsesøkonomi: Produktion, forbrug, kultur* (*The Experience Economy: Production, Consumption, Culture*), Fredriksberg: Forlaget Samfundslitteratur, pp. 27–50.

Klepp, I.G. (2009), 'Does beauty come from within? Beauty and well-being in Norwegian spas', *Medische Antropologie*, **21** (1), 39–51.

Lorentzen, A. (2009), 'Cities in the experience economy', *European Planning Studies*, **17** (6), 829–45.

Lorentzen, A. and C.J. Hansen (2009), 'The role and transformation of the city in the experience economy: identifying and exploring research challenges', *European Planning Studies*, **17** (6), 817–27.

Lund, J.M., A.P. Nielsen, L. Goldschmidt, H. Dahl and T. Martinsen (2005), *Følelsesfabrikken: oplevelsesøkonomi på dansk*, København: Børsen.

Lyck, L. (2008), *Service- og oplevelsesøkonomi: i teori og praksis* (*Service and Experience Economy in Theory and Practice*), Århus: Academica.

Markusen, A. (2003), 'Fuzzy concepts, scanty evidence, policy distance: the case for rigour and policy relevance in critical regional studies', *Regional Studies*, **37** (6–7), 701–17.

Marshall, J.N. and P.A. Wood (1995), *Services and Space: Key Aspects of Urban and Regional Development*, New York: Longman Scientific and Technical.

Miles, I. (1993), 'Services in the new industrial economy', *Futures*, **25** (6), 653–72.

Nielsen, T. (2004), *Understanding the Experience Industry. A Swedish Perspective on Creativity*, Gothenburg: Tobias Nielsen and QNB Analys & Kommunikation AB.

Page, S.J., W. Steele and J. Connell (2006), 'Analysing the promotion of adventure tourism: a case study of Scotland', *Journal of Sport and Tourism*, **11** (1), 51–76.

Pine, B.J. and J.H. Gilmore (1998), 'Welcome to the experience economy', *Harvard Business Review*, July–August, 97–105.

Pine, B.J. and J.H. Gilmore (1999), *The Experience Economy: Work is Theatre and Every Business a Stage*, Boston, MA: Harvard Business School Press.

Porat, M.U. (1977), *The Information Economy: Definition and Measurement*, Office of Telecommunications, Special Publication, 77-12, Washington, DC: US Department of Commerce.

Salamon, L.M. and H.K. Anheier (1992), 'In search of the non-profit sector. I: The question of definitions', *Voluntas: International Journal of Voluntary and Nonprofit Organizations*, **3** (2), 125–51.

Salamon, L.M. and H.K. Anheier (1997), 'Toward a common classification', in L.M. Salamon and H.K. Anheier (eds), *Defining the Nonprofit Sector: A Cross-national Analysis*, Manchester: Manchester University Press, pp. 51–100.

Sayer, A. (1992), *Method in Social Science: A Realist Approach*, 2nd edn, New York: Routledge.

Schulze, G. (1992), *Die Erlebnisgesellschaft: Kultursoziologie der Gegenwart* (*The Experience Society: The Cultural Sociology of the Present Time*), Frankfurt: Campus Verlag.

Selstad, T. and S.E. Hagen (1991), 'Servicenæringene til besvær' ('The "trouble" of the service industries'), ØF rapport 30/91, Lillehammer: Østlandsforskning.

Selstad, T. and P. Sjøholt (1990), 'Regional development and the service sector: the post-industrial challenge' (Editorial introduction), *Norsk Geografisk Tidsskrift*, **44**, 1–5.

Smidt-Jensen, S., C.B. Skytt and L. Winther (2009), 'The geography of the experience economy in Denmark: employment change and location dynamics in attendance-based experience industries', *European Planning Studies*, **17** (6), 847–62.

Sointu, E. (2005), 'The rise of an ideal: tracing changing discourses of wellbeing', *Sociological Review*, **53** (2), 255–74.

Statistics Norway (2008), *Standard Industrial Classification*, NOS D 383, Oslo: Statistisk sentralbyrå.

Sundbo, J. (2009), 'Innovation in the experience economy: a taxonomy of innovation organisations', *The Service Industries Journal*, **29** (4), 431–55.

Sundbo, J. and J.O. Bærenholdt (2007), 'Inledning: Den mangfoldige oplevelsesøkomi' ('Introduction: the many-sided experience economy'), in J.O. Bærenholdt and J. Sundbo (eds), *Oplevelsesøkonomi: produktion, forbrug, kultur* (*The Experience Economy: Production, Consumption, Culture*), Frederiksberg: Forlaget Samfundslitteratur, pp. 9–25.

Thomsen, K. (2012), 'The experience as a difference to service and personal development', Paper presented at the conference Innovating the Experience Economy – Design, Consumption and Concepts, Roskilde University Centre, 11 June.

Toffler, A. (1970), *Future Shock*, New York: Bentam Books.

Toffler, A. (1981), *The Third Wave*, London: Pan Books.

Voigt, C., G. Howat and G. Brown (2010), 'Hedonic and eudaimonic experiences among wellness tourists: an exploratory enquiry', *Annals of Leisure Research*, **13** (3), 541–62.

Walker, J.A. and J.B. Murphy (2001), 'Implementing the North American industry classification system at BLS', *Monthly Labor Review*, 5–21 December.

Walker, R.A. (1985), 'Is there a service economy? The changing capitalist division of labor', *Science and Society*, **49** (1), 42–83.

Weber, K. (2001), 'Outdoor adventure tourism: a review of research approaches', *Annals of Tourism Research*, **28** (2), 360–77.

5. The economic value of experience goods

David Emanuel Andersson and Åke E. Andersson

5.1 INTRODUCTION

All consumer goods (including consumer services) are at least to some extent experience goods. There is no clear-cut distinction between a category of goods that is experienced and another category that is 'non-experienced'. Even a standardized and relatively homogeneous consumer good such as a sugar cube gives rise – at the very least – to an experience of 'sweetness'. But this does not mean that all goods are the same regarding their ability to engender consumer experiences. They are not. But instead of a dichotomy between experience and non-experience consumer goods, it is more realistic to think of a good's experiential nature as a multi-dimensional question. An increase in any one of a number of relevant attributes implies that a good becomes 'increasingly experiential'. There are at least five such experience-related attributes: learning by consuming; uniqueness; location and context dependence; interdependence; and non-storability.

Goods that exhibit high levels of several experience attributes differ from goods that combine low or zero levels across all five attributes. There are certain features that unite those goods that are commonly thought of as non-experience goods, but which – strictly speaking – should be referred to as low-experience goods. We may think of such goods as 'standard goods'.

There are obviously other factors associated with experiences that we will not be discussing in this chapter. Examples are those that are associated with love and other passionate relations between people as well as political, religious and mystical experiences. These types of experiences and their consequences have been analysed in depth by the neuroscientist W.J. Freeman (1995). We will also not discuss work experiences, thereby limiting our analysis to consumer goods (including consumer services) that are traded in markets.

A consumer buying a standard good has in the normal case accumulated sufficient information to evaluate the attributes of these goods, where an attribute refers to any utility-generating service that is subjectively valued by the specific individual consumer (Andersson, 2008a). Usually, the consumer can return such a good if it differs in any objective way from its standardized specification. For the most standardized goods (according to the definition used here), it is also possible to buy a great quantity at one point in time, after which the consumer gradually consumes the units of the good over an extended period of time. For example, if there is a temporary reduction in the price of sugar cubes, the consumer can decide to buy a few extra pounds to be stored for later consumption. Moreover, standard goods only require low levels of interaction with sellers and other buyers, since producers standardize the (objective) attributes of such goods; the goods are standardized in order to stabilize consumer expectations and to reach economies of scale in production. The installation of self-checkout machines in supermarkets is an illustration of the way such goods predominate in conventional shops.

Goods with high levels of experiential attributes can thus differ from standard goods in a number of ways. Such goods are in most cases intangible. This means that it is not easy to separate production from consumption, and that the characteristics of each consumer determine the outcome of the production process. Typical examples of experience goods are live concerts, records, books, dining in restaurants, walks, lectures and dental surgery. The following sections aim at a conceptualization and starting point for an economic theory of what makes some goods have greater 'experience content' than others.

There is a certain overlap between characteristics of experience goods and general services. One example of this overlap is 'learning by doing'. For example, in the analysis of productive services this is primarily an important aspect of the dynamics of employee interactions, while in the analysis of experience goods we focus on the consumer and the dynamic process of consumption.

5.2   EXPERIENCE CHARACTERISTIC 1: LEARNING BY CONSUMING

The first characteristic is associated with what we mean by the word 'experience' in normal language usage. We usually associate experience with a period of learning that precedes an action, which may be thought of as an act of consumption or production in economic terms. Although discussed by Adam Smith (1776 [1937]) and Alfred Marshall (1920), Kenneth Arrow (1962) was the first economist to formally analyse the role of 'learning by doing' as an endogenous factor. In Arrow's model, learning by doing determines production efficiency. It is the result of the accumulated experiences of the workforce in relation to the production of a specific good.

It is of course possible to extend this analysis to an understanding of the efficiency of the consumer in her enjoyment of different goods. It is rather obvious that the ability to enjoy reading books requires knowledge of a written language. But this is seldom enough. The enjoyment (or utility) of, say, a sonnet by Shakespeare requires much more, such as knowledge of literary conventions and the historical context. But a true connoisseur of Shakespeare's *oeuvre* would also have a history of learning by consuming, such as a regular habit of reading Shakespeare. There are numerous experience goods of this kind. Music, chess, computer games, photography, interior decorating and gardening are all examples of experience goods where the process of learning by consuming is of great importance. Addictive behaviour is also sometimes thought of as learning by consuming, but this is only true in a trivial sense. Consider the following example.

Wine is one of the least homogeneous goods to be found in supermarkets, which the high relative frequency of buyer–seller interaction reflects. Wine connoisseurs are able to distinguish several attributes of wine quality, sometimes referred to as the aroma and bouquet of the wine. The ability to distinguish aromas as well as bouquets is not primarily the result of a good sense of smell and taste; it is first and foremost the result of a long process of experiential learning (Andersson, 2008a; see also Earl, 1983). Becoming an increasingly sophisticated wine connoisseur implies that one becomes increasingly good at distinguishing between different consumption attributes, which usually affects the willingness to pay for a specific bottle. Thus high-quality wine is an experience good to a much greater extent than sugar, flour or ketchup.

One of the consumption attributes of wine is quite unrelated to its aroma or bouquet; it is its ability to produce 'intoxication services', which is directly related to its alcohol content. We may think of its intoxication services as something that is unequally valued by consumers of wine. Consumers who are addicted to alcohol usually derive more subjective utility from the intoxication services than the utility that they derive from the joint effect of all other perceived consumption attributes. While it is certainly true that there is a learning process associated with knowing the effects of intoxication, it is usually a short one. The fact that alcoholics demand more alcohol over time is not the outcome of increasing levels of connoisseurship; it is the effect of 'chasing the dragon'. This refers to the increasing amounts of alcohol that are required to achieve the same level of intoxication: the consumption attribute remains one and the same, but becomes increasingly elusive over time.

There is thus no learning process involved after a certain point in time; what one observes is instead repetitive behaviour and a 'household production function' that is increasingly inefficient in technological terms. A further consequence of addictive behaviour of this type is decreasing interest in other attributes over time, which may, for example, manifest itself as increasing demand for the least expensive type of alcohol. There is thus a decreasing number of perceived consumption attributes associated with a heterogeneous good over time, which implies 'forgetting by consuming' rather than learning by consuming. The same process is typical of all addictive consumption attributes where increasing objective quantities are needed to achieve the desired effect of temporary satiation (for example, heroin). It is not true of addictive attributes with a stable dose–response relationship, which do not as a rule lead to processes of 'de-skilling' in consumption.

Goods that require learning by consuming share the property of increasing returns to the scale of consumption, but it is important to remember that the increasing returns derive from observed quantities of objective goods; they do not derive from subjectively perceived consumption attributes. These consumption attributes are often correlated with objective quantities, but sometimes they are not, as the example of increasingly inefficient addictive behaviour illustrates.

Standard consumption theory is based on the assumption of diminishing marginal utility. Learning by consuming effects show that this is only true in a static sense as far as objective goods are concerned. However, a subjective interpretation of goods as open-ended bundles of consumption attributes preserves the validity of the decreasing returns assumption. There may thus be increasing utility associated with increasing consumption of a specific tradable good, even though the consumption attributes that together constitute the tradable good are all subject to decreasing returns in utility terms. The key to resolving the apparent contradiction is that the quantity of perceived attributes is an increasing function of time as long as a learning process is taking place (Andersson, 2008a). Static (cross-sectional) and dynamic (time-series) observations of individual consumption behaviour may therefore seem more contradictory than they are in reality.

5.3   EXPERIENCE CHARACTERISTIC 2: UNIQUENESS

Another characteristic that reinforces the experiential nature of a good is its uniqueness. Standard goods such as mass-produced foods, drinks and clothes can be tasted, touched and perceived in other ways before the consumer decides whether to buy them. Although it is sometimes possible to demonstrate goods with unique attributes, there is in general no way of forming a conclusive opinion about the story in a book or a play before the act of buying and consuming these services. A novel or an education can only be evaluated in advance to a very partial extent. Subjective and relatively unreliable expectations of the future are part and parcel of the consumption of goods with high experience content. The problem of rational decision-making as regards the purchase of experiences is therefore similar to the decision problems facing an investor in capital goods. Investors also have to take expected benefits and cost as well as risks of mistakes into consideration when deciding whether and in what to invest.

The suppliers of unique experiences therefore systematically exploit the fact that subjective expectations are important in their marketing and design activities. It is for this reason that entertainment firms develop global brand names such as Disney, EA Games or Play Station – it is a method that stabilizes consumer expectations to some extent. There are also similar 'brand-name individuals' in art and entertainment. They spend considerable amounts of money to market their personalities by the use of various marketing strategies. As a consequence, the expectation-derived price premiums of brand-name individuals such as Sir Paul McCartney, Meryl Streep and Lionel Messi are much greater than can be explained by the relative quality of their technical skills. In certain limiting circumstances 'winner-takes-all' phenomena can at least partly be explained by marketing-driven expectations associated with the perceived uniqueness of an experience.

An analogous example is universities, which nowadays try to stabilize the expectations of students and financiers by hiring Nobel laureates and other notable scholars in order to attract good students and faculty. Reputation-based marketing strategies have become increasingly common with the growing mobility of students and teachers. Global university league tables constitute one example of a new marketing tool that leading universities exploit. Examples include the rankings produced by *The Times Higher Education Supplement*, Quacquarelli-Symonds and Shanghai Jiaotong University, which in 2012 ranked Cal Tech, Cambridge or Harvard as the best university in the world (the exact ranking of each university tends to differ as a result of different quantitative criteria). These rankings reinforce the ability of the aforementioned universities to attract desired scholars and students from around the world.

5.4 EXPERIENCE CHARACTERISTIC 3: LOCATION AND CONTEXT DEPENDENCE

A cup of espresso at the Café Florian in Piazza San Marco in Venice is an example of an experience good with a high level of location dependence (Pine and Gilmore, 1999). Affluent tourists visiting Venice often end up at the Café Florian, where they sip coffee priced at 12 euros (US$15) per cup. A cup of coffee with identical flavour – but served to a standing consumer at a normal Italian café in a less celebrated town square – would cost only about a tenth as much. What the consumer at Florian is actually paying for is not primarily the coffee itself; for the most part she is paying for a combination of the ambience of the café, the view of the Basilica di San Marco and Piazza San Marco, and

Table 5.1   The ten best locations according to different criteria

Rank	Best tourist attractions for Americans, 2007[a]	Best tourist destinations according to global travellers, 2012[b]	Cities with best quality of life according to 30 objective indicators, 2012[c]
1	Times Square, New York, USA	London, UK	Melbourne, VIC, Australia
2	National Mall, Washington, DC, USA	New York City, USA	Vienna, Austria
3	Walt Disney World, Lake Buena Vista, FL, USA	Rome, Italy	Vancouver, BC, Canada
4	Trafalgar Square, London, UK	Paris, France	Toronto, ON, Canada
5	Disneyland, Anaheim, CA, USA	San Francisco, CA, USA	Calgary, AB, Canada
6	Niagara Falls, ON, Canada	Marrakech, Morocco	Sydney, NSW, Australia
7	Fisherman's Wharf, San Francisco, CA, USA	Istanbul, Turkey	Helsinki, Finland
8	Tokyo Disneyland, Tokyo, Japan	Barcelona, Spain	Perth, WA, Australia
9	Notre Dame, Paris, France	Siem Reap, Cambodia	Adelaide, SA, Australia
10	Disneyland Paris, Marne-la-Vallée, France	Berlin, Germany	Auckland, New Zealand

Source: [a] Forbes (2007), [b] Tripadvisor (2012) and [c] Economist Intelligence Unit (2012).

the ever-changing crowd in the square. All these attributes contribute to the willingness to pay for the experience associated with having coffee at that particular location.

This location dependence is even more obvious in the choice of tourist destinations. A tourist is the most obvious case of a pure experience consumer. Favoured tourist destinations among Europeans include both beach locations such as the Canary Islands, Cannes and Phuket and large cities such as London, Paris and Rome. The choice of location-dependent experiences is conditioned both by culturally influenced preferences as well as whether the experience refers to a short vacation or long-term quality of life. Table 5.1 gives three examples of location-specific rankings. The first column lists the top ten tourist sights according to a survey of the American population; the second column lists the top tourist destinations according to a global survey of frequent travellers; and the third column is a ranking of urban quality of life according to the Economist Intelligence Unit, which is based on 30 objective indicators of city-specific attributes such as environmental quality, education and infrastructure. All such location choices are heterogeneous bundles of consumption attributes, the valuation of which may vary across individuals according to their subjective preferences and expectations.

Most art and entertainment experiences require that you are present on the production site. Spatio-temporal location specificity typifies all live performances, ranging from concerts over theatrical performances to live sports. The uncertainty of consumers' expectations increases with the degree of improvisation that is associated with the performance. Stand-up comedy, jam sessions or football matches are therefore more uncertain than Shakespeare, opera or the 25th show of a rock band on its world tour. But even the most thoroughly planned live performances are less predictable than a pre-packaged recording of the same words or music.

In all these cases, there is no way of taking account of all the relevant attributes before-hand. The composition and response of the audience as well as the relative quality of the performance on a specific occasion are all inherently uncertain. The producers have an interest in inflating the consumers' expectations of product quality and ambience, while specialized critics sometimes cooperate in these efforts and sometimes moderate con-sumer expectations. A side-effect of the ambiguous relationship between critics' opinions and consumers' performance expectations is the existence of opportunities for mutual rent-seeking among producers, performers and critics.

In contrast to these interactions between professional critics, performers and produc-ers, the audience itself acts as an influential group of amateur critics. Their evaluations are often conveyed in conversations and on internet forums, thereby affecting the will-ingness to pay of potential consumers of later performances. The evolution of demand over time is therefore subject to a number of influences, including marketing efforts, the assessments of critics in the mass media, and audience feedback through word of mouth or through impersonal and perhaps anonymous web-based interaction.

5.5   EXPERIENCE CHARACTERISTIC 4: INTERDEPENDENCE

Interdependencies between producers and consumers are an important aspect of goods with pronounced experience characteristics. In the production of standardized tangible consumption goods, firms can attain efficiency by means of the spatio-temporal sepa-ration of production from consumption. A firm may make cars or shirts in a Chinese factory that its American or European consumers cannot even visit. The situation is different when consuming dental care, restaurant services or stand-up comedy. The con-sumers have to be present in 'the factory' during production.

In education the interdependencies between the buyer and the seller are even more important. In that case, the learner-buyer almost automatically becomes a co-producer of the resulting output. The situation is similar for online computer games, where the players' co-production is the key to success for the producers of the computer software.

The interdependence between consumption and production enters the analysis in many different ways. The spatial economic consequences were first analysed by Edward Chamberlin (1933) in his path-breaking book on monopolistic competition. The fact that many types of experience goods require frequent personal contacts between con-sumers and producers and/or between different consumers leads to price-inelastic con-sumer demand, even if there are low entry costs and a multitude of buyers and sellers. Each producer captures a local market as a consequence of high transaction and/or transport costs.

In Chamberlin's theory, the entry and exit of competing producers determine the size of each such market until the producers with the lowest average cost curve reach a point of tangency to the adaptive but downward-sloping demand curve. When all local firms have reached this equilibrium, they cannot attain any additional profits and each one has to operate with unexploited returns to scale in production. In practice, such an outcome is, however, never achieved since entrepreneurial innovation and consumer learning processes ensure that revenue and cost functions remain in a state of flux (Andersson, 2008a).

Interdependencies also enter the picture in other and more dynamic ways. Increasing returns to scale are not only important in production, as reflected in downward-sloping average cost functions. There are also economies of scale on the demand side. The fact that a telephone is useless unless there are also other telephones alludes to scale economies in the demand for communication experiences. The well-known logistic interaction function is a model of consumer economies of scale as an effect of self-reinforcing demand. For example, the increase in the use of the internet and its interactive applications usually features a period in which there are increasing returns to scale in consumption. This can be shown with the following model:

$$X(t + 1) - X(t) = c \, X(t)(T - X(t)), \tag{5.1}$$

where $X(t)$ is the number of (interactive) consumers; T is the total number of potential consumers; and c is a contagion parameter. This model has two equilibria. The first – unstable – equilibrium occurs when $X^*(u) = 0$. A small addition to this value would set in motion an (initially) accelerating growth process that does not cease until the other equilibrium has been reached, which occurs when $X^*(s) = T$, at which point all (previously) potential consumers have become actual ones.

The interactive growth of some experience services is driven by the fact that the probability of forming interacting pairs increases with the size of the crowd up to the capacity limit of the service-specific infrastructure. Examples abound in discotheques, bars, museums and other interactive agorae.

In some experience services – for example, many music events – the perceived quality of the performance improves with the size of the audience, even if there are no identifiable formations of new linkages between distinct individuals. In those cases, the effect is a kind of crowd effect, where the presence of one more individual typically generates a minuscule positive increment to the perceived utility of each individual in the crowd. The increment is occasionally more substantial, as when a particularly loud and extroverted person joins the audience.

5.6   EXPERIENCE CHARACTERISTIC 5: NON-STORABILITY

The impossibility to store certain goods is a central economic problem for their producers. A hotel or restaurant guest who does not show up on time creates excess capacity that cannot be set aside for later use.

The Santa Fe economist Brian Arthur (1994) has modelled the dynamics of this type of experience market in his El Farol model. El Farol is a bar in Santa Fe, New Mexico, that specializes in the Irish beer-drinking experience. In his model, Arthur assumes that the consumer of the El Farol experience neither enjoys being in the bar when it is overcrowded nor when it is deserted. He also assumes that the decision to visit El Farol on a given night is based on the consumer's expectation as to the number of other bar patrons on the same night. In the model, a large number of different sub-models of expectation formation are tried out in simulations. It turns out that there is no system of expectation formation that ever converges on correct predictions of the number of customers. Instead, chaos is the typical outcome of these simulations.

Some evenings offer ample room for new guests. Because of the bar's perceived emptiness, the guests that do show up tend to leave after a short while. Most of the capacity of the bar and its personnel therefore remains unused. On other nights the place is overcrowded. Nevertheless, the average demand and its volatility (standard deviation over time) for this kind of experience service can be predicted with this type of model. The average number of customers in Arthur's simulation models was predicted to be approximately two thirds of the bar's capacity, but with large unpredictable fluctuations around this average. This is similar to the difference of predicting the average temperature in March and the actual temperature on a specific day in the same month.

The non-storability of many experience goods has led to the development of sophisticated systems of temporal price discrimination, with the aim of reducing the variability in demand and capacity utilization. It is, for instance, quite common to have lower prices of event tickets for early birds and latecomers. Similarly, hotel rates at tourist destinations differ between low and high seasons.

5.7   THE MULTIDIMENSIONALITY OF EXPERIENCE GOODS

As the preceding sections make clear, a good may be an experience good in one or more dimensions. We can therefore conclude that consumer goods range from goods with minimal experience content across the five dimensions to goods that have substantial experiential content on each dimension. Table 5.2 illustrates this by listing ten different consumer goods according to whether they score high or low on each of the five dimensions. One of the dimensions – uniqueness – is divided into two sub-dimensions, since a good may be unique in its composition and/or be a unique unit. A sonnet by Shakespeare and a painting by Picasso are both unique (literary or visual) compositions, but a text by Shakespeare is considered 'authentic' even if it is a mass-produced copy, whereas a painting by Picasso is only considered 'authentic' if it is an original rather than a reproduction.

As Table 5.2 makes clear, some goods can be considered as (almost) pure experience goods, whereas other goods combine high experience levels on some dimensions/attributes with low levels on others. Mass-produced generic goods, finally, can be considered approximations of pure standard goods. Socks and sugar are the examples of standard goods that are used in the table, but there are many others, such as petrol, (non-erotic) underwear, ketchup, light bulbs and ATM services. A telephone is an example of a good that combines one strong experience attribute (interdependence) with standard good characteristics in the other four dimensions. This is especially true of conventional landline telephones; cell phones with internet connectivity, global positioning system (GPS) and a built-in camera may necessitate more learning on the part of the consumer.

Table 5.2 also shows that there is some ambiguity concerning the consumption of certain goods. The relevant examples in the table are bottles of vintage wine and opera compact discs. These goods can certainly be appreciated by a single individual in the privacy of her home, but for many consumers there is a considerable utility gain associated with consuming wine or music together with others. This is partly related to the

Table 5.2   The five experience dimensions with ten examples

Dimension	Low (or zero) level: examples	High level: examples
1 Learning by consuming	1. Socks 2. Sugar 3. Telephone	4. Book by Shakespeare 5. Vintage wine 6. Opera CD 7. Cricket game 8. Jazz jam session 9. Research seminar 10. Urban environment
2A Uniqueness (unit)	1. Socks 2. Sugar 3. Telephone 4. (Copy of) book by Shakespeare 5. (Bottle of) vintage wine 6. (Copy of) opera CD	7. Cricket game 8. Jazz jam session 9. Research seminar 10. Urban environment
2B Uniqueness (design)	1. Socks 2. Sugar 3. Telephone	4. Book by Shakespeare 5. Vintage wine; 6. Opera CD 7. Cricket game 8. Jazz jam session 9. Research seminar 10. Urban environment
3 Location and context dependence	1. Socks 2. Sugar 3. Telephone 4. Book by Shakespeare 5. Vintage wine 6. Opera CD	7. Cricket game 8. Jazz jam session 9. Research seminar 10. Urban environment
4 Interdependence	1. Socks 2. Sugar 4. Book by Shakespeare 5. Vintage wine (?) 6. Opera CD (?)	3. Telephone 5. Vintage wine (?) 6. Opera CD (?) 7. Cricket game 8. Jazz jam session 9. Research seminar 10. Urban environment
5 Non-storability	1. Socks 2. Sugar 3. Telephone 4. Book by Shakespeare 5. Vintage wine 6. Opera CD	7. Cricket game 8. Jazz jam session 9. Research seminar 10. Urban environment

'conversation value' that is generated when a consumption experience can be discussed with friends and acquaintances (Hargreaves Heap, 2002).

Four of the examples exhibit high levels of all five experience attributes, including both of the uniqueness sub-attributes. They are the consumption of cricket games, jazz jam sessions, research seminars and – particularly – urban (and rural) environments. Let us consider the example of urban environments in more depth.

An urban environment can certainly be enjoyed to some extent by all users of urban space. But learning processes may result in value being added to the consumption experience. A tourist in Venice who has studied the history of Western architecture and art is likely to find the experience much more rewarding than someone who has no idea what the Renaissance signifies. This also means that a skilled consumer will be able to differentiate between many more consumption attributes in a given city than a consumer with limited knowledge of history, culture or art.

In addition, an urban environment is to a greater or lesser extent unique, although some elements of its infrastructure and behavioural patterns may be replicated elsewhere. This alludes to the fact that cities such as Venice or Paris offer a more unique experience than cities that are (relatively speaking) lacking in distinctive architectural styles or cultural habits, for example, Wichita, Kansas or Cleveland, Ohio. In all cities, however, it is the case that the composition of the city and the unit of consumption coincide, which is the reason that we chose not to classify the uniqueness of the copy and the uniqueness of the composition as separate experience dimensions.

By definition, a city is spatially delimited, which points to its location specificity. An urban environment is, in other words, an immobile asset. It is also normally the case that an urban environment is not equally attractive or interesting in all its constituent parts. This fact points to the importance of intra-regional accessibility and neighbourhood character.

Consumption interdependencies operate on two levels: there is both the interdependence that may arise when interacting with local residents, such as shopkeepers, waiters and restaurant patrons. There is also the conversation value of discussing the experience with fellow travellers or – after the event – with friends and acquaintances back home.

As regards non-storability, the assessment is perhaps not as unambiguous. It is admittedly true that the urban infrastructure of streets, museums and churches tends to remain the same for long periods of time; in some cases, there are only minor changes in the course of a normal human life span. But infrastructural stability is true of the consumption of all goods: concerts are performed in concert halls; football matches are played in stadia; and petrol is conveyed between less changeable filling stations and cars.

What is more important in this context is that the interactions between people that are supported by the infrastructure are changing continuously. The conversations, cultural events, business transactions or muggings that take place at one point in time never repeat themselves in exactly the same way. An urban environment therefore offers an inherently unpredictable succession of interactive events. It is in this way similar to cricket games, jam sessions or research seminars, although the urban environment may include all of these 'micro events' along with numerous others. An urban environment can therefore be seen as the experience good par excellence, although it shares high experiential levels across all five relevant dimensions with various types of interactive and spontaneous art, entertainment and scientific exchange.

A noteworthy difference between goods that are high in experience content and standard goods is the valuation of uncertainty. For standard goods, uncertainty is perceived as bad, and is associated with a price discount. Branded goods such as Coca Cola, Nike sneakers and Heinz baked beans thus command higher market prices than their unbranded substitutes. For true experience goods, the uncertainty of consumption outcomes frequently yields a utility gain. A live transmission of a football match is more popular than a recording of the same match because the result is still uncertain. Jazz improvisers are considered substandard if they repeat themselves and become predictable. And participants in research seminars want to make serendipitous discoveries and learn something new.

On a more aggregated level, cities are considered exciting and lively if unexpected meetings take place and they host unusual artists, subcultures and minorities (Florida, 2002). The uncertainty of experience that is inherent in a creative global metropolis such as London or New York typically yields greater utility gains for the urban tourist than the comfortable but bland certitudes of a Basingstoke or Buffalo.

5.8   WILLINGNESS TO PAY FOR EXPERIENCE GOODS

The willingness to pay for a good of whatever kind depends on the subjective preferences, knowledge and expectations of the consumer. What the consumer values is not the objective good in itself, but the expected services that the good is perceived as capable of producing (Andersson, 2008a). This means that most consumer goods are heterogeneous, and should be conceived of as bundles of consumption attributes. According to a specific consumer, shirts may, for example, be decomposed into the relevant attributes 'beauty', 'comfort', 'durability' and 'warmth', each of which impacts the overall willingness to pay. Goods with higher experience content, for example, housing, music or restaurant meals, tend to be associated with a much greater number of relevant attributes. The most standardized goods, such as petrol or sugar, only consist of one attribute for most consumers. Market prices are therefore easier to interpret for standard than for experience goods.

The process of learning by consuming leads to a continually increasing ability to differentiate among more attributes as well as finer gradations within each attribute. An example is that a generic experience of music can become subdivided into genres and sub-genres, and musical attributes such as rhythm, pitch, speed, timbre, instrumentation and personal 'sound' may become increasingly evident as the consumer becomes more skilful. Some economists have modelled this as a dynamic preference string that becomes increasingly well specified as a result of increasing connoisseurship (for example, Potts, 2000). For the most sophisticated experience goods, there is an enormous difference between the number of attributes that an expert and a novice is able to perceive. The willingness to pay is therefore a function of many more attributes among skilled than among unskilled consumers.

For the skilled consumer, the uniqueness of the composition may also influence the willingness to pay. Studies have shown that most consumers want an optimal level of surprise, but this optimal level is associated with increasing complexity as the consumer becomes more skilful (Andersson and Andersson, 2006). The willingness to pay for the unique features of a composition therefore increases with increasing connoisseurship.

Since mass markets are associated with consumers who have only a minor interest in the mass-produced good, such goods offer a level of complexity that suits the unskilled consumer but which is disappointing to the connoisseur. Soap operas, top 40 hits and tabloid newspapers elicit a small but positive willingness to pay among a multitude of consumers, whereas Andrei Tarkovsky films, atonal music and mediaeval philosophical treatises trigger a substantial willingness to pay among small and exclusive groups of connoisseurs.

The uniqueness of a copy is much less related to learning processes, and in this case the willingness to pay often reflects evaluations of expected re-sale profit (that is, speculative entrepreneurship). The relevant learning process is therefore in this case about market knowledge, rather than product knowledge.

The willingness to pay for location and context dependence is closely related to the concept of agglomeration economies. Consumers exhibit a high willingness to pay for what they consider to be attractive environments and good accessibility. The effect of such preferences on market prices has been extensively studied by means of hedonic price functions for housing and other real estate markets. By way of illustration, Andersson and Andersson (2006) estimated a hedonic price function for the European hotel market. One of their conclusions was that hotel rooms in cities that are rich in architectural sights and museums command a significant price premium over cities that lack such cultural infrastructure, other things being equal. For example, the difference between the cultural attractiveness of Barcelona and Birmingham corresponded to rooms that were twice as expensive in the former as in the latter city, controlling for population size, level of economic development, intra-regional accessibility and the qualitative attributes of individual hotels.

Such price effects obviously reflect the level of connoisseurship of the highest bidders, but in this case the process is speeded up through the determination of land prices as the joint effect of transactions in the housing, hotel, retail and office markets. It is also the case that location preferences that are idiosyncratic or that reflect unique knowledge on the part of the consumer can engender a substantial consumer surplus since only relatively widespread preferences will be reflected in the price of land.

The effect of interdependence on the willingness to pay is interesting because it often gives rise to skewed income distributions (Andersson, 2008b). The reason why brand-name personalities such as Dan Brown, Lionel Messi, Jack Nicholson or Bruce Springsteen earn so much more than the median income of their occupations is primarily the effect of consumption interdependence. It is only secondarily due to superior occupation-specific skills. Most consumers of mass-market experience goods such as popular novels, professional football, Hollywood movies and rock music have only a minor interest in the product type. Moreover, their skills as product evaluators tend to be rather modest. They therefore rely on fame as an indicator of product quality. For those with only a minor interest – which will be most people in mass markets due to their average time constraints – it is not worthwhile to keep track of more than a handful of famous individuals producing each of the numerous experience goods in which they are mildly interested.

For profit-seeking experience-producing firms such as Manchester United or Real Madrid, this means that they can expect a big boost to their revenues if they sign up a brand-name individual such as Wayne Rooney or Christiano Ronaldo as opposed to footballers who are only slightly less skilled but much less recognized by the population at large. This puts the brand-name individuals in a strong bargaining position. This is true of all experience industries where there is a much larger population of mildly interested consumers than of knowledgeable connoisseurs. The effects are magnified when the good can be conveyed at negligible marginal cost to a global audience, as is the case for television transmissions, video or audio recordings, books and newspapers.

The interdependence effect is reinforced by social interaction effects, such as the utility that is derived from having a topic of conversation among friends and acquaintances. Being knowledgeable about the fortunes of Manchester United and its stars offers conversation utility in all countries where (European) football is popular; following the matches of Swindon Town is (at most) a useable conversation starter in Swindon. And being interested in less popular experience goods, such as Brazilian poetry or Vietnamese films, will offer scant utility gains that derive from their social interaction effects (although this may change with the proliferation of ever more specialized internet forums).

The non-storability of some experience goods may also generate a separable willingness to pay for a live as opposed to a recorded experience. The difference is greatest for experiences of nature and cities as there are few people who would think that a book or film about Paris or the Himalayas is a close substitute to actually visiting the places. Whenever uncertainty about the outcome is a valued consumption attribute, non-storability comes to the fore as an important partial determinant of the willingness to pay, as is illustrated by the much greater interest in live transmissions than recordings of competitive sports. If the interaction between the performers and the audience is important, there will be a special value increment associated with live attendance as opposed to live electronic transmission. This is also true of many sports as well as of live music, theatre and educational events.

The willingness to pay for experience goods is therefore a much more complex phenomenon than that for standard goods. The stronger the experience characteristics of a good are, the more difficult it becomes to disentangle the numerous components that contribute to consumers' willingness to pay. For experience goods more than for standard goods, the eventual market price reflects the interaction of consumers with heterogeneous preferences, skills and expectations, on the one hand, and producers with heterogeneous goods and production technologies, on the other.

5.9   CONCLUSIONS

Experience goods are more complex than standard goods. A number of different characteristics have to be taken into account in the economic theory of experience goods.

There are at least five such experience-related characteristics: learning by consuming; uniqueness; location and context dependence; interdependence; and non-storability.

For the most sophisticated experience goods, there is a substantial difference between the number of attributes that an expert and a novice is able to perceive. The willingness to pay for the quality of an experience good is therefore a function of many more attributes among skilled than among unskilled consumers.

Uniqueness, context dependence and interdependence (among both consumers and producers) lead to uncertain benefits and costs. These uncertainties are of great importance in the design and marketing of experiences. In order to reduce consumers' perceived risks, the producers tend to allocate substantial resources to branding and celebrity endorsements.

The effect of interdependence on the willingness to pay is interesting because it often gives rise to skewed income distributions. The reason why brand-name personalities such as Dan Brown or Bruce Springsteen earn so much more than the median income of their occupations is primarily the effect of consumption uniqueness and interdependence. It is only secondarily due to superior occupation-specific skills. Most consumers of mass-market experience goods have only limited skills as product evaluators. They therefore rely on fame as an indicator of product quality.

In our analysis, we have singled out a few examples that have all the five characteristics central to the economic analysis of experience goods, such as football matches, improvised music and urban environments. The multi-dimensional nature of such goods makes the willingness to pay a much more complex phenomenon than in the case of standard goods. Analogously, market prices become fuzzier and less reliable measuring rods of relative scarcity than the price of sugar or salt.

REFERENCES

Andersson, Å.E. and D.E. Andersson (2006), *The Economics of Experiences, the Arts and Entertainment*, Cheltenham, UK and Northampton, MA, USA: Edward Elgar.

Andersson, D.E. (2008a), *Property Rights, Consumption and the Market Process*, Cheltenham, UK and Northampton, MA, USA: Edward Elgar.

Andersson, D.E. (2008b), 'The double-edged nature of the Hayekian knowledge problem: systemic tendencies in markets and science', *Studies in Emergent Order*, **1**, 51–72.

Arrow, K.J. (1962), 'The economic implications of learning by doing', *Review of Economic Studies*, **29** (3), 155–73.

Arthur, W.B. (1994), 'Inductive reasoning and bounded rationality', *American Economic Review*, **84**, 406–11.

Chamberlin, E.H. (1933), *The Theory of Monopolistic Competition: A Re-orientation of the Theory of Value*, Cambridge, MA: Harvard University Press.

Earl, P.E. (1983), *The Economic Imagination: Towards a Behavioural Theory of Choice*, Brighton, UK: Wheatsheaf.

Economist Intelligence Unit (2012), 'The liveability ranking and overview', *The Economist*, August.

Florida, R. (2002), *The Rise of the Creative Class*, New York: Basic Books.

Forbes (2007), http://www.forbes.com/travel/ (accessed 22 October 2007).

Freeman, W.J. (1995), 'Chaotic state transitions in brains as a basis for the formation of social groups', in A. Albert (ed.), *Chaos and Society*, Quebec: Les Presses de l'Université du Québec, pp. 119–32.

Hargreaves Heap, S.P. (2002), 'Everybody is talking about it: intersubjectivity and the television industry', in E. Fullbrook (ed.), *Intersubjectivity in Economics: Agents and Structures*, London: Routledge, pp. 123–36.

Marshall, A. (1920), *Principles of Economics*, London: Macmillan.

Pine, B.J. and J.H. Gilmore (1999), *The Experience Economy*, Cambridge, MA: Harvard University Business Press.

Potts, J. (2000), *The New Evolutionary Microeconomics*, Cheltenham, UK and Northampton, MA, USA: Edward Elgar.

Smith, A. (1776), *The Wealth of Nations*, London: Random House, reprinted in 1937.

Tripadvisor (2012), http://www.tripadvisor.com/TravelersChoice-Destinations (accessed 22 August 2012).

6. The experience market
Gerhard Schulze

6.1 EXPERIENCE MARKET, EXPERIENCE SUPPLY, EXPERIENCE DEMAND

Since the ending of World War II, the social significance of the experience market in Europe has constantly grown. The term experience market here denotes the meeting of experience demand and experience supply. Experience demand as well as experience supply are subject to a particular rationality – this is the starting point of analysing the experience market in the following sections. By demanding experiences one is acting in quite another field than consuming material goods. Experience suppliers have to account for the particular rationality of experience demand. This holds, with some modifications, also for cultural policy administrating public events and opportunities.

On the experience market, experience offers are exchanged for money and/or attention. In the following, the concepts of experience offers and experience supply will comprise all products, the use of which is predominantly defined in aesthetical terms (nice, exciting, comfortable, stylish, interesting and so on). The concepts of experience demand or inwardly oriented consumption refer to the use of experience offers. Admittedly, this is merely a particular case of experience-oriented action, but the increased significance of this particular case requires a sociological analysis. Aesthetic episodes, whether everyday or not, unfold more and more in the framework of market relations.

It is clear that the terms experience market, experience supply and experience demand presuppose the reconstruction of meanings of products. Usually, this is easier than may appear at first. In regards to, for example, TV shows, magazines, folksong hours on the radio, rock concerts, clothes, packaged tours or innumerous internet offers and facilities, no great hermeneutic effort is required to identify these products as experience offers. It is the normal, predominant consumer motivation that defines supply as experience supply, regardless of differing individual cases. A tractor will not become an experience supply even if someone buys it for mere pleasure. Conversely, a meal in a specialty restaurant does not become mere food because for once it is devoured without culinary pleasure but only to satisfy one's hunger.

As a tiny detail of an enormous assortment of experience offers, the meal is in competition not only with other meals, but also with stylish shoes, books, sporting goods, flower bulbs, "The Marriage of Figaro," yoga courses, chrome hub caps, big sport events, trips, pornography, exhibitions or a new hairdo. Whether an offer is an experience offer or not might not always be as clear as with these examples. However, what is sociologically significant is not the border zone, but the undisputed core area of experience supply that is constantly expanding. There is a long list of products that, over the last decades, have lost their use value in objective terms to gain experience value: furniture, household appliances, foods, clothes, vehicles, car accessories and others. Between pure experience supply and offers like industrial goods, tools, staple foods and the like an area of products with blended meanings is to be observed, the experience component of which coming to the foreground more and more.

Only in a partial area of the experience market does the consumers give nothing but money in return. Seeing this market as a purely economic phenomenon we would not determine its sociological substance. Besides money other values for which experience suppliers stand in fierce competition are desired too: time, attention, appreciation, reputation, fame or followership. Television and radio programs or communal cultural policy sometimes are just as much part of the experience market as canned music or nerve-racking pop-ups. The distinction between commercial and non-commercial culture sometimes seems like an attempt to endow non-commercial experience offers with a magic of authenticity.

Experience offers are made available by a ceaselessly producing infrastructure. The dynamics of current everyday aesthetics is brought forward through the interaction between the experience production network and the public, in which each side influences the other. Both sides act according to their own rationality. The knowledge of each other corresponds to Coleman's analysis in *The Asymmetric Society* (1982): it is one-sided. While the experience suppliers have to try to capture their clientele's goal horizon as detailed as possible, those demanding experiences merely have to know where what is offered to them is from and for what purpose. However, the supplier's understanding of the wishes of the customers does not lead to a mutuality of interests. Comparable to information about interest rates, fixed costs, chains of distribution, employees' qualifications and so on, the consumer's need is only one of many parameters that are integrated into the experience suppliers' planning of actions. What finally precisely results from the collaboration of supply and demand – the actual experience market – can neither be described through set phrases of culture criticism about the consumer's total manipulation nor through the naïve counter-image of the public's aesthetical autonomy: after all, everyone could really do exactly what he or she wants to do.

Hardly any consumers would come up with the idea that through their simple, ever more casual act of experience consumption – buying a magazine, turning on the television, vacationing in the South and so on – they are contributing to the existence of an enormous production network. However, the relevancy of the individual's experience consumption is too low, the product supplier too intangible and the focus on planning actions for the small experience success in the near future too strong that those demanding experiences could ever consider controlling the experience market. In their rationality, the consumers act on the assumptions of given experience supplies, as if it were a reality not influenced by them.

Conversely, experience suppliers try to fit their customers into a different goal horizon, for instance, corporate survival, profits, artistic self-fulfillment, prestige or cultural-political utopias. Whatever their final intention might be, the whole lot has to be prepared to compete against each other on the experience market, struggling for shares of a total capacity of experience demand. To mobilize those demanding experiences for their own plans, all competitors have to get involved with similar strategies: the rock star's manager, the sneakers' company, the municipal cultural consultant, the producer of gummy bears, the concert pianist and the cultural worker at the community center. All of them have to consider what might catch on and arrange their offers accordingly.

With finesse and empathy they try to channel the public's money, time and attention into their own direction.

Those supplying and those demanding experiences symbiotically coexist in a social relation of rationalities that are interlaced with each other – incommensurable yet harmonizing. Producers and consumers are only effective in their aggregation; as individual participants in the experience market, they are facing conditions without possibilities of influencing them. One cannot control the experience market; only leave it, at the most. Whoever takes part in it, no matter on what side, makes a vanishingly small contribution (hardly relevant in terms of responsibility) for the cultural interaction of collectives that are well attuned to each other.

The long-term effects of these interactions arise without knowledge or intention of those acting, comparable to the gradual changes of nature triggered by millions of people who incessantly "just quickly" have to drive somewhere, turn on the washing machine or use refrigerators, hairspray, warm water and so on. However, while unintended changes in nature someday might set a signal for action, cultural changes that result as side-effects of everyday life imperceptibly retroact on inner lives, although perhaps not without unknown losses.

This chapter belongs to a sociological tradition, the origins of which can be traced back to Georg Simmel's phenomenological work on subjectivity in modernity (1900 [2004], 1908). In retrospect, with regards to the twentieth century, we see a line of milestones alongside a track we are still are following. Despite all differences, the books of David Riesman (1950), John Kenneth Galbraith (1958), Daniel Bell (1973), Ronald Inglehart (1977) and Neil Postman (1985) – to mention only some famous examples – reflect the same process: a shift of the main focus of action and thinking from objective circumstances to culture and the self. With his trilogy, Manuel Castells (1996, 1997, 1998) continued the series of sociological studies on subjectivity.

The following text is meant to pursue this sociological tradition. Methodologically, it is based on the thinking of Simmel and Weber, governed by a phenomenological perspective, following the approach of interpretative sociology, trying to achieve a holistic description of social reality, oriented on Weber's concept of rationalization. It is based on a chapter in my research study on experience society (Schulze, 1992 [2005]) and it corresponds to a number of surveys dealing with the whole field of the economization of experience, such as Keat and Abercrombie (1991), Lash and Urry (1994), Roberts (2004), Bagdikian (2004) and Hesmondhalgh (2007).

6.2   ACTION ROUTINES ON THE EXPERIENCE MARKET

As chaotic as the experience market may often appear to be, the actions of suppliers and consumers follow certain patterns, which in the following are depicted as rationality types. What is a rationality type? In our context, it denotes a conglomerate of action strategies that refer to ever recurring goals. Action strategies and goals have a hierarchical relationship. On both levels, rationality types have to be analysed separately: first, one has to deal with the integrating nucleus – goals that have solidified and become self-evident; then with the deadlocked action routines that are supposed to lead to those goals. Whether they are really adequate for this purpose or not is not fixed in the rationality type concept – it is focused on empirically found actions and reasons, not on their adequacy.

For a temporary classification of the sociological meaning of a rationality type, one can orient oneself by three dimensions: collective spreading, stability and frequency of actualization. According to all three aspects, the rationality type of experience demand stands out when compared to other rationality types: it is nearly universal, solidifies itself more and more and is a matter of course in everyday life. Only since the postwar era did this rationality type attain such an eminent position. It was established as a new life technique against the background of a new, inwardly directed view of life, apparently necessary for orientation in the expanding space of everyday aesthetic opportunities.

The goal to experience something is the core of the present rationality of experience demand. This goal is not as clear as people assume as a matter of course and the assumption that it could be easily attained is self-delusional: choose the appropriate experience offer available to be fully satisfied! But my analysis of strategies combined in the rationality of experience demand will show that the correspondence principle – the matching of wishes and selected products – is merely appropriate to compensate for the lack of clarity in the definition of means and goals, like the other strategies still to be described: abstraction, accumulation, variation and autosuggestion.

On the other side, that of experience suppliers, a rationality type has also emerged. The integrated goal here is public appeal, but other goals also play an important role, usually a superordinate one: profit, long-term survival of corporations, creative self-fulfillment and cultural-political ambitions. A necessary requirement for this and other goals, however, is public appeal, so this is the crucial point for understanding the strategies of experience suppliers. Even if the most important of these strategies – schematization, profiling, modification and suggestion – merely appear like a reflex to the rationality of experience demand, they do lead to a new situation that affects the public. Experience suppliers and demanders learn from one another.

There are inwardly and outwardly oriented rationality types. In the former, the definition of the integrating goal refers to the inner life of the person: his knowledge, skills, basic views, feelings and experiences. In contrast, the goal of outwardly oriented rationality types can be defined independently of the acting subject: money, product features, system statuses of organizations, attribute distributions in social collectives.

With this distinction, a gradation of difficulties with respect to planning action efficiently can be marked. As a general rule, we can state that outwardly oriented rationality types are easier to optimize than inwardly oriented ones. Outwardly oriented action usually refers to clearly definable and measurable goal states; the current state and target state are comparable to one another; instrumental actions are evaluable. On the other side, if the goals lie within us, everything becomes unclear. It is difficult enough to develop an unambiguous conception of inwardly oriented goal states. Additionally, psychic effects cannot be measured independently of the one who observes them in himself. Whether someone actually is feeling a psychic effect, whether that effect is merely suggested or whether one is suggesting it to oneself cannot be said with certainty.

In contrast to inwardly oriented action types, outwardly oriented ones can be technically perfected. If both action types encounter each other – as is the case on the experience market – the outwardly oriented type will, after a short while, take over the law of action, while the inwardly oriented one will react and create confusion through unpredictable, apparently irrational changes of course and leapfrogging. But even this can be planned in the outwardly oriented accounting of risks.

As Heiner (1983) has shown, ambiguity is a condition that brings forward the development of predictable behavioral patterns. If established information is at hand – clear cost-benefit criteria, broad subjective probabilities of success or failure – the behavior will fluctuate with the situations. The less one knows in how the alternatives differ and what one really wants, the more one is inclined to do the same thing over and over again. For example, it seems at least intuitively plausible that the annual pilgrimage to the Mediterranean Sea has to do more with helplessness than with efficient experience planning. Different aspects of the product "vacation in the South" within reach of lower middle income rather indicate uncertainty than adequate realization of experience dreams (unsightly architecture, noise, four-lane motorways near the beach, tasteless accommodation, concentration of crowds, the wearisome journey there and back and so on). An inwardly oriented rationality type tends toward regularity, not necessarily toward usefulness.

How the ideal rational experience planning of actions should look like is not the aim of this chapter. If, following Elster (1989), one looks at experiences as "incidents that are actually by-products," rational experience planning seems to be part of an absurd utopia. Quite the contrary, rationality of experience could consist in the avoidance of explicit experience planning, so as not to disturb the sensitive process of experiencing through the intention of bringing it about. It is not without reason that this philosophy has a long tradition to the heart of which Schopenhauer gets in his *The Wisdom of Life* (1851 [2005]). This philosophical insight did not catch on. Instead, methodic and complex experience work is characteristic for a growing number of societies. What strategies can be observed are analysed in the following.

6.3   FROM OUTWARDLY ORIENTED TO INWARDLY ORIENTED CONSUMPTION

The distinction of outwardly oriented and inwardly oriented consumption makes it easier to understand the rationality of experience demand. If one buys a pair of glasses as a means to better vision, a car as a set of wheels, flour as carbohydrate-rich food and so on, one acts outwardly oriented. The inwardly oriented consumer, in contrast, looks for glasses he feels good with, a car that fascinates him and flour of a certain brand in order to experience something: experience flour. What might still seem absurd today can become totally normal tomorrow. Each product can be supplied and demanded inwardly oriented; flour may simply be awaiting the change in meaning that has long since happened to glasses and cars. "Inward" is the subject. Phrases used to justify inwardly oriented consumption refer to processes that take place in the subject: "because it amuses me," "because I like it" or "because it suits me." In outwardly oriented consumption, the product's quality is defined independently from the consumer. It's about objective properties of products, irrespective of their reference to the subject's needs and however wrong the consumer might perceive them. Whether a used car is "good" can usually be determined better by an expert than by the outwardly oriented consumer himself. The inwardly oriented consumer, on the contrary, looking for a "nice" used car, cannot hand over the quality inspection to anybody else. He defines the product's wanted qualities in terms of reactions it triggers in his inner life.

In contrast, Bourdieu's *Distinction* (1984) basically refers to an objective dimension of things and situations seen from the perspective of the consumer. The distinctive demander is not oriented on desired experiences but on desired perceptions in the eyes of his observers. The supposed capacity of a new car or going to the opera to impress his neighbors is a social phenomenon beyond his experiences, whether he is feeling bored or fascinated by, say, the music of Richard Wagner. Bourdieu is talking about the symbolic manifestations of human pecking orders, not primarily about desired experiences (which nevertheless might occur as side-effects).

Many offers are demanded nearly exclusively out of inwardly oriented motivation: television and radio programs, canned music, magazines, vacations, stylish accessories, exhibitions, theaters, concerts, literature and a lot more. In other products, outwardly and inwardly oriented components combine, although the inwardly oriented components have significantly increased: clothing, vehicles, a privately owned house, furniture, food, to just name the major ones. It is difficult to still find any products that are consumed merely for outward orientation – aside from shoe polish, salt, fertilizer or other such sundries, there is hardly anything left. But the process of aestheticization – the arrangement of products for experiences – goes on and on. Product developments over the last decades show that even light bulbs, matchboxes, paper clips, thumbtacks or car tires can be aestheticized, to say nothing of notebooks, tabloids, smart phones, iPods and other terminal devices. The market for producer goods is the last reserve of economic relations that can be understood by merely exploring outwardly oriented motivations. The corporate demander of goods and services acquires products for their functions in an outwardly oriented context; the experience-oriented private consumer because of their appeal to his inner life.

If one would explain to the average consumer with which models economists try to describe his behavior, his reaction would be disbelieving surprise, not only because of his supposed type of rationality but also because of the trust in his calculation skills and abilities of processing information. For television viewers playing with their remote control, for shoppers in the pedestrian area, for tourists, concert goers, guests in a restaurant and so on, this model of purposive action planning according to rational choice theory would cause a great deal of laughter.

It might be the case that traditional economical decision models provide useful explanations under certain conditions: resource constraints, high significance of affecting subjective goals, long-time training in end-means thinking including the calculation of side-effects and only moderate diversification of products. All these conditions are untypical for our society's consumption situation. The motive for a strict benefit calculation becomes irrelevant if the consumed good has only an insignificant effect on one's resources of time and money, so that a bad investment only causes minor damage. Outwardly oriented motives, for instance, in the consumption areas of food, housing, transportation or clothing, are given a new meaning. The motives are turning inward increasingly: it is a question of "good" food, "stylish" living, transportation as an experience, clothing as self-staging. Basic needs are not perceived as misery but as a minimal deviation from a satiated state, the restoration of which is considered as a matter of course. More important than the satiated state is the slight deprivation as a premise for consumption to be fun: "I had a terrific appetite."

With the increasing multiplicity of products with the same outwardly oriented purpose more and more inwardly oriented motives come into the fore. When, for example, only a single glasses frame is available, the only need that plays a role in buying this product is to see better. However, if one can choose from hundreds of frames, the original need is only sufficient to make one go see an optician. When deciding what to buy, these other goals are superficially indicated with "good looking."

Inwardly oriented consumption is a special case of experience-oriented action that is defined through being integrated into market relations. New action routines have developed that in their totality form the rationality type of experience demand. In the two following sections this rationality type are described.

6.4   EXPERIENCE AS AN ACTION GOAL

How do we act facing a great amount of experience offers that we can acquire for no other purpose but to make nice experiences? The reason that rationality of experience action has not found a similar intensive interest in sociology like outwardly oriented action is due to the misleading equation of both action types. Experience-oriented action, however, cannot be subsumed as a special case under traditional models of rational action.

Experience orientation has long since pervaded our everyday life, just as the situation in which we choose from experience offers has become standard. Even potential partners for long-term relationships are perceived and presented as experience offers, as it were. The internet is used to find the person most familiar to one's experience desires – hopefully (Becker and Lois, 2010). But whether our behavior in the situation of choice can be described in a theoretically meaningful manner – for example, as "maximization of experience benefits" according to cost-benefit comparisons of different alternatives on the basis of subjective value expectations – seems doubtful for several reasons: because experience-oriented action often is not deliberative but actually staged with accentuated spontaneity; because experience benefits are incalculable; because the subject is confronted with great uncertainty. How will offer A affect me? How, in comparison, the countless competing offers? Will my benefit calculation on the basis of my current likes and dislikes still hold up in the future when I will have made my choice? And, more fundamentally, what do I really like and what not?

Experience rational acting aims at a center that lies within the actor himself. Whatever the experience goal might be, inwardly oriented consumer motivation is aiming at a subjective process. However, we find ourselves amidst incessant subjective processes in any case, whether we want to or not. Especially when we think we're experiencing nothing, when we feel bored to death, we experience our life especially intensely, albeit unpleasantly. As human beings we are condemned or privileged to experience, depending on what is currently going on. We are not able to just "switch off." To experience something per se, we do not have to act rationally in pursuit of this goal. We definitely have the alternative, however, to see what is always taking place within us anyway either as a side-effect – consciousness, inner life, self-awareness, subjective reactions to the world – or make it the main issue. We can systematically plan our action in service to very special experiences, but we are not forced to do so, if we want to experience something.

As soon as we no longer put up with the inescapable flow of experiences just as it comes but try to regulate it ourselves, we act experience-rationally. Our actions can then be understood as attempts of arranging our immediate experience environment in a way that an intended psycho-physical process takes place, for instance, by traveling into certain regions or providing optical and acoustic stimuli by pushing a button.

It is surprising at first how indistinct the information on concrete experience goals is even with those who have put their energy largely into the service of experience rationality. Experiences should be "interesting" or "nice"; one is looking for "fascination"; one does this or that to not get "bored." Afterwards, things are a lot clearer: one can (in the best case) at least say whether a desired experience has taken place even if one usually fails to describe the experience itself.

Even professional experience communicators like novelists, lyricists, scriptwriters, reporters or conductors of an orchestra can only partially overcome this speechlessness. The public is looking for a description of itself. Everyone who tries to describe experiences without exception reaches the borders of communicability. We construct our experiences in a universe of meaning that was established by a subject with a singular genetic disposition in a unique life story. Nobody can put oneself completely in somebody else's shoes, so the communication about our experiences is accordingly superficial.

The communication about experiences we want to have is even more limited. Here, language is restricted even more. The incongruity between words and subjective diversity of meanings not only has interpersonal but also intrapersonal effects. It results in a restriction of our imagination. A person acting experience-rationally takes the position of a DJ who has all possible records available but does not know what his audience likes. We are our own audience, but we often do not know exactly what catches on with us.

Outwardly oriented and inwardly oriented consumption differ by their degree of subjectively felt uncertainty. An outwardly oriented consumer can give clear specifications of what he needs the demanded product for. He can also deduce clear quality criteria out of it. He can distinguish goods and services by their usefulness for defined requirements and finally make a rational decision. To buy a pair of "good" shoes is easier in comparison to finding a pair of "nice" shoes. The consumer can only define tautologically what is nice or ugly: "It is nice just because it is nice." The existence of advertisements, fashion, feature pages and other manifestations of aesthetic definitions largely is due to a public in search of self-understanding. Most people can neither clearly say in what their experiences precisely consist nor are they at least able to define their own aesthetic quality criteria. This uncertainty is in no way a sign of stupidity, lack of education or superficiality, but an inevitable by-product of inwardly oriented consumption. Seen by the arguments of logic, one is on the last level of values, as soon as something nice is sought for its own sake. Here, decisions are only possible as spontaneous emotional acts, not as rational calculations. The only quality criteria of inwardly oriented consumption are the psycho-physical effects on the consumer himself. What these effects are exactly and why they should be just like this and not otherwise, whether a certain offer promises greater experience benefits than a competing offer, whether these benefits actually take place in the moment of consumption – all this is much harder to distinguish than whether a pair of shoes is waterproof.

6.5   THE RATIONALITY OF EXPERIENCE DEMAND

The rationality of experience demand as characteristic for our society is due to the premise that one can cause nice experiences by choosing the right and fitting one out of a mass of experience offers. With this assumption – which most people simply take for granted – a double deficit is overridden, but not eliminated. First, it is often unclear what kind of experiences the person is aiming at. But even if he knows exactly what he wants, the second question is whether he will succeed in producing this experience, because on the experience market he will only get the necessary ingredients. However, nobody can provide the subjective experience construction as everyday aesthetic service. The experience-rational consumer typically ignores both of these problems – the risks of insecurity and disappointment – only to keep himself explicitly occupied with a third one: which offer should he choose to reach his experience goal?

Who knows how participation on the experience market would decline if it became popular to pay more attention to preliminary questions. They certainly don't become insignificant by excluding them. Often enough the experience demander in his consumption activism gets to feel that he does not have clear experience goals and that consumption alone is not enough to experience. Strategies of product choice that in our society have consolidated into a rationality type are noticeably shaped by such feelings. Five principles are principally characteristic for this rationality type: correspondence, abstraction, accumulation, variation and autosuggestion. It is these principles that help to understand the mass audiences in the focus of Webster and Phalen (1997), trends, sales figures, bestsellers, charts or mass phenomena in the internet. In the following, these five principles are explained.

6.5.1   Correspondence

To procure experience offers one feels in the mood for seems to be, at first sight, the only possible and meaningful strategy of experience demand. It results in establishing a correspondence of accepted experience demands and acquired goods and services and shall therefore be termed as the correspondence principle. Though it is difficult for the consumer to make his experience demand explicit (if at all), at least he can vaguely feel interest, indifference or dislike when he is flooded with experience offers. This is his benchmark when operating with the correspondence principle. However, the consumer cannot consider anew in every situation which offers correspond to his own needs. He develops correspondence routines that combine into a personal consumption style. Only when guided by a kind of aesthetic basic program are we able to find our way in the experience market's chaos.

Theoretically, it seems possible that everybody maintains his very own consumption style but in reality collective elements dominate. Partially this can be explained by the rationality of experience supply. As the suppliers are forced to take public appeal into account, they react specifically to frequent and repeated demand. Both groups of actors on the experience market attune themselves to one another; their symbiosis leads to an everyday aesthetic evolution, the selection principle of which favors such complexes of signs and meanings on which many can agree. Everyday aesthetic schemas evolve that lead to the parallelization of the correspondence principle in large consumer subpopulations. A younger housewife with little education typically reacts to other experience stimuli than an older academic. The basic meanings of everyday aesthetic schemas can be combined with countless signs. The suspense schema, for example, is kept up-to-date by particular musical genres, reading matter, television shows or behavioral patterns when going out at night or during travel; it becomes evident in clothing styles, driving styles, movement styles and so on. The subject's position concerning innumerable experience offers is roughly predefined by his position concerning everyday aesthetic schemas.

Two features make the correspondence principle the most popular compass consumers use in the flood of experience supplies: first, they think it's easy to implement and second, they believe it to be experience-rational. Both assumptions are questionable.

The correspondence principle does not give clear orientation at all because experience needs don't make themselves as noticeable as hunger, thirst, fatigue and other physiological-based needs. Certainly, time and again it happens that a particular experience project dominates, for example, to go on a vacation. But even if the goal is reasonably clear, the handling of the correspondence principle gets difficult as soon as one has to decide on a particular offer. The product class "vacation," like all other classes of experience supply, conveys a confusing variety, so it is difficult to choose the offer most adequate to one's wishes, even if one really knows what one wants. Whether the consumer wants to spend his holidays in the mountains, in the Far East or at the Mediterranean Sea, in the end, he is faced with a large number of possibilities that are so similar that his final choice cannot be accomplished with the correspondence principle alone. There are many offers that fit a given pattern. To solve the problem of making his life nice, the experience demander needs further strategies.

6.5.2   Abstraction

The correspondence principle is seldom adequate to clearly distinguish a certain product from all the others. Only through abstraction can it be made applicable for everyday use. What is meant by that? The concrete everyday aesthetic episode – the pleasure of here and now – is pushed into the background of attention. Not singular consumer acts but habits are the focus of rational experience demand. Although pleasure always grows out of the details of specific situations and unique objects, consumers orient themselves more by abstract selection principles than by what they experience in particular moments. Accordingly, the correspondence principle's only function is often to merely make a diffuse pre-selection in creating selective receptivity for certain product classes and blanking out others from the beginning.

The closer consumption acts succeed one another, the less important it becomes to work out the correspondence of everyday aesthetic wishes and given products from situation to situation; rather it becomes important to rationalize consumer choice referring to whole classes of offers. To think about whether one really wants this or that, there is neither enough time nor energy. The average consumer is attuned to average experiences; he tries to maximize the probability of satisfaction in a continual consumption sequence and, in the process, accepts failures here and there. It is not the individual everyday aesthetic episode that matters to him, but the experience-optimal regulation of product streams. The consumer automatizes his demand through the abstraction principle that predefines acceptance and rejection in reference to an unlimited bulk of offers.

The abstraction principle manifests itself, for instance, through consuming serial offers (TV series, magazine subscriptions, light fiction series, bestseller series from famous literary writers, concert series, rock stars' series of hits and so on), through frequenting certain pubs and bars, through preferring certain radio channels that provide an all-day acoustic background, through preferring certain types of shopping environments, through selection patterns in networks (Facebook, blogs, twitter and so on). Many such abstractions are included in the hyper-abstraction of everyday aesthetic schemas. Enormous masses of objects, places, persons, offers, artifacts are interpreted as signs for only one meaning: a general experience expectation that often fulfills itself (see subsection below on autosuggestion).

6.5.3   Accumulation

With the growing habituation of inwardly oriented consumption, one can observe a trend of accumulating experiences and increasing their frequency, not only because it is difficult to keep finding effective experience offers but also in order to minimize the amount of energy used. To be fascinated, elated or deeply satisfied every day or hour is too much for most people. For intensive experiences one needs time in between them. Experiences take place in episodes. It is impossible to transform experiences from processes into states – they come to an end and have to be set in motion again and again. So the consumers at least try to reduce the intervals between experiences. Making the extraordinary ordinary – this paradoxical intention of habitual experience consumption leads to an increase of experience speed at the expense of experience depth.

In the fully developed routine of experience demand, not even experience needs are required for activating the willingness to consume. Well-tried or promising new experience offers are taken up in the expectation that these will perhaps entail small satisfactions (abstraction principle). Through the permanent contact with masses of experience offers, at last even the necessity to define one's own vague experience goals will disappear. The less you search, the more you find. Under the condition of the fully developed experience market, it is an experience-rational strategy to access offers constantly and in quick succession. Incidental fascinations arise with high reliability. It is enough to merely leave the radio on, to play around with the TV, to surf the web, or to stroll through the town or cruise around in an area. When the appeal to clarify experience intentions disappears because one can act at random, the aspiration level is reduced to a minimum. The action strategy (accumulation) scales down the action goal (experience) in a way that retrospectively the strategy seems to be justified despite the moderate success.

6.5.4   Variation

To be able to even feel each next stimulus when accumulating experience offers, the actor has to develop variety strategies. The more he shifts the responsibility for experiences from the inside to the outside, from himself to offers, the more his experiences depend on the differences between successive stimuli. However, if these differences exceed the subjective tolerance threshold, the risk of disorientation arises. Radical changes are seldom. The variation strategy is employed within the same general framework. One changes the bar, not the milieu. One changes the TV channel until one finds a program that is similar to the offer consumed so far. One looks for a radio station to listen to new tracks time and again that all belong to the same everyday aesthetic schema. One buys new clothes but stays true to one's style. To experience something new, one books a stay on Rhodes after having spent the last vacation on Crete.

6.5.5   Autosuggestion

Typical for the rationality of experience-oriented consumption is, finally, the auto-suggestive maximization of certainty. It is a rare exception that certainty is gained exclusively by one's own opinion and experience. Experience expectations before con-sumption decisions as well as reflections afterward ("nice," "interesting," "boring," "tasteless" and so on) usually come about only with massive social support when interpreting. To know whether something is nice or worth the money, time and atten-tion, one looks around for other people who seem to have that certainty or at least can contribute to it: fans, critics, bored people, fellow consumers, anti-consumers, model consumers.

Not all of those are significant for everybody. An experience offer radiates all the more certainty the more a consumer realizes that it is consumed by others that apparently are similar to him. Therefore, especially consumers in the alleged individualized society observe their social milieu – no longer out of the nineteenth-century fear of disgracing oneself but out of the contemporary fear of not enjoying one's life. Autosuggestion is a strategy to fight this fear. The same purpose is served by the subjective receptiveness of advertisements, which is usually larger than one admits. To let oneself be convinced is experience-rational. A notorious demand for demonstrations of aesthetic success is the result of the consumer's uncertainty, whether he actually achieved what he wanted and of the impossibility of exact inner quality control.

Uncertainty can be reduced by letting oneself be persuaded to aim (or have aimed) at a certain experience. The sales potential of an experience offer is all the higher the more it meets the demand of certainty and is charged with suggestions. Often the reference to an offer's objective qualities has the sole purpose to reassure the customer in light of an unsettling circumstance: whether the product keeps its aesthetic promise cannot be judged independently from the one who believes that promise. Other than when search-ing for a "good" pair of shoes (outwardly oriented consumption) it can be a reasonable strategy, when searching for a "nice" pair (inwardly oriented consumption), to trust what the shop assistant says because it is exactly under these conditions that the reason for consumption can realize itself (a nice experience or at least the idea of having one). Getting wet feet later on is irrelevant.

The rational experience consumer does not fight suggestion (as the rational outwardly oriented consumer has to), he looks for it: the virtuoso's reputation, the rush to the rock concert, the currency of stylish fashion details in one's own milieu, the labeling of a movie as cult, the romanticizing of travel destinations through enthusiastic descriptions, literary elevations in feature pages, defining experience content of offers through adver-tisements or creating an aura of specialty through exorbitant prices.

This rationality of experience demand was, in the last decades, an essential condition necessary for growth of experience-supplying organizations which, hardly launched, did everything to boost this action type. Experience suppliers have long developed their own corresponding rationality types. It is out of the interaction of both these action structures that the macro-sociological dynamic of the experience market develops.

6.6   PUBLIC APPEAL AS AN ACTION GOAL

With their strategies, the experience suppliers try to exploit the experience demanders' action patterns as much as possible for their own goals – "desperately seeking the audience" (in the case of TV) and often misled by false assumptions (Ang, 1991), but learning in the course of time (Murdock and Golding, 1999). They have developed a thoroughly outwardly oriented rationality type that appears to be inevitable, but is really just specific for our culture. There are alternatives for this rationality type as former centuries have shown.

Nothing is more apparent than that the current experience production is not considered as an end in itself – *l'art pour l'art*, brought into the world by self-sufficient artistry where the work alone counts and the public's favor is merely a convenient side-effect. Of course, such unwillingness to compromise has always been jeopardized by vanity and profit seeking, the alleged duty to artistic intention often merely concealed a pretense to use the experience wishes of others for the own totally profane ends. Nevertheless, the rationality type of inwardly oriented experience supplies was, after all, a guiding principle that many tried to approach.

The unadorned, functional supplying of experiences first became acceptable in the era of industrialized experience production. Even if once in a while a primarily subjectively, artistically motivated work makes its way to the experience market – a novel, a movie, a picture and so on – the traditional inwardly oriented rationality of experience supply stays limited to private niches. The experience market is dominated by a rationality type that doesn't define experience supply as an end in itself but as an end for something else. Inwardly oriented consumption, characteristic for the rationality of experience demand, is intertwined with outwardly oriented production of experience supplies. Demanders and suppliers move in different frames of reference – here inner life, there public appeal. The goal of public appeal is also concerned with the inner life, yet only with that of others, the demanders, not with the experiences suppliers.

On the experience market the suppliers fare better than the demanders. This is due, first, to the outwardly oriented rationality type being easier to optimize than the inwardly oriented one. It is easier to control effects outside one's own subjectivity – public appeal, profit, corporate survival, social appreciation – than obtaining psycho-physical inner effects: steering one's own experience in certain directions, provided one even knows which. Second, the experience suppliers' advantage results from their predominantly corporative structure. In a corporation's framework – whether it is a picture frames company, a media corporation or a municipal theater – a stronger pressure to optimize the action strategies exists as if an individual plans his actions. If action is experience oriented, the difference of effort between corporations and individuals is especially great, because experience-oriented action usually has the character to bring about small pleasures and because failure (boredom, dislike, experience deficits) can quickly be pushed aside by further experiences.

It is part of the experience market's dynamics that the production of experience supply increasingly passes into the hands of corporations. The private experience supplier (artist, writer, musician and so on) for whom the freedom of institutionalized practical constraint is a self-evident prerequisite to his work has long become an exception. Certainly there are creative individuals who produce inwardly oriented, or at least try to, but it is just as certain that most of their productions stay outside the experience market, banished in drawers, archives, storerooms or depots, reduced to the public of an only small, private circle. On the experience market, the original geniuses are mostly needed only in the framework of cooperating in the production, as furnishers of ideas without influence as to which idea will be picked, as communication talents to whom the contents are provided, as designers of details whose opinions of the whole are not asked for.

Individuals, if they are strong enough, can subordinate the calculation of their effect on the audience to their artistic intentions; corporations, in contrast, cannot. As soon as experience production is organized, it gets sucked into the rationality of corporal survival. Individual people, buildings or machines do not matter in this process – corporate identity is metastable when its personal and material concretization is changing. The goal is rather to secure a social construct with replaceable personnel and alterable material basis, but unchanged overall intention: the future of the company, the magazine, the disco and so on. Inwardly oriented goals – even if they refer to the experience offer itself – are subordinate to the inherent necessity to keep long-term corporative existence going. Success is ranked before artistic ambition, which leads, at best, to a compromise that artistic ambition is allowed as long as it is successful.

Inwardly oriented motivation of experience supply production is not necessary for corporate survival, but it must often be suggested to the public so that success materializes. Corporations that ignore the primacy of popular success deserve all respect, but they will go down with all respect when all other corporations are primarily survival oriented. Private and public experience suppliers come together in the interest of public appeal. Municipal theaters, cultural centers, publicly funded independent groups, adult education centers, libraries, museums, broadcasting corporations, leisure and cultural offices and so on also need public demand. But ensuring corporal existence in the public sector depends on different conditions than on the free market. Furthermore, the goal structure is more complex, as three levels have to be considered: corporation goals (including the goal of survival), general cultural-political goals and personal goals of artists and cultural workers. But as public appeal is an indispensable milestone in each of these goals, public experience suppliers have to work with similar strategies as private suppliers.

The contrast in which public experience suppliers see themselves to private ones, despite different goals and survival conditions, is slighter than it may seem. The survival of private suppliers certainly depends on economic aspects while public experience suppliers can even afford the luxury of mismanagement if they meet other demands, especially public recognition, good informal relations to administrations, institutional stabilization. However, both categories of experience suppliers do not get around popular success. Whether an experience-supplying corporation is fighting for survival on the free market or in public promotion of culture, it will only win this fight if it knows how to market its products.

6.7   THE RATIONALITY OF EXPERIENCE SUPPLY

Everyone who wants to sustain his position on the experience market has to pass through the needle's eye of demand, so this is where the heart of the current rationality of experience supply is to be sought. To attract the public, the experience suppliers have to consider the rationality of those demanding experience. Assumptions about their clientele, based on expert knowledge, have led to the development of many different strategies.

The suppliers' thoughts range in a triangle, the corners being product features, distribution and public. Two of these corners are clearly visible parameters for the supplier as observer of his own market: the product with all its attributes (including the way in which it is offered – packaging, advertisement and atmospheric details of the supply situation) and its distribution. Out of the analysis of stability and fluctuation of both parameters over time, the supplier constructs the image of the big unknown – the public. Whom am I reaching? Why were consumers catching on at point 1 in time and why were consumers lost at point 2? In the course of time, regularities emerge in the relation of product variations and sales variations. These regularities are the material out of which suppliers make their assumptions about their special public. Despite all support of market research, the suppliers' image about social reality is certainly often incomplete and distorted.

Under the pressure of competition, suppliers have to bring their strategies of collective experience management to perfection to ensure their survival. How can experience demands be mobilized? Suppliers on the experience market have reacted to the rationality of experience demand with the development of a rationality of experience supply that can be described by four strategies: schematization, profiling, modification and suggestion.

6.7.1   Schematization

Consumers are split into different subcultures of taste, comparable to fields that are cultivated by different beneficiaries. As the seeds have to be adjusted to the condition of the soil, the appeal has to be adjusted to the consumers' special experience demands. Despite the apparently chaotic dynamic of the experience market there are stable elements. Experience demands can be assigned to special schemas that are similar in large population groups and stay the same over the years. With the trial and error method, the market teaches sociology to every supplier. The paradox content of the lecture: who wants to achieve a lot has to offer aesthetically specialized products. Those suppliers who appeal to these schemas with their products are most likely to survive.

To "open up" new groups of buyers is an expression that describes the actual process rather fittingly: the product is equipped with a semantic code (for example, "individuality," "aspiration level," "harmony" and so on) that functions like a key and opens a door to those whose general experience disposition correspond to the same code. What schematization of a product means can be demonstrated with almost any product. A simple example would be the music market with its schematizations of (1) art music (for example, symphonies), (2) traditional or folk music (for example, brass music, country music) and (3) modern popular music (pop, rock, jazz and so on). It would never cross a producer's mind to mix all genres together into one single product. Why? The offer's schematization would be destroyed, the product absolutely unsalable. It is a strategic matter of course to avoid crossing genres to keep the products classifiable as groups of signs as clearly as possible. The visual presentation is used as backup: for example, classical music is usually portrayed by pictures of conductors or soloists, old instruments, altarpieces and art reproductions; traditional music by people in national costumes, mountains, snuggeries, warm-heartedly smiling singers; pop, rock, jazz and similar genres are often represented by demonic or ecstatic poses, eccentric styles, provocative or unusual titles, odd designs emanating unconventionality. The programmatic and visual product schemas are complemented by the development of different departments when displaying the products in a shop or by different buttons on the web. The spatial or visual separation of products emphasizes the semantic one.

6.7.2 Profiling

To achieve something on a market sub-segment, however, it is not enough to generate the product's design after the aesthetic schema of the sub-segment. This is also done by others who want to attract demand as well. Therefore, every supplier has to try to equip his offers with an aura that makes it unique: the product image. The aesthetic code of products therefore contains a general and a specific component. While the classification to an everyday aesthetic sign group is to be made clear through the schematization of experience supply, the strategy of profiling aims at highlighting individual signs. All market sub-segments are flowed by offers that are similar in use value, quality, technical standard and basic cultural schematization – only the image is different. To attain this difference as a necessary condition for consumption decisions, the experience impulse has to be complemented within the basic schema. Suppliers construct their market identity as a brand-specific experience promise that they stay true to over a longer period of time.

The less products differ in their objective attributes, the more suppliers have to create symbolic differences through profiling. There's hardly a product line that is better suited for research of profiling techniques than cigarettes. The basic schematization that profiling is based on has to do predominantly with the suspense schema, probably in connection with the psychology of smoking and the smokers. Experience scenarios, assigned to the product by advertisement impulses as a symbolic attribute, denote specific codes within the general schema for specific brands. This way, objectively same offers become subjectively distinguishable: cowboy ambience, engines and speed, sex, jungle and adventure. Lately, the originality theme has been emerging more frequently: laid-back bar atmosphere, peculiar guys, self-confident career women. Just like cigarettes, other products are marketed the same way. We come across the phenomenon of profiling everywhere, only schema frameworks and profiling topics differ. Let us examine, as another class of examples, conductors, pianists and opera singers. In the area of the high-culture schema, the density of signs is high; often only experts can keep the individual offers apart. Therefore, profiling through personal attributes and interpretative characteristics is indispensable: volcanic temperament, Italian flair, staying true to the original obsessively, revolutionary breakthroughs of routines, specializing in particular composers, physiognomy, poses when performing and so on. Around the artist, an aura comes into existence that has the same strategic significance as the image of a cigarette brand – profiling.

6.7.3   Modification

Even if a supplier only considers the first two principles, it is not enough to guarantee the sales of a sequence of products, because the consumption stimulus declines when getting used to the consumers. It is part of the distinction of the experience-oriented economy that familiarity, as constituted by basic schema and product image, has to be combined with the stimulus of novelty. On the one hand, the demander has to be offered certainty; on the other, a dosed stimulus of something new. Modification hence is the norm, transformation or introduction of totally new products the exception. Lopos (1992), for instance, shows how major record companies systematically produce innovation and diversity in American popular music to achieve market control.

In the age of outwardly oriented consumption, the dominating modification strategy was an improvement of utility value features, for example, technical enhancements of apparatuses, increasing the comfort of hotels rooms or increasing food quality. That consumption became more and more inwardly oriented is also recognizable in the appearance of absurd excesses of utility features, where further "improvements" can only be of a symbolic nature. Utility value increases arrive in the sphere of uselessness more and more often: increasing the maximum speed of cars, the sound level on speaker boxes or the accuracy of wristwatches. If before the product modification the cars were already faster than one could drive, the speakers louder than one could bear or the watches more accurate than one could arrange one's time, the increase in use value has an illusionary character. What matters is merely the evocation of new experience expectations, while the objective product modification is irrelevant. It is part of the rationality of experience supply to focus on any possible subjective relevancy that might consist in irrational exaggeration of functions.

More and more, supply modification has nothing to do with utility value features. "Improvements" through modification are inwardly oriented, only calculated for the consumers experience horizon. For this purpose, a number of possibilities exist: new packaging for tangible products, change in design, unaccustomed accessories, alterations of product descriptions (by adding words like "deluxe," "super," "comfort," "special" or through simple numbering of model succession); real-time up-to-dateness of information supply; apparent changes in style and interpretational revolutions in the area of the high-culture schema; replacing entertainers and making minimal changes in show structures of television entertainment; labeling routinized spring and fall collections as fashion novelties in clothes shops; redesigning the interior decorations of bars, cafés, discos; introducing new recreational sports equipment (hang gliders, snowboards, various stationary bicycles, mountain bikes and so on); and remodeling of sports equipment (skis and ski boots, cycling wear, tennis rackets, sports shoes and so on).

6.7.4   Suggestion

When products whose utility value have stayed nearly unchanged are thrown back onto the market as "new" after their modification, the only thing new about them is this labeling. It has symbolic quality and must be suggested. Suggestion then is no longer a lie if it is believed by the consumers because it is the inner life that counts on the experience market. The quality of experience supply depends less on the products' objective features but on the subjective constructs of experience demanders. To aid them in this process of construction is part of the indispensable supplier strategies. As soon as demanders believe the product to be new, it is, in a subjective sense, actually new. Suggestions do not, however, remain constricted to the assurance that a product is new. Everything that could be relevant for experience appears in suggestive messages – that the supply is preferred by a certain milieu, that it causes a certain type of pleasure, that it distinguishes the consumers of specific social groups, that it is an expression of certain life philosophies and existential views.

Relations are seen too one-sided if one criticizes the suppliers' suggestion tactics as seduction, as this implies the demanders are being deceived. This implication would only be legitimate on an outwardly oriented market. What counts for the inwardly oriented consumer is that his intention for consumption is achieved when he has an experience that he sees as satisfying. The mere goods without symbolical meaning are seldom sufficient for this as most consumers are either incapable or unwilling to construct the whole psycho-physical reactions necessary for experiencing by themselves. The supplier's answer to the consumer strategy of autosuggestion is external suggestion. Both work together; suggestions are part of the service. The terms "lie" and "truth" are useless where all market players are in agreement to provide the consumers with demanded psycho-physical processes. What holds under these conditions is the more effective the suggestions, the better the product. It is chiefly the consumer's belief in promised product features that make these features come into existence.

6.8   DYNAMICS OF THE EXPERIENCE MARKET

These reflections lead to another view of Bourdieu's *The Field of Cultural Production* (1993) – not a contradiction, rather an extension to general patterns of constructing experience goods and their long-term development. Demanders and suppliers have developed their rationalities in close relation to each other. After a couple of decades, people have got used to the cooperation of both rationalities in so far that they can hardly imagine a different society. One hand washes the other; one party wants its amusement, the other its public. The suppliers adjust their strategies to the patterns of action of the demanders, whereby both rationality types constantly affirm each other. The enormous, still increasing exchange of experience offers for the consumers' money, time and attention follows a self-perpetuating pattern of action referring to each other – unconcerned about critics or dropouts, not endangered by dissatisfaction but rather stabilized and immune against attempts of cultural-political course corrections. All are being pulled into the intertwined rationality types.

But the relation of both types of actors on the experience market is asymmetrical. Only the producers make calculations about the other side while consumers hardly ever waste a thought on the experience suppliers. Normally, the demanders' horizon ends with the products. The seldom cases where producers appear in the consumers' thoughts so that they are able to construct strategies (as would be the case with a consumer boycott, for example) are insignificant to the experience market's dynamics. The asymmetry of corporate and individual social relations (Coleman, 1982) results in an asymmetry of the processes of assimilation. The suppliers' strategies aim explicitly at influencing the demanders;

Table 6.1   Rationality correspondence of experience supply and experience demand

Experience suppliers' strategies	Experience demanders' strategies
Schematization	Correspondence, abstraction
Profiling	Correspondence, abstraction, variation
Modification	Variation
Suggestion	Autosuggestion
	Accumulation

in contrast, the demanders' influence on the suppliers does not take place through tactical actions, but through the aggregation of individualized acts of demand alone.

When comparing both sides' action strategies, the asymmetry becomes obvious: it is always the suppliers who tactically adjust to the demanders. Their schematization strategy is an answer to correspondence and abstraction strategies of the consumers. The same is true for the strategy of profiling that is nothing else than a product-related schematization. Profiling corresponds to the demanders' variation principle as it leads to a symbolic diversification of the products. Modification strategies serve the same purpose. The analogy of suggestion and autosuggestion is especially obvious. The demanders' accumulation principle does not need a single strategy on the supplier's side – it suffices that the suppliers are there and pursue their business. As they want to sell as much as possible, they enable accumulation to any extent. Table 6.1 shows how the strategies of both sides refer to each other.

The dynamics of the experience market results from the interplay of rationalities. Five main aspects are described in the following: (1) experience-oriented change of product structure; (2) expansion of trading volume; (3) territorial expansion of distribution areas and deregionalization; (4) corporatization and concentration; (5) progression.

6.8.1   Experience-oriented Change of Product Structure

The qualitative development of the total supply of experiences in the past decades can be described through three trends of increasing experience orientation: innovation, diversification and reinterpretation. Different types of products appear absolutely new in long-term comparison: movie theaters, radio, television, canned music, mass tourism, discos, slot machines, product-oriented new sports, cultural centers, computer games, internet offers. As soon as a supply category exists, a process of diversification into more and more competing products with similar schematizations begins, in which the suppliers according to their profiling strategies try to make the differences appear as big as possible. The product structure of the experience market is finally enhanced through the reinterpretation of products that had so far been offered as outwardly oriented consumer goods into experience goods: groceries, sportswear, kitchen furniture and a lot more.

6.8.2   Expansion of Trading Volume

If the population's experience capacity were constant, the economical appeal for the diversification of products would be low, because average sales volumes would decline with the increase of the number of competitors. Certainly, the experience market has experienced stagnation and negative growth time and again, but the overall tendency was constant growth over the years. More and more offers could be distributed to more and more consumers – magazines, radio stations, TV programs, travel, books, clothes, furniture, gastronomy, self-awareness and so on.

The suppliers react according to their *raison d'être* and economic logic to the demand strategy of accumulation with additional offers, without an ending foreseeable. The development can be illustrated by the concept of the trading volume of the experience market, related to society as a whole. It is defined by two dimensions: (1) the number of inwardly oriented consumption acts in the population per time unit and (2) the cash value of these consumption acts (which on the private experience market is to be determined through the price, on the public experience market through effort). In both dimensions, the trading volume grows; there is no endogenous mechanism on the experience market that would trigger stagnation or negative growth. Only exogenous factors like wars, natural disasters or recessions that evolved somewhere beyond the experience market can turn these developments around. It lies in the rationality of both types of actors on the experience market to increase the trading volume constantly.

The trading volume's upward trend on the experience market is possible through constant intensification of experience consumption. At first, this intensification took place by causing everyday aesthetic episodes to succeed more frequently: per time unit, the average consumer traveled more often, went to more bars and restaurants, drank more glasses of champagne, leafed through more magazines, changed his wardrobe more often, made more pictures, slides, movies, listened to more music and so on. Gradually, there is no more time left between the experience episodes. Now experience intensification reaches its next level: the average experience length becomes ever shorter. Zapping through TV programs is a symptom of a general development that manifests itself in numerous manners: in the growing trend of short vacations, the decrease of the average time spent at a club, the trend of TV stations shortening their shows or the decreasing lifecycle of products like clothes, furniture or cars.

A further level of intensification is the overlapping of experience episodes. While the television is running, one leafs through a magazine and talks on the phone with an acquaintance at the same time, to make an appointment for playing squash. For more and more vacationers, travel no longer just means experiencing landscapes and cultures. They move through foreign countries with an arsenal of experience instruments, the use of which is just as important as traveling itself: sport utility and recreational vehicles, sports equipment, water vehicles, photography and film equipment or experience wear purchased especially for time off. Music often is merely background music – there is always a radio, tape recorder or CD-player running somewhere, whether one is driving in the car, sitting in a bar, strolling through stores, at the fitness center or at home solving crossword puzzles. On this last level, the experience market participators have a last possibility to intensify experience consumption: refinement, enrichment, upgrading. A trend toward luxury has long started in that direction and the options of increase are endless.

6.8.3   Territorial Expansion of Distribution Areas and Deregionalization

To stay in business on the experience market, the suppliers have to reach as many people as possible. With strategies like schematization, profiling, variation and suggestion they try to elicit as much demand as possible from a given public. But what public is "given"? Modern communication and transportation techniques as well as the abolition of trade barriers have made more and more areas accessible. The suppliers can therefore pursue the additional strategy of expanding their distribution areas. In the process, they are backed by the growing regional mobility of the demanders. Experience market trends diffuse over the globe.

A consequence of this development is the disintegration of traditional relations such as regional closeness and familiarity. Small-scale social milieux with their own traditions and distinctive flair are fading. The fact of two people being neighbors or living in the same neighborhood does not give them a higher degree of familiarity than between any two strangers. On the other hand, one can come across people everywhere, whom one doesn't know but who seem familiar because of their consumption behavior. The multitude of regionally separated milieux with high familiarity has been replaced by few regionally diffuse milieux of the unknown. Still there are clearly visible tendencies toward spatial anchorage and particularization of milieux, for instance, in the metropolitan bar and club scene. However, these are usually branches of super-regional groupings that sprout at many areas at the same time and show similar patterns.

Through the expanding dynamic of the experience market, regional specialties of everyday aesthetic schemas have degenerated. Formerly, differences in local color were highly visible between neighboring communities. Now they are distributed more widely and reduced to less areas of everyday life. With proceeding concentration the suppliers become less while the distribution areas grow. Discos in Europe more or less play the same songs and visitors dance in a similar style, television stations broadcast the same series, people dress similarly, smoke the same cigarettes and so on.

The expansion of distribution areas only comes upon a natural border in the worldwide distribution of experience supply. Several market sub-segments have already drawn near to this border (Burnet, 1995; Castells, 1996;Miller et al., 2005). For example, the establishment of cable and satellite TV has merely continued the internationalization of program offers that had long before been started by importing and exporting movies and series and that comes to an end in the internet. Big sporting events and current sensation reports are offered worldwide by the media. Less and less areas in the world have not yet gained access to the latest hits. Fashions, magazines, foods, drinks, cars, motorcycles, hair styles, cigarettes, furniture designs, wristwatches, perfumes, symphony orchestras and chocolate bars – everything strives for large areas. All these globalization tendencies are topped by the World Wide Web.

6.8.4   Corporatization and Concentration

Suppliers which practice the above-mentioned rationality of experience supply are more successful on the experience market than others. The probability that a supplier will follow this rationality efficiently is higher with corporations (especially large corporations) than with individuals, loose groupings or small corporations, as can be seen comparing big show business and the independent sector (Bilton, 1999). In the course of time, the rationality of experience supply itself establishes the social structure of its professional consolidation by corporatization and concentration. Suppliers organize themselves in the form of apparatuses that have programmed the rationality of experience supply from the beginning, independent of what individuals want. It is difficult to seek out individual products on the market that do not owe their existence to a complex organization. The increase of corporations similarly affects all branches of experience products: television, radio, music production, publishing, media, tourism, gastronomy, consumer goods industry, film industry and internet. Communal cultural and educational policy is also subject to corporatization. In the last decades, new bureaucratic structures and new facilities offering culture have emerged in many places. Although special conditions apply to this sphere beyond the market, they do not take away the pressure of following the rationality of the experience market at least partially.

Corporatization means long-term consolidation of contexts of action: buildings, machines, installations, established posts, division of work, development of manufacturing routines, professionalization (designers, advertising experts, animators, market researchers, directors, writers and so on). Market research is also part of the corporatization development: how do viewer ratings, attendance numbers or the flow of customers change in reference to product changes and what can be learned by it to secure the apparatuses' existence as much as possible?

6.8.5 Progression

The experience market's dynamic does not contain self-generated dynamic equilibrium or even retrogressions. Neither an endpoint of collective saturation nor a general reorientation toward asceticism is coming into sight. The developments described in the preceding points are progressive: they only move forward, unless they are stopped by conditions arising beyond the experience market enforcing a return to outwardly oriented consumption. "Beyond the experience market" merely means beyond the rationality of its typical actors. But possible side-effects of experience-rational actions could indeed lead to the experience market's collapse – ecological consequences, distraction from problems of survival or decline of productivity.

What does one do when stranded on a desolate island that provides everything needed for survival, but nothing else – no television, no magazines, no hi-fi system, no discos, no events, no internet access and so on? Whether one likes it or not, one has to create the condition for experiencing the world on one's own authority in an environment that has not been professionally arranged for it. Seeing the inconspicuous as an aesthetic phenomenon, inventing games, keeping oneself busy is a personal challenge. "A person's free time is worth as much as he is" (Schopenhauer). The fear of boredom and the problem of defeating it without resources have led, as it were, to a collective flight from this island, as soon as the means for it were available. Having arrived at Disneyland, one might wish oneself back to simple and self-made pleasures, but it seems impossible. Tedium especially is a growth factor of the experience market.

We live in an environment that has been carefully prepared for the miscellaneous pleasure demands. The island metaphor clarifies the enormous extent of preparing the world for experience means. That we are moving away from the primal situation of a world without experience supply has to do with the difficulty of autonomous experience production. Every experience offer relieves the pressure of the task of entertaining oneself and takes the fear of failing at it. Experience supply exerts a nearly irresistible pull. The road of distancing oneself from experience supply is long and stony; it requires self-discipline and own effort. Who doesn't oppose the pull of experience supply, chooses the path of least resistance and many little satisfactions. These may often be troubled by uncertainty and disappointment. However, the subjective calamities of experience orientation do not slow down experience demand, but increase it more and more. The fear of missing the opportunity to enjoy one's life is an inexhaustible resource of the experience market.

The demanders' insatiability corresponds to the tirelessness of the suppliers. Who wants to survive on the experience market cannot waste his time with questions whether he likes the depicted strategies of supplier rationality or not. The market forces him to accept them; whoever ignores them goes down. This also applies to cultural-political experience supply, although in a moderated degree due to the granting of subsidy. Under the protection of public law, it is possible to break out of the experience market's constraints time and again. But this should not distract from the predominant tendency. When dealing with the acquisition of public resources for cultural offers, the public's interest as indicated by visitor frequency or viewing and circulation figures is an important argument. The cultural demander is indifferent to whether an offer is publicly subsidized or produced by the private sector – he only cares about what pleases him. That is why cultural and educational policy is constantly under the pressure of also practicing the rules of the experience market.

The experience market's progression is explained only inadequately with the increase of free time and financial possibilities. One additionally has to comprehend the rationality of suppliers and demanders. Experience demand cannot be compared to being hungry or thirsty. By and by, one has eaten and drunk enough. Experiences, however, do not satiate, but stimulate the appetite for more experiences. They fade away and leave only memories and the wish for a new psycho-physical activation: "What will I do now?" To the infinite experience demand, suppliers react with infinite product quantity.

REFERENCES

Ang, I. (1991), *Desperately Seeking the Audience*, London: Routledge.
Bagdikian, B.H. (2004), *The New Media Monopoly*, Boston, MA: Beacon Press.
Becker, O.A. and D. Lois (2010), 'Selection, alignment and their interplay: origins of lifestyle homogamy on couple relations', *Journal of Marriage and the Family*, **72**, 1234–48.
Bell, D. (1973), *The Coming of Post-industrial Society: A Venture in Sociological Forecasting*, London: Heinemann.
Bilton, C. (1999), 'Risky business: the independent production sector in Britain's creative industries', *Cultural Policy*, **6** (1), 17–39.
Bourdieu, P. (1984), *Distinction*, Cambridge, MA: Harvard University Press.
Bourdieu, P. (1993), *The Field of Cultural Production*, Cambridge: Polity Press.
Burnett, R. (1995), *The Global Jukebox*, London: Routledge.
Castells, M. (1996), *The Rise of Network Society*, Oxford: Blackwell.
Castells, M. (1997), *The Power of Identity*, Oxford: Blackwell.
Castells, M. (1998), *End of Millennium*, Oxford: Blackwell.
Coleman, J.E. (1982), *The Asymmetric Society*, New York: Syracuse University Press.

Elster, J. (1989), *Solomonic Judgments: Studies in the Limitation of Rationality*, Cambridge: Cambridge University Press.

Galbraith, J.K (1958), *The Affluent Society*, Boston, MA: Houghton Mifflin.

Heiner, R.A. (1983), 'The origins of predictable behavior', *American Economic Review*, **73**, 560–95.

Hesmondhalgh, D. (2007), *The Cultural Industries*, London: Sage.

Inglehart, R. (1977), *The Silent Revolution*, Princeton, NJ: Princeton University Press.

Keat, R. and N. Abercrombie (eds) (1991), *Enterprise Culture*, London: Routledge.

Lash, S. and J. Urry (1994), *Economies of Signs and Space*, London: Sage.

Lopes, P.D. (1992), 'Innovation and diversity in the popular music industry', *American Sociological Review*, **57** (1), 56–71.

Miller, T., N. Govil, J. McMurria, R. Maxwell and T. Wang (2005), *Global Hollywood 2*, London: British Film Institute.

Murdock, G. and P. Golding (1999), 'Common markets: corporate ambitions and communication trends in the UK and Europe', *Journal of Media* Economics, **12** (2), 117–32.

Postman, N. (1985), *Amusing Ourselves to Death: Public Discourse in the Age of Show Business*, New York: Viking-Penguin.

Riesman, D. (1950), *The Lonely Crowd: A Study of the American Character*, London: Yale University Press.

Roberts, K. (2004), *The Leisure Industries*, Basingstoke: Palgrave Macmillan.

Schopenhauer, A. (1851), *The Essays of Arthur Schopenhauer, Vol. 7. The Wisdom of Life*, Pennsylvania, PA: Pennsylvania State University, reprinted in 2005.

Schulze, G. (1992), *Die Erlebnisgesellschaft* (*The Experience Society*), Frankfurt am Main: Campus, reprinted in 2005.

Simmel, G. (1900), *Philosophy of Money*, London and New York: Routledge, translated in 2004.

Simmel, G. (1908), 'Das Problem des Stiles' ('The problem of style'), *Dekorative Kunst*, **7**, 307–16.

Webster, J.G. and P. Phalen (1997), *The Mass Audience*, Mahwah, NJ: Lawrence Erlbaum.

7. Experience as the DNA of a changed relationship between firms and institutions and individuals
Anna Snel

7.1   INTRODUCTION

Based on the argument that goods and services have become or are rapidly becoming commoditized, Pine and Gilmore (1998) claim that companies need to focus more on the customer and offer experiences as distinct economic offerings to be able to differentiate themselves and gain competitive advantage. Although attention for the importance of experience has increased enormously in the last decade, the idea that the customer and how he or she experiences things as a very important aspect of consumption has existed for much longer (for example, Levy, 1959; Boorstin, 1964; Toffler, 1970; MacCannell, 1976; Hirschman and Holbrook, 1982).

The *raison d'être* of the experience economy is the need to decommoditize economic offerings, thereby maintaining or increasing profit margins and making sure that customers choose economic offerings not solely based on price. The main reason that is given for entering a new economy is that since many economic offerings are nowadays similar in characteristics, features, quality and price, the importance of other differentiating aspects as an opportunity for competitive advantage in the marketplace increases (Dumaine, 1991). This development lies behind the current focus on experiences.

The purpose of this chapter is to explain how the relations between individuals and firms and institutions should change if the latter truly want to enter the experience economy to counter commoditization. I first explain that experiences consist of three elements, and that most scholars and practitioners mainly focus on one of these elements at the cost of the other two. The choice of one element and thus taking a specific approach of experience leads to a biased perspective of the experience economy. Furthermore, I argue that within the approaches the dominant objectivist organizational perspective is also a problem. Firms and institutions are seen as the entities that determine and manage what experiences should consist of, what effects the individual should experience and which values the individual should invest. I shall indicate that this perspective is problematic because it doesn't lead to the intended decommoditization and give recommendations for how this problem can be resolved by changing the way firms and institutions relate to individuals.

7.2   WHAT IS EXPERIENCE? THREE ELEMENTS AND APPROACHES

To get a grasp of what experiences entail, most current literature on the experience economy does not suffice. According to Poulsson and Kale (2004), the area of experience creation suffers from poor conceptualization and fuzzy directions. There is a lack of understanding of what experiences exactly are, how they differ from services and goods and in what way they deliver value to companies and customers. It is difficult to extract a clear and concise definition of what exactly is an experience from business literature on experiences. Some authors even claim that a definition of an experience is nowhere to be found in marketing literature and that no attempt has been made to systematically define what exactly constitutes an experience (Poulsson and Kale, 2004).

Without a clear definition of what an experience is and what it is not, the term can suffer from inflation. The problem is not that there is no definition to be found but that with all the definitions and descriptions given in the literature and all the different distinctions made between different types and kinds of experiences based on many different dimensions, it is not clear what experiences are and what they are not. An extensive analysis of definitions of the term 'experience' in various dictionaries, thesauri and encyclopaedias (Snel, 2011) shows that there are three elements that make up an experience: something in the environment that is experienced, someone who experiences some kind of effects and some type of encounter between this someone and the something (Figure 7.1). These are the three elements of an experience, and while one can try to distinguish between them, they cannot be separated for together they form what I call experiences. 'An experience is always what it is because of a transaction taking place between an individual and what, at the time, constitutes his environment' (Dewey, 1938 [1977], p. 43).

To be able to speak of experience all three elements should be present, so, for example, an event or occurrence per se cannot be counted as experience, only when it has one or some of the conditions mentioned in the other columns of Figure 7.1. To be able to call them experiences, they should affect one in some way, cause someone to learn something and/or have been personally lived through. Not every event, activity, occurrence or thing in the individual's environment should be called an experience according to these sources, but only those that satisfy the conditions.

One problem of the current experience economy discourse in the fields of marketing and business is that scholars and practitioners often seem to focus mainly on one of these three core elements. Since a focus on one of the elements means that one is approaching experience from a specific angle, I argue that there are three approaches that can be distinguished in the current discourse.

One approach is focused on the 'experienced being', or 'what' it is that is experienced in the individual's environment, for example, events, activities, occurrences, things and so on. I have named this approach the environment-centred approach. The second approach is focused more on the 'experiencer', and the effects that he or she experiences, hence I have called this approach the effect-centred approach. The third approach is focused on the characteristics of the encounter of the individual and his or her environment. This approach is called the encounter-centred approach.

The bias resulting from taking one specific perspective on experience, one of the three approaches, does not necessarily lead to problems if one consciously makes this choice and is aware of the consequences of the choice made. However, given the theoretically ill-founded nature of the subject, one may doubt whether this choice is always made intentionally.

Although the choice for one approach or the other may have unintended consequences,

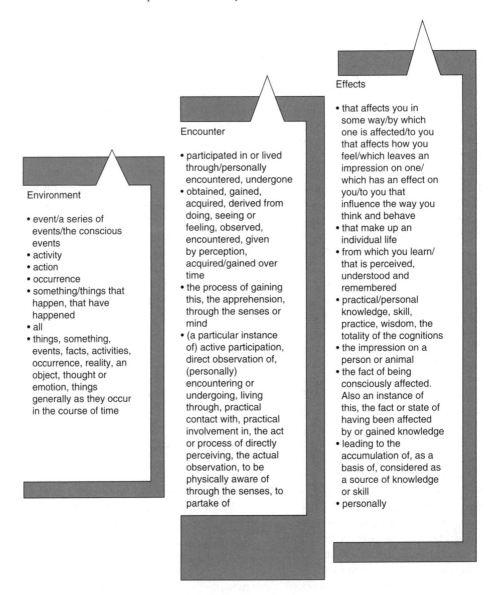

Environment

- event/a series of events/the conscious events
- activity
- action
- occurrence
- something/things that happen, that have happened
- all
- things, something, events, facts, activities, occurrence, reality, an object, thought or emotion, things generally as they occur in the course of time

Encounter

- participated in or lived through/personally encountered, undergone
- obtained, gained, acquired, derived from doing, seeing or feeling, observed, encountered, given by perception, acquired/gained over time
- the process of gaining this, the apprehension, through the senses or mind
- (a particular instance of) active participation, direct observation of, (personally) encountering or undergoing, living through, practical contact with, practical involvement in, the act or process of directly perceiving, the actual observation, to be physically aware of through the senses, to partake of

Effects

- that affects you in some way/by which one is affected/to you that affects how you feel/which leaves an impression on one/ which has an effect on you/to you that influence the way you think and behave
- that make up an individual life
- from which you learn/ that is perceived, understood and remembered
- practical/personal knowledge, skill, practice, wisdom, the totality of the cognitions
- the impression on a person or animal
- the fact of being consciously affected. Also an instance of this, the fact or state of having been affected by or gained knowledge
- leading to the accumulation of, as a basis of, considered as a source of knowledge or skill
- personally

Figure 7.1   Three components of the definition of experience

there is yet another bias in the discourse on a different level, namely the level of the approaches themselves. Even within the specific approaches marketing and business scholars take a restricted and objectivist view since the theory is often defined from an organizational perspective. This shouldn't surprise anyone, given the fact that the assumption is that commoditization is the main reason for the emergence of an experience economy. This causes a search for new ways to add value to economic offerings, so that one can differentiate one's offerings from those of the competition as explained earlier. Since the assumption seems to be that it is always the firm or institution that has to add value to the economic offerings, the organizational perspective is highly dominant in current literature.

In the environment-centred approach, for instance, the view of what is experienced according to marketing and business scholars is often restricted to treating experiences as if they are products or environments with objective characteristics that can be produced and managed. The objectivist perspective can be recognized in this approach in many ways. Experiences are staged, produced, sold, managed and so on, as if they are separate objects in the individual's environment. In the effect-centred approach, the marketing and business scholars' focus usually lies on how effects can or should be invoked and managed. Also here one can notice a clear objectivist perspective, since the effects, be they, for example, emotions, feelings or moods, are dealt with as if they are entities separate from the individual that can be given or sold to him or her. Thirdly, the role of the individual in the encounter-centred approach in marketing and business literature is primarily restricted to the investment of money. The encounter is often described as a transaction between a firm or institution that functions as 'experience-provider' and a customer, in which the provider gives something of value to the customer and the customer gives something of value, usually money, in return. The way in which these 'somethings-of-value' are discussed resembles a discussion of objects, separate from the firm or institution and separate from the individual, which are transacted. Again one can recognize the objectivist perspective. In the discussion of the three approaches the objectivist perspective is explained in more detail.

7.3   THE ENVIRONMENT-CENTRED APPROACH

In business and marketing literature on experience, experiences are often seen and dealt with as if they are products. The focus then is on the features and internal processes within the organization that can be managed in order to produce an experience. Literature is, for example, focused on connecting product features to experience, creating elaborate checklists with criteria describing the experience contexts, and practical ways in which experiences can be defined, distinguished, designed, evaluated and produced. Books that belong within this approach, for example, contain self-assessment tests (for example, Shaw, 2005) or tests and 'lessons learned' sections at the end of each chapter (for example, Ford and Heaton, 2000). Other books present a toolkit that readers can use to design an experience (for example, Smith and Wheeler, 2002) and subdivide the experience into manageable stages (for example, the Driving Improved Customer Experience model (Shaw and Ivens, 2002), levels (for example, the Customer Experience Pyramid™ (Shaw and Ivens, 2002; Shaw, 2005), touch points (for example, the Experience Touchpoint Charts and Pallettes (Millet and Millet, 2002) or moments (for example, Moment Mapping® (Shaw, 2005)). In a way, firms and institutions are doing what they have always done: they try to avoid commoditization and create new ways of differentiating themselves from competitors.

According to many authors, every time a customer comes into contact with a product or a company, he has an experience; the only thing that has changed is that firms and institutions should now focus on managing the experience and all elements, or clues, that are part of it (O'Sullivan and Spangler, 1998; Carbone, 1999, 2004; Jones, 1999; Schmitt,

1999; Millet and Millet, 2002; Shaw and Ivens, 2002; Adcox and Wittenstein, 2003; Shaw, 2005). The more phases of the experience that are managed and the more clues that are incorporated, the better the experience will be.

However, a problem with this way of dealing with experiences is that if exceptional experiences can be offered to people by exceptional management of experience clues and features, then knowledge of these clues and how to manage them would give everyone the same advantage in the experience economy and destroy the differentiating function of experiences. Benchmarking, checklists and blindly copying elements from competitors in practice rarely help in becoming successful in the experience economy (Carbone, 2004). Indeed, success of economic offerings will also be dependent on what the customer finds important in the specific situation and context he finds himself in.

In some situations consumers are primarily interested in what they can gain from the physical characteristics or technical performance of a product, from the so-called objective features of the product that are under the control of the organization providing the product. Products that primarily provide this type of value are called utilitarian, since it is their use, their utility, that motivates individuals to buy and consume them. Examples are many use products, such as cooking oil, detergent and cartridges. Functionality is mainly dependent on the objective features of the product and the subjective response of the individual usually has little or no influence. 'If we are upset about something or especially nervous or unusually happy, our feeling has no impact on the way the flashlight works' (Addis and Holbrook, 2001, p. 59). When the only element that is focused on is the environment, by taking the environment-centred approach, this is the line of reasoning. However, the encounter between the individual and the environment is then left out of the equation.

The techniques used for gaining an understanding of the individual's perspective are also radically different from the ones that are used in traditional inward-focused organizations (Levy, 1981; Zaltman and Higie, 1993; Zaltman, 1997; Carbone, 1999, 2004; Adcox and Wittenstein, 2003), which lead to self-referential results (Fornell, 1976; Baudrillard, 1983). 'Customers don't break their experiences down into twenty-seven different operational-based processes, analyze the execution of each process, and tabulate and average the results to determine whether they've had a great customer experience' (Millet and Millet, 2002, pp. 42–3). Customers don't care about the fact that 'we can build multiattribute models that predict preference toward toothpaste; we can generate complex multidimensional spaces that represent perceptions of cigarettes; we can construct devilishly clever procedures that trace the acquisition of information on cereal brands; we can – with our bare hands – construct mighty regression analyses that relate detergent usage to 300 separate life-style variables. In short – when it comes to factors of least importance to the consumer's emotional, cultural, and spiritual existence – we excel' (Holbrook, 1981, p. 36).

According to the literature in the environment-centred approach, organizations in an experience economy should be focused on producing experiences as economic offerings with the 'right' objective features and experiences are seen and dealt with as products by focusing inward on production processes. Within this perspective, the focus remains on the firm or institution that offers the experience, that manages all elements of the experience and that creates value. When one focuses exclusively on the elements that are under the control of the firm or institution, a large part of what makes an experience valuable is not recognized. Experiences are not under the complete control of the organization and therefore one should doubt the usefulness of how-to guides for producing, staging and building experiences with the goal of combating commoditization.

7.4   THE EFFECT-CENTRED APPROACH

The effect-centred approach focuses primarily on the effects the individual experiences and the role of firms and institutions in managing and producing predetermined hedonic effects neglecting the influence that the individual has on the effects he or she experiences (for example, in terms of the intensity of the effects, the type of emotions and the meaning attached to what happens to the individual).

For services, the customer's perception of value is seen as a trade-off between the quality of the obtained result and the service process and, on the other hand, the price he has to pay and the effort the customer has to make to obtain the service, as expressed in Heskett et al.'s (1997) customer value equation. For experiences, the customer's perception of value consists of more than this trade-off. According to many authors, there is a lack of attention for the emotional and irrational aspects involved in experiences and an excessive focus on functional and utilitarian aspects (Sheth et al., 1991; Schmitt, 1999; Snowden, 1999; Mathwick et al., 2001). Satisfiers, aspects of products or services that, when present, should cause satisfaction, have become dissatisfiers, aspects that are expected and taken for granted and can only cause dissatisfaction when absent (for example, Green and Jordan, 2002). Quality, reliability, pricing, brand or for that matter any of the traditional differentiators 'have become unspoken requirements, tickets to entry' (Shaw and Ivens, 2002, p. viii).

In search of new differentiators, many assumptions have been made about what individuals value and what their desires are. A review of the literature on this subject provides a myriad of potential, mostly hedonic, differentiators. Individuals allegedly want to be surprised, mesmerized, seduced, enhanced, enriched, pampered, entertained, inspired, scared, touched, amused, shocked, stimulated, dazzled, enthralled (de Cauter, 1995; Jensen, 1999; Wolf, 1999; Goossens, 2000; Mommaas, 2000; Scheerder, 2000; Schulze, 2000; Dagevos, 2001; Poulsson and Kale, 2004; Postman, 2005) and this list is not exhaustive.

De Cauter (1995) sums up the growing concern with hedonic effects by stating that the late modern society we live in is characterized by 'experience hunger'. Even in churches people are claimed to be looking for kicks, events and entertainment, and reading the Bible should be fun and personally engaging (Oevermans, 1999). Agritainment, edutainment and entertailing are some of the other terms that show that entertainment is pervasive nowadays. Everything seems to revolve around entertainment, 'If it isn't fun, cute, or packaged in a ten-second sound bite, then forget it. If it can't be presented with a smiling, cheerful, sexy face, then it ain't worth attending to' (Mitroff and Bennis, 1989, p. 7).

Besides this focus on hedonic effects, firms and institutions are perceived as providers of stimuli that in the encounter with an individual are transformed into effects in a seemingly black box way. However, especially now that firms and institutions are more and more recognized as cultural producers of symbolic goods (for example, Levy, 1959; Hirschman and Holbrook, 1982; Featherstone, 1991; Rifkin, 2000; Schulze, 2000;

Richards, 2001; Ter Borg, 2003), there is an increased need for a better understanding of the workings of this black box, of how meaning is created and how effects come about. There appears to be much concern about the neglect of this process of meaning making. 'With an ever quickening turnover time, objects as well as cultural artifacts become disposable and depleted of meaning . . . People are bombarded with signifiers and increasingly become incapable of attaching "signifieds" or meanings to them' (Lash and Urry, 1994, pp. 2–3). Falk and Dierking (2000) refer to William James (1890), when they describe that people are continuously bombarded with stimulations and that 'interest' is their filter. 'Millions of items in the outward order are present to my senses which never properly enter into my experience. Why? Because they have no interest for me. My experience is what I agree to attend to. Only those items which I notice shape my mind – without selective interest, experience is an utter chaos' (James, 1890, p. 403). This chaos caused by overstimulation or the excessive supply of disorganized, pattern-less and chaotic sensory stimuli can lead to confusion, bewilderment and impairment of the ability to think and act clearly (Toffler, 1970). 'It is for this reason that practitioners of political or religious brainwashing make use . . . of sensory bombardment involving flashing lights, rapidly shifting patterns of colour, or chaotic sound effects – the whole arsenal of psychedelic kaleidoscopy' (Toffler, 1970, p. 310).

In consumption experiences, the relative weight of the individual's subjective response is greater than that of the objective features of the product. While 'If we are upset about something or especially nervous or unusually happy, our feeling has no impact on the way the flashlight works' (Addis and Holbrook, 2001, p. 59), our feelings do have an impact on our consumption experiences when consuming, for example, products like ice cream or dinners in one's favourite restaurant. In cases like these, speaking of managing the effects of an experience or giving people certain emotions or feelings is a too simplistic way of explaining what is actually a quite complex process. If there were a simple way to give individuals emotions and feelings, then where would the decommoditizing function of the experience economy be, since everyone could or would be doing the same things? The problem that is pointed out is that there is an abundance of stimuli, but also a lack of attention for the capacities that people need to make sense of them. When experiences are not considered as mere hedonic effects that are causal effects of the individual's encounter with stimuli in his environment, then attention should be paid to the process of meaning making.

7.5   THE ENCOUNTER-CENTRED APPROACH

From the perspective of scholars and practitioners adhering to the encounter-centred approach the main role of individuals in the encounter is that of paying money in exchange for experiences, which causes a neglect of the other values that individuals invest. The individual's role does not just consist of investing money, but what seems to have happened in the encounter-centred approach of the experience discourse is that at first the encounter was perceived in terms of utility provided by firms and institutions in exchange for money provided by customers (Figure 7.2). When commoditization of goods and services urged firms and institutions to think about other ways to add value to their offerings besides offering mere utility, let's call this utility+, for some reason

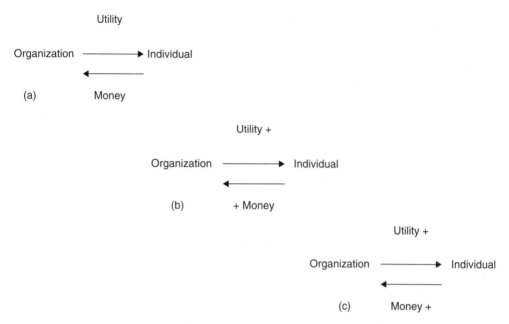

Figure 7.2   Development in value exchanges between organizations and individuals

most scholars' reasoning consisted of charging higher prices to the customer (+money) rather than thinking about what other values besides money (money+) were or could be invested by customers in exchange and recognizing that individuals are active partici- pants in an experience.

The interaction of individuals with products during consumption is one of the research areas that is receiving much attention. It is becoming more difficult to stick with this traditional 'produce and sell' attitude. Individuals resist being treated as a sales target anymore and demand dialogues with firms and institutions as valid interlocutors (Vavra, 1995; Duijvestein, 2001; Adcox and Wittenstein, 2003) and a more active role in the experience itself as co-producers (Ford and Heaton, 2000; LaSalle and Britton, 2003). This active role in production by individuals is not entirely new; after all, self-service concepts have been around for quite some time. However, there is now more recognition for the fact that consumers do not just get involved because they have no choice or to save time or money, but that they can also reap personal benefits from the activity and increase their enjoyment (Lewis and Bridger, 2001). People allegedly do not only use con- sumption to actively produce meanings (Csikszentmihalyi and Rochberg-Halton, 1981; Hirschman and Holbrook, 1982; Bengtsson, 2002) but this sense making capacity is even claimed to be the primary function of consumption nowadays (Douglas and Isherwood, 1979; Ter Borg, 2003).

There are, however, scholars who argue that businesses are defined by that for which they collect revenue. 'You're not truly selling a particular economic offering unless you explicitly ask your customers to pay for that exact offering' (Pine and Gilmore, 1999, p. 62) so organizations are not active in the experience economy unless they charge a fee for the experiences they offer.

On the other hand, by focusing merely on the market value of experiences and the financial value that the individual should invest, marketing and business scholars are claimed to be responsible for the commodification of experience. Rifkin (2000), for example, describes the experience economy as 'a world in which each person's own life becomes, in effect, a commercial market' (p. 7). Today many aspects of life have come under the influence of commodification, such as time, signs and symbols, human practices, culture, human relationships, shopping and identity and even happiness and life itself (Falk and Campbell, 1997; Rifkin, 2000; Dagevos, 2001; Richards, 2001; Hackley, 2003; Galle, 2004). Schumacher (1973) describes the risks of this singular focus on financial values for the environment, the culture, social structures and the like, but also for business itself. As the experience economy is growing, and more people will pay to participate, issues like rationalization, efficiency and economies of scale will become more important. This will inevitably lead to 'disenchantment', as Ritzer (1999) calls it, causing the loss of 'something of great, if hard to define, value' (p. 96). Enchantment has more to do with the qualitative aspects of experiences than with the quantity of experiences. 'An emphasis on producing and participating in a large number of experiences tends to diminish the magical quality of each of them . . . The mass production of such things is virtually guaranteed to undermine their enchanted qualities' (Ritzer, 1999, p. 98).

Contrary to enchantment, rationalization, efficiency, economies of scale and mass production are not typically the terms one associates with decommoditization. The focus on other values instead of or besides financial values may help to overcome the risk of commoditization

7.6   A DIFFERENT PERSPECTIVE ON EXPERIENCE

As the descriptions of these three approaches have shown, one cannot only recognize a bias towards one of the three essential elements of experience in the discourse, but also within the approaches there is a bias towards the objectivist and organizational perspective. In the environment-centred approach, there is a bias towards producing experiences with certain objective characteristics. The effect-centred approach suffers from a bias towards the management of certain pre-specified, usually hedonic, effects. And finally, the encounter-centred approach shows a clear bias towards the values that the organization decides should be invested by the individual, in most cases financial value. These biased perspectives do not help firms and organizations in overcoming the effects of commoditization, which was the *raison d'être* of the experience economy as I indicated earlier, but they even pose a risk for more commoditization (Snel, 2011). After all, if there exists a checklist of the right objective characteristics one should incorporate in an experience (the bias in the environment-centred approach), then every organization could implement these and we would again all be doing the same thing, leaving the individual with just one criterion to base his decision on: price. In the same way, if it were possible to determine which effects should follow from an experience and to manage these (the bias in the effect-centred approach), or which values the individual should invest in the experience and to manage these (the bias in the encounter-centred approach), then organizations would be able to follow the prescribed steps and again be doing the same things, leading to commoditization.

A different, broader perspective on experiences can help in overcoming the biases and indicate what firms and organizations could do to truly incorporate the experience discourse in their relationships with individuals.

7.6.1 Offsetting the Bias in the Environment-centred Approach

In the environment-centred approach, there is a bias towards producing experiences with certain objective characteristics. The idea behind this approach is that one can explain what a good experience consists of by giving information on the 'right' objective features that should be implemented in the experience. However, by understanding the difference between different meanings of the word 'experience', *Erlebnis* and *Erfahrung*, one can see that the core of experience does not consist of objective features but of meaning that is constructed by individuals. Instead of trying to understand experiences by consulting third-party explanations of experience in the form of information, one has to focus on grasping the meaning of the experience, which cannot be transferred by mere information as I shall explain.

Erlebnis and *Erfahrung* have come to imply two very different notions of experience (Jay, 2005).

Erlebnis generally connotes a more immediate, pre-reflective and personal variant of experience (Jay, 2005), with a focus on instantaneity and the totality of sensorial experience (Mommaas, 2000). The immediacy of *Erlebnis* is reflected in a focus on intensity (Goodman, 2003) but also in a focus on the immediate gratification of needs (Mommaas, 2000). In fact, the modern selling of experiences, and their commodification, has primarily to do with *Erlebnissen*, leading to the immediate gratification of individuals who 'buy' experiences (Schulze, 2000; Goodman, 2003).

When individuals exert mental activities on an *Erlebnis*, for example, by distancing themselves from it, contemplating or reflecting on it and making sense of it, it can become an *Erfahrung* (Mommaas, 2000; Jay, 2005). The individual is not just taking in or absorbing stimuli from her environment and neither does she merely have feelings of pleasure; there is some kind of cognitive processing involved, in the context of a long-term learning process, and the focus is not or not just on the immediate gratification of needs (Mommaas, 2000). *Erfahrung* connotes a creation or restoration of the coherence or narrative of an individual's life (Goodman, 2003), in the sense that a series of events in the past, present and hypothetical future are meaningfully connected in a temporal way and with a point of view (Georgakopoulou, 2004).

Erfahrung does not consist of mere sensations or subjective responses, but 'involves at least a potential learning process produced by an encounter with something new, an obstacle or a challenge that moves the subject beyond where it began' (Jay, 2005, p. 403). There are several theories on how individuals learn from their experiences, such as the Experiential Learning Cycle (Kolb, 1984), the Experiential Learning Model (Luckner and Nadler, 1997) and the Reflective Teacher Model (Ashcroft and Foreman-Peck, 1994). '(E)very experience enacted and undergone modifies the one who acts and undergoes, while this modification affects, whether we wish it or not, the quality of subsequent experiences. For it is a somewhat different person who enters in them . . . every experience both takes up something from those which have gone before and modifies in some way the quality of those which come after' (Dewey, 1997, p. 35). The discrete encounters with the environment over time leave some sort of permanent residue for the individual (Jay, 2005, pp. 61, 330). In this sense, an experience has a temporal dimension as accumulated learning, and memory has a central position in experience. The experiences from the past and the knowledge the individual already has play a part in experiences in the present and since no one has experienced the exact same things and accumulated the exact same knowledge as another person in the world, experiences are highly personal.

Compared to a layperson, an art critic sees an artwork differently, a professional musician listens to music in a different way, a head chef tastes food differently, a doctor perceives the human body in a different way and so on. These people have accumulated experience and knowledge, which enables them to learn more and make more sense of their experience.

For Gadamer (2004), genuine experiences function to provide the individual with 'a new horizon within which something can become an experience for him' (p. 348). The meaning an experience has for an individual not only depends on her prior knowledge and experience but also on this 'new horizon', and the impact the experience has on the life of the individual (James, 1902; van Saane, 1998).

The experience becomes part of the individual and can now be used in every context it is needed. The individual can now see things that, although they existed before, were not perceived by her, 'thus leaving us and the world itself irrevocably changed' (Jackson, 1998, p. 33).

The mental agency exerted and the temporal dimension involved make experiences inherently personal and unique. Because of this one can hardly expect someone else to fully understand one's experience, let alone determine and manage the objective characteristics of an experience for someone else. The other person has a different narrative and life horizon, has different knowledge and experience, and will therefore interpret events in a different way. This is what makes it so hard, or even impossible, to truly share an experience with someone who has not had the experience.

One can try to gain information on someone else's experience by asking her questions about it and having her tell about it, but the information shared consists of 'secondary experience.' Secondary experience means that 'information is processed – selected, modified, packaged, and presented' (Reed, 1996, p. 3), 'externalized' in Sveiby's terms (1997, pp. 81–2), providing at best second-hand or indirect knowledge (Reed, 1996). The person telling about her experience determines what to tell and what to leave out, and many aspects of her experience cannot be externalized and expressed at all. To truly understand what the person has experienced, the secondary experience or information is not enough; one needs to have primary experience for oneself. Primary experience is defined as 'the information . . . that all human beings acquire from their environment by looking, listening, feeling, sniffing, and tasting –the information, in other words, that allows us to experience things for ourselves' (Reed, 1996, pp. 1–2).

In terms of experience, it would be good if the people in charge of designing experiences would have primary experience of the situation they are dealing with and not just secondary experience of certain objective characteristics. However, this is not always possible. One cannot experience everything for oneself. If, for example, the task is to design solutions for the elderly, one cannot expect students in their twenties to have primary experience of what life is like as an elderly person. Fortunately, one can make use of what is called 'vicarious' experience. What distinguishes vicarious experiences is that (1) the individual is not in direct contact with the raw material of the experience (not having a primary experience) and (2) although there is no direct contact of the individual with the raw material and the experience can therefore be considered to be secondary, something is done to create the illusion of contact with the raw material in a less filtered and framed way than in a pure secondary experience (Snel, 2011, p. 119).

Based on the degree to which the primary experience is filtered and framed and based on the proximity of the actual raw material to the individual having the vicarious experience, one can distinguish various forms of vicarious experiences. One can, for example, talk with individuals who have or have had the primary experience, observe them, create and participate in a simulation of the primary experience, use role play; the list can go on and on. The most important point is to find a method that takes one as close as possible to the primary experience of the people having the experience. Research, to provide meaningful results, should make use of techniques found in, for example, ethnography (Adcox and Wittenstein, 2003; Berthon et al., 2003) and most importantly, it should view the experience as a whole, as a Gestalt, not as a series of distinct and isolated components or objective features (Holbrook, 1986; Chartrand, 1987). Experiences consist of encounters between individuals and their environment and so to gain valuable insights from the experience, this whole constellation should be taken into account from as close to a first-person perspective as one can get.

7.6.2   Offsetting the Bias in the Effect-centred Approach

The effect-centred approach suffers from a bias towards the management and direction of certain pre-specified, usually hedonic, effects. Scholars and practitioners who take the effect-centred approach of experience view the effects of experiences as being directed and evoked one-sidedly, from the side of the firm or institution, and neglect the interpretive framework of the individual and the process of meaning making that is involved in the emergence of effects. Two errors in relation to the construction of meaning may occur when holding this view: a syntactic error and a semantic error (MacCannell and MacCannell, 1982). In the case of a syntactic error, the signifier is taken at face value and there is no recognition of the fact that it refers to or represents something else, resulting in an uncritical absorption of the stimuli and impressions. McLuhan (1967) has coined the phrase 'the medium is the massage', to indicate that we have so many stimuli that we encounter day by day, that we become numb to them, we don't have the mental capacity to interpret them all and give them meaning. They are presented to us in this information-overloaded society and we don't even consciously register them. In the case of a semantic error, the signified is taken at face value, leaving the individual with a flawed understanding of the actual or complete meaning of it. Highlighting one specific detail of a complex situation and presenting the situation as if that detail is the whole picture is an example of a semantic error. The semantic error consists of not recognizing that a sign may mean different things under different circumstances. The assumption is that the sign will be interpreted in the same way by anyone confronted with it. However, perspectives work like filters or lenses and just like there are lenses that work better for looking at the stars, there are also lenses that are fit for looking at bacteria. Every perspective in isolation gives us a partial, limited or even distorted view of reality, and only by taking into consideration various perspectives and contexts will we gain a better understanding of the nature of reality.

When a perspective limits the view of available possibilities, this can have serious implications for the process of meaning making. Perspectives can 'limit people's choice sets by indicating what is likely to be seen as viable or productive, and define the implications of their choices. They affect what people try to understand, what problems they attempt to address, and how they direct their imagination and learning toward the yet unknown' (Huizing, 2002, p. 163). In this context, Tyrrell (1947) distinguishes 'convergent' and 'divergent' thinking. Convergent thinking starts with the end-state or the desired goal as a starting point and is focused on reaching that end-state or goal in the most efficient and effective way. The description of the effect-centred approach of experiences clearly refers to convergent thinking: desired effects are determined and the focus is on how to make the individual experience those effects. In the case of divergent thinking, choices have to be made related to which goal or end-state to strive for. There are many possible options and one first has to decide on which option to choose. The concepts thus refer to two different modes of operation; one narrows the mental focus until it converges into a solution, the other broadens the mental focus in many different directions.

Tyrrell (1947) further claims that convergent problems do not exist in reality, but are created by a process of abstraction. 'The true problems of living . . . are always problems of overcoming or reconciling opposites. They are divergent problems and have no solution in the ordinary sense of the word' (Tyrrell, 1947, p. 89). Although a process of reduction and abstraction of reality can translate all divergent problems into convergent problems, the price of doing so in terms of knowledge is high.

The construction of meaning is clearly a divergent problem, for which there is not one right solution. The individual interprets and relates to his environment within a certain context and by using his inherently personal interpretive framework. There is an unlimited quantity of possible contexts and unique interpretive frameworks since each person has a unique collection of existing knowledge, prior experience, concerns, motivations and goals. This makes the management of the interpretive process, with the aim of controlling the meaning that the person will attach to whatever happens to him and the effects that he will experience, a difficult, if not impossible, task.

Most people have been educated within a discipline, that has taught us to view the world in a certain way, from a certain perspective, in line with and prescribed by that discipline. To prevent the limitation of possibilities and choices it would therefore be wise to bring people with different perspectives, different knowledge and different experiences together in order for them to learn from each other. Developments in the areas of co-creation and democratized innovation in fact indicate a need for firms and institutions that want to understand experiences to disembed from their own viewpoint and incorporate the view of customers and users, since these may have very different but valuable perspectives. Customers may, for example, 'intuitively look at a function being performed, such as checking in at an airport, and ask themselves why their supermarket will open another checkout if there are more than three people queuing, but the airline does not: a reasonable question. This means you have to look across industries' (Shaw and Ivens, 2002, pp. 31–2).

Deductive thinking doesn't help us in situations like these, we need more abductive reasoning: using the insights gained divergently from our primary and vicarious experience to discover and explore valuable possibilities and frames of the situation, with the goal of finding valuable ideas (Dorst, 2011).The confrontation of a variety of perspectives offers more opportunities to abductively find a useful frame with which to view the situation and to discover possible ideas for dealing with it that would not come to the front if we keep on trying to engage with it from our conventional mono-disciplinary perspective.

The one-sided determination and management of effects is an example of convergent thinking, leading to semantic and syntactic errors. One doesn't and cannot know whether and, if so, how individuals are going to interpret signs, so the idea that firms and institutions can determine and manage the effects they want individuals to experience is an illusion. Can they influence the individual's process of meaning making? Of course, but given the inherently personal nature of interpretive frameworks and experiences this should not be done in a convergent way. To grasp the effects that individuals experience and the meanings they construct, one needs to grasp how the effects come about and how the meaning is constructed. One therefore needs to incorporate different viewpoints and perspectives in the thinking process to incorporate possibilities, alternatives and options that one would cut off if one were to engage in convergent thinking.

7.6.3 Offsetting the Bias in the Encounter-centred Approach

The encounter-centred approach shows a clear bias towards the values that firms/ institutions decide should be invested by the individual, in most cases financial value. To determine the value that they can expect individuals to invest, firms and institutions need to have an idea of what value individuals expect in return. Traditionally, in the service economy, customers were expected to determine what to invest in a transaction based on what they expected to receive in return. A well-known and often-used model for measuring the quality of services is SERVQUAL, which is based on the premise that a customer's evaluation of a service depends on the comparison of his perception of what was received with what was expected, leading to a confirmation or disconfirmation of pre-consumption standards (Zeithaml et al., 1990; Fournier and Mick, 1999). If perception and expectation can be measured on a scale of 1 to 10, one can imagine that an offering with a score of 7 for perceived value results in a different experience of value if a score of 9 was expected than if a score of 5 was expected. However, for experiences these 'pre-consumption standards' or expectations are often not as clear as they are for services. The product classification theory, also called the Search-Experience-Credence (SEC) framework (Animeshet al., 2005), explains why expectations for experiences are usually vague and why it is therefore difficult to use traditional expectation-based models for determining perceived value for the evaluation of experiences.

Search, experience and credence characteristics indicate the moment in the purchase process when consumers can accurately assess whether the good actually possesses the expected level of attributes (Animesh et al., 2005). Search characteristics are qualities a consumer can determine by inspection prior to purchase (Nelson, 1974; Aldrich, 1999; Animesh et al., 2005) or use (Girard et al., 2002). The information needed to be confident about one's purchase decision, in other words, the information needed to form clear expectations and be able to assess whether the product will satisfy the expectations, can easily be obtained prior to buying or using it. Examples of such search characteristics are price, size of package or colour. Experience characteristics are qualities a consumer cannot determine prior to purchase (Nelson, 1974) or use (Wright and Lynch, 1995). Examples of these characteristics are taste, durability or maintenance needs (Aldrich, 1999). Objective information on how someone will like the taste or smell or comfort of something does not exist and only the experience of the experience characteristics will help in determining whether the experience lives up to one's expectations (Andersen and Philipsen, 1998; Aldrich, 1999). Credence characteristics are characteristics of which the quality cannot be inferred before, during or sometimes even after the purchase or use of a product (Darby and Karni, 1973; Aldrich, 1999). Not only can consumers never know, verify or be certain of the level of credence characteristics they receive, they do not even know what level or extent of the characteristics supplied they actually need (Darby and Karni, 1973; Emons, 1997; Dulleck and Kerschbamer, 2006). Consumers therefore have to rely on outside experts (Ford et al., 1988), a role often taken on by the sellers themselves (Emons, 1997). Examples of credence characteristics are the benefits of dietary supplements, the expertise of a doctor or the honesty of a car repair shop (Aldrich, 1999).

For experiences the experience and credence characteristics are dominant. One will not know what something looks, sounds, feels, tastes or smells like or how someone is going to feel about something before one actually experiences it (experience characteristics). Learning experiences and experiences that change the individual's interpretive framework or life horizon will often be characterized by credence characteristics. After all, the impact of these types of experiences may not emerge for a very long time and one will never know for sure what someone will learn from the experience or in what ways he or she will change. Especially the presence of experience and credence characteristics makes it difficult or even impossible to form expectations of experiences and therefore to evaluate them, let alone put a price tag on them. To know what to expect, the customer at the very least needs to have the possibility to try the product, to experience it for himself or herself. The idea that firms and institutions can one-sidedly and upfront determine what type of value and how much of this value the individual should invest then seems illusory.

Yet another problem with determining the value that the individual should invest is that in the case of services, the role of individuals in the encounter consists of them investing money and dealing with costs to acquire or get access to the service (Heskett et al., 1997); in other words, the effort someone has to make to gain access. For experiences, there appear to exist three different types of effort that have to be distinguished to be able to make sense of what happens in the context of values during the encounter.

The effort a person has to make to get access to the experience is determined by decisions made by the provider. Are the opening hours convenient? Is the store or venue located conveniently? Are convenient options available for the consumer to contact the provider? This type of effort is provider-based since the choices involved are choices that the firm or institution makes. Of course individuals may perceive the required effort in different ways but it is the provider that can influence this type of effort. The second type of effort also has to do with getting access to the experience but in a different meaning, having more to do with the individual herself. Because of the fact that the individual plays an active role in the experience, she first and foremost has to be able to have the experience. Schumacher speaks of 'adaequatio' in this context, defining 'knowledge as *adaequatio rei et intellectus*: the understanding of the knower must be adequate to the thing to be known' (1978, p. 50). Being adequate means that a certain endowment has to be present and a certain effort has to be made to grasp the experience in full. 'Some people are incapable of grasping and appreciating a given piece of music, not because they are deaf, but because of a lack of *adaequatio* in the mind. The sense of hearing receives nothing more than a succession of notes; the music is grasped by intellectual powers' (Schumacher, 1978, p. 51). Of course effort is not some objective characteristic of the experience; it depends on the individual. The amount of effort needed depends on the knowledge and experience, or 'human capital' as Ratchford (2001) calls it, the individual has, and even on her emotional state (Cosmides and Tooby, 2000). This type of effort is more or less 'experience-based' in the sense that the nature of the experience determines what the required effort should be and the individual can only react to this by trying to comply with the requirement or by choosing a different experience. The third type of capital has to do with the fact that individuals who have made the effort that is required for access to the experience have the choice to invest even more effort in it. From an efficiency perspective, this behaviour would seem irrational: why would someone invest more than is required? In fact, this perhaps is one of the main differences between services and experiences. In an experience context, some investments actually cause an increase in value to the customer. In general, people gladly invest more time in activities they enjoy (Holbrook and Gardner, 1998).

The third type of effort, the investment of more human capital than is required for access, is not under the control of the provider. However, by providing opportunities for individuals to try the experience out, firms and institutions can explore which elements of the experience individuals seem to enjoy most and are most involved in. The other two types of effort are at least partially under the influence of the provider. The first type, access, is determined and designed by the provider so a try-out session can deliver feedback on whether the right choices have been made in the design. With the second type of effort, the adaequatio, individuals can be supported by the provider since this is influenced by the experience that is created by the encounter of the individual with whatever the firm or institution has designed for them.

A try-out session, which can take the form of testing out a prototype, literally a first ('protos') impression ('typos'), or providing a simulation of the experience, can also help in solving the problem with expectations. Because of the dominance of experience and credence characteristics, inherent in experiences, it is difficult for individuals to form expectations. Firms and institutions should make sure that the right information is available related to the search characteristics and try to be as reliable and transparent in relation to the credence characteristics, but trying out the experience can be especially helpful in communicating the experience characteristics. Also here one could make use of various forms of primary and vicarious experience. Abstract information on experiences is hard to grasp, so a tangible representation of the experience can help the communication process immensely. Not only can experience characteristics be communicated this way but the individuals can also communicate their feedback on the tangible representation, which can be very valuable information for the final design of the experience. The sooner in the process mistakes are discovered, the lower the risk of incurring high costs for adapting things later in the process (Thomke, 2003)

The idea of using a tangible object for communication reasons, to get feedback based on a first impression of what the firm or institution has thought up for the individual, can be related to theories on socio-materiality. Especially because the prototype is intentionally unfinished and meant to be adapted based on feedback, individuals will want to actively deal with it, because of the lacks it displays while it unfolds (Knorr-Cetina and Bruegger, 2000). Because of the interaction between the individuals and the objects, in which the objects influence the actions of the individuals and the individuals in their turn influence the objects, we can speak of socio-materiality, the constitutive entanglement of the social and the material in everyday life (Orlikowski, 2007).

The value that individuals are prepared to invest related to search characteristics can for the greater part be researched. The value individuals are willing to invest in credence characteristics is most difficult to estimate since it may take years or forever before the individual knows how he perceives the value of what he has experienced and what it was worth to him. It cannot be determined upfront, not by the individual, let alone by the firm or institution providing the experience. The value that individuals may invest for experience characteristics can't be estimated upfront either. Individuals have to be able to 'experience the experience' to know how much they value the encounter and how much and which types of effort and investment they are willing to make to have the experience. Providing individuals with the possibilities to have (a part of) the experience so they can get clearer expectations may help in this regard.

7.7   CONCLUSION

To recapitulate, in this chapter, I have shown that experiences consist of three elements, an individual, something in the environment and an encounter between these two, and that a dominant focus on one of these leads to a biased view of experience and problems related to commoditization, which was allegedly the *raison d'être* of the experience economy. I have also shown how even within the approaches of experience one can see a bias towards the objectivist perspective of the firm or institution, again with consequences in terms of commoditization. If firms and institutions maintain these biases, they will have a hard time changing their perspectives and assumptions, and therefore have a hard time changing their relationships with individuals, be these customers, patients, citizens, students and so on. Offsetting the biases and taking a different perspective on experience helps in changing these relationships. To conclude this chapter, I want to use the etymological root of the word experience to show how firms and institutions can give the individual a different and more meaningful role in the mutual relationship and diminish the risk of commoditization.

The root of the word experience can also be recognized in the words 'periculum' (danger, peril) and 'expereri' (to try). I shall start with experience.

7.7.1   Experience

To gain deep insights into the individual's experience one has to connect with the individual's experience. The ideas on primary and vicarious experience can be used in this stage. Ethnographical principles but also phenomenology and grounded theory can be very valuable in this respect. To understand what individuals experience, one has to step into the shoes of the individual and not rely so much on objective characteristics that have been determined from the outside. The mental agency and temporal dimension involved in experiences make every experience unique and personal. A focus on secondary information on the experience will not help much in this respect; one needs to have more subjective and primary insights into the experience. The attention paid to quantitative research in market research and reports should at least be complemented by qualitative research focused on the individual's experience. Whether this research should take the form of deep interviews, role play or simulations and so on depends on the questions at hand and the context in which one operates, but the most important point is that one should try to get as close to the primary experience as possible. Scholars and practitioners with an objectivist perspective, who look at experiences from the outside to find the 'right' objective characteristics that should be implemented, try to find universal rules for a quality experience. The downside is that universal rules make for a certain degree of sameness, resulting in more and not less commoditization. Although paying more attention to the personal and unique characteristics of specific experiences of individuals may require more time and effort, the flipside is commoditization.

7.7.2   Periculum

Firms and institutions should not focus on determining and managing effects in a convergent way but take into account a variety of interpretive frameworks. Effects involve meaning and the determination and management of this meaning increases the risk of semantic and syntactic errors. Therefore, to understand how effects originate one should gather different people: people from different disciplines, people with different experiences, people with different worldviews, talents, intelligences and so on. This is where the periculum or danger becomes apparent because where in situations of convergent thinking from one perspective one knows what the intended goal or end-state will be, we now invite people with other ideas in the process, leading to uncertainty of where the process may lead us (Van Loon, 2001). Although this uncertainty may not receive a warm welcome in every firm or institution, one should contemplate on the fact that by forcing real-life divergent questions and problems in a convergent straight-jacket, one loses many opportunities to create value. Diverse people, of course including the individuals who have the experience or for whom the experience is intended, can inspire and build upon each other's ideas, leading to new insights that may result in valuable and unique innovations in terms of what firms and institutions do and how they do it. The openness of this divergent process may feel uneasy for firms and institutions that are used to determine and manage what they do and how they do it, but it is necessary to avoid doing the same as other parties in the market resulting in commoditization.

7.7.3   Expereri

Firms and institutions cannot determine upfront which and how much value(s) the individual should invest if the individual himself doesn't even know what to expect. He

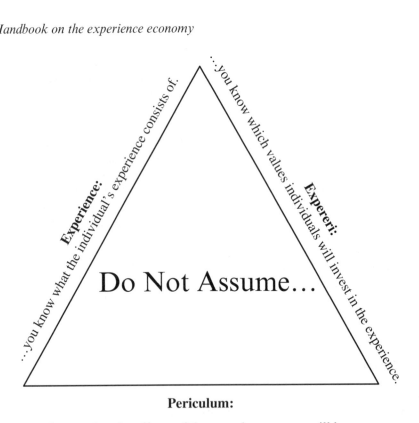

Periculum:

…you know what the effects of the experience are or will be.

Figure 7.3   Changing assumptions in the experience economy

therefore should be provided with opportunities to try out and experiment (expereri) at least the experience characteristics. Experiments with tangible representations of the experiences and trying these out have benefits for both the individuals involved and the firm or institution. Individuals can now better know what to expect from the experience since they can form expectations on the experience characteristics; the firms or institutions can get insight into how their idea of required invested effort would work out in practice: are the access costs acceptable, do individuals have enough adaequatio and are individuals willing to invest more human capital in the experience than required? If individuals do not know what to expect, all they have to base their decisions on are the search characteristics, like price, leading to commoditization. By giving them primary or vicarious experience of what to expect, firms and institutions provide the individuals with different information, based on which more informed decisions can be made.

The acronym DNA may help as a mnemonic device for organizations that are serious in trying to focus on experience and changing their relationships with individuals. DNA in this context stands for Do Not Assume, since the changes that entering the experi-ence economy entail are not superficial but truly have to do with a change in the basic assumptions of firms and institutions (Figure 7.3). As described above, they have to let go of the assumption that they can determine and manage certain things upfront and from the sideline and be open to the individual's perspective, to uncertainty about where the process will lead them and to first giving something to the individual to experiment with before he enters into the relationship so firms and institutions can learn from the individual.

It cannot be over-stressed: although explained in words and a three-letter acronym this may seem a straightforward story; one cannot overestimate its complexity. Most of us have been educated in a completely different way and the assumptions we have because of our training, our experience with the status quo, with incentives in organizations and so on will in some cases have to change 180 degrees. We have been used to the ideas of control, direction, determining, but if we really want to change our relationship with our customers, we will have to get used to the finite nature of our influence as firms and institutions. The decommoditizing power of experience can only result from this changed relationship, in which the individual takes centre stage.

BIBLIOGRAPHY

Adcox, J. and M. Wittenstein (2003), 'Beyond personalization: experience architecture', in N. Pal and A. Rangaswamy (eds), *The Power of One: Gaining Business Value from Personalization Technologies*, Victoria, Canada: Trafford Publishing, pp. 82–102.

Addis, M. and M.B. Holbrook (2001), 'On the conceptual link between mass customisation and experiential consumption: an explosion of subjectivity', *Journal of Consumer Behaviour*, 1 (1), 50–66.

Aldrich, L. (1999), *Consumer Use of Information: Implications for Food Policy*, Washington, DC: Food and Rural Economics Division, Economic Research Service, US Department of Agriculture.

Andersen, E.S. and K. Philipsen (1998), 'The evolution of credence goods in customer markets: exchanging "pigs in pokes"', Paper presented at the DRUID Winter Seminar, Middelfart, 8–10 January.

Animesh, A., V. Ramachandran and S. Viswanathan (2005), 'Online advertisers' bidding strategies for search, experience, and credence goods: an empirical investigation', in *Proceedings of the First Sponsored Search Workshop Held in Conjunction with the ACM Conference on Electronic Commerce in Vancouver, Canada*.

Ashcroft, K. and L. Foreman-Peck (1994), *Managing Teaching and Learning in Further and Higher Education*, London: Falmer Press.

Baudrillard, J. (1983), *Simulations*, New York: Semiotext(e).

Bengtsson, A. (2002), 'Unnoticed relationships: do consumers experience co-branded products?', *Advances in Consumer Research*, 29, 521–7.

Bernardini, O. and R. Galli (1993), 'Dematerialization: long term trends in the intensity of use of materials and energy', *Futures*, 25, May, 431–48.

Berthon, P., M.B. Holbrook and J.M. Hulbert (2003), 'Understanding and managing the brand space', *MIT Sloan Management Review*, Winter, 49–54.

Boorstin, D. (1964), *The Image: A Guide to Pseudo-events in America*, New York: Harper and Row.

Carbone, L.P. (1999), 'Leveraging customer experience in the twenty-first century', *Arthur Andersen Retailing Issues Letter*, 11 (3), 1–6.

Carbone, L.P. (2004), *Clued In: How to Keep Customers Coming Back Again and Again*, Upper Saddle River, NJ: FT Prentice Hall.

Chartrand, H.H. (1987), 'The arts: consumption skills in the post-modern economy', *Journal of Art and Design Education*, 6 (1), 35–50.

Christensen, L.T. and G. Cheney (2000), 'Selfabsorption and selfseduction in the corporate identity game', in M. Schultz, M.J. Hatch and M.H. Larsen (eds), *The Expressive Organization – Linking Identity, Reputation and the Corporate Brand*, Oxford: Oxford University Press, pp. 246–70.

Colombo, U. (1988), 'The technology revolution and the restructuring of the global economy. Globalization of technology: international perspectives', *Proceedings of the Sixth Convocation of the Council of Academies of Engineering and Technological Sciences*, Washington, DC: National Academy Press, pp. 23–31.

Cosmides, L. and J. Tooby (2000), 'Evolutionary psychology and the emotions', in M. Lewis and J. Haviland-Jones (eds), *Handbook of Emotions*, 2nd edn, New York: The Guilford Press, pp. 91–115.

Csikszentmihalyi, M. and E. Rochberg-Halton (1981), *The Meaning of Things: Domestic Symbols and the Self*, Cambridge, MA: Cambridge University Press.

Dagevos, J.C. (2001), 'De verruimde speurtocht naar aantrekkelijke belevenissen' ('The extended search for appealing experiences'), *Vrijetijdstudies*, **19** (1), 90–94.

Darby, M.R. and E. Karni (1973), 'Free competition and the optimal amount of fraud', *Journal of Law and Economics*, **16** (1), 67–88.

Davenport, T.H. and J.C. Beck (2001), *The Attention Economy: Understanding the New Currency of Business*, Boston, MA: Harvard Business School Press.

De Cauter, L. (1995), *Archeologie van de kick* (*Archaeology of the Kick*), Amsterdam: De Balie.

Dewey, J. (1938), *Experience and Education*, New York: Touchstone, reprinted in 1997, New York: Collier Books.

Dorst, K. (2011), 'The core of "design thinking" and its application', *Design Studies*, **32**, 521–31.

Douglas, M. and B. Isherwood (1979), *The World of Goods: Towards an Anthropology of Consumption*, New York: Basic Books.

Duijvestein, H. (2001), *Emotiemarketing: Vijf marketingstrategieën voor de eenentwintigste eeuw* (*Emotion-marketing: Five Marketing Strategies for the Twenty-first Century*), Den Haag: Stichting Maatschappij en Onderneming.

Dulleck, U. and R. Kerschbamer (2006), 'On doctors, mechanics and computer specialists –the economics of credence goods', *Journal of Economic Literature*, **XLIV** (1), 5–42.

Dumaine, B. (1991), 'Design that sells and sells and..', *Fortune*, 11 March, 86–94.

Emons, W. (1997), 'Credence goods and fraudulent experts', *RAND Journal of Economics*, **28** (1), 107–19.

Falk, J.H. and L.D. Dierking (2000), *Learning from Museums: Visitor Experiences and the Making of Meaning*, Walnut Creek, CA: AltaMira Press.

Falk, P. and C. Campbell (eds) (1997), *The Shopping Experience*, Part of the series Theory, Culture and Society, London: Sage.

Featherstone, M. (1991), *Consumer Culture and Postmodernism*, London: Sage.

Ford, G.T., D.B. Smith and J.L. Swasy (1988), 'An empirical test of the search, experience and credence attributes framework', *Advances in Consumer Research*, **15** (1), 239–43.

Ford, R.C. and C. Heaton (2000), *Managing the Guest Experience in Hospitality*, Albany, NY: Delmar.

Fornell, C. (1976), *Consumer Input for Marketing Decisions: A Study of Corporate Departments for Consumer Affairs*, EFL Research Report,, Lund: The Foundation for Economic Research.

Fournier, S. and D.G. Mick (1999), 'Rediscovering satisfaction', *Journal of Marketing*, **63** (4), 5–23.

Gadamer, H.-G. (1975), *Truth and Method*, New York: The Seabury Press, reprinted in 2004, London: Continuum.

Galle, M. (2004), 'Alle tijd' ('All the time'), in M. Galle, F. Van Dam, P. Peeters et al. (eds), *Duizend dingen op een dag: Een tijdsbeeld uitgedrukt in ruimte* (*A Thousand Things in One Day: An Image of Time Expressed in Space*), Rotterdam: NAi Uitgevers.

Georgakopoulou, A. (2004), 'To tell or not to tell? Email stories between on- and offline interactions', *Language@Internet*, **1** (1).

Girard, T., R. Silverblatt and P. Korgaonkar (2002), 'Influence of product class on preference for shopping on the internet', *Journal of Computer-Mediated Communication*, **8** (1), available at http://jcmc.indiana.edu/vol8/issue1/girard.html (accessed 6 February 2011).

Goodman, D.J. (2003), 'Dream kitsch and the debris of history: an interview with Martin Jay', *Journal of Consumer Culture*, **3**, 109–20.

Goossens, C. (2000), 'Zit er business in een belevenis?' ('Is there business in an experience'), *Vrijetijdstudies*, **18** (3–4), 87–92.

Green, W. and P. Jordan (eds) (2002), *Pleasure with Products: Beyond Usability*, New York: Taylor and Francis Group.

Hackley, C. (2003), '"We are all customers now. . ."': rhetorical strategy and ideological control in marketing management texts', *Journal of Management Studies*, **40** (5), 1325–52.

Herman, R., S. Ardekani and J. Ausubel (1989), 'Dematerialization', in J. Ausubel and H. Sladovich (eds), *Technology and Environment*, Washington, DC: National Academy Press, pp. 50–69.

Heskett, J.L., W.E. Sasser and L.A. Schlesinger (1997), *The Service Profit Chain: How Leading Companies Link Profit and Growth to Loyalty, Satisfaction, and Value*, New York: Free Press.

Hill, D. (2007), *Emotionomics: Winning Hearts and Minds*, Edina, MN: Adams Business and Professional.

Hirschman, E. and M. Holbrook (1982), 'Hedonic consumption: emerging concepts, methods and propositions', *Journal of Marketing*, **46**, Summer, 92–101.

Holbrook, M.B. (1981), 'Introduction: the esthetic imperative in consumer research', in E.C. Hirschman and M.B. Holbrook (eds), *SV – Symbolic Consumer Behavior*, New York: Association for Consumer Research, pp. 36–7.

Holbrook, M.B. (1986), 'Progress and problems in research on consumer esthetics', Paper presented at the Fourth International Conference on Cultural Economics and Planning, Avignon, France.

Holbrook, M.B. and M.P. Gardner (1998), 'How motivation moderates the effects of emotions on the duration of consumption', *Journal of Business* Research, **42**, 241–52.

Huizing, A. (2002), *On Organization: Looking Back on Reengineering and Ahead to Learning*, Amsterdam: Ard Huizing.

Jackson, P. (1998), *John Dewey and the Lessons of Art*, New Haven, CT: Yale University Press.

James, W. (1890), 'The principles of psychology', available from Classics in the History of Psychology, an internet resource developed by Christopher D. Green, http://psychclassics.yorku.ca/James/Principles/index.htm (accessed 6 February 2011).

James, W. (1902), *The Varieties of Religious Experience: A Study in Human Nature*, London and Bombay: Longmans, Green and Co.

Jay, M. (2005), *Songs of Experience: Modern American and European Variations on a Universal Theme*, Berkeley, CA: University of California Press.

Jensen, R. (1999), *The Dream Society: How the Coming Shift from Information to Imagination Will Transform Your Business*, New York: McGraw-Hill.

Jones, M.A. (1999), 'Entertaining shopping experiences: an exploratory investigation', *Journal of Retailing and Consumer Services*, **6** (3), 129–39.

Knorr-Cetina, K. and U. Bruegger (2000), 'The market as an object of attachment: exploring postsocial relations in financial markets', *Canadian Journal of Sociology*, **25** (2), 141–68.

Kolb, D.A. (1984), *Experiential Learning: Experience as the Source of Learning and Development*, Englewood Cliffs, NJ: Prentice-Hall.

LaSalle, D. and T. Britton (2003), *Priceless: Turning Ordinary Products into Extraordinary Experiences*, Boston, MA: Harvard Business School Press.

Lash, S. and J. Urry (1994), *Economies of Signs and Space*, London: Sage.

Levy, S. (1959), 'Symbols for sale', *Harvard Business* Review, **37**, July–August, 117–24.

Levy, S. (1981), 'Interpreting consumer mythology: a structural approach to consumer behavior', *Journal of Marketing*, **45**, Summer, 49–61.

Lewis, D. and D. Bridger (2001), *The Soul of the New Consumer: Authenticity – What We Buy and Why in the New Economy*, London: Nicholas Brealey Publishing.

Luckner, J. and R. Nadler (1997), *Processing the Experience: Strategies to Enhance and Generalize Learning*, Dubuque, IA: Kendall/Hunt Publishing.

MacCannell, D. (1976), *The Tourist: A New Theory of the Leisure Class*, London: Macmillan.

MacCannell, D. and J.F. MacCannell (1982), *The Time of the Sign: A Semiotic Interpretation of Modern Culture*, Bloomington, IN: Indiana University Press.

Maes, R.E. and B. Parson (2001), 'Pleidooi voor de emotie-economie' ('Plea for the emotion economy'), available at http://imwww.fee.uva.nl/%7Emaestro/PDF/Pleidooi_voor_de_emotie-economie.PDF (accessed 6 February 2011).

Mathwick, C., N. Malhotra and E. Rigdon (2001), 'Experiential value: conceptualization, measurement and application in the catalog and Internet shopping environment', *Journal of Retailing*, **77** (1), 39–56.

McLuhan, M. (1967), *The Medium is the Massage*, New York: Bantam Books.

Millet, G.W. and B. Millet (2002), *Creating and Delivering Totally Awesome Customer Experience: The Art and Science of Customer Experience Mapping*, Salt Lake City, UT: Customer Experience Inc.

Mitroff, I.I. and W. Bennis (1989), *The Unreality Industry: The Deliberate Manufacturing of Falsehood and What it is Doing to Our Lives*, New York: Carol Publishing.

Mommaas, H. (2000), *De vrijetijdsindustrie in stad en land: Een studie naar de markt van belevenissen* (*The Urban and Rural Leisure Industry: A Study of the Experience Market*), Den Haag: Sdu Uitgevers, Wetenschappelijke Raad voor het Regeringsbeleid.

Nelson, P. (1974), 'Advertising as information', *Journal of Political Economy*, **82** (4), 729–54.

Nussbaum, B. (2005), 'The empathy economy', *Business Week*, 7 March, available at http:// www.businessweek.com/bwdaily/dnflash/ mar2005/nf2005037_4086.htm (accessed April 2013).

Oevermans, H. (1999), 'De behoefte aan kicks is een maatschappelijk verschijnsel geworden: Kerk en geloof in het tijdperk van de beleving' ('The need for kicks has become a societal phenomenon: church and belief in the era of experience'), *Wapenveld*, **49** (6), 207–15.

Orlikowski, W.J. (2007), 'Sociomaterial practices: exploring technology at work', *Organization Studies*, **28** (9), 1435–48.

O'Sullivan, E.L. and K. Spangler (1998), *Experience Marketing: Strategies for the New Millennium*, State College, PA: Venture Publishing.

Piët, S. (2003), *De emotiemarkt: De toekomst van de beleveniseconomie* (*The Emotion Market: The Future of the Experience Economy*), Amsterdam: Pearson Education Benelux.

Pine, B.J. and J.H. Gilmore (1998), 'Welcome to the experience economy', *Harvard Business Review*, July–August, 97–105.

Pine, B.J. and J.H. Gilmore (1999), *The Experience Economy: Work is Theatre and Every Business a Stage*, Boston, MA: Harvard Business School Press.

Porat, M.U. (1977), 'The information economy: definition and measurement', available at http://eric.ed.gov/PDFS/ED142205.pdf (accessed 6 February 2011).

Postman, N. (2005), *Amusing Ourselves to Death: Public Discourse in the Age of Show Business*, New York: Penguin Books.

Poulsson, S.H. and S.H. Kale (2004), 'The experience economy and commercial experiences', *Marketing Review*, 4 (3), 267–77.

Prast, H. (2010), *Alles draait om geld: Over emotie en economie* (*Everything Revolves Around Money: About Emotion and Economics*), Amsterdam: Business Contact.

Ratchford, B.T. (2001), 'The economics of consumer knowledge', *Journal of Consumer Research*, 27 (4), 397–411.

Reed, E.S. (1996), *The Necessity of Experience*, New Haven, CT: Yale University Press.

Richards, G. (2001), 'The experience industry and the creation of attractions', in G. Richards (ed.), *Cultural Attractions and European Tourism*, Wallingford, UK: CABI Publishing, pp. 55–69.

Rifkin, J. (2000), *The Age of Access: The New Culture of Hypercapitalism, Where All of Life is a Paid-for Experience*, New York: Tarcher/Putnam.

Ritzer, G. (1999), *Enchanting a Disenchanted World: Revolutionizing the Means of Consumption*, Thousand Oaks, CA: Pine Forge Press.

Scheerder, J. (2000), 'Fysieke gezondheid, verschijning, ervaring en het hedendaagse vrijetijdslichaam' ('Physical health, appearance, experience and the leisure-body nowadays'), *Vrijetijdstudies*, 18 (3–4), 5–20.

Schmitt, B.H. (1999), *Experiential Marketing: How to Get Customers to Sense, Feel, Think, Act, and Relate to Your Company and Brands*, New York: Free Press.

Schulze, G. (2000), *Die Erlebnis-Gesellschaft: Kultursoziologie der Gegenwart (The Experience Society: Cultural Sociology of Value)*, New York: Campus Verlag.

Schumacher, E.F. (1973), *Small is Beautiful: A Study of Economics as if People Mattered*, London: Blond and Briggs.

Schumacher, E.F. (1978), *A Guide for the Perplexed*, London: Abacus.

Shaw, C. (2005), *Revolutionize Your Customer Experience*, Basingstoke: Palgrave Macmillan.

Shaw, C. and J. Ivens (2002), *Building Great Customer Experiences*, Basingstoke: Palgrave Macmillan.

Sheth, J.N., B.I. Newman and B.L. Gross (1991), 'Why we buy what we buy: a theory of consumption values', *Journal of Business Research*, 22, 159–70.

Smith, S. and J. Wheeler (2002), *Managing the Customer Experience: Turning Customers into Advocates*, Edinburgh: FT Prentice Hall.

Snel, J.M.C. (2011), 'For the love of experience: changing the experience economy discourse', PhD thesis, Faculty of Economics and Business, Amsterdam: University, Amsterdam.

Snowden, D.J. (1999), 'The paradox of story: simplicity and complexity in strategy', *Journal of Strategy and Scenario Planning*, 1 (5), 16–20.

Sveiby, K. (1997), *The New Organizational Wealth: Managing and Measuring Knowledge-based Assets*, San Francisco, CA: Berrett-Koehler.

Ter Borg, M. (2003), *Zineconomie: De samenleving van de overtreffende trap (The Economy of Meaning: The Society of Superlatives)*, Schiedam: Scriptum.

Thomke, S. (2003), *Experimentation Matters: Unlocking the Potential of New Technologies for Innovation*, Boston, MA: Harvard Business School Press.

Toffler, A. (1970), *Future Shock*, New York: Random House.

Tyrrell, G.N. (1947), *Grades of Significance: The Dependence of Meaning on Current Thought*, New York: Rider.

Van Loon, P.P.J. (2001), 'Collaboration in complex building projects through open design management', *International Journal of Architectural Management Practice and Research*, May, 69–82.

Van Saane, J. (1998), *De rol van gevoelens en emoties in de religieuze ervaring: Een theoretisch-psychologische benadering (The Role of Feelings and Emotions in the Religious Experience: A Theoretical-Psychological Approach)*, Amsterdam: Vrije Universiteit.

Vavra, T. (1995), *Aftermarketing: How to Keep Customers for Life through Relationship Marketing*, Chicago, IL: Irwin Professional Publishing.

Wernick, I.K., R. Herman, S. Govind and J. Ausubel (1996), 'Materialization and dematerialization: measures and trends', *Daedalus*, 125 (3), 171–98.

Wolf, M. (1999), *The Entertainment Economy: How Mega-media Forces Are Transforming Our Lives*, New York: Times Books.

Wright, A.A. and J.G. Lynch (1995), 'Communication effects of advertising versus direct experience when both search and experience attributes are present', *Journal of Consumer Research*, 21 (4), 708–18.

Zaltman, G. (1997), 'Rethinking market research: putting people back in', *Journal of Marketing Research*, **XXXIV**, November, 424–37.

Zaltman, G. and R. Higie (1993), *Seeing the Voice of the Customer: The Zaltman Metaphor Elicitation Technique*, Cambridge, MA: Marketing Science Institute.

Zeithaml, V.A., A. Parasuraman and L.L. Berry (1990), *Delivering Quality Service: Balancing Customer Perceptions and Expectations*, New York: Free Press.

Zuboff, S. and J. Maxmin (2002), *The Support Economy*, New York: Penguin Group.

8. Experiencing and experiences: a psychological framework
Christian Jantzen

8.1 EXPERIENCES IN EVERYDAY LIFE

Experiences are mental and corporeal phenomena. As such, they are psychological. This chapter sketches a framework for understanding the psychological issues implied in dealing experientially with products. This framework is based on two assumptions. Firstly, experiencing is a coherent structure of present sensing and feeling informed by past experiences. Secondly, experiencing is a specific structure by making us aware of the act of sensing and feeling and by questioning the validity of past experiences.

When asked to recount an experience, people readily reproduce stories from their immediate or long bygone past. A friendly smile in a crowded bus after a day at work, a sudden noise disturbing the serenity of the moment, a walk in fresh snow with one's parents many years ago, an anxiously anticipated rendezvous or a dramatic split-up all qualify as experiences. Experiences occur, whether they are planned, designed and marketed or not. They are incidents, imposing themselves on the ordinary routines of everyday life. As such, incidents may be easy to remember. They might even become core elements in people's life stories like, for example, a rendezvous or a divorce.

These considerations have important implications for understanding the experience economy. Firstly, experiences are not just goods and services to be produced or consumed. Experiences are neither bought nor sold. They are generated as a consequence, intended or not, of people's more or less quotidian dealings with the world. Users or consumers are the producers of the experiential quality and value of products. Designers, manufacturers, marketers, entertainers or retailers are at best merely providers of the frames and elements of a specific experience. Many personally valuable experiences actually occur without commercial intermediaries partaking in the process.

Secondly, an experience stems from people's interactions with their surroundings and is, as such, situated and subjective. Experiences are generated in concrete circumstances. The quality and value of an experience thus relies on how physical and social aspects of the situation influence the acts and perceptions of the experiencing person. Furthermore, the generation of experiences depends on the mood, goals, expectations, attitudes and capabilities of the experiencing person. These states of mind differ from one person to the next. They may even fluctuate from one moment to the next. This is the subjective component of experiencing. Experiencing should hence be analysed in psychological terms in order to understand how to design products that contribute to the generation of experiences. The process of experiencing is not a black box phenomenon nor a simple response to a stimulus. With few exceptions (for example, Mikunda, 2004; Boswijk et al., 2007; Hassenzahl, 2010; Boswijk et al., 2012), psychological approaches are nonetheless absent in current literature on experience design and economy.

Thirdly, experiences are mentally and physically significant. In many everyday situations, a smiling face or a sudden noise will unexpectedly affect our wellbeing. Such experiences regulate our mood. They may focus our attention on other aspects of the situation than those we perceived just a moment ago. They increase our awareness of the situation and direct our attention towards potential joys and dangers. In line with mood management theory, which stresses the significance of entertainment in maintaining balance, these modulating effects of experiencing could be labelled 'entertaining qualities' (Zillmann, 1988; Vorderer, 2001). But experiencing may also have 'developmental qualities'. Experiences may help people improve their capabilities by having their current presuppositions, expectations and abilities challenged. Such developing aspects are at the core of experiential learning (Kolb, 1984) and of 'flow-experiences', where people are immersed in a strenuous activity that demands the utmost of their skills (Csikszentmihalyi, 1975, 1990). Even negative experiences (for example, a dramatic split-up) may in the longer run lead to positive outcomes (for example, a better understanding of own wants and longings). Developmental experiences are thus crucial for identity formation. Memory of the challenges and crises that spurred development do in such cases typically become part of episodic memory: that is, that part of long-term memory where experiences of past events are recorded and stored.

Fourthly, experiences are psychologically complex. They range from split seconds of miniscule physiological modulations and fleeting emotional states to the memory of generalized events constructed throughout life (for example, what hot coffee tastes like). The first aim of this chapter is to uncover the psychological coherence behind this complexity. This should also clarify the intricate connections between entertaining and developmental qualities of experiencing.

Fifthly, although part of everyday life, experiences foreground extraordinary moments in the ordinary flow of occurrences. Experiences are surprising, sometimes overwhelming in that they deviate from the expected, thereby creating an altered awareness and a new understanding of the situation. The second aim of this chapter is to elaborate on the specificity or the extraordinary character of experiencing compared to 'ordinary life'. By changing physical states and challenging mental states, experiencing is part of the aesthetics of everyday life.

8.2 A BRIEF HISTORY OF THE PSYCHOLOGY OF EXPERIENCES

Together with behaviour, experiencing was recognized by the founders of modern psychology as fundamental for understanding mental life. The leading figure in the Leipzig School of psychology, Wilhelm Wundt (1832–1920), who developed psychology as an empirical science based on researchers' direct experiences, viewed psychology as a science of immediate experience. In this respect, psychology differed from the natural sciences, which focused on mediated experiences: that is, on the objects of experience, conceived of as independent of the perceiving subject (Wundt, 1896, p. 3). Wundt thus contended that psychology should be seen as the very foundation of the humanities (*Geisteswissenschaften*), because it had the universal laws of immediate subjective experiences as its field of study (Wundt, 1896, p. 4).

In the same spirit, William James (1842–1910), pragmatist philosopher and founding father of American psychology, in his later works argued for a psychology based on neither metaphysics nor rationalism, but on radical empiricism. This empiricist view implies that reality 'is created temporarily day by day' (James, 1911, p. 100). Reality is not based on a priori concepts, as rationalists would have it. 'Particular experiences' make up the 'facts' of sensed reality. And these 'facts' are not only disjunctive and discernable from each other, as traditional empiricism would posit. 'Radical' empiricism implies that 'particular experiences' are also conjunctive, continuous and overlapping. They emerge in a 'stream of thought': that is, in the immediacy of volatile feelings and sensations. Mixed sensations, for example, of anxious excitement or repulsive attraction, bear evidence of the overlapping, non-discrete character of particular experiences.

This flow of feelings and sensations is made up of 'pure experiences', described as 'the immediate flux of life which furnishes the material of our later reflection with its conceptual categories' (James, 1912, p. 117). Experiencing in this pure form is, according to James, a stream prior to the concepts of reflective thought such as mind and body or subject and object. Such distinctions only emerge in retrospect. Our ordinary experience of various things and relations is thus an a posteriori construction consisting of innate pure experiences and classifications based on prior experiences and temporary purposes.

James's theory of experience distinguishes between immediate experiencing in a volatile presence and developed experiences. In these ordinary experiences, the raw material of experiencing is retrospectively transformed into conscious shapes. This transformation is a construction by past experiences and future purposes upon the flux of ever emerging and waning feelings and sensations. Everyday experiences thus consist of a realm of undifferentiated, not yet fully conscious experiencing and a realm of conscious, but no longer immediate experiences.

James's theory lacks an explanation of how this transformation from pure experiencing to developed experiences micro-genetically is brought about. Moreover, the purity of 'pure experiences' may only – and even then only hypothetically – be found in newborn infants and is hence highly improbable in everyday life. The quotidian stream of thought is more aptly characterized by impurity. Immediate experiencing and the memory of prior experiences are always intersected with one another and they are mixed up with the experiencing person's hopes and worries for the future. James's seminal contribution is nonetheless that he emphasized the tension between the volatile presence of immediate and indistinctive experiencing and the retrospectively constructed states of conscious experiences.

This tension is perpetual, which explains the dynamics of experiencing. Experiencing is an ongoing and ever changing process connecting the yet unknown and hence surprising fact with an already known and therefore presupposed state. The unknown is understood in retrospect. But it may at the same time upset and alter existing understandings, thereby opening up new possibilities for the future.

Experiences should therefore be conceived of as a whole larger than the sum of its elements. This idea was put forward by successors of Wundt in the so-called Second Leipzig School between the two world wars. Rejecting the atomistic position that experiences consist of distinctive perceptions, responses or associations, they developed a *Ganzheitspsychologie*, crudely translated as 'holistic psychology'

(Sander and Volkelt, 1962). Experiencing is a non-reducible whole of immediate feelings, personal dispositions and structural realities. It should thus be understood in its totality and not dissected in its individual parts (Krueger, 1924, 1928). Such partition neglects the dynamics by which people develop through instant-by-instant experiences (Diriwächter, 2008).

This school of thought fell apart after the dismissal of Krueger for political reasons in 1938 and Klemm's suicide in 1939 (Loosch, 2008). Other members were compromised after the Second World War, having collaborated with National Socialism. Actually, in the post-war era, the very idea of holistic science became politically incriminated in Germany (Geuter, 1985; Harrington, 1999). But other factors may also have hampered the further development of a holistic psychology of experience. One of them is the advance of behavioural research in the beginning of the twentieth century propelled by the famous experiments by the Russian physiologist Ivan Pavlov. American behaviourism (Thorndike, Watson, Skinner), disregarding the intermediary role of experiences in the processing of stimuli, is the most obvious example of this. This shift coincided with the rise of ideals imported from the natural sciences. Psychology started to favour objective experiences and therefore methods used in traditional empiricism. Focusing on disjunctive and discernable facts, Anglo-Saxon psychology followed a highly atomistic path, which after the war became mainstream in other Western countries too (cf. Métraux, 1985).

Psychology branched out in an array of specialized psychologies, each having its own subdisciplines. Cognitive science especially has produced an enormous body of knowledge on detailed and sometimes miniscule aspects of human experiences. The coherence of experiencing, however, has been ignored. As a side effect of the computational allegory, which since the 1960s drove cognitive psychology forwards, the psychology of emotions was considered a relatively minor field. Ironically, it was not until the 1990s with spectacular advances in neuropsychology, on the face of it the most measurable and hence 'objective' of all psychologies, that research in emotions again gained prominence. Neuroscientists could actually demonstrate the role of emotions in decision-making (Damasio, 1994; LeDoux, 1996)

Despite its success, it is unlikely that neuroscience will help re-establish a holistic theory of experiences in the foreseeable future. Neuroscience focuses on physical brain processes and is apparently closing down the gap between brain and mind, understood as a complex of cognitive faculties, by materialistically explaining the latter as a function of the former: for example, reassessing the 'free will' as just an illusionary shadow effect of neurological processes (Dennett, 1991; Churchland, 2002). But from there, it is still a very long way to explaining the developmental dynamics between sensing and emotions, on the one hand, and meanings and understandings, on the other.

I would therefore suggest a framework for understanding the coherence of experiences based on the holistic approaches of Wundt, James and Krueger, but taking advantage of a wide range of contributions from contemporary psychology. The core of this framework is the impurity of pure experiences: namely the inherent and dynamic tension between the here-and-now of experiencing and the developed and developing experiences not only prior to and following after this immediacy, but also actively implicated in this here-and-now.

8.3   SEMANTICS MATTERS

According to the Merriam-Webster online dictionary, a range of slightly different meanings define the noun 'experience'. It may denote:

1.   'direct observation of or participation in events as a basis of knowledge';
2.   'practical knowledge, skill, or practice derived from direct observation of or participation in events or in a particular activity';
3.   'the conscious events that make up an individual life';
4.   'something personally encountered, undergone, or lived through';
5.   'the act or process of directly perceiving events or reality'.

Experience (1) stands for the methods by which we find evidence for facts about the world. The truth of a proposition or a fact is determined by our own experience of it. Having seen an unidentified flying object (UFO) gives us evidence of the existence of aliens. Until somebody else proves that the object was a fraud or an illusion, we will stick to our newly acquired knowledge. Experience (2) is tacit knowledge, practical dispositions or *savoir faire*. It is learned throughout the span of life having encountered many similar situations. People living close to the sea may without being particularly conscious of it become experienced beach goers, whereas more unexperienced people have a higher risk of drowning. Experience (3) is about knowing how to apply general rules in prototypical situations. The gist of an original experience (5) is blended with experiences of similar events to form a general image of what to expect and how to tackle the event.

Experience (4) is our own evaluation of an experience (5). When we experience something repulsive (experience 5), we report the situation as being terrible (experience 4). Experience (5) may be an accidental event: for example, dropping my ice cream while distracted by the glimpse of another beach goer. It might be reported as an anecdote soon to fade from memory (experience 4). But reports can also be based on lasting impressions of specific events. Thereby they become part of my autobiography telling myself and others who I really am. I may remember the first time my father offered me an ice cream (experience 4). Having eaten ice creams on many previous occasions, I will be able to activate a vast body of knowledge on how, what, where and when to order an ice cream (experience 3). The act of eating ice creams has furthermore become tacit knowledge of how to handle ice creams in general (experience 2).

Experience (5) differs from experience (1) in one important aspect. Experience (1) gives us evidence of objective features. The truth is 'out there' for us to perceive. This is the mediated experience of empirical science. Experience (5) on the other hand is Wundt's immediate experience, which bears evidence of our own subjective feelings in the situation. Regardless of whether it is falsifiable or not, the truth is 'in here', emerging from our presence in the event. Miracles are high-impact events uniting experience (1) and (5). They are interpreted as evidence of objective existence, when a deity reveals himself or herself (experience 1). At the same time, this event only occurs to a chosen one. It is subjective evidence of his or her devote character (experience 5). The apparition of Madonna at Lourdes (France) in 1858 was interpreted as a token of her real existence (experience 1), but it also proved to the 14-year-old girl for which she appeared that she had a very special blessing (experience 5). She was later canonized as Saint Bernadette Soubirous.

Table 8.1   Comparison between the English 'experience' and its German equivalents

'Experience'	German equivalents
Experience (1): Knowledge through observation	*Erfahrung*
Experience (2): Practical skills	
Experience (3): Conscious knowledge	
Experience (4): Autobiographical knowledge	*Erlebnis*
Experience (5): The act of sensing and feeling	

In a more pagan vein, seeing UFOs, whether a fraud or not, tends to turn people into ardent believers.

Translating the composite meanings of 'experience' to other Germanic languages is not straightforward. In these languages, there is not a single noun that translates the whole range of meanings of 'experience'. The German *Erfahrung*, the Dutch *ervaring* and the Danish *erfaring* roughly stand for experience (1), (2) and (3). The German *Erlebnis*, Dutch *belevenis* and Danish *oplevelse* approximate experience (4) and (5). The concept 'experience economy' is usually translated into *Erlebnisökonomie, beleveniseconomie* and *oplevelsesøkonomi*, which points to the fact that the 'fantasies, feelings and fun' (Holbrook and Hirschman, 1992) of experiences (that is, its entertaining aspects) are being emphasized to the detriment of more developmental aspects. These semantic differences are illustrated in Table 8.1.

Immediate experience (experience 5) may be recounted as an evaluation of the event (experience 4), it may blend with other experiences of similar events, thereby forming a memory of prototypical situations (experience 3) or it may form a habit or skill to be used in practical situations (experience 2). The merging of experience (1) and (5) in epiphanies blends the objective and subjective qualities of experiencing. These intricacies are in line with my emphasis on the coherence of experiences and an argument for broadening our understanding of the 'experience economy'. When dealing with experiences we should look at both *Erlebnisse* and *Erfahrungen*.

8.4   *ERLEBNIS* AND *ERFAHRUNG, ERLEBEN* AND *ERFAHREN*

From these semantic differences between the English 'experience' and its twin equivalents in some Germanic languages, five further considerations follow. Firstly, the impurity of immediate experiences implies that *Erfahrungen* have already informed an *Erlebnis*. *Erfahrungen* are not only outcomes of *Erlebnisse*, they are also sources of *Erlebnisse*. Our memory sets expectations guiding us towards certain events, which appear especially promising for having interesting experiences. They are motivating. In addition, our experience-based knowledge frames such events. Memory helps us interpret what is going on and supports us in finding an appropriate attitude.

Secondly, experience (2), (3) and (4) are part of long-term memory that comes in two main categories. The first category is called declarative or explicit memory, because its content can be explicitly retrieved by consciousness (for example, facts and conscious knowledge). The second category is procedural or implicit memory: learned skills and habits that can be automatically reproduced without the help of consciousness (Graf and Schachter, 1985). In fact, consciousness may impair the performance of these skills. Thinking about how to steer makes biking a more strenuous job, actually increasing the risk of having accidents. The skills and habits included in experience (2) are procedural memory. We acquire them by practicing: that is, in the process by which new experiences through repetition are turned into routines.

Declarative memory comes in two subcategories: semantic and episodic memory (Tulving, 1983). Semantic memory is event-independent concept-based knowledge. Our recollection of Lisbon being the capital of Portugal or of 2 and 2 adding up to 4 are examples of knowledge reproduced without the underlying memory of an event.

Episodic memory, however, is founded in experienced events. Entering a new restaurant activates memories of previous experiences with restaurants in general. This gives us a degree of certitude as to what is going to happen. Such memories of general events are part of experience (3). Our recollections of an evening at a particular restaurant is specific autobiographical memory: that is, highly subjective and often charged with feelings. This is experience (4), an *Erlebnis*. If this experience deviates significantly from our generalized episodic memory of what restaurants are about, we may learn something new about restaurants in general (experience 3). This is episodic learning: development spurred by having to cope with experiences deviating from past events (Terry, 2008). *Erfahrung* and *Erlebnis* are thus related to different categories of memory:

- Procedural memory enabling us to do things automatically (that is, without being specifically aware of this) simply because we are experienced through practice. The knowledge used is implicit and does not require conscious thinking. Instead, it is the hand doing the thinking (Pallasmaa, 2009).
- Episodic memory of a generalized type enabling us to interpret and adjust our appearance so it fits prototypical situations. Confronted with such events we retrieve appropriate cognitive resources from memory, for example, in the form of 'scripts' being the cognitive structure describing the expected sequence of acts in an event (Schank and Abelson, 1977; Schank, 1999) or 'schemata' being a well-integrated chunk of knowledge about how things, events, people or actions are generally connected (Bartlett, 1932; Piaget, 1985).
- Episodic memory of an autobiographical type enabling us to recall and recount specific events as formative of our social and personal identity and as the subjective foundation of our present values and attitudes. This recollection is often far from precise, omitting certain aspects, overemphasizing others and blending the specific event with other ones in order for the memory to fit the current situation (Berntsen and Rubin, 2012).

These types of memory are learned from experience. This makes memory dynamic in two respects. New experiences may expand, revise or refine our practical or conscious knowledge. And secondly, the repeat experiencing of similar events may alter the quality of the remembered content. What was once a highly personalized and hence autobiographical experience (experience 4) may by repetition become episodic memory of the generalized type (experience 3). Being knowledgeable of what restaurants in general are about but visiting McDonald's for the first time may disturb established knowledge of restaurants (experience 3). Memories of 'first times' are autobiographical (experience 4). If these events recur several times, we may forget the 'first time' and learn a general rule of what to expect and how to behave in this prototypical situation (experience 3). Becoming a knowledgeable McDonald's visitor implies learning the scripts and schemata of fast food catering (Jantzen et al., 2011, pp. 193 ff.). Learning to eat fast food without the use of fork and knife may go from autobiographical memory to procedural memory (experience 2). In such a case, conscious knowledge is transformed into automatic skills. Episodic memory (experience 3 and 4) may also be transformed into semantic memory (Baars and Gage, 2010, p. 327). Learning to add 2 and 2 at primary school may once have been an autobiographical memory. Today such knowledge is typically reproduced without any remembrance of the learning experience. To sum up: *Erlebnis* is the origin of *Erfahrungen*.

Thirdly, having been learned, semantic memory might also qualify as *Erfahrung*. It resembles experience (2) by being skills put to practice when such activity is required. But it is distinguished from implicit memory by being explicitly declarative. Semantic memory is a body of retrievable conscious knowledge like experience (3). Knowing that Lisbon is the capital of Portugal is exclusively part of semantic memory only as long as this knowledge is treated as a mere fact. As soon as this fact is combined with more elaborate subjective knowledge it also becomes episodic memory. For people having been to Lisbon the very concept 'Lisbon' may likely retrieve a mental map of parts of this city from memory (Lynch, 1960). This map is experience (3). It contains not only objective knowledge of streets, squares, buildings and so on but also subjective knowledge of places I like or loathe in this city and thus what (not) to do next time. Being subjective there is a feeling quality in episodic memory, remnants of *Erlebnis* revived by the mere 'doing' of the concept.

When 'Lisbon' activates autobiographical memory of specific events having occurred in the past, this feeling quality is pertinent (experience 4, an *Erlebnis*). But the 'doing' of practical skills (experience 2) may also generate such feeling qualities. A carpenter carving a piece of wood may derive pleasure from her effortless execution of the skill without having to activate any episodic memory. Me writing this text or (albeit more unlikely) you reading it may find the mere 'doing' of the task inherently enjoyable. The very act of crafting words, putting them together, watching sentences grow and sections emerge is, irrespective of the vast body of semantic and episodic knowledge implied, part of 'the pleasure of the text' (Barthes, 1973). The 'doing' of *Erfahrung* may thus in itself be an *Erlebnis*.

In the fourth place, episodic memories raise expectations as to the quality of coming events. *Erfahrungen* are also the sources of new *Erlebnisse*. They motivate us to seek out particular opportunities for new experiences. This has some important consequences for experiential entrepreneurs:

1. The higher these expectations are, the harder it is to meet them. Disappointment seems to be part and parcel of the striving for new experiences (5).
2. Episodes not only consist of events but also integrated feelings and sensations. In memory, this integration misleadingly blurs these distinct elements so that the role of moods can be overlooked. In a bad mood, even the most well-crafted event will seem disappointing.

3.   The more experienced a person is (experience 3), the more likely will she or he have a blasé attitude towards new offers on the experiential market.
4.   A repetition of once extraordinary experiences may turn them ordinary (experience 2 and 3). Routinization decreases the quality and value of experience (5).
5.   People cherish memories of events personally undergone (experience 4). If these events turn out to be mass produced and marketed this may diminish their value.

In this respect, the experience economy is also an *Erfahrungsökonomie* capitalizing on past experiences. But these resources may very well be the source of present disappointments (cf. Schulze, 1992, pp. 424 ff. for more on this topic). To avoid disappointment the event should either exceed expectations (that is, being even better than expected) or deviate from expectations (that is, being different than expected). The first strategy will have difficulties reaching an experienced target group. The second strategy runs the risk of alienating its target group from the event.

Fifthly, and returning to the semantics of the noun 'experience', the five meanings of the word identified by the Merriam-Webster online dictionary invite further ramifications. Some of the meanings denote states of mind. An experience is the outcome of past experiencing. Practical skills (experience 2), cognitive capabilities (experience 3) and autobiographical memory (experience 4) are all states following from 'having been' experiencing something. In contrast, the process or method by which some objective truth is asserted (experience 1) and the process of sensing and feeling (experience 5) are nouns for the verb 'to experience' something. These two meanings stand for the present act of 'experiencing', whereas the states of mind (experience 2, 3 and 4) are representations of previous acts of experiencing. They are mental images of past experiencing albeit sometimes with an almost magical power to rekindle the feeling qualities of experiencing when activated (or 'done').

Experiencing, that is, the present, volatile act of having an experience, comes in different qualities. One of them has the German equivalent of *Erleben*. *Erleben* is the present moment of sensing and feeling where life is intensified and awareness of the situation becomes acute (Stern, 2004). It equals Wundt's immediate experiences and James's pure experiences. Such moments may last but some seconds. Nonetheless, sometimes a profound subjective truth about existence may emanate from such an occurrence. The conversion of Saul to Saint Paul after having been blinded by divine light on the road to Damascus is an extreme case. In everyday life, the smile of your kid momentarily reveals a deeper meaning of existence. And in ordinary interactions, a slight change in the pitch of your partner's voice, a twinkling in her eye or a sudden gesture may create a proximity or distance exposing a hidden or forgotten truth about the relationship.

In such instances, *Erleben* turns into *Erfahren*: that is, a coming to know a fact. This fact can either be subjective concerning the perceived truth about myself or about my intimate or social relations, or it can be objective concerning the perceived truth about things and relations in the world. In the first case, it is *Erfahren* as experience (5). In the latter case, it is *Erfahren* as experience (1). This type of *Erfahren* can be dispassionate, for example, when facts are simply registered and counted. If this activity adds up to an unexpected result, it might become involving. This is a token of *Erleben*, physiologically identifiable by, for example, an increase in heart rate.

8.5 THE COHERENCE OF EXPERIENCE

If we take *Erleben* to be the immediacy of sensing and feeling, then *Erfahren* is the presence of fact-finding. These facts may be either subjective or objective, thus constituting different subtypes. Experience understood as representation or a state of mind is either *Erlebnis* or *Erfahrung*. *Erlebnis* is more or less reliable remembrance of a specific event of experiencing. An *Erlebnis* can either be short-lived or more permanently become part of autobiographical memory. *Erfahrung* comes in different categories of memory. Declarative memory is explicitly retrievable by consciousness when called upon. Non-specific episodic memory is experience-based declarative recollection without exact recollection of any of the past experiences constitutive of the learned content. Semantic memory is declarative recollection where the very experience of learning does not count. On the other hand, procedural memory is implicit and automatic (that is, without consciousness). It is performing a task in a skilled manner without having to think about it. Past experiences have provided the necessary skills but the ontology of acquiring such practices is forgotten and superfluous in the actual performance. This may be illustrated in the Table 8.2.

This whole gamut of experiences and experiencing is implied in those experiences that experiential economists attempt to market. As stated above, the experience economy is not only about *Erleben* and *Erlebnis*. *Erfahrung* is what motivates consumers to seek out certain products and ignore others. This has been plain market wisdom for over a century. The best way to gain new customers is to let them try the product. In addition, the expectations that stem from past experiences and are the drivers of motivation might critically impair the actual experience (*Erlebnis*) of the product. To be evaluated positively the experiencing (*Erleben*) has at least to level these expectations. Expectations are the yardstick measuring the quality and value of the actual experience. As for *Erfahren*, this act is at the core of the 'transformation economy', which has been prophesized as the imminent and perhaps final stage of economic value creation (Pine and Gilmore, 1999 [2011], p. 244). Experiencing the truth about who I really am or what I really like might quite simply change me dramatically.

Designing for experiences or marketing experiential products ought to be done with

Table 8.2 Erleben, Erfahren, Erlebnins *and* Erfahrung *compared to the five meanings of the noun 'experience' identified by Merriam-Webster and to categories of memory in cognitive psychology*

'Experience'	German equivalents	Categories of memory
Experience (1): Knowledge through observation	*Erfahren*	
Experience (2): Practical skills	*Erfahrung*	Implicit procedural memory
Experience (3): Conscious knowledge	*Erfahrung*	Generalized episodic memory
Experience (4): Autobiographical knowledge	*Erlebnis*	Autobiographical episodic memory
Experience (5): The act of sensing and feeling	*Erleben*	

the totality of experiencing in mind. Experiencing is a *Ganzheit* in which all aspects of experiences and experiencing potentially intersect. It is therefore 'impure': namely fundamentally non-sequential. This impure and non-linear totality is the first distinctive feature of the coherence of experience.

Experiencing does not necessarily start with the processing of an external input or stimulus. An *Erfahrung* containing feeling qualities may just as well elicit the process. Such *Erfahrungen* are not exclusively activated on demand: that is, only when the cognitive system is posed with a problem and therefore retrieves possible solutions from memory. They may also be triggered on their own (that is, involuntarily). The pleasures in executing practical skills come from performing these skills. Thoughts may start wandering, activating a network of associations from which enjoyable daydreams emerge. Such fantasies may be highly motivating for having actual experiences (for example, for shopping). Autobiographical memories may also pop up spontaneously. Not only traumatic but also pleasurable events are remembered involuntarily (Berntsen, 2009). The intricacy of experiencing is furthermore demonstrated by the intertwining of *Erleben* and *Erfahren*. Whereas *Erleben* may lead to subjective *Erfahren* transforming the experiencing person's existential perspective, objective *Erfahren* may lead to *Erleben* engaging the experiencing person sensually and emotionally in the act of experiencing.

Experiencing may start at several points: by responding to an external input; by voluntarily or not remembering a past experience; by flights of fancy; or by simply doing a practice. From this starting point there is no single chain of causes and effect. *Erleben* could branch out to *Erlebnis*, *Erfahren* or *Erfahrung* in the next instance. A new moment of *Erleben* could also be the sequel, either reversing or reinforcing the previous instant. But the second distinctive feature of the coherence of experience is this: it always implies *Erleben*, that is immediate sensing and feeling. The coherence of experience is materialistic or corporeal. It is defined by bodily activity.

This activity occurs in a here-and-now instant. Experiencing, understood as *Erleben*, is presence. But this volatile presence blends with the remembrance of previous experiences, with *Erfahrungen*. *Erfahrungen* are developed experiences prior to the instant of experiencing. The present moment is also the germ of future remembrance, of *Erlebnis*. *Erlebnisse* are those experiences to be carried over into the future. They potentially have an explanatory power telling us and other's stories about who we really are. Through recurrence, specific *Erlebnisse* may be transformed into non-specific *Erfahrung*. Moreover, in the moment of experiencing *Erleben* and *Erfahren* may merge. Presence is thus informed by the past and formative for the future.

This leads to a further classification of experiences. *Erfahren* and *Erleben* are presence (acts), whereas *Erlebnis* and *Erfahrung* are mental representations of past presence (images). Furthermore, *Erfahren* and *Erfahrung* are aspects of development. The latter is a result of previous development. The former is related to the process of change and transformation (for example, as a crisis) implied in identity formation throughout life. The unity of *Erleben* and *Erlebnis* I would call 'entertainment'. 'Entertainment' understood not solely in its common usage as 'amusement' but in its broader etymological sense of 'holding together' (from the French *entretenir*). What entertains us is thus what maintains us, what keeps up a certain frame of mind and what allows certain notions, ideas and so on to come into consideration (Online Etymology Dictionary). Apart from

Table 8.3   The structural distinctions of the four categories of experience

	Entertainment	Development
Presence	*Erleben*	*Erfahren*
Representation	*Erlebnis*	*Erfahrung*

being recreation and maintenance, entertainment supports a notion or sense of self (hence *Erlebnis*) and attunes us to the situation, making us aware of our own presence in it (hence, *Erleben*) (Vorderer, 2001; Jantzen and Vetner, 2010). These distinctions are shown in the grid in Table 8.3.

For the experienced individual, previous development is implied in all acts of experiencing. *Erleben* being the first distinctive feature of 'experiences' also means that development without entertainment – that is, without bodily involvement – does not count as an experience. Such development is new knowledge apprehended without sensing it consciously. Developing through the imitation of others is an example of such an apprehension (Tarde, 1890 [1903]). The recent, but contested, hypothesis on neurological imitation via so-called 'mirror neurons' is a theory on this kind of development. 'Mirror neurons' are thought to enable empathy and the understanding of others' intentions, thus leading to development by mere participation in social groups (Rizzolatti and Sinigaglia, 2008).

The implication of consciousness in experiencing pinpoints the third distinctive feature of the coherence of experience. Experiencing is more than just sensing and feeling. It is awareness of sensing and feeling. As long as we are alive, our bodies are constantly sensing and feeling something. Experiences are generated when we become conscious of these physiological processes. In experiences, the presence of experiencing is represented in our mind. Thus, a minimal form of *Erlebnis*, not necessarily leading to more permanent autobiographical memory, is required. This minimal form is noticing that we are actually sensing and feeling something. Like in the case of the carpenter, attention is diverted from what we are doing (the task) to how we are doing it (the performance in itself).

I shall elaborate on this aspect when dealing with the specificity of experience. To sum up: an experience is coherent because it is a totality of experiential modes active in the moment of experiencing. The distinctive features of this coherence are:

1. The non-sequential or impure nature of the totality marking it as a dynamic tension between now, past and future.
2. Bodily activity in the form of sensing and feeling is prerequisite for having an experience.
3. The consciousness of being engaged in sensing and feeling is also a prerequisite for having an experience.

Having dealt with the cognitive aspects of experience (*Erfahrungen* and *Erlebnis*) at some length, I shall now turn to the bodily substance of experiencing, towards sensing and feeling.

8.6   EXPERIENCING

Sensing and feeling are elementary physiological processes caused by the trivial fact that we are living organisms interacting with our environment. They stem from the more primitive parts of our brain. But they are literally vital for maintaining life. Experiencing is thus generated by the way we adjust to our environment, how we respond to it and what we do in order to adjust the environment to our purposes. This bodily activity implies undergoing changes in the environment as well as doing acts that change our interactions with the environment. Undergoing changes is a response in the form of perceptions. Such changes alter the level of arousal, which is the 'engine' that keeps the rest of the brain, that is, emotions and cognitive functions like consciousness, attention and information processing, running (Pfaff, 2006). Doing acts changes our relatedness to the environment. This doing can be intentional and hence voluntary or impulsive and hence involuntary. In the last case, our organism alters its activity in order to change the level of arousal. For example, we fall asleep because the organism demands a lower level of arousal (that is, relaxation).

As pointed out by Scitovsky (1976), building an economic theory based on the concept of arousal revises some of the tenets of microeconomic thinking based on the concept of demand. The accepted principle underlying consumer demand is that consumers buy goods to satisfy needs. These needs are caused by a felt lack. As soon as this lack is met the need is supposed to disappear. Demand is thus an on/off mechanism switching between lacks and needs (on), on the one hand, and satisfaction (off), on the other. After satisfaction nothing happens until a new lack becomes manifest.

Applied to the experience economy satisfying a need either obliterates the urge to experience or lifts this urge to a higher stage in a pyramid of needs as sketched in a strictly non-commercial vein by Maslow (1943). This line of thinking may seem alluring but the problem is identifying the number of needs, the differences between 'natural' and 'artificially created' needs (for example, is the need for toothpaste natural or artificial?) and the nature of truly experiential needs: that is, are only self-actualization needs truly experiential or may fulfilling basic needs also elicit experiences?

Viewing demand as steered by ongoing fluctuations in the level of arousal, which by the way is only switched off when life is over, points instead to the both volatile character and perpetual nature of demands. An important early contribution to this field came from the physiologists Yerkes and Dodson (1908). Their behaviourist experiments showed that test-persons (white mice) performed a given task best when the level of arousal was neither to high nor to low. This led to the following hypothesis: the optimum level of arousal is dependent on the difficulty of the task at hand. As known from sport psychology, a high performance in an apparently easy match requires high arousal as the optimum level. The team has to be extra stimulated to get a good result against a weaker opponent. A match against a stronger opponent requires the opposite approach. The team has to be brought to a state of relaxation in order not to lose its head – and the match. The optimum level is here not a medium level but a low level of arousal.

The logic in this is that both high and low levels have quite adversary effects. A low level of arousal promotes relaxation, which is good for a weak and therefore stressed team, but it also diminishes attention and concentration, which might prove fatal for the stronger team. A high level of arousal increases attention and vigilance, which is

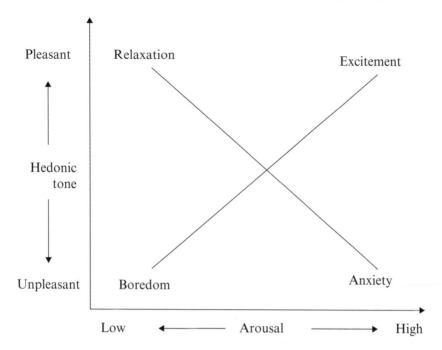

Figure 8.1   The relationship between levels of arousal and hedonic tone

beneficial for the stronger team, but it might also lead to anxiety and stress, reducing the possibility of reacting adequately to the environment. This may prove fatal for the weaker team.

High and low levels of arousal may both be pleasant: the first is exciting, the second relaxing. But they are also both unpleasant: the first is stressing, the second boring. These opposite hedonic tones are illustrated in the graph in Figure 8.1 (cf. Apter, 1989, p. 18).

The optimum level depends on the performance that is required. This optimum is comforting. What goes for sport teams goes for the organism as well. It is programmed to maximize the chances of survival and therefore to minimize the dangers inherent in too high or low levels of arousal. It therefore attempts to optimize arousal, adjusting it to the level that the environment seems to require. Changes in the level of arousal towards an optimum generate pleasure. The faster and the more profound this change, the more pleasurable it will be (Hebb, 1955), which can be represented as shown in Figure 8.2.

Comfort is a temporary equilibrium, whereas pleasure is the movement towards – and beyond – this line (Scitovski, 1976). Precisely because pleasure is hedonically gratifying it may become a goal in itself. This is seminal for understanding experiencing. Firstly, this explains the pleasures derived from doing seemingly simple tasks. When the job is re-framed from fulfilling a job to the process of fulfilling it, that is, the art of reaching an optimum result, it becomes pleasurable. Secondly, and in a much more critical vein, we may consume beyond the satisfaction of needs, that is, beyond optimum, to the point where pleasure turns into discomfort and unpleasantness. Compulsive eating, shopaholism and other deviant habits are neurologically the result of habituation to the neurotransmitter of pleasure, endorphin. By habituation the effect decreases. Addiction

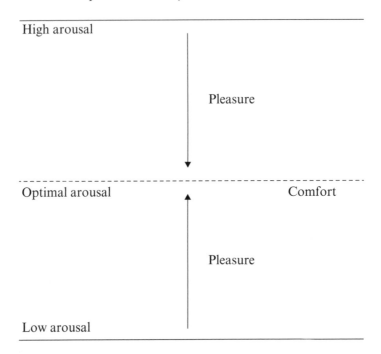

Figure 8.2   Comfort and pleasure

thus implies increasing the doses of this endogenous morphine in order to experience a pleasurable effect.

Thirdly, pleasure can be reversed. Prolonged excitement may become distressing, prolonged relaxation boring, thus reversing the hedonic tone. But more importantly, reversing the activity from, for example, arousal-avoidance to arousal-seeking may add to the pleasure (Scitovski, 1976, pp. 75 ff.). Going for a walk after a copious meal is an example of such a reversal. Eating has diminished the stress generated by hunger. The quantity of food eaten is beyond the optimum, leading to a state of relaxation close to drowsiness (that is, discomfort). Physical exercise reactivates the system, thereby producing a reversed pleasure. In media fiction, the opposite reversal is common. Firstly, there is an increase in arousal but a happy ending ensures relaxation. What we remember afterwards are the ending and the peaks in the sequence of experiences (cf. Kahneman, 2000). When these peaks occurred, they might have been experienced as anxiety provoking. In the *Erlebnis* after the fact, they will probably be evaluated as exciting.

These shifts in arousal and their reversals are entertaining in the sense that they maintain a notion of us being present in the situation. All this is in line with mood management theory that hypothesizes that people try to arrange their environment so that the chance of pleasure (excitement or relaxation) is maximized and the risk of pain (anxiety or boredom) is minimized (Zillmann, 2000; Oliver, 2003): 'So what exactly is entertainment? It's an experience that helps ... users cope with their everyday life' (Vorderer, 2001, p. 258). According to this theory, people are motivated to seek out pleasurable events either consciously (intentionally) or involuntarily (that is, by impulse). In the latter case, mood management is at the service of organic self-interest in sustaining life.

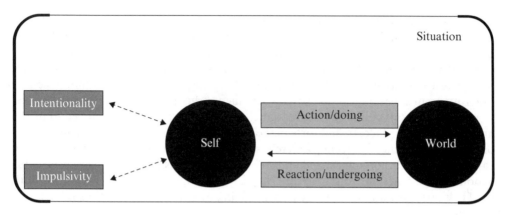

Figure 8.3   The rudimentary form of human experiencing

Changes in the level of arousal may occur as a result of the self's actions in the world as well as reactions to the world. These changes are motivated both consciously and involuntarily. They may as well affect these intentional and impulsive motivations, thus setting new directions for behaviour. This complexity is demonstrated in Figure 8.3.

The philosophical underpinning of this line of thought is quantitative hedonism. As a moral philosophy this branch of utilitarianism stresses pain and pleasure as the 'sovereign masters of mankind': 'It is for them alone to point out what we ought to do, as well as determine what we shall do' (Bentham, 1780 [1907], p. 1). The basic goal of existence is hence minimizing pain and maximizing pleasure. This morality may be alluring in its simplicity. But as noted by Nozick and many others, such a goal is a shallow representation of human strivings, reducing the individual to 'an indeterminate blob' in a pleasure machine (Nozick, 1974, p. 43).

Nozicks's first argument against this crude form of hedonism is that we do not want pleasure in itself. Instead we want to experience ourselves as a specific person having these pleasures. They must mean something to us: that is, be an *Erlebnis* and potentially contributing to our autobiography. His second argument is that we not only do things for obtaining pleasure or having experiences. Pleasure is just as often derived from the act of doing itself: 'It is only because we first want to do the actions that we want the experience of doing them' (Nozick, 1974, p. 43). In other words, quantitative hedonism in Bentham's version fails to appreciate the full extent of pleasure and experiencing.

Thus, a theory of experiencing should take account of reversals from one form of pleasure to another one (for example, from relaxation to excitement) but also explain reversals from pain to pleasure and vice versa (Apter, 1989). Furthermore, such a theory should, as I have already discussed at some length, view experiencing as just an aspect albeit a seminal one in the coherence of experience, thereby emphasizing the personal and social meanings derived from or inherent in experiencing. And not least, it should stress the auto-telic experience of doing: that is, the experiencing derived from the performance of an action.

A new contribution to the latter issue is research in vitality (Stern, 2010). Vitality is here viewed as a dynamic whole emerging from movement, force, time, space and intention. Time and space relate to the perception of the concrete situation, in which a specific form of vitality becomes manifest. Arousal is the force behind vitality, because quantitative alterations of the level of arousal have qualitative effects in terms of dynamic vitality forms. Beyond the crude mechanisms of either pain or pleasure, vitality forms are miniscule changes in the flux of sensing. Changes in rhythm, pace and intensity seem especially important for producing this kind of experiences. Phrased in musical terms, it could be the gradual changes of crescendo or diminuendo or the abrupt changes of staccato and forte piano. Vitality forms are the effervescent, pulsing or fading experience of feeling oneself saddening, enraging, anguishing, relieving, calming (down), becoming excited and so on. These effects manifest themselves in our actions in and reactions to the world. They capture us, move us, overwhelm or sooth us. They carry us away from what we were doing or undergoing and thus refocus our attention.

Vitality forms pre-empt emotions. Emotions stem like arousal from the primitive parts of the brain. Among emotional psychologists there is considerable disagreement on the status of emotions. The dominant paradigm used to be the appraisal theory (Lazarus, 1991). This is a cognitive theory arguing that emotions are produced by cognitive assessments of changes in the environment ('appraisals'). This cues an emotion preparing the body physiologically (for example, increased heart rate) to respond to this assessment. From this the person chooses how to react and an action follows. Emotion is 'activation readiness': emotions are an alarm system telling the body to interrupt its current activities and start responding to the change (Frijda, 1986, 2006). Seeing a bear makes us aware of danger. This cues an emotion of fear with all of its corresponding neurological processes. We decide to fight or flight.

Neuroscientists have recently challenged this paradigm, thereby reverting to the so-called James-Lange hypothesis (Öhman and Wiens, 2004). James (1884 [2010]) argued that we feel fear because we start running when seeing a bear. Emotions are secondary to physiological phenomena. And cognition is the result of an emotion. At first glance, this seems counter-intuitive but it makes for rapid decisions. When we start crossing a street we may step back onto the pavement before consciously noticing the truck progressing towards us at high speed.

The James-Lange hypothesis matches findings in neuropsychology. LeDoux (1996) posits a twin road in processing a fear stimulus. The low and faster road activates only primitive parts of the brain leading to an immediate response. The high and slower road also activates consciousness (neocortex), thus producing a conscious impression of what the stimulus is. The two roads are taken simultaneously with the result that the physical response is triggered before the conscious reaction. The somatic marker hypothesis (Damasio, 1994) posits that the brain associates particular bodily reactions and emotions with particular events. This association is created due to conditioning: that is, by the repeat exposure and reaction to an event. When a particular bodily change is felt (a somatic marker) this will activate an immediate response. The emotion is an effect of this response, felt independently of cognitive appraisal.

In the appraisal theory, it is cognitive awareness that triggers bodily response. According to the followers of the James-Lange hypothesis, awareness is triggered by our bodily response. Both paradigms assert that emotions belong to the primitive parts of the brain, that they are implied in a behavioural change and that they presuppose

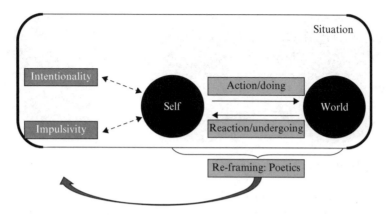

Figure 8.4   The elementary form of human experiencing

awareness. The controversy between these paradigms is on the precise sequence of events, which might be reconciled by the 'embodied appraisal theory' (Prinz, 2004). This emphasis on awareness in the theory on vitality forms as well as in different theories of emotion confirms the third distinctive feature of the coherence of experience: that is, the consciousness of being engaged in sensing and feeling as a prerequisite for having an experience. On this basis we can sketch a more complete picture of experiencing as shown in Figure 8.4.

Only in the newborn infant or in a semi-comatose state connected to some hedonic pleasure machine (cf. Nozick, 1974) will experiencing be pure *Erleben*. All other cases of experiencing will involve awareness and hence *Erlebnis* and *Erfahrungen* from which the conscious categories of awareness are derived. Awareness makes experiencing a specific way of sensing and feeling. I shall now deal with the specificity of experience, which makes it extraordinary compared to other everyday events.

8.7   THE SPECIFICITY OF EXPERIENCE

Two operations make experience stand out from ordinary sensing and feeling. Firstly, it represents a change in behaviour and secondly, it presents a challenge. The first operation is constitutive for entertaining experiences. Such experiences are based on:

- Alterations in the level of arousal inducing pleasure and/or pain or a broad spectre of vitality forms.
- Emotions connected to changes in behaviour: either inducing these changes (as appraisal theory would have it) or reporting on these changes (according to the James-Lange hypothesis).

The challenging operation is a prerequisite for developmental experiences. What is being challenged is namely the valence and completeness of existing habits, values and disposi-tions. This challenge may urge the individual to develop new *Erfahrungen* and perhaps even a new perspective on her or his existence. The presentation of a challenge is thus

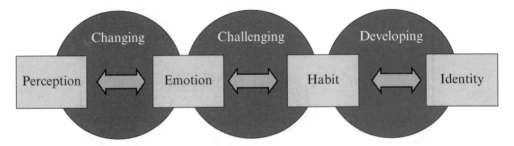

Figure 8.5   The elaborated field of human experiencing

what links entertaining experiences to developmental ones. This link expands the field of experiencing. Experiencing not only concerns bodily phenomena but may as well involve mental ones. This is illustrated in Figure 8.5.

Habit denotes practical skills as well as mental presuppositions: that is, *Erfahrungen* or procedural and non-specific episodic memory (for example, schemata and scripts). The tension between perception (sensing) and emotion is constitutive for bodily experiences. Experiences may contribute to identity formation by supplying new perspectives on existence. The challenges posed force the individual to reconsider previous assumptions. A 'crisis' or a breakthrough 'insight' (*Erfahren*) sometimes accompanies this development. This could be in the form of an 'epiphany' (Denzin, 1989 [2001], pp. 34 ff.), an ecstatic 'peak experience' (Maslow, 1964) or a 'transformative' experience (Pine and Gilmore, 1999 [2011]). Development is rarely that dramatic. In most cases, a challenge leads towards more refined habits or towards autobiographically remembered exceptions to the rules of habit.

To understand the principle underlying these two operations we need a detour around aesthetics understood as the philosophy of sensual or sensory-based knowledge (German *sinnliche Erkenntnis*). In the first half of the twentieth century, scholars of literature and linguistics in the tradition of Russian formalism and Czech structuralism attempted to make the knowledge generating potentials of aesthetically crafted messages scientific (Striedter, 1989). Their objective was to identify the distinctive features of literature. Although they failed to reach this goal, this tradition produced interesting insights, applicable also outside the domain of literature. I shall deal briefly with this tradition here, merely outlining its tenets.

A core concept is that of 'the aesthetic function' (Mukarovsky, 1936 [1970], 1940 [1976]; Jakobson, 1960). This function denotes the sensual qualities intrinsic in messages. When this function becomes dominant attention is directed from what is being said (or done), that is, from the content, purpose or context of the message, to how it is being said (or done). The handling of the message becomes auto-telic, focusing not on the meanings of the message but instead refocusing on the style of the message. This creates awareness. And that is precisely what occurs in experiencing. When a craftsman starts noticing his own performance his attention is redirected from the routines of the task or from all kinds of quotidian preoccupations towards his own way of doing (form). Suddenly these routines appear afresh, exciting or soothing – pleasurable.

In such incidences, a habit is being de-contextualized. It is removed from its ordinary context and placed in a different one. It is re-contextualized: made sensual and arousing again (Bauman and Briggs, 1990). Experiencing is the de-contextualization of ordinary actions and reactions re-contextualizing them as something outside the realm of ordinary life, as momentarily extraordinary. This produces presence (Gumbrecht, 2004) or the heightened awareness of being alive, which are 'vitality affects': 'the subjectively experienced shifts in internal feeling states' (Stern, 2004, p. 64). The change implied in bodily experiencing is hence not only quantitative (that is, alterations in the level of arousal); it is first and foremost qualitative.

When experiences become challenging, it is due to the awareness generated by these qualitative changes. They may make us wonder what exactly is going on. A challenging experience is characterized by a prolongation of this astonishment. The meaning of the message does not perfectly fit our expectations. Such a misfit either leads to disappointment, as explained above, or to an uncertainty regarding the appropriateness of our own *Erfahrungen*. Challenging experiences capitalize on this instability. In this, they benefit from the bodily involvement in the message created by the aesthetic function.

Challenging operations proceed along lines similar to those of changing operations. The existing frames of interpretation (for example, the schemata and scripts) prove insufficient to understand the message fully. This is a 'de-familiarization', that is, a 'making strange' of what seemed familiar (Shklovsky, 1917 [1965]; Crawford, 1984). Visiting McDonald's for the first time is an example of de-familiarization: existing knowledge about restaurants seems insufficient. The result is a de-stabilization of established knowledge, a concept known as 'disequilibration' in developmental psychology (Piaget, 1985). To reach a new stability, 'equilibration', it is necessary to re-frame *Erfahrung*. The existing schemata are adapted to fit the information generated by new experiences. This is called 'accommodation' (Piaget, 1985). The challenging operation thus questions the mental organization of our knowledge (the frame) of the world. And accommodation (re-framing) is a developmental response to this challenge.

The specificity of experience is hence double. Firstly, it attunes us to the environment by making us focus on the sensual qualities of our actions in and reactions to the world. This is the changing operation, setting the experience aside from ordinary sensing, intensifying our presence and re-enchanting the world. The world is 'made special', endowed with beauty (Dissanayake, 1992). Currently, the burgeoning field of neuroaesthetics, uniting neuroscientists, art historians and psychologists, is exploring the universal laws guiding the perception of beauty. These laws are founded in evolved brain functions, which are considered to be specific for the human race (Ramachandran and Hirstein, 1999 Zeki, 2008; Skov and Vartanian, 2009).

Secondly, the awareness of being present and experiencing re-enchantment may induce reflexivity: what is going on? This is the challenging operation of de-familiarizing our knowledge of the world. Coming to grips with this disturbance holds prospects for future development. The field of cognitive semantics combining linguistics and cognitive science has provided formalizations of how this challenging operation is brought about mentally (Lakoff and Johnson, 1980; Turner, 1996; Fauconnier and Turner, 2002). Especially promising is research in cognitive poetics, which links the changing operation (that is, style) with the challenging one (that is, the generation of new meaning) (Tsur, 1992).

8.8   CONCLUSION AND PERSPECTIVES

This chapter has presented a psychological framework outlining the complexity of experiences. If experiences are to be understood as more than mere sensing and feeling, then experiences are complex for two reasons. The first one being a paradox: experiencing is an everyday phenomenon, but it is at the same time extraordinary. Experiencing is ordinary, because sensing and feeling serve to maintain life and to uphold the organism's relations with its environment. It has entertaining features. Experiencing is extraordinary in creating awareness of the organism's own sensing and feeling. This potentially elaborates and expands capabilities. It has developmental features. I have dealt with this first complexity by stressing the specificity of experience. Experiences depart from other everyday acts by aesthetic operations, which not only produce change but awareness of change and which in addition utilize awareness of bodily changes to instigate mental development by challenging pre-existing cognitive structures.

Experiences are secondly complex, because of a tension between the immediate, but volatile present of experiencing, the past of prior experiences and the future of imminent experiences. Past and future are implicated in this present, making the tension dynamic. I have dealt with this second complexity by stressing the coherence of experience. By reconceptualizing the concept of 'experience' with the help of its twin equivalents in other Germanic languages, I have argued for the non-sequential nature of experience. This operation, by the way, also reconceptualizes the almost exclusive focus on *Erlebnis* in dealing with the 'experience economy' in these other languages.

Awareness of being bodily involved is seminal for experiences. Awareness links the coherence with the specificity of experience, the psychology with the aesthetics of experiencing. It combines a corporeal (that is, physiological and emotional) substratum with cognitive aspects of experiences. I have dealt with the various cognitive categories of memory implicated in experience. In explaining the bodily aspects I have focused on arousal. Experiencing is characterized by transforming quantity (that is, the level of arousal) into quality (that is, aesthetical awareness of change), and style into new meanings. The coherence of experience is corporeal (matter), the specificity of experience is style (form).

The significance of positive everyday experiencing is thus that it maintains the integrity of existence in a perpetually changing environment. It does this both on a bodily and a mental level. It attunes us to the environment, involves us pleasurably and emotionally in our (re)actions and encourages us to learn in challenging and playful ways. Positive experiences are events, which we had not foreseen but that we afterwards cannot imagine that we could ever have been without.

Having a new experience could thus be defined as an awareness of experiencing, from which our capabilities for understanding and acting in the world may develop. Questioning the relevance of existing habits (that is, practices and/or remembered knowledge) induces this link between sensing and feeling, on the one hand, and development, on the other. The crux of experiences is the coherence of mental structures and bodily involvement in the world in the here-and-now of experiencing.

As noted throughout this chapter, this psychological framework has implications for entrepreneurs and designers in the experience economy. Firstly, experiencing is not a simple response to a stimulus. An experiential product is thus not only an object to react to, but also an object to act upon. The physical and mental activity of the user is seminal in generating experiences. The product should therefore allow for active participation in the event. Co-creation, the heralded 'future of competition' (Prahalad and Ramaswamy, 2004), is a pronounced way of designing for user participation. But experiences are also produced as a side effect of doing. A simple way of generating experiences is thus to instigate bodily movement by diverting the body from everyday routines, changing its field of perception and involving it in unexpected ways.

Secondly, good experiences are not simply a matter of providing pleasure. The issue is rather to modulate the levels of arousal, creating peaks of excitement and relaxation (that is, reversals) that end up in an emotionally gratifying way. These peaks do not necessarily have to be pleasurable in their own right. A peak could, for example, be a saddening sentiment. It is the outcome and the effervescing, pulsing or fading of various vitality forms in an impure string of moments that sum up to a pleasurable experience.

Thirdly, disappointment about expectations not fulfilled seems part and parcel of the experiential market. Expectations stem from previous experiences. Entertaining experiences should at least meet these expectations. Developmental experiences should, however, de-stabilize them. By breaking expectations events become memorable and by having to deal with the unexpected, new meanings and memories are produced. The real challenge for experiential products is therefore de-stabilizing without becoming disappointing. This chapter has pointed at aesthetic operations that can solve this dilemma by involving individuals actively in sensing and cognition.

Treating experiences psychologically means dealing with them as extraordinary incidents in everyday life whether these phenomena have been marketed or not. Experiences are a universal feature of human existence. Nonetheless, this psychological perspective may also contribute to understanding the rise of the experience economy. The emergence of experiential markets is not only caused by demographic changes, a significant increase in wealth, a dramatic shift towards service and knowledge-intensive industries, globalization, the dynamics of corporate competition and other factors at a macro level in Western societies. These longitudinal changes interact with slowly changing ideas about the 'the good life'. On the micro level of an individual's daily life such changes are backed by a set of new techniques to bring about experiences, a discourse to verbalize the ways of experiencing and an ideology that turns experiencing into a legitimate existential goal for the sake of self-actualization (Jantzen et al., 2012).

One survey has documented the emergence of a significant cultural shift in Western societies during the last decades (Inglehart, 1990; Inglehart and Welzel, 2005). Since the 1970s secular values and self-actualizing goals have become predominant in a number of highly developed countries. In a self-actualizing culture, experiences are not just pleasurable goals to be obtained. To a great extent experiences serve as evidence (*Erfahren*) of the truth and sincerity of the self-actualizing endeavour. Existential or political goals may seem true simply because the acts of thinking about them, fighting for them or bringing them about feels good. Moreover, in a secular setting devoid of superstition but also thoroughly disenchanted (Weber, 1904 [1930]), being carried away while experiencing may produce small moments transcending the profanity of everyday life and re-enchanting the world once again (Ritzer, 1999 [2010]). A bold interpretation of such consumer practices is that the experiential market is attractive in late modern culture because it offers the means for deifying the individual in an otherwise utterly profane world. But this is undeniably a sociological rather than a psychological topic.

BIBLIOGRAPHY

Apter, M.J. (1989), *Reversal Theory: Motivation, Emotion and Personality*, London: Routledge.

Baars, B.J. and N.M. Gage (2010), *Cognition, Brain, and Consciousness*, Amsterdam: Elsevier.

Barthes, R. (1973), *Le Plaisir du Texte* (*The Pleasure of the Text*), Paris: Édition du Seuil.

Bartlett, F.C. (1932), *Remembering: A Study in Experimental and Social Psychology*, Cambridge: Cambridge University Press.

Bauman, R. and C.L. Briggs (1990), 'Poetics and performance as critical perspectives on language and social life', *Annual Review of Anthropology*, **19**, 59–88.

Bentham, J. (1780), *An Introduction to the Principles of Morals and Legislation*, Oxford: Clarendon Press, reprinted in 1907, London: T. Payne & Son.

Berntsen, D. (2009), *Involuntary Autobiographical Memories: An Introduction to the Unbidden Past*, Cambridge: Cambridge University Press.

Berntsen, D. and D.C. Rubin (eds) (2012), *Understanding Autobiographical Memory: Theories and Approaches*, Cambridge: Cambridge University Press.

Boswijk, A., T. Thijssen and E. Peelen (2007), *The Experience Economy: A New Perspective*, Amsterdam: Pearson Education.

Boswijk, A., E. Peelen and S. Olthof (2012), *Economy of Experiences*, Amsterdam: European Centre for the Experience Economy.

Churchland, P. (2002), *Brain-wise: Studies in Neurophilosophy*, Cambridge, MA: MIT Press.

Crawford, L. (1984), 'Viktor Shklovskij: difference in defamiliarization', *Comparative Literature*, **36**, 209–19.

Csikszentmihalyi, M. (1975), *Beyond Boredom and Anxiety*, San Francisco, CA: Jossey-Bass.

Csikszentmihalyi, M. (1990), *Flow: The Psychology of Optimal Experience*, New York: Harper and Son.

Damasio, A. (1994), *Descartes' Error: Emotion, Reason, and the Human Brain*, New York: Putnam.

Dennett, D.C. (1991), *Consciousness Explained*, Boston, MA: Little, Brown.

Denzin, N.K. (1989), *Interpretive Interactionism*, Thousand Oaks, CA: Sage, 2nd edn reprinted in 2001.

Diriwächter, R. (2008), 'Genetic *Ganzheitspsychologie*', in R. Diriwächter and J. Valsiner (eds), *Striving for the Whole: Creating Theoretical Syntheses*, New Brunswick, NJ: Transaction Publishers, pp. 21–46.

Dissanayake, E. (1992), *Homo Aestheticus. Where Art Comes From and Why*, New York: Free Press.

Fauconnier, G. and M. Turner (2002), *The Way We Think: Conceptual Blending and the Mind's Hidden Complexities*, New York: Basic Books.

Frijda, N. (1986), *The Emotions*, Cambridge: Cambridge University Press.

Frijda, N. (2006), *The Laws of Emotion*, New York: Psychology Press.

Geuter, U. (1985), 'Nationalsozialistische Ideologie und Psychologie' ('National-socialist ideology and psychology'), in M.G. Asch and U. Geuter (eds), *Geschichte der deutschen Psychologie im 20. Jahrhundert* (*History of German Psychology in the 20th Century*), Opladen: Westdeutscher Verlag, pp. 172–200.

Graf, P. and D.L. Schacter (1985), 'Implicit and explicit memory for new associations in normal and amnesic subjects', *Journal of Experimental Psychology: Learning, Memory, and Cognition*, **11**, 501–18.

Gumbrecht, H.U. (2004), *Production of Presence: What Meaning Cannot Convey*, Stanford, CA: Stanford University Press.

Harrington, A. (1999), *Reenchanted Science: Holism in German Culture from Wilhelm II to Hitler*, Princeton, NJ: Princeton University Press.

Hassenzahl, M. (2010), *Experience Design: Technology for All the Right Reasons*, San Francisco, CA: Morgan and Claypool.

Hebb, D.O. (1955), 'Drives and the C.N.S.', *Psychological Review*, **62**, 243–54.

Holbrook, M.B. and E.C. Hirschman (1982), 'The experiential aspects of consumption: consumer fantasies, feelings, and fun', *Journal of Consumer Research*, **9**, 132–40.

Inglehart, R. (1990), *Culture Shift in Advanced Industrial Society*, Princeton, NJ: Princeton University Press.

Inglehart, R. and C. Welzel (2005), *Modernization, Cultural Change, and Democracy: The Human Development Sequence*, Cambridge: Cambridge University Press.

Jakobson, R. (1960), 'Closing statements: linguistics and poetics', in T. Sebeok (ed.), *Style in Language*, Cambridge, MA: MIT Press, pp. 350–77.

James, W. (1911), *Some Problems of Philosophy*, London: Longmans, Green and Co.

James, W. (1912), *Essays in Radical Empiricism*, London: Longmans, Green and Co.

James, W. (1884), 'What is an emotion?', *Mind*, **9** (34), April, 188–205, reprinted in R.D. Richardson (ed.) (2010), *The Heart of William James*, Cambridge, MA: Harvard University Press.

Jantzen, C. and M. Vetner (2010), 'Entertainment, emotions and personality: why our preferences for media entertainment differ?', in F. Pons, M. de Rosnay and J.P. Doudin (eds), *Emotions in Research and Practice*, Aalborg: Aalborg University Press, pp. 39–64.

Jantzen, C., M. Vetner and J. Bouchet (2011), *Oplevelsesdesign: Tilrettelæggelsen af unikke oplevelser* (*Experience Design: Crafting Unique Experiences*), Copenhagen: Samfundslitteratur.

Jantzen, C., J. Fitchett, P. Østergaard and M. Vetner (2012), 'Just for fun? The emotional regime of experiential consumption', *Marketing Theory*, **12** (2), 137–54.

Kahneman, D. (2000), 'Experienced utility and objective happiness: a moment-based approach', in D. Kahneman and A. Tversky (eds), *Choices, Values and Frames*, Cambridge: Cambridge University Press, pp. 673–92.

Kolb, D. (1984), *Experiential Learning as the Science of Learning and Development*, Englewood Cliffs, NJ: Prentice Hall.

Krueger, F. (1924), *Der Strukturbegriff in der Psychologie* (*The Concept of Structure in Psychology*), Jena: Fischer.

Krueger, F. (1928), *Das Wesen der Gefühle. Entwurf einer systematischen Theorie* (*The Essence of Feelings: Outline of a Systematic Theory*), Leipzig: Akademische Verlagsgesellschaft.

Lakoff, G. and M. Johnson (1980), *Metaphors We Live By*, Chicago, IL: Chicago University Press.

Lazarus, R.S. (1991), *Emotion and Adaptation*, New York: Oxford University Press.

LeDoux, J.E. (1996), *The Emotional Brain: The Mysterious Underpinnings of Emotional Life*, New York: Simon and Schuster.

Loosch, E. (2008), *Otto Klemm (1884–1939) und das Psychologische Institut in Leipzig*, Berlin: LIT Verlag.

Lynch, K. (1960), *The Image of the City*, Cambridge, MA: MIT Press.

Maslow, A.H. (1943), 'A theory of human motivation', *Psychological Review*, **50** (4), 370–96.

Maslow, A.H. (1964), *Religions, Values, and Peak Experiences*, Columbus, OH: Ohio State University Press.

Merriam-Webster, *Experience*, http://www.merriam-webster.com/dictionary/experience.

Métraux, A. (1985), 'Der Methodenstreit und die Amerikanisierung der Psychologie in der Bundesrepublik 1950–1970' ('The disagreement on methods and the Americanization of psychology in the Federal Republic 1950–1970'), in M.G. Asch and U. Geuter (eds), *Geschichte der deutschen Psychologie im 20. Jahrhundert* (*History of German Psychology in the 20th Century*), Opladen: Westdeutscher Verlag, pp. 225–51.

Mikunda, C. (2004), *Brand Lands, Hot Spots and Cool Places: Welcome to the Third Place and the Total Marketing Experience* London: Kogan Page.

Mukarovsky, J. (1936), *Estetická funkce, norma a hodnota jako sociální fakty*, Praha: F. Borovy, reprinted in 1970, *Aesthetic Function, Norm and Value as Social Facts*, Ann Arbor, MI: University of Michigan Press.

Mukarovsky, J. (1940), 'O jazyce básnickém', *Slovo a slovonost*, **VI**, 113–45, reprinted in 1976, *On Poetic Language*, Lisse: Peter de Ridder.

Nozick, R. (1974), *Anarchy, State, and Utopia*, New York: Basic Books.

Öhman, A. and S. Wiens (2004), 'The concept of an evolved fear module and cognitive theories of anxiety', in A. Manstead, A. Fischer and N. Frijda (eds), *Feeling and Emotion. The Amsterdam Symposium*, New York: Cambridge University Press, pp. 58–80.

Oliver, M.B. (2003), 'Mood management and selective exposure', in J. Bryant, D. Roskos-Ewoldsen and J. Cantor (eds), *Communication and Emotion. Essays in Honor of Dolf Zillmann*, Mahwah, NJ: Lawrence Erlbaum, pp. 85–106.

Online Etymology Dictionary, *Entertainment*, http://www.etymonline.com/index.php?term=entertain.

Pallasmaa, J. (2009), *The Thinking Hand: Existential and Embodied Wisdom in Architecture*, Chichester: John Wiley and Sons.

Pfaff, D.W. (2006), *Brain Arousal and Information Theory: Neural and Genetic Mechanisms*, Cambridge, MA: Harvard University Press.

Piaget, J. (1985), *The Equilibration of Cognitive Structures: The Central Problem of Intellectual Development*, Chicago, IL: University of Chicago Press.

Pine, J.B. and J.H. Gilmore (1999), *The Experience Economy*, Boston, MA: Harvard Business Review Press, reprinted in 2011.

Prahalad, C.K. and V. Ramaswamy (2004), *The Future of Competition: Co-creating Unique Value with Customers*, Boston, MA: Harvard Business School Press.

Prinz, J.J. (2004), *Gut Reactions: A Perceptual Theory of Emotion*, Oxford: Oxford University Press.

Ramachandran, V.S. and W. Hirstein (1999), 'The science of art: a neurological theory of aesthetic experience', *Journal of Consciousness Studies*, **6** (6–7), 15–51.

Ritzer, G. (1999), *Enchanting a Disenchanted World: Revolutionizing the Means of Production*, Thousand Oaks, CA: Sage, 3rd revised edn printed in 2010, *Enchanting a Disenchanted World: Continuity and Change in the Cathedrals of Capitalism*.

Rizzolatti, G. and C. Sinigaglia (2008), *Mirrors in the Brain: How We Share Our Actions and Emotions*, Oxford: Oxford University Press.

Sander, F. and H. Volkelt (1962), *Ganzheitspsychologie*, Munich: Beck.

Schank, R.C. (1999), *Dynamic Memory Revisited*, Cambridge: Cambridge University Press.

Schank, R.C. and R.P. Abelson (1977), *Scripts, Plans, Goals and Understanding: An Inquiry into Human Knowledge Structures*, Mahwah, NJ: Lawrence Erlbaum.

Schulze, G. (1992), *Die Erlebnisgesellschaft: Kultursoziologie der Gegenwart* (*The Experience Society: Cultural Sociology of the Present Time*), Frankfurt am Main: Campus.

Scitovski, T. (1976), *The Joyless Economy: The Psychology of Human Satisfaction*, Oxford: Oxford University Press.

Shklovsky, V. (1917), 'Iskusstvo, kak priëm', in V. Shklovsky (ed.), *Sbornik på Teorii Poeticheskogo Yazyka* (*Collection on the Theory of Poetic Language*), Petrograd: OMB, pp. 8–23, reprinted in 'Art as technique', in E.L.T. Lemon and M.J. Reiss (eds) (1965), *Russian Formalist Criticism: Four Essays*, Lincoln, NE: University of Nebraska Press.

Skov, M. and O. Vartanian (eds) (2009), *Neuroaesthetics*, Amityville, NY: Baywood.

Stern, D.N. (2004), *The Present Moment in Psychotherapy and Everyday Life*, New York: Norton.

Stern, D.N. (2010), *Forms of Vitality: Exploring Dynamic Experiences in Psychology, the Arts, Psychotherapy, and Development*, Oxford: Oxford University Press.

Striedter, J. (1989), *Literary Structure, Evolution, and Value: Russian Formalism and Czech Structuralism Reconsidered*, Cambridge, MA: Harvard University Press.

Tarde, G. (1890), *Les lois de l'imitation*, Paris: Alcan, reprinted in *The Laws of Imitation* (1903), New York: Henry Holt.

Terry, S. (2008), *Learning and Memory: Basic Principles, Processes and Procedures*, London: Pearson.

Tsur, R. (1992), *Toward a Theory of Cognitive Poetics*, Amsterdam: Elsevier.

Tulving, E. (1983), *Elements of Episodic Memory*, Oxford: Oxford University Press.

Turner, M. (1996), *The Literary Mind*, Oxford: Oxford University Press.

Vorderer, P. (2001), 'It's all entertainment – sure. But what exactly is entertainment? Communication research, media psychology, and the explanation of entertainment experiences', *Poetics*, **29**, 247–61.

Weber, M. (1904), *Die protestantische Ethik und der Geist des Kapitalismus*, Tübingen: Mohr, reprinted in 1930, *The Protestant Ethic and the Spirit of Capitalism*, London: Allen and Unwin.

Wundt, W. (1896), *Grundriss der Psychologie* (*Outline of Psychology*), Leipzig: Engelmann.

Yerkes, R.M. and J.D. Dodson (1908), 'The relation of strength of stimulus to rapidity of habit-formation', *Journal of Comparative Neurology and* Psychology, **18**, 459–82.

Zeki, S. (2008), *Splendors and Misery of the Brain: Love, Creativity, and the Quest for Human Happiness*, Chichester: John Wiley and Sons.

Zillmann, D. (1988), 'Mood management: using entertainment to full advantage', in L. Donohew, H.E. Sypher and E.T. Higgins (eds), *Communication, Social Cognition, and Affect*, Hillsdale, NJ: Lawrence Erlbaum, pp. 103–23.

Zillmann, D. (2000), 'Mood management in the context of selective exposure theory', *Communication Yearbook*, **23**, 103–12.

9. The power of the economy of experiences: new ways of value creation
Albert Boswijk

9.1 INTRODUCTION

An essential shift is taking place in Western economies, a switch from agricultural and industrial production to a service economy, and towards an economy of experiences (Pine and Gilmore, 1999). Actually, we find ourselves in a transitional stage from a service economy towards an economy of experiences or an economy of meaning. In general terms, we can speak of dematerialization (Hilty, 2006), which also refers to the relative reduction in the amount of physical materials required in order to perform economic functions (Herman et al., 1988). There are three areas in which dematerialization finds expression: digitalization, eco-efficiency and intangible aspects of consumption. This chapter describes the interrelationships between societal shifts taking place at present, from a business context and from the context of individuals or citizens.

The growing transparency of society and businesses, added to the sheer abundance of peer-to-peer total connectivity, leads to a power shift that will eventually lead to the democratization of our society (Green, 2010) and economy (Pralahad and Krishnan, 2009). According to De Ridder (2012), the world is opening up. The economy of experiences is developing into a serious field of entrepreneurship with new forms of value creation – in the domain of intangible value – driven by innovative and creative industries and by co-creative efforts.

Rifkin (2000) argued that we are moving from an age of possession to the age of access. The physical economy (muscle industry) is changing from an age of industrial power into a digitalized economy (flow industry). The balance of economic power is shifting from producing parties towards users and user networks. The networked economy, based on communities of practice, communities of interest and peer-to-peer production, is growing and finding its way in society as grassroots untouched by traditional governmental parameters. Relevance and meaning based on fair and shared value are emerging as the opposites of purely transactional focus and share of wallet. An economy of meaning is unfolding, where the centricity of individuals will become the key differentiator.

A shift of values is taking place in people's mindsets and values are also changing in the business context (Brand and Rocchi, 2011). Traditional institutions and their hierarchies are no longer trusted. According to Cornelis (1988), we are going through a revolutionary process from a social regulatory system to a system of deep communicative self-regulation. This is taking place at all levels of society, for example, the institutional level, business level, community level and the level of individuals.

Technological innovations and structural societal developments are facilitating and forcing people to find new ways of identification and meaning in order to find stability in their lives. The logic of feeling and emotional expression are becoming the new navigators in our lives, replacing the former navigators, that is, religion, institutions and big brands. In a business context, this shift in value orientation is forcing corporations to refocus their business models. Businesses and the media have discovered the arena of emotion and meaning. Competition will grow in the fields of relevance, identity and meaning. This growing economy of meaning demands that suppliers give up their traditional role patterns.

9.2   THE DYNAMICS: CHANGING ROLES AND RELATIONSHIPS

The traditional roles of suppliers and customers, as well as the relationships between citizens and governments, are changing rapidly. New technologies and the internet are creating space and environments for individuals to connect and link up with one another 'en masse'. We are living in a time that is abundant with information and networks. Information can be found everywhere by everybody. Having grown up with all the opportunities of information technology, Generation Y is giving an extra impulse to the use to which that technology is being put in our present society. This generation wants to be engaged and is less passive than older generations and does not take things for granted. The percentage of citizens involved in co-creating and co-producing is increasing. We are moving towards a situation where the moment will come that citizens themselves self-regulate and self-determine with whom they do business and what they will produce and trade in. In terms of energy, for example, in the very near future citizens will become merchants and start selling their surplus solar energy. They will be able to produce ten times as cheaply as the large energy companies. Most of the large energy suppliers have been insufficiently alert to these developments.

Traditional and incremental improvements are constantly being initiated and are taking place in the supply chain to create more value and better revenue and cost structures for those engaged, but it is only when suppliers and their stakeholders really become customer- or patient-centric that economic systems and structures are reversed! A pacemaker supplier will focus not only on improving his device but also enlarging the user's world. He will use noodle networks to engage and organize local and global doctors in hospitals in order to enlarge the patient's world and make it possible for the patient to feel safe no matter where he goes.

In this way, production units are no longer the central focus, but the quality of life of a patient or client, the nature of which is predominantly immaterial. In order for companies to prepare for a different game and mindset, innovation is needed at the level of business models and new ways of organizing our businesses. Within the business context, organizations need to give up their traditional roles even though new business models and frameworks are not yet available. The new partners who are needed to participate in the new value creation processes are not well known and therefore do not generate sufficient confidence. New business models are moving towards alternative fee structures involving access to an experience instead of paying a price for a product.

9.3   THE PROCESS OF EXPERIENCING, THE LOGIC OF FEELING

Experiences are inherent to the basic human condition. Without experiences we do not feel and there is no conscious life. Experiences are unique and deeply personal and may be social. Experiences determine who we are: they form our characteristics, shape our personality and determine what we believe in, what makes us happy and how satisfied we manage to be about ourselves in relation to others and our environment. During our lives we all encounter turning points that set us thinking and lead to a re-evaluation of what we consider valuable. We may become stronger and enriched as a result. According to Cornelis (1988), it is through our feelings that we discover and unfold our individual learning programme. Our feelings are our feedback mechanisms in relation to the world.

Cornelis differentiates three layers of cultural stability in society:

1. The 'natural system' made up of family and friends; here, the human being is 'hidden'.
2. The 'social regulatory system'; this system comprises the agreements we make with one another about social interactions, which roles we fulfil and how we derive our social identity from these. Here, the position of the human being is to be 'obedient'.
3. 'Communicative self-direction': people have more opportunities for self-knowledge, self-reflection and self-direction. In this third layer, people act upon values instead of obeying rules. The reality is too complex to be understood by one person. Here, the human being is 'creative'.

In our understanding, experiences are personal and per definition not of an economic character (Boswijk and Peelen, 2007). The most valuable experiences are not economically driven. Experiences that have the greatest impact on our lives are deeply emotional and in many cases will form turning points in our lives. Personal experiences help us to create meaning and identity, and to go about realizing a respectable life and career. Innovative and progressive research in this realm is continually being undertaken by philosophers, sociologists and psychologists, like Kahnemann (1999) who identified two different functions of the brain: the experiencing self and the remembering self. Positive psychology will lead the way for further research. A lot of extremely constructive research has already been done and does not need to be repeated by experience professionals.

It is at this edge and threshold that personal meaning and the social–cultural context and dynamics described in Section 9.1 come together and these movements will join forces to form a powerful tsunami of change. This is the dawning of the age of the self-directed and creative human being, with total interconnectedness of peer-to-peer networks and technologies that make it possible to break the world open.

9.4   SHIFTS IN VALUE

There is a tendency to believe that people's values are changing fast because of our fast-changing society. However, a study by Seekles et al. (2006) suggests that traditional

		1950>>	1980>>	Unfolding	Future
		Industrial economy	**Experience** economy	**Knowledge** economy	**Transformation** economy
People mindset	Captivating idea	Product ownership	Experience	Self-actualization	Meaningful living
	View	Local	Global	Contextual	Systemic
	Quest	Moderning one's life	Explore lifestyle identities	Individual empowerment	Address collective issues
	Effect	Productivity and family life	Work hard play hard	Develope your potential	Meaningful contribution
	Skills	Specialization	Experimentation	Creativity	Transformative thinking
	Approach	Follow cultural codes	Break social taboos	Pursue aspirations	Empathy and cooperation
Business mindset	Economic driver	Mass production	Marketing and branding	Knowledge platform	Value networks
	Focus	Product function	Brand experience	Enabling creativity	Enhancing meaning
	Qualities	Products	Product-service mix	Enabling open-tools	Inclusive value networks
	Value proposition	Commodities	Targeted experiences	Enable self-development	Ethical value exchange
	Approach	Persuade to purchase	Promote brand lifestyle	Enable participation	Leverage coperation
	Goal	Profit	Growth	Development	Tranformation

Source: Brand and Rocchi (2011).

Figure 9.1   Rethinking value in a changing landscape

values such as trust, love and friendship remain steady. New values can be defined, as global citizenship, self-direction and co-creativity seem to be emerging alongside traditional values. Brand (2010) attempted to compare business values and people's mindsets and postulated a pattern in the development of values and interests. His findings indicate six social values and parallel aspirations that characterize people in Western society today as shown in Figure 9.1 above.

From a people perspective, we are currently moving from modernization to the discovery of new lifestyles, from self-actualization to integration and the creation of meaning. Viewed from a business context, we are moving from industrialization and product-driven orientation to a market-driven economy, and from there to a network-based and person-oriented economy. Brand anticipates that we will then move towards an economy driven on the basis of worldwide responsibility. The unfolding of the 'creative industries' and the network economy is forcing businesses to examine why they have been successful so far and whether this will enable them to survive in the future.

Old traditional business models may have come to the end of their life cycle. Their strategies are barely working. A new economy is evolving that is digitalized and intangible in nature. We may be moving towards a more 'social' society in which interest in the good of us all becomes an important emerging value.

9.5   HOW TO CREATE MEANINGFUL EXPERIENCE VALUE IN THE BUSINESS CONTEXT

We have adapted the competing values framework of Quinn (1988) to form a model for experience value creation (Boswijk et al., 2012) in order to help organizations create value propositions that are robust enough for the future and customer-centric instead of being firm-centric. This framework applies both to a digital and a physical environment.

1.   The first step relates to the capacity to loosen up traditional ways of thinking and to innovate.
2.   The second step encompasses the design and creation of an experience value proposition. Can we create a meaningful dialogue? Where can we grant our clients access to our organization in a way that makes sense to them?
3.   The third step is designing the processes in order to deliver the experience value proposition and to make sure the processes are efficiently organized.
4.   The fourth step concerns employee competences and the function of the corporate culture in delivering the value proposition.
5.   The fifth step involves taking a look at how you capture the value, the design of the revenue model; where are the margins created and the revenues earned that will guarantee your continuity and what cost structures do you have?

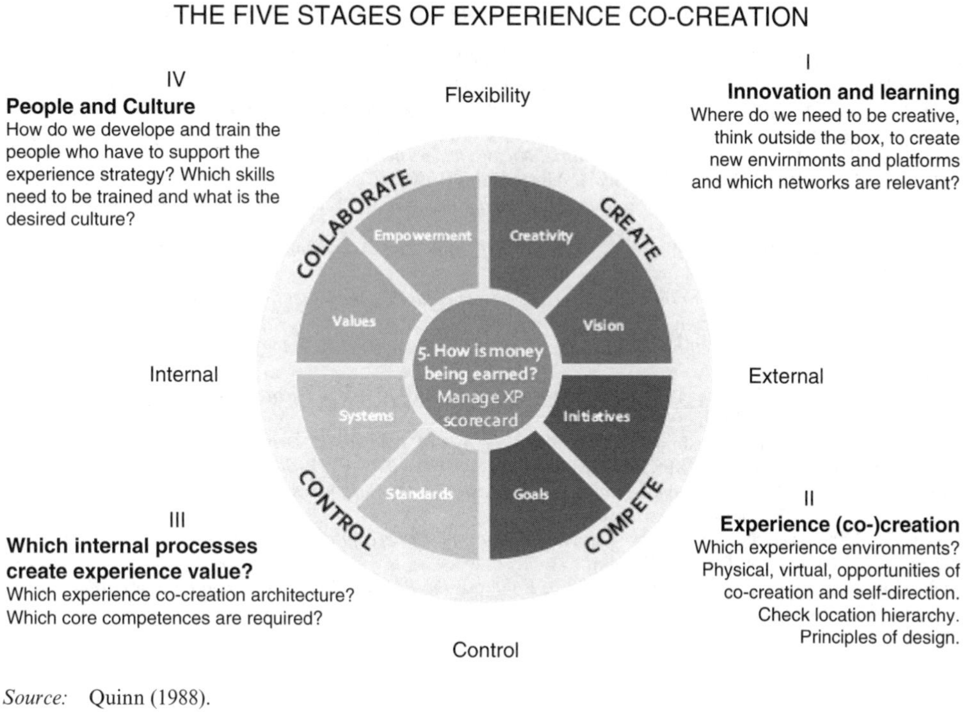

THE FIVE STAGES OF EXPERIENCE CO-CREATION

IV
People and Culture
How do we develop and train the people who have to support the experience strategy? Which skills need to be trained and what is the desired culture?

Flexibility

I
Innovation and learning
Where do we need to be creative, think outside the box, to create new envirnmonts and platforms and which networks are relevant?

Internal

External

III
Which internal processes create experience value?
Which experience co-creation architecture? Which core competences are required?

Control

II
Experience (co-)creation
Which experience environments? Physical, virtual, opportunities of co-creation and self-direction. Check location hierarchy. Principles of design.

COLLABORATE — Empowerment, Values, Systems, Standards — CONTROL
CREATE — Creativity, Vision, Initiatives, Goals — COMPETE
5. How is money being earned? Manage XP scorecard

Source: Quinn (1988).

Figure 9.2   Competing values framework for experience value creation

These five steps are continuously followed through. They do not need to be applied in this specific order on every occasion. The ultimate goal is to keep delivering.

9.6   SUBSEQUENT STEPS

We have described the shifts taking place in society from a business point of view and from the point of view of individuals. These changes, which are moving in the same direction, will result in a powerful change in the way the economy develops. What we need in order for the economy of experiences to develop are new parameters for governments to work with because the present parameters are still those of the industrial economy.

Before we can take the theory of the 'economy of experiences' a step further, we will need a 'common' language and a shared terminology, followed by a shared research agenda. Our theory is still too fragmented and lacking in coordination. We need economists to understand the economy of experiences and – in a collaborated effort – we need to study and develop the parameters of the future.

REFERENCES

Boswijk, A. and E. Peelen (2007), *A New Look at the Experience Economy*, Amsterdam: Pearson Education.
Boswijk, A., E. Peelen and S. Olthof (2012), *The Economy of Experiences*, Amsterdam: European Centre for the Experience Economy.
Brand, R. and S. Rocchi (2011), *Rethinking Value in a Changing Landscape: A Model for Strategic Reflection and Business Transformation*, Eindhoven: Philips Design.
Cornelis, A. (1988), *Logica van het gevoel: Stabiliteitslagen in de cultuur als nesteling der emoties* (*The Logic of Feeling: Layers of Stability in the Culture as Nestling of Emotions*), Diemen: Stichting Essence.
De Ridder, W. (2012), *De Strategische Revolutie: Nieuwe leiders nemen het stuur over* (*The Strategic Revolution: New Leaders are Taking the Drivers Seat*), Amsterdam: Kluwer.
Green, J. (2008), *Democratizing the Future: Sensemaking and Making Sense of the Future*, Eindhoven: Philips Design.
Herman, A. and J.H. Ausubel (1988), *Dematerialization and Materialization*, New York: Rockefeller University.
Hilty, L. (2006), *The Relevance of Information and Communication Technologies for Environmental Sustainability: A Prospective Simulation Study*, Zurich: Elsevier.
Kahnemann, D. (1999), *Well-being, the Foundations of Hedonic Psychology*, New York: Russell Sage Foundation.
Pine II, B.J. and J.H. Gilmore (1999), *The Experience Economy: Work is Theatre and Every Business a Stage*, Boston, MA: Harvard Business School Press.
Pralahad, C.K. and M.S. Krishnan (2009), *The New Age of Innovation: Driving Cocreated Values through Social Networks*, New York: McGraw-Hill.
Quinn, R.E. (1988), *Beyond Rational Management: Mastering the Paradoxes and Competing Demands of High Performance*, San Francisco, CA: Jossey-Bass.
Rifkin, J. (2000), *The Age of Access: The New Culture of Hypercapitalism Where All of Life is a Paid-for Experience*, New York: Penguin Putnam.
Seekles, P., A. Boswijk and P. Adriaans (2006), *Values of the Past are No Guarantee for Values in the Future*, Amsterdam: Renaissance Group.

PART II

TOPICS

10. IT and experiences: user experience, experience design and user-experience design
Jens F. Jensen

10.1 INTRODUCTION

Experiences created and shaped by information technology (IT) and digital media are often called 'user experience'. They can include both genuine IT-based experiences, that is, products and services whose primary purpose is to create an experience for the user or consumer, and experience-enriched products and services, that is, products and services whose main purpose is not the experience per se, but to which experience aspects are added that create additional value to the primary function. In this way, user experience and user-experience design can be viewed as the specific implementation of the experience economy and experience design within the domain of IT and technology.

The purpose of this chapter is to present, discuss and also develop a number of central concepts related to user experience in connection with IT and digital media, primarily the concepts user experience, experience design and user-experience design. These concepts are related and in some contexts closely interlaced, but they also have separate meanings. In this chapter, we discuss user experience, experience design and user-experience design both as a common field and the individual terms separately. User experience will be seen as the central term, that is, the term in focus in this specific context, while experience design and user-experience design will be seen as related concepts. Experiences related to IT will, for the same reason, be the main focus, but the chapter will also examine IT-based experiences' relationships to experiences in general as well as to general experience design. User experience is often abbreviated to UX or UE; experience design is often abbreviated to XD, while user-experience design is abbreviated to UXD or UED.

10.2 DEFINING THE PROBLEM

The terms user experience, experience design and user-experience design are used frequently, but they can be difficult to comprehend. This is not because the concepts have not been defined but rather because there are so many different definitions of and perspectives in relation to the terms, that is, definitions and perspectives that are disintegrated and denote many different contexts and many different subject fields (Law et al., 2008). Forlizzi and Battarbee write, for example: 'The term "user experience" is associated with a wide range of meanings, and no cohesive theory of experience exists for the design community' (2004, p. 261).

If the term 'user experience' is looked up, several completely different definitions can be seen.

1. 'All the aspects of how people use an interactive product: the way it feels in their hands, how well they understand how it works, how they feel about it while they're using it, how well it serves their purpose, and how well it fits into the entire context in which they are using it' (Alben, 1996).
2. 'A result of motivated action in a certain context' (Mäkelä and Fulton, 2001).
3. 'An activity of encounter by a computer user with the auditory and visual presentation of a collection of computer programs. It is important to note that this includes only what the user perceives and not all that is presented' (Microsoft).
4. 'UX is a momentary, primarily evaluative feeling (good-bad) while interacting with a product or service' (Hassenzahl, 2008).
5. 'User experience stands for the quality of a global experience as perceived by a person (user) interacting with a system' (Use design).
6. 'User experience = Convenience + Design − Cost' (Nyman, 2005).
7. 'UX = the sum of a series of interactions' (Fatdux).

The above is only a small selection of existing definitions of user experience, which serves to demonstrate how different such definitions can be – in terms of focus, in relation to the field they define and in relation to approach. The definitions are all taken from the website All about UX (www.allaboutux.org), which lists 27 different definitions of user experience. As can be seen, the examples of user-experience definitions stretch from the specific interaction with a computer interface, on the one hand (1, 3 and 5), to the general interaction with and perception of products and services in general, on the other (2, 4 and 7), from a given user's perception of a product, on the one hand (3 and 5), to objective attributes linked to the product, on the other (6), and from momentary feelings while interacting with a system, on the one hand (4), to a global experience of the interaction with the product or the system, on the other (5).

'User-experience design', for its part, has been defined as everything from: 'A holistic, multidisciplinary approach to the design of user interfaces for digital products, defining their form, behavior, and content' (Gabriel-Petit), over 'a broad term used to explain all aspects of a person's experience with the system including the interface, graphics, industrial design, physical interaction, and the manual' (Wikipedia entry 'User experience design') to in short 'The cult of the cute' (Marcus, 2002, p. 29).

Nevertheless, user experience, experience design and user-experience design as terms have quickly become widespread and accepted within several different fields. The terms have become buzzwords in human–computer interaction (HCI) and interaction design (Hassenzahl and Tractinsky, 2006, p. 91). They have gained a foothold in marketing, consumer behaviour and experience economy in broad terms, as consumer experience, customer experience and experiential design (Schmitt, 1999). And they have spread within the design field; not least in connection with user-centred design or human-centred design (see, for example, the Usability Professionals' Association (UPA) website).

Within all these fields, it can even be said that 'the experience turn' has taken place over the past decade, that is, a general trend in the form of a turn towards experience and experience design. Oppelaar et al. (2008), for instance, write 'Where in the past century a great emphasis was on products (20th century is called the "product age"), in the current age products are just vehicles to construct an experience', with the latter being an explicit reference to Pine and Gilmore's (1998) article 'Welcome to the experience economy'.

And they continue: 'this move cannot stay without consequences: the design process has certainly changed and moved from the original perspective of functionality, cognition and usability to a much broader perspective, with new "experience factors"' (Oppelaar, 2008).

This breakthrough and this turn are evident in many different ways and at many different levels. Over the past ten years, several conferences and seminars on user experience, experience design and user-experience design have been arranged (for example, 'Design and Emotion'; 'DUX: Designing for User Experiences'; 'DUXU: Design, User Experience and Usability'; 'uxlx/User Experience-lx'; 'MX/Managing Experience'; and 'MEX/Mobile User Experience'). Numerous books have been written (for example, Jordan, 2000; Shedroff, 2001; Garrett, 2002; Buxton, 2007; Hassenzahl, 2010) and several anthologies and article collections on the fields have been compiled (Blythe et al., 2003; Helander and Tham, 2003; Law et al., 2007b). Several resource sites with references to literature, websites, activities and studies have been launched (for example, Nathan Shedroff's Nathan, Peter Morville's Semantic Studios, All about UX, UX Magazine and A list apart). Several blogs on the subjects have been established (for example, Adaptive Path Blog, UX Booth: User Experience and Usability Blog, Inspire UX, Everyday Blog UX and Whitney Hess's Pleasure and pain). Several manifestos – UX manifestos – have been prepared for the field (Law et al., 2007a; Law et al., 2007b; André, 2008), as well as white papers (Roto et al., 2011) and green papers (Blythe et al., 2007), and, in addition, an 'Experience design for dummies' (Oppelaar et al., 2008) has been issued. Correspondingly, many former usability experts now write user-experience designer on their business cards, new roles and new job titles are created such as User-experience Researcher, Experience Manager and Experience Modeller (Forlizzi and Battarbee, 2004, p.261), and what were previously typically called Usability Labs are now called User Experience Labs and the like.

But experience and user experience as the focus points for design are also reflected directly in the market, for instance, in the marketing campaigns and slogans chosen by leading brands. In 2004, Philips changed its slogan 'Let's make things better' to 'Sense and simplicity'. In 2005, Apple marketed its iPod shuffle under the slogan 'Enjoy uncertainty'. In 2006, Nike launched the campaign 'Joint product eXperience' (Oppelaar et al., 2008). In the automobile sector, BMW has used slogans such as 'Sheer driving pleasure' and 'The ultimate driving experience', and Peugeot focused on 'Peugeot. Live the pleasure'. The South African computer brand Mecer chose the slogan 'Experience IT'. Husqvarna selected the motto 'Husqvarna. Great experience'. And the shopping centre Santa Maria Town Center in California was launched with the catchphrase: 'Transforming shopping into an experience' (Textart).

Thus, user experience, experience design and user-experience design are a quickly growing paradigm, which has attracted more and more attention over the past 10–15 years.

Naturally, efforts such as conferences, publications, websites and blogs have been introduced more or less directly with the aim to find a common understanding and to create a shared viewpoint on user experience, experience design and user-experience design. However, it cannot be said that such shared definition and common understanding have been found. Law et al. write, for instance: 'One obvious outcome of these activities is a number of diverse definitions and viewpoints on UX, but a shared definition is still lacking' (2008, p.2396). Donald Norman writes that since the mid 1990s, the term user experience has 'spread widely, so much so that it is starting to lose . . . [its] meaning' (UX Design, 2010). In 2007, he says in a comment to the same statement that user experience with other related terms 'just sort of entered the vocabulary and no longer have any special meaning. People use them often without having any idea why, what the word means, its origin, history, or what it's about' (Merholz, 2007). Hobbs et al. (2010) state that user-experience design 'although professionally successful and widespread is not weaved into a common or coherent discipline'. And based on an empirical quotation analysis of contributions to a workshop on user experience in 2007, Blythe et al. conclude that the results indicate 'a severe lack of overlap in the underlying theoretical basis and emphasizes the need for a shared view', and they also mention 'the still fragmentary status of the domain UX' (Blythe et al., 2007, p. 3).

This means that some kind of paradox situation has been created where the recognition rate and penetration rate of the concepts are inversely proportional to their precision and fixed, shared definition (Law et al., 2008).

Presumably, there are several reasons why it is difficult to reach a shared understanding of user experience, experience design and user-experience design:

- Firstly, user experience, experience design and user-experience design are a complex multidisciplinary field, which means that there are many different perspectives, approaches and definitions (Roto et al., 2011, p. 4). To put it differently, the field of user experience research is fragmented, informed by knowledge from many different disciplines with many different foci and compiled by many different theoretical models (Law et al., 2008). To integrate all these disciplines and perspectives is a challenge (Forlizzi and Battarbee, 2004, p. 261).
- Secondly – and consistent with the above – user experience, experience design and user-experience design have been linked to a very broad range of weakly defined concepts related to the emotional, affective, hedonistic and aesthetic fields, for example, to concepts and human values such as pleasure, fun, joy, pride, beauty, website appeal, 'wow effect', surprise, intimacy and so on, where inclusion or exclusion of the concepts in the individual context seems to depend on the specific author's background and interest (Hassenzahl and Tractinsky, 2006, p. 91).
- Thirdly, the analysis unit for user experience seems to vary significantly, stretching from a single factor of an end-user's interaction with a system to a full life cycle of touch points between user and product or to all aspects of many end-users' interaction with a product, service or business.
- Finally, user experience as a theoretical and methodological discipline is still a relatively new phenomenon and, therefore, it has not reached a sufficient degree of maturity and coherence. In 2007, Law et al. wrote: 'Theoretically UX is incoherent; methodologically UX is not yet mature either' (Law et al., 2007a, p. 206).

The absence of a common, shared definition and understanding of user experience, experience design and user-experience design causes inexpediencies and problems.

- It makes it difficult to develop common, shared standards for the field, and generally, it makes it difficult to create a coherent view on the principles of user experience (Law et al., 2007a, p. 205).

- It makes it difficult for users and consumers to know and assess what to expect and demand from products and services in relation to user experience.
- It makes it difficult for designers to know what to design towards if they want to achieve good quality of user experience.
- It makes it difficult for researchers to research in and deal with and discuss the field scientifically, especially when representatives from different disciplines and scientific traditions are to communicate with each other; consequently, it is also difficult in general to promote user experience as a research field (Roto et al., 2011, p. 4).
- It makes it difficult to develop sound research methods to analyse, design and evaluate user experience.
- It makes it difficult to teach systematically in the field and identify efficient teaching strategies (Law et al., 2008).
- It makes it difficult to consolidate the work with user experience in commercial, industrial and public organizations (Roto et al., 2011, p. 4).
- It makes it difficult to clarify different user-experience perspectives between researchers and practitioners (Roto et al., 2011, p. 4), for instance, the difference between validated knowledge, on the one hand, and know-how and opinions, on the other (Hobbs et al., 2010).
- It makes it difficult to explain the meanings of the terms to persons who are not already familiar with them (Roto et al., 2011, p. 4).
- It makes it difficult to classify user experience in a landscape with related concepts such as usability, human factors, interaction design, software engineering, marketing and so on (Law et al., 2007a, p. 205).
- And finally, it leads to weak concepts, since, as applies to all definitions, the more precise and widespread, the more influence (UX Design, 2010).

This chapter seeks to examine and map the concepts and fields of user experience, experience design and user-experience design in order to account for their origins and meaning, to outline their interaction with one another and their interaction with other fields and concepts and to find a common understanding and definition. Because as mentioned by Law et al. (2008, p. 2396), for instance, it should be possible to converge the various understandings and perspectives towards a shared definition and an integrated viewpoint on user experience: 'While reaching a shared definition is not a panacea for resolving a number of problems pertaining to UX, it serves as an initial and crucial step towards an integrated framework of UX' (Law et al., 2008, p. 2396). In short, the aim is to map user experience, experience design and user-experience design and to establish a shared understanding, a shared language and a shared definition.

However, it should not be expected that definitions and delimitations of user experience, experience design and user-experience design will find their final forms within a short time horizon, let alone remain stable in the longer term. The field and the perspective are still so new and dynamic that they will continue to develop. Shedroff, for instance, writes that 'Experience Design as a discipline is . . . so new that its very definition is in flux.'

10.3   BACKGROUND

There are several development trends that form the basis of the emergence of and the fast increasing interest in the phenomena user experience, experience design and user-experience design.

Due to the development of IT, digital media have moved from being a primary tool in a work-related context to support and rationalize tasks. Now digital media are used in the spare time, at home, in everyday life and so on. With this move, the focus has moved from efficiency and performance in relation to solving work-related tasks to user satisfaction with and experience of the product. In parallel to this, technologies have moved from being helpful and useful only to being fashionable, fascinating products that can be desired. The narrow focus on interactive products as tools could therefore no longer encompass the emerging, very differentiated elements of technology usage in which aspects such as identity creation, cultural meaning, personal branding and so on are also comprised. This was where user experience as an approach started to appear as a more attractive alternative at the backdrop of traditional HCI (Hazzenzahl and Tractinsky, 2006, p. 91).

Furthermore, HCI researchers and practitioners have gradually become more conscious about the limitations of the usability paradigm. Traditionally, usability has focused on efficiency, effectiveness and subjective satisfaction, of which the latter has in practice often been interpreted and handled as the absence of dissatisfaction. Correspondingly, usability has primarily been task and work related, and the focus has been on user cognition and user performance in human–machine interaction. Usability is still important but according to consumers, it is no longer sufficient. Gradually, usability is being expected, and therefore it is only noticed when it is absent. Patric Jordan writes, for example: 'Human factors . . . have been seen to add value to products by helping to make them easy to use. However, because, customers have come to expect products to be easy to use, usability has moved from being what marketing professionals call a 'satisfier' to being a 'dissatisfier'. In other words, people are no longer pleasantly surprised when a product is usable, but are unpleasantly surprised by difficulty in use' (Jordan, 2000, p. 3). In this context, the user-experience paradigm offers an approach that goes beyond pure usability and also focuses on the consumers' feelings, motivations, values and so on – what Jordan calls '"pleasure-based" approaches' (2000, p. 4). This has supported a shift in perspective away from usability and usability engineering to the much broader and richer scope of user experience, experience design and user-experience design in academic environments as well as among designers and in the corporate sector.

Furthermore, user experience, experience design and user-experience design matched an emerging and growing need for a more integrated and interdisciplinary approach. Usability experts, for instance, saw an increasing need to incorporate elements such as marketing, branding and the aesthetic dimension. Marketing and branding people, on the other hand, saw a growing need to enter the interactive world in which usability is important. In this world, user experience was a unifying platform that could combine and cover the needs of the various interested parties from marketing, branding, visual design, usability and so on, and that could make IT products easier to use and more valuable and richer in experience for the user (Hazzenzahl and Tractinsky, 2006, p. 91).

More specifically, on the one hand, the latest developments in IT and digital media –

mobile media, social media, ubiquitous computing, pervasive computing – mean that the computer and the media as such disappear as a manifest object, and, on the other hand, that the computer and digital media are present everywhere. This means that HCI moves into largely all areas of human activity. In an article with the characteristic title 'From information design to experience design: smart artefacts and the disappearing of the computer', Strietz et al. point to a trend they call 'the notion of the "disappearing computer"' (Strietz et al., 2005, p. 21), which is, paradoxically, linked to an opposing trend that IT penetrates and controls our lives to an increasing extent. So while the computer and technology disappear from our lives as immediately manifest and sensuous objects, on the one hand, they become increasingly dominating and all-pervading on the other. According to Strietz et al., this is related to another trend that they call a shift from 'information worlds to experience worlds' (Strietz et al., 2005, p. 21) or, more precisely, a shift in focus 'from developing not only information worlds' but also 'experience worlds', that is, 'complementing information design by experience design' (Strietz et al., 2005, p. 22). This is, for example, reflected in expressions such as 'extension and augmentation of our perception and experience of the physical and social environment' (Strietz et. al., 2005, p. 22) – and therefore as a general development trend towards experience, experience worlds and experience design.

Finally, the increasing use of user experience, experience design and user-experience design is also – more generally – a consequence of the recognition that, to an increasing extent, the success of a technology is dependent on one thing only, that is, how the user perceives it: Does it add value to the user? Does it have cultural meaning for the consumer? Is it easy to use? Such questions arise in the minds of the users when they interact with products, and they form the basis of their decision to buy, decision to return to the product, decision to become a regular user and so on (Gube, 2010) – and these very questions are at the centre of user experience, experience design and user-experience design as approaches.

10.4   CONCEPTUAL PARADOXES

Various authors have pointed to different conceptual paradoxes in connection with the terms user experience, experience design and user-experience design. These paradoxes stretch and unfold between a number of different pairs of contrast.

1. One paradox concerns the domain marked by user experience, experience design and user-experience design. At one end of the spectrum, there are relatively narrow definitions linking user experience, experience design and user-experience design to HCI and digital media in a narrow sense and, at the other end, there are broad definitions, linking experience design to a number of traditional fields and activities within the experience and entertainment fields. Shedroff writes, for instance: 'Many see it [that is, experience design] as a field for digital media, while others view it in broad-brush terms that encompass traditional, established, and other such diverse disciplines as theater, graphic design, storytelling, exhibit design, theme-park design, online design, game design, interior design, architecture, and so forth. The list is long enough that the space it describes has not been formally defined' (Shedroff, 2001).

2. Shedroff also points to another paradox related to that mentioned above, which concerns the temporal and historical dimensions, that is, experience design is both a very old tradition and a very new phenomenon. It is a very old tradition in the sense that experience design can be said to have existed as long as experiences and people's conscious use of experiences have existed. And it is a very new and recent phenomenon in the sense that it has not been until recent years that experience design has been named and defined as a formal discipline of its own. 'The design of experiences isn't any newer than the recognition of experiences', writes Shedroff and continues: 'As a discipline, though, Experience Design is still somewhat in its infancy. Simultaneously, by having no history (since it is a discipline so newly defined), and the longest history (since it is the culmination of many, ancient disciplines) experience design has become newly recognized and named.' So the discipline in itself is not new, but so is the opportunity of combining and integrating ancient disciplines into a simple formally recognized discipline, argues Shedroff.

3. A third paradox is – as already mentioned above – the relation between the concepts user experience, experience design and user-experience design, on the one hand, and concepts such as usability and usability engineering, on the other. In this respect, there are definitions that see usability as an integrated and constitutive element of user experience, experience design and user-experience design, and definitions that position user experience negatively with respect to usability, that is, in differentiation to usability. The International Organization for Standardization (ISO) – an international standard-setting body comprised of representatives of various national standard organizations, working for and announcing worldwide industrial, commercial and other standards – claims, for example, that 'usability criteria can be used to assess aspects of user experience'. On the other hand, there are definitions that see user experience as something different to, and more than, usability. The website UX Design, for instance, has a very direct and unambiguous wording in that it says: 'Given the persistent level of confusion about the meaning of User-experience design, defining it by *what it is not* can be useful. It is *not* a trendy new name for, or in any way synonymous with . . . Usability testing' (UX Design, 2010).

4. A fourth paradox concerns the experience concept's focus or reference. In everyday speech – and often within research as well – the term 'experience' actually refers to two completely different things. On the one hand, it refers to the external event: the incident, the object that is the basis of the experience, what is *being* experienced. On the other hand, it refers to the internal process: the mental and emotional processes going on in the subject, the individual *experiencing* it. The same concept therefore refers to two different things – the external object/event and the internal process – in the subject–object interaction and the context forming the framework of the 'experience' (see the experience model below). Naturally, this gives rise to a number of contradictions or paradoxes in the discussion of user experience, experience design and user-experience design.

5. A fifth paradox concerns the concepts experience design and user-experience design. Literally, the concepts indicate that experience is designable. On the other hand, it has been specified a number of times in the literature that experience is not designable. Experience designer and blogger Bob Jacobson writes: 'there is no way to design experience' (2007). And Jacob Gube writes: 'we can't design a user experience . . .

we can't manufacture, impose or predict the actual experience itself' (Gube, 2010). That it is impossible to design experience is primarily due to the fact that experience is eventually a product of the mental and emotional work of the individual experiencing it. In principle, experience only appears in the head or in the body of the individual experiencing it. It is not possible for the experience designer to directly affect the individual person or the individual user and form and create a specific experience. Therefore, a central paradox is embedded in the concepts experience design and user-experience design in relation to what is designed and what is actually designable.

6. A sixth paradox concerns – as already indicated above – the fact that the framing of and hence the analysis unit of user experience may vary significantly, in principle from a single moment or a spot check of an end user's interaction with a system to a full life cycle of interactions and touch points between the user on the one hand and a product, business or brand on the other.

7. Finally, a seventh paradox – which has also been mentioned in the introduction – concerns the relation between the degree of recognition of the concept and its precision or accuracy. Hazzenzahl and Tractinsky, for instance, point to the fact that the concept user experience has been adopted early by the HCI community, by practitioners as well as researchers, but at the same time, it has been criticized repeatedly 'for being vague, elusive, ephemeral' (Hazzenzahl and Tractinsky, 2006, p. 91).

As illustrated, there are a number of paradoxes linked to the concepts user experience, experience design and user-experience design. Therefore, it is no wonder that it has been difficult to find a common understanding and definition of the concepts. In the following, these paradoxes are addressed, and we shall even seek to solve them.

10.5 CONCEPT MAPPING

There are at least two methods to approach concept mapping, the historical approach and the methodological approach. The historical approach examines where the concepts derive from, how they arose, in which contexts they emerged and the meaning layers that are therefore historically embedded in the concepts. The methodological approach examines how the concepts are defined and delimited logically. Often, the latter approach will be seen in a contemporary perspective according to which various interpretations and variations of the concepts will be examined to see what elements are encompassed in the concepts, how they relate to each other and what the core and secondary meanings of the concepts are. In this context, both approaches are examined. Firstly, the history of the concepts are analysed, their origins, their genealogy; then their logical definitions and methodological components are investigated.

10.6 CONCEPTUAL HISTORY

Historically, the concepts user experience, experience design and user-experience design can be said to have at least three important backgrounds and origins, which have in part converged into a common tradition today. The first originates from HCI, human factors, informatics or the usability tradition; the second originates from the mercantile context within the marketing and business school traditions; and the third from the design tradition, including user-centred design or human-centred design in particular. In the following, these three traditions are analysed separately.

10.6.1   The HCI Tradition: User Experience

Obviously, the tradition of HCI, human factors and usability focuses primarily on experiences in the context of interactive products and software. In this context, it will be referred to as the HCI tradition, since this is the more comprehensive term that includes the other terms.

Compared with other disciplines and traditions within HCI, user experience is a relatively new phenomenon. The origin of the term can in fact be dated and localized quite precisely. It was implemented by cognitive science researcher Donald Norman in the mid 1990s, while he was Vice President of the Advanced Technology Group at Apple. One of the first times the term appears is in a CHI proceedings paper from 1995, in which Norman and a couple of his colleagues wrote an organizational overview in which they 'cover some of the critical aspects of human interface research and application at Apple or, as we prefer to call it, the "User Experience"' (Norman et al., 1995).

Reportedly, the reason why Donald Norman implemented the term 'user experience' back then is that he would not have his group at Apple 'relegated to pushing pixels in the "user interface"' (Merholz, 2005a), that is, only working with interface design. He writes: 'I invented the term because I thought Human Interface and usability were too narrow: I wanted to cover all aspects of the person's experience with a system, including industrial design, graphics, the interface, the physical interaction, and the manual' (mail from Donald Norman to Peter Merholz, quoted from Merholz, 2007). In other words, Norman wanted to extend the perspective in relation to usability and interface design to cover the entire user experience of the system and other touch points between user and product. But, as appears from the listing, the touch points considered by Norman are all relatively close to the product and the interface. Consequently, Norman's concept remains largely within the framework of 'product user experience'.

This origin is also the historical reason why, later on, the term 'user experience' has been so closely related to IT, the design of interactive systems and web design. This issue has puzzled several authors. For example, writes Andrew in a reply to a blog article by Peter Merholz of 20 March 2005: 'I never quite understood how, in a world with . . . [sensuous] Vegas casinos, Cirque du Soleil, Harry Potter cross-merchandising, and Target, a bunch of web designers ever decided what they did should be called "user experience design"' (post from Andrew, 21 March 2005, quoted in Merholz, 2005b). Andrew thus emphasizes the paradox that in a world full of sensuous experience design, it is a group of web designers who – at that time hardly representing what is most sensuous and rich in experience – monopolize the term 'user-experience design'.

This first tradition in user experience and user-experience design therefore directly originates from HCI, human factors, usability studies, interaction design, interface design, web design and so on, in a movement that has increasingly focused on the human side of HCI and that has extensively focused on the soft, more qualitative sides of the human factor. Later, user-experience design as a professional discipline has also been practised and developed extensively in the context of IT and especially web-based systems such as websites and web applications. Therefore, user experience and user-experience design are also historically related to and dependent on web design in a narrow sense and IT in a broader sense.

10.6.2   The Marketing Tradition: Customer Experience

While using the term user experience within the HCI tradition, the parallel term used in the more mercantile environments and more commercial contexts has been customer experience (often abbreviated to CX), consumer experience, brand experience or experiential marketing. In this context, customer experience is often defined as all experiences of a customer or user across all touch points between a business and the product, where touch points can be the product itself, the shop in which the product is bought, engineer work, people, sale, follow-up service, after-sale service, call centres and so on. In Wikipedia, 'customer experience' is, for example, defined as 'the sum of all experiences a customer has with a supplier of goods or services over the duration of their relationship with that supplier. From awareness, discovery, attraction, interaction, purchase, use, cultivation and advocacy' (Wikipedia entry 'Customer experience'). Further down, the elaboration follows: 'In short, customer experience meaning a customer journey . . . start from first contact and through the whole relationship' (Wikipedia entry 'Customer experience').

Here and later in the chapter, Wikipedia is not used as a scientific authorized source with the purpose to clarify a definition but it is, in fact, because it is a user-generated website, read as a source that reflects and represents the unofficial, immediate, broad consensus about and perception of the meaning and cultural understanding of the concepts. In other words, Wikipedia is read as expressing present collective social intelligence.

In parallel, Idris Mootee defines 'customer-experience design' as follows: 'Customer experience design is taking the customer views of the interaction to understand the emotional bond between the brand and customers. It requires a common understanding of the customer journey, then align[s] the company actions to build emotional bonds' (Mootee, 2007, p.11).

This tradition has many representatives (for example, Shaw et al., 2010), but one of the most predominant among them is Bernd H. Schmitt. In 1999, he published the book *Experiential Marketing. How to Get Customers to Sense, Feel, Think, Act, Relate to Your Company and Brands*. In fact, the same year that Joseph Pine and James Gilmore published *The Experience Economy: Work is Theatre and Every Business a Stage* (1999), Rolf Jensen published *Dream Society: How the Coming Shift from Information to Imagination will Transform Your Business* and Michael J. Wolf published *The Entertainment Economy: How Mega-media Forces are Transforming Our Lives*. Therefore, there are indications that, at the threshold of the new millennium, there were several related phenomena linked to the experience field that simultaneously and apparently independently of each other became visible to several different authors.

Experiential Marketing focuses on the experimental part of marketing, and the main point is that this experimental part has become the dominating trend in marketing, which will gradually replace the more traditional approaches to marketing. Whereas traditional

Table 10.1   Comparison between traditional marketing and experiential marketing

Traditional marketing	Experiential marketing
Narrow definition of product categories and competition	Investigations of the consumption situation – consumption of a holistic experience
Focus on functional features and advantages	Focus on customer experience
Consumers as rational and logical decision makers	Consumers as rational and emotional beings, i.e. also emotional and irrational aspects
Analytical, quantitative methods	Eclectic methods

marketing attempts to market products and brands through the placement of advertisements, experiential marketing is based on the principle of marketing a product or brand through experiences, where the intended result is an emotional relation between the customer and a brand, product or idea. Or to put it more precisely, experiential marketing is a special approach to marketing goods and services that integrates elements of emotions and general, logical thought processes to relate to the customer. In other words, the aim of experiential marketing is to establish a connection to the consumer so that he or she will respond to a product offer based on a combination of emotions and rational response levels.

The differences between traditional marketing and experiential marketing may be outlined as shown in Table 10.1.

According to Schmitt, the most significant backgrounds for the emergence of the new trend during the period leading up to the new millennium are: '(1) the omnipresence of information technology, (2) the supremacy of the brand, and (3) the ubiquity of communications and entertainment' (Schmitt, 1999, p. 3). Also in this mercantile tradition for the use of the concept, IT and the ubiquity of communications and entertainment play a role, but in this case as a background explanation.

Traditionally, customer handling has been dealt with under customer relationship management (CRM), with a focus on the product, the price and the businesses' processes in relation to customer management with maximum efficiency. In that respect, customer experience management (CEM) encompasses a shift in perspective, where the focus is instead on the needs, wishes and expectations of the customers – and preferably the individual customer. To put it differently, business models, support systems and so on are seen from the customer's viewpoint. In principle, the aim is to move the customer up the loyalty ladder from 'prospects' over 'customer', 'client', 'supporter' and 'advocate' to 'partner'.

While the concepts 'user experience' and (product) 'user-experience design' as trends are primarily targeted at products, 'customer-experience design' is targeted at products, services as well as touch points encircling products and services. Thus, it may be said that whereas Donald Norman with the concept user experience attempted to extend the limits as to what the usability approach could concern, but with the concept in reality staying within the framework of 'product–user relationship', the concept customer experience has to a larger extent come to represent this broad, extended perspective on the relation between user and customer, on the one hand, and the product, business, brand and so on, on the other.

However, the two concepts are closely related, and also they seem to have converged towards each other in recent years. For example, the Wikipedia definition of 'experience design' also includes the mercantile meaning and the marketing tradition when it says, with the inclusion of terms such as 'commercial context', 'experiential marketing', 'customer experience design' and 'brand experience': 'In its commercial context, experience design is driven by consideration of the moments of engagement, or touch points, between people and brands, and the ideas, emotions, and memories that these moments create. Commercial experience design is also known as customer experience design, and brand experience. In the domain of marketing, it may be associated with experiential marketing' (Wikipedia entry 'Experience design'). The convergence of the concepts is reflected in the HCI tradition as well, for instance, when in 2007 Nielsen-Norman – that is, the firm and partnership established by Jacob Nielsen and Donald Norman in 1998 – defined 'user experience' by means of a wording very close to the mercantile tradition's understanding of 'customer experience': 'All aspects of the end-user's interaction with the company, its services, and its products' (Nielsen-Norman Group, 2007), that is, as all touch points between the end-user and the business.

Consequently, there is close affinity between the concepts 'experience design' and 'user-experience design' in the HCI tradition, on the one hand, and 'customer experience' and 'customer-experience design' in the commercial and mercantile traditions, on the other. However, there are also sources primarily emphasizing the difference between the two concepts, although the mutual influence is still recognized. For example, Roto et al. write 'UX differs from the broader concepts of brand/consumer/customer experience, although UX affects them and vice versa' (2011, p. 6).

10.6.3   The Design Tradition: User-centred Design

The third important origin of 'user experience' and 'user-experience design' is represented by the design tradition, or more specifically the tradition in user-centred design (UCD) or human-centred design (HCD).

To understand experience has always been an important aspect for the design profession. Therefore, design has a long history when it comes to supporting specific experiences, for example, in connection with the interaction with products. Forlizzi and Battarbee write: 'What is unique in design research relative to understanding experience is that it is *focused on the interaction between people and products, and the experience that results*. This includes all aspects of experiencing a product – physical, sensual, cognitive, emotional, and aesthetic' (Forlizzi and Battarbee, 2004, p. 261, emphasis in the original).

UCD can be defined as an approach to design, according to which the main focus of the design process, that is, the solution of a given design problem, is on the end-user's wishes, needs, preferences and limitations. Rather than forcing the user to change behaviour to adapt to the product, as can be seen in other design philosophies, UCD attempts to optimize the product in relation to what the user can, wishes and needs to use the product. UCD asks questions to the users, their tasks and targets, and uses the answers to make decisions in the design and development processes.

According to ISO, design can be called 'user centred' if it meets six criteria, as stated in the ISO standard that is not, however, called 'User-' but 'Human-centred design for interactive systems':

1. The design is based upon an explicit understanding of users, tasks and environments.
2. Users are involved throughout design and development.
3. The design is driven and refined by user-centred evaluation.
4. The process is iterative.
5. The design addresses the whole user experience.
6. The design team includes multidisciplinary skills and perspectives. (Human-centred design for interactive systems, ISO 9241-210, 2010)

A central issue in UCD is therefore that the explicit point of departure is the user and that the design is seen from the user's viewpoint, that focus is on the user experience as a whole and that the approach is multidisciplinary – as is also the case with user-experience design.

UCD is often linked to interface design or IT system design, but in principle it can be used for all products and services.

The user's role and involvement may vary from, at one end of the spectrum, being imaginary content for the designer in the form of empathic design (that is, the designer takes the user as his point of departure and analyses, predicts or imagines what the user might wish and think about a product or how the user might wish to use a product); over design processes, where representatives of the users take part in continuing tests of prototypes and products or in co-creation processes, in which the designer and the user work together on equal terms on the design; to, at the other end of the spectrum, being purely UCD processes, in which the designer merely has the role of facilitator and executor of the user's wishes in relation to design.

In that way, UCD is related to 'cooperative design', the Scandinavian approach to designing IT systems in an equal partnership between designers and users, which has developed continuously since the 1970s; 'participatory design', the US tradition of user involvement and participation, which is inspired by cooperative design and which has developed since the early 1990s; and 'customer-centred design' or 'contextual design', which is design in the specific context that also makes use of approaches and methods from cooperative design and participatory design.

In their 'user experience manifesto', Roto et al. point explicitly to the fact that 'The roots of user-experience design (UXD) can be found in the principles of Human Centred Design . . . HCD . . . Often referred to as UCD, User Centred Design' (Roto et al., 2011, p. 11). They describe the relation in the following way: 'In principle, UXD is not different from HCD. However, UXD adds important dimensions to the challenge of implementing HCD in a mature form. These additions are not trivial. The main dimensions distinguishing UXD from a traditional view of HCD include UX factors; methods, tools and criteria used in UX work; representation of the UX idea; and UX positioning in the organization' (Roto et al., 2011, p. 11). According to this understanding, user-experience design is HCD plus something more.

There are also a number of definitions of 'user experience' that use UCD as their point of departure. Robert Rubinoff (2004) defines, for example, 'user experience' based on the focus on the consumer, describing it as 'a concept that places the end-user at the focal point of design and development efforts, as opposed to the system, its applications or its aesthetic value alone. It's based on the general concept of user-centered design.' The website UX Design defines user-experience design as follows: 'professionals use the term User Experience Design to refer to the judicious application of certain user-centered design practices' (UX Design, 2010). On the other hand, the experience aspect has also become a main theme within UCD. Oppelaar et al. (2008) write: 'Experience is currently a key concept in literature on user centered design.'

Donald Norman was the first to define 'user experience' and 'user-experience design' within the HCI tradition, and he was also one of the first to describe the importance of UCD within the broad design approach (Gube, 2010), that is, the perception that design decisions must be based on the needs and wishes of the user or consumer, for example, in the book *The Psychology of Everyday Things*, published in 1988, in which Norman uses the term 'user-centred design' to describe design approaches based on the needs of the user rather than other criteria such as aesthetics. In that way also, there is a close connection between, on the one hand, the design tradition and UCD in particular and user-experience design, on the other.

10.7   METHODOLOGICAL DEFINITIONS

To find a definition of the concepts user experience, experience design and user-experience design based on a logical, methodological and perhaps also a temporary perspective rather than on a historical, genealogical approach, the ISO is a good point of departure, because this is presumably the closest we get to an official, authoritative definition and understanding of the concepts (see the introduction of ISO above).

ISO 9241-210 with the title *Ergonomics of Human-System Interaction – Part 210: Human-centred Design for Interactive Systems* defines 'user experience' as 'a person's perception and responses that result from the use or anticipated use of a product, system or service' (ISO, 2010). Accordingly, the ISO lists three fundamental factors that affect 'user experience': user, system and context. Or, more specifically: the state of the user, the characteristics of the system and the situation or context of use. These three factors can be said to comprise the essential and necessary components in every user experience. Graphically, the model can be presented in two ways as shown in Figures 10.1 and 10.2.

The first graphical representation shows a relatively abstract relation between the elements in which user experience is the intersection where user, system and context meet, while the other graphical representation shows a more specific relation where system and user are included in, that is, are subsets of, the context. The latter graphical representation is therefore preferable. Furthermore, it should be emphasized that the model is viewed through the user, that is, from the perspective of the user.

In the ISO 9241-210 notes, the individual elements are elaborated further:

- State of the user comprises among other things: 'the user's internal and physical state resulting from prior experiences, attitudes, skills and personality', that is, 'all the users' emotions, beliefs, preferences, perceptions, physical and psychological responses, behaviours and accomplishments that occur before, during and after use' (p. 9).
- Characteristics of the system comprise, for example: 'brand image, presentation, functionality, system performance, interactive behaviour and assistive capabilities of the interactive system' (p. 9),
- And context comprises, for example: 'the context of use' (p. 9).

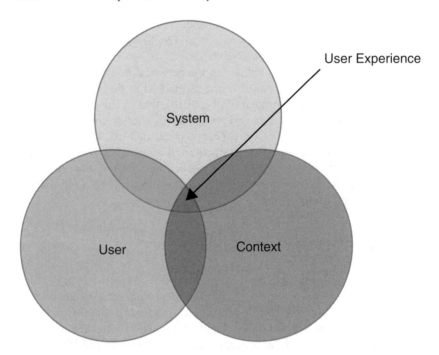

Figure 10.1   *Graphical representation of the three constitutive elements of 'user experience' – user, system and context – where user experience is the intersection of the three elements*

Although the definitions of 'user experience' vary – as shown in the introduction to this chapter – convergence is seen towards a definition of this type in the literature on user experience, that is, a definition emphasizing that: (1) user experience should be interpreted with the user and more specifically the user's perception or sensory apparatus as the point of departure; (2) user experience is based on interaction between user and product; and (3) the three fundamental elements in the understanding of user experience are: user, system and context.

As regards the former, experience designer Nathan Shedroff defines user experience as 'The overall experience, in general or specifics, a user, customer, or audience member has with a product, service, or event ... However, the experience encompasses more than merely function and flow, but the understanding compiled through all of the senses' (Shedroff, n.d.). As regards the system, Nielsen-Norman Group defines user experience as 'All aspects of the end-user's interaction with the company, its services, and its products' (Nielsen-Norman Group, 2007). And as regards the latter, there is broad consensus that these three elements – user, system and context – encompass the central defining features of user experience. In their *User Experience White Paper*, Roto et al. define 'user experience' as 'the experiences that people have through the use of (or encounter with) a system. This use takes place in a specific context, which has an impact on, or contributes to, the UX' (Roto et al., 2011, p. 5). Oppelaar et al. (2008) write correspondingly: 'An experience is a result of, both, the artefact, the individual experiencing it, the context and the culture of the audience to which the individual feels engaged.' And Hassenzahl

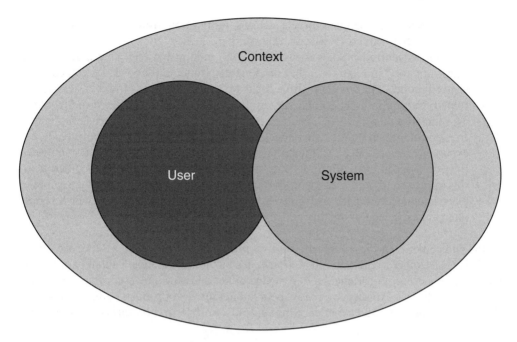

Figure 10.2   Graphical representation of the three constitutive elements of 'user experience', where user experience arises from the interaction between user and system in context

and Trantinsky (2006) too agree to the main content of the ISO definition when they define user experience as conditional upon three elements: 'UX is a consequence of a user's internal state (predispositions, expectations, needs, motivation, mood, etc.), the characteristics of the designed system (e.g. complexity, purpose, usability, functionality, etc.) and the context (or the environment) within which the interaction occurs (e.g. organisational/social setting, meaningfulness of the activity, voluntariness of use, etc.)' (Hassenzahl and Trantinsky, 2006, p.95). Parallel definitions based on these three elements may also be found in, for example, Forlizzi and Ford (2000).

At a more general level – in a macro perspective – Forlizzi and Battarbee (2004) divide the temporary theoretical approaches and models at hand to understand experience into three perspectives that are defined by their focus on one of the three above-mentioned key components. They denote the three theoretical approaches or models: 'product-centred', 'user-centred' and 'interaction-centred' models:

● Product-centred models focus on the product and often provide information about how to design products that generate convincing experience. Frequently, they are guidelines for design practice, design guidelines in the form of subject indices or criteria that can be used as checklists in design, or they are criteria to assess experience quality (Forlizzi and Battarbee, 2004, p.262).
● User-centred models focus on users, and often they aim to help designers and developers understand people who use their products. They can be theoretical

models describing people's targets, actions, motivations and experience when they interact with products (Forlizzi and Battarbee, 2004, p. 262).

● Interaction-centred models focus on the interaction between user and product. These are not – in relation to the components pointed out above – direct 'context-centred models', but models with a focus on the interaction. However, it is accentuated that the interaction and the resulting experience are situated in a context. This includes all aspects of experiencing a product – the physical, sensuous, cognitive, emotional, aesthetic experience and so on. Consequently, this approach sees experience as a totality encompassing user and system and the interaction between them in a specific situation or context. In accordance with the focus on context, this approach accentuates the importance of the fact that the experience can take place in connection with social interaction and in a social context, in which people interpret experiences together and create meaning.

In the choice between these three alternative approaches, Forlizzi and Battarbee (2004, p. 261) argue explicitly that 'an interaction-centered view is the most valuable for understanding how a user experiences a designed product'. Just as they accordingly end with a definition of user experience as 'how people interact with products, other people and the resulting emotions and experience that unfold' (Forlizzi and Battarbee, 2004, p. 266).

10.8   EXPERIENCE AND USER EXPERIENCE: TOWARDS A NEW, SHARED DEFINITION

We consent to Forlizzi and Battarbee's assessments that an interaction-based approach will offer the most adequate understanding of experience. The product-centred approach and the user-centred approach represent particular perspectives with a focus on one of the factors but they both establish blind spots with respect to the other factors, that is, user, product, interaction and context, respectively. An interaction-based approach, on the other hand, may encompass user, product, the interaction between them and the context of the interaction.

Inspired by Forlizzi and Battabee's understanding of user experience's, 'how people interact with products, other people and the resulting emotions and experiences that unfold' (Forlizzi and Battarbee, 2004, p. 266) and their selection of key components, we now propose revised definitions of experience at first and then of user experience, experience design and user-experience design (see also Jensen, 2006, p. 192). Definitions that will both further accentuate the interaction dimension and emphasize that experience is viewed with the user or subject as the point of departure, and finally they will emphasize the most important elements that are a precondition for the experience. Experience may now be defined as follows:

Experiences (understood as particular instances of or the processes or facts of personally observing, encountering or undergoing something) are sensory-based effects that humans get in interaction with products/objects, services, events, processes, other people, surroundings and so on, which are reflected in the form of emotional impressions and/or meaningful experiences (understood as the knowledge or practical wisdom gained from

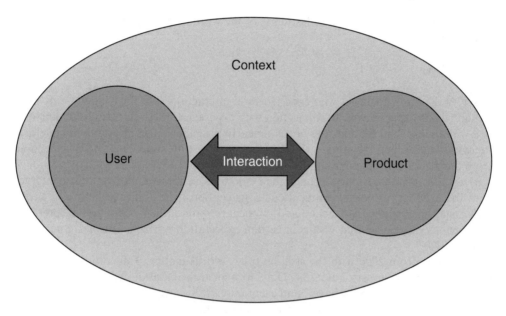

*Figure 10.3   Model of experience based on the interaction between user and product in
context*

*what one has observed, encountered or undergone). Experiences are a consequence of the
experiencing individual's internal state (for example, needs, wishes, motivations, personality traits, emotions, convictions, values, culture, knowledge, skills, expectations, mood/
spirits/sentiment and so on), characteristics of the product/object, service and so on (for
example, functionality/utility, usability, accessibility, design, brand and so on) and the
context in which the interaction takes place (for example, environment/physical context,
social context, cultural context, technological context, temporal context, organizational
context, task-related context and so on).*

To emphasize the interaction between user and product as the central point for the
understanding of experience, we suggest the graphical presentation shown in Figure 10.3.

This means that the paradox regarding the double reference of the experience concept
to the thing being experienced and the individual experiencing it (no. 4) outlined in the
earlier section 'Conceptual paradoxes' has been solved by means of an interaction model
for experience and the emphasis that experience is localized at the user, but that it occurs
as an effect of an interaction between user and product.

10.9   USER, PRODUCT AND INTERACTION/SOCIAL
     CONTEXT

In the following, the three fundamental elements: user, system and interaction/social
context are discussed in further detail. However, we use the denotation 'product' instead
of system or artefact as above, since this term is considered more generic. In this context,

product should be seen in the widest sense of the word as object, service, activity, event and so on.

10.9.1   User

'User' is the human subject who experiences in interaction with the product – the individual who is experiencing. In connection with experience, users can also be understood in a wider sense than the end-user or customer. In principle, it can be everybody interacting with the product, the service, the event and so on: staff, suppliers, specialists, people from the media, entrepreneurs and so on.

Users affect the experience through their emotions, sentiment, motivations to interact with the product, values, cognitive models, perceptions (the ability to hear, see, smell, feel, taste), their immediate mental and physical resources, their ability to interpret and all previous experience that results in certain expectation horizons (Forlizzi and Ford, 2000, p. 420).

In a paper from 2006 with the striking title: 'Words matter. Talk about people: not customers, not consumers, not users', Don Norman argued that the words we use control the way we think, act and behave – and eventually the way we design. When using words such as 'customers', 'consumers' or 'users' about a target audience, they are marked as objects rather than personified as human beings. Consequently, the people we design for are degraded and depersonalized, and the ability to create good design is reduced. These terms 'take us away from our primary mission: to help people', writes Norman and continues: 'If we are designing for people, why not call them that: people, a person, or perhaps humans. But no, we distance ourselves from the people for whom we design by giving them descriptive and somewhat degrading names, such as customer, consumer, or user. Customer – you know, someone who pays the bills. Consumer – one who consumes. User, or even worse, end-user – the person who pushes the buttons, clicks the mouse, and keeps getting confused'. He concludes: 'It is time to wipe words such as consumer, customer, and user from our vocabulary. Time to speak of people' (Norman, 2006). Norman's point is therefore that designers should design for human experience and not design simply to serving 'uses'. We recognize Norman's argumentation and point, but decide to maintain the original concepts such as user, user experience and so on – to avoid unnecessary terminological confusion – noting that user should be perceived in the wide sense of the word and without degrading and depersonalizing connotations.

10.9.2   Product

'Product' is the object with which the user interacts – the thing being experienced – and which generates the user's experience through the interaction. Product and object must be understood in the broad sense as an artefact, service, activity, event, place, environment, media, other people and so on.

It is important to emphasize that product does not equal experience; it only represents the source of the experience. This links to the paradox mentioned in the introduction, which is embedded in the terms experience design and user-experience design. Contrary to what is immediately indicated by these terms, it is accentuated several places that, in principle, experience is not designable. Experience designer and blogger Bob Jacobson writes: 'there is no way to design experiences. Experiences occur by definition only in the minds of those who have them, not at a designer's behest. There is no way to reach into the head of individuals and implant or create particular experiences' (Jacobson, 2007). And Jacob Gube agrees: 'we can't design a user experience . . .', 'The best we can do is design for specific experiences and promote certain behaviors, but we can't manufacture, impose or predict the actual experience itself ' (Gube, 2010).

Contrary to traditional designs of external material objects in the physical world – a chair, a vase or a house – it is not possible to design experience directly. This is due in part to the fact that experience is a product of the experiencing individual's own mental and emotional work that the designer cannot directly affect in a controlling way, and in part to the fact that the experience designer cannot sufficiently control all relevant elements in the experience context so that a controllable and predictable result will be seen in the form of a specific predetermined experience.

But what can be done is to design *for* experience. Oppelaar et al. (2008) write: 'Because it is not possible to design an experience, designing for experience is the way to go.' And Bob Jacobson explains further in continuation of the above quotation: 'Many designers and critics have thoughtfully argued that there is no way to design experiences . . . However, the same designers and critics do endorse designing for experience. Designing for experience means creating the conditions by which target audiences can be made, persuaded, or encouraged to have desired experiences' (Jacobson, 2007).

To design *for* experience means to design the product – the thing being experienced – (as well as the context) in a way that, through affordances, functionality, story of use, design language, structure, attributes, degree and form of interactivity, responsiveness, aesthetic qualities, accessibility, brand, image and so on, it is likely to trigger a certain interaction with the consumer and thus to produce a certain experience – although the specific experience cannot be guaranteed (Forlizzi and Ford, 2000, p. 420). Folizzi and Ford elaborate: 'As designers trying to craft an experience, we can only design situations, or levers that people can interact with, rather than neatly predicted outcomes. A product offers a story of use that invites engagement. If the product happens to be encountered in an unfamiliar context for a user, the product may be experienced in ways other than the designer intended' (Forlizzi and Ford, 2000, p. 420).

In experience design, it is therefore not the actual end product that is designed, that is, the experience. Instead, it is the product, the system, the object (and to some extent the context) that are subject to design – and hence represent the 'designable'. From approximately 2007 and onwards, this approach has been denoted DUX as an abbreviation for designing for user experience.

However, the designable should not be neglected for that reason. According to experience designer Nathan Shedroff, it is fruitful to realize that 'great experiences . . . are based upon principles that have been proven'. And he continues: 'the elements that contribute to superior experiences are knowable and reproducible, which make them designable'. To some extent, the factors producing experience are thus substantiated and well known and therefore, they can be reproduced. In other words, they are designable. In this specific meaning, it is therefore possible (indirectly) to design experience – or to design for experience – and with a certain degree of likelihood to control and predict the experience that is produced as effect. And naturally, this is the entire rationale behind experience design as an activity and a profession.

This also means that the paradox (no. 5) outlined in the earlier section 'Conceptual paradoxes' between the term experience design and the fact that experience is not designable has been solved by clarifying what is designable.

10.9.3   Context

'Context' or 'context of use' is the surroundings or the situation in which the user–product–interaction takes place. The reason why context is important is that experience cannot be isolated from the context in which it takes place. To put it differently, user experience can change if the context is changed although user and product are the same. Context of use is shaped by, for example, social and cultural factors such as social, cultural and organizational patterns of behaviour (Forlizzi and Ford, 2000, p. 420). It is important to emphasize that context – in addition to product – can be subject to design. Context is therefore also designable to some extent.

Roto et al. (2011) pay attention to the fact that context may assume several different forms or be described at different levels. At this point, we suggest that context is broken down to the following major dimensions: physical context/environment; social context; cultural context (values); temporal context; technological context (technological infrastructure); organizational context (work/spare time, voluntary work); and so on.

10.9.4   Summary: User, Product and Context

All three factors – user, product and interaction/context – are dynamic and change and develop over time. Users develop because they are affected by, for example, related experience in their context, culture or personal history. Context or culture develops and changes as a result of, for example, the development of individuals (and products) who are part of it. This means that products too, which represent the point of departure for the experience, must develop if they are to keep up with users and the context and not become obsolete (Oppelaar, 2008).

In this respect, it is important to stress that user experience cannot be reduced to these factors: user, product and interaction/context, and, on the other hand, that the factors alone cannot explain user experience. Roto et al. write: 'UX itself cannot be described by describing the UX factors, but UX factors and their main categories can be used to describe the situation in which a person felt a particular UX. UX factors also help identify the reasons behind a certain experience' (2011, p. 10).

10.10   EXPERIENCE DESIGN AND USER-EXPERIENCE DESIGN: TOWARDS A NEW, SHARED DEFINITION

Incorporating the points on DUX – designing for user experience – and the three fundamental elements in experiences, experience design can now be defined as follows:

Experience design is an integrated design practice that designs for experience – in the form of products, services, events, processes, surroundings and so on, with a focus on the quality of the experience, i.e. with the goal of producing successful, engaging and relevant experiences – based on considerations of (1) the needs, wishes, convictions, knowledge, skills, experiences, values and so on of the given human individual (user, consumer, customer, guest and so on) or social group; (2) the potentials and limitations in the design material for the source of the experience (product, service, event and so on); and (3) the interaction and the context for the interaction between the experiencing individual or social group and the source of the experience.

The difference between experience and user experience, and the difference between experience design and user-experience design can now be specified.

While experience is a basic and innate element in our existence as human beings, since 'Experience in general covers everything personally encountered, undergone, or lived through' (Roto et al., 2011, p. 6), the definition of user experience is much narrower. Wikipedia, for example, defines user experience as follows: 'User eXperience (UX) is about how a person feels about using a system' (Wikipedia entry 'User experience'), where the term 'system' is interpreted in a relatively wide sense of the word.

Correspondingly, Wikipedia defines experience design as 'the practice of designing products, processes, services, events, and environments with a focus placed on the quality of the user experience and culturally relevant solutions' (Wikipedia entry 'Experience design', the definition refers to Aarts and Marzano, 2003, p. 46), that is, as a specific approach or a specific design focus in which the user and especially the quality of user experience are the pivotal points, while user-experience design in the parallel Wikipedia entry is defined as 'a subset of the field of experience design that pertains to the creation of the architecture and interaction models that impact user experience of a device or system . . . The scope of the field is directed at affecting "all aspects of the user's interaction with the product: how it is perceived, learned, and used"' (Wikipedia entry 'User experience design'; the quotation is from Donald Norman, 1999).

So user-experience design is seen as a subset of experience design, which focuses especially on the interaction models and architecture of a device or system. Or the other way around: while the term experience design addresses general product and service experience, the term user experience more specifically addresses the IT field. This understanding is confirmed by others. Paluch writes, for example: 'Most commonly, however the specific term "user experience" is applied to that of software, web applications and digital devices whereas the more general user-product experiences are referred to as "experience design"' (Paluch, 2006). And further down it says correspondingly that user-experience design takes the same approach as experience design 'and applies it to a specific set of products – computer-related ones' (Paluch, 2006).

In this understanding, user experience and user-experience design are therefore narrower than experience and experience design, since the former focuses solely on experience related to HCI. The difference in meaning between experience design and user-experience design naturally originates from the word user and this word's historical link to the computer field. Paluch writes: 'We refer to a person as a user particularly in the case where he/she is operating a computer or similar device. Thus the "user experience" refers to the overall impression, feelings, interactions that a person has while operating these systems . . . the term in practice has been specifically associated to the direct interactions with devices operated by specific peripherals and providing an interface for feedback via a screen' (Paluch, 2006). This is also in accordance with Roto et al., who in their *User Experience White Paper* unlike 'experience in a general sense' explicitly define user experience as 'the experience(s) derived from encountering systems' (Roto et al., 2011, p. 6), where, in this context, system should denote 'products, services, and artefacts – separately or combined in one form or another – that a person can interact with through a user interface' (Roto et al., 2011, p. 6). Further down it says directly: 'UX is a subset of experience as a general concept. UX is more specific, since it is related to the experiences of using a system' (Roto et al., 2011, p. 6).

Although this distinction is not clear-cut – and not at all, if systems are interpreted in a wide sense as products, services and artefacts – we will nevertheless stick to the concepts, since in many cases, it may make sense to separate IT supported experience from non-IT supported experience. However, we will sharpen up the definition. User experience and user-experience design should thus refer to IT-based or IT-supported experience, where experience substantially presupposes interaction with a IT system, device or product interface, while experience and experience design refer to experience where this is not the case. To put it differently, user experience and user-experience design are linked exclusively to interactive digital media or technologies.

This means that the paradox (no. 1) outlined in the earlier section 'Conceptual paradoxes' between experience design as a relatively narrow domain, on the one hand, and a very wide domain, on the other, has been (dis)solved. The same applies to the paradox (no. 2) between experience design as a very new tradition, on the one hand, and a very old tradition, on the other. Both paradoxes are dissolved through the differentiation between experience and user experience and between experience design and user-experience design, where experience and experience design can be seen as the wide domain and the long tradition, and user experience and user-experience design as the narrow domain and the relatively new tradition.

10.11   USER EXPERIENCE VERSUS USABILITY

In the following, a couple of more specific aspects of user experience, experience design and user-experience design are discussed. They concern the remaining paradoxes mentioned in the earlier section 'Conceptual paradoxes', which have not been examined yet. What remains to be examined are the paradoxes between user experience versus usability (no. 3) and the temporal extent of the experience: user experience and temporality (no. 6), respectively. The former is dealt with in this section, the latter in the following section. The last paradox (no. 7) will not be discussed until the conclusion.

As has been mentioned several times above, there is a complicated, unclear and unclarified relation between user experience and usability. Some sources see usability as an integrated, fundamental element of user experience; other sources differentiate between user experience and usability, viewing the former as something other and more than the latter.

In the ISO standard (9241-210), it is indicated – as already mentioned – that 'usability criteria can be used to assess aspects of user experience' (ISO, 2010). Unfortunately, the standard does not describe the relation between user experience and usability further.

According to Robert Rubinoff (2004), user experience consists of four factors, branding, usability, functionality and content, which cannot individually create a positive experience, but in combination they constitute what he understands as 'user experience' – primarily used in web design, the domain or media mainly addressed and worked with by Rubinoff. Paluch emphasizes that 'User-experience design is a complex field that is not exactly discrete from all the others mentioned (e.g.: Usability, User Interface Design, Interaction design, Information Architecture, Human-Computer Interaction, Human Factors Engineering). In essence, user experience draws from each of these fields in order to address the various aspects of a user's experience' (Paluch, 2006). And he continues further down: 'User experience is the culmination of all of these parts into one field' (Paluch, 2006).

On the other hand, we find positions emphasizing that user experience is something else and more than usability. As already mentioned, UX Design writes directly, for instance: 'Given the persistent level of confusion about the meaning of User Experience Design, defining it by *what it is not* can be useful. It is *not* a trendy new name for, or in any way synonymous with . . . Usability testing' (UX Design, 2010). And Hassenzahl and Roto also define user experience negatively in relation to usability, when they describe their understanding of the former as 'addressing needs beyond the instrumental' (2007, p. 12) or 'addressing needs beyond the mere practical level' (2007, p. 10).

To solve the paradox, it is important to stress that the two concepts both overlap and show differences. There is an overlap in the way that usability aspects will normally be comprised as factors in user experience. But at the same time, there are significant differences between the two concepts. While usability focuses on pragmatic aspects, user experience focuses on both the pragmatic and the hedonistic and affective aspects of the product. And while traditional usability factors primarily relate to performance and problem-free interaction – where typical targets are to minimize time consumption and the number of errors in problem solutions – user experience relates to broader and more differentiated factors such as affect, interpretation, meaning and social and aesthetic aspects. In this perspective, user experience is therefore a broader term than usability since user experience absorbs and encompasses usability.

However, there is one important point that is not encompassed in this perspective, which is the fact that user experience concerns the personal, subjective perceptions of and feelings in relation to the product, that is, user experience takes place inside the user, while usability is a feature or attribute of the product, which is of a relatively objective nature (Roto, 2007, pp. 31–2). In brief: user experience is subjective and linked to the user; usability is objective and linked to the product. This means that they are two essentially different perspectives. Therefore, the right thing to say would be that usability and user experience are two different phenomena, but that 'perceived usability' or 'experienced usability' – that is, usability as perceived by the user – is encompassed as one of more elements in user experience, thus contributing to the overall user experience (Roto et al., 2011, p. 6).

This means that the paradox between user experience and usability (no. 3) has been solved too.

10.12   MOMENT VERSUS LIFE CYCLE: USER EXPERIENCE AND TEMPORALITY

As shown from the above, experience has been understood and interpreted as everything from a momentary or a spot event nature to something extending to a full life cycle of interaction with a product, business or brand.

Experience always stretches over time. Therefore, the understanding of experience should always be framed in terms of temporality. As such, none of the above-mentioned positions are wrong. It is possible to see experience both with different foci on given moments in time during the various phases of the experience process and under different time frames or extents in relation to the process.

Often, the core element of user experience will be the actual experience of use. But there are other relevant aspects of user experience as well. Users may experience something before the first meeting or first use. It may be expectations shaped by previous experience with related technology or brands; it may be advertisements, presentations or demonstrations; or it may be other persons' utterances about the product. Correspondingly, experience may stretch to after use, for example, through reflections on previous use, social negotiations with other users or through changes of assessments of use (Roto et al., 2011, p. 8).

Furthermore, the focus can be on user experience in different time frames. At one end of the continuum, the focus can be on what somebody experiences over a very short period of time, and at the other end of the continuum, the focus can be on what the user experiences over a long period of time, perhaps both including the use and non-use of the given system, object, service and so on. Based on these two dimensions – focus and the time frames for user experience – Roto et al. (2011) suggest a division into four different possible positions in relation to studies of user experience:

- 'Anticipated UX', which relates to the period before the first use and before the experience, concerning the imagination or expectation of the experience – 'imagining experience' – which can in principle address all the three time periods mentioned below (Roto et al., 2011, p. 8).
- 'Momentary UX', which relates to the period during use and while experiencing, which is of a short spot event nature. It could be 'a specific change of feeling during interaction' (Roto et al., 2011, p. 8).
- 'Episodic UX', which relates to the period after use and consists of a reflection on a specific experience. It could be 'appraisal of a specific usage episode' (Roto et al., 2011, p. 8).
- 'Cumulative UX', which takes place over time and reflects several periods of use, that is, 'views on a system as a whole, after having used it for a while' with experience 'formed through a series of usage episodes and periods of non-use, that might span months of usage, or longer' (Roto et al., 2011, p. 8).

For a graphical illustration of the four foci on and time frames for studies of user experience, see Figure 10.4. The different temporal foci have various strengths and weaknesses. To focus on the momentary may, for example, give information about the user's emotional reactions to details of the system or object; to focus on longer time periods

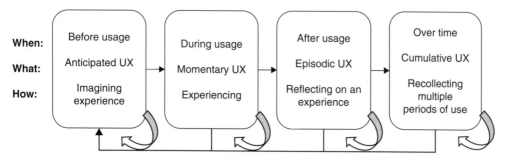

When:	Before usage	During usage	After usage	Over time
What:	Anticipated UX	Momentary UX	Episodic UX	Cumulative UX
How:	Imagining experience	Experiencing	Reflecting on an experience	Recollecting multiple periods of use

Source: Based on Roto et al. (2011).

Figure 10.4   Various foci and time frames for investigations of user experience

may give access to information as to how momentary and episodic user experience is synthesized to cumulative user experience and assessments. Different choices of focus on anticipated, momentary, episodic or cumulative user experience may therefore also have implications in relation to the demands made on design.

Consequently, no specific focus or time frames for the perception of experience are more correct than others. It is different positions, with different strengths and weaknesses. This means that the paradox (no. 6) regarding the understanding of experience as something momentarily at one end of the spectrum and as a full life cycle of interactions at the other end also has been (dis)solved.

10.13   CONCLUSION

In this chapter, we have described the background for the increasing use of the concepts user experience, experience design and user-experience design and we have discussed the paradoxes apparently embedded in them. Through concept mapping in a historical, genealogical perspective and in a logical, methodological perspective, we have worked our way forward to a number of new understandings and a number of new and more precise definitions of user experience, experience design and user-experience design.

Throughout this chapter, several conceptual paradoxes related to user experience, experience design and user-experience design outlined in the introduction have been solved or dissolved. The paradox addressing the at once both narrow and wide domain (no. 1) has been solved through differentiation between experience and user experience and between experience design and user-experience design. Consequently, the related paradox regarding experience design as a very old tradition as well as a very new tradition (no. 2) has also been solved. The paradox related to the inclusive or exclusive relation between user experience and usability (no. 3) has been solved by emphasizing that user experience includes 'experienced usability' or 'perceived usability', that is, the user's perception of the product's usability. The paradox relating to the double reference of the experience concept to the thing being experienced and the individual experiencing it (no. 4) has been solved through the interaction model and the emphasis that the product can only encompass the source of the experience itself. The paradox relating to the term experience design and the fact that experience is not designable (no. 5) has been solved by specifying that it is the product or the source that can be designed, not the experience directly. And the paradox relating to the analysis unit of the experience – both focus and time frame (no. 6) – has been solved through a taxonomy of approaches to view and analyse experience.

Finally, the last paradox regarding the relation between the increasing use and recognition of the user experience, experience design and user-experience design concepts, on the one hand, and their lack of precision, on the other (no. 7), has hopefully become solved by means of this chapter's overall discussion – since the chapter has sought to specify the concepts and to converge the various perspectives to a complete, integrated framework for the field and to common, shared definitions of user experience, experience design and user-experience design.

BIBLIOGRAPHY

Aarts, E.H.L. and S. Marzano (eds) (2003), *The New Everyday. Views on Ambient Intelligence*, Rotterdam: 010 Publishers.

Alben, L. (1996), 'Quality of experience', *Interactions*, **3** (3), 11–15.

André, B. (2008), 'Experience design manifesto', available at http://www.brazandre.com/manifesto/ (beta version) (accessed 22 September 2012).

Blythe, M., C. Overbeeke, A.F. Monk and P.C. Wright (eds), (2003), *Funology: From Usability to Enjoyment*, Dordrecht: Kluwer.

Blythe, M., M. Hassenzahl, E.L.-C. Law and A.P.O.S. Vermeeren (2007), 'An analysis framework for user experience (UX) studies: a green paper', in E. Law, A. Vermeeren, M. Hassenzahl and M. Blythe (eds), *Towards a UX Manifesto*, Lancaster: COST294-MAUSE Affiliated Workshop, COST, pp. 3–5.

Buxton, W. (2007), *Sketching User Experience: Getting the Design Right and the Right Design*, Amsterdam: Morgan Kaufmann.

Forlizzi, J. and K. Battarbee (2004), 'Understanding experience in interactive systems', in *Proceedings of the 2004 Conference on Designing Interactive Systems (DIS 04): Processes, Practices, Methods, and Techniques*, 1–4 August, 2004, New York: ACM, pp. 261–8.

Forlizzi, J. and S. Ford (2000), 'The building blocks of experience: an early framework for interaction designers', in *Proceedings of the 3rd Conference on Designing Interactive Systems (DIS 2000): Processes, Practices, Methods, and Techniques*, New York: ACM, pp. 419–23.

Gabriel-Petit, P. (n.d.), 'UX matters', available at http://www.uxmatters.com/glossary/ (accessed 3 December, 2012).

Garrett, J.J. (2002), *The Elements of User Experience: User-centered Design for the Web*, Indianapolis, IN: New Riders Publishing.

Gube, J. (2010), 'What is user experience design? Overview, tools and resources', available at http://uxdesign. smashingmagazine.com/2010/10/05/what-is-user-experience-design-overview-tools-and-resources/ (accessed 4 December 2012).

Hassenzahl, M. (2008), 'User experience (UX): towards an experiential perspective on product quality', in *IHM 2008 Proceedings of the 20th International Conference of the Association Francophone d'Interaction Homme-Machine*, Metz, France: ACM, pp. 11–15.

Hassenzahl, M. (2010), *Experience Design: Technology for All the Right Reasons*, San Rafael, CA: Morgan and Claypool.

Hassenzahl, M. and V. Roto, (2007), 'Being and doing: a perspective on user experience and its measurement', *Interfaces*, **72**, 10–12.

Hassenzahl, M. and N. Tractinsky (2006), 'User experience – a research agenda', *Behaviour and Information Technology*, **25** (2), March–April, 91–7.

Helander, M.G. and M.P. Tham (2003), 'Hedonomics – affective human factors design', *Ergonomics*, **46** (13–14), 1269–72.

Hobbs, J., T. Fenn and A. Resmini (2010), 'Maturing a practice', *Journal of Information Architecture*, **2** (1), available at http://journalofia.org/volume2/issue1/04-hobbs/ (accessed 22 April 2013).

ISO (International Organization for Standardization) (2010), *ISO FDIS 9241-210: 2010. Ergonomics of Human System Interaction – Part 210: Human-centred Design for Interactive Systems*, Switzerland.

Jacobson, R. (2007), quoted from 'Obstáculospara el diseño de experiencias', available at http://experiential-design.blogspot.dk/2009/11/obstaculos-para-el-diseno-de.html (accessed 4 December 2012).

Jensen, R. (1999), *Dream Society. How the Coming Shift from Information to Imagination Will Transform Your Business*, New York: McGraw-Hill.

Jensen, J.F. (2006), 'ExCITe – forskning, uddannelse og formidling i oplevelsesøkonomien' ('ExCITe – research, education, and communication in the experience economy'), in C. Jantzen and J.F. Jensen (eds), *Oplevelser: Koblingerog transformationer* (*Experience Connections and Transformations*), Aalborg: Aalborg University Press.

Jordan, P. (2000), *Designing Pleasurable Products: An Introduction to New Human Factors*, Boca Raton, FL: Taylor and Francis.

Law, E.L, A.P.O.S. Vermeeren, M. Hassenzahl and M. Blythe (2007a), 'Towards a UX manifesto', in *Proceedings of the 21st BCS HCI Group Conference*, Lancaster: Lancaster University, pp. 205–6.

Law, E., A. Vermeeren, M. Hassenzahl and M. Blythe (2007b) (eds), *Towards a UX Manifesto*, Lancaster: COST294-MAUSE Affiliated Workshop, COST.

Law, E., V. Roto, A. Vermeeren, J. Kort and M. Hassenzahl (2008), 'Towards a shared definition of user experience', in *CHI 2008 Proceedings*, 3–10 April, Florence, Italy, pp. 2395–8.

Mäkelä, A. and S.J. Fulton (2001), 'Supporting users' creativity: design to induce pleasure experiences', in *Proceedings of the International Conference on Affective Human Factors Design*, London: ASEAN Academic Press, pp. 387–94.

Marcus, A. (2002), 'The cult of cute: the challenge of user experience design', *Interactions*, **9** (6), November–December, 29–34.

Merholz, P. (1998), 'Interaction design', available at http://www.peterme.com/index112498.html, 24 November (accessed 3 December 2012).

Merholz, P. (2005a), 'User experience is a quality, not a discipline', available at http://www.peterme.com/archives/week_2005_04_17.html (accessed 26 October 2012).

Merholz, P. (2005b), 'Is "user experience", for all intents and purposes, dead?', available at http://www.peterme.com/archives/000467.html (accessed 3 December 2012).

Merholz, P. (2007), 'Peter in conversation with Don Norman about UX and innovation', available at http://www.adaptivepath.com/ideas/e000862, 13 December (accessed 3 December 2012).

Mootee, I. (2007), 'Customer experience design', available at http://www.slideshare.net/imootee/customer-experience-design-talk-idris-mootee (accessed 3 December 2012).

Morville, P. (2004), 'User experience design', available at http://www.semanticstudios.com/publications/semantics/000029.php (accessed 28 April 2010).

Morville, P. (2007), 'User experience strategy', available at http://www.semanticstudios.com/publications/semantics/000029.php (accessed 28 April 2010).

Nielsen-Norman Group (2007), *User Experience*, available at http://www.nngroup.com/about/userexperience.html (accessed 3 December 2012).

Norman, D. (1988), *The Psychology of Everyday Things*, New York: Basic Books, reprinted in D. Norman (1998), *The Design of Everyday Things*, Boston, MA: MIT Press.

Norman, D. (1999), *Invisible Computer. Why Good Products Can Fail, the Personal Computer is So Complex and Information Appliances are the Solution*, Boston, MA: MIT Press.

Norman, D. (2006), 'Words matter. Talk about people: not customers, not consumers, not users', available at http://jnd.org/dn.mss/words_matter_talk_about_people_not_customers_not_consumers_not_users.html (accessed 29 August 2012).

Norman, D., J. Miller and A. Hendersen (1995), 'What you see, some of what's in the future, and how we go about doing it', available at http://www.sigchi.org/chi95/proceedings/orgover/dan_bdy.htm (accessed 4 December 2012).

Nyman, N. (2005), 'The user experience equation', available at http://www.nnyman.com/personal/2005/11/18/the-user-experience-equation/ (accessed 3 December 2012).

Oppelaar, E.-J.R.G., E.-J. Hennipmann and G.C. Var der Veer (2008), 'Experience design for dummies', in *ECCE 2008 Proceedings of the 15th European Conference on Cognitive Ergonomics: The Ergonomics of Cool Interaction*, New York: ACM, pp. 1–8.

Paluch, K. (2006), 'What is user experience design', available at http://www.montparnas.com/articles/what-is-user-experience-design/ (accessed 3 December 2012).

Pine, B.J. and J.H. Gilmore (1998), 'Welcome to the experience economy', *Harvard Business Review*, **76** (4), 97–105.

Pine, B.J. and J.H. Gilmore (1999), *The Experience Economy. Work is Theatre and Every Business a Stage*, Boston, MA: Harvard Business School Press.

Roto, V. (2007), 'User experience from product creation perspective', in E. Law, A. Vermeeren,

M. Hassenzahl and M. Blythe (eds), *Towards a UX Manifesto*, Lancaster: COST294-MAUSE Affiliated Workshop, COST.

Roto, V., E. Law, A. Vermeeren and J. Hoonhout (2011), 'User experience white paper. Bringing clarity to the concept of user experience', Paper presented at the Dagstuhl Seminar on Demarcating User Experience, 15–18 September 2010.

Rubinoff, R. (2004), 'How to quantify the user experience', available at http://www.sitepoint.com/quantify-user-experience/ (accessed 13 November 2012).

Schmitt, B.H. (1999), *Experiential Marketing: How to Get Customers to Sense, Feel, Think, Act, Relate to Your Company and Brands*, Hoboken, NJ: John Wiley and Sons.

Shaw, C., Q. Dibeehi and S. Walen (2010), *Customer Experience: Future Trends and Insights*, Basingstoke: Palgrave Macmillan.

Shedroff, N. (2001), *Experience Design 1*, Indianapolis, IN: New Riders Publishing.

Shedroff, N. (n.d.), 'Experience design', 'Glossary of experience design terms', available at http://www.nathan.com/ (accessed 3 December 2010).

Strietz, N., C. Magerkurth, T. Prante and C. Röcker (2005), 'From information design to experience design: smart artefacts and the disappearing computer', *Interactions*, **12** (4), July–August, 21–5.

Wolf, M.J. (1999), *The Entertainment Economy: How Mega-media Forces Are Transforming Our Lives*, Harmondsworth: Penguin.

Web Resources

A List Apart, available at http://www.alistapart.com/ (accessed 10 November 2012).

Adaptive Path, Adaptive Path Blog, available at http://www.adaptivepath.com/ (accessed 28 November 2012).

All About UX, available at http://www.allaboutux.org (accessed 10 November 2012).

Everyday UX Blog, available at http://everydayuxblog.tumblr.com/ (accessed 4 December 2012).

Fatdux, *Designing Valuable User eXperiences*, available at http://www.fatdux.com (accessed 28 November 2012).

Hess, W., 'Pleasure and pain', available at http://whitneyhess.com/blog (accessed 10 November 2012).

Inspire UX, available at http://www.inspireux.com/ (accessed 4 December 2012).

Microsoft, *Glossary of MMC Terminology*, available at http://msdn.microsoft.com/en-us/library/windows/desktop/bb246417(v=vs.85).aspx (accessed 28 November 2012).

Montparnas, Intelligent Experience Design, User Experience Design Blog, *Commentary on Strategy and Design of Interactive Products*, available at http://www.montparnas.com (accessed 3 December 2012).

Peterme (Peter Merholz), available at http://www.peterme.com/ (accessed 28 November 2012).

Morville, P., 'Semantic studios', available at http://semanticstudios.com (accessed 4 December 2012).

Nathan (Nathan Shedroff), available at http://www.nathan.com (accessed 3 December 2012).

Textart, available at http://www.textart.ru/ (accessed 28 November 2012).

UPA (Usability Professionals' Association), available at http://www.upassoc.org/usability_resources/about_usability/what_is_ucd.html (accessed 28 November 2012).

Use Design, available at http://www.use-design.com (accessed 28 November 2012).

UX Booth, User Experience and Usability Blog, available at http://www.uxbooth.com (accessed 4 December 2012).

UX Design (2010), available at http://uxdesign.com (accessed 28 November 2012).

UX Design Defined, available at http://uxdesign.com/ux-defined (accessed 28 November 2012).

UX Magazine, available at http://uxmag.com/ (accessed 4 December 2012).

UX quotes, available at http://www.uxquotes.com/ (accessed 28 November 2012).

Wikipedia entry 'Customer experience', available at http://en.wikipedia.org/wiki/Customer_experience (accessed 28 November 2012).

Wikipedia entry 'Experience design', available at http://en.wikipedia.org/wiki/experience_design (accessed 24 September 2012).

Wikipedia entry 'Relationship marketing', available at http://en.wikipedia.org/wiki/Experiential_marketing (accessed 17 October 2012).

Wikipedia entry 'User experience', available at http://en.wikipedia.org/wiki/user_experience, (accessed 28 November 2012).

Wikipedia entry 'User experience design', available at http://en.wikipedia.org/wiki/User_experience_design (accessed 28 November 2012).

11. Consumer immersion: a key to extraordinary experiences

Ann H. Hansen and Lena Mossberg

11.1 INTRODUCTION

> I didn't really think of anything else . . . I was in the most amazingly, beautiful remote place . . .
> It brings you in one with nature and so you get those moments of where you are just caught up
> in it, and you are not thinking about anything else or anyone else – you are just experiencing it.

These are the words of a 46-year-old female tourist from London describing how she became immersed during a three-day dog sledging trip in Svalbard in the arctic region of Norway. What is immersion, and what role does it play? The concept of immersion has gained visibility as a result of the growth of the experience economy, and it appears to be one of the key elements of an unforgettable consumer experience. Immersion has also become a theme in the psychology (Mainemelis, 2001) and consumer behaviour literature (Carù and Cova, 2007) as well as in gaming and virtual reality research (Jennett et al., 2008), and the concept has been applied to settings such as creativity at work (Mainemelis, 2001), artistic experiences (Carù and Cova, 2006) and computer games (Calleja, 2011). However, it remains unclear what exactly immersion is and what causes it (Jennett et al., 2008). How can immersion be defined and understood? Should it be understood as a unique concept, or is it an element of other related concepts such as flow or peak experience? Is the idea of immersion relevant to nature-based tourism experiences such as the one referenced above?

The purpose of this chapter is to conduct an explorative and conceptual discussion of the concept of immersion within a consumer experience context. We begin by comparing different definitions of immersion and discuss how immersion is related to other concepts such as extraordinary experiences, peak experiences, peak performance and flow. Is immersion a relevant concept within the experience economy? We continue by discussing the existing theory regarding the different underlying foundations for the consumer immersion process and the factors necessary for this process to succeed. We propose a new integrated model for understanding the relational and liminal aspects of immersion in the tourism context. Finally, we discuss the issues with the existing theories on the complex and dynamic process of immersion. The aim is to continue the discussion of how to develop a conceptual foundation that can be used to define immersion in experiential marketing theory.

The chapter features examples from an extraordinary tourist experience context. We have chosen this case because it provides extreme examples of extraordinary experiences that can help us to understand immersion in this type of activity-based context. In addition, tourism theory has a long tradition of addressing issues of relevance to consumer immersion in experiences. Wang (2002) has argued that tourists can be defined as peak consumers in pursuit of dreams that are difficult to realize in daily reality. Vacations represent a contrast to everyday life in a spatial sense (allowing tourists to get away from home), a temporal sense (providing more free time) and financial capacity (given their association with surplus consumption and freedom to spend). The essence of tourism consumption is deviation from routines and engagement in non-ordinary or extraordinary experiences. Therefore, the tourist becomes a peak consumer oriented towards realizing fantasies and dreams and seeking peak experiences. This contrast to everyday life and the newness of the activity and/or context heighten the potential for awareness and high emotional involvement and, in turn, are likely to engender moments of immersion. It is likely that immersion will result in more memorable and satisfying experiences for the consumer. Therefore, immersion is an interesting concept both within research on the tourist experience and, more generally, within the experience economy.

The data used in our examples were gathered from a commercial three-day dog sledging trip in Svalbard in the arctic region of Norway during the 2012 winter season. These data are based on participatory observation and interviews with participants that were conducted within a week following the trip. The tourists are active participants, as they drive the sledges. The example illustrates the immersion process in an experiential context in which physical participation is required in a risky environment (see also examples from similar dog sledging trips at Svalbard used by Eide and Mossberg in Chapter, 13, this volume).

11.2   EXPLORING THE CONCEPT OF IMMERSION

11.2.1   Immersion and Relevance for Extraordinary Experiences

How can immersion be defined? Although there is some consensus regarding the importance of immersion to consumers' extraordinary experiences, it is apparent that different perspectives have generated divergent views of how immersion should be defined and characterized (Table 11.1).

Within the social sciences, Carù and Cova have written several articles on immersion in aesthetic consumer experiences based on data from classical music concerts (Carù and Cova, 2005, 2006, 2007). Although they do not provide a concrete definition of immersion, the authors argue that immersion is important to the individual meaning-making process and to consumers' ongoing identity project (Carù and Cova, 2007, p. 35). They view immersion as the process of accessing an experience and one in which the consumer becomes one with the experience by 'being plunged in a thematized and secure spatial enclave where they can let themselves go' (Carù and Cova, 2006, p. 5). Therefore, the authors do not define the concept of immersion itself, instead focusing on the qualities of the context in which consumers can become immersed.

Pine and Gilmore (1999) regard absorption as being on the opposite side of the continuum from immersion and define absorption as 'occupying a person's attention by bringing the experience into the mind', while immersion is defined as 'becoming physically (or virtually) a part of the experience itself' (p. 31). Their use of absorption and immersion as two poles on one scale has resulted in confusion (Holbrook, 2000) as the concepts are positioned as opposites but are not defined as such. Other researchers use absorption and immersion as synonyms for one another or describe them as having

Table 11.1   *Definitions of immersion*

Author(s)	Context	Definition
Carù & Cova (2006)	Classical music concerts	Being plunged in a thematized and secure spatial enclave where they can let themselves go (p. 5).
Pine & Gilmore (1999)	Experience economy in general	Becoming physically (or virtually) a part of the experience itself (p. 31).
Jennett et al. (2008)	Computer games	Immersion involves a lack of awareness of time, a loss of awareness of the real world, involvement and a sense of being in the task environment (p. 657).
Abuhamdeh & Csikszentmihalyi (2012)	Daily activities	Attentional involvement represents the degree to which one's attention is devoted to the activity at hand (p. 258).
Mainemelis (2001)	Creativity at work	The feeling of being fully absorbed, surrendered to, or consumed by the activity, to the point of forgetting one's self and one's surroundings. (Dewey, 1934; May, 1994; Pöppel, 1988). Immersion is an accurate representation of the fact that, during the state of engrossment, one is not self-conscious, as one's attention resources are totally captivated by the task (p. 557).

another relationship, for example, in the phrase 'immersion as absorption' (Brown and Cairns, 2004) and in the definition of immersion as 'the feeling of being fully absorbed' (Mainemelis, 2001, p. 557).

Researchers within gaming and virtual reality use the terms immersion, engagement and involvement interchangeably (Calleja, 2011), which does not make the task of clarifying these terms easier. Jennett et al. (2008, p. 657) state that 'immersion involves a lack of awareness of time, a loss of awareness of the real world, involvement and a sense of being in the task environment'. In the gaming context, involvement is one dimension of immersion. Presence can also be related to experiences in both virtual and actual environments (Calleja, 2011), and sometimes the terms presence and immersion are used interchangeably (Calleja, 2011). Calleja states that the two concepts have been formulated in different disciplines (technologists, media psychologists) and that human–computer interaction researchers refer to the phenomenon as presence, whereas researchers in the humanities and social sciences refer to the same phenomenon as immersion. At other times, the two terms are given specific and complementary meanings (Ijsselsteijn and Riva, 2003), and still other researchers view presence as a combination of involvement and immersion (Slater and Wilbur, 1997; Witmer and Singer, 1998).

Instead of referring to presence or immersion, other researchers within psychology use the concept of attentional involvement (Abuhamdeh and Csíkszentmihályi, 2012). Attentional involvement is argued to be necessary to derive enjoyment from an activity or to access an experience. Experiences may become strong and rewarding when a consumer allocates attentional resources to them. When attentional involvement is high, a large amount of attentional resources is devoted to the activity, and activity engagement can therefore be fully experienced. The feeling of timelessness occurs because the consumer does not have the attentional resources to think about the time that is elapsing during periods of high concentration on the activity at hand (Abuhamdeh and Csíkszentmihályi, 2012, p.265).

Mainemelis (2001) describes the phenomenon of timelessness in the context of environmental psychology and creativity at work. He views immersion as one of four characteristics of timelessness, the other three being a sense of mastery, transcendence and time distortion. Mainemelis defines immersion as 'the feeling of being fully absorbed, surrendered to, or consumed by the activity, to the point of forgetting one's self and one's surroundings (Dewey, 1934; May, 1994; Pöppel, 1988). Immersion is an accurate representation of the fact that, during the state of engrossment, one is not self-conscious since one's attention resources are totally captivated by the task' (Mainemelis, 2001, p.557). Therefore, timelessness can only be described in retrospect (Mainemelis, 2001, p.557) and is one of the memorable and multifarious experiences that people have during immersion. Again, the timeless intensity of being in the present moment is described as a gateway to creativity and joy.

What is common to all these definitions of immersion is that they describe a special temporal state of belonging in the world. Experiences can generally be argued to be dynamic and to involve different temporal aspects. They are influenced both by the past (for example, former experiences) and factors related to the future (for example, our expectations). Immersion is described as a state of being in the world that is characterized by a complete and deep involvement in the present moment and here-and-now-directed activity. In this respect, one can argue that immersion, absorption and engrossment, as used in the definitions above, all describe the deepest type of present-moment involvement. Immersion can be focused on the activity (Mainemelis, 2001) or the environment and can occur in relation to the real world (Carù and Cova, 2006) or a virtual world (Jennett et al., 2008). Because the person's attentional resources are focused on the activity or environment, his or her awareness of other aspects can be lost. Examples include lack of awareness of time (Jennett et al., 2008) and loss of self-consciousness (Mainemelis, 2001). Common to some of these definitions is the concept of a 'letting-go process'. Mainemelis (2001) describes this process as one of surrendering to the activity, whereas Carù and Cova (2006) emphasize the creation of a thematized and secure spatial enclave in which consumers can 'let themselves go'.

We have chosen to combine some of these ideas to create an understanding of immersion that is relevant to consumer experiences. Immersion can be defined as a form of spatio-temporal belonging in the world that is characterized by deep involvement in the present moment. Immersion involves a lack of awareness of time and a loss of self-consciousness.

How can this understanding of immersion be related to other relevant concepts? Most consumption is hedonic and, according to Hirschman and Holbrook (1982), concerns fantasy, feeling and fun. Several concepts have been discussed as related to these consumer experiences, including extraordinary experiences (Arnould and Price, 1993), peak experiences (Maslow, 1964), peak performance (Privette, 1983) and flow (Csíkszentmihályi, 1990). One might argue that immersion is a pivotal part of all of these related concepts.

Extraordinary experiences can be defined as experiences that stand out from what is normal as special and particularly memorable moments (Abrahams, 1986). These experiences have two distinct features: they can be recalled many years later and they have the ability to be transformative (Arnould and Price, 1993). According to research conducted by Arnould and Price (1993, p.41), these experiences are characterized by 'absorption and integration, personal control, joy and valuing, a spontaneous letting-be of the process, and a newness of perception and process'. The concept of absorption and that of 'letting be' are similar to that of immersion.

Peak experience can be viewed as powerful and transient moments of intense joy that are personally meaningful, highly valued and transformational (Privette, 1983; Lipscombe, 1999; Schouten et al., 2007). Peak experience can also be defined as 'moments of great awe, intense happiness, even rapture, ecstasy or bliss – moments of pure, positive happiness when all doubts, all fears, all inhibitions, all weaknesses were left behind' (Maslow, 1967 p.9, quoted in Lipscombe, 1999, p.269). Some of the elements of peak experience (Lipscombe, 1999, p.270) are also characteristics with immersion. Examples of these characteristics are total attention, rich perception, unity of the world, the fusion of dichotomies, ego transcendence, a lack of consciousness of time and space and fusion of the individual. In addition, peak experience has religious qualities: it may involve feeling godlike as well as awareness of the absolute and the unique being of the individual. These characteristics are also associated with some types of immersion.

Flow theory addresses the optimal combination of skills, challenges and high mental focus on an activity. Csíkszentmihályi defines the concept of flow as 'the state in which people are so involved in an activity that nothing else seems to matter' (Csíkszentmihályi, 1990, p.4). The intensity of flow can vary from deep to micro level, and flow results in an intrinsically rewarding experience (Privette, 1983, p.1362) that has the power to motivate people (Schouten et al., 2007). Csíkszentmihályi refers to eight qualities that are important to flow (Csíkszentmihályi, 1990, pp.49–67). One might argue that several of these are characteristics that flow shares with immersion, for example, the merging of action and awareness, concentration on the task at hand, loss of self-consciousness and the transformation of time.

Peak performance is another concept that is similar to immersion in some ways. In peak performance, humans use their full potential and power. This phenomenon has, for example, been studied in relation to sports activities (McInman and Grove, 1991; Jackson and Roberts, 1992). Peak performance can be defined as 'behavior which exceeds typical behavior' (Privette, 1983) or as 'an episode of superior functioning' (Privette 1983, cited in Thornton et al., 1999, p.254). Like immersion, peak performance requires strong focus and is high intensity. Privette (1983) argues that peak performance has strong similarities to both flow and peak experience. However, the emphasis on goal achievement and performance is stronger than in definitions of immersion.

The common feature of all these concepts is that they describe positive or even optimal human experiences. These experiences are subjective, affective and interpretive, and they vary across individuals and social situations. In addition, these experiences all stand out from ordinary life, and, thus, we notice them and can easily recall them for a long time. The presence of intense emotions allows these experiences to have significant meaning and value for the individual. According to Arnould and Price (1993), peak experience, peak performance, flow and extraordinary experiences are all examples of a special class of hedonic consumption activities. What these experiences have in common is that they

Table 11.2   Immersion compared to related concepts

Concept	Author(s)	Definition	Qualities shared with immersion
Extraordinary experiences	Arnould & Price, 1993	The provision of absorption and integration, personal control, joy and valuing, a spontaneous letting-be of the process, and a newness of perception and process (p. 41).	Absorption, integration, valuing, letting-be process
Peak experience	Maslow, 1967	Moments of great awe, intense happiness, even rapture, ecstasy or bliss – moments of pure, positive happiness when all doubts, all fears, all inhibitions, all weaknesses were left behind (p. 9).	Total attention, rich perception, unity of the world, fusion of dichotomies, ego transcendence, no consciousness of time and space, fusion of the individual
Flow	Csíkszentmihályi, 1990	The state in which people are so involved in an activity that nothing else seems to matter (p. 4).	The merging of action and awareness, concentration on the task at hand, loss of self-consciousness and transformation of time
Peak performance	Privette, 1983	Behavior that exceeds typical behavior (p. 1362).	Clear focus

are 'intense, positive, intrinsically enjoyable experiences' (Arnould and Price, 1993, p. 25) (Figure 11.2). Despite the overlapping descriptions of these phenomena, it appears that all of these concepts can be examined both in isolation and in combination with each other. Several authors have argued that these concepts are interconnected. Schouten et al. (2007) view both flow and peak experience as aspects of extraordinary experience. They argue that the interconnected aspects of peak experience and flow are important to consumers' relationship with and loyalty to brands and brand communities. In addition, Jackson et al. (2001, p. 130) claim that flow generally occurs in peak experiences. Privette compares the concepts of flow, peak experience and peak performance and concludes that the 'important attributes shared by all three include absorption, valuing, joy, spontaneity, a sense of power and personal identity and involvement' (Privette, 1983, p. 1361). She also concludes that peak experience appears to trigger peak performance and vice versa.

The different features of these concepts can also be observed. Extraordinary and peak experiences are described as effortless and spontaneous, whereas both flow and peak performance emerge from situations where individuals are using all of their abilities at the optimal level (for example, at work, in sports, in music). Therefore, a superior skill level and the task of mastering challenges add a level of focus to performance and goal orientation that is absent or not required in extraordinary and peak experiences. Flow and peak performances can also be planned to a certain degree and involve a strong internal drive to use one's own abilities to the fullest (Thornton et al., 1999). Csíkszentmihályi (1990) argues that even familiar and repetitive activities can facilitate flow as long as they have an element of personal growth and development. This characteristic makes flow different from extraordinary and peak experiences, which often require something out of the ordinary and an element of surprise (Mossberg, 2007) and thus can be difficult to predict or plan for. Peak experience and extraordinary experiences seem to have a stronger ability to transform people than flow and peak performance as they are normally understood. Peak performance is the only one of these concepts that does not involve loss of self. On the contrary, control, clear focus and a strong sense of self are important characteristics of peak performance.

One can argue that immersion is a pivotal part of all the above types of hedonic experiences. However, these concepts can also be regarded as different origins or types of immersion. Immersion during flow can be regarded as challenge-based immersion, where the focus and involvement are on the activity, whereas immersion during peak experience is effortless and is not necessarily oriented towards any specific activity. Immersion in situations with a performative focus is similar to peak performance, and the feeling of timelessness can be regarded as one of the characteristics of immersion. Therefore, we find the concept of immersion interesting and worth further investigation as a singular concept.

11.2.2   Underlying Foundations for Immersion

> Going places like Paris or Milan doesn't take me to another dimension . . . At Svalbard you are so in the wilderness and just taken out of your everyday life. That was one of the most exciting parts of it . . . For me it requires effort I think to get to that point of relaxation. If I just go and lay on a beach, I will still be thinking about work. (Female, 46 years, London)

What are the underlying foundations of immersion? Carù and Cova (2007) suggest that for consumers to become immersed, the experiential context must contain three interrelated qualities. More specifically, the context must be enclavized, secure and thematized (see also Firat and Dholakia, 1998). The concept of the enclavized context has been extensively discussed. In tourism, it has been argued that the destination is an extension of the tourist's home culture. The destination has thus been described as, for example, a 'home plus' (Theroux, 1986), a 'scene of dreams' (Shaw and Williams, 1994), a 'tourist bubble' (Smith, 1978), a 'tourist space' (Cohen, 1979), an 'enclave of familiarity' (Farrell, 1979), an 'activity enclave' (Graburn, 1978) and a 'creative space' (Richards and Wilson, 2006). When the context is enclavized with specific boundaries (a 'start' and 'stop'), the consumer is better able to contrast the experience with his or her daily life (Quan and Wang, 2004). The enclave also reduces the likelihood of elements that interfere with the experience, which, in turn, enhances its intensity (Firat and Dholakia, 1998).

A sense of security is paramount to focusing attention on the experience and eliminating distractions such as one's belongings, one's children or one's own behaviour (Carù and Cova, 2007). The same authors suggest that when consumers step outside the ordinary, they get 'into a separate world of enhancement where all the worries and hardships that they face in their ordinary lives disappear' (Carù and Cova, 2007, p.41). In the enclave, the consumers give up some control (Boswijk et al, 2007) and expect the commercial firm to take control instead (Jackson et al., 1996). The enclave provides safety in a strange place (Schuchat, 1983, p. 472) and is often thought of as risk free (Goulding et al., 2002, p. 281). The guides, the programme and the time schedule are factors that help the consumers to perceive themselves as having control, even though the environment is new, different from home and potentially dangerous. Safety, security, risk and fear are all important concerns (Larsen et al., 2011), and a vast number of studies (Roper et al., 2005; Wong and Wong, 2004; Ladwein, 2007) appear to agree that a guide can reduce risk and fear and increase participants' perceived safety and security.

The theme acts as symbolic packaging for the context (Carù and Cova, 2007, p. 41). It can also be regarded as a (re)constructed symbolic site or a dramaturgical space (Edensor, 2000). The theme communicates the relevant content and values to the consumer in an understandable, meaningful and memorable way. The consumption experience in a themed environment represents something different from consumers' everyday life and is designed to stimulate consumers' senses, to help them escape and to smooth meetings with other consumers.

'If I go somewhere where I am in an different environment to what I am used to – everything is new, so everything is interesting and everything makes you in the moment' (female, 38 years, London). This quotation from one of the tourists who participated in the dog sledging trip at Svalbard exemplifies the importance of the contrast between tourism and everyday life and the need to experience something extraordinary to become immersed in the experience. According to Arnould and Price (1993), ritual aspects such as rites of passage and rites of integration may assist in the transition between ordinary and extraordinary experiences and hence may help the consumer to become immersed. Rites of passage involve the process of separation, transition and reintegration, whereas rites of intensification increase the emotional intensity of the links between the persons sharing the experiences (Arnould and Price, 1993, p. 27). These rites are often associated with important life events such as birth, puberty, marriage and death, but, in principle, they may accompany any change from one state to another (Turner, 1987). Turner (1969) described leisure tourism as a liminoid situation because it is an activity with liminal attributes even though it lacks ritual associations (Gyimóthy and Mykletun, 2004). Jafari's tourist model (1987) emphasizes this transformational aspect of tourism but can in principle also be applicable to other experience contexts. Using a springboard metaphor, the model describes how the consumer (in this case, the tourist) leaves the ordinary world and leaps temporarily into the extraordinary liminal world before returning to the ordinary world again. This transformative process involves six stages: corporation (the need to get away from it all); emancipation (the distance from the ordinary world); animation (being immersed into 'touristhood'/the non-ordinary, including its spatial, temporal and cultural dimensions); repatriation (the return to the ordinary); incorporation (tourism subsumed in the ordinary mainstream); and omission (the ordinary current that flows despite the tourist's absence from home). A successful transformation into the 'bubble' may increase the likelihood of immersion.

Within the gaming literature, involvement is seen as a prerequisite for higher-order cognitive processes, such as presence or immersion, in much the same way that attention is a prerequisite of involvement (Calleja, 2011, p. 35). Focus is diverted from context and space to time and involvement as a pivotal foundation for immersion. It is insufficient to create a liminal virtual world in which to immerse; the gamer must be involved in the game as well. The same could be said about other consumer experiences. The consumer must be involved in the extraordinary liminal world. This requirement may partly explain why some consumers become immersed and others do not despite their participating in the same activity.

Another theory that focuses on the temporal aspects of immersion is the reversal theory within psychology. This theory claims that behaviour cannot be fully understood unless we understand the motive and personal meaning driving behaviour for the person who is performing it. The theory emphasizes the changeability of human nature and can be used to explain why we might behave differently at different times, even in the same situation. Reversal theory has been used in adventure tourism to explain emotions and behaviour (Gyimóthy and Mykletun, 2004; Mackenzie et al., 2011). The means/end domain is especially interesting within hedonic experiences, as is the transition in which the individual switches between the serious state (which is telic, goal and future oriented) and the playful state (which is paratelic, fun and arousal oriented, focused on enjoying the moment). It is the playful state that triggers immersion and physical or intellectual arousal. To be in the playful state, one must feel protected from danger. This perceived feeling of safety in potentially dangerous situations is called a protective frame (Gyimóthy and Mykletun, 2004). Risk, fear and penalties are removed from the setting, and the individuals feel free to participate in the activity, take the risk or engage in something novel.

Therefore, we can argue that fundamental elements of space and time are the underlying foundation for immersion. An enclaved, thematized and secure extraordinary context that represents a protective frame and a liminal world is essential to the spatial dimension. Likewise, deep involvement is argued to be pivotal to the temporal dimension of immersion. Like timelessness (Mainemelis, 2001), immersion requires the creation of a psychological and sometimes physical space (at least in tourism) in which one can become totally involved.

11.2.3   Facilitators for Immersion

> I guess it was a bit unexpected how attached I got to the dogs. I really did love my dogs by the end. I could have taken Franklin [one of her dogs] home if I was allowed . . . You were out there against the elements and these were like five little helpers that got you through that. (Female, 46 years, London)

Addis and Holbrook (2001) argue that consumption can be regarded as interaction and that interactions vary depending on the consumption context. As the quotation above indicates, bonding with the dogs became a significant and unexpected part of the trip. From a holistic and relational perspective, one can argue that individuals always have several relationships with the world around them (Hansen et al., 2011). Therefore, interactions and relations may be regarded as facilitating immersion. Different relationships constitute different sources of immersion, for example, relationships with nature, activities or animals. Mossberg (2007) has identified four major interactions that facilitate tourists' extraordinary experiences in the enclave, presenting an example of a relational model within the tourism context (Figure 11.1). These principles are also relevant to other contexts within the experience economy.

The tourist experience, which is regarded as differentiated from daily routines and daily consumption (with the enclave as an underlying foundation), can be understood

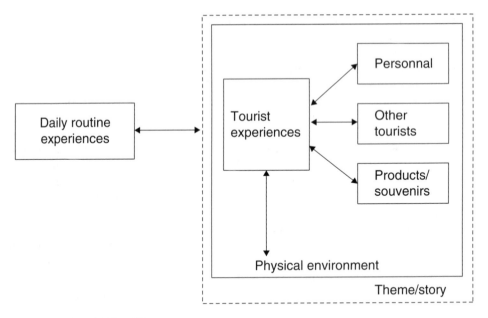

Source: Mossberg (2007, p. 65).

Figure 11.1   Factors influencing the consumer experience within the tourism context

as a combination of both supporting and peak consumer experiences (Quan and Wang, 2004). Peak consumption refers to the intensified use of time and funds during holidays, whereas supporting experiences are daily routines such as eating, sleeping and playing. The consumer experience must be understood holistically and in relation to the lived life of the consumer. This idea is consistent with Carù and Cova's discussion of the enclavized context. However, the borders around the enclave are often obvious in tourism, for example, in the case of an all-inclusive resort as compared to retail contexts such as shoe stores in the consumer's home environment. In the case of dog sledging, the activity had a clear beginning and end. The remoteness of Svalbard also created a contrast between that environment and the participants' urban everyday lives, and the participants were all novices at arctic dog sledging.

First, the physical environment is one of the main elements that facilitates the tourist experience. The physical environment includes the tourist's interaction with ambient conditions (for example, music, colour, lightning, odours), spatial layout and functionalities, as well as sign, symbols and artefacts. The physical environment can enhance the activities, promote socialization and differentiate the environment from other environments (Mossberg, 2007, p. 66). In nature-based tourist activities such as dog sledging, the participant's relationship with nature and his or her natural surroundings is essential. 'It is easier to become immersed in a landscape. I think it makes you feel small – it makes you realize that you are human scale. In London you never see the horizon . . . Svalbard made you feel very small and quite vulnerable' (female, 46 years, London).

Second, the effect of personnel is apparent in all service and consumer encounters and is well acknowledged in the strand of service management/marketing literature that focuses on the service encounter. The importance of guides in an activity-based tourist experience has long been recognized (Arnould and Price, 1993), but interactions with other personnel are also important and facilitate the consumer experience. In our example, the guides represented safety (for example, they wore rifles to protect the participants from potential polar bear attacks), knowledge (for example, of the environment, of dogs) and opportunities for socialization (through interaction with the guests).

> I think both of the guides were very good. They both got on very well with each other and they had excellent knowledge on nearly all subjects which we talked about, whether it'd be on the island or navigation and dog sledging or things to do with the stars and just being outdoors. So I think they showed a great, wide range of knowledge. (Male, 43 years, London)

It was obvious that no one in the group would have been able to manage the trip without the guides' assistance.

Third, the participants relate to other actors, whether human beings (for example, fellow participants, other consumers or locals) or even animals. Other consumers affect the experience both through direct interaction and as part of the audience, providing social interaction and positive aspects of togetherness. Social interaction can be both positive and negative. During some activities, the participants may bond in strong communitas during the experience (for example, Arnould and Price, 1993), whereas in other situations, participants with different personalities or mindsets may create social tension. Other consumers may also make the individual aware of his or her role as a consumer.

> We actually only saw one other tour group with dogs on the first day. People going to work on skidoos actually felt like you were part of Svalbard – this is what people do when they live here. If we had seen other tour groups, then I would have felt a bit more like being in a tourist environment. But it didn't feel like that because it was just us. (Female, 38 years, London)

Fourth, during consumption experiences, consumers relate to different products and physical objects, which will also have an effect on the experience. Such objects could include the sledge during dog sledging, the paddle during kayaking, the cutlery during meals or the souvenirs that tourists bring home as symbols of the experience. The participants' relationship to clothing was also important in the dog sledging example; for example, they experienced limited movement because they were wearing several layers of clothing or were able to keep warm because of their clothing. Some of the participants also deliberately turned off their mobile telephones because they represented a stressful connection to their everyday lives and thus a potential distraction.

> I was glad to turn my mobile phone off because I didn't want to take phone calls there. I remember [one of the other personnel] had a phone call in the middle of the dinner – and you're thinking 'I want to pretend that I am in this place where no one can . . . [laughter] you know, that I am on the edge of the Earth . . .'. (Female, 46 years, London)

Relationships that may facilitate immersion can also hinder immersion. Some relationships may become dominant and require an increasing share of the consumer's awareness, pushing other relationships to the background. One example from the Svalbard case is the influence of bodily needs such as the need for warmth, the need to use the bathroom or the need to eat, which sometimes prevented the participants from enjoying and focusing on their relationship to the beautiful landscape. Lack of information about the remaining distance also made them worry about when they would arrive at the cabin. Better information from the guides could have prevented this orientation towards the future, which hindered the participants' enjoyment of the experience and their immersion in the present moment.

Theories within the gaming literature also focus on relationships and interactions as facilitating immersion. The player involvement model (Calleja, 2011, p. 38) identifies six aspects of involvement: kinaesthetic involvement (all types of avatar or game piece control); spatial involvement (engagement with the spatial qualities of the virtual reality); shared involvement (awareness of and interaction with other agents in a game environment); narrative involvement (engagement with elements of the story); affective involvement (emotional engagement); and ludic involvement (engagement with choices and the repercussions of these choices within the game). All of these dimensions exist in relation to each other. They are experienced unconsciously during the interpretive and communicative process of playing the game and thus influence where attention is directed during different phases of the game-playing experience. Involvement is defined at two temporal levels: in the micro-involvement phase, which entails deep involvement during game play, and the macro-involvement phase, which includes offline thinking about playing and the player's ongoing motivation to interact with the game.

Therefore, one might argue that immersion is facilitated (or hampered) by individual relationships and interactions with the world. The relevant relationships will vary according to the context. We have presented two examples, one from a real-world tourism context and one from a virtual reality gaming context. Using this holistic and relational perspective, it is possible for providers to identify, discuss and pay special attention to the most relevant interactions associated with their products. Immersion can be facilitated through a focus on the multi-relational aspect of experiential design.

11.2.4   The Process of Becoming Immersed

> I think the first day I was focusing on holding on to the thing [sledge] and controlling it and not going off and hurt myself. But the second day I felt much more comfortable when we went on the really big, long 70 kilometre ride. And then, I felt absolutely part of nature. (Female, 46 years, London)

When do we become immersed? Are there different levels of intensity of immersion? How can the different phases of the consumer immersion process be described? Carù and Cova (2007) discuss whether immersion is immediate or progressive. They argue that this depends on the consumer's distance from the situation. Expert consumers, who possess the necessary skills and the most important knowledge about the theme and context, are able to dive straight into that context and become immediately immersed in it. Novice consumers, however, feel more distanced from the theme or context and must involve themselves in a process of appropriation to become immersed. The concept of the appropriation process is based on environmental psychology and consists of three stages, and where immersion only can be achieved during the deepest phase of involvement. Carù and Cova (2006) argue that consumers experience immersion through a complex combination of the three stages.

The first stage is called nesting and includes familiarity, comfort and group membership. Nesting is characterized by 'the consumer's perception of an array of physical and mental sensations and by the search for (and identification of) anchorage points' (Carù and Cova, 2005, p. 47). In this phase, the consumer feels at home, the context is sufficiently familiar and the consumer has sufficient control and comfort not to feel disoriented by the situation. The second stage is the investigation stage, in which the tourists feel the urge to extend their territory. 'Starting from the nest . . . the individual explores new elements in order to develop her/his points of anchorage and control (signposts)' (Carù and Cova, 2005, p. 44). The final stage is called stamping and involves consumer creativity and the attribution of meaning to the experience. Stamping is characterized by 'the relationship between the development of impressions about the situation being experienced and the meaning ascribed to it' (Carù and Cova, 2005, p. 49). According to the authors, it is in this stage that the consumer is in a position to truly access the experience, either in whole or in part, thereby becoming immersed.

The appropriation process is argued to have a cyclical dynamic in which one moves from nesting to investigating and then to stamping and back to nesting. This dynamic may progress during the experience based on the intensity of the various elements of the experience. In Carù and Cova's investigation of artistic experiences (more specifically, classical concerts), some of the participants struggled to connect with the experience (that is, to reach the stamping phase), and various distractions reverted the consumer back to the nesting phase. The research also reports that brief sequences of appropriation led to episodes of mini-immersion and that all moments characterized as immersion resulted in feelings of well-being, growth and gratification for the consumers.

Other theories involve some of the same concepts as the appropriation process. Varley (2011) argues that it is in periods of reflective tranquillity, after adventurous activities (such as sea kayaking as liminoid and transcendent experiences), satisfaction and deep meaning of activities can be experienced. Varley discusses the tension between Dionysian values (communitas, emotional expression, transcendence and bodily reinvigoration) and Apollonian values (comfort, predictability, security and planning). The richest experiences are lived in the liminal zones between these values. According to Varley, the notion of liminality is essential to adventure, as it creates a separation and a 'becoming other' (through a new environment or way of living or through new social norms). The Dionysian spirit emphasizes living in the present, the here and now and ecstatic communion (Varley, 2011, p. 94). Inspired by this approach, one could argue that the process of immersion may be viewed in connection with theories of liminality. Thereby, one might focus on the transition between everyday life and the phenomenon of 'becoming other' in the liminal spaces that the traveller temporarily visits during the experience (as well as the transformation back to everyday life). Furthermore, the transitions between different experiencescapes within the liminal world have an impact on the process of immersion.

It is important to consider whether immersion always implies strong emotional arousal or whether immersion may vary between high and low intensity in this respect. The most intense experiences must be relatively short given that 'our organisms have not been built to undergo intense, personality-shaking experiences all the time' (Carù and Cova, 2003, p. 277, referring to Schmitt, 1999). Can we move in and out of different levels of immersion intensity? Calleja (2011, p. 35) argues that 'the various forms of experience that make up involvement need to be considered on a continuum of attentional intensity rather than as a binary on/off switch'. We found indications of different levels of immersion intensity in our data from Svalbard. The informants reported short moments of intense immersion that resembled peak experience (for example, the effortless enjoyment of beautiful natural surroundings) and flow (for example, in managing challenging situations). They classified these moments as extraordinary experiences. 'I think it [moments of strong immersion] is rare, I mean I don't think you get them very often in your life at all' (female, 46 years, London). At the same time, they describe being involved and focused for the entire day while engaging in the activity. 'I thought it felt pretty intense all that day. It was definitely achieving my level of excitement for pretty much the entire day' (male, 49 years, London). These comments could be interpreted as encouraging a broader and more inclusive perspective on immersion and a means of becoming deeply involved in the present moment. Perhaps it is easier to become immersed in a physical activity such as dog sledging than in a physically passive activity such as attending a classical concert. More research should explore these aspects of the immersion process.

Individuals can move in and out of immersion, but how can this dynamic element of immersion be illustrated? Carù and Cova (2006) discuss a cyclical process in which immersion can only be experienced during the stamping phase and in which familiarity and sufficient control are important elements. Our empirical data from an extraordinary nature-based tourism context give us reason to question whether this assertion is valid for all experiential contexts. Several of the participants on the dog-sledging trip had actively sought an unfamiliar context that contrasted with their everyday lives and deliberately avoided pre-trip information because they felt that the novelty of the situation would enable them to be more focused and involved in the moment.

> It is just something I have never seen before, so it brings me right into that particular point in time. If it is something that is more familiar, then I don't take as much notice of it. I don't have to, because I already know what it's going to be like. (Female, 38 years, London)

This finding indicates that the need for appropriation may vary across contexts and that a lack of control may encourage immersion in contexts such as adventure tourism. Harnessing the dogs for the first time was challenging and unfamiliar and could thus be categorized as belonging to the nesting phase in the appropriation process. However, this step was described as a very intense activity in which visitors felt fully focused on the present moment and deeply involved in what they were doing: using no awareness to think about work-related problems or the time or to be self-conscious. As we have argued in this chapter, these are characteristics of immersion.

Another challenge that arises when we apply the appropriation process to some consumer experience contexts is the one-way cyclical movement assumed in the model. The stamping phase, in which immersion can occur, is followed by a return to the nesting phase. In the Svalbard case, we found that this was not the only possible progression. More intense phases of immersion were followed by less intense phases of deep involvement, indicating the possibility of moving from the stamping phase back to the investigation phase. However, we also observed situations in which the participants were 'thrown out of immersion'; their experience did transition from the stamping phase back to the nesting phase, and was more consistent with the typical appropriation process. One example from our tourist experience case occurred when we arrived at the cabin at night and the participants had to cope with unorganized sleeping arrangements.

> What you don't want is mundane things, like how many pillow cases there are, to encroach upon the romance and the excitement of being on the expedition. It brings you back down to earth, and you don't want to be. You still want to be in that slightly wild surreal space. (Male, 49 years, London)

This statement indicates that the dynamic process of becoming immersed may be more variable, with the participants moving into and out of immersion. In short, the process may be more flexible, complex and multifarious than the theory of the appropriation process suggests.

11.3 CONCLUSION

> To live in the moment, for the moment, is an amazing thing if you can find some way to do it ... I think this is one of my top five experiences for sure. Absolutely, yeah! Just staying in an extraordinary landscape, and I loved the bonding with the animals and experiencing of something that was just so different from my everyday life. (Female, 46 years, London)

Consumer immersion is an important concept within the experience economy, as it is often regarded as a key element of unforgettable consumer experiences. In Carù and Cova's study of classical music concerts (2007, p. 36), consumers identified brief moments of immersion that led to a feeling of well-being, growth and gratification, whereas not experiencing these short moments led to feelings of frustration or a lack of appreciation for the experience. The value of immersion is also clear within other consumer contexts, and immersion can be argued to be especially relevant within tourism as a type of peak consumption (Wang, 2002).

The underlying foundation for immersion can be found in the spatio-temporal dimensions of the consumer experience. A thematized, enclaved and secure context is necessary to create a small and manageable liminal world that contrasts with the consumer's everyday life and in which the consumer can more easily become immersed. Within the temporal dimension, deep involvement is a prerequisite for immersion. Involvement is facilitated through individuals' multiple, dynamic relationships to the world around them. We have argued that different relationships can facilitate immersion. The main relationships must be identified according to the specific context and experiencescape. However, in a holistic perspective, these relationships must be understood in relation to the individual's everyday life and not merely as a part of the current activity.

The underlying foundations for consumer immersion and the factors that facilitate that experience can be summarized in an integrated model based on Jafari (1987) and Mossberg (2007). The enclaved, thematized and secure context is related to what Jafari and others call the liminal world in the springboard metaphor. Consumption occurs within this 'bubble', which has an entry and exit in time and space. Inside the liminal world are facilitators who help (or hinder) consumer immersion. In our example, such facilitators include the personnel (that is, guides), other consumers (in this case, the other participants who engaged in the activity together for three days), the tangible products

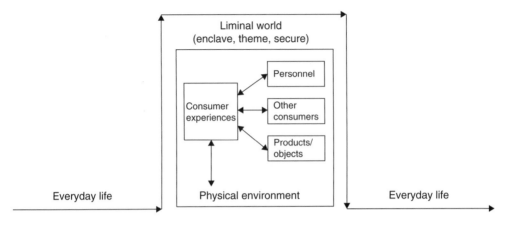

Figure 11.2   Underlying foundations and facilitators for immersion in a tourism context

involved in the experience (which, in this case, included sledges and warm clothing) and the physical environment (for example, the landscape, the weather and the cabin that served as the participants' accommodations). All of the activities were framed within a theme (arctic adventure and husky dog sledging). The contrast between this experience and the participants' everyday life is obvious, and the context is facilitated and ready for the consumer to 'dive in'. The consumers' everyday lives, interests and previous experiences both tacitly and explicitly influenced their relationships and thus their level of involvement and immersion. We believe this model to be generalizable to different consumer experience contexts (Figure 11.2).

The process of immersion appears to be dynamic and complex. The existing theory of appropriation as applied by Carù and Cova (2005) argues that the consumer must be comfortable with the situation to become immersed. An enclave and risk-free context provides the necessary conditions (a protective frame) in which the tourist can investigate, challenge, contrast and extend his or her territory, away from everyday life. This level of security and comfort is argued to be essential to the deepest level of involvement, in which travellers 'let themselves go' and become immersed. How rapidly this process occurs depends on the individual's emotional involvement, knowledge and skills as well as the length, type and interactive qualities of the activity. There may also be examples of alternative processes of immersion within other consumption contexts. Unfamiliarity and newness to a situation can prove stimulating and result in deep involvement and a total focus on the activity as a result of the consumer's experience coping with and mastering challenging situations. In addition, we argue that immersion should be seen as a continuum of attentional intensity that includes both short moments of high-intensity immersion and longer periods of less intensive immersion. More research in different experiential contexts will be needed to further illuminate the immersion process.

This study has been an attempt to explore the concept of consumer immersion. We argue that immersion is an important concept for us to consider if we wish to understand experience in general. Further research is needed to properly develop the theory on immersion. Both conceptual and empirical studies from different experiential contexts within the experience economy should be conducted. Methodological limitations and challenges should also be addressed, for example, the use of participant observation, several methods of empirical data gathering, different methods of data interpretation and different aspects of timing. We must keep in mind that it is difficult to study immersion directly during immersion itself because of the loss of self-consciousness that occurs during the experience (Mainemelis, 2001, p. 553).

We believe that this holistic approach to the analysis of immersion within consumer experiences has potential positive implications. A better understanding of the factors that facilitate immersion and the dynamic immersion process itself will enable companies that function within the experience economy to improve the experiences they offer. The organization and sequencing of different experiencescapes could, for example, be adjusted for different market segments to facilitate transformations and to optimize the experience. Elements that are believed to trigger immersion should be encouraged, and potential hindrances should be eliminated. Some experiencescapes have a greater potential for consumer immersion (for example, experiencescapes representing 'start', 'stop' or climax/peak) and should therefore be given special attention. More information about the customer's everyday life, skills and motivations may also be essential for us to understand the relational aspects of the customer's experience in a particular context. In addition to good planning, awareness and flexibility during the activity are vital facilitators of consumer immersion. We believe that the conscious application of the concept of immersion has the potential to enhance customer satisfaction and thus to increase corporate long-term profitability.

> One of the barometers to me of how good it was, was the fact that we didn't really see anything overly exciting apart from that ice cave. We didn't stay on the ship in the ice, we didn't see the Northern Lights – and yet I still think of it as a really remarkable experience. So despite the fact that actually on paper it doesn't seem that thrilling, it really was! (Male, 49 years, London)

ACKNOWLEDGEMENT

The chapter is written as part of the research project Northern InSights (www.opplevelserinord.no), which is partly financed by The Research Council of Norway.

REFERENCES

Abrahams, R.D. (1986), 'Ordinary and extraordinary experience', in V.W. Turner and E.M. Bruner (eds), *The Anthropology of Experience*, Urbana, IL: University of Illinois, pp. 45–72.
Abuhamdeh, S. and M. Csíkszentmihályi (2012), 'Attentional involvement and intrinsic motivation', *Motivation and Emotion*, **36** (3), 257–67.
Addis, M. and M.B. Holbrook (2001), 'On the conceptual link between mass customisation and experiential consumption: an explosion of subjectivity', *Journal of Consumer Behaviour*, **1** (1), 50–66.
Arnould, E.J. and L.L. Price (1993), 'River magic: extraordinary experiences and the extended service encounter', *Journal of Consumer Research*, **20** (1), 24–45.
Boswijk, A., J.P.T. Thijssen and E. Peelen (2007), *The Experience Economy: A New Perspective*, Amsterdam: Pearson Prentice Hall.
Brown, E. and P. Cairns (2004), 'A grounded investigation of game immersion', Paper presented at the CHI '04 Extended Abstracts on Human Factors in Computing Systems, Vienna, 24–29 April, pp. 1297–300.
Calleja, G. (2011), *In-game: From Immersion to Incorporation*, Cambridge, MA: MIT Press.

Carù, A. and B. Cova (2003), 'Revisiting consumption experience: a more humble but complete view of the concept', *Marketing Theory*, **3** (2), 267–86.

Carù, A. and B. Cova (2005), 'The impact of service elements on the artistic experience: the case of classical music concerts', *International Journal of Arts Management*, **7** (2), 39–54.

Carù, A. and B. Cova (2006), 'How to facilitate immersion in a consumption experience: appropriation operations and service elements', *Journal of Consumer Behaviour*, **5** (1), 4–16.

Carù, A. and B. Cova (2007), 'Consumer immersion in an experiential context', in A. Carù and B. Cova (eds), *Consuming Experience*, London: Routledge, pp. 34–47.

Cohen, E. (1979), 'Rethinking the sociology of tourism', *Annals of Tourism Research*, **6** (1), 18–35.

Csíkszentmihályi, M. (1990), *Flow: The Psychology of Optimal Experience*, New York: Harper Perennial.

Dewey, J. (1934), *Art as Experience*, New York: Perigee.

Edensor, T. (2000), 'Staging tourism: tourists as performers', *Annals of Tourism Research*, **27** (2), 322–44.

Farrell, B.H. (1979), 'Tourism's human conflicts: cases from the Pacific', *Annals of Tourism Research*, **6** (2), 122–36.

Firat, A.F. and N. Dholakia (1998), *Consuming People: From Political Economy to Theaters of Consumption*, London: Routledge.

Goulding, C., A. Shankar and R. Elliot (2002), 'Working weeks, rave weekends: identity fragmentation and the emergence of new communities', *Consumption, Markets and Culture*, **5** (4), 261–84.

Graburn, N.H.H. (eds) (1978), *Tourism: The Scared Journey*, Oxford: Basil Blackwell.

Gyimóthy, S. and R.J. Mykletun (2004), 'Play in adventure tourism: the case of Arctic trekking', *Annals of Tourism Research*, **31** (4), 855–78.

Hansen, A.H., F. Lindberg and D. Eide (2011), 'A multi-relational approach to the study of tourist experiences', Paper presented at the Advances in Hospitality and Tourism Marketing and Management Conference, Istanbul, 19–24 June, pp. 305–10.

Hirschman, E.C. and M.B. Holbrook (1982), 'Hedonic consumption: emerging concepts, methods and propositions', *Journal of Marketing*, **46** (3), 92–101.

Holbrook, M.B. (2000), 'The millennial consumer in the texts of our times: experience and entertainment', *Journal of Macromarketing*, **20** (2), 178–92.

Ijsselsteijn, W.A. and G. Riva (eds) (2003), *Being There: The Experience of Presence in Mediated Environments*, Amsterdam, IOS Press.

Jackson, M., G. White and C. Schmierer (1996), 'Tourism experiences within an attributional framework', *Annals of Tourism Research*, **23** (4), 798–810.

Jackson, S.A. and G.C. Roberts (1992), 'Positive performance states of athletes: toward a conceptual understanding of peak performance', *The Sport Psychologist*, **6** (2), 156–71.

Jackson, S.A., P.R. Thomas, H.W. Marsh and C.J. Smethurst (2001), 'Relationships between flow, self-concept, psychological skills, and performance', *Journal of Applied Sport Psychology*, **13** (2), 129–53.

Jafari, J. (1987), 'Tourism models: the sociocultural aspects', *Tourism Management*, **8** (2), 151–9.

Jennett, C., A.L. Cox, P. Cairns et al. (2008), 'Measuring and defining the experience of immersion in games', *International Journal of Human-Computer Studies*, **66** (9), 641–61.

Ladwein, R. (2007), 'Consumption experience, self-narrative, and self-identity: the example of trekking', in A. Carù and B. Cova (eds), *Consuming Experience*, London: Routledge, pp. 95–108.

Larsen, S., T. Øgaard and W. Brun (2011), 'Backpackers and mainstreamers: realities and myths', *Annals of Tourism Research*, **38** (2), 690–707.

Lipscombe, N. (1999), 'The relevance of the peak experience to continued skydiving participation: a qualitative approach to assessing motivations', *Leisure Studies*, **18** (4), 267–88.

Mackenzie, S.H., K. Hodge and M. Boyes (2011), 'Expanding the flow model in adventure activities: a reversal theory perspective', *Journal of Leisure Research*, **43** (4), 519–44.

Mainemelis, C. (2001), 'When the muse takes it all: a model for the experience of timelessness in organizations', *Academy of Management Review*, **26** (4), 548–65.

Maslow, A. (1964), *Religions, Values and Peak-experience*, Columbus, OH: Ohio State University Press.

Maslow, A. (1967), 'Lessons from the peak experience', *Journal of Humanistic Psychology*, **2**, Spring, 9–18.

May, R. (1994), *The Courage to Create*, New York: Norton.

McInman, A.D. and J.R. Grove (1991), 'Peak moments in sport: a literature review', *Quest*, **43** (3), 333–51.

Mossberg, L. (2007), 'A marketing approach to the tourist experience', *Scandinavian Journal of Hospitality and Tourism*, **7** (1), 59–74.

Pine, B.J. and J.H. Gilmore (1999), *The Experience Economy: Work is Theatre and Every Business a Stage*, Boston, MA: Harvard Business School Press.

Pöppel, E. (1988), *Mindworks: Time and Conscious Experience*, trans. T. Artin, Orlando, FL: Harcourt Brace Jovanovich.

Privette, G. (1983), 'Peak experience, peak performance, and flow: a comparative analysis of positive human experiences', *Journal of Personality and Social Psychology*, **45** (6), 1361–8.

Quan, S. and N. Wang (2004), 'Towards a structural model of the tourist experience: an illustration from food experiences in tourism', *Tourism Management*, **25** (3), 297–305.

Richards, G. and J. Wilson (2006), 'Developing creativity in tourist experiences: a solution to serial reproduction of culture?', *Tourism Management*, **27** (6), 1209–23.

Roper, A., Ø. Jensen and R.-H. Jegervatn (2005), 'The dynamics of the Norwegian package tour industry', *Scandinavian Journal of Hospitality and Tourism*, **5** (3), 193–211.

Schmitt, B.H. (1999), *Experiential Marketing: How to Get Customers to Sense, Feel, Think, Act and Relate to Your Company and Brands*, New York: Free Press.

Schouten, J.W., J.H. McAlexander and H.F. Koenig (2007), 'Transcendent customer experience and brand community', *Journal of the Academy of Marketing Science*, **35** (3), 357–68.

Schuchat, M.G. (1983), 'Comfort of group tours', *Annals of Tourism Research*, **10** (4), 465–77.

Shaw, G. and A.M. Williams (1994), *Critical Issues in Tourism: A Geographical Perspective*, London and New York: Routledge.

Slater, M. and S. Wilbur (1997), 'A framework for immersive virtual environments (FIVE): speculations on the role of presence in virtual environments', *Presence Teleoperators and Virtual Environments*, **6** (6), 603–16.

Smith, V.L. (1978), *Hosts and Guests: The Anthropology of Tourism*, Oxford: Basil Blackwell.

Theroux, P. (1986), *Sunrise with Seamonsters, Travels and Discoveries 1964–1984*, Harmondsworth, UK: Penguin.

Thornton, F., G. Privette and C.M. Bundrick (1999), 'Peak performance of business leaders: an experience parallel to self-actualization theory', *Journal of Business and Psychology*, **14** (2), 253–64.

Turner, V.W. (1969), *The Ritual Process*, Chicago, IL: Aldine.

Turner, V.W. (1987), 'Betwixt and between: the liminal period in rites of passage', in L.C. Mahdi, S. Foster and M. Little (eds), *Betwixt and Between: Patterns of Masculine and Feminine Initiation*, La Salle, IL: Open Court Publishing Company, pp. 3–19.

Varley, P.J. (2011), 'Sea kayakers at the margins: the liminoid character of contemporary adventures', *Leisure Studies*, **30** (1), 85–98.

Wang, N. (2002), 'The tourist as a peak consumer', in G.M.S. Dann (ed.), *The Tourist as a Metaphor of the Social World*, Cambridge, MA: CABI Publishing, pp. 281–95.

Witmer, B.G. and M.J. Singer (1998), 'Measuring presence in virtual environments: a presence questionnaire', *Presence*, **7** (3), 225–40.

Wong, C.-K.S. and W.Y.Y. Wong (2004), 'Outbound tourists' selection for choosing all-inclusive package tours', *Tourism Management*, **25** (5), 581–92.

12. Innovation in the experience sector

Jon Sundbo, Flemming Sørensen and Lars Fuglsang

12.1 INTRODUCTION

We might suppose that innovation in the experience sector is as important as in any other but that the sector has its own innovation logic. However, given the newness of the topic little research has been undertaken in this area. This chapter presents the first investigation of innovation in the experience sector that is based on a general survey.

When the service sector was discovered as a specific phenomenon (for example, Gadrey et al., 1993; Sundbo, 1998; Gallouj, 2002), the question of whether this newly defined sector innovates and whether it does so in the same way as the old sector became relevant (for example, does the service sector innovate in the same way as the manufacturing sector?). When we investigate the experience sector, we may ask the same questions: do experience firms innovate and, if so, do they do so in the same way as service and manufacturing firms? To answer these questions requires comprehensive research that must be carried out in the future. However, we might start our investigation by asking how much firms in the experience sector innovate compared to other sectors, and if the characteristics of innovation are similar to or different from those of other sectors. This implies that we need to engage in methodological considerations about whether or not it is possible to measure innovation in the same way in the experience sectors as in other sectors and, thus, if comparisons between sectors can be made. In the service innovation literature it has, for example, been debated as to whether or not innovations in services share characteristics with innovations in manufacturing or if they are fundamentally different (for example, Toivonen and Tuominen, 2009; Fuglsang and Sørensen, 2011).

Thus, the purpose of the chapter is to discuss the questions: Are experience firms innovative in comparison with firms in other sectors? Is innovation in experiences different from that in (other) services? And can innovation in experiences be measured in the same way as has been done in (other) services? It is important to answer these questions if we want to understand experience production in a business perspective and include experience industries in innovation policies. These questions are also relevant if we want to develop theories about innovation in experience industries and firms.

In order to seek answers to the research questions, this chapter presents a statistical survey-based explorative investigation on innovation in the experience sector. The survey was carried out in Denmark in 2007. The survey can in some respects be compared to the European Community Innovation Surveys (CIS) (Eurostat, 2004) as several questions from the CIS survey were included in the Danish survey with a view to enabling comparisons between the experience and the service and manufacturing sectors.

In the following we first discuss, theoretically, different issues concerning innovation in the experience sector. This is followed by a description of the method applied in the investigation after which the findings of the analysis are presented. Finally, in the conclusion, the main results of the investigation are emphasized and new theoretical issues arising from the findings are discussed.

12.2 THEORETICAL FRAMEWORK

Before we investigate the research questions empirically, we will discuss a theoretical framework, or state-of-the-art, for understanding the character of experience innovations, and an evaluative framework for understanding the empirical results from the survey.

When we discuss innovation in the experience sector, it is important to distinguish between creativity and innovation. Creativity has often been connected to art, culture and other activities that can be included in the experience sector. Thus, the experience sector and creative industries have often been considered particularly creative. This issue opens an important theoretical and empirical field about what creativity is and how more creative experience sub-sectors, the so-called creative industries, are compared to other industries. A comprehensive literature discusses these questions (for example, Amabile, 1996; Sternberg, 1999; Jeffcut and Pratt, 2002; Weisberg, 2006; Gahan et al., 2007; Rickards et al., 2009). The outcome of the discussion is that creativity is, of course, a complex phenomenon. Arts and culture are often based on creativity, but creativity is also important in other sectors, for example, high-tech manufacturing sectors where creative problem-solution is a precondition for the innovation of new, usable technologies. Creativity may be a feature of innovation, but innovation is not the same as creativity. It involves additional factors. Innovation can be defined as the realization of a business idea, that is, one that either introduces a product that is accepted by the market or a process or market innovation that increases productivity and thus gives the firm a better position in terms of price competition or which improves the firm's market position (Tidd et al., 1997). Innovation may also be defined more broadly as the realization of an idea. Innovation, even if it is not narrowly defined as a business activity, is about having other people accept and use the idea (or the product, process or market behaviour), not to create the idea. Innovation does not need the innovator to be creative. He or she can imitate other peoples' ideas. Thus, creativity and innovation must be seen as two different phenomena even though they are often connected. Creativity in itself does not create business or solve peoples' problems, but innovation does. In this analysis we focus on innovation, not creativity, but accept that creativity may be an important factor influencing innovation in the experience sector.

As mentioned, a parallel can be drawn between the current theoretical situation concerning the explanation of experience innovation and the attempt to theorize service innovations. This was also a new field 20 years ago. Within the last two decades research has tried to describe the specificities of innovation in services (for example, Gadrey et al., 1993; Andersen et al., 2000; Sundbo, 2001; van den Aa and Elfring, 2002; Gallouj, 2002; Tidd and Hull, 2005; Gallouj and Djellal, 2010), and several empirical studies of innovation in services have been conducted (for example, Brentani, 1993; Gadrey et al., 1993, Finch et al., 1994; Sundbo, 1996, 1998; Evangelista and Sirilli, 1998; Gallouj, 2000, 2002; Vermeulen, 2001; Fuglsang, 2002; Howells, 2004; INNO-Studies, 2004; Hipp and Grupp, 2005).

As a consequence of this work, an understanding of the special character of service innovation has emerged. Innovations in services are often small improvements integrated in day-to-day work. The innovation process in services is generally very interactive involving many managers and employees. It involves both employee bottom-up and top-down strategy-making (Sundbo, 1996). The latter means that a firm's strategy is a guideline for as well as a limit to innovations. Service innovations are rarely research and development (R&D) based. By contrast, they are often market or customer based. The outcome of service innovation is often 'fuzzy' and can be hidden in service delivery (Toivonen and Tuominen, 2009). Furthermore, generally speaking, service innovations seem less technology-driven than manufacturing innovations (Sundbo 1996; van den Aa and Elfring, 2002). However, information and communications technology (ICT) is an exception that becomes increasingly important to service innovations (Evangelista and Sirilli, 1998). Additionally, service companies' innovations are more often based on organizational cooperation than in manufacturing (Tether and Tajar, 2008).

Service innovation research has also stated that the different categories of innovation that studies of manufacturing have revealed can also be applied to services (Sundbo, 1998; van den Aa and Elfring, 2002; Drejer, 2004; Gallouj and Djellal, 2010). These categories include product, process, organizational and market innovation as well as radical and incremental innovation. One may assume that these categories are also applicable to the experience sector (cf. Sundbo, 2009; Fuglsang et al., 2011). However, innovation in experiences has not been investigated generally, only partially. For example, innovation in tourism including hospitality (hotels and restaurants) has been investigated and discussed in theoretical terms, albeit to a limited extent (for example, Sundbo et al., 2007; Hall and Williams, 2008; Martinez-Ros and Orfila-Sintes, 2009; Hjalager, 2010; Hjalager and Nordin, 2011). Entrepreneurship in tourism has also been investigated and theorized (Shaw and Williams, 1994, Mattsson et al., 2005; Ateljevic and Page, 2009), but even that has been limited. An emerging literature of innovation in design and architecture (Verganti, 2009; Hobday et al., 2011, 2012) is mostly normative and attempts to provide usable tools for innovation activities, including other sectors (for example, information technology (IT)-based services, such as Yoon et al., 2012). Some experience industries are included in analyses of service innovation, however, it varies as to which and they are often not separated out in the results. Furthermore, some innovation studies have focused on creative industries, however, this is not a large field, and it is primarily based on case studies (for example, Sunley et al., 2008; Cunningham, 2011) or are policy-oriented (for example, Innovation-Management Policy and Practice, 2009). It has been argued that the creative and culture industries are important because they feed other industries with basic experience innovations (Bakhshi and Throsby, 2009), but not that much innovation in creative industries is, for different reasons, included in innovation statistics or in general innovation surveys, thus the innovation rate in creative industries is underestimated (Miles and Green, 2008).

Of the few investigations of innovation in experiences one article emphasizes experience innovation as a situated process that is partly open (cf. Chesbrough, 2006), and partly closed (Fuglsang et al., 2011). The closed aspect in manufacturing is internal R&D (for example, Freeman and Soete, 1997). In arts and similar creative industries the closed innovation process may be said to be the artistic creative activity. In some case studies it is emphasized that culture producers consider the innovation process push-oriented and closed (Sundbo and Hagedorn-Rasmussen, 2008). The artists' ideas are considered the input to the process compared to R&D in manufacturing innovation. Innovating experience organizations can be placed in different categories depending on the character and aim of the organization (Sundbo, 2009).

Entrepreneurship in experience industries has been treated in some literature (Andersson and Andersson, 2006; Henry, 2007; Hjort and Kostera, 2007; Sundbo, 2011), but only qualitatively. The degree and character of entrepreneurship specifically relating to experiences has not been measured in surveys or statistics. The literature shows that entrepreneurship defined as the establishment of businesses based on innovative ideas is as common in experience industries as in other industries. Even artists are often good innovators, meaning that they can realize their creative ideas as business projects (Sundbo, 2011). The so-called creative industries have an advantage in their tradition for artistic creativity, but that does not in itself create business and innovation.

Thus, studies on innovation in experiences constitute a highly fragmented and immature research area and no particular theory or even theory discussion exists about experience innovation. Generally, one may assume that innovation in the experience sector is carried out in the same way as in services. Both result from people-intensive processes that provide an immaterial product. Experiences have until recently been considered part of the service sector and innovation treated just as other service innovation. However, the theoretical discussion of service innovation suggests that service innovation uses the same theories as manufacturing innovation, but has specific characteristics. It might be that experience innovation should be considered the same way compared to service innovation. However, as argued, creativity may be a special factor affecting experience innovation. Furthermore, one might argue that technology, particularly IT, is more important in experiences than in services. Much experience is currently produced and provided via IT networks such as the Internet and mobile phones. This might suggest that technology and technological innovation, or at least software, R&D is more important in experiences than in services. Experience innovation thus might be closer to the manufacturing technology laboratory and R&D than we have observed in services generally.

Consequently, we are left with a number of unanswered questions, or theoretical assumptions, about the character of innovations and innovation processes in experiences. For example, it remains unclear whether or not the description of services as customer-driven, interactive and strategic apply to the experience sector and if there are further particularities of experience innovation that need to be taken into account. In our research we start to investigate and theorize this. As the research referred to in this chapter is groundbreaking, we seek to answer our research questions in a mainly explorative manner by presenting the results from the survey of experience firms, and in the concluding section of the chapter we discuss the general theoretical perspectives of the results.

12.3 METHOD

The survey on which this chapter is based investigates innovation in the primary experience sector, that is, firms that have the production of experiences as their core activity.

These firms have never been studied separately in innovation surveys and therefore we do not know much about their innovation activities, except from case studies. There is no authorized and generally accepted definition of the primary experience sector. Here, we have applied a definition that has been used in an investigation of the Danish experience sector made by the Danish Ministry of Industry (Erhvervs- og byggestyrelsen, 2008). The primary experience sector as defined here includes, for example, restaurants, travel agencies, publishers of discs and CDs, cinemas, theatres, amusement parks and museums (see Appendix). The primary experience sector has earlier been considered part of the service sector; however, Pine and Gilmore (1999) have defined it as a sector of its own. The Danish primary experience sector contributed 10.4 per cent of the total value added in Denmark in 2006. In 2008 this had increased to 11.8 per cent (Erhvervs- og byggestyrelsen and Centre for Culture and Experience Economy, 2011). It contributed more to the total value added in Denmark than in most other European countries and its productivity was also higher in 2008 than in most European countries. In 2006 10 per cent of all jobs were in the primary experience sector, which is about average for European countries. The 'secondary experience sector' – including firms where experiences is a side-activity, or add-ons to goods or services – was not included in the survey since it requires a different methodology to measure innovation in the secondary sector where experience innovation is only a smaller part of service or goods innovation and often is integrated in these. Innovation in the secondary experience sector should be investigated in future research to get a full picture of the experience innovation pattern. However, in this first investigation of innovation in the experience sector we limit ourselves to analysing innovation in the primary experience sector.

The web-based survey on which this chapter is based was carried out in Denmark in autumn 2007. A population of all firms in Danish experience industries with at least one employee and with an e-mail address was contacted by e-mail and invited to answer the questionnaire. Firms without employees were excluded because many of these are not really firms, but only small side-businesses or hobbies where people for some reason have been registered as a firm. This delimitation compares to the one of the Danish CIS, thus we can compare our results with results from that survey. The survey population included 4500 firms out of a total population of 14000 firms in the selected industries. The response rate was 29 thus 1315 firms are included in the population that is analysed. This response rate is normal for surveys to firms and therefore may be thought satisfactory.

The representativeness of the population (the 1315 responding firms) in relation to the total population of 14000 firms has been analysed. The analysis shows that tourist firms are slightly under-represented while firms within design, image and branding are slightly over-represented. Small firms with less than five employees are under-represented (50 per cent of the analysed population while they are 68 per cent of the total population). This must be kept in mind when the results are interpreted. The bias of the sample is not very serious; however, it might lead to a slight overestimation of innovation, since large experience firms are more often innovative than small ones. Besides this, the selected population is representative for the total population. On that basis we find that the results are sufficiently valid to be used for a general analysis of innovation tendencies in the Danish experience sector.

The results of the Danish survey about innovation tendencies in the primary experience sector are compared to the results of the European CIS surveys about innovation tendencies in services and industry (manufacturing) to assess whether the level of innovation in the experience sector is high or low. The CIS surveys, carried out by Eurostat and national agents (Dansk center for forskningsanalyse, 2004, 2006; Eurostat, 2004), provide representative results on innovation tendencies in industry and, for recent years, also services. In particular, we compare our results to the Danish CIS results to eliminate national variations. Additionally, we also compare them to European results.

The following analysis focuses particularly on comparing the innovativeness of experience firms (and of firms in different experience sub-sectors) with the innovativeness of firms in other sectors and discusses the importance for innovation of different sources, technology, firm size, innovation barriers and the nature of experiences. In this way the analysis offers knowledge about some of the unanswered questions concerning innovation in experience firms that the theoretical discussion above emphasized, for example, whether or not the description of services as customer-driven, interactive and strategic applies to the experience sector and if there are further particularities of experience innovation that need to be taken into account.

12.4   INNOVATION IN THE DANISH EXPERIENCE SECTOR COMPARED TO OTHER SECTORS

In both our survey and the CIS surveys innovation has been measured in a simple way by asking if the firm has innovated within a two-year period. In our survey of the experience sector we have asked about product and process innovations. We have compared our findings to the CIS results about these two forms of innovation. However, the results concern different time periods. Further, the CIS surveys distinguish between innovation activities and successful innovators. The latter are firms with product innovations that have been successfully launched on the market or process innovations that have been implemented. In our survey of experience firms we have only asked about innovation activities. This makes comparison more complicated. However, the differences between firms with innovation activities and firms that are successful innovators are not large. For example, 44 per cent of all firms in Europe have undertaken innovation activities in the period 1998–2000 while 41 per cent were successful innovators (Eurostat, 2004, p. 18).

In Table 12.1 we compare the type of innovation (product and process) between sectors. The results are not completely comparable because the CIS results concern successful innovators while we measure innovation activities, but we may assume that the differences are very small (see the statement above).

According to this comparison, the experience sector is clearly more innovative than other sectors. In particular, experience firms combine product and process innovations to a greater extent. As said, different time periods are compared and thus should be taken into consideration when making conclusions.

However, variations of the innovativeness of different experience sub-sectors can be expected. One hypothesis could be that a creative, and perhaps a particular, entrepreneurial spirit in the experience sector leads to more innovation. Another might be that the management of innovation and entrepreneurship in experience firms has not been

Table 12.1   Firms with innovation (percentages)

	Our survey Denmark experience 2004–06	CIS3 Europa All firms 1998–2000	CIS3 Denmark All firms 1998–2000	CIS3 Europe industry 1998–2000	CIS3 Denmark industry 1998–2000	CIS3 Europe services 1998–2000	CIS3 Denmark services 1998–2000
Firms that have innovation activities	69	44	44	47	52	40	37
Succesful innovators	n.a.	41	42	44	49	36	34
Only product innovation	16	10	16	10	18	11	14
Only process innovation	9	7	5	8	6	5	5
Product and process innovation	44	23	21	25	26	20	16

Source: Eurostat (2004) and authors' own results.

Table 12.2   Innovation in experience sub-sectors Denmark. Percentage of firms that had innovated 2004–06

Sub-sector	Have had innovation activities
Tourism	68
Art and culture	73
Entertainment and leisure	78
Design, image and branding	59
Total	69

Source: Authors' own results.

very professional (dominated by artistic non-business orientation) and is less oriented towards innovation than in other sectors. These two hypotheses could be investigated by looking at different sub-sectors within the experience sector.

Table 12.2 compares the innovation activity in different experience sub-sectors based on the results of our survey.

The different sub-sectors have different levels of innovation activities. Entertainment and leisure (sports, amusement parks, museums, fair organizers and so forth) is the most innovative sub-sector and design, image and branding the least. This might seem a little surprising since entertainment and leisure might not traditionally have been considered the most creative sub-sector. However, this sector has probably been the most business-oriented including large communication, movie and TV corporations. It has therefore probably been influenced by a more systematic industrial approach to innovation. More surprisingly, art and culture is number two in terms of innovativeness. These results do not support the second hypotheses of artists and cultural institutions as absent-minded and not business-oriented, neither do they support the first hypothesis that creative people per se leads to innovation. The least innovative sub-sector, design, image and branding might, on the other hand, traditionally have been considered *the* creative part of traditional manufacturing. This result again supports the conclusion that creativity per se neither leads to innovation nor is a barrier to it.

Tourism is placed in the middle, which reflects that this sector has traditionally not been very innovative, but innovations in this sector are increasing.

12.5 SOURCES OF INNOVATION

A central issue in innovation research is where the innovation ideas come from and who develops the innovation. In particular, questions concerning whether or not ideas come from 'in-house' activities or if they arise in collaboration with external partners have become relevant because of the discussions of open versus closed innovation (Chesbrough, 2006) within services. In Table 12.3 we look at the main sources of innovation in the primary experience sector. This source analysis is related to the theoretical discussion of artistic or some other particular experience creativity as something special to the experience sector. We have not measured creativity specifically, but employees as a source of innovation may express a creativity factor.

The table indicates that employees and their creativity are an important source of innovation and may be considered a push phenomenon, but management is a slightly more important source of innovation. This result shows that experience innovation is at least as much top-steered and strategic as it is based on an artistic or another type of creativity. Even customers or users are an important source of innovation, thus experience innovation often seems to be market- or pull-oriented. Also, other external sources are important, however to a lesser degree. The pattern of innovation sources within experience innovation is similar to that in manufacturing and services (Eurostat, 2004; Dansk

Table 12.3   Main sources of innovation in the experience sector. The main source to a high degree/to some degree

	Per cent
Management	97
Employees	90
Customers or users	77
Suppliers of technology and services	55
Other companies	44
Journals, newspapers, TV	42
Expositions, conferences	35
Consultants	27
Universities and educational institutions	17
Industrial organizations or trade unions	13

Source: Authors' own results.

Table 12.4   Primary developer of product and process innovations. CIS and the experience sector distributed according to primary developer of product and process innovation (percentages)

	Product innovation		Process innovation	
	CIS	Experience firms	CIS	Experience firms
Primarily the company	73	64	60	63
Primarily the company in collaboration with other companies or institutions	22	32	30	33
Primarily other companies or institutions	5	4	10	4
Total	100	100	100	100

Source: Dansk center for forskningsanalyse (2006) and authors' own results

center for forskningsanalyse, 2006), thus the experience sector does not in that respect seem to present special features.

Table 12.4 compares who the primary developers of product and process innovation are and thus how important cooperation with other actors is for innovation. Here it is seen that the pattern in the experience sector, generally, is similar to other industries. However, in the case of product innovations experience companies collaborate more with other companies, which indicates that networking and open innovation is important for experience companies' product innovation activities.

12.6   INNOVATION DETERMINANTS

A few determinants for new products or processes have been much emphasized in the quantitative research of innovation in services (for example, SIC, 1999; Djellal and Gallouj, 2001; Drejer, 2004; Eurostat, 2004). These are characteristics that are special to service firms compared to manufacturing ones or are those that correlate most with the degree of innovation. When we now enter the experience sector, which in many respects is close to the services sector, it is natural to see if the same characteristics are central to understanding innovation in the experience sector. In this section we shall emphasize a few of these main characteristics as well as some characteristics that are supposed to be special to experiences.

12.6.1   Technology-enabled Innovation

In contrast to manufacturing innovations, service innovations are rarely technological (Sundbo, 1998; Gallouj, 2002; INNO-Studies, 2004). However, service innovations seem to increasingly become technological, or technology enabled, particularly because of the increased use of ICT (Miozzo and Soete, 2001; INNO-Studies, 2004). Experience firms have also traditionally been characterized as (for example, art and sport) being technological only to a limited extent, but they are becoming more enabled by new technological

Table 12.5   ICT and innovation. Firms with different uses of ICT distributed according to whether they have innovation activities (percentages)

Has innovation activities	Use of IT			
	Not at all	Not very many	To some degree	Very many
No	47	45	28	24
Yes	53	55	72	76
Total	100	100	100	100

Source: Authors' own results.

Table 12.6   Enterprise size and innovation. Percentage of enterprises that have introduced product and/or process innovations

Size: number of employees	Our survey* Denmark experience 2004–06	Size: number of employees	CIS4 Denmark All firms 2002–04	Size: number of employees	CIS3 Europe industry 1998–2000	CIS3 Europe services 1998–2000
2–9	66	2–9	38			
10–49	73	10–49	43	10–49	40	36
50+	86	50–249	47	50–249	63	54
		250–999	64	250+	80	69
		1000+	68			

Note: * Only enterprises with two and more employees included.

Source: Eurostat (2004 figure 2.1.2), Dansk center for forskningsanalyse (2006, table 2b) and authors' own results.

innovations, particularly as ICT presents possibilities for providing experiences on the Internet, mobile phones and so on. According to the survey results, technology is apparently important for experiences, particularly ICT, but also other types of technology. ICT has some or much importance for about 80 per cent of the experience firms, and other technology has some or much importance for about 65 per cent. One may presume that this is reflected in the product and process innovations in experiences, which thus may be assumed to be rather technological or at least based on technology. Table 12.5 indicates how experience companies to whom the use of ICT is important are also more innovative than those companies to whom the use of ICT is of less importance. Thus, ICT is of importance in experience firms and ICT is intertwined with innovation in such firms.

12.6.2   Enterprise Size

The size of enterprises is the factor that most clearly correlates with innovation in services (SIC, 1999). The CIS surveys also demonstrate a correlation between size and innovativeness in service and industry. In Table 12.6 we have compared our results about innovation in the Danish experience sector with the CIS results about services and industry.

Table 12.7   Characteristics (entertaining, learning, improve social gathering) of
experience products distributed according to whether the firms have
innovation activities or not (percentages)

Has innovation activities	Characteristics	
	All three aspects, completely or partly agree	None or only some of the three aspects, completely or partly agree
No	19	40
Yes	81	60
Total	100	100

Source: Authors' own results.

The different surveys have slightly different categories concerning size, however, the trends may be compared in Table 12.6. For all sectors it is clear that the larger the enterprise is, the more innovative it tends to be and experience firms are no exception.

12.6.3   Types of Experience

In the discussion of experiences there has been a focus on the nature of experiences: whether they are always entertaining or can also be educational (Pine and Gilmore, 1999; Sundbo and Darmer, 2008). Some experiences (for example, rock festivals; Sundbo, 2004) seem – although they have one obvious aim (for example, music) – in reality to satisfy the social need to get together. This factor concerns the aim of new experience products – which types of customer need they should satisfy. In the survey we asked what characterizes the firms' experience products: 61 per cent of the firms said they are entertaining, 65 per cent that they promote learning and 75 per cent that they improve social gathering. In Table 12.7 the characteristics of experience products of experience firms that are innovative are compared to those that are not innovative.

The survey data indicate that experience products are generally entertaining, learning and support social gathering. The last factor seems to be the most important. This result suggests that experience products are complex and must satisfy several of the customers' needs. This multi-dimensionality of experiences must be taken into consideration when one innovates new products. The strong emphasis on the products' social tasks should particularly be kept in mind when firms develop new ICT media-based experiences such as computer games, TV series and amusement products for mobile phones. Furthermore, Table 12.7 indicates how experience firms whose products are more complex and satisfy more needs are also more innovative experience firms. Thus, this is a particular aspect of experiences that influences and can explain the innovativeness of experience firms.

12.6.4   Innovation Barriers

Barriers to innovation are often emphasized in innovation research. If one wants to enhance innovation activities, it is important to know the barriers. Table 12.8 compares the barriers in the primary experience sector with those found in other business sectors.

Table 12.8   Innovation barriers. CIS and the experience sector distributed according to innovation barriers with great importance for the company's innovation activities (percentages)

	Innovation barriers	CIS	Experience firms
Cost factors	Lack of external financing	9	21
	Too high innovation costs	8	28
Knowledge factors	Lack of qualified personnel	5	22
	Lack of information about technology	3	3
	Lack of information about market	2	5
Market factors	Market is dominated by other companies	8	6
	Uncertainty about demand	9	7

Source: Dansk center for forskningsanalyse (2006) and authors' own results.

Financial matters such as high costs of innovation activities and difficulties in procuring investment capital are a much larger barrier in experience innovation than in business in general. This result can be supported by preliminary case studies that we have done that show that many venture capitalists have difficulties in assessing experience innovation processes because they have no experience with these. They therefore tend to decide not to take the risk associated with financing experience innovation projects. This is an important result to be taken into consideration in policies. Furthermore, lack of qualified personnel is a significant barrier to innovation. From other case studies we know that this factor particularly has an effect in tourism and other experience industries not characterized by a high degree of artistic, creative employees or academics.

12.7   CONCLUSION AND THEORETICAL DISCUSSION

12.7.1   Conclusion of the Empirical Study

Experience firms are very innovative. Their innovation rate is significantly above other sectors. The innovations are more often new to the market. The experience sector is not only populated with creative and artistic people that develop ideas, the enterprises also have the ability to transform the creative ideas into business projects. This survey demonstrates that experience firms are fully able to innovate in terms of launching new products on the market or implementing process changes in the organization. The innovation capability (Teece and Pisano, 1994) of experience firms seems to generally be higher than that of service and manufacturing firms.

The innovation rate varies between different experience industries. Entertainment and leisure has the highest innovation rate, which may be explained given this sector has always been the most business-oriented and includes large communication, movie and TV corporations. Design, image and branding is the least innovative experience industry. This sector is the one that is closest to the manufacturing and service sectors and the secondary experience sector (see Chapter 1). It is of little surprise that it is the least innovative industry, but this might be explained by the fact that it is a mature industry that maybe faces a need for radical changes in the way of thinking and its core products in the future.

The characteristics of the innovations and of innovative experience firms are similar to those found in services (and to a large degree in manufacturing). Large firms are more innovative than small ones and experience firms introduce product and process innovation as much as service and manufacturing firms. Furthermore, experience firms often introduce combined product and process innovations, which suggests that experience firms are similar to services in that the production and delivery process is difficult to separate from the product. Exceptions to these similarities are that experience firms collaborate more with external partners and that the difficulties in getting venture capital and qualified employees are larger barriers than in other businesses. Experience innovations are thus more difficult to finance. This may be because it is more difficult for experience enterprises to make their ideas clear to the venture market. Experience products are more fuzzy and the market more difficult to evaluate, and maybe also less lucrative in some cases.

Conversely, creativity may be an advantageous factor for, at least some, experience industries. The creativity factor may be that which determines the higher innovation rate and innovation capability of experience firms, but we cannot, empirically, establish that from this survey-based analysis.

Additionally, technological innovations are quite important in experiences. ICT in particular means much for experience products. Technological innovations enable new experience innovations. Nevertheless, we cannot conclude from this analysis whether experience innovations are more technological than service innovations.

Our attempt to create a survey of experience firms in Denmark demonstrates that it is possible to measure innovation in experiences with general measures that are also suitable for measuring innovation in the manufacturing and service sectors. Experience production is not only a domain of the core experience firms analysed in this chapter, but also becoming increasingly important in other sectors – service or manufacturing – which provide experiences as an addition to goods and services. Therefore, it can be suggested that some of the new issues dealt with in this chapter can also be of relevance for such sectors.

12.7.2   Theoretical Discussion

We started by asking the questions: Are experience firms innovative in comparison with firms in other sectors? Can innovation in experience be measured in the same way as has been done in (other) services? And is innovation in experiences different from that in (other) services?

We have observed that experience firms innovate in the way traditionally defined in innovation theory (for example, Freeman and Soete, 1997; Tidd et al., 1997): the market realization of a business idea (or solving a social problem). Experience innovations can be defined as product and process innovations just as goods and service innovations can. Categories such as organizational and market innovations that have been applied to service innovations (van den Aa and Elfring, 2002) could also be applied to experience innovations. Our analysis has also shown that innovation in experiences can be measured in the same way as has been done in services and manufacturing. This, for example, implies that experience industries could be included in general innovation statistics and surveys such as the European CIS (Eurostat, 2004).

Our survey analysis indicates that innovation in experiences, including entrepreneurship (Henry, 2007; Hjort and Kostera, 2007), is similar to that in services, which is also supported by some of the few other analyses of experience innovation (for example, Hjort and Kostera, 2007; Sundbo, 2009; Hjalager, 2010; Fuglsang et al., 2011). The service innovation theories (for example, Sundbo, 1997; van den Aa and Elfring, 2002; Gallouj, 2002; Tidd and Hull, 2005; Gallouj and Djellal, 2010; Howells, 2010) can be used to explain innovation in the primary experience sector, and probably also in the secondary experience sector. It would thus be obvious to base the development of a theory on experience innovation on the assumption that experience innovation can be explained by service innovation theories, however with some particularities that make it different.

This means that experience innovation is characterized by the following:

● It is often decided by the management and is strategic (that is, the strategy is a framework for deciding which ideas to carry out, cf. Tidd et al., 1997; Sundbo, 2001). Sundbo and Hagedorn-Rasmussen (2008) show in case analyses how experience innovation becomes increasingly 'back-staged': managerial and strategic decided).
● It is often user-based, which means that it is based on market possibilities ('pull-oriented') (which also characterizes service innovations, cf. Sundbo and Toivonen, 2011).
● It implies the involvement of employees – which may be creative as well as other employees (technicians, service personnel and so on) – which has also been shown to be an important innovation determinant in services (Boden and Miles, 2000; Fuglsang, 2008).
● Technology, particularly ICT, has great importance for innovation (as it has in services, Barras, 1986; Miles, 2008). Experience innovations are enabled by technological innovations.

However, experience innovation also has certain peculiarities when compared to service innovation. From our analysis we can point to four that can be the basis for further theorization.

One is the particularly creative basis that some experience industries have. This basis often relies on artistic work, but may also exist as a competence tradition in industries such as design, mobile phone or Internet entertainment and computer games that are not traditionally seen as culture or arts industries. High creativity can be important in the idea phase of innovation processes (for example, Amabile, 1996; Sternberg, 1999; Weisberg, 2006; Gahan et al., 2007) and may thus be an advantage in innovation. It might be assumed that the creative factor is a particular innovation determinant in some experience industries. However, it is not a determinant in all experience industries; research, for example, indicates that it is not a determinant in tourism and hospitality (Hjalager, 2010). Furthermore, creativity is not sufficient in itself; it must be combined with the ability to convert the creative ideas into business projects, that is, new products that are launched on the market or new processes that may increase productivity, which is also an important competition factor in experience industries. Artistic creativity may theoretically be suggested to be equal to natural and technical science in manufacturing. Both are fundamental activities that are not directly related to production, but kinds of basic laboratory activities, which might be the basis for innovations. One might further suggest that both natural science and artistic creativity may be the basis for radical innovations, which are rare in services (Howells, 2010). Certain experience industries may thus, just as high-tech manufacturing industries, be more characterized by radical innovations than services because of the artistic creative potentials.

Another specific feature that can be discussed is the importance of ICT. We have in this analysis observed that ICT is important for many experience innovations. We also know from other studies that much experience is based on ICT (for example, Bartle, 2004). For example, experiences on the Internet and mobile phones, TV, movies and music delivered via different ICT networks are growing rapidly and are innovative fields. One may theoretically suggest that ICT-based experience may be the, or one of the, fastest growing economic sectors in the near future. ICT may be assessed to be of greater importance to experiences than to services, even knowledge services, which seem to have difficulties in really realizing the potentials for ICT network-based self-service and other new service forms. ICT is also an important factor in experience innovation of location-based ICT applications, for example, as the basis for radically new museum concepts (Tallon and Walker, 2008). Artistic and more manual experience competencies may be mixed with technical competencies as the basis for future experience innovations such as those we have seen, for example, in the computer game industry (Kristiansen, 2008). Technical experience laboratories might be common in the future, perhaps combined with artistic ateliers, thus approaching the traditional manufacturing innovation organization with its R&D laboratory. Experience production also requires other technologies, for example, light and sound technology. However, this is not different from services that also are dependent on different technologies (for example, chemicals in cleaning services, transport technology in transport and so forth).

A third feature is the character of experiences. Many experiences are a combination of entertainment, learning and social gathering. These three are included in Pine and Gilmore's (1999) scheme of different experiences forms. Our analysis has indicated that experiences often seem to be multi-dimensional. This is important to have in mind when firms attempt to innovate experience products and processes. Our findings indicate that the more multi-dimensional experiences are, the more innovative the experience firms. Thus, multi-dimensionality of experiences and innovativeness of experience firms are related.

A final particularity is related to financing. We find that there are characteristics of experience innovations that make them difficult to finance, perhaps because they are fuzzier than goods. This raises a question of how experience providers can codify their offerings better and make them more visible and clear to the financial market.

BIBLIOGRAPHY

Amabile, T.M. (1996), *Creativity in Context: Updating the Social Psychology of Creativity*, Boulder, CO: Westview Press.

Andersen, B., J. Howells, R. Hull, I. Miles and J. Roberts (eds) (2000), *Knowledge and Innovation in the Service Economy*, Cheltenham, UK and Northampton, MA, USA: Edward Elgar.
Andersson, A. and D. Andersson (2006), *The Economics of Experiences, the Arts and Entertainment*, Cheltenham, UK and Northampton, MA, USA: Edward Elgar.
Ateljevic, J. and S.J. Page (2009), *Tourism and Entrepreneurship: International Perspectives*, Oxford: Butterworth-Heinemann.
Bakhshi, H. and D. Throsby (2009), *Innovation in Arts and Cultural Organisations*, London: NESTA.
Barras, R. (1986), 'Towards a Theory of innovation in services', *Research Policy*, **15** (4), 161–73.
Bartle, R.A. (2004), *Designing Virtual Worlds*, London: New Riders.
Boden, M. and I. Miles (eds) (2000), *Services and the Knowledge-based Economy*, London: Continuum.
Brentani, U. (1993), 'The new product process in financial services: strategy for success', *International Journal of Bank Marketing*, **11** (3), 15–22.
Chesbrough, H. (2006), *Open Innovation*, Boston, MA: Harvard Business School Press.
Cunningham, S. (2011), 'Soft innovation: economics, product aesthetics and creative industries', *Journal of Cultural Economics*, **35** (3), 241–5.
Dansk center for forskningsanalyse (Danish Centre of Research Analysis) (2004), *Innovation i dansk erhvervsliv. Innovationsstatistik 2002. Tabelsamling* (*Innovation in Danish Business. Innovation Statistics 2002. Tables*), Århus: Dansk center for forskningsanalyse.
Dansk center for forskningsanalyse (Danish Centre of Research Analysis) (2006), *Dansk erhvervslivs innovation 2004. Tabelsamling* (*Innovation in Danish Business 2004. Tables*), Århus: Dansk center for forskningsanalyse.
Djellal, F. and F. Gallouj (2001), 'Innovation in services, patterns of innovation organisation in service firms: postal survey results and theoretical models', *Science and Public Policy*, **28** (1), 57–67.
Drejer, I. (2004), 'Identifying innovation in survey of services: a Schumpeterian perspective', *Research Policy*, **33** (3), 551–62.
Erhvervs- og byggestyrelsen (Danish Enterprise and Construction Authority) (2008), *Vækst via oplevelser* (*Growth via Experiences*), Copenhagen: Erhvervs- og byggestyrelsen.
Erhvervs- og byggestyrelsen (Danish Enterprise and Construction Authority) and Centre for Culture and Experience Economy (2011), *Vækst via oplevelser 2011* (*Growth via Experiences 2011*), Copenhagen: Erhvervs- og byggestyrelsen.
Eurostat (2004), *Innovation in Europe, 2004 Edition*, Luxembourg: Eurostat.
Evangelista, R. and G. Sirilli (1998), 'Innovation in the service sector: results from the Italian Statistical Survey', *Technological Forecasting and Social Change*, **58** (3), 251–69.
Finch, R., J. Fleck, R. Procter, H. Scarbrough, M. Tierney and R. Williams (1994), *Expertise and Innovation*, Oxford: Clarendon Press.
Freeman, C. and L. Soete (1997), *The Economics of Industrial Innovation*, 3rd edn, London: Pinter.
Fuglsang, L. (2002), 'Systems of innovation in social services', in J. Sundbo and L. Fuglsang (eds), *Innovation as Strategic Reflexivity*, London: Routledge, pp. 164–80.
Fuglsang, L. (2008), *Innovation and the Creative Process: Towards Innovation with Care*, Cheltenham, UK and Northampton, MA, USA: Edward Elgar.
Fuglsang, L. and F. Sørensen (2011), 'The balance between bricolage and innovation: management dilemmas in sustainable public innovation', *The Service Industries Journal*, **31** (4), 581–95.
Fuglsang, L., J. Sundbo and F. Sørensen (2011), 'Dynamics of experience service innovation: innovation as a guided activity – results from a Danish survey', *The Service Industries Journal*, **31** (5), 661–77.
Gadrey, J., F. Gallouj, S. Lhuillery, O. Weinstein and T. Ribault (1993), *Etude effectuée pour le ministère d e l'enseignement superieure et de la recherche* (*Research Conducted for the Ministry of Higher Education and Research*), Lille: IFRESI CNRS.
Gahan, P., S. Minahan and H. Glow (2007), 'A creative twist: management theory, creativity and the arts', *Journal of Management and Organization*, **13** (1), 41–50.
Gallouj, F. (2000), *Economie de l'innovation dans les services*, Paris: Harmattan.
Gallouj, F. (2002), *Innovation in the Service Economy*, Cheltenham, UK and Northampton, MA, USA: Edward Elgar.
Gallouj, F. and F. Djellal (eds) (2010), *The Handbook of Innovation and Services*, Cheltenham, UK and Northampton, MA, USA: Edward Elgar.
Hall, C. and A. Williams (2008). *Tourism and Innovation*, London: Routledge.
Henry, C. (ed.) (2007), *Entrepreneurship in the Creative Industries*, Cheltenham, UK and Northampton, MA, USA: Edward Elgar.
Hipp, C. and H. Grupp (2005), 'Innovation in the service sector', *Research Policy*, **34** (4), 517–35.
Hjalager, A. (2010), 'A review of innovation research in tourism', *Tourism Management*, **31** (1), 1–12.
Hjalager, A.M. and S. Nordin (2011), 'User-driven innovation in tourism – a review of methodologies', *Journal of Quality Assurance in Hospitality and Tourism*, **12** (4), 289–315.

Hjort, D. and M. Kostera (eds) (2007), *Entrepreneurship and the Experience Economy*, Copenhagen: Copenhagen Business School Press.
Hobday, M., A. Boddington and A. Grantham (2011), 'An innovation perspective on design: part 1', *Design Issues*, **27** (4), 5–15.
Hobday, M., A. Boddington and A. Grantham (2012), 'An innovation perspective on design: part 2, *Design Issues*, **28** (1), 18–29.
Howells, J. (2004), 'Innovation, consumption and services: encapsulation and the combinatorial role of services', *The Service Industries Journal*, **24** (1), 19–36.
Howells, J. (2010), 'Services and innovation and service innovation: new theoretical directions', in F. Gallouj and F. Djellal (eds), *The Handbook of Innovation and Services*, Cheltenham, UK and Northampton, MA, USA: Edward Elgar, pp. 68–83.
INNO-Studies (2004), *Innovation in Services: Issues at Stake and Trends*, INNO-Studies 2001, Lot 3 (ENTR-C/2001), Brussels: European Union Commisssion.
'Innovation-management policy and practice' (2009), *Special Issue: Creative Industries and Innovation Policy*, **11** (2).
Jeffcutt, P. and A. Pratt (2002), 'Managing creativity in the cultural industries', *Creativity and Innovation Management*, **11** (4), 225–33.
Kristiansen, E. (2008), 'Designing innovative video games', in J. Sundbo and P. Darmer (eds), *Creating Experiences in the Experience Economy*, Cheltenham, UK and Northampton, MA, USA: Edward Elgar, pp. 33–59.
Martinez-Ros, E. and F. Orfila-Sintes (2009), 'Innovation activity in the hotel industry', *Technovation*, **29** (9), 632–41.
Mattsson, J., J. Sundbo and C.F. Jensen (2005), 'Innovation systems in tourism: the role of the attractors and scene-takers', *Industry and Innovation*, **12** (3), 357–81.
Miles, I. (2008), 'Patterns of innovation in service industries', *IBM Systems Journal*, **47** (1), 115–28.
Miles, I. and L. Green (2008), *Hidden Innovation in the Creative Industries*, London: NESTA.
Miozzo, M. and L. Soete (2001), 'Internationalization of services: a technological perspective', *Technological Forecasting and Social Change*, **67** (7), 159–85.
Pine, J.B. and J.H. Gilmore (1999), *The Experience Economy*, Boston, MA: Harvard Business School Press.
Rickards, T., M. Runco and S. Moger (eds) (2009), *The Routledge Companion to Creativity*, London: Routledge.
Shaw, G. and A.M. Williams (1994), *Critical Issues in Tourism: A Geographical Perspective*, Oxford: Blackwell.
Shaw, G. and A.M. Williams (1998), 'Entrepreneurship, small business culture and tourism development', in D. Ioabbides and K. Debbage (eds), *The Economic Geography of Tourism*, London: Routledge, pp. 235–55.
SIC (Service development, Internationalisation and Competence development) (1999), *Danish Service Firms' Innovation Activities and Use of ICT, Based on a Survey*, Report No. 2, Roskilde: Centre of Service Studies, Roskilde University Press.
Sternberg, R.J. (ed.) (1999), *The Handbook of Creativity*, Cambridge: Cambridge University Press.
Sundbo, J. (1996), 'Balancing empowerment', *Technovation*, **16** (8), 397–409.
Sundbo, J. (1997), 'Management of innovation in services', *The Service Industries Journal*, **17** (3), 432–55.
Sundbo, J. (1998), *The Organisation of Innovation in Services*, Copenhagen: Roskilde University Press.
Sundbo, J. (2001), *The Strategic Management of Innovation*, Cheltenham, UK and Northampton, MA, USA: Edward Elgar.
Sundbo, J. (2004), 'The management of rock festivals as the basis for business development: an example of the growing experience economy', *International Journal of Entrepreneurship and Innovation Management*, **4** (6), 587–612.
Sundbo, J. (2009), 'Innovation in the experience economy: a taxonomy of innovation organisations', *The Service Industries Journal*, **29** (4), 431–55.
Sundbo, J. (2011), 'Creative artists and entrepreneurship', in K. Hindle and K. Klyver (eds), *Handbook of Research into New Venture Creation*, Cheltenham, UK and Northampton, MA, USA: Edward Elgar, pp. 328–43.
Sundbo, J. and P. Darmer (eds) (2008), *Creating Experiences in the Experience Economy*, Cheltenham, UK and Northampton, MA, USA: Edward Elgar.
Sundbo, J. and P. Hagedorn-Rasmussen (2008), 'The backstaging of experience production', in J. Sundbo and P. Darmer (eds), *Creating Experiences in the Experience Economy*, Cheltenham, UK and Northampton, MA, USA: Edward Elgar, pp. 83–110.
Sundbo, J. and M. Toivonen (eds) (2011), *User-based Innovation in Services*, Cheltenham, UK and Northampton, MA, USA: Edward Elgar.
Sundbo, J., F. Orfila-Sintes and F. Sørensen (2007), 'The innovative behaviour of tourism firms – comparative studies of Denmark and Spain', *Research Policy*, **36** (1), 88–106.

Sunley, P., S. Pinch, S. Reimer et al. (2008), 'Innovation in a creative production system: the case of design', *Journal of Economic Geography*, **8** (5), 675–98.

Tallon, L. and K. Walker (eds) (2008), *Digital Technologies and the Museum Experience*, Plymouth: AltaMira.

Teece, D.J. and G. Pisano (1994), 'The dynamic capability of firms: an introduction', *Industrial and Corporate Change*, **3** (3), 537–56.

Tether, B.S. and A. Tajar (2008), 'The organisational-cooperation mode of innovation and its prominence amongst European service firms', *Research Policy*, **37** (4), 720–39.

Tidd, J. and F. Hull (2005), *Service Innovation*, London: World Scientific Publishing.

Tidd, J., J. Bessant and K. Pavitt (1997), *Managing Innovation*, Chichester: Wiley.

Toivonen, M. and T. Tuominen (2009), 'Emergence of innovations in services', *The Service Industries Journal*, **29** (7), 887–902.

Van den Aa, W. and T. Elfring (2002), 'Realizing innovation in services', *Scandinavian Journal of Management*, **18** (2), 155–71.

Verganti, R. (2009), *Design-driven Innovation*, Boston, MA: Harvard Business School Press.

Vermeulen, P. (2001), *Organizing Product Innovation in Financial Services*, Nijmegen: Nijmegen University Press.

Weisberg, R. (2006), *Creativity: Understanding Innovation in Problem Solving, Invention, and the Arts*, New York: Wiley.

Yoon, B., S. Kim and J. Rhee (2012), 'An evaluation method for designing a new product-service system', *Experts Systems with Application*, **39** (3), 3100–108.

APPENDIX 12.A: THE EXPERIENCE SECTOR AND SUB-SECTORS

Experience industries included in the survey are listed below.

12.A.1   Tourism

Hotels
Conference centres
Youth hostels
Camping sites
Other facilities for leisure
Restaurants
Cafeterias, grill bars and so on
Banqueting rooms
Pubs
Discotheques and nightclubs
Cafes
Catering
River transport
Land passenger transport
Tourist information
Travel agencies
Tourist guide enterprises
Holiday residence renting bureaus
Marinas

12.A.2   Arts and Culture

Publishing companies
Book editors
Publishers of discs and CDs
Publishers of other kind
Gold- and silversmiths
Producers of music instruments
Picture and video production
Picture and video wholesale
Cinemas
TV companies
Radio companies
Theatres and concert organizers
Independent artists
Culture houses

12.A.3   Entertainment and Leisure

Producers of sport equipment
Producers of toys and games
Fair organizers
Amusement parks
Other amusement enterprises
Museums
Botanical and zoological gardens
Sport and swimming pool installations
Other sport installations (stadiums and so on)
Sports clubs
Other sport activities
Lotteries
Beauty salons
Sun, motion and health care centres
Other leisure activities

12.A.4   Design, Image and Branding

Development of software
Architects
Public relations and advertising agencies
Photographers
Industrial design

13. Towards more intertwined innovation types: innovation through experience design focusing on customer interactions

Dorthe Eide and Lena Mossberg

13.1 INTRODUCTION

Innovation is vital in the experience economy and the saying 'innovate or die' seems highly relevant for the experience economy as it operates within global, competitive and changing markets, where customers often seek something new (Pine and Gilmore, 1999; Hall and Williams, 2008; Sundbo, 2009; Fuglsang et al., 2011). If we are to facilitate positive innovations, we need to understand what 'innovation' means and how it can be facilitated.

The dominant theories on innovation are mainly based upon studies within manufacturing since these sectors traditionally were assumed to be the most innovative and productive (Gallouj and Djellal, 2010). The knowledge about innovation in the service sectors has increased significantly over the last two decades; while knowledge about innovation in the experience sectors is embryonic but is on the increase (Eide and Ljunggren, forthcoming). There is an ongoing discourse concerning whether or not the characteristics and measurement of innovation pertaining to the manufacturing sectors are relevant to the service and experience sectors. Some authors see an assimilation and argue for transferring both theory and measures; others argue for divergence and context sensitivity; while a third group argues for a mix (Hjalager, 2002; Hipp and Grupp. 2005; Miles, 2005; Vence and Trigo, 2009; Gallouj and Savona, 2010; Sundbo et al., 2010). There are both similarities and differences regarding innovations across manufacturing, service and experience sectors (see, for example, Sundbo et al., Chapter 12, this volume), a fact that can support the mix-perspective mentioned above in which one seeks to combine pre-understanding and context sensitivity. With regard to context sensitivity, researchers studying service innovations have focused on the core characteristics of service sectors (Edvardsson et al., 2000). Gustafsson et al. (2002, p. 141) maintain that 'New service development and innovation concepts, theories and models must be based on an understanding of the service logic.' We suggest a parallel argument; that is, that an increased in-depth understanding of innovation in experience sectors depends on understanding and beginning with the core characteristics of the experience logic.

This chapter addresses the debate on how to understand and conceptualize innovation types in the experience economy. We seek to contribute with a more holistic and in-depth understanding of innovation types in experience sectors. In particular, we offer an understanding of how the types can be related and intertwined. Innovation types can be talked of in different ways (Hall and Williams, 2008); we address the focus/object of innovation, that is, what is innovated. We suggest a new theoretical framework involving conceptual grids, ideal-types and propositions (main assumptions) that focus on customer interactions and show how ideal-types can structure experience designs and how innovation types can be intertwined.

The chapter is structured as follows. Section 13.2 elaborates on the theoretical concepts of innovation and some core characteristics of the experience economy. Section 13.3 explores experience design by focusing on customer interactions, and suggests a conceptual grid of ideal-types (that is, combinations of interaction types). Section 13.4 explores innovation types through experience designs focusing on customer interactions, and suggests a second grid that also includes innovation-types. Section 13.5 summarizes the main arguments and briefly discusses them in a broader context.

This is an explorative, conceptual chapter in which we use empirical examples not as 'evidence' but to illustrate what we mean. Our main examples are taken from nature-based experiences and, in particular, from dog sledging at Svalbard. However, we also, indirectly, draw upon other empirical studies relating to nature, cultural and food-based experience sectors. We selected the subsector of dog sledging as our main example as it offers different types of experience products that illustrate our points. The dog sledging examples are based on fieldwork carried out in August 2011, which was supplemented in March 2012. The main phase included interviews with management, employees and others working in relation to tourism; and five researchers undertook group reflections. The supplementary phase included interviews with customers (see Hansen and Mossberg, Chapter 11, this volume). Both phases used participative observations and ongoing interactions/conversations with customers and employees; and gathering of documents. Svalbard differs from the mainland of Norway due to the polar bears and arctic climate, which has implications for work with innovations. Since all new outdoor products must be accepted by the governor, they must go through risk analyses, and care for safety and the environment must be accounted for. An extra licence is required if someone wants to go outside the least restricted area.

13.2   INNOVATION AND CUSTOMER EXPERIENCES

The experience economy seeks to create positive, mentally and bodily, memorable experiences, that is, experience products are largely intangible and subjective. This can briefly be illustrated by the following quote written in Enterprise 'X's guest book, in Svalbard almost ten years ago: 'very exciting the interplay with the dog, man and nature. Our guide was exceptional.' The customer addresses the importance of customer interactions for value creation. She points to interactions with animals, humans (this can include customers and the personnel) and nature. In particular, she mentions the guide. When diverse types of interactions are significant for customers' perceived value creation, we argue they are (and should be seen as) important when designing or redesigning commercialized/organized experiences and probably also innovation types. Enterprise 'X' was ambitious when starting up; it wanted to be different and innovative. The enterprise framed the total concepts of experience activities, the hotel, dog yard and most of the experiencescapes, around the theme of trapping, which has long traditions in Svalbard. They actively tried to involve and surprise customers through dramatizing and storytelling. During the early years they worked with radical and incremental innovations.

13.2.1   Innovation in Experience and Tourism

By innovation we mean something new or significantly improved that is implemented (for example, commercialized or put into practice). Open, multi-relational approaches to innovation can be seen as a Schumpeter-3 model in which one seeks to combine both internal and external ideas, knowledge and actors as sources and involved parts in processes (Fuglsang, 2008). We situate ourselves within Schumpeter-3, as we assume it fits recent business life, including the experience sectors. For a brief overview of how innovation can take place in experience sectors, see Sundbo et al., Chapter 12, this volume and Eide and Fuglsang, Chapter 15, this volume. Below we focus on what is innovated, that is, what is new.

Some choose to study innovation in service and experience sectors within the generic conceptual frame suggested by Sundbo and Gallouj (1999) and the Oslo Manual (2005) used by, for example, Community Innovation Surveys (CIS), European Innovation Scoreboard (EIS) and Eurostat. It involves four main types of innovations: product (physical, service or experience); process (how products are produced, for example, work with production productivity or quality); organization (for example, structure, culture, management, network and cooperation, competence or work environment); and market (for example, market segments, marketing and sale). Innovation takes place when one or more of the four areas become new or significantly improved. International surveys until recently only focused on process, product and patents; the inclusion of all four types was done to produce a better fit with service industries. However, Sundbo et al. (Chapter 12, this volume) focus on product and process innovations in their Danish study and argue that the two general concepts functioned well in experience sectors. But is something important veiled?

A brief literature review reveals alternative conceptualizations of innovation types. Schumpeter (1934) viewed innovations as new combinations of knowledge contributing to new goods, new processes, new markets, access to new sources of raw materials and intermediates, and/or reorganization of an industry. Hjalager (2002) conceptualizes innovation in tourism in terms of five types, namely product, process, management, logistics and institutional innovations. Johannessen et al. (2001) suggest six types (new products, new services, new methods of production, new markets, new distribution and new ways of organizing); the first two fall under the heading of 'product' in the Oslo Manual. Others address innovations of, or within, business models (Chesbrough, 2006, 2011; Furseth, 2008; Boswijk et al., 2012). For example, the Business Model Canvas suggested by Osterwalder and Pigneur (2010), which has nine building blocks (that is, customer segment, value proposition, customer relation, channel, price mechanism, key resources, key activities, key partners and the cost structure), which can span across firms. One innovation can involve some blocks or be supplemented with further blocks. One can argue that the business model approach is a more holistic way of working with innovation as all the elements involved potentially can be related and changed. Furseth (2008) argues that when using a business model one also tends to situate the organization within the larger ecosystem of the business. He describes this broader approach as the second wave in service innovation research, while the first wave is focused on the more unique characteristics of service compared to manufacturing (Furseth, 2008). It can be argued that more fundamental changes in the business model include a radical innovation of, and double loop learning for, the organization and perhaps even the sector (Gallouj and Savona, 2010). Others suggest defining if an innovation is radical or not depending on whether the service is new for the client or user (Barcet, 2010). The latter can be seen as a customer-oriented approach instead of the traditional product and technology focus when addressing innovation.

Since most literature has focused on product, process and technology innovations (Gallouj and Djellal, 2010), there is a lack of knowledge about market and organizational innovation (Fagerberg, 2005), and how innovation types relate to each other. Previous studies of innovation in services and tourism indicate that innovation types are not so divided as in manufacturing sectors, rather they seem complex, fuzzy and intertwined (Hall and Williams, 2008, p. 9; Toivonen and Tuominen, 2009). This difference seems to be a result of the core characteristics of service and experience sectors. Hjalager (2010, p. 4) also addresses complexity when arguing that 'Experience design will almost break down boarders between categories.'

Experience design is a young field, even though it is approached from multiple and separate disciplines (Jantzen et al., 2011). Experience design can be defined as the way one organizes and facilitates valuable experiences for a market segment; in particular, it is about 'facilitating the frames, develop objects, plan situations and the steps in events' (Janzen et al., 2011, p. 49, our translation). Design can be seen as one phase in the generic process of innovation (Edvardsson et al., 2000, 2006). We assume that design can take place at different steps of the iterative (non-linear) phases of the innovation process.

To sum up, we chose to start out with the four main innovation types in the Oslo Manual, combined with more holistic approaches such as the notion of total concepts and/or business models. These are tentative concepts, since there is both a need to be open and flexible towards new understandings, and at the same time to have some idea about what can be involved. As already argued, to get a deeper understanding we see the need to start with the core characteristics of experience sectors when studying innovation. We have chosen to focus on customer interactions as the main core characteristic in this chapter.

13.2.2 Customer Interactions within Experiencescapes

The environment where the consumption takes place has been illuminated and described as a 'scape' within the consumption and tourism literature, but with different meanings depending on whether or not one addresses service or experience-scapes. The experiencescape is a space of pleasure, enjoyment and entertainment, where interactions between people occur (O'Dell, 2005). In these experience environments, the visitors are directly influenced by the physical and social surroundings (Prahalad and Ramaswamy, 2004) in which both functional and emotional attributes play an important role (Kumar and Karande, 2000). Compared to a servicescape (Bitner, 1992), which covers service production in general, an experiencescape is seen as nested products of inputs from organizations and customers and argued to be more relevant in tourism settings (Mossberg, 2007). The experiencescapes can be framed through a main theme or story (for example, 'trapping' as in the example from Svalbard earlier in this section). Mossberg (2007) elaborates on customer experiences by focusing on the experiencescape and three main interaction types, that is, with personnel, with other customers and with physical objects (see more in Hansen and Mossberg, Chapter 11, this volume). Below we briefly focus on customer interactions with personnel and with other customers.[1]

Customer interactions with personnel can be viewed from many perspectives. Within consumer behaviour, as well as service marketing and management, the concept of the service encounter has frequently been used since the mid 1980s and is often linked to service quality. Some focus on actors' roles, scripts, symbolic interaction and dramaturgy; such studies add performance, conduct and communicative concepts to the field (Echeverri, 2000). The subtle role of the guide in the service encounter was pointed out by Arnould and Price (1993) in their study about river rafting. A tour guide can be regarded as one of the key frontline players in tourism (Ap and Wong, 2001) and several studies have shown that a tour guide's performance affects a tourist's satisfaction with both the tour as a whole and the tour operator (Mossberg, 1995).

Service encounters also occur in the presence of other customers (Baker, 1986) and these can increase or decrease tourist satisfaction and the perception of service quality (Lehtinen and Lehtinen, 1991; Grove and Fisk, 1997). When consuming the same services or experience at the same time, the concept of 'audience' (Celsi et al., 1993) can be used, and they can be recognized as 'co-producers' necessary for the performance and production. Lovelock (1996) argues that an exciting and stimulating audience can enhance the experience. Certain researchers point towards positive aspects of 'togetherness' with other consumers and how it influences their willingness to be co-producers (Celsi et al., 1993; Gummesson, 1993). Gustafsson et al. (2006) point out how service encounters influence the atmosphere and satisfaction in various hospitality contexts. Likewise, Andersson and Mossberg (2004) showing how important various aspects (cuisine, restaurant interior, service, dining company and other consumers) are for the dining experience and consumers' satisfaction. Despite the agreements that 'other consumers' influence service encounters, there is a lack of theory that explains this impact (Miao et al., 2011).

The research on consumer communities also elaborates on the importance of other consumers. For example, Schouten and McAlexander (1995) do so when studying consumer communities related to motorbikes. Studies in sport subcultures, such as diving, climbing, golfing, skiing and flying, or subcultures where the participants have a strong interest (for example, of nature and culture) in common, also show the importance of other customers for the value creation. This sense of belonging to the group and community was, for example, pointed out by Hallin and Mykletun (2006) in BASE jumping. The participants share the same consumption values and behaviours (Oliver, 1999). Another concept is brand community, a specialized, non-geographical linked community based on relationships between consumers who appreciate the same brand (Muniz and O'Guinn, 2001) and show similar lifestyles and identities.

Sundbo et al. (Chapter 12, this volume) address how experience products seem multidimensional since they often mix entertainment, learning and social gathering. One can argue that innovations should be related to customers' reasons to go/buy, and that experience designs should facilitate customer interactions so that they contribute towards what customers seek and what creates positive value for the customers.

13.3   EXPERIENCE DESIGN FOCUSING ON CUSTOMER INTERACTIONS

This section explores how we can understand experience design through a focus on customer interactions.

13.3.1   The Importance of Different Interaction Types

Building on the experience literature discussed above, including Mossberg's model (2007), and our own ongoing empirical research, we argue that there are at least six main types of customer interactions that can be important during consumption (in addition to which there are pre- and post-consumption interactions that should also be addressed with regards to innovation activity). These are the customer's interactions with: (1) personnel (for example, tour guides and other staff within or across organizations that is part of the planned delivery); (2) other customers (in the same experience product/package); (3) other humans (more random meetings); (4) animals (for example, dogs, horses, birds); (5) objects (for example, kayak, dog sledge, water, snow); and (6) oneself. The interactions are situated in the experience-scape(s) that can be framed within a theme (main story).

Which of the six main types are most relevant at a particular time or most important for the co-production and experience quality varies with the experience sector, subsector, segment, product and not least the specific actors and conditions involved. Through studies of experience packages (sea kayaking, horse tourism and dog sledging) lasting for three to six days, we have found that customers on the same tour focus on and evaluate the quality and roles of the main interaction types differently. How the six types of interaction evolve, are related to each other and contribute to the value creation for the customers partly depend upon the theme framing of the experiencescape. How the mixed interactions can be situated in themed experiencescapes can briefly be illustrated by a four-day package tour that includes sea kayaking in Helgeland (near Vega, a World Heritage Area in Norway), where the product is designed under the theme 'The World Heritage Area of Vega' (Box 13.1).

Knowledge about customers' experiences, value creation and motives can be vital when making relevant and competitive experience designs. A specific experience product or the portfolio can be analysed by customers, the organization and/or researchers with regard to the degree that each main interaction type is involved and its importance (their roles). This can produce knowledge about the weaknesses and strengths of existing or planned experience designs and can visualize the need, or potentials for, redesign and new design. Based upon the above, we suggest the first proposition:

P1: Commercialized/organized experiences (for example, activities, packages, attractions) within one subsector can be designed in different ways depending on the different combinations of the six main types of customer interactions.

13.3.2   Ideal-types of Combinations when Involving Two Interactions

Above we briefly explored experience designs in relation to the six types of customer interactions; for simplification we narrow the focus to two of the main types of customer

BOX 13.1   THE WORLD HERITAGE AREA OF VEGA

The package tour provides consistent nature-culture-food experiences, though kayaking is still the core product. All of the six types of interactions (referred to in the main text) took place. Interactions with animals are a usual part of sea kayaking, but mainly in the form of watching (gazing) at, for example, birds, sheep and perhaps, from a distance, even whales. Getting close to, for example, whales or eagles when in the kayak can be a strong emotional and lifetime experience. Spontaneous interactions with 'other humans' (for example, local people living in the area or other tourists not in the group) are rare in this product. The guides and the other customers interact with the person during all four days, but the intensity and quality varies across periods and depending on the customer. Over long periods customers interact with objects (for example, kayak, water) and with their self. The wind and waves create different challenges, perhaps scaring or hard work for some, and fun for others. Also personnel from other enterprises co-produce parts of the package; in particular, the customers are amazed by the hospitality of these people. The local stories, it results in learning and gives the customers material for own storytelling when they get home. These customers appreciate and seek more varied activities (for example, combining kayaking with hiking, biking and perhaps horse riding if convenient) and multiple types of interaction when on holiday.

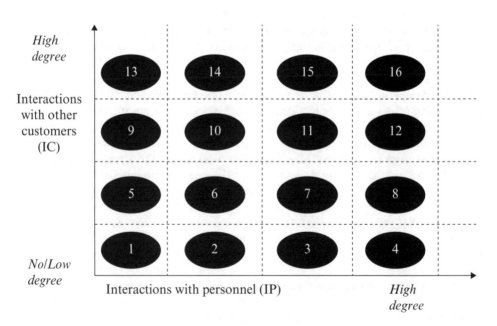

Figure 13.1   Ideal-types of customer interactions – different degrees of interaction

interactions, that is, interactions with personnel and with other customers. This does not mean that other types of interaction do not take place or are of less importance. We do this to develop conceptual frameworks and elaborate on experience design. The two types of interaction are chosen since both are involved in most tour packages offered by experience firms and they are also common in other experience sectors.

If combining a customer's interactions with other customers (IC) and with personnel (IP), we get a grid (matrix) of ideal-types of combinations. In the grid shown in Figure 13.1 we have involved four alternative degrees on each interaction type (variable), with IP on the horizontal line and IC on the vertical line.

By 'degree' we refer to a four-point scale ranging from no/very low to very high concerning the type of interaction involved in the experience-based product and production. We are aware that what is 'much' or 'little' is subjective and cannot be reduced to a number, and there may be contextual differences depending on subsector and geography. Whether a type of interaction positively or negatively influences customers' perceived value creation is also a subjective matter. These subjective aspects must be studied empirically within different subsectors and market segments. The scale is a simplification with limitations.

The grid shown in Figure 13.1 includes 16 ideal-types.[2] Below we describe and illustrate some of the ideal-types. Ideal-type 1: could include a tourist planning and booking a tour on the web, materials (for example, maps, keys to the cottage, written advice) arrive by mail and the person goes alone. The two types of interaction are not involved during this kind of consumption. Ideal-type 6: could include the case of going on a self-organized tour using the infrastructure of the Norwegian Hiking Association, with cottages/motels and personnel serving meals and providing information. It is likely that interaction with personnel and other customers/humans increases when at the cottages. Most of the daytime, when hiking from one place to another, there is no or little interaction with personnel and other humans, but the other four interactions types (described in Subsection 13.3.1) can be involved and significant for the total experience. If there are no other customers in the cottages, this can be an example of ideal-type 2. If there are no personnel at the cottages but other customers, we have an example of ideal-type 5. Ideal-type 11: could be a person going on a guided group tour in the same area, in which case interactions with both personnel and other customers increase in varying degrees depending on the tour guide, the others and the self. Ideal-type 3: this could be a short period of ski instruction. Ideal-type 4: could be a package with a personal ski instructor for a longer period, in which case the interactions are regular, probably increasingly relational and personal, and not only task oriented. Ideal-type 9: one example could be when a family or group of friends visit a water-land or museum; there is a great deal of interaction during the day, but almost none with the personnel. Ideal-type 10-11: could be exemplified by a cooking course, the personnel take the lead during some periods, but most of the time the person interacts with some of the others preparing the food. Ideal-type 12: could be a day of rafting on a river with strong streams and difficult passages, the tour guide takes a direct management approach telling customers what to do. Ideal-type 13: an example could be a survival camp with others, without tour guides, where the activity is largely based on regular interactions in regard to tasks and social gathering (bonding, identity), and perhaps conflicts and distancing from others. Ideal-type 7: could be exemplified by a guided tour in, for example, a church, where a story is dramatized with singing and reading from a book or a movie. The guide is dressed up accordantly, and the surrounding place fits with the story. If the customers also get directly involved in the dramatized activity using clothes and equipment, and appointed roles, then the design facilitate increase interactions with other customers (ideal-type 10), with personnel (ideal-type 12) or with both (ideal-type 11).

The examples from hiking and from cultural experiences indicate how enterprises can shift between alternative ideal-types when designing experiences for different and perhaps new segments. The narrowing down to two interaction types and the suggested grid with ideal-types of combinations support the following proposition:

P2: Commercialized/organized experiences (for example, activities, packages, attractions) within one subsector can be designed in different ways depending on the combinations (degree) of customer interactions with personnel and with other customers. The different combinations make up ideal-types.

Alternative grids can be made by using combinations of other main interaction types, for example, customers' interactions with personnel and with animals. The use of other grids can reveal other challenges and opportunities for experience designs. Combining the six main types of interactions, with only two of them in a grid at a time, produces 15 different grids. We suggest that researchers, managers or others working with experience design should, as a first sub-step, start with the grid introduced here and analyse one existing or planned experience design. The next sub-step may be to do this with a second grid that mixes the two interaction types that seem most important seen from the perspective of the customers or the organization/subsector. To use all 15 in experience design, or when studying experience design, is probably too extensive, and the result uncertain. A third sub-step could be to analyse the portfolio of designs that the enterprise is involved in. This could give an overview and visualize how the different designs fit different segments, and localize if there are areas and moves in the grid that are not covered but worth exploring and exploiting.

P3: The grid(s) with ideal-types of combinations of two customer interactions can be used:
(a) To study and analyse existing or planned experience designs.
(b) To study, visualize and construct opportunities for new experience designs.

Analysing single experience designs, or a portfolio, with grids has limitations since it offers a partial and static overview. Experience products often involve combinations of the six main interaction types, and tend to be dynamic. By dynamic we mean that the degree of involvement and importance of each interaction type can change during the consumption of the product (that is, different ideal-types can be involved in different parts of the product and production), and there can be shifts between experiencescapes. Complex and time-spanning products we suggest should be analysed in greater depth, that is, also day by day in relation to the chosen grid(s), and perhaps even by the main phases or events of each day. The reason is that such analysis can visualize whether or not the product has adequate combinations of interactions (ideal-types) or if redesigns or other innovation types are needed.

13.4 RELATED AND INTERTWINED INNOVATION TYPES

In this section we explore how we can understand innovation types through experience design focusing on customer interactions. The brief literature review in Section 13.2 showed that scholars and empirical studies traditionally have focused on product and process innovations. This rather narrow focus has gradually been expanded by multiple innovation types (for example, Oslo model) or the business model innovation approach, but still the knowledge and practice are underdeveloped. There are at least three main arguments for not using a narrow focus. Firstly, it can veil and devalue other innovation types. Secondly, it has been argued by scholars that innovation in service and tourism is complex, fuzzy and difficult to sharply separate. Thirdly, practitioners within experience sectors report difficulties in separating the innovation types in surveys, which creates frustration as well and can give rather biased survey results. All three reasons we see as supporting the need of more in-depth understanding of innovation types in experience sectors. The conceptual framework and approach suggested in Section 13.3 is narrow, but not in the traditional way. It focuses on customer interactions as the interpretive 'window' when exploring experience designs. We use this 'window' also in this section when exploring innovation types.

13.4.1 From Ideal-type of Customer Interactions to Innovation Types

The first grid expressing ideal-types of customer interactions (Figure 13.1) can be developed into a new framework that also includes innovation types. We have integrated the two customer interaction variables in Figure 13.1 with a third variable 'innovation types' (focus area/objects of the innovation); this is illustrated three-dimensionally in Figure 13.2.

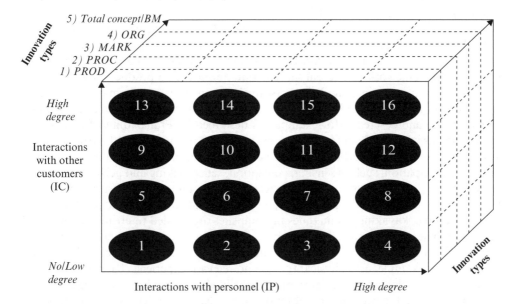

Figure 13.2   From ideal-types of customer interactions to holistic innovations

The four first numbers of innovation types in the upper part of the figure are in accordance with the Oslo Manual (2005), that is, (1) Product innovation; (2) Process innovation; (3) Market innovation; and (4) Organizational innovations. Alternative (5) are other elements involved in the total concept or business model (BM) that are not covered by the first four (1–4) areas. The five alternatives were briefly introduced in Section 13.2.

In Section 13.3 we argued that one can study, analyse or visualize and construct experience designs (existing, planned or potential) with a focus on customer interactions. We suggest that the next main step is to use the framework in Figure 13.2 to study, analyse and visualize consequences and opportunities for innovations in the five focus areas.

P4: The grid (Figure 13.2) with ideal-types (combinations of two customer interaction types) and innovation types can be used to study, analyse and visualize:
(a) *The need of, or potentials for, innovation types when working with experience designs.*
(b) *How innovation types can be related and intertwined when working with experience designs.*

13.4.1.1 How can the ideal-types help when exploring innovation types?
Customer interactions are one of the core characteristics in the experience logic. The ideal-types can bring awareness to, and more careful work with, this core characteristic. The grids when related to a context can be used as an interpretation 'window' starting with a focus on customer interactions. This does not mean that the innovation work ends with this focus. An experience design, when contextualized, often involves other types of customer interactions and aspects (for example, smell, food, stories), and the customer interactions are situated within experience-scapes perhaps framed by a theme. When using the frameworks in a context, the other aspects supplement the analysis, while the customer interactions are the starting point.

The ideal-types give clues about the experience design. The clues, we argue, are not only about the product but also the production process, customers, personnel, organizing and so on, and how they are related. In particular, the analysis of experience designs by using the framework can reveal information about the co-production and involvement of both the customers and the personnel. It can provide information about, for example, how much/little and what ways the involved actors are assumed and facilitated to participate and co-create (for example, as described by Prahalad and Ramaswamy, 2004), such as whether the interaction concerns rather passive external participation or a highly active external participation. In addition, there are different degrees of more internal participation, such as sensing, perception, sense making and perhaps even more critical reflections. Both internal and external participation more or less depends on the pre-understanding of the activity, topic, context and so on that the product relates to (for example, kayaking); sometimes prerequisites are needed to create meaning and/or coping. The analyses can give information about who can or cannot do the activity, which can be the start of developing understanding and criteria (access barriers) in regard to, for example, age, physical fitness and relevant experience background. It can be the start of exploring the question of who the likely and unlikely customers are, that is, it can visualize the need of market innovation. Also the analyses can give clues with regard to the framing of other customer interactions, experiencescapes, dramaturgy and so on, that is, other sides of product and process innovation. Further, the exploration of the ideal-types can give clues regarding demands and prerequisites for employees, that is, it can visualize the need for organizational innovation. For example, if the experience design involves a great deal of involvement of the personnel during a four-day tour, it is far from enough to be highly competent in, for example, kayaking. The guide is also expected to be able and willing to interact with the customers, to manage the group, to have local knowledge and share it, to tell stories, take the main responsibility for safety and so on. Some guides, or personnel, fit better with certain ideal-types than others. To sum up, the focus on the ideal-types, and the use of the frameworks (Figures 13.1 and 13.2) when contextualized at the level of a geographic area (for example, Svalbard) or an enterprise, seems to reveal some of the holistic connections and overlaps between the areas of innovation types.

Further, we suggest that a pilot test or the implementation of a planned experience product can be seen as a pilot test or implementation also of the experience designs' production process, marketing, organization and potentially other elements in the concept/ business model, that is, it is related to the more holistic experience design and not only the product. The pilot test or implementation of the latter areas can be rather careless and coincidental if the enterprise's preparation is made solely with regard to the product. All the areas may need careful and conscious focus and innovation, therefore we suggest analysing consequences or opportunities also for the other areas (1–5) when working with experience design and innovations.

13.4.1.2 How to use the frame?
The first main step (with sub-steps) was suggested in Section 13.3 (using Figure 13.1) when addressing the concept of experience design through a focus on ideal-types. The second main step is to address the concept of innovation types by using Figure 13.2, that is, to expand the focus from the ideal-type and experience design to also include the innovation types. This can be done as an analysis and visualization of the implications and opportunities for potentially all the areas (1–5) of innovation types when working with an experience design. A stepwise in-depth analysis, by researchers or practitioners, can give a more holistic and careful approach to innovations in experience sectors.

A first sub-step could be to analyse an idea or planned design. For example, the analysis could produce insights about what is new and what differs from the enterprise's or subsector's previous activities; what might be reused and what must be developed or acquired other ways (for example, investments, recruiting and outsourcing). Also it could create insights about what could or should be done before and after consumption, and not only during it (about transformation and three main time-phases described by the springboard metaphor, see, for example, Hansen and Mossberg, Chapter 11, this volume). Our empirical studies (in progress) focusing on customer interactions indicate that there are large potentials for innovations not only related to the consumption of products but also before and after consumption. One example is the need to develop new matching practices (for example, matching of customer to the best product, or to a suitable kayak, horse, other customer to share a double kayak with and so on), when selling demanding experience designs (we shall return to this later).

A second sub-step could be to analyse and visualize potentials for innovation types in relation to existing experience designs in the portfolio of an enterprise. It could give an overview of how products, people, objects, animals and so on can be related within and perhaps across organizations. For example, such an overview could provide ideas and trigger the innovation of new practices concerning how one cares for equipment, animals, personnel, marketing and so on. An example that shows how organizational and process innovation can be intertwined is the issues of quality and competence that are critical issues in the tourism sectors. It is often a challenge both to recruit and keep enthusiastic and competent personnel. Guides in nature-based subsectors are often lifestyle workers, doing their hobby and trying to satisfy their desires, and seek exciting trips. Their desires might be too exotic and demanding for most customers, and can also be so for guides if they engage in them for a long time. Quality is not only constructed during production and consumption. The grid, when related to the portfolio, can be used to analyse and visualize aspects of the guides' work conditions (or the animals), the insight can be used in the planning and making of new practices of work schedules (that is, organizational inno-vation). The overview can prevent a guide (or animal) from having too many long trips in a row, or weeks of short standardized routine trips; both can be draining but in different ways. It can help create variations and rest that motivate and care for the employees (or animals) too, which can make them do a better job with customers, and reduce risks. Care is multi-relational and dynamic, in need of continual (re)constructions (Eide, 2007).

13.4.2 Move-pattern from Low-low to High-high

> It is genuine experiences when people get to feel, think and be like a trapper through dog sledg-ing. To drive your own team, to stand there on the sledge alone but still in the group, and to get the feeling of coping with the activity. To participate is vital, if one wants to understand what dog sledging is about. It is very different from just sitting passively in a sledge and watching. (Ex guide)

An enterprise and a subsector can move between alternative ideal-types in the grid when innovating on experience designs to attract different customer segments. We illustrate a move-pattern from low-low degree towards high-high degree of the two customer inter-actions (that is, ideal-types 1, 6, 11 and 16) with examples from dog sledging in Svalbard.

Ideal-type 1 is exemplified by a single customer going on a tour of about one to two hours with up to seven other customers not knowing each other. They are seated in a wagon or sledge being dragged by the team of dogs, and the guide's main activity is to drive and communicate with the dogs. For the tourist, this experience design involves no direct interactions with the dogs, at least not while on the ride. If the guide starts telling about the dogs and the places they pass, the increased interaction becomes more like ideal-type 2. If the customers start interacting more with each other when gazing at the nature, the experience becomes more like that of ideal-type 5; or almost ideal-type 6 if both the interaction types are increasing. This move during the consumption can happen spontaneously or it can be facilitated by the guide. Ideal-type 1 requires very little exter-nal activity by the customer, it is mainly about seeing, and interpreting and constructing meaning concerning what is seen. It demands rather little of the employee as well, and it can be an example of standardizing within experience economy (an organizing logic focusing on productivity and standardizing rather than tailoring and care, similar to what has been described in the service economy; see, for example, Ritzer, 1998; Ritzer and Stillman, 2001; Eide, 2007).

Ideal-type 6 can be exemplified by a half day trip where customers harness and drive themselves, two customers share a team of dogs (winter with sledge, summer with wagon). The tour guide must inform, instruct and help customers with the dogs and the equipment, particularly before and after they do the driving, but also during it if something happens, and during pauses. This design requires more of both customers and employees, and can give them more; still, it can be rather standardized. Easier and more standardized products like half day tours can also be constructed so they become more unique designs, through situating the interactions within designed experiences capes within a suitable theme (for example, 'Be a trapper for a day'). For some customers, this ideal-type can be demanding enough. For example, one female customer left all the har-nessing and driving to her husband; he thereby actively co-produced, while she watched and felt as if she was active. After she claimed that they had been on real dog sledging with harnessing and driving. This was her construction and narration, and hence positive memorable experience.

Exemplifying ideal-type 11, some customers want to go on longer tours and live almost like the famous explorers and trappers, but with some comfort. One example is a three-day tour to a ship in the ice (Box 13.2).

Every day, customers get a unique combination of comfort and the exotic in this expe-rience package. The comfort with prepared food, sleeping inside in a warm bed, a shower and other hotel facilities on the boat, on the one hand, and the exotic experience of being in the total wilderness with the weather, landscape and wild animals, on the other. The interactions with the dogs and the equipment are much higher than in ideal-type 6, as they harness, feed and play with the dogs in addition to driving for hours each day (this has similarities with what is described in Hansen and Mossberg, Chapter 11, this volume, although our example has a higher level of comfort). Also interactions with personnel and other customers are significantly higher and more significant than in ideal-type 6. This is so partly due to the increasing complexity of the activity and partly the longer time-span. When back at the trappers' hotel they debrief through narrating and sense making, spontaneously or perhaps organized. If the personnel do not participate, they miss the feedback that could lead to learning and innovations.

Ideal-type 16 is exemplified by some customers wanting even more exotic and chal-lenging experiences where they sleep and live more like explores. They might choose a four to ten day tour as briefly described in Box 13.3.

Such a dog sledging tour can be interpreted by customers and others as more authen-tic (within the expedition theme), there is less comfort and they have to take the roles and tasks of 'expedition members'. The product is more demanding for the customers, one has to take responsibility and co-produce more fully during consumption. Also the product has (should have) higher requirements (for example, relevant background, physical fitness and will to struggle) in order to get access to the product. It is not for everybody, but still people can take part without experience of dog sledging. This is an example of experience products that may involve going through 'hell before getting to heaven'. These customers often seek to get out of their comfort zone to do/learn new things and become different. The good feelings can come in phases during the tour, but are perhaps strongest at the end of it and shortly after. Personal meaning and identity seem particularly important; the tour can be transformative even for later practice in daily life. If people go on such a tour without the necessary prerequisites, then the tour

---

BOX 13.2   LIKE FRITJOF NANSEN, ALLOWS YOU TO
FORGET THE REST OF THE WORLD FOR A FEW
DAYS

Arriving at the trappers' hotel on the first night, customers meet the reception-
ists. They meet the tour guides and the other guests after breakfast for information. The customers have been put into the experience-scape of trappers, as
the hotel is designed in accordance with this theme. They go by car to the trappers' station meeting the dogs. The wilder the nature, the more direct the tour
guides become, yelling commands if needed, expecting the customer to be part
of a team working together with the tour guide and partly also with the other
customers so the teams of dogs are not getting in each other's way (fighting and
stopping the sledge). Most of the direct interactions with the other customers
take place during pauses and in the morning and evening when they express,
narrate and make sense of what they have experienced and their pains, worries
and joys. Their social gathering and outdoor activities make them a social group.
Part of this product is also the personnel on the ship who serve food, drinks,
facilities and perhaps entertainment and learning through stories. On the ship
or during the tour, they might meet other people, which can influence the value
of the experience product. They pass by an old hunting cottage and see some
remaining objects, perhaps talk with the hunter. The day between the two nights
on the boat, they drive to a glacier, seeing seals and other animals. The last day
on their way back, the tour guides take them to a frozen waterfall with frozen
fish and spectacular ice formations. The guides show the customers what to do
and talk when they want to, but there could have been more guiding both when
outdoors and indoors. When back at the trappers' station it is time for more
pictures and a goodbye to the dogs and people. Most of the customers seem to
bond with their dogs, even identifying with them and would not have liked it if
they had to switch dogs.

---

can be risky and reduce the value creation for the person, as well as for the other customers and the employees. These issues also have some relevance for the example of
ideal-type 11 above. This ideal-type can be more demanding for employees as they have
the main responsibility 24 hours each day, which also gives clues about tasks and prerequisites with regard to them.

The four dog sledge examples illustrate a move (upper right) in the grid that involves
increasing degree of both interaction types in the experience designs. The examples reveal
a second point, that is, this move-pattern coexists with an increase in what is required,
and perhaps gained by the customer and personnel during the experience. Such coexisting patterns (high degree of interactions and increase in demands) have been observed in
other nature-based subsectors too, and were briefly indicated in the hiking and culture
examples earlier (Section 13.3). These move-patterns can increase the need or potential
for innovations related to the phases before and after the experience and not only during

---

BOX 13.3   BE ACTIVE EXPEDITION PARTICIPANTS

Live in tents and participate not only with the dogs, but also in the camp life getting tents up and down; make water and food, clean and do other team tasks at the arctic camp such as night shifts watching for polar bears.

---

the experience. The contextualized examples of designs (not least of ideal-type 16) and moves in the grid reveal that the product and production get increasingly intertwined during consumption since the co-production increases. When working with innovation of such a product, one at the same time works with process innovation (the main structures of the process), which can also give premises towards market (type of segment), organization (competence, routines for security), equipment and perhaps more. In sum, it shows how innovation types can be related and intertwined.

What about other move-patterns, for example, down-left in the grid: would that have large or small consequences or potentials for innovation types? This needs to be explored more somewhere else. It seems risky and less likely that an enterprise offering designs of ideal-type 1 move directly to ideal-type 16. However, there are enterprises that start at ideal-type 16 (for example, hiking, ski tours and glacier tours) but these are people with a great deal of experience with non-commercial tours as part of their lifestyle and leisure time. Nevertheless, the move could be a giant step to take, since now paying customers are to participate. How radical a design and innovation are depends partly on the portfolio of the enterprise, that is, where the experience designs are in the grid, and where a firm tries to move in the grid when creating new designs. Also it depends partly upon the local destination or the subsector one competes within. Further, and not least, it depends upon the customers' view as to whether a design is seen as radical or not. When Enterprise 'X' was established during the 1990s, it was the first firm in Svalbard to let customers drive a team of dogs by themselves. It created a storm of critique from competitors and in the local newspaper, it was argued that it was crazy and risky since the dogs could run into reindeer, or be attacked by polar bears. However, the three people running the firm had experience from letting customers' drive in mainland Norway, and they had brought with them trained huskies that were suitable for this while competitors were using another type of dog that were less tame. The design was new in this local area, but not on the mainland. Customers liked it, and soon the competitors started doing the same (that is, imitating this part of the experience, for example, see Rogers, 1995). Getting ideas from other firms or copying is a challenge within experience sectors, it influence the competition and can make products seem similar to customers. However, if framing the activity within an experience-scape to facilitate certain interaction types and within a main theme/story, then the design can become different in content and meaning.

When Enterprise 'X' started up they designed dog sledge tours within experience-scapes framed within the theme of trapping, and conscious use of stories and dramaturgy. They did not offer the design of ideal-type 1. They offered half day and whole day tours within ideal-type 6. They also offered tours lasting three to seven days, in particular they had tours on which customers slept and ate within house tents or snow caves. The house tents where often warmed up before the customers arrived, they had wooden floors, five to six beds in each and a stove. A tour could have three house tents and one sanitary tent. The snow caves were also prepared in advance, and two customers shared one. But the comfort was lower in these caves and it was a great deal of work to make them (the concept was used for only two seasons). The customers preferred greater comfort combined with the exotic. This gave the idea of freezing a boat into the ice. The concept with the boat is much more expensive than house tents or snow caves; still more customers preferred it. The concept was introduced in 1999 and has been recognized internationally as innovative and unique, for example, by the *Guardian*: 'The idea is so simple, so beautiful, that you can't believe it was not thought of before' (Rushby, 2010). Not all drive to the boat by dog sledging, some go by snowmobiles with Enterprise 'X' or with other enterprises. The concept of using house tents has not been practised for many years, but during 2011 was brought up again as an idea. Other ideas for longer trips were also explored and some have been exploited. They have started to combine sleeping in cottages, expedition tents, boat and/or house tents. The changes in weather have forced them to improvise; several of the tours to the boat were cancelled during the winter of 2012 as the ice was unstable. Since the business started, a part of the business model related to accommodation has been to move customers between different camps since there are rather few rooms at the main camp.

The above elaborations support the following propositions:

P5: The higher degree of customer interactions (on one or both interaction types), the more the product and production process get intertwined during consumption (as co-production) and during innovation (as intertwined product and process innovations). This also seems to increase the potential of other intertwined innovation types.

P6: Being able to see, explore and exploit different ideal-types of experience designs and moves in the grid (Figure 13.2) can improve:

(a)   Innovations of products and portfolios through more varied products and deeper understanding of what the product involves.

(b)   Process innovations, as one gets a deeper understanding of the different types of co-productions and involvements.

(c)   Market innovations (segmentation and matching), due to increased understanding of what the product and production demands of, and can contribute to, the customer before, during and after the co-production.

(d)   Organizational innovations due to the increased understanding of what the product and production demands of, and can contribute to, the employees and the management before, during and perhaps after the co-production.

13.5   CLOSING REMARKS

We started this chapter by arguing that it is important to understand and focus on core characteristics of the experience logic in order to get a deeper understanding of innovation in experience sectors. We have chosen to explore customer interactions as the main core characteristic of the experience logic. The chapter contributes a theoretical framework that includes grids, ideal-types of customer interactions and suggested propositions about experience design and innovation types. The main arguments and elaborations are concluded below.

Six main types of customer interactions were outlined as potentially important for customer value. The customer interactions are situated within experience-scapes and perhaps framed by theme or story. It was first argued that commercialized/organized experiences (package, activity, attraction) can be designed in different ways depending on the different combinations of the six main types of customer interactions. This argument can be developed further to the point that different combinations of the six can visualize and give clues with regard to what innovations types (focus areas) are likely to be involved in the innovation process.

Due to the need for simplification, two main types of customer interactions were chosen for elaboration, that is, interactions with personnel and with other customers. A grid (Figure 13.1) focusing on the two types of customer interactions was developed making up 16 ideal-types of combinations. We elaborated and illustrated how commercial/ organized experiences can be designed in different ways depending on the ideal-types.

The first grid was developed into a second grid (Figure 13.2) by combining it with innovation types. In particular, we argued that ideal-types give clues for experience design and innovation not only about the product but rather the ideal-types focus on the co-production that can have implications for the other areas that innovation types address too. The grids, ideal-types and elaborations offer a new understanding of experience design and how innovation types can be related and intertwined. However, this is a start that needs further research. We have not developed new innovation types, but have shown and theorized how innovations can be complex, fuzzy and intertwined as suggested earlier in the literature on innovation in service and tourism (Hall and Williams, 2008; Toivonen and Tuominen, 2009). Our focus on the core characteristic 'customer interaction' through the use of ideal-types opened up a more holistic approach to innovation. When trying to measure or support innovations this is important, since it can be difficult for the stakeholders involved in innovations to say exactly what type and numbers of innovations have taken place, for example, the last year. Questions can arise: What type of innovation types should be registered in the survey? What if there were intertwined types, should they be registered as one innovation or one of each type, or as new types not asked for? This can make the registrations biased due to their random practice. Even the word 'innovation' may be unfamiliar to stakeholders in these sectors. This makes it difficult to measure innovation in terms of numbers in surveys, and even in interviews, which calls upon more complex and narrative approaches when trying to study or measure (that is, it has methodological implications). The theoretical framework suggested in this chapter contributes a new and deeper understanding of innovation types related to experience design. However, it was not our aim to elaborate on all the ways that innovation types can be related and intertwined; rather, we have tried to suggest one approach focusing on customer interactions that can reveal some of them. It may also be the case that a focus on one of the other core characteristics of the experience logic can reveal a new and deeper understanding of how innovation types can be related and intertwined.

The frames and arguments suggested in this chapter need to be studied empirically. There is also a need for further theorizing and studying other combinations of interaction types than the two that we have focused on and, hence, for work on other and perhaps extended grids that can handle more than two main types in a grid. This might be done by using spider-webs to show the degree to which each interaction type can be explored with regard to innovation types. The grids can be used by researchers and/ or practitioners to explore and analyse existing designs or new ideas more critically, and to work more holistic and carefully with innovation types before and during pilot testing and implementation of experience designs. Although we have focused on innovation types in the meaning of what is innovated, we have also addressed some aspects of how to interpret if an innovation is radical or not, which also can be useful in later studies.

Getting knowledge about how different customers or other actors perceive the involvement and significance of different interaction types and their mix (combinations) for the total experience can result in knowledge that opens up avenues for redesigns or new designs and other innovation types (for example, new markets and marketing, new ways of producing, organizing and so on). Regular involvement of customers and other stakeholders (for example, employees, cooperators) in evaluations and learning can be important steps in the innovation processes. Doing so through conversations/interviews, focus groups or pilot testing can give deeper and more interactive learning from and together with customers (Mannervik and Ramirez, 2006) and with other stakeholders.

ACKNOWLEDGEMENTS

The chapter is written as part of the research project Northern InSights (http:// www. opplevelserinord.no/), which is partly financed by The Research Council of Norway. We are grateful to the anonymous informants contributing with vital data. This chapter has benefited from constructive feedback on earlier versions at the 20th Nordic Symposium in Tourism and Hospitality Research, Rovanjemi in 2011, at the Innovating the Experience Economy: Design, Consumption and Concepts Conference, Roskilde in 2012, at a project seminar not least by Ann Jorid Pedersen and by the editors of this book, Jon Sundbo and Flemming Sørensen.

NOTES

1. Chosen since we focus most on them later in the chapter.
2. The number of types is not a point in itself; we could have chosen a five-point scale that would have given 20 ideal-types.

BIBLIOGRAPHY

Andersson, T.D. and L. Mossberg (2004),'The dining experience: do restaurants satisfy customer needs?', *Food Service Technology*, **4**, 171–7.
Ap, J. and K.K.F. Wong (2001), 'Case study on tour guiding: professionalism, issues and problems', *Tourism Management*, **22**, 551–63.
Arnould, E. and L. Price (1993), 'River magic: extraordinary experience and the extended service encounter', *Journal of Consumer Research*, **20**, 24–45.
Baker, J. (1987), 'The role of the environment in marketing services: the consumer perspective', in J. Czepiel,

C. Congram and J. Shanaham (eds), *The Services Challenge: Integrating for Competitive Advantage*, Chicago, IL: American Marketing Association, pp. 79–84.

Barcet, A. (2010), 'Innovation in services: a new paradigm and innovation model', in F. Gallouj and F. Djellal (eds), *The Handbook of Innovation and Services: A Multi-disciplinary Perspective*, Cheltenham, UK and Northampton, MA, USA: Edward Elgar, pp. 49–67.

Bitner, M.J. (1992), 'Servicescapes: the impact of physical surroundings on customers and employees', *Journal of Marketing*, **56**, 57–71.

Bitner, M.J., B.H. Booms and L.A. Mohr (1994), 'Critical service encounters: the employees' viewpoint', *Journal of Marketing*, **58**, 95–106.

Boswijk, A., E. Peelen and S. Olthof (2012), *The Economy of Experiences*, Amsterdam: Peason Education Benelux.

Celsi, R.L., R.L. Rose and T.W. Leigh (1993), 'An exploration of high-risk leisure consumption through skydiving', *Journal of Consumer Research*, **20**, June, 1–23.

Chesbrough, H. (2006), *Open Business Models: How to Thrive in the New Innovation Landscape*, Boston, MA: Harvard Business School Press.

Chesbrough, H. (2011), *Open Service Innovation*, San Fransico, CA: Jossey-Bass.

Echeverri, P. (2000), 'Servicemötets kommunikation' ('Service encounter communication'), PhD dissertation, Business School, Gotenburg Univerisity, Gotenburg.

Edvardsson, B., A. Gustafsson, M.D. Johnson and B. Sanden (2000), *New Service Development and Innovation in the New Economy*, Lund: Studentlitteratur.

Edvardsson, B., A. Gustafsson, P. Kristensson, P. Magnusson, and J. Matthing (2006), 'Introduction', in B. Edvardsson, A. Gustafsson, P. Kristensson, P. Magnusson and J. Matthing (eds), *Involving Customers in New Service Development*, Series on Technology Management, Vol. 11, London: Imperial College Press, pp. 1–13.

Eide, D. (2007), 'Knowing and learning in-practice in service: a relational and collective accomplishment', Doctorial thesis, Tromsø University, Tromsø.

Eide, D. and E. Ljunggren (forthcoming), 'Towards a framework for studying gendered innovations', Unpublished paper in review.

Fagerberg, J. (2005), 'Innovation: a guide to the literature', in J. Fagerberg, D. Mowery and R. Nelson (eds), *The Oxford Handbook of Innovation*, Oxford: Oxford University Press, pp. 1–26.

Fuglsang, L. (2008), 'Innovation with care: what it means', in L. Fuglsang (ed.), *Innovation and the Creative Process: Towards Innovation with Care*, Cheltenham, UK and Northampton, MA, USA: Edward Elgar, pp. 3–21.

Fuglsang, L., J. Sundbo and F. Sørensen (2011), 'Dynamics of experience service innovation: innovation as a guided activity. Results from a Danish survey', *The Service Industries Journal*, **31** (5), 661–77.

Furseth, P.-I. (2008), 'Serviceinnovasjon: nye perspektiver og anvendelser' ('Service innovation: new perspectives and application'), *Magma*, **11** (5), 1–10, available at http://www.magma.no/serviceinnovasjon-nye-perspektiver-og-anvendelser (accessed April 2013).

Gallouj, F. and F. Djellal (2010), 'Introduction: filling the innovation gap in the service economy – a multidisciplinary perspective', in F. Gallouj and F. Djellal (eds), *The Handbook of Innovation and Services: A Multidisciplinary Perspective*, Cheltenham, UK and Northampton, MA, USA: Edward Elgar, pp. 1–23.

Gallouj, F. and M. Savona (2010), 'Towards a theory of innovation in services: a state of the art', in F. Gallouj and F. Djellal (eds), *The Handbook of Innovation and Services: A Multi-disciplinary Perspective*, Cheltenham, UK and Northampton, MA, USA: Edward Elgar, pp. 27–48.

Grove, S.J. and R.P. Fisk (1997), 'The impact of other customers on service experiences: a critical incident examination of 'getting along'', *Journal of Retailing*, **73**, 63–85.

Gummesson, E. (1993), *Quality Management in Service Organizations*, New York: St Johns University and International Service Quality Association.

Gustafsson, A., B. Edvardsson and B. Sande'n (2002), 'Mapping customer behavior: a key to successful new service development and innovation', in J. Sundbo and L. Fuglsang (eds), *Innovation as Strategic Reflexivity*, London: Routledge, pp. 140–63.

Gustafsson, I.-B., Å. Öström, J. Johansson and L. Mossberg (2006), 'Five Aspects Meal Model – a tool for developing meal services in restaurants', *Journal of Food Service*, **17**, 84–93.

Hall, C.M. and A.M. Williams (2008), *Tourism and Innovation*, Oxon: Routledge.

Hallin, C. and R. Mykletun (2006), 'Space and place for BASE: on the evolution of a BASE-jumping attraction image', *Scandinavian Journal of Hospitality and Tourism*, **6**, 95–117.

Hipp, C. and H. Grupp (2005), 'Innovation in the service sector: the demand for service-specific innovation measurement concepts and typologies', *Research Policy*, **34** (4), 517–535.

Hjalager, A.M. (2002), 'Repairing innovation defectiveness in tourism', *Tourism Management*, **5**, 465–74.

Hjalager, A.M. (2010), 'A review of innovation research in tourism', *Tourism Management*, **31**, 1–12.

Jantzen, C., M. Vetner and J. Bouchet (2011), *Oplevelsesdesign (Experience Design)*, Fredriksberg: Samfundslitteratur.
Johannessen, J.A., B. Olsen and G.T. Lumpkin (2001), 'Innovation as newness: what is new, how new, and new to whom?', *European Journal of Innovation Management*, **4** (1), 20–31.
Kumar, V. and K. Karande (2000), 'The effect of retail store environment on retailers' performance', *Journal of Business Research*, **49**, 167–81.
Lehtinen, U. and J. Lehtinen (1991), 'Two approaches to service quality', *The Service Industry Journal*, **11**, July, 287–303.
Lovelock, C.H. (1996), *Service Marketing*, Upper Saddle River, NJ: Prentice Hall.
Mannervik, U. and R. Ramirez (2006), 'Customers as co-innovators: an initial exploration of its strategic importance', in B. Edvardsson, A. Gustafsson, P. Kristensson, P. Magnusson and J. Matthing (eds), *Involving Customers in New Service Development*, Series on Technology Management, Vol. 11, London: Imperial College Press, pp. 57–75.
Miao, L., A. Mattila and D. Mount (2011), 'Other consumers in service encounters: a script theoretical perspective', *International Journal of Hospitality Management*, **30**, 933–41.
Miles, I. (2005), 'Innovation in services', in J. Fagerberg, D.C. Mowery and R.R. Nelson (eds), *The Oxford Handbook of Innovation*, New York: Oxford University Press, pp. 433–58.
Mossberg, L. (1995), 'Tour leaders and their importance in charter tours', *Tourism Management*, **16**, 437–45.
Mossberg, L. (2007), 'A marketing approach to the tourist experience', *Scandinavian Journal of Hospitality and Tourism*, **7** (1), 59–74.
Mossberg, L. (2008), 'Extraordinary experiences through storytelling', *Scandinavian Journal of Hospitality and Tourism*, **8** (3), 195–210.
Muniz, A.M. and T.C. O'Guinn (2001),'Brand community', *Journal of Consumer Research*, **27**, 412–32.
O'Dell, T. (2005), 'Experiencescapes: blurring borders and testing connections', in T. O'Dell and P. Billing (eds) *Experiencescapes – Tourism, Culture, and Economy*, Copenhagen: Copenhagen Business School Press, pp. 11–33.
Oliver, R. (1999), 'Whence consumer loyalty', *Journal of Marketing*, **63** (Special Issue), 33–44.
Oslo Manual (2005), *Guidelines for Collecting and Interpreting Innovation Data*, 3rd edn, Paris: OECD.
Osterwalder, A. and Y. Pigneur (2010), *Business Model Generation: A Handbook for Visionaries, Game Changers, and Challengers*, Hoboken, NJ: Wiley.
Pine, B.J. and J.H. Gilmore (1999), *The Experience Economy. Work is Theatre and Every Business a Stage*, Boston, MA: Harvard Business School Press.
Prahalad, C.K. and V. Ramaswamy (2004), 'Co-creating unique value with customers', *Strategy and Leadership*, **32** (3), 4–9.
Ritzer, G. (1998), *The McDonaldization Thesis*, London: Sage.
Ritzer, G. and T. Stillman (2001), 'From person – to system-oriented service', in A. Sturdy, I. Grugulis and H. Willmott (eds), *Customer Service*, London: Palgrave Macmillan, pp. 102–16.
Rogers, E.M. (1995), *Diffusion of Innovation*, 4th edn, New York: Free Press.
Rushby, K. (2010), 'A hotel like no other in Arctic Norway', *Guardian*, 6 November, available at http://www.guardian.co.uk/travel/2010/nov/06/arctic-adventure-spitsbergen-ship-frozen (accessed April 2013).
Schouten, J.W. and J.H. McAlexander (1995), 'Subcultures of consumption: an ethnography of the newbikers', *Journal of Consumer Research*, **22**, June, 43–61.
Schumpeter, J.A. (1934), *The Theory of Economic Development: An Inquiry into Profits, Capital, Credit and the Business Cycle*, Cambridge, MA: Harvard University Press.
Sundbo, J. (2009), 'Innovation in the experience economy: a taxonomy of innovation organizations', *The Service Industries Journal*, **29** (4), 431–45.
Sundbo, J. and F. Gallouj (1999), *Innovation in Services in Seven European Countries*, Report No. 1, Roskilde: Center of Service Studies, Roskilde University.
Sundbo, J., F. Sørensen and L. Fuglsang (2010), *Innovation in the Experience Sector*, Research Report No. 10:7, Roskilde: Centre of Service Studies, Roskilde University.
Toivonen, M. and T. Tuominen (2009), 'Emergence of innovations in services', *The Service Industries Journal*, **29** (7), 887–902.
Vence, X. and A. Trigo (2009), 'Diversity of innovation patterns in services', *The Service Industries Journal*, **29** (12), 1635–57.

14. Entrepreneurship in the experience economy: overcoming cultural barriers
Lars Fuglsang and Flemming Sørensen

14.1 INTRODUCTION

This chapter sets out to investigate the success factors for entrepreneurship in the experience economy. It shows how entrepreneurship in the experience economy can be described as an open process that can come into conflict with different cultural barriers, but also shows how entrepreneurs can succeed in spite of the existence of such barriers.

Among the central topics in entrepreneurship studies is the question of how entrepreneurs behave (Gartner, 1985, 1988) and also the cultural and emotional encouragement of entrepreneurship has been investigated (see, for example, Choueke and Armstrong, 2000; George and Zahra, 2002; Hayton et al., 2002; Jayasinghe et al., 2007). However, the social and cultural barriers that entrepreneurs face within a social community have been less investigated and are generally less understood. Also in innovation studies, especially in innovation surveys (OECD, 2005), there is a long tradition of studying the barriers to innovation. However, cultural barriers and issues have been explored in less detail (see, for example, Dougherty, 1992; Filson and Lewis, 2000; Scozzi et al., 2005). Nevertheless, understanding the nature of these barriers and how entrepreneurs deal with them is of central relevance because entrepreneurship and innovation can be seen as an activity that comes into conflict with everyday life, what Schumpeter called the 'circular flow' of the economy (Schumpeter, 1934 [1969]).

In relation to the concept of the experience economy, entrepreneurship has received little attention (see Hjorth and Kostera, 2007 for an exception). However, studies of different experience economy subsectors indicate that entrepreneurship is an important aspect of change and development in such subsectors (for example, Darmer, 2008; Henry, 2007; Ateljevich and Page, 2009; Sundbo, 2011). In this chapter we shall argue and illustrate how cultural norms can pose particular obstacles for entrepreneurs in the experience economy because experiences often are rooted in local cultures and because open innovation is central for entrepreneurship and development in the experience economy. We shall also explore how entrepreneurs in the experience economy can creatively overcome cultural barriers. We do so through a case study of a number of experience entrepreneurs in a local community. These entrepreneurs have been responsible for developing different experiences such as tourist attractions, different events and a youth culture house in a municipality characterized by different cultural barriers to experience development. The study indicates how experience entrepreneurs can be successful, in spite of the strong presence of cultural barriers.

The chapter is structured as follows. We first theoretically discuss the cultural barriers that may conflict with entrepreneurship and especially with entrepreneurship in the experience economy. Secondly, we present the empirical method applied. Thirdly, the analysis is presented and a model of successful entrepreneurship in the experience economy is developed and illustrated. Finally, we come to some conclusions in the chapter about how successful experience entrepreneurs can overcome cultural barriers.

14.2   CULTURAL BARRIERS TO ENTREPRENEURSHIP

Schumpeter (1934 [1969]) originally defined entrepreneurs as individuals motivated to run the risk of introducing new ideas made from new combinations of materials and forces. Entrepreneurship theory generally tends to define entrepreneurs in a positive and functional way as individual people 'who perform the function of reforming or revolutionising the productive system' (Bruyat and Julien, 2001) or as individuals who discover and exploit opportunities (Shane and Venkataraman, 2000). However, in management and business studies, entrepreneurs are often associated with creating firms rather than bringing about change (Benneworth, 2004). Other entrepreneurs may sustain alternative development paths but tend to stress self-reliance rather than growth. Examples include certain types of lifestyle entrepreneurs in tourism (Ateljevich and Doorne, 2000). In what follows, entrepreneurship is understood as being related to change and innovation rather than simply the creation of new firms.

Places and regions characterized by entrepreneurship and development (for example, industrial districts, innovative milieus and so on) have been seen as being characterized by a common culture, shared norms and an 'entrepreneurial spirit' (Maskell and Malmberg, 1999). In contrast, certain regions may become locked-in and 'static' if people continue to do things in the 'usual way' (Grabher, 1993; Capello, 1999). This indicates how culture can both be a resource and a barrier to entrepreneurship and development. As a starting point to understand what kind of cultural norms can present barriers to entrepreneurship in the experience economy, it is relevant to look at what in the Scandinavian countries is known as the 'Law of Jante'. The Law of Jante is not a real law, but rather a number of tacitly shared norms and codes of conduct that were described by the Norwegian/Danish novelist Axel Sandemose in his 1933 novel *A Refugee Crosses his Track*. The Law of Jante states that one should never try to be, or consider oneself to be, different or more valuable than others in a community (Silvera and Austad, 2004). The law consists of ten commandments, including: Don't think you are anything special, that you are smarter than us, better than us, know more than us or can teach us anything. Although Jante is a fictional Danish town in a novel, it is recognized that societal norms in Denmark today continue to tacitly function on the premises of this law. Furthermore, although the Law of Jante has developed in a Danish context, traces of it can be found more or less universally. For example, the law is often referred to in the other Scandinavian countries to describe their societal norms and elements of the law can also be recognized in other parts of the world (see Peterson, 1988 for examples). The 'Tall Poppy Syndrome' in Anglophone countries is also an example of this (Kirkwood, 2007). This indicates that social and cultural norms may be maintained in many places as a way to justify and enable actions of certain kinds, and to avoid others. These are universal phenomena, though their intensity and impact varies across space and various social groups. As discussed later, because experiences are often related to and rooted in local culture, such cultural norms may be particularly strong barriers to entrepreneurship in the experience economy.

Cultural norms, such as those expressed in the Law of Jante, are often referred to as cultural barriers for those who believe in the possibility of creating new and different ways of doing things. In this way, cultural norms work as protection against entrepreneurs breaking with tradition or – using Schumpeter's terms – 'the circular flow'. The cultural barriers can be perceived as tacitly shared norms and codes of conduct that are in contrast to those of cultures in which entrepreneurs have typically been described as 'heroes'; cultures in which individualism is praised and in which the traditional entrepreneurial paradigm seems to fit well. Thus, Schumpeter (1934 [1969]) defined entrepreneurs as individuals motivated to run the risk of introducing new ideas mainly for egoistic reasons (that is, with profit in mind). In contrast, the emphasized cultural norms encourage (or rather demand) people to put the community before the individual (Silvera and Seger, 2004) and they are rooted in a communitarian and egalitarian culture in which traditional individualistic entrepreneurship is received negatively (Peterson, 1988). Thus, they can be perceived as a barrier towards successful entrepreneurship (in its original sense) in more communitarian-oriented societies. The norms preserve a sense of egalitarianism in which standing out in a crowd through high performance or self-promotion is unacceptable (Jackson and Gharavi, 2006).

The cultural norms are socio-cultural modes of existence and justification that can lead to lock-in. This has been illustrated to be the case in the 'industrial district' of the Swedish Gnosjö Region (Johannisson and Wigren, 2006). In this case, Jante Law was perceived as a socio-cultural expression of people's negative responses to deviant behaviour in a static community where people were used to doing things in a familiar and safe way and where the principle of rational behaviour worked well (Swedberg, 2006). A referent for entrepreneurship in the ideal typical Schumpeterian sense is exactly the opposite: deviation from norms (Lindgren and Packendorf, 2006) and decisions based on intuition rather than on rational behaviour (Swedberg, 2006). In local communities such as the one mentioned, indigenous entrepreneurs who play by the rules of the local culture can be considered 'insiders' acting as caretakers of the past, the present and the future. The Schumpeterian entrepreneurs (understood as an ideal type in the Weberian sense), on the other hand, are 'outsiders' who challenge the established norms and practices (Johannisson and Wigren, 2006). Thus, for 'insiders', the cultural barriers can be seen as a way to protect existing cultural norms. 'Outsiders' have to violate the norms in order to promote change.

Successful entrepreneurship has also been argued to depend on the entrepreneurs' social embeddedness (that is, being an 'insider'), which facilitates access to social and economic resources (Jack and Anderson, 2002). However, becoming embedded is, as indicated, complicated for ideal typical Schumpeterian entrepreneurs in a community dominated by cultural barriers. It is also equally important to stress that being too embedded will constrain change. In conclusion, as Lindgren and Packendorf (2006) argue, it is important for the success of the entrepreneur to be an 'outsider' while still being connected to and involved in the community. The entrepreneur must see cultural norms as a justificatory regime and understand how they work in general. But they must also be able to depart from this and play with other justificatory orders. Thus, a tension between entrepreneurship and cultural norms must be allowed. This will be a balancing act between deviation and belonging, being an 'insider' and an 'outsider'. This corresponds somewhat with Peterson's (1988) argument that the Jante Law does not prevent the emergence of entrepreneurs, but that entrepreneurs must play by the rules of the law, they must know its norms and codes of conduct. According to Johannison (cited in Peterson, 1988), to succeed in a Jante culture, the entrepreneur should not consider the community as a means for attaining personal goals but rather – as a sort of social entrepreneur (for example, Swedberg, 2006; Garud et al., 2007) – consider the development of the community to be a personal goal. These entrepreneurs resemble the ideal typical Schumpeterian entrepreneur, but they are not necessarily or not only motivated by the prospects of personal profits (Peterson, 1988).

14.3   EXPERIENCE ECONOMY AND CULTURAL BARRIERS TO ENTREPRENEURSHIP

Entrepreneurs must manage change as a 'delicate balance' between innovation and not breaking the given cultural norms. We shall argue that this balance becomes even more delicate when entrepreneurs operate within the experience economy, which is often related to local culture and cultural norms and which is under the influence of open innovation, where external ideas play an important role.

Entrepreneurship in the experience economy has until now received little direct attention from the academic world (see, however, Hjorth and Kostera, 2007). Nevertheless, examples of entrepreneurship in different subsectors of the experience economy have been discussed, such as in music (Darmer, 2008), film production (Soila-Wadman, 2007), tourism (Ateljewich and Page, 2009), among artists (Sundbo, 2011) and more broadly in the creative industries (Henry, 2007). These studies indicate how entrepreneurship in the experience economy is widespread and of crucial relevance for the dynamic development of the different experience economy subsectors. A lack of entrepreneurship can ultimately result in the demise of experience economy clusters (for example, in the case of British coastal resorts; Shaw and Williams, 1998) whereas dynamic experience entrepreneurship can lead to the rise of others (see, for example, Cooke, Chapter 20, this volume) or can define new possibilities for entire subsectors of the experience economy (Ateljevich and Doorne, 2000). Entrepreneurs are important for disembedding and re-embedding the concept of the experience economy in a local context (Hjorth and Kostera, 2007). It is through the entrepreneurs and entrepreneurial networks that the concept of experience is brought to life and can be performed in the local context.

While the above-mentioned cultural barriers and inertia may be relevant to entrepreneurship in general, matters are complicated further in the experience economy. Firstly, this is because many experiences are rooted in local areas and in their cultures and they are targeted at local markets. Thus, experiences are often directly anchored in local cultural phenomena to which people are emotionally tied. Thus, acceptance from local consumers of a particular experience and of the entrepreneurs themselves is indispensable. However, experiences are cultural phenomena that can rouse emotions, especially when the experiences break the circular flow of local cultural habits and traditions (which can, for example, be the case in the arts) the entrepreneurs may be faced with cultural constraints. Thus, the balancing act between being an 'insider' and an 'outsider' and between conforming to and deviating from the cultural norms becomes particularly delicate for entrepreneurs in the experience economy.

Secondly, the experience sector is a dynamic sector characterized by dynamic processes of change and development (Fuglsang et al., 2011). In such dynamic and changing sectors in particular, there can be more impatience towards the cultural barriers that prevent entrepreneurs from pushing new ideas. In static sectors where efficiency and rational behaviour are more important for competitiveness, cultural stability may be better sustained by economic actors and entrepreneurs. In static sectors, cultural barriers to change can help guide businesses' and other actors' behaviour in already known and efficient ways. On the other hand, in dynamic sectors such as the experience economy, cultural barriers may prevent entrepreneurs from introducing the required changes and development. The result will be a loss of competitiveness and stagnation. Thus, in a dynamic sector such as the experience economy, overcoming cultural barriers is not only more complicated for entrepreneurs but, at the same time, also more important because overcoming the barriers is required if individual actors and regional and local areas are to develop and remain competitive.

Thirdly, open processes of entrepreneurship and open innovation play a central role in creating change in the experience economy (see Sundbo et al., Chapter 12, this volume), which can exacerbate possible confrontations between the entrepreneur who is bringing in external ideas and local cultural barriers. Open innovation is an interactive process that actively scans and uses ideas external to the firm and the community; ideas that need to be accommodated to internal resources and ideas. In open innovation, inputs to the entrepreneur come from many sides: suppliers, competitors, entrepreneurial spin-offs from large firms, new start-ups, knowledge-intensive service firms, other services or advanced user groups. In his later work, Schumpeter recognized that innovation had become a routinized and automated activity that was taken care of by trained specialists in research and development (R&D) departments (Schumpeter 'II'; for a discussion see Phillips, 1971). But today the case can be made that innovation has become a more differentiated, dispersed and 'open' activity (Bessant, 2003; Chesbrough, 2003; von Hippel, 2005; Fuglsang, 2008). Furthermore, entrepreneurship may have regained its importance today because of open innovation as it requires entrepreneurial types that can pick up external ideas and use them in a new context. Open innovation means that the involvement of many inputs and ideas become critical to entrepreneurship, which requires the mobilization of actors that are both internal and external to a firm and a region. The experience economy can be understood as an area of development that involves a great deal of open innovation and therefore requires entrepreneurship. Fuglsang et al. (2011), for example, show how users and other external actors are critical in creating innovations in experiences. This is partly because many actors need to coordinate their interests in order to benefit from innovation in experiences. For example, in tourism in particular, where destinations have different elements such as attractions, hotels and restaurants, many actors must coordinate their activities and experiences in order for a single entrepreneur to enact change.

Therefore, open processes of innovation and entrepreneurship are central for experiences but if entrepreneurs operate locally under strong cultural barriers, this may represent a fundamental obstacle for them as they and their ideas will have to be accepted by the local community in which their businesses are unfolding.

Thus, entrepreneurship is central to the experience economy and its development. However, in cultures dominated by cultural barriers and conservatism, such entrepreneurship may be complicated. In what follows, this is illustrated empirically.

However, also discussed is how entrepreneurs, in spite of cultural barriers in the experience economy, can become successful.

14.4   METHOD

In order to explore how entrepreneurs in the experience economy perceive and deal with cultural barriers, the critical incident technique was applied, though in a somewhat modified form.

The critical incident technique was developed by Flanagan (1954) and has been applied to service research (see Bitner et al., 1990; Roos, 2002; Gremler, 2004; Fuglsang, 2007) including studies of public services (see, for example, Urquhart et al., 2003) and public health (see, for example, Ölvingson et al., 2002) in order to explore incidents or events that have a positive or negative impact on given situations. Flanagan studied, among other things, critical incidents for successful flight crew performance during war expeditions, by asking about events that were especially important for success or failure in that situation. In that way, it was possible to uncover actions that were crucial for coping with a situation, such as the ability to deal with vertigo during a flight and how the design of the cockpit was affecting the situation. The method presumes that a situation can be distinguished and that incidents in the situation can be remembered and described in detail by participants. Quantitative as well as qualitative data can be used for this, but qualitative data are often preferred because the researcher looks for action-oriented data and descriptions of how individual persons experience the situation.

In this investigation, the basic situation is that the entrepreneur is faced with cultural barriers, while the focus is on positive ways in which the entrepreneur can deal with them. The approach is, however, not directly an application of Flanagan's method, where incidents are seen as hard ontological facts. Instead, the approach is inspired by the more phenomenological approach of Chell (1998) who proposes that the method can be used to uncover incidents as they are perceived by respondents, that is, perceptions of problems, and strategies for coping with them, in a given situation. Following this, the method used here explores how entrepreneurs perceive cultural barriers and how they deal with them. Also, rather than looking for 'incidents', which are normally understood as human behaviour linked to specific individual persons, the analysis looks for broader success factors in the situation, hence incorporating more structural aspects in the analysis such as organizational, institutional or strategic factors. For example, 'trust' is not really an incident but more a factor that is important for success. This corresponds to the tradition of critical success factor analysis that has been important to business system research (see, for example, Rockart, 1979; Bullen and Rockart, 1981; Shank et al., 1985; Nah et al., 2003). According to Bullen and Rockart (1981), 'Critical success factors are the few key areas of activity in which favourable results are absolutely necessary for a particular manager to reach his goals.' Critical success factor analysis thus aims to identify a limited set of factors that are important for success in an enterprise and its resource planning, such as, for example, management support, business plans and vision. Bullen and Rockart also argue that five general sources of critical success factors can be distinguished: (1) the industry; (2) competitive strategy and industry position: (3) environmental factors; (4) temporal factors; and (5) managerial position.

However, the method applied in this chapter is largely inspired by Flanagan in the sense that the critical factors are uncovered through qualitative interviews by collecting subjective, action-oriented information. The factors we identify are not limited to the five sources but are distinct factors that respondents have observed and that are then grouped into certain themes in accordance with Flanagan's method. According to Flanagan, 'The critical incident technique outlines procedures for collecting observed incidents having special significance and meeting systematically defined criteria' (Flanagan, 1954, p. 327).

In the empirical study, more than 20 semi-structured interviews were made with public and private actors in a Danish municipality who in different ways were related to public and private experience economy activities. These interviews helped in building up a picture of the business environment of the municipality and in identifying interesting experience entrepreneurs. From the interviews, four exemplary experience entrepreneurs were identified who had been successful in innovating and introducing change in spite of meeting significant cultural barriers to experience entrepreneurship. They were selected because they represented different types of entrepreneurs, enabling us to study cultural barriers in different dimensions. These were a business entrepreneur, an entrepreneurial consultant, a subcultural entrepreneur and a political entrepreneur. Partly following Flanagan's guidelines, the entrepreneurs were asked to report the events or factors that they remembered as important during entrepreneurship. These were then interpreted and grouped into broader themes that were then hypothesized to be critical incidents; each representing critical problem-solution strategies of the entrepreneur that in retrospect appeared important; including events, processes and issues. This also implies that in general we chose to focus on positive critical incidents and thus identify incidents leading to success. The four entrepreneurs described had been either business entrepreneurs or entrepreneurial types working with policy and administration. A description of the entrepreneurs and their activities is provided in Table 14.1, by which they have been categorized according to the different dimensions of entrepreneurship in the experience economy that they cover: public versus private as well as profit versus non-profit oriented.

14.5　ANALYSIS

14.5.1　The Local Cultural Context

The municipality in which the identified entrepreneurs performed their activities has about 65000 inhabitants, of which approximately 25000 live in its central town. The municipality is considered to belong to a semi-peripheral area in which unemployment rates are higher than the national average, the educational level lower and health conditions worse. Apart from a smaller tourist destination located in the municipality, it has never been known for its experience economy.

The four entrepreneurs all feel they have met cultural barriers in the municipality. In the case of the business entrepreneur A (here and elsewhere, 'A' to 'D' refer to the entrepreneurs listed in Table 14.1), the development of experiences, which for the local population were new and unfamiliar, included encountering obstacles. A was met by a

Table 14.1   The entrepreneurs and their entrepreneurial activities

Entrepeneur	Entrepreneurial activities
(A) The business entrepreneur	Created a Go-Kart attraction later replaced by a Golf and Fun Park, an attraction offering 'adventure golf' (large-scale mini-golf), football and frisbee golf, a driving range, bumper boats, electric cars, radio-controlled cars and an American style baseball batting cage. The Golf and Fun Park opened in 2005. Since then, new activities have been introduced and visitor numbers have been growing.
(B) The entrepreneurial consultant	Employed by the municipality as cultural consultant, her professional background is from 'the world of theatre'. She has created different networks and various new events such as the one-week long annual Culture Clash Festival, presenting local and non-local alternative cultural expressions.
(C) The subcultural entrepreneur	Manager of the Culture Factory, an independent youth house financially supported by the municipality. The Culture Factory is located in an old factory outside the centre of the main town in the municipality. Its services are targeted at young musicians, climbers, kick boxers, skaters and the municipality's youth council. It functions as a busy concert club for non-mainstream artists.
(D) The political entrepreneur	Politically active for 25 years, and chairman of the cultural council for a number of years before he was mayor of the municipality from 1990 until February 2007. He has for many years been the main political actor responsible for the cultural policy of the municipality's main town, which has resulted in different projects, e.g. the building of a new leisure and residential harbour area, a culture house and the development of other different cultural experiences such as a festival week.

lack of trust by the population, and by economic and political actors who were not receptive to his ideas:

> When I made the Go-Kart track, it was almost the first new thing that had happened in the last 20 years . . . When I went to the municipality and told them I would like to make a Go-Kart track they thought I was an idiot! . . . When you come with completely new ideas such as adventure golf, frisbee golf, football golf, you have an explanation problem.

Similarly, the cultural entrepreneur (B) met several obstacles to developing experiences, especially because of the limited willingness to change in both local cultural actors and the local population.

> The area is a bit conservative compared to a big city. It is easier to present 'Candis' [a mainstream pop-group for the middle aged] on the square for the 16th, 17th, 18th year in a row, because you know that there is a large group of people who want that. (B)

She was also met with the attitude that what she was trying to do was nothing special, or nothing to be proud of. The subcultural entrepreneur (C) also fought against lack of trust in the idea of the culture factory: 'I don't think many believed we would last many years when we started.' Furthermore, due to the focus on unconventional youth cultures, the support from the local population was not strong:

I think there was a reason that we were put out here [in the industrial outskirts of the central town] . . . I think they liked it to be a bit invisible . . . There are a lot of prejudices about what this place is like.

The appearance of C as a hybrid of a punk rocker and a biker – surely not an 'insider' – may have sustained such prejudices.

Finally, D felt lack of trust in his projects in a similar way. For example, when suggesting the creation of a new large-scale residential area including all the service infrastructure that was needed, he was met with scepticism, laughter and lack of support because 'It is not usual "in this part of the country".'

The entrepreneurs relate their experiences to the general (non-) innovative atmosphere in the municipality. Firstly, a lack of ambition and a lack of belief in innovative capabilities pose barriers to change: 'You were afraid to be ambitious. Because we do after all come from [the municipality] . . . If you create something, you almost excuse yourself: "Sorry we come from [the municipality]"' (D). Lack of ambition and belief is indicated as being rooted in the agricultural history of the area: 'We don't have a development gene, a desire to develop. Because from the dawn of times we have been a rich agricultural society with no need to create anything' (D). Both of the above statements indicate the presence of the Jante Law: people stick to traditions and if not then they humbly excuse themselves. This becomes explicit in the next statement:

Sandemose could have written the Jante Law down here. It is a bit up hill normally: 'That is never going to work out' . . . But when they see that it is a good business they say: 'now you are making too much money'. (A)

The result is that the local population is considered by the entrepreneurs to be unsupportive towards new experience initiatives and that tradition poses a barrier to change that breaks the circular flow: 'It is hard to move people from what they are used to' (C). Thus, the municipality is described as a milieu that has mentally eliminated its own capabilities to introduce and accept change. The milieu is not 'open to open innovation'. It has its own culture that depends on the Jante Law not supporting, but restricting entrepreneurship. Therefore, there is a need for new entrepreneurs: 'You need somebody to put on the yellow jersey. Somebody who doesn't care about what the others say' (D).

14.5.2 Critical Incidents for Entrepreneurship in the Experience Economy

In spite of being met by cultural barriers, the four entrepreneurs have developed and implemented experiences breaking with tradition. The following emphasizes five incidents described during the interviews, consisting of five critical problem-solution strategies for the entrepreneurs that were vital for the entrepreneurial activities. Together, the incidents point at the crucial role of balancing between being an 'insider' and an 'outsider'. This is illustrated in Figure 14.1, which summarizes the entrepreneurs' actions in relation to the five critical incidents and to the 'balancing act'.

14.5.2.1 Incident 1: Networking innovation in a strategic arena

The first incident consists of networking innovation activities in a strategic arena (the municipality), where people with different perspectives, positions, morals and powers

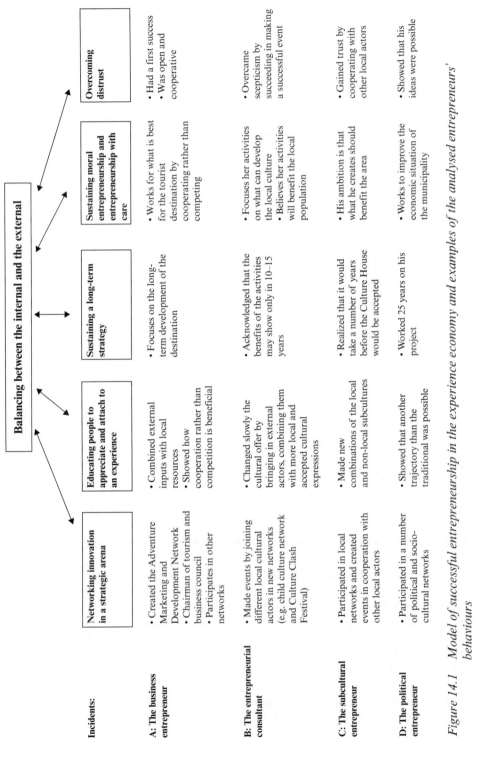

Balancing between the internal and the external

Incidents:	Networking innovation in a strategic arena	Educating people to appreciate and attach to an experience	Sustaining a long-term strategy	Sustaining moral entrepreneurship and entrepreneurship with care	Overcoming distrust
A: The business entrepreneur	• Created the Adventure Marketing and Development Network • Chairman of tourism and business council • Participates in other networks	• Combined external inputs with local resources • Showed how cooperation rather than competition is beneficial	• Focuses on the long-term development of the destination	• Works for what is best for the tourist destination by cooperating rather than competing	• Had a first success • Was open and cooperative
B: The entrepreneurial consultant	• Made events by joining different local cultural actors in new networks (e.g. child culture network and Culture Clash Festival)	• Changed slowly the cultural offer by bringing in external actors, combining them with more local and accepted cultural expressions	• Acknowledged that the benefits of the activities may show only in 10–15 years	• Focuses her activities on what can develop the local culture • Believes her activities will benefit the local population	• Overcame scepticism by succeeding in making a successful event
C: The subcultural entrepreneur	• Participated in local networks and created events in cooperation with other local actors	• Made new combinations of the local and non-local subcultures	• Realized that it would take a number of years before the Culture House would be accepted	• His ambition is that what he creates should benefit the area	• Gained trust by cooperating with other local actors
D: The political entrepreneur	• Participated in a number of political and socio-cultural networks	• Showed that another trajectory than the traditional was possible	• Worked 25 years on his project	• Works to improve the economic situation of the municipality	• Showed that his ideas were possible

Figure 14.1 *Model of successful entrepreneurship in the experience economy and examples of the analysed entrepreneurs' behaviours*

interact. Much of this pluralistic networking happens through the process of accommodating and negotiating compromise within the local community.

In the case of A, networks linking the entrepreneur to the strategic arena have been of crucial importance. A has, for example, created a local strategic 'Adventure Network' with three other local companies in the tourist destination (a bowling centre, a water activity centre and a go-cart and paintball centre). Several other local businesses have loosely enrolled in this network through cooperation agreements (for example, transport companies, accommodation and restaurants). Through this network, which has created increased business for the companies, different combined experiences are sold to private and business customers. Thus, combining resources in the network has provided new development possibilities. Furthermore, A has involved himself in other networks to gain influence over the development of the destination. He has been chairman of the destination's tourism and business council and has also been involved in the municipality's tourism council.

A networking strategy has also been central to B's success. She has been the network entrepreneur behind different networks in the municipality, such as formal networks (for example, a child culture network) as well as informal social networks. One network is particularly remarkable: the Art-in-Time Network. Through this, B has joined actors from different experience sectors from the local community with the result that new innovative experiences have been created, 'When different perspectives cross each other and change each others' usual ways of seeing things, that's where I see that new things are created.' The one-week long yearly Culture Clash Festival is an example of this.

Entrepreneur C's Culture Factory can be considered a strategic platform for young people, musicians and others in the municipality. C is simultaneously a member of the Art-in-Time Network and participates in other networks with local actors. This has resulted in different experiences, for example, a mobile nightclub (Kazoo) representing an alternative to mainstream discotheques in the central town, and a bingo-lightshow-nightclub in the swimming centre. C considers the networks as central to experience innovation because they combine different cultural resources: 'We are not afraid of combining things, finding playmates and creating something that we don't know where will end. It is the idea of trying out things.'

Finally, for D, networks of a political/municipal character have been of central importance. These networks are of a direct and indirect political character as well as having a more socially oriented style. D is, for example, an active member of the football club, the business council and more. He also promotes networking with other municipalities in order to break down the typical competition among neighbouring municipalities as he considers cooperation to be the only way to improve the situation of the individual municipalities as well as the entire area.

The four entrepreneurs' activities depend, to a large degree, on the entrepreneurs' networks – the innovations would not have been possible without them. Furthermore, they weave together different ideas and interests so that different groups that must be involved in the experience are prepared to be so. All in all, networking the innovation in the strategic arena serves the purpose of connecting the entrepreneurs ('outsiders') with the local community ('insiders') so that they and their entrepreneurial activities can become more easily accepted. This helps the entrepreneurs to balance their role as 'insiders' and 'outsiders'. This is further sustained because networking in the strategic arena also influences the other critical incidents in Figure 14.1. For example, the networks provide a context for learning about an experience (incident 2), and they increase the ability to mutually benefit from innovation (incident 4).

14.5.2.2   Incident 2: Educating people to appreciate and attach to an experience

There is seldom a clear need for a new experience. People cannot initially see the use of it, as shown by the cases of the Go-Kart track (initially considered a mad idea), the Culture Factory (which was hidden away), the Culture Clash Festival (which was seen as nothing special) or the Northern City (conflicting with 'how we usually do things'). Therefore, the entrepreneur has the task of educating people to want the experience. This means that he or she must try to develop people's tastes. For example, A had to show that the Go-Kart track was not an idiotic idea. In the case of the Culture Clash Festival, B needed to show the population that 'it *was* special!' In the case of the Culture Factory, C had to demonstrate its potential, while D had the difficult task of educating people to see that it is possible to create something new 'in this part of the country'. Part of the entrepreneurial role is thus to teach people to appreciate and understand an experience and see it in the right proportion so that they become attached to it. This corresponds somewhat to the role Becker, in a famous article (1953), assigned to people who teach other people to become marijuana users by continuously showing users how they could appreciate and get attached to the drug. In the same vein, entrepreneurs can teach people to appreciate what they are doing in a given environment.

One strategy applied by entrepreneur B is to make the population see the potential in a new experience by introducing it in a way that gradually makes people receptive to its cultural value. A describes this strategy as a 'sugar makes the art go down' strategy; a way of introducing a new cultural experience in a format that does not 'threaten' or intimidate the local population. In order to achieve this, while drawing inspiration for new experiences from other places, it has been B's aim to apply such experiences in ways that 'fit' the local population. The Culture Clash Festival is an example. The festival 'clashes' different cultural expressions to introduce the local population to unknown arts (punk-rock, drag-show and so on) and combines local and non-local cultural resources:

> We have a festival that is different from what you see in any other place in the country because you can experience a combination of a local peculiarity – subcultures from the local area – and some very different cultural expressions that come from the outside, within the frame of the same festival.

Thus, external cultural ideas and resources are combined with local ones in order to attach the local population to new cultural experiences. C and the Culture Factory applied a similar strategy. C possesses networks with other youth culture houses in the country and abroad and an extensive social/professional network within the music sphere. Apart from receiving ideas, knowledge, inspiration and access to resources from these, they cooperate in creating events, such as the yearly Gutter-Island Garage Rock Festival. Thus, entrepreneur C has also brought in new experiences in the shape of alternative, subcultural events that are combined with local subcultures and other local cultural actors' activities. D directly describes the process of getting acceptance as an educational process: 'You need to create an excitement that it is possible to create something. It is an educational process.' D feels he has influenced the mentality of the population due to the cultural policy, but that it has been a long effort. D also finds inspiration from other places to do things in another way than one is used to 'in this part of the country'.

Incident 1 facilitated and educated people to appreciate an experience. This is also the case for entrepreneur A, who in a less strategic manner introduced new experiences for which he found inspiration abroad and which were combined with local resources through networking. It is through local networks that the entrepreneurs may gain acceptance for their ideas, while networks are also used to combine the old with the new and thus create gradual changes that induce dynamism in the static community. Educating people to appreciate the experiences also helps the actors to balance attention between the inside and the outside and maintain a delicate balance between the local and the non-local; that is, local tradition and cultural input from the outside.

14.5.2.3   Incident 3: Sustaining a long-term strategy

From the interview with D, it soon became clear that he has attempted to pursue a long-term strategy for experience development. This long-term strategic approach is critical because experience development, according to D, requires leaders and champions that can show the way, and because it takes time to build a capacity for the development of experiences. This approach leads to the employment of new entrepreneurial types, such as the role of the cultural consultant (B). She herself sustains such a long-term perspective as she is aware that the results of her efforts may not show tomorrow, but only in 10 or 15 years time. A also has such a long-term strategic perspective, which results in his involvement in different networks 'for the good of the destination'. Finally, C indicates how it takes many years to teach the population about the qualities of the Culture Factory, but he is prepared for this and does not intend to give up, so he also takes a long-term perspective.

Thus, acknowledging that getting entrepreneurial activities accepted by the local community takes time is a crucial characteristic of the entrepreneurs. It does not make them give up but instead makes them engage in the other necessary activities such as building networks and educating people. In this way, the entrepreneurs accept that introducing new ideas requires considerable time, within which internal and external inputs are delicately balanced. This is further helped on the way by the next critical incident.

14.5.2.4   Incident 4: Sustaining moral entrepreneurship and entrepreneurship with care

It follows from the earlier incidents that the entrepreneurs are not, strictly speaking, entrepreneurial individuals in the Schumpeterian sense. Individual economic benefits are not the only driving engine. They are more like composite entrepreneurs who possess different drives and capabilities that make them fall under concepts such as social, moral, lifestyle, political and network entrepreneurs. Not being strictly focused on economic benefits turns out to be one central critical incident for succeeding despite the presence of cultural barriers.

For example, A's different network activities are related to an almost patriotic localness: 'We are some that think in the area. We love this area and we would like to see some development.' This 'love of the place' is characteristic for the Adventure Network in which the collaborators know that only by complementing each other rather than offering the same products will they benefit from the destination. The network is characterized by a collaborative approach to business and local development:

> It is clear that it demands that each company sees it as a plus for the area and does not see the others as direct competitors, but has the point of view that there is room for all of us. (B)

B has a focused view on creating experiences that benefit the area: 'If what I create is good for the area, then I'm satisfied'. Although, in this case, it may be a result of a professional localism rather than local patriotism, it is a central aspect of her activities. Also, C has a clear geographical focus. This is somehow expected from his employment but is also expressed in C's desire to create an offer of experiences that are beneficial for the area, and to be a cultural dynamo that moves the local culture and initiates other initiatives. D of course has a geographical approach that, due to his political position, has naturally been central. His mission is to improve the economy of the municipality, partly by attracting citizens to the municipality by developing an attractive cultural offer.

Thus, the four entrepreneurs have developed a capacity to care for the local community. This helps them and their ideas to become accepted by 'insiders' and seen as embedded in the local community. As a result, their deviant behaviour is more easily accepted. The geographical point of view may be a way of 'showing good intentions', which also makes trust building (the following incident 5) and networking (see incident 1) easier.

14.5.2.5   Incident 5: Overcoming distrust

A final critical challenge for the entrepreneurs is overcoming the distrust of the local population of economic and political actors. The above described incidents themselves sustain this. Participating in local networks (incident 1), educating people to appreciate the new experiences (incident 2) and carrying out activities for the good of the local geographical area (incident 4) are all steps towards overcoming distrust. For example, trust is a central aspect of the Adventure Network as a forum where ideas can be discussed without the fear that they are stolen: 'We are very open about our plans.' The network as such breaks the traditional pattern of competition among businesses in the destination where distrust and competition are rooted in old controversies, free-riding and a lack of coordination.

A fundamental way to overcome distrust is for the outsider to actually demonstrate in practice that their ideas are successful. For example, A, having managed to convince the relevant actors that they should support his project of developing the Go-Kart track, could also demonstrate that the new experience actually became successful. This meant that new entrepreneurial activities have become easier: 'The municipality has been positive after things began to move.' Thus, having created one success, A gained trust and subsequent projects have been easier to carry through. For B, creating the first successes has also been essential: 'People said, "That is not anything special." But it was something special! And the next time you have more friends with you.' This has also meant that while the Culture Clash Festival was originally met with scepticism from the population, it has now become a yearly event that the inhabitants are generally proud to host.

The importance of trust may partly be explained by the notion of trust developed in a much-quoted article by Mayer et al. (1995) in which trust is defined as 'The willingness of a party to be vulnerable to the actions of another party based on the expectations that the other will perform a particular action important to the trustor, irrespective of the ability to monitor and control that other part' (p. 712). The authors argue that trust depends on four dimensions: the trustor's propensity to trust, and the trustee's demonstration of ability, integrity and benevolence. We have no reason to doubt that people in the municipality also have a high propensity to trust. As for the three other dimensions, succeeding with innovation can certainly demonstrate ability, but in the four cases we also observe that the two remaining dimensions of integrity and benevolence are important to trust building: the entrepreneur must be reliable (long-term strategy, incident 3) and he must demonstrate that he wants the best not just for himself – or herself – but also for the whole of the local community (incident 4).

14.6   DISCUSSION AND CONCLUSIONS

The above incidents all point to one general central rule for successful entrepreneurship in the experience economy above all the others when cultural barriers are present – that of keeping a delicate balance between the internal and the external in a process of open innovation involving local and non-local resources. On the one hand, 'outsiders' are needed to create change and generate new values. On the other, localized control seems critical and 'insiders' need to learn to relate to the new experiences. The various critical incidents all support this in an interdependent way. Innovations must be networked in a local setting (incident 1), appreciation and attachment must be established (incident 2), this must happen in the context of reliable long-term strategies (incident 3) that are backed by moral entrepreneurship (incident 4) and trust creation (incident 5). Thus, the actions of each of the entrepreneurs, as summarized in Figure 14.1, sustain change in a local culture where cultural barriers to experience entrepreneurship can be identified. This shows that patterns of innovation can be constructed by a strategizing process that gradually accommodates the internal and the external worlds. In this way, entrepreneurial activities have the potential to break the circular flow and create change and regional development in the long run in areas dominated by cultural barriers to entrepreneurship.

Cultural barriers to entrepreneurship have been little explored. Overcoming cultural barriers by accommodating the different worlds of the 'insider' and the 'outsider' can be an important local development strategy. Cultural barriers such as those discussed in this chapter favour community and indigenous culture over individual initiatives and entrepreneurship in an open market economy. Therefore, overcoming these barriers is critical for entrepreneurship, especially when entrepreneurs (in conditions of open innovation, as described in the theory section of the chapter) need to mobilize local people. The experience economy is particularly sensitive to such cultural barriers. For one thing, experience innovations are often linked to a community and its traditions. They are sometimes directly anchored in local cultural phenomena to which people are emotionally tied. This may constitute both a resource and a strong barrier to change.

The approach of the chapter leads to a slight revision of the Schumpeterian view of entrepreneurship. Under conditions of open innovation in the experience economy where entrepreneurs become dependent on inputs and ideas from external actors, destroying cultural barriers in the Schumpeterian sense of 'creative-destruction' is not an issue. The notion of creative-destruction seems insufficient as a way to describe entrepreneurship under such conditions. Instead, we notice that people accommodate different worlds. Cultural barriers mean that people do not want to become involved in change for cultural reasons. Again, this problem cannot be solved by a Schumpeterian entrepreneur acting on her own. It must be solved by experience entrepreneurs that are able to overcome the barriers and work with them in a constructive, justificatory way. This can be seen as a process of 'creative-accommodation' rather than 'creative-destruction'.

The chapter also contributes an understanding of how entrepreneurship in an experience economy must justify itself in relation to cultural barriers in a local context. The entrepreneur can be seen as someone who translates the idea of the experience economy into practice (Hjorth and Kostera, 2007), yet in this case study translation also means justification in relation to a cultural framework of a local community.

The cultural barriers discussed in this chapter are not equally strong everywhere and they may in some places be absent, and even rejected. Furthermore, certain subsectors of the experience economy are not as closely attached to local cultures and markets as those dealt with in this chapter. This is, for example, the case in the video games industry. Cultural barriers may be less important for the success of entrepreneurs in such subsectors. Also, the specific forms of behaviour of the studied entrepreneurs cannot be generalized. The theoretical contribution of this chapter is instead to analytically understand the experience economy as antagonistically performed by entrepreneurs in localized settings where they must seek justification for introducing external ideas. To understand how the experience economy is created requires, we would argue, more context-sensitive and process-oriented approaches that explore the complex conditions under which entrepreneurs operate and the attitudes and claims they must continuously adopt. There is no general recipe for creating the experience economy but entrepreneurs must find their way through, be sensitive to the rationality of local cultural barriers and realize that there is certainly no guarantee of success.

REFERENCES

Ateljevic, I. and S. Doorne (2000), 'Staying within the fence: lifestyle entrepreneurship in tourism', *Journal of Sustainable Tourism*, **8** (5), 378–92.

Ateljevic, J. and S.J. Page (2009), *Tourism and Entrepreneurship: International Perspectives*, Oxford: Butterworth-Heinemann.

Becker, H.S. (1953), 'Becoming a marijuana user', *American Journal of Sociology*, **59** (3), 235–42.

Benneworth, P. (2004), 'In what sense "regional development?": entrepreneurship, underdevelopment and strong tradition in the periphery', *Entrepreneurship and Regional Development*, **16** (6), 439–58.

Bessant, J. (2003), *High-involvement Innovation: Building and Sustaining Competitive Advantage through Continuous Change*, Chichester: Wiley.

Bitner, M.J., B.H. Booms and M.S. Tetreault (1990), 'The service encounter – diagnosing favourable and unfavourable incidents', *Journal of Marketing*, **54** (1), 71–84.

Bruyat, C. and P.A. Julien (2001), 'Defining the field of research in entrepreneurship', *Journal of Business Venturing*, **16** (2), 165–80.

Bullen, C.V. and J.F. Rockart (1981), A primer on critical success factors, Working paper No. 69, Massachusetts Institute of Technology, Cambridge, MA.

Capello, R. (1999), 'Spatial transfer of knowledge in high technology milieu: learning versus collective learning processes', *Regional Studies*, **33** (4), 353–65.

Chell, E. (1998), 'Critical incident technique', in G. Symon and C. Cassell (eds), *Qualitative Methods and Analysis in Organizational Research: A Practical Guide*, London: Sage, pp. 51–72.

Chesbrough, H.W. (2003), *Open Innovation: The New Imperative for Creating and Profiting from Technology*, Boston, MA.: Harvard Business School Press.

Choueke, R. and R. Armstrong (2000), 'Culture: a missing perspective on small and medium sized enterprise development?', *International Journal of Entrepreneurial Behaviour and Research*, **6** (4), 227–38.

Darmer P. (2008), 'Entrepreneurs in music: the passion of experience creation', in J. Sundbo and P. Darmer (eds), *Creating Experiences in the Experience Economy*, Cheltenham, UK and Northampton, MA, USA: Edward Elgar, pp. 111–33.

Dougherty, D. (1992), 'Interpretive barriers to successful product innovation in large firms', *Organization Science*, **3** (2), 179–202.

Filson, A. and A. Lewis (2000), 'Cultural issues in implementing changes to new product development processes in a small to medium sized enterprise', *Journal of Engineering Design*, **11** (2), 149–57.

Flanagan, J.C. (1954), 'The critical incident technique', *Psychological Bulletin*, **51** (4), 327–58.

Fuglsang, L. (2007), 'Critical incident teknikken' ('The critical incident technique'), in L. Fuglsang, P. Hagedorn-Rasmussen and P.B. Olsen (eds), *Teknikker i samfundsvidenskaberne*, Frederiksberg: Roskilde Universitetesforlag, pp. 260–77.

Fuglsang, L. (ed.) (2008), *Innovation and the Creative Process: Towards Innovation with Care*, Cheltenham, UK and Northampton, MA, USA: Edward Elgar.

Fuglsang, L., J. Sundbo and F. Sørensen (2011), 'Dynamics of experience service innovation: innovation as a guided activity', Results from a Danish survey, *The Service Industries Journal*, **31** (5), 661–77.

Gartner, W.B. (1985), 'A conceptual framework for describing the phenomenon of new venture creation', *Academy of Management Review*, **10** (4), 696–706.

Gartner, W.B. (1988), '"Who is the entrepreneur?" is the wrong question', *American Journal of Small Business*, **12**, 11–32.

Garud, R., C. Hardy and S. Maguire (2007), 'Special issue on "institutional entrepreneurship"', *Organization Studies*, **28** (7), 957–1140.

George, G. and S.A. Zahra (2002), 'Culture and its consequences for entrepreneurship', *Entrepreneurship Theory and Practice*, **24** (4), 5–7.

Grabher, G. (1993), *The Embedded Firm: On the Socioeconomics of Industrial Networks*, London: Routledge.

Gremler, D.D. (2004), 'The critical incident technique in service research', *Journal of Service Research*, **7** (1), 65–89.

Hayton, J.C.J., G.G. George and S.A.S. Zahra (2002), 'National culture and entrepreneurship: a review of behavioural research', *Entrepreneurship Theory and Practice*, **26** (4), 33–52.

Henry, C. (ed.) (2007), *Entrepreneurship in the Creative Industries*, Cheltenham, UK and Northampton, MA, USA: Edward Elgar.

Hjorth, D. and M. Kostera (2007), *Entrepreneurship and the Experience Economy*, 1st edn, Copenhagen: Copenhagen Business School Press.

Jack, S. and A. Anderson (2002), 'The effects of embeddedness on the entrepreneurial process', *Journal of Business Venturing*, **17** (5), 467–87.

Jackson, P. and H. Gharavi (2006), 'Technologies of the self: virtual work and the inner panopticon', *Information Technology and People*, **19** (3), 219–43.

Jayasinghe, K., D. Thomas and D. Wickramasinghe (2007), 'Bounded emotionality in entrepreneurship: an alternative framework', *International Journal of EntrepreneurialBehaviour and Research*, **14** (4), 242–58.

Johannisson B. and C. Wigren (2006), 'The dynamics of community identity making in an industrial district: the spirit of Gnosjö revisited', in C. Steyaert and D. Hjorth (eds), *Entrepreneurship as Social Change*, Cheltenham, UK and Northampton, MA, USA: Edward Elgar, pp. 188–209.

Kirkwood, J. (2007), 'Tall Poppy Syndrome: implications for entrepreneurship in New Zealand', *Journal of Management and Organization*, **13** (4), 366–82.

Lindgren, M. and J. Packendorf (2006), 'Social constructionism and entrepreneurship: basic assumptions and consequences for theory and research', *International Journal of Entrepreneurial Behaviour and Research*, **15** (1), 25–47.

Maskell, P. and A. Malmberg (1999), 'Localised learning and industrial competitiveness', *Cambridge Journal of Economics*, **23** (2), 167–85.

Mayer, R.C., J. H. Davis and F.D. Schoorman (1995), 'An integrative model of organizational trust', *Academy of Management Review*, **20** (3), 709–34.

Nah, F.F.-H., K.M. Zuckweiler and J.L.-S. Lau (2003), 'ERP implementation: chief information officers' perceptions of critical success factors', *International Journal of Human-Computer Interaction*, **16** (1), 5–22.

OECD (2005), *The Measurement of Scientific and Technological Activities. Oslo Manual. Guidelines for Collecting and Interpreting Innovation Data. Third edition. A Joint Publication of OECD and Eurostat*, Paris: OECD.

Ölvingson, C., N. Hallberg, T. Timpka and R.A. Greenes (2002), 'Using the critical incident technique to define a minimal data set for requirements elicitation in public health', *International Journal of Medical Informatics*, **68** (1–3), 165–74.

Peterson, R. (1988), 'Understanding and encouraging entrepreneurship internationally', *Journal of Small Business Management*, **26** (2), 1–7.
Phillips, A. (1971), *Technology and Market Structure: A Study of the Aircraft Industry*, Lexington, MA: Lexington Books.
Rockart, J.F. (1979), 'Chief executives define their own data needs', *Harvard Business Review*, **57** (2), 81–93.
Roos, I. (2002), 'Methods of investigating critical incidents: a comparative review', *Journal of Service Research*, **4** (3), 193–204.
Schumpeter, J. (1934), *The Theory of Economic Development: An Inquiry into Profits, Capital, Credit, Interest and the Business Cycle*, Cambridge, MA: Harvard University Press, reprinted in 1969, Oxford: Oxford University Press.
Scozzi, B., C. Garavelli and K. Crowston. (2005), 'Methods for modelling and supporting innovation processes in SMEs', *European Journal of Innovation Management*, **8** (1), 120–37.
Shane, S. and S. Venkataraman (2000), 'The promise of entrepreneurship as a field of research', *Academy of Management Review*, **25** (1), 217–26.
Shank, M.E., A.C. Boynton and R.W. Zmud (1985), 'Critical success factor-analysis as a methodology for MIS planning', *MIS Quarterly*, **9** (2), 121–9.
Shaw, G. and A. Williams (1998), 'Entrepreneurship, small business culture and tourism development', in D. Ioannides and K. Debbage (eds), *The Economic Geography of the Tourist Industry*, London: Routledge, pp. 235–55.
Silvera, D.H. and B. Austad (2004), 'Factors predicting the effectiveness of celebrity endorsement advertisements', *European Journal of Marketing*, **38** (11–12), 1509–26.
Silvera, D.H. and C.R. Seger (2004), 'Feeling good about ourselves – unrealistic self-evaluations and their relation to self-esteem in the United States and Norway', *Journal of Cross-Cultural Psychology*, **35** (5), 571–85.
Soila-Wadman, M. (2007), 'Film producer entrepreneurship and the experience economy', in D. Hjorth and M. Kostera (eds), *Entrepreneurship and the Experience Economy*, 1st edn, Copenhagen: Copenhagen Business School Press, pp. 55–71.
Sundbo, J. (2011), 'Creative artists and entrepreneurship', in K. Hindle and K. Klyver (eds), *Handbook of Research into New Venture Creation*, Cheltenham, UK and Northampton, MA, USA: Edward Elgar, pp. 328–43.
Swedberg, R. (2006), 'Social entrepreneurship: the view of the young Schumpeter', in C. Steyaert and D. Hjorth (eds), *Entrepreneurship as Social Change*, Cheltenham, UK and Northampton, MA, USA: Edwards Elgar, pp. 21–34.
Urquhart, C., A. Light, R. Thomas et al. (2003), 'Critical incident technique and explicitation interviewing in studies of information behavior', *Library and Information Science Research*, **25** (1), 63–88.
Von Hippel, E. (2005), *Democratizing Innovation*, Cambridge, MA: MIT Press.

15. Networking in the experience economy: scaffolded networks between designed and emerging regional development

Dorthe Eide and Lars Fuglsang

15.1 INTRODUCTION

The experience economy is a new setting for local and regional development and planning that may prove more sensitive to local conditions and hedonistic perspectives than previous approaches (Lorentzen, 2012). Enterprises and other local actors can participate in the experience economy in a diverse and lifestyle-inspired way using niche strategies of innovation (Fuglsang et al., 2011), for example, within the fields of local food, sea kayaking or cultural heritage. Yet, there are barriers preventing local enterprises from participating in innovative activities. In particular, experience-based enterprises are often small and have limited resources.

In adopting a practice-based approach we argue that successful networking in experience sectors and tourism is dependent on 'scaffolding structures' (Orlikowski, 2006), that is, external resources and guidance that help actors create a focus and move beyond their immediate practice and reach a wider goal. The concept of experience is such a focus that can be created through scaffolding. In this chapter we seek to understand what this means by identifying three scaffolding structures: mobilizing actors, focusing attention and creating infrastructure and activities. The main contribution is to show how scaffolding structures and interactions can be important for successful network formation and innovation.

The chapter is based on case studies of two rural tourism networks, one in Northern Norway (the network Arena Innovative Experience) and the other in Southern Denmark (the Small Tourism network); both mainly consist of small enterprises. The enterprises are involved in attendance-based experiences within various fields including nature-, culture- or culinary-based experiences that people seek during their leisure time. The target groups are regional business sectors or travellers (tourism, business conferences and business groups).

The chapter is structured as follows. Section 15.2 starts with a brief review of network theory, and then goes on to discuss the concept of scaffolding structure and relates it to innovation and networks. Section 15.3 accounts for the methodology. In Section 15.4 we present the two case studies. The first of these is an in-depth study of the Norwegian tourism network, which, we argue, is an 'open', scaffolded network. Then we present a shorter description of a Danish case, namely the development of a 'domestic' network, thereafter we compare the cases. In Section 15.5 we summarize and discuss the main findings.

15.2 THEORY

15.2.1 Towards a Dynamic Approach to Networking

Industrial network studies have multiplied over the past decades and our knowledge about the role of networks of innovation in and between enterprises has increased significantly. Yet there are still important areas that we know little about, not least within the services and experience sectors. In a special issue of *Organization Science* on the genesis and dynamics of networks Ahuja et al. (2012) argue that there is a lack of knowledge concerning how and why networks emerge and evolve. Static, passive and premature approaches to networks dominate. Further, they argue that without understanding the dynamic nature of networks, the understanding of the outcomes of networks will suffer. One reason for the lack of dynamic perspectives is that evidence of them requires a complex and longitudinal methodology. In a 2013 (deadline) call for papers for a special issue of *Organizational Studies* Clegg et al. (n.d.) also address knowledge gaps related to networks and their dynamic and complex nature, and consequently call for more complex and longitudinal studies in which networks are seen not only as structures but also as actors. They emphasize the question of the manageability of networks, and hence the importance of emerging versus design characteristics and approaches to networks, a topic that is also addressed by others focusing on networks, learning and innovations (Powell and Grodal, 2005; Thompson, 2005).

Some studies have begun to explore, empirically, the dynamics of network formation and the interaction of designed and emergent characteristics. Doz et al. (2000) show how network formation processes can be both emergent and engineered. Sydow (2004) explores how evaluation can be a means of network development. Browning et al. (1995) have studied how the building of moral community can be important for network formation. Capaldo (2007) investigates how different network architectures evolve into weak, strong or dual network architectures. Berends et al. (2011) investigate the interaction of inter-organizational and interpersonal networks over time. These and other related studies (Bizzi and Langley, 2012) help us to understand the complexity of network formation and how networks evolve around social relations and social structures (Berends et al., 2011). Still, we know little about how these processes and dynamics support learning and innovation, and how design and emergent characteristics interact.

Innovative milieu theories (Camagni, 1991a, 1991b; Maillat, 1998a, 1998b; Crevoisier, 2004), which have a local and regional focus, have argued that local production 'milieus' composed of informal multifaceted relationships among people may evolve over time in a specific geographical area. The 'milieu' concept denotes how networks create synergies between enterprises and exploit them in informal ways. An innovative milieu is

> the complex network of mainly informal social relationships on a limited geographical area . . . which enhance the local innovative capability through synergetic and collective learning processes. (Camagni, 1991a, p. 3)

The concept of 'milieu' suggests how informal emerging social structures are important for mastering rules, standards, values and capital (Maillat, 1998a, p. 117). A milieu includes 'trust and convergence of viewpoints' and a 'chemistry of cooperation . . . that prompt firms to transcend the usual barriers of competition' (Maillat, 1998a, p. 118). A milieu is based on a 'collective and socialised process' (Camagni, 1991b, p. 130).

But milieu theories of innovation have been criticized for their emphasis on proximity. The concept has clear limitations when trying to explain innovative networks in an era of globalization. Research shows that even in rural areas, enterprises participating in such structures seek to broaden, deepen and reground their resources (van der Ploeg et al., 2002; Kitchen and Marsden, 2009). They become increasingly multi-locational and open as they draw on interactions and inspiration from other regions. They evaluate and specify their value chains and business models (Crevoisier and Jeannerat, 2009).

Network studies in experience sectors are scarcer, though some studies can be found in tourism research in particular, which is the main focus of this chapter. Networking, cooperation and proximity among tourism enterprises have been stressed as assets of competiveness, knowledge transfer and innovation (Buhalis and Cooper, 1998; Weidenfeld et al., 2010). Yet, at the same time, there is little evidence in the literature that tourism firms and tourism networks can be characterized by concepts like localized learning, agglomeration or industrial districts, all of which have been seen as relevant when explaining dynamics in manufacturing (Camagni, 1991a; Storper, 1995; Maskell et al., 1998). Hjalager (2000) finds little evidence for the industrial district approach in tourism. One reason for this is that many tourism firms are small. They may tend to erode network activities (Sørensen, 2007) because they are occupied by day-to-day activities. Further, the owners of some micro-tourism firms can be described as lifestyle entrepreneurs (Ateljevic and Doorne, 2000) for whom the love of place and quality of life is their prime motivation. They may be difficult to mobilize for large-scale network activities. In addition, local tourism networks can be ambiguous concerning whether they pursue community development or commercial values or not (Gibson et al., 2005).

Furthermore, some tourism firms, such as hotels, participate in global networks and chains rather than local networks in order to attract customers. In such cases participation in local networks tends to create redundancy and stagnation rather than improving market positions. Network relations that go beyond local bonds and present a larger diversity of inputs are required to ensure competiveness and innovation (Bærenholdt et al., 2004). Sørensen (2007) provides a case study to show that local networks may be dense and weak while non-local networks may be strong and sparse. The former focus on exploration and the latter on exploitation.

Tourism enterprises can hardly be blamed for this lack of localized learning (Bærenholdt et al., 2004). Rather, research should develop more complex, dynamic, contextual and evolutionary approaches in order to understand how tourism and experience networks evolve over time (Tremblay, 2000; Bærenholdt et al., 2004; Sørensen, 2007). Our argument here is that practice-based approaches to network formation can shed light on network formation and innovation in tourism and experiences. Practice-based approaches take their starting point in everyday actions and investigate their consequences for social and economic structures (Feldman and Orlikowski, 2011) rather than the other way round. This seems a relevant approach in rural tourism where day-to-day actions are often important.

15.2.2   The Concept of Innovation

Innovation can be defined as 'the effort to develop an element that has already been invented, so that it has a practical-commercial use, and to gain the acceptance of this element' (Sundbo, 1998, p.12). Innovations must be realized successfully in practice to count as innovations, but success does not necessarily mean commercial success. In service and experience-based sectors innovations are often incremental and intertwined with customer encounters, making it difficult to observe successful realization in practice. The outcome of innovation can be fuzzier than in the manufacturing of goods (Toivonen and Tuominen, 2009).

We know from research that innovation is not something that happens in isolation, undertaken by single entrepreneurs or research and development (R&D) departments, but in interaction among many actors. Open, multi-relational approaches to innovation are sometimes called Schumpeter III approaches to innovation, emphasizing how the knowledge applied to innovation is distributed and interactive (Fuglsang, 2008; Sundbo, 2008). Actors collaborate and draw on knowledge from other sources beyond their immediate context in order to innovate. Hence, the formation of networks and interactive systems of innovation can be important resources of innovation and represent innovations themselves.

15.2.3   The Concept of Managed Network Community and Scaffolding

We situate our approach to network formation in a practice- and process-based theoretical perspective (Bizzi and Langley, 2012). A practice- and process-based perspective stresses how everyday actions are 'consequential in producing the structural contours of social life' (Feldman and Orlikowski, 2011, p.1241; see also Fujimura, 1988; Carlile, 2002; Gherardi, 2006). This does not mean that structural elements and design are not important to everyday action or practice. Practice evolves around and responds to plans, structures, designs and so on. There is no fundamental contradiction between design and emerging.

Practice-based approaches to learning and knowing have mainly addressed interactions and learning within organizational contexts, and in self-organized communities of practices. Thus, there has been a call for studies that investigate processes across organizational boundaries, since combinations of knowledge and resources can create important innovations and learning (Brown and Duguid, 1991; Nonaka and Takeuchi, 1995; Gherardi, 2000, 2006; Lam, 2000). The potential for more radical innovations seems highest when resources and ideas are combined across boundaries (Brown, 1999; Wenger, 2003). Further, one can argue that cross-boundary collaboration can be important since collective practices are not limited by organizational boundaries.

Focusing on the concept of scaffolding structures is one way to explore how cross-boundary relations are constructed in a practice-based approach. The notion of scaffolding structures has been applied in practice- and process-based studies to explain how actors extend their knowledge beyond their immediate context (Orlikowski, 2006). It grows out of theories of child development and theories of distributed knowledge (Orlikowski, 2006). In child psychology (Vygotsky) it refers to the phenomenon that guidance/scaffolding can help children learn beyond what they can otherwise learn by focusing attention on certain concepts. While child psychology, in the tradition of Vygotsky, focuses on adult guidance in interaction with children and their practice, we argue for the importance of taking a more interactive and equal relational approach where actors may mutually guide each other and co-construct the focal points. Our context is adults, working in the experience sectors, and the actors participating in networks are often managers in the enterprises they represent. Nevertheless, the actors may need facilitating processes and structures in order to succeed with networks. We find that this approach is particularly relevant with regard to experiences because 'experiences' is a focus often co-constructed by many actors and it may help them to extend their practice in a dynamic way. Scaffolding is the activities that help them focus attention and innovate.

Clark (in Orlikowski, 2006, p. 462) defines scaffolding as 'a broad class of physical, cognitive, and social augmentations – augmentations that allow us to achieve some goal that would otherwise be beyond us'. Lane and Maxfield (2005, p. 37) refer to 'interaction loci' as an example of a scaffolding structure that includes 'user groups and trade fairs, trade and professional organizations, standards bodies, and communication media like trade and professional journals, company and organizational newsletters, and websites'.

In this chapter we emphasize scaffolding as interactive and mutual guidance that helps actors focus attention on the concept of experiences. This facilitates learning and new practices beyond those that the involved actors can undertake without mutual help and conceptual focus. Scaffolding structures are emerging structures that are provided by many actors and mutual cooperation. But in contrast to Orlikowski (2006), we argue that they must also, at least partly, be seen as designed structures.

According to Newell et al. (2009), social networks related to learning and innovations have been studied from two main perspectives. First, networks have been studied as 'channels' for knowledge/resource flow. Here the focus has been on nodes (for example, individual, community) and ties (relations between nodes, weak or strong, for example, Granovetter, 1973; quantitative or qualitative, connectivity) and often studied through a Social Network Analysis (SNA) approach (Cross and Parker, 2004). Second, networks have been studied as 'network communities', which tend to focus less on form and structure and more on relational quality, identity and activity. There are at least three main types of communities: (1) emerging communities like Communities of Practice (CoPs) that tend to be informal, self-organic and develop bottom-up; (2) managed (network) communities, created top-down to increase performance; and (3) online communities, for example, Facebook groups.

The networks we study in this chapter seem to have most in common with network communities (Newell et al., 2009, p. 169). They are experience-based tourism networks that evolve and emerge over time in an undetermined way. Yet they are not simply emerging communities but emerging through focusing and elaborating experiences. In this they draw on conceptual input helping them to develop, share and systematize their knowledge. We propose that experience networks create innovation and learning through scaffolding activities that provide focus and direction.

15.3   METHODOLOGY AND DATA

The study uses a hermeneutical-phenomenological and processual research method (Pettigrew, 1990; Langley, 1999; Van de Ven, 2007), which means that we seek to understand experience-based enterprises and their development in their particular business context. The study therefore uses a case design (Flyvbjerg, 2001) and the method is qualitative. We try to investigate some of the critical issues, perspectives and processes for network formation in two experience networks (Flanagan, 1954; Chell and Pittaway, 1998). In this respect, this chapter extends a previous study (Fuglsang and Eide, 2012) where we explored the bandwagon effect in the networks. In this chapter we analyse and compare the empirical cases by taking the starting point in the structural input they receive and how they evolve around this structural input.

The Norwegian and Danish experience cases were selected by using the strategic choice method (Fuglsang and Eide, 2012) to ensure both similarities and differences. The level of regional network is the analytical unit of the study. However, the networks are not seen in isolation; they are embedded in social relations and structures. Using a multi-level logic (Gherardi, 2006), we see the networks from the point of view of individuals, groups/sub-projects and regional innovation systems, yet our main focus is the network at the meso level between micro and macro.

The Danish case is based on in-depth interviews with three key informants following a semi-structured interview guide, and on documents, web pages and a Master's thesis (Petterson, 2010) supervised by one of the authors. In the latter nine network members were interviewed.

The Norwegian case has been studied over a longer period (in time and retrospectively), it is more in-depth, uses various analytical levels and mixed methods: in-depth interviews with six informants were undertaken (following almost the same semi-structured interview guide as in the Danish case). Follow-up interviews have been made with some of these informants and with other informants on special topics. Diverse documents (for example, project applications and reports) and web pages have been studied. Observations, interactions and conversations have been made. In addition, one of the researchers has conducted case studies in some of the firms, also employing mixed methods. She has also worked on sub-projects together with some of the actors.

Interviews lasted between 45 minutes and three hours, but most of them took about 1.5 hours. They were recorded and transcribed. Early phases of data analysis moved between a more open approach searching back and forth in the data, reflecting upon them (Kvale, 1996; Czarniawska-Joerges, 1997), looking for patterns of activities that led to experience network formation, learning and innovation. Later phases were more framed by the interview guide and theoretical perspectives using an approach similar to content analysis (Miles and Huberman, 1984).

A short introduction of the cases is outlined in Table 15.1.

15.4   CASE FINDINGS

The presentation of findings starts with the Norwegian case, which is more complex and involves more scaffolding structures.

Table 15.1   The two networks

	Arena Innovative Experiences (AIE)	Small Tourism
Number of enterprises	33 in 2012	Almost100 in 2011
Typical size of enterprise	Mainly micro or small in low seasons (fewer than ten employees); some medium sized	Micro (in many cases just a one-man company)
Year of creation	2007	1999
Experience label	Together we will excite our guests with world-class nature, culture and culinary experiences.	Give tourists a good experience so they return. Refer tourists to other network members.
Situatedness	Northern Norway, the county Nordland. Four of five sub-regions in Nordland are involved (Vesterålen, Lofoten, Ofoten and Salten). Plus Svalbard	South of Denmark, the sub-regions Lolland and Falster
Leadership	Project management and board from the start. Bottom-up approach with enterprises in the front seat, but also structure given top-down.	Coordinator; coordination group; later a chairman and a board.

15.4.1   Arena Innovative Experiences Case: An Open Experience Network

Arena Innovative Experiences (AIE) is a formalized business network among experience enterprises situated in Norway. It is part of the 'Arena programme', a national programme for long-term development of regional business clusters. The objective is to strengthen regional businesses' ability to innovate through dynamic interactions across enterprises, R&D institutions and universities and public facilitators, that is, so-called 'triple helix' interactions. Each arena project must have a unique business idea as well as develop and share knowledge with non-members of the network. In addition to a pre-study and pre-project period, the main projects are normally supported for three years (www.arenaprogrammet.no/).

AIE (www.innovativeopplevels.no) is situated mainly in the county of Nordland, which is the most southern of the three counties in Northern Norway. The enterprises are located in four of five sub-regions in the county (that is, Ofoten, Vesterålen, Lofoten and Salten). Two enterprises are situated in Svalbard, an integral overseas territory and archipelago. All enterprises are situated above the Arctic Circle.

The development of the network can be described in six phases (Table 15.2), in addition to which there was a background period during 2002–06 where the way was paved for the network. The enterprises decided to continue the network after finishing the Arena programme in November 2012.

The case findings are structured in terms of three scaffolding structures that we discovered: (1) focusing attention; (2) mobilizing actors; and (3) creating infrastructure and activities.

Table 15.2　The focus of attention throughout time

Pre-study (spring 2007)	Pre-project (fall 2007 to spring 2008)	Main year 1 (October 2008 to September 2009)	Main year 2 (October 2009 to September 2010)	Main year 3 (October 2010 to September 2011)	Exit phase (November 2011 to October 2012)
Increasing focus on experiences by firms plus is there a foundation for a regional network?	Vision: Create world-class experiences Sub-focus: Create commitment, application (main project), competence development and boundary objects	Vision continues Sub-focus: Four strategic action areas, with priority on MA1 and MA3	Vision continues Sub-focus: Four strategic action areas, with priority on MA1, MA3 and increase on MA2	Vision continues Sub-focus: Four strategic action areas, priority on MA2 and MA4	Vision continues Sub-focus: Do remaining tasks, particularly MA2 and MA4; secure sustainability of the network

15.4.1.1　Scaffolding structure 1: focusing attention

The main focus of the network was to innovate and produce experiences. This focus emerged from the firms' activity before the network formation, and provided an umbrella, energy and direction for the actors in different phases. The sub-focus at different stages is described in Table 15.2.

During the 2002–06 period different destination development projects in the region showed that (1) an increasing number of firms focused on experience production and (2) these projects did not focus enough on innovation. Further, other regions involved with Arena projects inspired public facilitating organizations to explore the potential for an Arena project focusing on experience innovation and production. During a pre-study and pre-project phase a vision was created: 'Together we shall inspire our guests with world-class experiences'. The firms recruited were involved in experiences production as a primary or secondary activity in one or more of the following main areas: nature, culture and food. The pre-project developed an application for the main project with a designed strategy in four main action (MA) areas: MA1: Renew and develop experience production; MA2: Increase internationalization and improve market development; MA3: Competence and network development; and MA4: Improve conditioning factors. MA four was not at first suggested by the project management and facilitators, but was argued increasingly important by some of the firms (that is, an example of a bottom-up process). The four areas with sub-projects were given different weights in different phases of the main project as shown in the table, starting with a focus on MA1 and MA3. In the exit phase the focus was also on creating sustainability for the network after finishing the formal programme as an Arena project. The strategic areas have structured the need for involving more actors, relations, activities and supporting infrastructure.

The focus on experiences has been ambitious as well as a significant 'glue', creating the basis for commitment and collective development with room for flexible tailoring to the individual firm and more emerging developments and co-developments of individuals, firms, networks and other actors.

15.4.1.2 Scaffolding structure 2: mobilizing actors

The number and nature of stakeholders increased significantly during the project period. This broadening of stakeholders was important for scaffolding the firms, but also for developing an innovation system within the experience economy. Below the actors are grouped into two main types.

Main actors According to the project manager, the main participants of the network have been the network members, that is, the firms, the network management, Nordland research Institute (NRI) and Nordland County Administration (particularly through the VRI Programme for Regional R&D and Innovation). In addition, we argue that Innovation Norway (IN) at the regional level has played a central role. These five main types of actor have been involved throughout the phases.

The number of firms has been rather stable at about 30 after entering the main project stage. During the first years most were micro or small in size; later a few medium-sized firms became involved. It was important that the network was not dominated by larger firms. About half of the firms participated in all phases. In the pre-study mature firms that focused on experiences were invited, and 18 firms signed an agreement of intent. During the pre-project phase 25 firms were involved (two exited). Recruitment was carried out in the exit phase as well. This is a demanding network, it is not for all:

> AIE is a network for the more experienced. As the CEO in one of the enterprises put it, 'AIE can be seen as a common development department, the operative running of the enterprises must be good, we do not use the network on things that have to do with the daily running [of a business], we use it to work with the areas we shall develop' . . . But it has been other enterprises that have tried, perhaps being in a building up phase and thinking they should get help with other things, perhaps with other ambitions or without the capacity. Some felt it was not what they expected, and they exited. That is OK. (Interview with N-2)

The project management consists of people from Mimir, a consultancy and development firm situated in the south. At first, only the manager was involved but later other employees participated in the network management and as knowledge providers and developers in specific sub-projects. In addition, the project management included a project administrator from Nordland Destination Marketing Organization (DMO). Getting an Arena project is difficult, a good grounding and application and access to a highly competent project manager were critical. The project and process manager of two successful destination projects in the county had also been in the management of an Arena network in tourism situated in the south. Getting him as a core partner for the new Arena project was considered a scoop:

> He has been very central all the time, because Mimir in the shape of consultant 'Z', has been the strongest professional supplier of these process management tools in tourism within Norway, and no one has been able to compete with them . . . If we were to 'to pick from the top shelf' there is none else . . . he knows the sector and how the society works with its many actors, he has the personal attributes. (Interview with N-1)

Interviews with other actors, not least firms, address the vital role of the project management and the project leader in particular.

When the idea of the Arena project came up, a public committee on tourism in Nordland County (with four public organizations) pointed at IN as the main public facilitating actor, and later the firms wanted IN as a more active facilitator in the early phases than IN used to be. IN and Nordland County Administration (NCA) have been represented on the network board and they have thereby created alliances and facilitation at the strategic level.

Nordland Research Institute (NRI) was member of the board from the start. In addition, NRI has been the main R&D partner involved at operative levels at network gatherings and in several sub-projects. However, when starting up this relation, NRI mainly had competences within entrepreneurship and innovation at a more general level, and little within tourism or the experience economy.

Other actors   The number of other actors increased significantly due to the network's searching and requests for expertise knowledge, co-operators to do activities with or funding. The relational developments took place through both designed and emerging approaches. Some of 'the others' (for example, the firm Human Factors and the film specialist Govertsen Film) have been involved in many sub-projects over several phases, interacting directly with the network management and the firms. While some actors were involved only in more narrow activities and periods, perhaps mainly at a distance and/or sharing knowledge in the form of reports/books and oral presentations.

Further examples of actors involved are:

1. Other clusters (also from other countries) and the National Center of Expertice (NCE)-Fjord Norway. One example is a new Arena project, that is, Arena Profitable Winter Experiences (APWE). So far, this new relation has created two formal subprojects aimed at learning from each other and working on shared problems. This has opened up the possibility for involvement of Troms County Administration and an R&D institute from Troms, in addition to increasing the cooperation with the University of Nordland (UiN) and the research project Northern InSights (see below).

2. Involvement of researchers from different regional, national and international R&D institutes and universities in a research project called Northern InSights (with focus on experience-based tourism). The Arena programme expected AIE to establish closer relations with R&D and educational institutions, and the network proactively searched for such possibilities. They became part of the resource group of the research project Northern InSights and suggested research questions when the research application was made. Later, the network developed its interactions with researchers. They have created spin-offs, for which Nordland County Administration often gave financial support. The large research project, however, emerged at a very convenient time for the network that could not be foreseen or designed by the network.

3. Interactions with local networks. Some of the firms are active members in local networks too, and some networks, for example, Winter Lofoten, developed in parallel and/or somehow intertwined with AIE. The learning has gone both ways: 'Like

the business network Winter Lofoten, where one gets a mutually interdependent learning, where it is not as with many of the other networks where AIE is the sole contributor of knowledge. A network like Winter Lofoten can contribute to AIE, because it is a good network' (Interview with N-1). Some local networks seem to be spin-offs from the knowledge and relational creations in the AIE network (for example, in Salten and in Vesterålen).

15.4.1.3 Scaffolding structure 3: creating activities and infrastructure

The rather stable involvement of the main actors contributed to regular and tighter relations, which increased mutual trust and mutual knowledge amongst the members. Cooperation had to be practised and emerged over time; it could not only be designed top-down. Yet, certain designed activities could 'scaffold' the emerging practices of cooperation and interaction.

One example of this third type of scaffolding structure is the representation of main actor types in the network board dealing with strategic choices such as sub-focus, sub-projects, recruiting and financing of activities not already financed by the Arena programme.

Another example is the yearly activities that took place during all four years after the pre-project. These were: (1) four network gatherings with a focus on the vision and chosen sub-focuses; (2) one study trip to other regions in the country or abroad; and (3) one larger open conference with a focus on experiences, with the aim to share knowledge and develop relations with actors not part of the network. These yearly activities (1–3) were vital scaffolding structures for the network development and creating new experiences. The designed main action areas (MA1–MA4) and sub-areas became concrete and implemented through sub-projects, first through design and then through emerging approaches as part of in-use activity. New challenges and opportunities emerged from practising and learning, which the main actors had less control over and little knowledge of when developing the main strategy. A vital undertaking in the pre-project phase was the experience course and later work with a specific tool of experience design called the LEO Experience Pyramid Model (developed by Lapland Center of Expertise). It gave a competence lift through shared language, knowledge and a tool that all could relate to (that is, boundary object, see for example, Wenger, 2003). It also became a 'glue' that tightened the relations and gave positive useful results for the firms. The network management summarizes it as follows:

> It stimulates innovation and advances, it strengthens the relations between the members and gives a more dynamic development of the cluster activities . . . a setting created in the cluster where many initiatives and spin offs are generated. (NGPExcellence, 2011, p. 37)

The LEO Experience Pyramid Model was developed into more usable toolkits and new or improved experience products were created in most of the firms.

Examples of other innovations and results of the network are 54 YouTube films involving 25 firms, profile design innovations, start-up and mid-phase measuring of innovations (Samuelsen and Clausen, 2008; Clausen et al., 2010), a foresight study (Løvland and Samuelsen, 2009), knowledge gathering in seven countries, new local networks and/or sale organizations, books for the sector, a new formal course on experience design at the university and so on.

Far from all sub-projects and activities were financed through the Arena programme of IN and the firms only. Other funds came from IN and the County Administration (the last year also by Troms), as well as, for example, the APWE, the Business School at the University of Nordland through Northern InSights and actors interested in the same topics (for example, Hanen, NCE). In the exit strategy the work with a sustainable infrastructure was argued to be vital, and funding for further R&D and education were regarded critical parts of this.

Many things have been designed when making the applications for the project phases, but opportunities and challenges emerged and become less or more important. Activities within MA2 (internationalization and marketing) were most challenging. The firms were too different in market segmentation and most of them too small and immature for more heavy internationalization. This also challenged some of the other actors (for example, IN) involved, starting internal development processes. The development of YouTube films is an example of an activity that became more important than originally assumed.

Another challenge was the unfamiliar specialized language and knowledge of R&D actors, not least in the beginning. Some enterprises experienced challenges due to their own competence development, which created difficulties in interactions with their own employees or external cooperating firms. These challenges hampered the innovation process and collective learning in or across the firm, and needed careful coping strategies.

15.4.1.4   Open co-development with both design and emerging elements

Networks (clusters) financed through the Arena programme of IN are supposed to develop triple helix relations. Further, they must share knowledge with actors who are not members of the network (for example, through open conferences, publications, interactions/cooperation). Above we have shown many examples of how knowledge and relational development and sharing is scaffolded, helping the actors to achieve goals otherwise beyond them. These examples involve both external and internal network interactions. For example, during the pre-project a start-up mapping showed that only 6 per cent of the 17 respondents considered universities/colleges, and 12 per cent considered R&D institutions, as medium/important sources in innovation (Samuelsen and Clausen, 2008). Two years later the mid-phase mapping showed an increase, 15 per cent of the 20 respondents considered both these two types of sources medium/important (Clausen et al., 2010). The positive trends increased further in 2012, as 39 per cent versus 29 per cent of the 28 respondents had such considerations (Flatnes and Furre, 2012). The triple helix effect of scaffolding can be illustrated by this quote written by one of the organizers of the experience conference in November 2011: 'Research, public facilitating organizations and firms in a perfect "dance" . . . Wow how it swings when triple helix works' (quoted on Facebook, 2011). The evaluation of the conference showed that participants were very satisfied, and one main reason was the scaffolding effects of professional organizing, and the way of involving researchers (from the Northern InSights project) as participants. By scaffolding openness and interaction with new kinds of actors in new ways, learning and innovations have increased (as indicated by, for example, Wenger, 2003). Facilitating a triple helix is an approach that originated in other sectors; this case shows that it can be very useful also in experienced-based sectors.

The scaffolding structures helped the firms to meet challenges that would otherwise have been impossible:

> I do think the project manager has been important in coping with emerging challenges and creating value of the potential . . . But it would not have been such a success if not all had been working toward it. And I think that VRI, the research project Northern Insights, the R&D environment and the county administration have all created positive synergic processes that improved the results. (Interview with N-3)

Another important achievement was the ability and will to 'voice' the experience firms' opinions: 'One has developed an arena as a partner [that is, the network] that one wants to listen to, its opinions about industry development. They are asked to participate in important projects, outside of Northern Norway' (Interview with N-4).

The experience-based tourism sector consists largely of small and rather fragmented enterprises that often have problems with coordination and 'voicing' their opinions. The ability of collective mobilizing and voicing improved significantly and can be seen as an innovation outcome in itself.

Looking back, not only did the firms co-develop, the other main actor's involved in the network (that is, NRI, NCA, IN and the network management) did so too. Emerging challenges and interactions have also created learning and innovation within these organizations, and learning following from network activity has been used in interactions with other actors not in the network.

> Competence developed through AIE on experience economy and knowing how to create good experiences we bring back to the public facilitating organizations. One learns together with the firms in the network, and we see that when we interact with other environments, other networks and firms, we use the experience from AIE and give the others suggestions based upon that. And we try to connect firms from AIE, for example, firms from Lofoten and firms not in AIE like from Vega in the southern Helgeland. (Interview with N-3)

In addition, several regional and national actors have contributed to the activities, and co-developed. It seems reasonable to conclude that the network has been open and interactive. Further, we argue that an innovation system in the experience economy has been developed, operating mainly at a regional level, but being at the front at the national level. The emerging innovation system is, however, not just due to the Arena project and its main actors. The VRI projects and Northern InSights project, with its involved actors and activities, have also created positive synergies with the Arena project.

15.4.2 Small Tourism Case: A Domestic Network

The Danish network called Small Tourism (www.den-lille-turisme.dk/) can be seen as an internally oriented 'domestic network', because it is oriented towards endorsing local cultural values rather than growth and change. It has a lower degree of policy support and a higher degree of proximity between the companies than the Norwegian network. It is justified by the attempt to make local tourism values more visible to tourists.

The Danish network tended to start with the actors, their values and social worlds rather than with a specific focus on development and innovation as in the Norwegian case. Therefore, we describe this network in a slightly different order.

15.4.2.1   Scaffolding structure 1: mobilizing actors

The owner of a local consulting firm took the initiative to start the network. He felt that travellers coming to Lolland-Falster were informed about three or four major tourist attractions only. But he also found that there was a great variety of many 'invisible' small tourist-related enterprises in the countryside, which could be given much more attention.

The businessman asked one of his employees to go around Lolland-Falster by car and identify such enterprises, and the employee asked the owners to come to a meeting. In this way, the businessman was able to identify small tourist-related enterprises on Lolland-Falster that were willing to attend a meeting and pay more attention to local tourism. And he made them aware of each other's existence, value and needs.

However, the way members were recruited also tended to constrain the scaffolding.

> We are very aware of who we take in as members. We need to understand each other and be serious . . . There is a group that talks to those who want to be members. You must have solidarity towards the network and its members. (Interview with D-3)

Therefore, mobilization both helped the network participants to move beyond existing practices but was also structured to keep up a high level of solidarity and mutual trust. It tended to be a social movement based in voluntary work more than a business network.

15.4.2.2   Scaffolding structure 2: focusing attention

Following the first meeting a network was formed. The businessman asked the members about their most urgent needs. They realized that their weak point was marketing. If they could improve marketing, they could attract more tourists to each enterprise.

They agreed to develop a brochure in which all members were represented. This was placed at strategic places around Lolland-Falster such as local tourist offices and in each member's enterprise. Furthermore, the members of the network agreed to refer and recommend tourists to each other.

> A common idea was worked out, which was to provide tourists with a good experience and make them desire to come here again . . . We demand that members should want to give tourists a good experience when they are down here. We believe that the right way to make tourists come here again and again is that they get good experiences . . . I think there is a common approach: give a good experience. (Interview with D-1)

Focusing attention was very dependent on previous experiences of common needs:

> We have talked about how it is important to give some little extra thing. Many times these small sites actually do it. Actually, before they come along with us. So it turns out that they have already found out that this is the way to get the tourists, or guests, inside. (Interview with D-1)

In 2011 there were almost 100 members of the network. Members were, among others, small eateries, ceramists, farm shops, museums and bed and breakfasts with special identities and competencies. Small common projects of management and innovation were financed by Leader+, the Danish Rural Community Development Programme and the European Union's Social Fund.

However, the network was not so ambitious with respect to scaffolding activities. As one member says:

> The idea is that it should be a self-managed network. You lose something of the network thinking when you have to create the network yourself . . . I think it will be difficult, because it consists of very small companies that are located in different places with different thoughts. (Interview with D-2)

The network was oriented towards local culture and it was self-organized. Therefore, there was a lower degree of focus on structural input and scaffolding. This was a conscious choice and important for mutual trust in the network. But it was also experienced as a problem by some of the members for whom it was difficult to find time and resources for the network activities.

15.4.2.3   Scaffolding structure 3: creating activities and infrastructure

The network has published a common brochure every year, and shared a website. Other activities include the designing of two bicycle routes, an open door project, yearly assemblies have been organized, and some of the members have formed networks within the network or small collaborative projects such as gourmet dinners and outdoor events. The businessman organized several short courses for the members about, for example, business accounting or how to develop a hobby business (for example, ceramics) into real business. Some of the innovations were created more spontaneously and unpredictably by small networks in the network through co-development.

In 2010 the network was turned into a more formal association. Previously it was just a loose network with a coordination group, but with no clear legal status. In 2010 it was a registered association with a board. This made it possible to apply for financial support from the municipality fo smaller cultural funds that better fitted the purpose and size of the network. It also helped to define a narrower workspace:

> now that we are a registered association, you get an insight into the budget, and you get an insight into the accounts. Now the possibilities are much better to argue, hey, this is not wise what the board is doing. And you can elect some other people to administer the network. (Interview with D-1)

The Statutes of Small Tourism (www.den-lille-turisme.dk/DLT-FK-medlem/2010/ Vedtaegter].pdf) stipulated that the purpose was 'promoting tourism on Lolland-Falster, by exposing and assembling the variety of exciting and unique tourist-related businesses that exist on Lolland-Falster' and 'creating a forum where members of Small Tourism can get to know each other, share knowledge and back up each other'.

15.4.2.4   Domestic emerging network with increasing design elements

As previously mentioned, networks can be constituted through everyday actions that are 'consequential in producing the structural contours of social life' (Feldman and Orlikowski, 2011, p. 1241). Everyday actions were important to this network that had a strong cultural and local orientation. Everyday actions and interventions including actions by the network coordinator were important in maintaining the values of the network, for example:

> There was a case where someone had not been particularly friendly when they opened the door [for a tourist]. So I [the coordinator] went down and talked with them. It turned out that it was her husband who had opened the door [for the tourists]. He had nothing to do with her

enterprise. But, if she wanted to remain a member of the network, she simply had to tell her husband that he needed to be friendly to the tourists. (Interview with D-1)

The coordinator, who was only partly funded, struggled to launch initiatives outside the emerging approach. An example was the creation of bicycle routes between the enterprises for tourists. But the design of this route mainly had to be made by the coordinator herself. Network and innovation activities that did not fit in closely with the pre-existing resources and practices of the enterprises were difficult to promote in the network. This is partly different from the Norwegian case, where many of the actors and the network goals where more ambitious.

Nevertheless, some initiatives that had a stronger design dimension proved useful for mobilizing actors, focusing attention and creating activities and infrastructure. The creation of the network was dependent on the local owner of a consulting firm who identified the needs and brought the relevant enterprises together. The brochure was in the beginning a simple A4 folder with some plastic pockets and a one-page presentation of each member. It developed into one with a professional layout. Furthermore, a website that presented the network and the network members was set up. And the whole network was developed into a more formal organization in order to make it more open and democratic and be able to apply for local funding.

Overall, the domestic network model is dependent on local pre-existing resources, practices and values and is in keeping with an emerging approach to co-development of firms. It is difficult to scaffold and scaffolding activities are justified mainly by marketing needs and small co-development initiatives that develop spontaneously and need help. There are limits to this kind of network for participating in larger projects because members are difficult to mobilize. The network coordinator plays a crucial role in facilitating the relations but she experienced constraints with regard to more ambitious goals beyond existing practices.

15.4.3   Comparison of Cases

The two networks are summarized and compared with respect to important factors in Table 15.3.

Both networks were characterized by scaffolding activities that helped the enterprises to focus attention around the concept of 'experiences' and develop beyond existing practices. AIE developed extensive scaffolding structures and processes that helped the enterprises to be open and relational, to integrate new relations and areas of expertise and to increase the web of actors and interactions. Four key activities characterized AIE: (1) a strong focus on experiences; (2) regional development through open and multi-levelled interactions; (3) ambitious firms were the main actors; and (4) scaffolding and engagement activities create action. Scaffolding activities were support structures for emerging activities and practices – which were partly emerging, partly designed also by external actors.

Small Tourism developed less extensive scaffolding structures. Although a conceptual focus on providing good experiences for tourists was developed, the conceptual focus and cultivation of 'experiences' was less developed. The connection to regional development strategies was underdeveloped and the firms were less ambitions. The scaffolding

Table 15.3   The two network cases compared

	Arena Innovative Experiences (AIE)	Small Tourism
Focus	Create experiences that inspire and are at world-class level. Different sub-focus in different phases.	Endorse local cultural values. Give tourists coming to the area good experiences. Refer tourists to other members.
Actors	Main: About 30 firms, the project management, Nordland County Administration (NCA); Innovation Norway (IN) and Nordland Research Institute (NRI). Others: Increasing number of organizations regionally, nationally and internationally within R&D, education, other networks/clusters, other counties, other tourism firms, other public facilitating units.	About 100 firms: small eateries, ceramists, farm shops, museums and bed and breakfasts with special identities and competencies. Local consulting firm.
Relations	Regular interactions between the main actors at yearly activities. Networks in the network. Many new relations with others. An innovation system in the experience economy emerges.	Yearly general assemblies; networks in the network; ensure a friendly approach to tourists.
Infra-structure	IN, NCA and other regional and national actors, including universities and The Research Council of Norway.	Leader+, the Danish Rural Community Development Programme and the European Union's Social Fund.
Activities	Yearly activities: four network gatherings, one study trip and an open conference. The four strategic areas involve many sub-projects, learning and innovations within MA1 (renew and improve experiences), MA2 (internationalization and marketing), MA3 (competence and network development) and MA4 (conditioning factors). Also spin-offs for other actors.	Common brochure, common website. Open door project, bicycle routes, small courses, small projects or networks in the network. Trading with each other.
Challenges/ opportunities	Internationalization and co-marketing is hard. R&D knowledge and language challenging for firms. The competence development of firms brings challenges and opportunities in meeting with employees and external co-operators.	Mobilizing actors. A more designed approach to co-development of innovation. A more transparent approach to organizing. Apply for funding on a small scale.
Design/emerging	The Arena programme demands a design and scaffolding structure. Interactions and experiences bring emerging aspects. New actors emerge.	Domestic network constrained by an emerging approach.
Co-development	Of firms, network, other actors and an innovation system. Both incremental and radical innovations.	Of small, incremental tourism innovations.

structures provided in this case were support structures for focusing activities – but they were less designed and more emerging structures than in the AIE case.

15.5   DISCUSSION AND CONCLUSION

Below we discuss the main findings and suggest implications.

15.5.1   Scaffolding

Most of the literature on networks tends to see networks as antecedents of development and innovation in a static way rather than investigating the network dynamics that lead to innovation and learning. Another group of studies, however, sees networks the other way round, emerging from cultural affinities and geographical proximities as rather closed innovative milieus or communities of practice with informal practice, culture and local synergies.

This chapter has argued for a new approach to network formation in experience sectors, what we have called the scaffolded approach to network formation. We have shown that successful network formation in experience sectors uses scaffolding structures to focus attention around the concept of 'experiences', and develops beyond existing practices. The concept of scaffolding implies that network formation must emerge from practice, yet practitioners are not trapped by practice or the internal environment of the milieu in which they operate. A conceptual focus on experiences through scaffolding can help them to develop further in a process that may be called emergence by scaffolding.

Scaffolding is not the same as strategy or vision. As we have described in this chapter, it is more comparable to a learning process, with no pre-existing clear strategy or vision but rather a conceptual focus being co-constructed along the way. 'Experiences' is a complex and blurred concept not comparable to a strategy or vision, but something that must be given meaning and filled in through mutual interactions and practicing.

Contrary to Orlikowski (2006), we argue that these scaffolding structures in experience sectors are, and probably need to be, at least partly deliberate and designed structures, though they also emerge and develop over time through feedback loops to those who provide them. Scaffolding structures are activities that augment the view of participants, enable them to extend their practice and knowledge and achieve goals that they would otherwise not achieve. The cases show that in the area of experiences it is possible to involve actors in scaffolded network formation in a rather diverse way. Yet, the Norwegian case in particular demonstrates that if companies are 'ready' for scaffolding inputs, these may appear in a rather designed form, co-existing with emerging processes. We found three scaffolding structures in the cases: focusing attention, mobilizing actors and creating activities and infrastructure around them. Focusing attention implies that participants together find out what they want to develop and how. Attention is focused on a complex concept of experiences. They develop and practice this concept with the help of external inputs that may include policy and network management. Mobilizing the actors means that participants seek to identify the relevant actors that may want to participate and can help augment further the views of the network. Creating activities and infrastructures involve a wide range of both emerging and designed elements that have an augmentation effect on the practice and knowledge of the participating actors by narrowing the work space and creating topical themes and activities for collaboration.

15.5.2 Network Types

The two case studies have also demonstrated that the relevance of, or conditions for, scaffolding activities in experience sectors were highly dependent on network types and context. In one of the studied networks the relevance of scaffolding was high, while the other network seemed much less interested in scaffolding and augmentation activities. The first network we characterized as an open network approach and the second by a domestic, internally oriented network approach.

Thus, the study shows that 'network' can mean different things in different contexts of experience sectors. In experience-based sectors like tourism the symbolic meaning of various ideas and concepts may sometimes be high in the sense that participants are fighting for a particular form of life that gives meaning to them. The tourism network may sometimes look more like a social network than an economic collaboration between companies and it may be targeted at other outcomes other than economic such as local development and culture. The contextual and processual approach may help us to distinguish different network types and different drivers, barriers and styles of networking with quite different outcomes and purposes.

The two cases studied in this chapter show how culture, purpose and scaffolding play an important role for networking and co-development in different ways. The Norwegian network started out with 18, later 33, committed mature enterprises together with a major funding institution (IN) and other co-operators. They were greatly interested in being guided and scaffolded because they wanted to extend their practice and draw in new knowledge. Although the network experienced many challenges, it was characterized by its ability to create experiences, create regional development through open and multi-levelled interactions, involve ambitious firms as the main actors and use structure, design and engagement to create action.

The Norwegian case also showed that triple helix interactions (among enterprises, R&D institutions and universities, and public facilitators) can be scaffolded in experience sectors. Participants were different types of cultural-, nature- and food-based experience organizations partly or fully involved in tourism or other attendance-based travel and leisure time experiences. The enterprises were mostly small, ambitious and innovative, the educational level and background in these enterprises were diverse. How triple helix networking across enterprises, R&D institutions and universities, and public facilitators can be scaffolded needs to be further studied.

The Danish network was quite different and much less interested in scaffolding activities. In 2011 it involved almost 100 micro-enterprises many of whom could be characterized as lifestyle entrepreneurs and people who were mainly oriented towards local culture and values. The network they formed had a more domestic, internal orientation. Domestic networks may exist in many places in the experience economy because many tourist enterprises like many other small enterprises are often less growth and innovation oriented, but lifestyle oriented and oriented towards local values and culture.

One can argue that the experience economy may offer special opportunities for involving companies in a more diverse and hedonistic way in scaffolded networks. Several of the enterprises in the Norwegian case are also lifestyle oriented in the sense that the manager and employees largely identify themselves with their experience activity (for example, kayaking, local food, cultural activity). They can practice their hobby and desires at work. They combine the dedication in the activity with a proactive and ambitious business style when it comes to cooperation, development and quality.

15.5.3   Co-development of Involved Actors

Networks are often assumed to be useful political/management tools to foster innovation (Swan et al., 2002). This chapter shows that different types of networks in experience sectors have different outcomes and may require different institutional solutions in order to survive, develop and contribute to enterprise and regional development. Sotarauta (2010) argues that public policy organizations (in Finland) seem to have changed their understanding of regional development and networks from a top-down planning approach towards an interactive approach where also regional policy making is involved in more interactive, practice-based and dynamic ways. Policy organizations must step down from their power position. Our study has confirmed the existence of an interactive, co-learning involvement of public policy organizations in experience sectors especially in the Norwegian case. In addition, our study has shown how the interactive approach also involves different R&D and educational organizations in co-learning and co-development with firms and policy organizations. It involves not only development of a network and the enterprises but is also intertwined with a development of an emerging experience-based innovation system.

Overall, we conclude that scaffolding structures (helping practitioners to conceptually focus attention towards experiences, mobilize actors and create activities and infrastructure) can help actors in experience sectors to achieve goals that they would otherwise not achieve. But this not only requires structural input, it also involves a change of culture at the level of all actors: policy makers must interact rather than govern, enterprise managers must scaffold emerging practices rather than only impose designed structures and network members must be willing to adopt a complex conceptual focus rather than simple strategies and visions. What the implications are in terms of policy, local social networks and economic culture should be studied further.

ACKNOWLEDGEMENTS

The chapter is written as part of the research project Northern InSights (http://www.opplevelserinord.no/), which is partly financed by The Research Council of Norway. It has also benefited from small projects supported by VRI Nordland. We are grateful to the anonymous informants contributing with vital data. Research colleagues have contributed with constructive feedback on an earlier version, not least participants at the conference Innovating the Experience Economy. Design, Consumption, Concepts, Roskilde in 2012, participants at the EGOS conference in 2012, sub-team 56: 'Practices of Inter-organizational Collaboration: Designed or Emerging?', Sara Carter and other participators at the workshop on Innovation in tourism organized by Northern InSights and the editors of this book, Jon Sundbo and Flemming Sørensen.

BIBLIOGRAPHY

Ahuja, G., G. Soda and A. Zaheer (2012), 'Introduction to the special issue: the genesis and dynamics of organizational Networks', *Organization Science*, **23** (2), 434–48.

Ateljevic, I. and S. Doorne (2000), '"Staying within the fence": lifestyle entrepreneurship in tourism', *Journal of Sustainable Tourism*, **8** (5), 378–92.

Bærenholdt, J.O., M. Haldrup, J. Larsen and J. Urry (2004), *Performing Tourist Places*, Aldershot: Ashgate.

Berends, H., E. van Burg and E.M. van Raaij (2011), 'Contacts and contracts: cross-level network dynamics in the development of an aircraft material', *Organization Science*, **22** (4), 940–60.

Bizzi, L. and A. Langley (2012), 'Studying processes in and around networks', *Industrial Marketing Management*, **41** (2), 224–34.

Brown, J.S. (1999), 'Foreword', in R. Ruggles and D. Holtshouse (eds), *The Knowledge Advantage*, Oxford: Capstone, pp. ix–xii.

Brown, J.S. and P. Duguid (1991), 'Organizational learning and communities-of-practice: toward a unified view of working, learning, and innovation', *Organization Science*, **2** (1), 40–57.

Browning, L.D., J.M. Beyer and J.C. Shetler (1995), 'Building cooperation in a competitive industry – Sematech and the semiconductor industry', *Academy of Management Journal*, **38** (1), 113–51.

Buhalis, D. and C. Cooper (1998), 'Competition or co-operation? Small and medium sized tourism enterprises at the destination', in E. Laws, B. Faulkner and G. Moscardo (eds), *Embracing and Managing Change in Tourism*, London: Routledge, pp. 324–46.

Camagni, R. (1991a), 'Introduction: from the local "milieu" to innovation through cooperation networks', in R. Camagni (ed.), *Innovation Networks: Spatial Perspectives*, London: Belhaven Press, pp. 1–9.

Camagni, R. (1991b), 'Local "milieu", uncertainty and innovation networks: towards a new dynamic theory of economic space', in R. Camagni (ed.), *Innovation Networks: Spatial Perspectives*, London: Belhaven Press, pp. 121–44.

Capaldo, A. (2007), 'Network structure and innovation: the leveraging of a dual network as a distinctive relational capability', *Strategic Management Journal*, **28** (6), 585–608.

Carlile, P.R. (2002), 'A pragmatic view of knowledge and boundaries: boundary objects in new product development', *Organization Science*, **13** (4), 442–55.

Chell, E. and L. Pittaway. (1998), 'A study of entrepreneurship in the restaurant and café industry: exploratory work using the critical incident technique as a methodology', *Hospitality Management*, **17**, 23–32.

Clark, A. (1998), 'Magic words: how language augments human computation', in P. Carruthers and J. Boucher (eds), *Language and Thought: Interdisciplinary Themes*, Cambridge: Cambrige University Press, pp. 162–83.

Clausen, T.H., E.L. Madsen and E. Vinogradov (2010), *Midtveisundersøkelse av bedriftene i ARENA Innovative Opplevelser* (*Midterm Evaluation of Companies in ARENA Innovation Experiences*), NF-notat No. 1010/2010, Bodø: Nordlandsforskning.

Clegg, S., E. Josserand, A. Mehra and T. Pitsis (n.d.), 'Call for papers. Special Issue on "The transformative and innovative power of network dynamics"', *Organizational Studies*, available at http://www.egosnet.org/organization_studies/special_issues_cfps__guidelines_for_proposal_submissions/call_for_papers (accessed 9 May 2012).

Crevoisier, O. (2004), 'The innovative milieus approach: toward a territorialized understanding of the economy?', *Economic Geography*, **80** (4), 367–79.

Crevoisier, O. and H. Jeannerat (2009), 'Territorial knowledge dynamics: from the proximity paradigm to multi-location milieus', *European Planning Studies*, **17** (8), 1223–41.

Cross, R.L. and A. Parker (2004), *The Hidden Power of Social Networks: Understanding How Work Really Gets Done in Organizations*, Boston, MA: Harvard Business School Press.

Czarniawska-Joerges, B. (1997), *Narrating the Organization: Dramas of Institutional Identity*, Chicago, IL: University of Chicago Press.

Doz, Y.L., P.M. Olk and P.S. Ring (2000), 'Formation processes of R&D consortia: which path to take? Where does it lead?', *Strategic Management Journal*, **21** (3), 239–66.

Feldman, M.S. and W.J. Orlikowski (2011), 'Theorizing practice and practicing theory', *Organization Science*, **22** (5), 1240–53.

Flanagan, J.C. (1954), 'The critical incident technique', *Psychological Bulletin*, **51** (4), 327–58.

Flatnes, A. and H. Furre (2012), *Evaluering av Arena Innovative Opplevelser. Sluttevaluering av Arena-prosjekt*

(*Evaluation of Arena Innovative Experiences. Final Evaluation of the Arena Project*), Oxford Research. Kristiansand.

Flyvbjerg, B. (2001), *Making Social Science Matter: Why Social Inquiry Fails and How it Can Count Again*, New York: Cambridge University Press.

Fuglsang, L. (2008), 'Innovation with care: what it means', in L. Fuglsang (ed.), *Innovation and the Creative Process: Towards Innovation With Care*, Cheltenham, UK and Northampton, MA, USA: Edward Elgar, pp. 3–21.

Fuglsang, L. and D. Eide (2012), 'The experience turn as "bandwagon": understanding network formation and innovation as practice', *European Urban and Regional Studies*, 5 July, doi: 10.1177/0969776412448090.

Fuglsang, L., J. Sundbo and F. Sørensen (2011), 'Dynamics of experience service innovation: innovation as a guided activity. Results from a Danish survey', *The Service Industries Journal*, **31** (5), 661–77.

Fujimura, J. (1988), 'The molecular biological bandwagon in cancer-research – where social worlds meet', *Social Problems*, **35** (3), 261–83.

Gherardi, S. (2000), 'Practice-based theorizing on learning and knowing in organizations', *Organization*, **7** (2), 211–23.

Gherardi, S. (2006), *Organizational Knowledge: The Texture of Workplace Learning*, Oxford: Blackwell.

Gibson, L., P.A. Lynch and A. Morrison (2005), 'The local destination tourism network: development issues', *Tourism and Hospitality Planning and Development*, **2** (2), 87–99.

Granovetter, M. (1973), 'The strength of weak ties', *American Journal of Sociology*, **78** (6), 1360–80.

Hjalager, A.-M. (2000), 'Tourism destinations and the concept of industrial districts', *Tourism and Hospitality Research*, **2**, 199–213.

Kitchen, L. and T. Marsden (2009), 'Creating sustainable rural development through stimulating the eco-economy: beyond the eco-economic paradox?', *Sociologia Ruralis*, **49** (3), 273–94.

Kvale, S. (1996), *Interviews: An Introduction to Qualitative Research Interviewing*, Thousand Oaks, CA: Sage.

Lam, A. (2000), 'Tacit knowledge, organizational learning and societal institutions: an integrated framework', *Organization Studies*, **21** (3), 487–513.

Lane, D.A. and R.R. Maxfield (2005), 'Ontological uncertainty and innovation', *Journal of Evolutionary Economics*, **15** (1), 3–50.

Langley, A. (1999), 'Strategies for theorizing from process data', *Academy of Management Review*, **24** (4), 691–710.

Lorentzen, A.B. (2012), 'The experience turn of the Danish periphery: the downscaling of new spatial strategies', *European Urban and Regional Studies*, 30 May, doi: 10.1177/0969776412441192.

Løvland, J. and R. Samuelsen (2009), *Rapportering fra foresight-prosessen for Arena-\klyngen 'Innovative Opplevelser'* (*Reporting from the Foresight Process of the Arena Cluster 'Innovative Experiences'*), NF-arbeidsnotat 1007/2009.

Maillat, D. (1998a), 'From the industrial district to the innovative milieu: contribution to an analysis of territorialised productive organisations', *Recherches Économiques de Louvain*, **64** (1), 111–29.

Maillat, D. (1998b), 'Innovative milieux and new generations of regional policies', *Entrepreneurship and Regional Development*, **10** (1), 1–16.

Maskell, P., H. Eskelinen, I. Hannibalsson, A. Malmberg and E. Vatne (1998), *Competitiveness, Localised Learning and Regional Development*, London: Routledge.

Miles, M.B. and A.M. Huberman (1984), *Qualitative Data Analysis: A Sourcebook of New Methods*, Beverly Hills, CA: Sage.

Newell, S., M. Robertson, H. Scarbrought and J. Swan (2009), *Managing Knowledge Work and Innovation*, 2nd edn, Basingstoke: Palgrave Macmillan.

NGPExcellence (2011), *24 proofs of Cluster Excellence – Successful Stories from Clusters in Northern Europe*, Copenhagen: Danish Agency for Science.

Nonaka, I. and H. Takeuchi (1995), *The Knowledge-creating Company: How Japanese Companies Create the Dynamics of Innovation*, Oxford: Oxford University Press.

Orlikowski, W.J. (2006), 'Material knowing: the scaffolding of human knowledgeability', *European Journal of Information Systems*, **15** (5), 460–66.

Petterson, J. (2010), 'Mikrovirksomheder & makroøkonomier: Turismens indflydelse på vækst i yderområder'('Micro companies and macro economies: the impact of tourism on growth in peripheral areas'), Unpublished Master's thesis, Roskilde University, Roskilde.

Pettigrew, A.M. (1990), 'Longitudinal field research on change: theory and practice', *Organization Science*, **1** (3), 267–92.

Powell, W.W. and S. Grodal (2005), 'Networks of innovators', in J. Fagerberg, D.C. Mowery and R.R. Nelson (eds), *The Oxford Handbook of Innovation*, Oxford: Oxford University Press, pp. 56–85.

Samuelsen, R. and T. Clausen (2008), *Arena forprosjekt Innovative opplevelser. Nullpunktsmåling og oppstartsanalyse* (*Arena Pilot Project Innovative Experiences. Zero Measurement and Startup Analysis*), NF-rapport 5/2008. Bodø: Nordlandsforskning.

Sørensen, F. (2007), 'The geographies of social networks and innovation in tourism', *Tourism Geographies*, **9** (1), 22–48.

Sotarauta, M. (2010), 'Regional development and regional networks: the role of regional development officers in Finland', *European Urban and Regional Studies*, **17** (4), 387–400.

Storper, M. (1995), 'The resurgence of regional economies, ten years later: the region as a nexus of untraded interdependencies', *European Urban and Regional Studies*, **2**, 191–222.

Sundbo, J. (1998), *The Organisation of Innovation in Services*, Frederiksberg: Roskilde University Press.

Sundbo, J. (2008), 'Innovation and involvement in services', in L. Fuglsang (ed.), *Innovation and the Creative Process. Towards Innovation with Care*, Cheltenham, UK and Northampton, MA, USA: Edward Elgar, pp. 87–111.

Swan, J., H. Scarbrough and M. Robertson (2002), 'The construction of "communities of practice" in the management of innovation', *Management Learning*, **33** (4), 477–96.

Sydow, J. (2004), 'Network development by means of network evaluation? Explorative insights from a case in the financial services industry', *Human Relations*, **57** (2), 201–20.

Thompson, M. (2005), 'Structural and epistemic parameters in communities of practice', *Organization Science*, **16** (2), 151–64.

Toivonen, M. and T. Tuominen (2009), 'Emergence of innovations in services', *The Service Industries Journal*, **29** (5), 887–902.

Tremblay, P. (2000), 'An evolutionary interpretation of the role of collaborative partnerships in sustainable tourism', in B. Bill and L. Bernard (eds), *Tourism Collaboration and Partnerships, Politics, Practice and Sustainability*, Sydney: Channel View Publications, pp. 314–32.

Van de Ven, A.H. (2007), *Engaged Scholarship: A Guide for Organizational and Social Research*, Oxford: Oxford University Press.

Van der Ploeg, J.D., A. Long and J. Banks (eds) (2002), *Living Countrysides: Rural Development Processes in Europe: The State of the Art*, Amsterdam: Elsevier.

Weidenfeld, A., A.M. Williams and R.W. Butler (2010), 'Knowledge transfer and innovation among attractions', *Annals of Tourism Research*, **37** (3), 604–26.

Wenger, E. (2003), 'Communities of practice and social learning systems', in D. Nicolini, S. Gherardi and D. Yanow (eds), *Knowing in Organizations: A Practice-based Approach*, New York: M.E. Sharpe, pp. 76–99.

16. Experiencing spatial design

*Connie Svabo, Jonas Larsen, Michael Haldrup and
Jørgen Ole Bærenholdt*

16.1   INTRODUCTION

A central feature of the experience economy is that places are designed for experience.
Place is a commodity for consumption and it is designed to stimulate growth (Urry,
1995). There is an attempt to boost cities and regions in development strategies' investment in cultural events and institutions while multinational firms construct dazzling
brandscapes to provide an entertaining and seductive environment for selling their
products. The touristic gaze is no longer reserved for spectacular or extraordinary space-
times, but has become part of an experience-seeking everyday life. Indeed, the central
arguments for an economy of experiences were prefigured by Lash and Urry (1994,
p. 259) who almost 20 years ago argued that in post-Fordist capitalism, touristic forms
of cultural consumption disseminate into the spheres of everyday life.

Towns, cities and municipalities, challenged by population decrease and lack of
commercial production, look to 'the experience economy' for revenue and potential
attraction of citizens and visitors. The reinvention, rebuilding and rebranding of
places (Nyseth, 2009) has become a (perceived) necessity in culturally driven urban
and regional development. Florida's work (2002, 2005) on creative labour and urban
competition has been particularly influential. Places are articulated as being in competition with each other for visitors, financial investment, residency and tourists.
Throughout the first decade of the new millennium, the idea of the experience economy
has spread into a broad range of commercial fields (Landry, 2006; Bell, 2007), and furthermore forms part of a wider policy interest in developing a new 'cultural economy'
(Löfgren, 2003; Gibson and Kong, 2005; O'Dell and Billing, 2005). When seeking to
revitalize decaying places and commercialize cultural institutions (such as theatres and
museums), policy makers, urban planners and architects attempt to create attractive
'experiencescapes' (Hayes and MacLeod, 2007). Cities and regions compete with one
another to attract tourists and they are evaluated for their 'experiental' qualities as
tourist destinations and as interesting places to live, work and locate businesses. So
places may stage events and performances and invest in new eye-catching buildings for
cultural consumption.

Given all this energy put into designing spaces for experiences, a crucial question
becomes one of how such places work in practice. This chapter is concerned with discussing how physical environments are designed to provide experiences and not least
how visitors in practice experience them. Section 16.2 briefly contextualizes the experience economy as part of a post-Fordist cultural economy of signs. Section 16.3 focuses
on what is distinctive about architecture and spatial design in the experience economy.
Section 16.4 moves from design to how places are actually experienced. Section 16.5

provides ethnographic accounts of how users experience three distinct places: a small city harbour, a museum and a mass tourism resort. Together these accounts show that experiences of a particular place emerge through the engagement with other designs and the specific social group that one travels with. Our overall argument is that while architects, designers and guides are powerful in framing experiences they do not determine how experiences actually take place.

16.2   THE EXPERIENCE ECONOMY

The experience economy forms part of a 'cultural economy of signs' where culture and commerce are intricately bound together. This 'economy of signs' is characterized by de-differentiation: borders have been erased between high and low cultures, as well as between various cultural forms, such as shopping, sports, architecture, music, television, photography, art, education and tourism. This effaces distinctions between culture and life, high and low culture, auratic art and popular pleasure, and between elite and mass forms of consumption (Lash and Urry, 1994).

This de-differentiation is evident with many new buildings. In 'Designing the experience city', urban design scholar Gitte Marling and co-authors (2008) write about hybrid buildings. A hybrid art museum, for instance, exhibits art, makes art and sells art and may be an architectural icon, a motor for urban renewal, a shop and a space for performance. This affects curatorial activity. In order to attract visitors and media attention, curation becomes less about documenting and communicating the topic on display and more about creating an attractive space for hanging out with an exhibition space as an appendix. Moreover, as urban environments are vitalized by constructing museums and galleries, museums are subjected to entrepreneurial imperatives to become cultural drivers of urban development. At the same time, museums themselves have become more like commercial businesses in which visitors treat their experiences as 'a matter for consumption – something akin to shopping and tourism' (Macdonald, 1995, p. 25). The growth of theme parks, shopping malls and heritage centres have forced museums to compete and become more market-oriented, with cool shops, trendy cafés and spectacular displays. Such processes may also be seen in de-differentiated exhibition aesthetics. Shops, for example, can now look like museums with elaborate displays of designer goods. One example is the Prada store Epicenter in New York designed by celebrity architect Rem Koolhaas (Klingmann, 2007, pp. 126–7).

In the next section, we discuss in more detail the symbolic and physical spatial design of de-differentiated experience environments.

16.3   SPATIAL DESIGN IN THE EXPERIENCE ECONOMY

Part of the experience economy is a scenographic approach to the physical or built environment. Architecture and interior design are strategically used for staging 'experiencescapes' that afford corporeally immersive experiences (Riewoldt, 2002; O'Dell, 2010). Urban design scholar Anna Klingmann links the experience economy and architecture: '[F]or architecture, in the experience economy, the relative success of design lies in the sensation a consumer derives from it – in the enjoyment it offers and the resulting pleasures it evokes' (2007, p. 19). Whereas modern architecture was largely concerned with forms and function, Klingmann argues that design in the 'experience economy' focuses on experiences and engenders affective sensations. It is no longer the formal design of a building that determines its quality but rather its powers of affecting and engaging users, emotionally, bodily and mentally. The key becomes what a building does rather than what it is (Klingmann, 2007, p. 317). The built environment is designed to be experienced by the senses and to generate affective and emotional impact. The transitional and performative powers of architecture are central, and architects increasingly come to think of themselves as choreographers of dynamic themes and situations (Klingmann, 2007, p. 214). Klingmann stresses that to consumers in the experience economy 'the value of a commodity is therefore appraised no longer by its actual use and exchange value, nor solely by its representational value, but by its ability to transform the sensation of the subject' (Klingman, 2007, p. 6).

In particular, the architectural style of what Urry and Larsen term 'consumerist postmodernism' demonstrates the design paradigm of the experience economy (Urry and Larsen, 2011, p. 120). This architectural style celebrates commercialism and postmodern 'theming' (Klingmann, 2007, pp. 194–205). Previous elements of high culture are resampled and no longer signify a single style; rather it is an architecture of surfaces and appearances, of playfulness and pastiche. It is mannerist – the past is an 'inexhaustible repertoire of forms, "styles" that everyone could re-cycle' (Ibelings, 1998, p. 21). Historical styles and conventions of architecture are endlessly drawn on, juxtaposed and fitted together at will. The consumerist postmodernist architectural style aims to 'learn from Las Vegas' (Venturi et al., 1972; Jencks, 1977; Ibelings, 1998), and Caesar's Palace, Luxor Las Vegas, The Bellagio and the Venetian Hotel in Las Vegas are icons of this architecture.

The visual spectacles of Las Vegas and many tourist sites show how architecture can be liberated from the deadness of modern architectures' 'pure forms' as well as local references, architectural styles or cultural icons. Postmodern theming no longer respects local 'semiotics' and styles but has become 'global'; what Castells calls 'an architecture of the space of the flows'. It expresses: 'in almost direct terms, the new dominant ideology, the end of ideology: the end of history and suppression of places in spaces of flows. Because if we are at the end of history we can now mix up everything we knew before. Because we do not belong any longer to any place, to any culture, the extreme version of postmodernism imposes codified code-breaking anywhere something is built' (Castells, 1996, p. 419).

The heightened symbolism of this architecture builds a fictional fantasy landscape. It is an architecture of signs, styles and materialized narratives that liberates architecture from its visual silence by turning it into an imaginary world of appearance. One lesson learned from Las Vegas is that pleasure-zone architecture should have a narrative structure with the power to engulf people in an imaginary role (Venturi et al., 1972, p. 53). We can take as an example the spectacular shopping mall, the Trafford Centre, near Manchester where there is a de-differentiation of the gaze of the shopper and the tourist as the visitor is invited on an imaginary world tour (see Urry and Larsen, 2011, pp. 129–32). This is how Urry and Larsen read the place as an example of 'consumerist architecture':

The Trafford Centre looks like a mix of a Classical Roman building and the Taj Mahal. Having stepped into a granite colonnaded atrium space with sculptures, fountains and decorated benches, palm trees and an ocean liner invite visitors to go on a 'great tourist escape'. The Trafford Ocean liner is no pale imitation of a 'real' ocean liner. It has all the appropriate props and set pieces: lifeboats, lifebelts, port holes, a swimming pool, and a white surface with reddish-brown spots showing many years at sea! The main deck is a 1600-seater food court where customers are entertained by live-performances, 'Trafford-TV' or gazing at fellow cruisers. There is a spectacular sky-effect ceiling that takes visitors from day to night and back again via dusk and dawn by-the-hour. From the leisure of the ocean liner, visitors can comfortably step into different worlds: China, Italy, New York and New Orleans. In the New Orleans French Quarter one is welcomed by a statue of four smiling black trumpeters and restaurants with 'outside' tables. Laundry is hanging out of the windows and the balconies proliferate with flowers and ornamentation. Once New Orleans is consumed (with no hurricanes in sight!), the journey continues into the shopping streets. Regent Crescent gives the feeling of Ancient Rome and Greece with its neo-classically inspired ornaments, while the Festival Village is themed as a traditional English market. (Urry and Larsen, 2011, p. 129)

Urry and Larsen (2011, p. 129) argue that:

The Trafford Centre has learnt lessons from Las Vegas and Disney. First, the Centre is virtually nothing but surface effects, images, decorations and ornaments. It is a glossy visual feast: an ecstasy of looking. Secondly, it quotes vicariously from historical forms. However, classical greatness is here invoked with touches of both nostalgia and humour – as part of a narrative. This is not architecture as art, but as popular storytelling, a story about the world as nothing but the 'tourist's oyster'.

What such postmodern experience architecture affords is staged environments, themed experiences and a particular ambience as much as consumer goods. To cite Klingmann: 'within a generation, shopping malls have gone from functional shopping machines to highly immersive environments where lighting, music, and a careful selection of materials not only displays the merchandise as such but provides the *right ambience*'(2007, p. 36, emphasis added). In contrast to the supposedly alienating and soulless architecture of the modern era, postmodern architecture is about providing the right ambience and affective state. Postmodern consumerist architecture is said to be an 'inclusive' architecture for 'real' people (Jencks, 1977, p. 8). Urry and Larsen cite the Public Relation Manager of the Trafford Centre:

We have gone out to create a building that is warm, where you feel protected, feel part of it. It is not somewhere that is contemporary or modern or clinical. The whole building has been built to be a huge stately home. The architectural details go back to neo-classical design that gives a sense of warm feeling . . . it has a nice ambience and a nice atmosphere.

Such postmodern ambience and 'inclusive public space' is arguably also seen in relation to the Sony Centre on Berlin's Potsdamer Platz. The geographer John Allen argues that this place is designed to attract people in seductive ways, through atmosphere:

Sony's forum . . . seems to be more about an emergent *economy of affect*, rather than the more familiar economy of commodity sales and profits. It is as if it is the *experience* of the space itself which provides the commercial offering . . . (Allen, 2006, p. 450, emphases in the original)

The brand space works through what Allen calls ambient power: 'This is a modest form of power, which is suggestive rather than directive, and utilizes elements of the built environment to soothe and guide people.' He describes it as affective: 'a particular atmosphere, a specific mood, a certain feeling – that affects how we experience [a space] and which, in turn seeks to induce certain stances' (Allen, 2006, p. 445). Allen's analysis points to how an urban space can work through difference, seduction and experience. He seems to find that the design is successful in encouraging combined activities of hanging out, browsing and shopping and that this form of 'ambient power' is becoming increasingly important in the management of urban spaces.

Neither Urry and Larsen nor Allen explore ethnographically how people experience, that is, 'do' and feel such designed places. There are few studies that explore how designed experience economy places are used and experienced. As Degen et al. (2008) point out: 'Although many authors acknowledge that, in theory, such encounters between human subjects and designed urban environments are richly various and unpredictable, few studies have examined this empirically and learnt theoretically from these encounters' (p. 1901). Degen et al. examine, ethnographically, the fissures and cracks between the design intent of a shopping mall in Milton Keynes, in the UK, and the experiences people have at this place. Rose et al. (2010) point to three co-existing practices: shopping, socializing and caring, and while Allen (2006) in his example of the Sony Centre at Potsdamer Platz does not account for how people 'opt out' or 'walk away' from the affect of a building, Rose and co-authors tackle this question explicitly. They make the point that the affective power of the building is not consistent. The intensity of affect varies and the building's affect is disturbed by other affective constellations: talk, food, laughter, phones, children (Rose et al., 2010, p. 344).

The mall's affect can be reduced, for example, by social interaction (Rose et al., 2010, p. 344). As Degen et al. (2008) write with regard to visiting the mall with children:

> When one is in the mall as a carer with children, eyes and bodies are responsively attuned to the bodies and movements of the children. The mall and its sensory stimuli (windows, music, street furniture) fall into the background as the children's bodies are followed and the mall's geography turns into a (sometimes dangerous, other times fun) playground . . . with two mobile kids, enjoying being with them, my eyes and ears and hands were tuned into them, focused on them, and not so much on the wider space. Where were they, what were they saying, what were they doing. This was in relation to many material objects, of course, and also to other people. Sometimes it is possible almost to see and sense through the eyes of the children. We attune our perceptions to those of a child and read anew the affordances of a place as we learn that a public sculpture becomes a skeleton to climb on, the edge of a fountain a running track. (Degen et al., 2008, p. 1911)

The experience of the mall's spatial design is transformed by the presence of children. The attention of the parent goes to the children, and the mall seems to be experienced almost through the children, through their eyes and bodies. The parent thus experiences the building through a kind of extended sensory engagement; through the perceptive and locomotive capabilities of the child. With children the design of the mall turns into a playground (Degen et al., 2008, p. 1911) – sometimes fun (you can climb sculptures), sometimes dangerous (you can fall off sculptures).

16.4   TOWARDS SPATIAL PRACTICES, RELATIONS AND PROCESSES (THEORETICAL INTERMEZZO)

We have discussed how spatial design in the experience economy stages symbolical and physical environments that afford experiences and guide people's movements, interactions, purchases and experiences. But architects, designers and planners do not exclusively decide how and whether such design actually works. We discussed the ethnographic work of Rose et al. (2010) to highlight how experiences emerge in practices of use, that is, how people actually 'do' these places, here-and-now and over time. There is no objective perception or evaluation of designed places and different people engage with them in different ways. Spatial design is interpreted, stretched and mutilated in practices of use; it is continuously (re)worked, negotiated and transformed. Although the 'real' version of a design may be presented as being the intended meaning and use of the design, ethnographic design research also highlights unintended meanings and practices as part of people's everyday life. Exploring how interactions take place and what users do is central in order to understand how spatial design works in practice. Such inquiries move focus from the perspective of the 'sensegiver' to the 'sensemaker' (Pratt and Rafaeli, 2006, p. 284) and, more broadly speaking, to spatial practices, relations and processes.

Many geographers argue that places are made and made sense of in relations and in processes of practice (Thrift, 1996; Murdoch, 1998; Massey, 2005; Simonsen, 2005). This understanding disturbs the understanding most people probably have of space: what we in everyday terms would understand to be one space, suddenly multiplies, it becomes many spatial practices and practised 'spatialities'. Space is generated in interactions, and for this reason one environment may be enacted in numerous coexisting spatial practices.

A practice-orientation brings together the mutual constitution of human and material objects (small or big) and furthermore considers bodily activity, mental activity, the use of things, knowledge, emotion, know-how and more. Space is viewed not as a container but a consequence, an emergent effect, 'the result of inter-action, *consequences* of the ways in which bodies relate to one another' (Latour, 1997, p. 176, emphasis in the original). Space becomes a consequence of the ways in which heterogeneous entities interact and relate. Space is practised, performed or enacted. As argued by a number of tourism scholars, this means that a shopping mall, a museum or a tourist site is co-practised or co-performed by visitors and the many objects and information (for example, cameras, guidebooks) that are part of performing places (for example, Edensor, 1998; Coleman and Crang, 2002; Bærenholdt et al., 2004). These studies show how visitors experience designs and portray experiences not as the effects of singular designs but enacted engagements with cross-combinations of designs, negotiated bricolages of design, intentions, forces and wills, between people and things. This is an important observation. For instance, the experience of a museum is affected by technologies (such as chairs, strollers, cameras, maps, guidebooks, footwear and clothing), atmospheres (for example, room temperature and noise) and fellow visitors such as one's companions (as shown below). This complexity of related objects and socialities is always at play, so we cannot push it to the background and talk simply of the relations between a, so to say, naked, solitary experiencing subject and a physical environment. Places, buildings and objects are constituted in complex and heterogeneous interrelations – as are humans. Focusing on the messy interconnectedness and entanglements of practice helps avoid a narrow-minded subjectivism or falling into the trap of either social or architectural/technological/material determinism (Latour, 2005). In contrast, we argue that the focus must be placed on the emergent relations between hybridized people and specific physical environments. This has implications for how experience is conceptualized and studied. What is inquired is not experience in the abstract, but specific, situated, enactments of experience. Experience is 'taken out' of the human subject and is stretched out as a relational occurrence constituted in the conjoint actions of heterogeneous entities (Crang and Thrift, 2000, p. 19). Experience does not *belong* to human beings, it is not located *in* the human, but is a relational accomplishment. Experience is a process where people undergo the influence of things, environments, situations and events, and a wide range of materials play active roles as mediators of experience (Svabo and Strandvad, forthcoming).

In relation to music, the sociologist Antoine Hennion discusses this understanding of experience. He suggests that seeking pleasure is an activity where we seek to make something affect us: 'It is an active way of putting oneself in such a state that something may happen to oneself' (2007, p. 109). Listening is an activity where the influence of the 'object' (music) is explicitly sought. This is in line with the tradition from the American pragmatist John Dewey (1934 [1959]) who describes the experience of art as a mix of doing and undergoing. Experience is a combination of engaging with and subjecting to an influence (Strandvad, 2012).This understanding may be related to experience as both active appropriation of the world and receptive sensory engagement (Löfgren, 1999, p. 95).

In this relational and processual approach to experiences of design, explicit attention is paid to the body, technology and place as they meet up in specific encounters, in doings and enactments (Bærenholdt et al., 2008, p. 178). For this reason, we now proceed to such doings and enactments involved in experiencing spatial design. The next section provides three ethnographic vignettes of engagements between people and places in order to unfold enacted experiences of spatial design in the experience economy. These ethnographies are constructed through in-depth participation observation and interviews with tourist staff and especially tourists. The three places reveal different aspects of spatial experience design and they are also performed in very different ways. The first study takes us to a quiet, romantic harbour, the second one visits a busy museum and the third one a themed beach resort. Together they give a sense of the variety of designs and experiences of spatial design in the experience economy.

16.5   EXPERIENCING SPATIAL DESIGN

16.5.1   Experiencing a Small Town Harbour

The central role of visitor performances in making places is found in an ethnography of Allinge harbour (*Allinge Havn*), a small intimate harbour on Bornholm, during the tourist season (this draws on Bærenholdt et al., 2004, chapter 3). While it used to be the base for many fishing vessels, producing an all-year-around sequence of life, it is now mainly a harbour for strolling tourists. While little spatial experience design has been carried out on the macro scale, there are, nonetheless, some smaller businesses with 'a nose for the experience economy'. So around the harbour, shops sell designer souvenirs, arts and clothing, big ice creams thrill children and cafés and restaurants afford a spectacular view over the harbour and the sea. The nearby smokehouse is an attraction in itself and people go there to eat the iconic open sandwich '*Sol over Gudhjem*' (an open sandwich with rubric, smoked herring, chives and a raw egg yolk ('the sun' on top), this can be literally translated as 'sun over Gudhjem'. Gudhjem is a town situated on Bornholm and the island Bornholm is very well known for its old-fashioned smoking houses. Allinge harbour is also the home to cultural events such as a well-established annual jazz festival and, since 2011, a much-hyped political weekend event where Danish politicians meet and debate with each other and ordinary people.

Tourists perform Allinge harbour as an embodied, social and remembered place. Tourists inhabit public benches, cafés and bars. Corporeal experiences involve eating iconic 'Sol over Gudhjem' open sandwiches and strolling around (often with an ice cream in one hand and a child or partner at the other). Middle-aged couples in particular say they 'browse around and look for an open sandwich . . . you know, a beer in a café, drifting around, isn't that what it's all about?' (quoted in Bærenholdt et al., 2004, p. 40). Particularly strong experiences occur when the 'tourist gaze' (Urry and Larsen, 2011) is performed with a beer or glass of wine and on a terrace or balcony with a view over the harbour and sea. Such embodied gazing, strolling around, shopping as well as in- and outgoing boats and ferries produce an ambient atmosphere that is supported by the close intimacy of the physical environment and the slow rhythms of the place. While Allinge harbour is not a spectacular place, the interviewed tourists enjoy its perceived authenticity and laid-back atmosphere and this makes this otherwise ordinary place somewhat extraordinary and therefore a place of touristic experiences (Bærenholdt et al., 2004, p. 41).

Allinge harbour also facilitates pleasurable sociality performed by tourists in various ways. People move around in relaxed ways, they come together collectively when events take place, they bump into old and new faces and meet up with friends and family members. People notice and talk about how the place has changed compared with earlier visits and they enjoy doing the same things as last year, such as buying fresh fish, interacting with shop workers or talking with the harbour master or 'known' local people. All of these social performances criss-cross and work 'in concert' to make the feeling of a comfortable crowd.

The sociality of place is highly connected to place as memory. There is the history of the place embedded in buildings and harbour structures. But memories are primarily associated with earlier visits. Many tourists to Bornholm tend to visit the same places again and again, assuring themselves that the place is still there. This is especially important when places are associated with childhood memories, or of family members who are no longer alive. Memories are associated with events, with eating 'Sol over Gudhjem', sea and weather conditions, shops opened and closed and trips by boat or ship. Every year, one middle-aged Swedish couple visits the island by yacht. This year they have brought friends with them in order to share Bornholm's attractions, which are described as 'the smoked herring, the quiet, the sea, small fine harbours, the picturesque' (Bærenholdt et al., 2004, p. 44). Performing memories along with such attractions are of great importance to people's experience of places.

Although Allinge harbour is very different from Berlin's Sony Complex at Potsdamer

Platz and the historical processes of their design are far from each other, both places owe their atmosphere to those visiting the place. These are places that people more or less take possession of, at least during a short visit and through memories, photographs and so on.

16.5.2   Experiencing a Museum Exhibition

The idea that experience emerges in the intersections between various affects, rather than as a blueprint of one overarching design intent, is also evident in the following study of visitor experiences of children in a modern museum of natural history (for more details, see Svabo, 2010). Naturama is designed to achieve a specific aesthetic. The name, Naturama, is a combination of nature and drama and the museum stages dramatized nature, predominately for children.

The permanent exhibition is divided into three levels: Air on the top floor, Land in the middle and Water on the ground floor. Exhibited animals are mounted on minimal podiums resembling catwalks. The exhibition design is the result of collaboration between the museum, a theatre scenographer, exhibition consultants and an architectural firm. Tools for scenic dramatization are built into the exhibition. Exhibition walls, floor and ceiling hold large amounts of audiovisual equipment providing multimedia possibilities equivalent to those of a well-equipped TV studio. The museum also uses dramatization in their guided tours and other education and communication activities. The management has considered employing actors and teaching them about nature, rather than – as has been the case until now – employing biologists and teaching them how to entertain visitors.

Experiences of dramatized nature can be enacted by using animal costumes: on their way through the museum, costumes and a sign invite young children to get dressed in animal costumes: 'Do you want to be . . . an unseen owl, a wild boar, an icy polar bear, a hopping hare, a brumming bear?' Costumes are highly successful in creating experiences of dramatized nature. Once bodies and costumes are fitted, animal children flesh their way through the exhibition. Costumes inspire visitors to be 'animal'. A boy wearing an orange fur fox head runs across Land. He spurts past the wild boar, the badger, the elk and the brown bear. He dashes for the stairs, the fur hanging down his back swings from side to side as he climbs the steps at an infernal pace.

When children wear animal costumes they possess the exhibition space. They make it into a territory for hunting down each other. The exhibition presents itself as spatial impulses; it is a landscape with a topography for movement, it goes up and down. The stairs assume the form of hills that one can run up, and winding paths that one can run down. The exhibition is experienced as a sensuous landscape where eyes, ears and skin are engaged and in movement; it is experienced kinaesthetically and as flows of sound and light. The children sense the 'natural' drama of the earth and sky, they are embedded in it and it becomes part of their imaginary world. Children are adorned, draped and veiled. They feel fur stroke against a cheek. The child disappears, dissolves and shimmers into animal form.

Costumes inspire children to use their bodies and imagination in performing what they perceive as nature and animal realities – and frequently this entails hard, physical meetings. Children scratch, push and butt each other and fellow visitors, and adult visitors frequently play along. An adult who is under continuous attack from a couple of bears playfully says:

> 'Ouch, ouch, ouch, you are scratching me', and later, 'Ouch, ouch, ouch, I want to go home to my Mommy, they scratch, these animals, Oh, Oh' – 'or maybe I will have to go down there and put on the wolves' clothes and then I will come after you!'.

Animal costumes permit a specific way of acting – also for grown-ups

The experience of the exhibition is supported by costumes. Costumes are mediators that help visitors experience dramatized nature, but these engagements do not stand uncontested. Considerable negotiation occurs about how the exhibition should be experienced. Museum staff do not equivocally support costumes. Costumes create wild animal children that affect how other visitors experience the exhibition – collisions take place. Furthermore, specific negotiations take place between costumes and another kind of experience mediator: family trails.

Almost one third of the children visit Naturama in the company of a family trail. Staff suggest that visitors purchase pamphlets (1.5 euros), which are designed to influence how children engage with the exhibition. Pamphlets direct users to find specific locations where they are instructed to find answers for facts-oriented questions about biology – either on computers, signs or by looking at exhibited animals. With such pamphlets, the exhibition takes on the form of information deposits and treasure hunts. Information is stored at different locations and the visitor moves information from one depository to another in performances of scholastic learning. Pamphlets are even used to dispossess visitors from the grasp of costumes; transforming them into more orderly beings.

Three children, nine-year-old Johannes, his sister Ann (aged 12) and their cousin Sara (aged 13) come across the row of costumes:

> 'Aah, do you wanna get dressed up Johannes?' Ann asks. No reply.
> 'Do you wanna get dressed?'
> 'Yeah.'

The children all work together on transforming Johannes into various forms of non-human animals.

> 'Now I am going to be an elk as well', says Johannes, as he is being clad in the third costume.
> 'Woawoo', he says, about to fall.
> 'Johannes, concentrate', says cousin Sara.
> 'These are my hooves, these are my hooves', says Johannes. His sister puts the headgear on him and closes the Velcro. The boy gets down on all four, crawls.
> Animal Andreas crawls around on the floor. He butts his sister Ann with his forehead.
> 'Aargh, my leg, man', she cries out.
> 'What is it?' asks the children's mother, who has just joined them.
> 'He bumped right into my leg', Ann says – and to this mother replies:
> 'We need to get an overview of how far you have gotten.'

POOOF. The exercise pamphlet that Johannes had been doing earlier, but had forgotten all about, is now brought into existence again. Bye, bye animal costume. Bye, bye animal child.

This example illustrates how experience emerges in combinations and cross-cuttings of designs and intentions. Experience emerges as sequences of interaction where visitors undergo the influence of different mediators. Experience is not constituted by a singular architectural or interior design but emerges as willing visitors undergo the influence of a variety of designs – small and large.

This we shall see as well the next case as we travel to a mass tourism beach resort in Egypt (this draws on Haldrup and Larsen, 2010).

16.5.3   Experiencing a Mass Tourism Resort

Naama Bay has also 'learned from Las Vegas' (Venturi et al., 1972). It has embraced the theming and reiterative quoting of architectural and cultural tropes to stage an exotic performance around sunbathing, shopping and consuming tourists. It is an example of what can be called a 'light Orientalism' that flavours tropical and sub-tropical mass tourist tourist sites with a particular local, yet recognizable and universal 'exotic' flavour (Haldrup and Larsen, 2010, pp. 97–8). One tourist we interviewed explicitly used the notion of an 'Arabian Las Vegas' to describe the atmosphere of this particular resort.

'Oriental Nights' belongs to the regular stock in trade of tourist entrepreneurs in Egypt and references to palm trees, Bedouins and belly dance are popular symbolic markers. The streets of this resort are full of 'Oriental'-styled restaurants (yet serving 'international' dishes such as pizza, pasta and steak) and open *shisha* cafés (brought to you by Bedouin dressed waiters) with Oriental-style plastic carpets and cushions around a bonfire and flashing 'palm leaves'. Materials such as plastic, concrete and neon lights used for staging the 'light Orientalism' of Naama Bay resonate more with Las Vegas than with an exotic 'Orient' (see illustrations in Haldrup and Larsen, 2010, pp. 98–103).

But why are tourist resorts such as this packed with tasteless concrete and plastic set pieces bathed in neon light? Are tourists cheated in their quest for authenticity and proximity with the Other? This overlooks the irony at play at the resort. 'Welcome to Disneyland Egypt' as a newspaper salesman at our hotel ironically greeted Michael on the first morning of his fieldwork in Namaa Bay. It seems that few tourists, workers, entrepreneurs and owners even attempt to escape the 'kitschy' character of an 'Arabian Las Vegas'. We argue that the set pieces of 'the Oriental show' (for example, camels, Bedouins, desert/oasis, 'Thousand and One Nights') should not be taken at (sur)face (or rather 'symbolic') value. Rather than being merely representational markers of 'the exotic', they are fragments and materials for staging improvised play and, often, ironic performances and representations of 'the Orient'. Moreover, the core of such performances is embodied enactment and experience. Thus, the performances of the Orient for and by tourists involve engagement and play rather than pure simulation.

The 'Bedouin Night Trip' – a 'must' for package tourists to Sharm el Sheikh – is illustrative. Here we 'shadowed' (Czarniawska, 2007) a group of tourists on their journey into the Sinai Desert to experience a 'real' Bedouin Night. During the pick-up routine, participants are introduced to the theme of 'real Bedouins'. The tour slowly enters into a blended geography of fiction and fact; myth and materiality. After a short drive, we leave the bus in the desert and children and camel drivers immediately offer us camels and to tie scarves around our heads – to avoid the sand or perhaps just for the fun of it! Once we all are safely placed on a camel, some wrapped in scarves, others trying to maintain balance in the saddle, we begin the ride. After a 30-minute ride, we approach the 'Bedouin desert camp', which turns out to be a concrete and steel construction, with makeshift shelters, carpets, cushions and low 'Bedouin-style' tables, and dismount the camels. A mint tea welcomes us and seductively wraps us in the 'different' fragrances and flavours, a bonfire is lit and flutes and drums entertain with an Oriental soundscape, perfect for dancing with the Bedouins and mind-travelling while gazing into the flames. The 'drama' of the Bedouin Night Trip then enables an embodied imagination of 'difference'.

Such 'sensuous geographies' enable tourists to take possession. By exposing oneself to 'different' moves, scents, flavours, sights and sounds, the tourist can enjoy and engage in 'difference' by incorporating it. Camel riding through the desert, Bedouin dances, belly dancing lessons and laid-back evenings at *shisha* cafés are all rich and colourful components of a fantasized Orient materialized in embodied performances. Thus, they are illustrative of tourism's entangled and blended geographies of the virtual and material, the fantasized and 'the real', the embodied and the poetic. Thus, the 'fantastic realism' (Bærenholdt and Haldrup. 2004) of the Orient involves scenes, set pieces and accessories that afford 'the Orient' to be inhabited by immersion and incorporation.

We have argued that such playful embodied performances do not require 'auratic' qualities. Bedouin desert camps may be in concrete and iron as well as crowded together (for logistic purposes) but they still afford the play of the 'Oriental Night' to be enacted; they are an 'authentic stage play' in which tourists can take part corporeally, by engaging in the dramaturgical environment afforded by the set pieces and accessories of the stage. This is further exemplified by the provisional character of many of the set pieces of 'light Orientalism', in bars, restaurants, hotel lobbies and streets. In that sense, notions of the 'Arabian Las Vegas' or 'Disneyland Egypt' may not only be read as derogative nicknames for a faked Orient but metaphors of performance of play and make-believe.

The props and set pieces of tourist sites are not 'blueprinted' by one overarching designer's intent. While the tourists that engage in the play may simply experience an overwhelming, smelling, glittering and noisy Disneyficated Orient, the creative scopes for creating the Arabian Las Vegas in plastic and concrete are wide. The spatial designs of the 'Orient Night' tour at Naama Bay enable tourists to experience another place and perform their own roles in the play. These experiences and roles do not emerge out of one single design processes – but rather through the contingent 'bricolage' of performative efforts by committed entrepreneurs and workers, also mobilizing the night environments, camels, fires and the like. Furthermore, it seems that the triggering aspects of the tour derives from these messy combinations and cross-cuttings of intentions, designs and projects, letting the tourist visitors escape for a while from the more standardized tourists resort props of Naama Bay, though this is of course not an escape but the fulfilment of the desired 'light Orientalism' of the whole destination.

16.6 CONCLUSION

We conclude with the argument that it is not possible to design experiences since they can never be fully predicted or controlled as they depend on co-producing the performance of visitors and the interrelations of heterogeneous entities. Yet it is possible to design *for* experiences: actual experience emerges as visitors (consumers/users) are engaged with spatial designs and with the social situations that ritualize and help shape experiences.

We have drawn these more general conclusions from a number of case studies, with a special emphasis on our own field studies from Allinge harbour, the Naturama museum and the tourist site of Naama Bay. We have shown that spatial designs for experience work through various forms of postmodern bricolage that enable visitors to perform a variety of experiences.

One could argue that all this is due to the successful 'supply' of postmodern designs, which has persuaded tourists, visitors, urban strollers and consumers at large to act in accordance with designers' intentions. But this is only partly right. The types of practices and performances we have examined have not only been produced from the supply side. In line with Pine and Gilmore (1999), we suggest that these changes are partly consumer and visitor generated. They represent a societal generalization of the demand for experiences, which has for long been the trademark of tourist practices.

For instance, in the tourist site of Naama Bay, we have shown how tourists expose themselves to many stimuli and designs. Camel riding, belly dancing and so forth crucially depend on tourists' own participatory performance. The liveability of the designs thus fully depends on the performance, partly scripted by tour organizers, but in the end only becoming a tourist experience through tourists' engagement.

The significance of tourist performances was also shown in our ethnography of Naturama natural history museum where we showed that the museum, so to say, is a facility that can be used, consumed or experienced in different ways. From fieldwork with children visitors, we showed how the very same spatial design is translated into different experiences, depending on the visitors' mediated engagements. The experience of the spatial design thus shifts when visitors alternate between experiencing the exhibition as it is mediated by pamphlets or costumes. These small-size mediators design the experience in instant time while visiting. This highlights the bricolage involved in experiencing spatial design. The experience of the exhibition is constituted by much more than the exhibition alone.

To finally conclude, we have pointed to the contingencies involved in making and especially experiencing spatial design. We have suggested an open-minded approach that allows us to take notice of and acknowledge the multiple dimensions involved. And we have highlighted the role of visitors, since the experience of spatial design is not given, scripted or programmed once for all but depends on the practices of use, remaking and remembering.

BIBLIOGRAPHY

Allen, J. (2006), 'Ambient power: Berlin's PotsdamerPlatz and the seductive logic of public spaces', *Urban Studies*, **43**, 441–55.

Bærenholdt, J.O. and M. Haldrup (2004), 'On the track of the Vikings', in M. Sheller and J. Urry (eds), *Tourism Mobilities: Places to Play, Places in Play*, London: Routledge, pp. 78–89.

Bærenholdt, J.O., M. Haldrup, J. Larsen and J. Urry (2004), *Performing Tourist Places*, Aldershot, UK: Ashgate.

Bærenholdt, J.O., M. Haldrup and J. Larsen (2008), 'Performing cultural attractions', in J. Sundbo and P. Darmer (eds), *Production of Experiences*, Cheltenham, UK and Northampton, MA, USA: Edward Elgar, pp. 176–202.

Bell, D. (2007), 'The hospitable city: social relations in commercial spaces', *Progress in Human Geography*, **31**, 7–22.

Bingham, N. and N. Thrift (2000), 'Some new instructions for travellers: the geography of Bruno Latour and Michel Serres', in M. Crang and N. Thrift (eds), *Thinking Space*, London: Routledge, pp. 281–301.

Castells, M. (1996), *The Rise of the Network Society*, London: Blackwell.

Coleman, S. and M. Crang (eds) (2002), *Tourism: Between Place and Performance*, Oxford: Berghahn Books.

Crang, M. and N. Thrift (2000), 'Introduction', in M. Crang and N. Thrift (eds), *Thinking Space*, London: Routledge, pp. 1–30.

Czarniawska, B. (2007), *Shadowing and Other Techniques for Doing Fieldwork in Modern Societies*, Copenhagen: Copenhagen Business School Press.

Degen, M., C. DeSilvey and G. Rose (2008), 'Experiencing visualities in designed urban environments: learning from Milton Keynes', *Environment and Planning A*, **40**, 1901–20.

Dewey, J. (1934), *Art as Experience*, New York: Minton, Balch and Company, reprinted in 1959, New York: Capricorn Books.

Edensor, T. (1998), *Tourists at the Taj*, London: Routledge.

Florida, R. (2002), *The Rise of the Creative Class. And How It's Transforming Work, Leisure and Everyday Life*, New York: Basic Books.

Florida, R. (2005), *Cities and the Creative Class*, London: Routledge.

Gibson, C. and L. Kong (2005), 'Cultural economy: a critical review', *Progress in Human Geography*, **29**, 541–61.

Haldrup, M. and J.O. Bærenholdt (2010), 'Tourist experience design', in J. Simonsen, J.O. Bærenholdt, M. Büscher and J.D. Scheuer (eds), *Design Research: Synergies from Interdisciplinary Perspectives*, London: Routledge, pp. 187–200.

Haldrup, M. and J. Larsen (2010), *Tourism, Performance and the Everyday: Consuming the Orient*, London: Routledge.

Hayes, D. and N. Macleod (2007), 'Packaging places: designing heritage trails using an experience economy perspective to maximize visitor engagement', *Journal of Vacation Marketing*, **13**, 45–58.

Hennion, A. (2007), 'Those things that hold us together: taste and sociology', *Cultural Sociology*, **1** (1), 97–114.

Ibelings, H. (1998), *Supermodernism: Architecture in the Age of Globalisation*, Rotterdam: NAI Publishers.

Jencks, C. (1977), *The Language of Post-modern Architecture*, New York: Academy Press.

Klingmann, A. (2007), *Brandscapes*, Cambridge, MA: MIT Press.

Landry, C. (2006), *The Art of City Making*, London: Earthscan.

Lash, S. and J. Urry (1994), *Economies of Signs and Space*, London: Sage.

Latour, B. (1997), 'Trains of thought: Piaget, Formalism, and the Fifth Dimension', *Common Knowledge*, **6** (3), 170–91.

Latour, B. (2005), *Reassembling the Social: An Introduction to Actor-Network-Theory*, New York: Oxford University Press.

Löfgren, O. (1999), *On Holiday: A History of Vacationing*, Berkeley, CA: University of California Press.

Löfgren, O. (2003), 'The new economy: a cultural history', *Global Networks*, **3**, 239–54.

Macdonald, S. (1995), 'Consuming science: public knowledge and the dispersed politics of reception among museum visitors', *Media, Culture and Society*, **17**, 13–29.

Marling, G., O.B. Jensen and H. Kiib (2008), 'Designing the experience city: the role of hybrid cultural projects', *Nordisk Arkitekturforskning*, **20** (1), 21–38.

Massey, D. (2005), *For Space*, London: Sage.

Murdoch, J. (1998), 'The spaces of actor-network theory', *Geoforum*, **29** (4), 357–74.

Nyseth, T. (2009), *Place Reinvention at the Northern Rim*, Farnham, UK: Ashgate.

Nyseth, T. and A. Viken (eds) (2009), *Place Reinvention*, Farnham, UK: Ashgate.

O'Dell, T. (2010), 'Experiencescapes: blurring borders and testing connections', in T. O'Odell and P. Billing (eds), *Experiencescapes: Tourism, Culture and Economy*, Copenhagen: Copenhagen Business School Press, pp. 11–34.

O'Dell, T. and P. Billing (eds), (2005) *Experiencescapes: Tourism, Culture and Economy*, Copenhagen: Copenhagen Business School Press.

Pine, B.J. and J.H. Gilmore (1999), *The Experience Economy: Work is Theatre and Every Business a Stage*, Boston, MA: Harvard Business School Press.

Pratt, A. and M.G. Rafaeli (2006), 'Artifacts and organizations: understanding our "objective" reality', in A. Pratt and M.G. Rafaeli (eds), *Artifacts and Organizations: Beyond Mere Symbolism*, Princeton, NJ: Lawrence Erlbaum Associates, pp. 279–88.

Riewoldt, O. (2002), *Brandscaping: Worlds of Experience in Retail Design*, Basel and Boston, MA: Birkhäuser.

Rose, G., M. Degen and B. Basdas (2010), 'More on "big things": building events and feelings', *Transactions of the Institute of British Geographers*, **35**, 334–49.

Simonsen, K. (2005), 'Bodies, sensations, space and time: the contribution from Henri Lefebvre', *GeografiskaAnnaler*, **87** (1), 1–14.

Strandvad, S. (2012), 'Attached by the product: a socio-material direction in the sociology of art', *Cultural Sociology*, **6**, 163–76.

Svabo, C. (2010), 'Portable objects at the museum', PhD thesis, Roskilde University, Roskilde, available at http://rudar.ruc.dk/bitstream/1800/5583/4/Svabo_Portable%20Objects%20at%20the%20Museum%20 (small%20file).pdf (accessed 19 November 2012).

Svabo, C. and S.M. Strandvad (forthcoming), 'Experience: under the influence of things', in E. Kristensen (ed.), *Engaging Spaces*, Copenhagen: Museum Tusculanum Press.

Thrift, N. (1996), *Spatial Formations*, London: Sage.

Urry, J. (1995), *Consuming Places*, London and New York: Routledge.

Urry, J. and J. Larsen (2011), *The Tourist Gaze 3.0*, London: Sage.

Venturi, R., D.S. Brown and S. Izenour (1972), *Learning from Las Vegas*, Cambridge, MA: MIT Press.

17. The essential role of community in consumption of a shared experience: lessons from youth sport

Laurence Chalip, Yen-Chun Lin, B. Christine Green and Marlene Dixon

17.1 INTRODUCTION

The notion that experiences associated with consumption are vital considerations when designing and delivering products and services became focal when Pine and Gilmour (1999) published their now classic treatise on the subject. The assumptions that undergird that work set the stage for what was to follow. Their model and their consequent descriptions of the experience economy focused on the individual consumer. When delineating their fundamental assumptions, they assert, "Services are intangible activities performed for a particular client" (p. 9). They go on to say, "Experiences are events that engage individuals in a personal way" (p. 12). They then proceed to develop a model for adding value to products and services by paying attention to the nature of experiences that individuals accrue during their interactions with and purchases of products or services.

The concern with individual consumers' experiences has thereby pervaded subsequent work. So, for example, Schmitt (2003) elaborated a framework for managing customer experience that required marketers to build a dynamic, multisensory, multidimensional experience platform by formulating a brand experience, structuring the customer interface, addressing the company's touch points with the customer and continuously innovating. Poulsson and Kale (2004) argued that the notion of experience required analysis. They built their analysis by defining experience as "the mental state that occurs in any individual, at a conscious moment" (p. 270), and by then characterizing novelty, surprise, engagement, learning and personal relevance as core qualities of experience. Both Schmitt (2003) and Poulsson and Kale (2004) began the task of elaborating relevant theory by describing the experience economy in terms of creating and managing the individual customer's experience.

Since theory has been built with reference to individual experience, empirical work has similarly treated experience as a matter that is ultimately obtained and evaluated at the individual level. Experiences are thought to engage people through their senses, thereby engendering cognitive and/or emotional engagement. Thus, Mehmetoglu and Engen (2011) compared learning during tourism with affective responses to tourism settings, finding that the relationship between each and satisfaction varied as a function of the tourism setting. Also in a tourism setting, Laursen (2008) showed that the five senses play a key role in the ways that a destination is experienced. Orth et al. (2012) then examined the ways that servicescape design affects sensory and consequent emotional response.

The individualist focus has extended to elements of the consumption experience that are avowedly social. The underlying insight is that experiences are actively constructed by those who obtain the experience. So, for example, consumers find value in planning, creating, enjoying and remembering experiences with others (Wikström, 2008). Consequently, although the *in situ* consumption experience has important social characteristics (Otnes et al., 2012), it is not limited to *in situ* consumption. It occurs both before and after, largely through interaction with others (Carú and Cova, 2006). Indeed, it has been argued that the experiences enabled by consumption play fundamental roles in the construction and maintenance of the consumer's social identity (Klein et al., 2009). Thus, the social nature of the experience is evaluated with reference to its impact on the individual as a consumer – a way of thinking that finds its way into the manners in which consumer experiences are generally measured (cf. Chang and Horng, 2010).

These examples are illustrative. They demonstrate that important advances have been enabled by a focus on the consumption experiences of individuals. Indeed, the analytic reduction to individual experience is consistent with the more general predisposition of Western social science to examine behavioral and even social phenomena from an individualist standpoint (Bhargava, 1992). So doing can certainly be useful; but by so doing we can miss phenomena that emerge at other levels of analysis, and that are not merely the sum of phenomena from a lower level of analysis (cf. Allison, 1971; Dixon and Bruening, 2005). Recent work in the context of sport observes that the social interactions enabled by shared viewing (Fairley and Tyler, 2012) and family involvement in youth sport (Glover and Bates, 2006) each render an intensity of social interaction that can be conducive to the formation of a sense of community. Other work demonstrates that the capacity to enable a sense of community among participants can be a source of sport's attraction, but the contingencies associated with different contexts cause the intensity and substance of a sense of community to vary among sport settings (Warner et al., 2012). This work suggests that a sense of community may represent a useful level of analysis for consumer experience.

The remainder of this chapter examines that proposition. The work on a sense of community is briefly reviewed to demonstrate its utility as a level of analysis for social behavior. Four sequential studies of a community-based competitive swimming league for children and adolescents are then summarized to illustrate the central role that a sense of community can play, as well as the means to build it into the experience of families who participate. Finally, implications are discussed.

17.2   SENSE OF COMMUNITY

Although notions of community can be traced back to early philosophers, it was Seymour Sarason's (1974) monograph that focused social scientists' attention on the distinctive nature of a sense of community, its collective character and the necessity of incorporating it into analyses of behavior. He described it as "the perception of similarity to others, an acknowledged interdependence with others, a willingness to maintain this interdependence by giving to or doing for others what one expects from them, [and] the feeling that one is part of a larger dependable and stable structure" (p. 157). Sarason's description clearly sits at the individual level, which reflects his training as a psychologist. However, he also argued for emergent properties by contending that social networks enable intimacy, diversity, usefulness and belonging. In other words, a sense of community is dialectical in the sense that it derives from and also contributes to social structures that foster a sense of mutual obligation, trust and connectedness.

Since that time community has been understood in relation to two points of reference (Gusfield, 1975; Hunter and Riger, 1986; McMillian and Chavis, 1986). The first is geographic, as it references the neighborhood, city or region. The second is relational, as it has to do with the social ties and interactions among people. Ultimately, therefore, people belong to multiple communities, some of which have to do with the places they live and work, some of which reference organizations and institutions to which people belong and some of which have to do with shared activities (McKeown et al., 1987). Ultimately, these may not be independent facets of community, as each can overlap with the other.

Theoretical models of a sense of community suggest that it has multiple facets, including membership, trust/influence, fulfillment of members' needs, emotional connection and a spiritual bond among members (McMillan and Chavis, 1986; McMillan, 1996). Whether these elements can validly and reliably be pulled apart for psychometric evaluation remains a matter of debate (Nowell and Boyd, 2010; McMillan, 2011), although quantitative measures typically incorporate items to represent each aspect, and qualitative studies incorporate each aspect as phenomenologically relevant to the holistic lived experience. It has recently been argued that these facets are manifestations of the intersubjectivity that emerges through shared meanings resulting from shared experiences (O'Donnell and Tharp. 2012) – another indication of emergent phenomena at the social/ group level.

To date, nearly all the work on a sense of community has focused on its relevance to psychological well-being and the effective functioning of organizations and social institutions. Its relevance to consumer behavior has not been a focus. However, the important role that a sense of community may play is suggested by studies of brand communities (for example, McAlexander et al., 2002; Algesheimer et al., 2005; O'Sullivan et al., 2011; Pongsakornrungsilp and Schroeder, 2011; Felix, 2012). Although brand community studies do not employ a sense of community as an explicit variable, brand community studies do demonstrate the vital roles of collective experience, the sense of shared group identity and the impact that consequent intersubjectivity has on the commitment of some consumers to particular product or brand choices.

17.3   FOUR STUDIES OF A SENSE OF COMMUNITY

Recent work on consumer expectations and satisfaction in the context of sport services demonstrates the vital role that a sense of community plays when families purchase sport services for their children. The sense of community that they and their children obtain is a pivotal driver of their satisfaction and their willingness to return in following seasons. A series of four studies demonstrating and exploring that effect are summarized below.

17.3.1   Study 1: The Essential Nature of a Sense of Community

A new competitive swimming league was formed in the southwestern region of the USA. The league would operate using public swimming facilities during the summer months.

(Swimmers seeking to train year-round could swim with their school teams or with a year-round club during the off season.) The league was created by three clubs that had broken away from a larger league. League administrators sought information about families in their clubs that would enable them to provide services in a manner that would be well received by member families.

Parents of swimmers from each of the three founding clubs were contacted by email prior to the start of the league's first season, and invited to participate in focus group discussions about the current state of their club, their past experiences with the previous league and their thoughts regarding formation of the new league. Five parents who responded from each club were then selected to participate in a focus group. Each came from a different family, and each was chosen so that parents of males and females as well as swimmers of different ages were represented. Focus groups were conducted five weeks prior to the start of the season, and each was recorded for subsequent transcription and analysis. The protocol was the same for each focus group, although probes were responsive to what was being said in each.

Although issues specific to each club emerged, there was substantial consistency across the three focus groups regarding the parents' most fundamental concerns. Two themes were clearly salient across all three focus groups. First, parents sought a strong sense of community from their swimming club – not just for their children, but generally. Second, they wanted that community to enable ongoing learning and improvement for their children.

Parents wanted their children to feel camaraderie. As one parent put it,

> My daughter wanted to go [to swimming club] every day . . . I think they got swim competitive spirit by just having fun [with other swimmers].

Parents also wanted a sense of community for themselves. As one parent described it,

> We have met so many people in the neighborhood [through our swimming club]. I think it really helps bring the community together – just seeing all the parents involved here . . . And there's something really special about that in a community . . . How you really build a community is by people in a community contributing to the community. And not just for your own child, but for the other children that are in your community.

Indeed, parents were adamant that they chose their club because they found competent coaching and a nurturing atmosphere. This was important, because it highlights that these parents felt that the development of swimming skills goes hand-in-hand with the club's sense of community. For these parents, the two are intertwined. One parent put it this way,

> It really impressed me on a daily basis how the coaches interacted with the children, and how [the children] came first. It wasn't really about the competition or the winning . . . I think if they have a really good sense of camaraderie, it's really important.

Although swimming skills were paramount for these parents, their reasons for requiring a sense of community also had to do with the adjunct training they were seeking for their young swimmers. They talked about the importance of teamwork and striving. One summarized it this way,

It's [good] because they need each other to do well in order for the team to do well . . . So, [each] kid sets goals and works to achieve them. That's just fabulous.

It is no surprise that parents wanted their children to improve their swimming, as that is the stated purpose of clubs like those in this league. The centrality of community was a surprise, however, as the literature on managing programs of this kind focuses entirely on instrumental considerations, such as coaching, equipment and facilities. Development of an enabling social climate has been only a tangential consideration, although previous work has suggested it can play a vital role in sport events (Green, 2001). Nor has the literature on coaching considered the centrality of coaching for fostering a sense of community. Yet, these parents felt that was an essential feature of effective coaching.

17.3.2 Study 2: Confirming the Centrality of a Sense of Community

Four weeks after the end of the league's first summer swimming season (almost five months after Study 1), parents from each of the 338 families that had competed in the league were contacted and asked to participate in a survey. Of those families contacted, 129 (38.2 percent) agreed to participate. One parent from each family (105 mothers and 24 fathers) completed the survey.

In order to examine the role that a sense of community played in their evaluation of the season, an eight-item scale was constructed. Since a sense of community is thought to require need fulfillment, membership, influence and emotional connection (McMillan and Chavis, 1986), two items were developed to represent each. These were taken from measures that had previously been shown to be reliable and valid (Obst and White, 2004; Peterson et al., 2008), and were worded to refer to "swimming club." In this study, these items were found to represent only a single dimension, as principal components analysis found that only the first eigenvalue exceeded unity, and the alpha for all eight items was 0.92. All eight items loaded comparably onto the first principal component, so the eight were averaged to render a measure of a sense of community.

In order to determine whether a sense of community played as vital a role as the focus groups had suggested, parents' satisfaction with the swimming club experience was measured using a previously validated three-item measure of parents' happiness with the swimming club experience (Nicolao et al., 2009). Other important dimensions that were measured included the likelihood that parents would enroll their children the next season (a six-point scale ranging from "definitely will not participate" to "will definitely participate"), learning (measured on three six-point scales with reference to swimming, teamwork and striving), communications (measured using three six-point scales with reference to club and league email, posted announcements and the league website) and the degree to which they and their children had obtained or strengthened friendships through the swimming cub (four six-point items – two for parents, two for children, one each for obtaining friendships and for strengthening friendships). The three communications items were averaged to yield a single measure of perceived communications quality (alpha = 0.70). Perceptions that friendships had been strengthened and that new friendships had been obtained were highly correlated for both parents and children ($r = 0.75$), so the two measures were averaged in subsequent analyses.

Parents' perceptions of the quality of coaching were also measured using six-point scales with reference to coaching freestyle, coaching backstroke, coaching breaststroke, coaching butterfly, coaching starts, coaching turns, managing, communicating with swimmers and communicating with parents. It was found that parents evaluated coaching globally, as these items together yielded only one eigenvalue above unity (representing 67.2 percent of the variance). Since the items loaded differentially onto the first principal component, they were not averaged; rather, the first principal component score was exported for use in subsequent analyses.

It was expected that parents' perceptions of coaching quality, friendships and communication would predict a sense of community, and a sense of community would predict (at least partially) perceived improvements in swimming, learning to strive, learning teamwork, satisfaction and the likelihood that parents would re-enroll their children the next summer season. These effects were tested using path analysis. Prior to pooling the data, tests for linear restrictions were undertaken to assure that none of the pathways varied as a function of club.

The final model is shown in Figure 17.1. Examination of Figure 17.1 shows that findings are remarkably consistent with expectations, including those stemming from the focus groups conducted months earlier. Parents' sense of community at their swimming club had direct and indirect effects on the likelihood that they would re-enroll their children in the program, and direct effects on their satisfaction and the sense that their children had improved their swimming. There was an added indirect effect of a sense of community on satisfaction through perceptions that swimming had been improved. Obtaining and/or strengthening friendships were particularly important, as those had direct effects on learning teamwork and learning to strive. A sense of community did not impact perceptions that children had learned teamwork or learned to strive. Club and league communications had a direct effect on the sense of community, and an indirect effect through parents' perceptions that they had obtained and/or strengthened friendships through their participation. Parents' and children's friendship development through the club and league played vital roles in their sense of community. Children's friendships were particularly important, as those also impacted their learning to strive and learning teamwork. These findings confirm that a sense of community plays a central and pivotal role in parents' evaluation of their family's involvement in a competitive swimming program.

17.3.3   Study 3: Enhancing a Sense of Community

Findings from the first two studies raised new questions about the ways that a sense of community might be fostered. Based on findings from the first two studies, research focused on creating and/or strengthening friendships, as well as communications among families, their club and the league. The use of space around each club's pool was also of interest, as observation during the previous season indicated that a great deal of social interaction could occur there before and after training, as well as during swimming meets. Finally, parents' experience as volunteers in support of the club and league was deemed important to include because volunteering had been mentioned in the original focus groups with reference to community, and it had been raised as a concern by the league's board of directors.

In-depth interviews were provided by 15 parents representing each of the three original

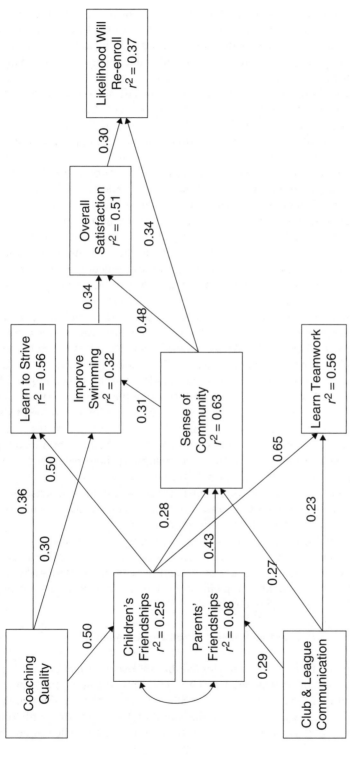

Note: Path coefficients are standardized beta weights from regression.

Figure 17.1 Path analysis showing precursors and outcomes of a sense of community

clubs (five fathers and ten mothers, each from a different family). Interviews were conducted during the two months preceding commencement of the league's second summer season. Research staff also visited the pools and facilities of the three clubs to observe the space and map potential uses. Resulting insights informed the interviews and analysis of interview transcripts.

As parents talked about the experience of friendships during the summer competitive swimming season, it became clear that the likelihood that new friendships would emerge or that existing ones would be strengthened was a function of distance. Some neighborhoods had multiple families on a club, while others did not. Families found it easiest to socialize, commute to and from swimming or share swimming-related tasks with other families in their neighborhood. Doing so with families from other neighborhoods was not as easy, but could be done. As distance increased, the likelihood of social interaction declined. The resulting model of league friendships is shown in Figure 17.2 (which reflects the expected addition of a fourth club to the league). It was concluded that friendships could be fostered if recruitment of members focused on neighborhoods. New families could be introduced especially to others from their neighborhood and nearby neighborhoods. Club and league social events could also reflect the hierarchical nature of friendships by including local or regional events drawing from neighborhoods near one another, as well as events for an entire club or the league.

Throughout the interviews, parents rarely talked about their club in terms of "we"; rather, they most commonly used "I" and "they." The word "we" was never used with reference to the league. This indicated a weak community feeling at the clubs, and a lack of community feeling for the league as a whole. The challenge, it seemed, would be to build a sense of "we" among members. It was concluded that this would require the sense that families are part-owners of their club and, through the club, the league. Following a review of data from the previous two studies and this one, along with the literature on communities (as reviewed in this chapter's introduction), the research team concluded that three strategies are essential: enhance communications, build a "brand community" and formalize the volunteer program. In order to support the three essential steps and optimize the overall effort, four additional strategies were thought to be facilitative: redevelop the system of social events, foster friendships, establish a sense of physical presence and link each club to its pool and community. The resulting system of recommended strategies and tactics is illustrated in Figure 17.3.

As examination of Figure 17.3 shows there is an array of tactical means to support each strategy, and each strategy can be leveraged against several others. The model suggests that the development of a sense of community can be fostered, at least to some degree, through formulation and implementation of a comprehensive strategy that makes use of multiple interlocking tactics.

17.3.4   Study 4: Volunteering Can Enhance a Sense of Community

Findings from the first three studies each hinted that the experience of being a parent volunteer for the club and/or the league played an important role in parents' experience of a sense of community. In the focus groups for Study 1, participants had noted that some parents resisted volunteering, even though the league and its clubs could only function if parents volunteered to fill key roles, especially at the competitions. The league's board of

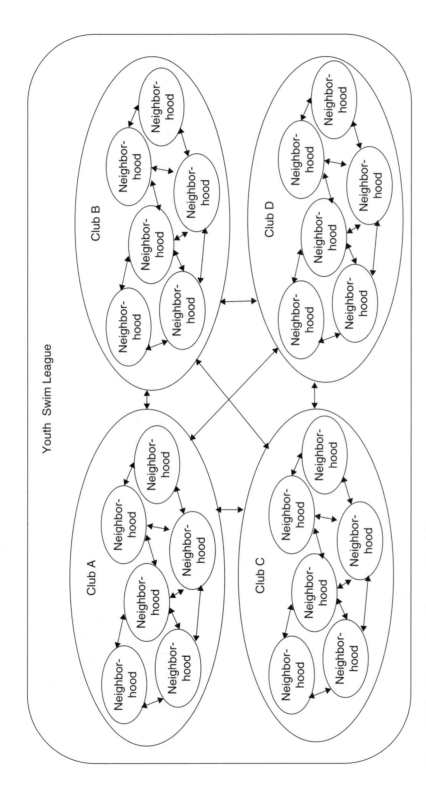

Figure 17.2 Geography of league friendships

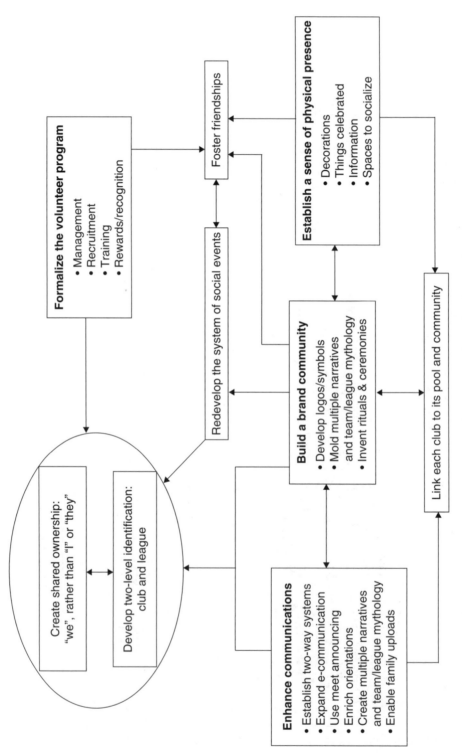

Figure 17.3   Tasks and objectives for enhancing a sense of community for a youth sport league

directors noted that the volunteer experience had been the single most common basis for complaints from parents. Yet, during Study 3 interviews, volunteer roles were consistently cited by parents as contexts in which they were particularly likely to feel that they were as essential to their club and the league as the club and league were to them. It was therefore particularly useful to test whether, in fact, the volunteer experience required of families did, in fact, affect a sense of community and/or other outcome variables.

Further, families have other choices for their children's activities during the summer. There are other competitive swimming programs within the same critical trading radius as the league under study. There were also alternative sports available, such as baseball and basketball. So, it was of some interest to determine whether the degree of comparative advantage offered by the club and league derived, at least in part, from the sense of community that parents obtained, and whether their sense of the comparative advantage mediated the relationship between a sense of community and satisfaction.

Study 4 took place four weeks after the end of the league's second season of competition. Procedures were comparable to those used for Study 2. One parent (22 fathers and 80 mothers) from each of 102 families completed the survey (31.3 percent response rate).

A sense of community, parental ratings of communications, parental ratings of coaching, perceptions that swimmers had improved, happiness with the experience (that is, satisfaction) and the likelihood that families would return for the next season were measured in the same way they had been at the end of the first season (in Study 2). Two new variables were added: parents' perception of the unique value and difference of their club and the league were measured using four six-point items, one each for the unique value of the club, the unique value of the league, difference of the club from other clubs, difference of the league from other leagues. These four items were highly intercorrelated (alpha = 0.82), and rendered only one eigenvalue exceeding unity. The items were averaged to form a single index. Parents' satisfaction with their experience volunteering for the club and/or the league during the preceding season was measured using three items drawn from previous work (Green and Chalip. 2004; Costa et al., 2006) that have been shown to be reliable and valid. The items were averaged for subsequent analysis (alpha = 0.88).

As in Study 2, path analysis tested the direction of effects. Relationships among variables in the model were expected to replicate those found in Study 2 with the exception that the meaning and reward parents obtained from their volunteer experience was added as a variable predicting a sense of community, and the distinct value of the club and league was added as a possible mediator of the relationship between a sense of community and overall satisfaction with the club/league experience. Prior to pooling the data, tests for linear restrictions were undertaken to assure that none of the pathways varied as a function of the club.

Results are shown in Figure 17.4. Examination of Figure 17.4 shows that the direction of effects is comparable to that found a year earlier. The two new variables had the predicted effects. Parents' perceptions of the value of the club and league were significantly affected by their sense of community with their club, and those perceptions of value partially mediated their overall satisfaction, which substantially increased prediction of overall satisfaction beyond that found the previous year when value was not included as a measure. The sense of meaning and reward that they obtained from their volunteer experience had a significant impact on their sense of community,

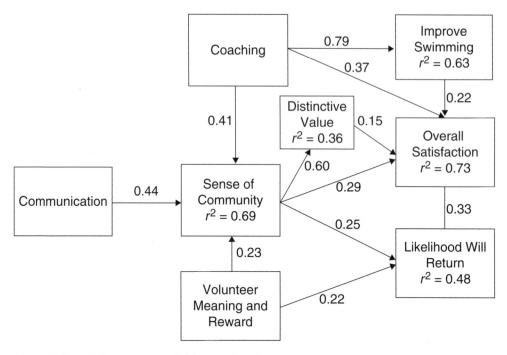

Note: Path coefficients are standardized beta weights from regression.

Figure 17.4   Model showing the effect of volunteering

and a further direct effect on the likelihood that their family would return the next season. Thus, volunteer programs that participants find meaningful and rewarding can enhance their sense of community and the consequent retention of families in a youth sport experience.

17.4   CONCLUSIONS AND IMPLICATIONS

Although previous work has demonstrated the importance of experience for individual consumers, there has been little consideration of the properties of experience that emerge at group or social levels. Previous work on brand communities (for example, McAlexander et al., 2002; Algesheimer et al., 2005; O'Sullivan et al., 2011; Pongsakornrungsilp and Schroeder, 2011; Felix, 2012) suggests, however, that social experiences associated with consumption can build consumer satisfaction and loyalty. Psychological research into effective group functioning indicates that a sense of community is conducive to effective group functioning (Sarason, 1974; Hunter and Riger, 1986; MacMillan, 1996). Studies 1, 2 and 4 reported here demonstrate that these two research traditions can be combined usefully, as a sense of community provides a relevant framework for examining the social/group level of experience associated with consumption of a shared service. Study 4 is also consistent with previous work (Green and Chalip. 2004; Costa et al., 2006) demonstrating the utility of a sense of community for examining the volunteer experience. Study 3 suggests that a sense of community can be managed and developed, at least to some degree, by the service provider.

The obvious question is whether these effects are unique to youth sport settings. The fact that social experiences have been shown to be important in other studies of consumption (for example, Carú and Cova, 2006; Wikström, 2008; Otnes et al., 2012) suggests that the social dynamics demonstrated in the studies reported here are, in fact, more general. Indeed, this competitive swimming league for children and adolescents may have provided a useful venue for exploring a sense of community in a service setting because a sense of community is particularly challenging to establish and maintain in sport organizations. Several studies have shown that the very competition that it is the purpose of sport clubs and leagues to provide renders social forces that complicate the task of retaining consumer commitment (Roberts and Chick, 1984; Sharpe, 2003; Chalip and Scott, 2005). In other words, the distinctive challenges associated with developing and retaining a sense of community in the competitive world of sport may make the need for a sense of community particularly salient. Future work on brand communities and the social dynamics of consumption, particularly consumption of shared services, will benefit by incorporating a sense of community as a conceptual framework and as a variable. Identification and tests of tactics for developing a sense of community, such as those recommended in Study 3, may help to make a sense of community a practical lens through which to develop the group-level experiences of consumers.

REFERENCES

Algesheimer, R., U.M. Dholakia and A. Herrmann (2005), 'The social influence of brand community: evidence from European car clubs', *Journal of Marketing*, **69** (3), 19–34.

Allison, G.T. (1971), *Essence of Decision: Explaining the Cuban Missile Crisis*, New York: Harper Collins.

Bhargava, R. (1992), *Individualism in Social Science: Forms and Limits of a* Methodology, New York: Oxford University Press.

Carú, A. and B. Cova (2006), 'How to facilitate immersion in a consumption experience: appropriation operations and service elements', *Journal of Consumer Behaviour*, **5** (1), 4–14.

Chalip, L. and E.P Scott (2005), 'Centrifugal social forces in a youth sport league', *Sport Management Review*, **8** (1), 43–67.

Chang, T.-Y. and S.-C. Horng (2010), 'Conceptualizing and measuring experience quality: the customer's perspective', *The Service Industries Journal*, **30** (14), 2401–19.

Costa, C., L. Chalip, B.C. Green and C. Simes (2006), 'Reconsidering the role of training in event volunteers' satisfaction', *Sport Management Review*, **9** (2), 165–82.

Dixon, M.A. and J.E. Bruening (2005), 'Perspectives on work-family conflict in sport: an integrated approach', *Sport Management Review*, **8** (3), 227–53.

Fairley, S. and D.B. Tyler (2012), 'Bringing baseball to the big screen: building sense of community outside of the ballpark', *Journal of Sport Management*, **26** (3), 258–70.

Felix, R. (2012), 'Brand communities for mainstream brands: the example of Yamaha R1 brand community', *Journal of Consumer Marketing*, **29** (3), 225–32.

Glover, T.D. and N.R. Bates (2006), 'Recapturing a sense of neighbourhood since lost: nostalgia and the formation of First String, a Community Team, Inc.', *Leisure Studies*, **25** (3), 329–51.

Green, B.C. (2001), 'Leveraging subculture and identity to promote sport events', *Sport Management Review*, **4** (1), 1–19.

Green, B.C. and L. Chalip (2004),'Pathways to volunteer satisfaction: lessons from the Sydney Olympic Games', in R. Stebbins and M. Graham (eds), *Volunteering as Leisure/Leisure as Volunteering: An International Assessment*, Wallingford, UK: CABI, pp. 49–67.

Gusfield, J.R. (1975), *The Community: A Critical Response*, New York: Harper Colophon.

Hunter, A. and S. Riger (1986), 'The meaning of community in community mental health', *Journal of Community Psychology*, **14** (1), 55–71.

Klein, R.E., S.S. Klein and G.J. Brunswick (2009), 'Transformational consumption choices: building an understanding by integrating social identity and multi-attribute attitude theories', *Journal of Consumer Behaviour*, **8** (1), 54–70.

Laursen, B. (2008), 'What makes Rome: ROME? A curious traveller's multisensory analysis of complex Roman experiences', in J. Sundbo and P. Darmer (eds), *Creating Experiences in the Experience Economy*, Cheltenham, UK and Northampton, MA, USA: Edward Elgar, pp. 60–81.

McAlexander, J.H., J.W. Schouten and H.F. Koenig (2002), 'Building brand community', *Journal of Marketing*, **66** (1), 38–54.

McKeown, C.T., R.A. Rubinsteein and J.G. Kelly (1987), 'Anthropology, the meaning of community and prevention', in L.A. Jason, R.E. Hess, R.D. Felner and J.N. Moritsugu (eds), *Prevention: Toward a Multidisciplinary Approach*, New York: Haworth, pp. 35–64.

McMillan, D.W. (1996), 'Sense of community', *Journal of Community Psychology*, **24** (4), 315–25.

McMillan, D.W. (2011), 'Sense of community: a theory not a value', *Journal of Community Psychology*, **39** (5), 507–19.

McMillan, D.W. and D.M. Chavis (1986), 'Sense of community: a definition and theory', *Journal of Community Psychology*, **14** (1), 6–23.

Mehmetoglu, M. and M. Engen (2011), 'Pine and Gilmore's concept of experience economy and its dimensions: an empirical examination in tourism', *Journal of Quality Assurance in Hospitality and Tourism*, **12** (4), 237–55.

Nicolao, L., J.R. Irwin and J.K Goodman (2009), 'Happiness for sale: do experiential purchases make consumers happier than material purchases?', *Journal of Consumer Research*, **36** (2), 188–98.

Nowell, B. and N. Boyd (2010), 'Viewing community as responsibility as well as resource: deconstructing the theoretical roots of psychological sense of community', *Journal of Community Psychology*, **38** (7), 828–41.

O'Donnell, C.R. and R.G. Tharp (2012), 'Integrating cultural community psychology: activity settings and the shared meanings of intersubjectivity', *American Journal of Community Psychology*, **49** (1), 22–30.

O'Sullivan, S.R., B. Richardson and A. Collins (2011), 'How brand communities emerge: the Beamish conversion experience', *Journal of Marketing Management*, **27** (9), 891–912.

Obst, P.L. and K.M. White (2004), 'Revisiting the sense of community index: a confirmatory factor analysis', *Journal of Community Psychology*, **32** (6), 691–705.

Orth, U.R., F. Heinrich and K. Malkewitz (2012), 'Servicescape interior design and consumers' personality impressions', *Journal of Services Marketing*, **26** (3), 194–203.

Otnes, C.C., B.E. Ilhan and A. Kulkarni (2012), 'The language of marketplace rituals: implications for customer experience management', *Journal of Retailing*, **88** (3), 367–83.

Peterson, N.A., P.W. Speer and D.W. McMillan (2008), 'Validation of a brief sense of community scale: confirmation of the principal theory of sense of community', *Journal of Community Psychology*, **36** (1), 61–73.

Pine, B.J. and J.H. Gilmore (1999), *The Experience Economy: Work is Theatre and Every Business a Stage*, Cambridge, MA: Harvard Business School Press.

Pongsakornrungsilp, S. and J.E. Schroeder (2011), 'Understanding value co-creation in a co-consuming brand community', *Marketing Theory*, **11** (3), 303–24.

Poulsson, S.H.G. and S.H. Kale (2004), 'The experience economy and consumer experiences', *Marketing Review*, **4** (3), 267–77.

Roberts, J.M. and G.E. Chick (1984), 'Quitting the game: covert disengagement from Butler County Eight Ball', *American Anthropologist*, **86** (3), 549–67.

Sarason, S.B. (1974), *The Psychological Sense of Community: Prospects for a Community Psychology*, San Francisco, CA: Jossey-Bass.

Schmitt, B. (2003), *Customer Experience Management: A Revolutionary Approach to Connecting with Your Customers*, Hoboken, NJ: John Wiley and Sons.

Sharpe, E.K. (2003), '"It's not fun anymore": a case study of organizing a contemporary grassroots recreation association', *Loisir et Societe (Society and Leisure)*, **26** (2), 431–52.

Warner, S., M.A. Dixon and L. Chalip (2012), 'The impact of formal versus informal sport: mapping the differences in sense of community', *Journal of Community Psychology*, **40** (8), 983–1003.

Wikström, S.R. (2008), 'A consumer perspective on experience creation', *Journal of Customer Behaviour*, **7** (1), 31–50.

18. Volunteering and user creation in communities of interests
Sune Gudiksen

18.1 INTRODUCTION

Three major reasons for the establishment of the experience economy have been proposed: (1) a wealth increase in Western countries; (2) the development within information and communications technologies; and (3) a change in consumer behaviour. A number of other reasons have also been mentioned, such as the introduction of new organizational structures, the effects of globalization and the political changes towards more liberalization (see Christensen, 2009), but they all seem to be effects caused by the three major reasons. Since the term experience economy was introduced and described in 1999 by Pine and Gilmore, the experience economy research has moved in many directions. A significant direction in the broadly defined experience economy is the focus on co-creation or community theory as a way to involve consumers or users (see Toffler et al., 1981; Prahalad and Ramaswamy, 2004; Boswijk et al., 2007; Jantzen et al., 2011). Here consumers, customers or users are seen as (co-)creators of the experience. Of the aforementioned references, it is only Boswijk et al. (2007) and Jantzen et al. (2011) who link it directly to the experience economy, which is probably because the user creation aspects originate from many different directions. What is central and new is that businesses such as LEGO, Build-a-bear and so on increasingly use it as a competitive advantage factor. A deeper understanding of how to approach the inner consumer desire to create some part of the experience is needed in order to explicate how organizations can choose to design, plan and structure community-based organizations and projects with growth or successful execution as goals.

The question is what characterizes the motivational factors behind this tendency in consumerism and how do experienced and successful organizations or project owners cope with the involvement of consumers or users at many levels. One can argue that to create something and feel part of a project is not a completely new issue. For example, festivals or local community projects have a long history of including users where they voluntarily use their spare time to do everything from overall planning work to low practical work tasks such as cleaning toilets. Similarly, in the online Internet world, thousands of different communities exist with users spending a lot of hours participating and creating a large amount of content. The organizations behind both physical and online community projects have different assets, structures and configurations in comparison with other organizations or businesses – traditional organizational structures simply do not function well with the involvement of users. To distinguish between different types of (co-)creations, a comparison of user involvement and volunteering in physical communities of interests versus those in online communities of interest from successful project owners can lead to an extraction of the fundamental, motivational factors and creation principles at play, making it possible for both public and private organizations to consider how to approach this inner consumer desire of creating experiences for themselves and other consumers.

The first part of the chapter explores the still existing physical communities of interest. The focal point is on volunteering and what makes people participate, create content and spend a lot of time and work on something that has no economic gain, while also looking at the organizational structure. Through 20 open-ended questionnaires with recognized industry experts, the chapter traces and explicates the volunteer experience and the fundamental organizational structure behind it. The respondents come from many different projects in cultural organizations like theatres, museums, libraries, nature parks, small and big festivals, culture houses and so on and the organizations have all made a name for themselves working with projects that have the involvement of volunteers as a major issue.

The second part moves to the online world and compares physical communities of interest with the online community of interest experience, through chosen online community cases. Here, three larger Danish online communities of interest are included to understand and explain what makes people create content and volunteer for community work tasks, while the organizational structures are compared to those that are used in physical communities of interest.

18.2   THE TENDENCY TOWARDS USER CREATION

To find the roots of what has led to the focus on people being interested in creating their own experiences, we need to look through different research traditions that have a strong link to the three major reasons for the experience economy or the society we have today.

18.2.1   Consumerism

Today, consumers want to a have a say in the experience they go through and many businesses are yet to recognize or acknowledge the human need in modern hedonism to influence a process and outcome – consumers want active roles. In 1981, the American futurist Alvin Toffler described a new phenomenon – he called it the prosumer, a contraction of the two words producing and consumer. Prahalad and Ramaswamy introduced the term co-creation through several articles and books at the beginning of the millennium in which they advocated for the importance of mutual firm–consumer value creation. They described the changing role of the consumer in this way:

> The most basic change has been a shift in the role of the consumer – from isolated to connected, from unaware to informed, from passive to active. The impact of the connected, informed, and active consumer is manifest in many ways. (Prahalad and Ramaswamy, 2004, p. 4)

An example of co-creation is the Build-a-bear stores. Here, consumers walk around the room and choose between different kinds of materials, thereby creating a personalized and unique bear. The bear comes to life in the child's hands (birth certificate) and the humanizing of the bear and personal relationship between the bear and child is born. Another example is the Mini cars where you can co-create your own car, influence interior style, outlook, elements, styling and so on and thereby end up having an individualized and unique car. A significant part of consumerism today (also because of the many types of communication technologies existing out there) is that people seek and to some extent demand active involvement if they are to open up their wallet.

18.2.2   Communication Technologies

The rise of the Internet gave us new communication technologies making it possible to communicate with each other across distances and borders. From the late 1990s, the human–computer nteraction research field focused on online communities. Emails, bulletin boards and chat systems are just some of the communication technologies that accommodate the many varieties of online communities we have today (Preece et al., 2003). To begin with, the focus on human–computer interaction was mostly on usability issues, but it was quickly followed by sociability concerns. Recently, considerations over new types of communities have occurred based on technology platforms, for example, mobile communities (Rhee and Lee, 2009) and ubiquitous communities, such as Google's new research project called Project Glass (Churchill et al., 2004; Google, 2012). For many years, mobile communication has been focusing on one-to-one connections, but what we will probably see more in the future is group communication, one to many and many to many. The things we can do may not differ from what we are already capable of in online communities – sharing, contacting and collaborating – but it will be interesting to see how the blend of physical spaces and communities with online and mobile communities will turn out.

18.2.3   Participatory Design

The Scandinavian tradition of participatory design is a design discipline that can be traced back to the beginning of the 1970s as a response to the very technology-focused processes, which were not linked with the people who were actually to use it. Workers were therefore invited to have a say and be a part of the creation of new technologies and workplace situations. Central themes in participatory design have been a democratization of design activities and attempts at equalizing power relations (Greenbaum and Loi, 2012). Ethics have played an important role with the notion that technologies and designs are completed in use (Ehn and Badham, 2002; Robertson and Wagner, 2012). The knowledge from participatory design about participation and what that means for a process is something that can inspire co-creation issues. Today, new terms like user-driven innovation, employee-driven innovation and co-design have also entered the literature but, in its essence, it relates to the more explored participatory design.

18.3   COMMUNITIES

From many research fields – with the three mentioned above as the most visible ones – there are strong tendencies towards user creation of some sort, but the type of creation and what it contains is something that is still inadequately elucidated. To dig deeper in the creation part, a definition of what is a community is appropriate. Many definition attempts exist with no definite consensus but, in past times, the term 'community' was defined as a group of people living in a common location (Newman, 2006).

But with the development of the Internet, we could suddenly connect to people not just within our own borders but also to people around the globe – it reduced the limitations of distance. It does not have to be face-to-face communication anymore or based on proximity. Therefore, communities today can be expanded to this definition: A group of people organized around common circumstances, values, interest, practices or purposes (Rhee and Lee, 2009).

In this chapter, the focus is first on what motivates people to participate and create in what could be termed communities of interest, which exclude many other types of online communities, for example, communities of circumstance, action, place, practice and purpose (though they sometimes overlap). Here, I define a community of interest as: A community of people who share a common interest or passion.

18.4 A MOTIVATIONAL AND EXPERIENCE THEORY FOUNDATION

Herzberg divided motivational factors into two categories, often called two-factor theory or the intrinsic-extrinsic divide: (1) motivators and (2) hygiene factors. He argued that while motivators are those such as challenging work, recognition, responsibility and so on that give positive satisfaction, hygiene factors are those such as job security, salary work conditions that give dissatisfaction if absent (Herzberg, 1968). Ryan and Deci (2000a) distinguish between intrinsic, which refers to doing something because it is inherently interesting or enjoyable, and extrinsic, which refers to doing something because it leads to a separable outcome. Over the last 50 years, the discussion of this division has turned in many directions. Some argue that one cannot separate motivators from hygiene factors, while most motivational theory researchers hold that they can. It is furthermore discussed that hygiene factors can only lead to dissatisfaction and that extrinsic motivation undermines the intrinsic motivators (Kohn, 1996). Herzberg among many shows that 'stick and carrot' only works for a short period, and in the long run will undermine the intrinsic motivational factors. He categorizes three types of kick in the ass motivators (KITA): (1) negative physical KITA – for example, in schools in the past; (2) negative psychological KITA – kick via psychological managing the employees; and (3) positive KITA – for example, status and rewards (Herzberg, 1968). He has a very apt example:

> I have a year-old schnauzer. When it was a small puppy and I wanted it to move, I kicked it in the rear and it moved. Now that I have finished its obedience training, I hold up a dog biscuit when I want the schnauzer to move. In this instance, who is motivated? – I or the dog? The dog wants the biscuit, but it is I who want it to move.

After illustrating a couple of attempts that used to install motivation, he ends up explaining that KITA in its essence is not motivation. An example could be reducing the time one spends at work, but he argues that motivated people seek more hours of work, not fewer. Intrinsic motivation has been investigated thoroughly by Deci and Ryan, at some point establishing a direction they call self-determination theory (SDT), which consists of three innate needs: (1) autonomy – the universal urge to be causal agents of one's own life; (2) competence – seek to control the outcome and experience mastery; and (3) relatedness – the universal want to interact, be connected to and experience caring for others (Deci and Ryan, 2000). They argue that if people are satisfied by these needs, it leads to optimal function and growth. Providing extrinsic motivation for an activity that is not intrinsically motivating can sometimes increase intrinsic motivation (Kohn, 1996), while if not used at the right moment or on already intrinsically motivated people, then it undermines motivation. The respondents' reflections and the online community cases are compared to these points:

- intrinsic versus extrinsic motivators;
- extrinsic motivators can undermine intrinsic motivators;
- SDT – autonomy, competence, relatedness.

If we switch to another theoretical field that has used psychology in a different way, it is experience theory. Many recent research publications on experience draw upon the philosopher John Dewey's work in the 1930s on experience in arts and education (Dewey, 1934, 1938 [1967]). His work lays out fundamental understandings on the meaning of experience. Today, several researchers and practitioners have tried to expand on what constitutes a good experience (see Pine and Gilmore, Chapter 2 and Jantzen, Chapter 8, this volume). The start of this could be said to be Pine and Gilmore's experience realm where the success of the experience offerings is determined by the ability to balance four factors, thereby reaching the so-called sweet spot: (1) entertainment; (2) educational; (3) escapist; and (4) aesthetic. Gilmore and Pine (2007) later expanded on this by saying that authenticity is also of major importance. Lund et al. (2009) took another angle, saying that a good experience is determined by the novelty value, repeatability (in the sense that it is not a good thing), unpredictability and personal engagement. Boswijk et al. (2007) collected 11 characteristics of a good experience. Having provided an industry perspective on the elements of good experiences, ending with ten elements and most recently having made a new attempt, Jantzen et al. (2011) also presented ten elements deeply relying on the cognitive processes of the individual (see also Have, 2008).

It seems very difficult to generalize which elements are the decisive ones and there are many overlaps. For example, Have (2008) and Jantzen et al. (2011) come extremely close to each other in choice of terms, but Jantzen et al. have most depth in their arguments and research spanning more literature. As one can see, there are plenty of practitioners and researchers who have considered the meaningful first-time experience but what is instead interesting, new and relevant for communities of interest is to look at which elements come into play when we talk about repeatable use or returning users. If the point of departure is Jantzen et al.'s ten elements we can move on and ask: What attracts people when we are over the first fascinating stages? What can make them come back again and again? What type of creation are we talking about?

An important experience theory to add comes from the flow term and model from Csikszentmihalyi (1997, 1998) that has often been cited in psychology literature. Flow is the state where an individual is fully immersed in an activity, not registering anything else. This state is reached by providing challenges according to the individual's skills, and if one comes outside the flow channel either anxiety or boredom enters. Therefore,

Table 18.1   Comparison of criteria for meaningful first-time experiences

Pine and Gilmore (1999), Gilmore and Pine (2007)	Lund et al. (2005)	Boswijk et al. (2007)	Have (2008)	Jantzen et al. (2011)
Entertainment	Novelty value	High concentration	Exciting	Interactivity
Educational	Non-repeatability	All senses involved	Meaningful	Intimacy
Escapist	Unpredictability	Perception of time	purpose	Closeness
Aesthetic	Personal	changed	Transparent	Authenticity
Authenticity	engagement	Touched emotionally	Uniqueness	Uniqueness
		Uniqueness	Positive	Inclusive
		The real thing	change	Vibrant
		A process of during	Identity	Learning
			creation	Interesting
			Authenticity	Relevance
			Intimacy	
			Closeness	
			Active	
			involvement	
			Valuable	

the goal is to create experiences that keep people in the flow 'channel' (see flow channel model in Csikszentmihalyi, 1997) – game designers are especially good at this, balancing every level the player reaches.

I initially considered flow to be a part of the meaningful first-time experience but the notion of skills and challenges could count for the prolonged experience as well.

18.5   ORGANIZATIONAL STRUCTURES AND CONFIGURATIONS

Many organizational structures exist but Professor in Business and Management, Henry Mintzberg, has theorized over six archetypes of organizational configurations that can be used as starting points for analysing the organizational structures of communities of interest (Mintzberg, 1983, 1988, 1989):

- The entrepreneurial organization – small staff, loose division of labour, little management hierarchy, informal, with power focused on the chief executive.
- The machine organization – highly specialized, routine operating tasks, formal communication, large operating units, tasks grouped under functions, elaborate administrative systems, central decision making and a sharp distinction between line management and staff.
- The diversified organization – a set of semi-autonomous units under a central administrative structure. The units are usually called divisions and the central administration referred to as the headquarters.
- The professional organization – commonly found in hospitals, universities, public

agencies and firms doing routine work, this structure relies on the skills and knowledge of professional staff in order to function. All such organizations produce standardized products or services.
- The innovative organization – this is what Mintzberg sees as the modern organization: one that is flexible, rejecting any form of bureaucracy and avoiding emphasis on planning and control systems.
- The missionary organization – it is the mission that counts above all else in such organizations; and the mission is clear, focused, distinctive and inspiring. Staff readily identify with the mission, share common values and are motivated by their own zeal and enthusiasm.

In a 2009 article, Mintzberg stated that companies should be rebuilt as communities and cites Peter Block's book *Community: The Structure of Belonging*:

> Most sustainable improvements in community occur when citizens discover their own power to act . . . when citizens stop waiting for professionals or elected leadership to do something, and decide they can reclaim what they have delegated to others. (Block, 2009, p. 4)

The co-author of the 1999 book *The Dream Society*, Rolf Jensen, mentioned in his follow-up book in 2005, *Fremtidsmagerne*, a radical new organizational form based on emotions and storytelling:

> The emotional diagram looks different. Its core is the stories. The Core is what creates energy and the energy is the story. Those who provide it with energy is the persons who is mostly connected to the story.

It seems like communities of interest have much in common with these newly proposed organizational configurations, but has it caught on within the industry? Does it correspond with industry practice?

When compared to the industry – physical and online – the two-factor theory and self-determination theory are used as a starting point to look for answers to the first two questions below, while Mintzberg's organizational configuration archetypes are used to shed light on the last question:

- What motivates people to have prolonged experiences?
- What characterizes creations in communities of interest
- How do organizations cope with the shared creation of value?

18.6   RESEARCH METHOD

For the examination of the physical communities, open-ended questionnaires were used followed up by correspondence with the respondents through shorter interviews as well as emails on further understandings, elaborations and interpretations of the incoming answers. Behind the selection of open-ended questions and interview, follow-ups were done with the intention of encouraging full, meaningful answers using the respondent's own knowledge and/or feelings as opposed to single-line, closed questions. By not including more statistically based questions, I de-selected the possibility of generalizing on a higher level, leading the research to focus exclusively on qualitative research aspects of the deeper understandings of the reasoning behind the experienced community creators' practice.

Online communities function in another way and it can be hard to access or get information from the community founders. On the other hand, more information is available merely by following the documents, rules/laws, actions, conversations and practices in general and by becoming a member for a certain period of time. Therefore, I chose to rely on the following three successful, larger Danish online communities (based on member size and amount of content created by users) during a couple of weeks looking at conversations, comments and the way users get involved in work tasks, while also analysing the available information from document sheets and interviews from the owners not conducted by myself. The data is still comparable with the physical community data as the focus is on the experts' opinions and practices, and the deeper understandings of these in a qualitative, motivational perspective.

18.7   THE USER AS CREATOR OF CONTENT IN PHYSICAL AND LOCAL EVENTS

To provide an experience offering is sometimes very expensive and to give a good experiential episode through every touch point the customers go through demands a lot of resources. In light of the financial crisis, the need to include volunteers and how to attract them seems even more pertinent. From regional and local politicians there seems to be a movement towards including volunteers as a strategic approach either as a component of the goal of economic growth or as a cheap resource within mostly public but also private organizations.

Cultural experiences are very often the first thing politicians see as a cutting down opportunity when the box is empty, because if the choice is between, on the one hand, a cultural event, a library or a museum and, on other hand, healthcare or day care then the latter draws the longest straw. Some employers fear the involvement of volunteers as they see it as a loss of professionalism or they simply fear for their own job, not having faith in the management ability to balance this.

To reach a better understanding of how to involve and cope with volunteers, politicians could turn to the managers within the cultural sector. The management and leadership of volunteers in the cultural sector has very much been a 'learning by doing' process where practitioners have received experience from multiple projects, but without verbal or written reflections on how they did it. This research challenged the practitioners to reflect upon their approaches and put the practice into words.

Being a volunteer in the experience economy, it is a given that you are not directly paid for doing the work, which is a major difference from work-related research where people have a paid job. So an organization does not have (to start) the payment as an extrinsic issue and just the use of the word 'volunteer' implies an expectation that one should be involved because of intrinsic values. This also gives rise to questions of how to attract people in the first place, where the use of extrinsic motivators may entice people, while, in the long run, one should work towards intrinsic motivations and keep extrinsic motivation on a fair level, without that being the central issue.

Volunteering in the experience economy is not about rescuing people in developing countries. This does not mean that a bigger purpose is necessarily missing. The values that an organization stands for and its practices (hopefully there is no discrepancy between those two) are a vital component and can be an attractive factor for volunteers. There is also a difference between public and private, as volunteers know that cultural institutions do not make an overall profit, while private businesses certainly pursue this goal. So how do practitioners work with these types of motivators in the cultural sector?

18.7.1   How to Enlist or Recruit Volunteers?

Many of the respondents mention different channels they use to come into contact with potential new volunteers such as, for example, social media, press announcements, through job sites devoted to volunteer jobs, in other events and so on. Word-of-mouth is often also mentioned as being very important and if one compares this with other channels it is most likely to be more used here:

> Through somebody who knows somebody. Volunteering for us is based on a tradition around a certain event. (Viking project leader)

As I touched on earlier, volunteering could be seen as an intrinsic motivation to begin with. This is also the case for some of the respondents:

> The recruitment depends on the nature of the assignment, but motivation comes from the individual having an interest in the area you are dealing with. (Cultural festival leader)

The difference here can be that it is much easier to reach those already known by the organizations from previous events, which they do through word-of-mouth, while it is harder to drag in potential newcomers this way. Several of the organizations are trying to establish websites or databases to keep people coming back or to reach them in an easy way.

18.7.2   How to Motivate Them Along the Way?

The list of motivational factors used is long including both intrinsic and extrinsic approaches. Some say it is not necessary to use any instruments, because when volunteers come they are already in a motivated state:

> It is not necessary, they are there because they really like to be a part of the play. (Theatre manager)

Others believe that praise – an extrinsic motivator – is the best way to motivate volunteers along the way, sometimes also using the phrase 'you do a good deed'. A clear issue mentioned by the respondents is the social relatedness, corresponding to Deci and Ryan, on the one hand, as being part of the community or group and, on the other, as an inclusive element in the sense that they would like to feel a part of the organization.

Answers from the respondents on what makes the individual want to be a volunteer can be divided into five major intrinsic reasons and one particular extrinsic motivator. The first one is about social aspects with comments like 'fun to be with others' or 'to be part of a social community', but in this case it is not only like a social network, because it is closely connected to interest-based motivations. As this library manager sums up:

> Through volunteering work that makes sense or gives meaning be that an interest for culture or libraries, the volunteer has the opportunity to – within a social network – strengthen the local library and the local society.

Apart from the social and interest-based motivators, there is also the local attachment and importantly that one can actually see what comes out of the effort. This is one of the main differences compared to aid organizations, because here one is not necessarily able to directly experience what comes out of one's effort and there maybe too many steps involved to actually turn things around. Furthermore, volunteers are also in it for the competencies and experience they get through being involved in the processes.

These five factors lead to the end goal, that is, 'a good or meaningful experience' – compared to the meaningful first-time experiences this does not equal the meaningful first-time experience motivational factors. On the extrinsic side, the only thing mentioned by the managers or project leaders are points or documentation to use later on in the volunteers' lives or to get access to certain education.

18.7.3   How Do They Reward Volunteers?

The respondents put forward six categories of rewards:

1. Social relatedness – this is, for example, networking, social events beforehand and so on.
2. Influence on the project and the process and being heard – some of the comments mentioned 'treated with respect', 'the same attention as paid to employees' and 'influence on the project outcome'.
3. Experience – some of the respondents simply wrote the word experience, others elaborated on it by saying they learn something and become part of a shared project.
4. Being part of something big – the respondents emphasized the importance of showing the volunteers that they are part of a bigger purpose.

The first four are intrinsic motivations corresponding with Deci and Ryans's relatedness competence and Herzberg's recognition, responsibility and growth. On the extrinsic side, two categories are highlighted as equally important compared with the intrinsic motivators.

5. Education or CV – the paper that documents that one has experience in the field through courses and the process.
6. Access and discount – this is, for example, free drinks, free access to all events, all kinds of products from the events such as t-shirts and caps, food and so on.

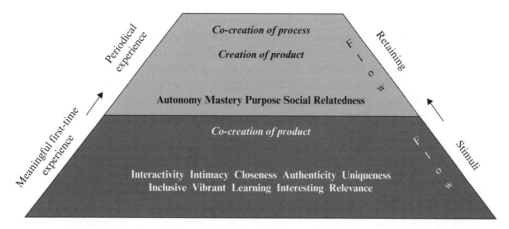

Figure 18.1   The first part of the pyramid of creation types

One could argue that if these factors were absent, the volunteers would quickly be annoyed, similar to Herzberg's argument about absent extrinsic motivators leading to dissatisfaction. Either the respondents do not mention money as a reward or they explicitly say that they were not offered money.

18.7.4   Volunteers as Co-creators

If we relate the above discussion to the prolonged experience pyramid model, we may already now illustrate the different kinds of creation needs. Volunteers want to influence both the process and the final product, so they become co-creators of the process and creators of the product directly. 'Mastery' is a term closely connected to this, a deeper wish to show that the volunteers are capable of doing something more than first-time experiencers. The same goes for purpose and autonomy – having been involved in projects before, volunteers want something new out of the process often through new responsibilities but also a bigger purpose.

18.7.5   Organizational Structure in Physical Communities of Interest

The cultural leader respondents agree that there are both positive and negative issues when including volunteers as part of the organization. They find the structure relatively decentralized in the meaning that the volunteers are authorized to make some decisions. While seen as a positive element, the managers sometimes find it hard to steer towards common goals. The respondents underline the importance of not considering volunteers as a free resource. From the management board and down the organization, there resources should be made available to coordinate volunteers. This national park has this as an upcoming issue:

> It takes continuous attention to get a volunteer to work over a longer period and take responsibility. Our park is a new institution where volunteering is a central issue – both in executive orders, in the management board and the administration. That can be seen in the decision to hire a volunteer coordinator from the beginning.

There is – at first glance – much in common with the organizational configurations of the missionary organization, and the manager often highlights the mission or purpose as the driver for getting volunteers to take responsibilities. However, going deeper into the answers from the respondents, the innovative organization configuration is the one that has most in common with these characteristics. An important characteristic is the delegation of decision making competences. As this library manager says, much is based on trust and commitment:

> The organizational structure is characterized by a high degree of trust-based delegation. The volunteers can be seen as teams being facilitated by a professional.

Herzberg (1968) elaborates on the innovative organization by saying that it builds upon network structures for authority, control and communication and the work tasks are redefined and adapted based on needs in the projects. One of the jobs that facilitators or network coordinators have is to clearly define the individual's role many times as it changes along the way, so communication and dialogue are of major importance both vertically and horizontally in the organizational structure. A manager of a creative craftsmanship house brings forth another important issue:

> We have tried different adjustments and, in general, we believe that projects with volunteers function best with few rules and barriers to overcome and with as little bureaucracy as possible.

While the managers emphasize the importance of creating lesser bureaucracy, a very visible hierarchy sometimes exist but it is mostly between the volunteers themselves (those who have been involved before and have a certain status). In a newer, but already successful indie rock festival, the management chose to hire a selected team of volunteers, giving them status by highlighting them on the website and explaining the role they play in the organization:

> NorthSiders is the term for the forty persons who have been chosen to participate in the development of NorthSide over the next two years. The staging of tomorrow's festival should happen in close dialogue with the target group, musicians and partners and therefore the forty selected persons now have the opportunity to participate in strategic development projects that could lead to concrete products or services at the festival.

So they are the selected ones, but what about all the other volunteers? This is a clear example of the hierarchy that can emerge over the years between the volunteers. The ones who have been involved before have a certain status and if they are not given that status, the chances are that they will not return.

The last characteristic is that the typical support staff that exist in most organizations (besides entrepreneurial) to some extent become part of the volunteer work. Volunteers work because they have a strong interest in the project or the purpose. The coordinators become the middle line or middle manager. The coordinators are sometimes volunteers themselves or at least have been, but now have more responsibility and can even be paid as this theatre manager puts it:

> The project leader has the responsibility, but he has support by a paid educator who we found among the volunteers.

Therefore, one of the things the managers in these organization typically try to balance is when to give work tasks with higher responsibility (intrinsic motivator) and when that is not enough, so they have to pay a salary (extrinsic motivator). The organizations risk losing people with high competences who have been involved in organizational projects before. Based on the answer, the following characteristics can be outlined:

● A minor top management (or at least fewer top management people who are connected to the projects).
● A large operating core consisting of all the volunteers and none or few paid members.
● Middle line or managers – typically with a coordinator role – are sometimes paid, sometimes not.
● Supporting staff are limited as far as volunteers are willing to do this work.
● The techno structure is needed and depends on project size. The employers are seldom volunteers, unless for small projects and volunteers have very high trustworthiness.

In general, a tendency towards giving volunteers responsibilities is that it has a strong impact on some of the traditional elements that in a sense merge or intermingle.

18.8 THE USER AS CREATOR OF CONTENT IN ONLINE COMMUNITIES OF INTERESTS

From the expanded definition of communities highlighted in the introduction, we already now know that it is not about local attachment in online communities of interest, but instead a common interest or passion. Sociologist Barry Wellman introduced the word 'glocalization', meaning the ability the Internet has to extend participants' social connections to people around the world while also aiding them in further engagement with their local community (Wellman and Hampton, 1999).

18.8.1 Online Communities

In the early 1990s, the sociologist Ray Oldenburg argued for so called 'third places'. The internet has later been proposed as being a significant third place that replaces some of the physical third places. Some of the characteristics of a third place are that it is a neutral ground (or at least to begin with) where occupants have little to no obligation to be there; it is a kind of leveller in the sense that it puts no importance on an individual's status in society; and conversation is the main focus of activity, but seldom the only one (Oldenburg, 1989, 2001). Professor in Information Studies, Jenny Preece has noted that an online community can be characterized by the following elements (Preece and Maloney-Krichmar, 2005):

● whether they have physical as well as virtual presence;
● purpose;
● software environment supporting them;

- size;
- duration of their existence;
- stage in their life cycle;
- culture of their members;
- governance structure.

If we go through statistics on the most visited websites in Denmark, a pattern becomes apparent (see, for example, September 2012 statistics from fdim.dk).The most visited sites are the bigger media houses, national television stations, weather sites and so on but clear examples of communities of interest are ranked highly and challenge the traditional media-consuming platforms.

For a population with around five million people, BaZoom.dk ranked 18th on the most visited sites with a very high number of monthly users and is in the top five on page views. So what do online community firms do to convince users to have a prolonged experience?

If we take a closer look at BaZoom.dk, it has many different forums for conversations about cars, trucks, boats, dogs and houses with new ones like tractors and gardens. With all these forums, there should be a good chance of catching a big portion of the Danish Internet users out there and that is exactly what is happening. In an illustration, the car section is highlighted showing the many kinds of discussions going on from general discussions to very specific ones about styling, tuning and so on. Another example is number 31th, a website for soccer news and people interested in that. Both these websites are very niche oriented and only work as a business because it is the users who create the content, not the owners.

In every section, there is an off-topic forum, not a shared forum across all the sections, but one in each one of them. So even though one would like to discuss something else than, for example, horses one wants to do so with the same people. Hence, everyone creating content in the forums is more or less also looking for social relatedness and if one becomes a regular user it is about social status within the group of people who often visit the forums.

18.8.2   Mastery and Responsibility

Mastery in an online community comes in different forms as users are looking for mastery of the different subjects within a certain interest, like knowing what kind of materials are needed for a specific car, but also mastery of the forum and knowledge about the people who often visit the site.

In online communities, responsibility is given to people for different reasons not unlike the volunteer projects – sometimes the choice is based on interest and engagement from the persons themselves, sometimes people are randomly chosen, while for others how long one has been a member or maybe selected through a collection point system. Take, for example, computer hardware forums where one can earn points by answering questions in a good way, while it is very often the questioner who decides to whom they will give points based on the most useful answer. In physical communities, it is the users when, for example, becoming volunteers that begin to have an impact not only on the product but also the process.

Amy Jo Kim has developed a framework in which she explains what she calls the membership life cycle (Kim, 2000). Here, users go from peripheral – visitors and lurkers – to inbounds providing a little bit of content, to insiders providing content regularly, to veterans providing content and have some kind of status until they, at some point, become elders and retire from the community because of conflicts with the direction it takes, not being motivated to participate anymore or simply because of new interests.

18.8.3 Status and Acknowledgement

Women who are pregnant or have just given birth go through a very emotional time looking for support anywhere in their surroundings but in their physical surroundings, it can be hard to find someone who understands their emotions. The founder of Min-mave. dk, Birgit Larsen, mother of six children, had an idea to make an online community for those going through that period of their life. It is now one of the most visited online communities in Denmark. Here, women can discuss everything from which types of diapers to use to more dramatic and emotional issues about the process they go through. In the online community, these women have a greater chance of finding someone who will give them the answers they need and understand what they are going through other than their neighbour, colleague or even husband. Online community researchers have theorized over strong ties being the family and closest ties being friends and weak ties, which, in this case, could be online community members, but at certain points in time it might be the other way around: members from the community become strong ties and the family becomes weak ties.

In an online community like Min-mave.dk, experienced mothers are suddenly acknowledged more widely for their competencies and understanding of the whole process of having a child. It is possible to give advice to a large group of people, not just a sister or colleague. In online communities, users can take on different kinds of responsibilities and thereby also move around the membership cycle to becoming a veteran. It could be responsibilities given out by agreement in a group, for example, you can be in charge of making a termination list for your group in Min-mave.dk or it is possible to become an administrator, securing a certain dialogue approach style or law and order in general. In some online communities, there are strict rules about both how to become an administrator and how to act when you are in that role. Wikipedia is an example of this:

> If you are interested in requesting adminship, you should first read the guide to requests for adminship and the nomination instructions. When you are ready to apply, you may add your nomination to the Wikipedia: Requests for adminship page according to the aforementioned instructions. A discussion (not a vote) will then take place among fellow editors about whether you should become an administrator. After seven days, a bureaucrat will determine if there is consensus to approve your request. (http://en.wikipedia.org/wiki/Wikipedia:Administrators)

Wikipedia wants to secure a high quality of content and a knowledge that is as close to the truth as possible. In BaZoom.dk, it is not an issue to have high quality discussions – that is not something the organization interfere in. The owners of the online communities have to create the platform, the guidelines, the rules and the awareness to begin with but, when established, it is sometimes also the administrators or users who become co-creators of new platform elements, guidelines and rules. Therefore, there can be a very high degree of creation by users on community frames, process and product and a high degree of self-control.

What the best and most successful online communities do is to secure awareness of not only the website and community platform but also the content made by users. Take, for example, the Danish newspaper *Information* (one of the last newspapers not yet struggling with low profit) – they know that the customer segments they are targeting are looking for long, intellectual articles with a great deal of substance. They also provide comments – often long ones – and like to have a good intellectual discussion and given the opportunity to speak about the subject addressed in the article. The website shows and ranks the most recommended articles by users, but not only that. Comments from users can also be recommended, which means that if you deliver a comment that is liked by many users, your name appears on the front page. People want to be recognized for the skills they have and through the online communities they can create awareness of them that they cannot in physical communities.

18.8.4   User Creation Types in Online Communities

In online communities, users are rewarded by the attention they get from responses on a post (or the now famous Facebook-like feature) and the responsibility they are given. If they are to return to the community and keep on delivering content they want to be recognized for their competencies through either their expertise in relation to a certain interest or in managing or understanding how the community works. They create both process and product (or forum-post outcome) and co-create the frames, constraints and boundaries that the community evolves in, be that guidelines, rules or platform elements (Figure 18.2).

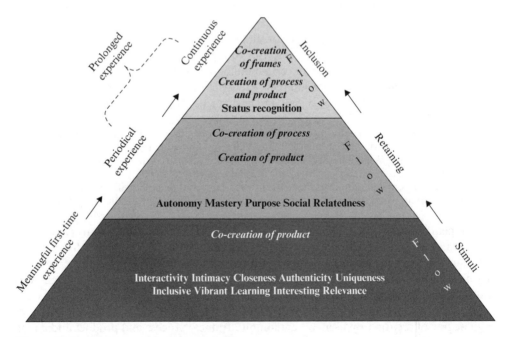

Figure 18.2   The pyramid of creation types

18.8.5   Organizational Structures of Online Communities of Interest

In an interview with *Business Insider*, founder of Wikipedia, Jimmy Wales, revealed that they only had 35 paid employees (in 2010). This is a very small group of paid staff for a website size with so much content (reportedly one of the world's five biggest websites) and so widely used. What kind of competences do the paid staff need? The first competences have to do with legal issues, accounting and fundraising, because they are a non-profit organization. Technical staff members provide other important competencies such as carrying out work tasks on usability issues and development of software. Asked about how many of the paid staff focuses on content, he responded none, besides maybe himself and a volunteer coordinator who has the role of being the link to the community (*Business Insider*, 2010).

What is highly interesting is the notion that many of the online communities have few details on the organization and simple information about who is employed in the firm is not visible. Searching around BaZoom.dk you will only find emails or telephone numbers for the support staff about technical matters or a telephone number for those who want to advertise. As a business, they can offer advertisers even more precisely targeted ads to a customer segment than, for example, Google. Searching information about who is behind the founding of BaZoom.dk only leads to the name of the founder. The same goes for Min-mave.dk. There are no descriptions of the organization behind the community. By asking the founders directly it turns out that they are very small organizations with only a few paid employees with the same tasks as the ones Jimmy Wales lists – only on a minor scale. From big firms like LEGO or Apple, we know that the visibility and signals from top management to the consumers are very important – this might also be the case for communities of interest but it is through messages direct to the community not other media channels. The important issues to highlight are the users, the content and the opportunities available through the platform and, if profit-oriented, also the ads. The organizational structure of communities of interest is clarified and explicated through the online community examples. The insights from the physical organizational examples still count here, but there is an even higher degree of users or volunteers doing the work tasks that the supporting staff usually do, simply because they are motivated by passion towards the subject or because there is nobody else to do it. There is also a visible and sometimes manifested hierarchy, not in the paid staff but within the users and coordinators. One way of illustrating the organizational configurations in communities of interest is to illustrate it in a Mintzberg style (Figure 18.3).

These organizational configurations in communities of interest are exemplified by the following:

- Operating core: characterized by a large or huge number of users or volunteers creating all the operations besides technical-related platform issues or planting advertisers.
- Techno structure: all the work tasks that have to do with securing community creation, for example, accounting, legal issues, fundraising, charity and so on.
- Support staff: can be both paid and unpaid, but it is usually unpaid administrators

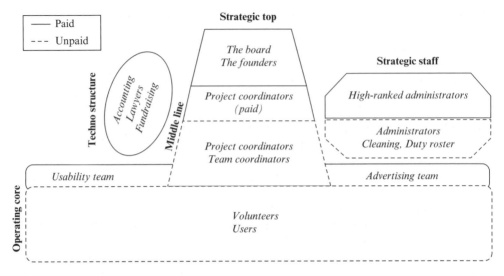

Figure 18.3   Organizational configuration in communities of interest

or those working in physical communities who do tasks such as cleaning, prepare food and so on.

- Middle management line: project or team coordinators based on experience and competencies. They can be paid or unpaid.
- Strategic top: often no more than three or four people including the founder – they make the strategic decisions that sometimes go straight to the users or volunteers in direct messages.

18.9   CONCLUSION

Throughout this chapter and the empirical data from the respondents as well as the online cases, several arguments have been put forth illustrating that the prolonged experience does not have the same parameters as the meaningful first-time experience. When we talk about a returned use of a place, product, platform or in short the prolonged experience, different motivational factors come into play. In the volunteer experience in the physical community, it was about social relatedness – we want to be part of a community, a belongingness one might call it. We also want to master something new, which relates to the balance in the flow channel. If going through a similar type of experience again, both the surprise element and the mastering element are not taking place. New or different purposes and new competences given are important for the volunteers. Firms can provide these by inviting volunteers into the creation of not only the product but also the process. So, they co-create the process and create products or maybe co-create products with the consumers.

While local attachment is important in physical communities, it is different in the online communities. Here one is only attached to groups, but as users get more responsibilities according to a certain group or in the community at large, they start to become more dependent on the place. It becomes a duty – you cannot turn down the group or the community. To keep users coming back again and again, they even have the chance of influencing the framing of the community by co-creating new guidelines, rules and proposing new platform elements.

The innovation in communities of interest lies in figuring out what can make users create more and the model of pyramid creation types functions as an initial understanding of how to motivate users for prolonged experiences. The organizational structures build upon Mintzberg's archetype of the innovative organization, but many of the work tasks are done by volunteers and smaller teams and therefore a high degree of delegation of decision making occurs.

In online communities, it is interesting that users, who are not being paid at all, do many of the traditional functions in firms. Future research could expand on decision making in such communities – who actually makes decisions? Is everyone allowed to take action? Or is everyone willing to or capable of making decisions? A focus point for firms will be to consider how to work with co-created value and dealing with the loss of control – communities of interest should be the first place to visit.

BIBLIOGRAPHY

Block, P. (2009), *Community: The Structure of Belonging*, San Francisco, CA: Berrett-Koehler Publishers.

Boswijk, A., T. Thijssen and E. Peelen, E. (2007), *The Experience Economy: A New Perspective*, Amsterdam: Pearson Education.

Buxton, W. (2007), *Sketching User Experiences: Getting the Design Right and the Right Design*, San Francisco, CA: Morgan Kaufmann.

Christensen, J. (2009), *Oplevelsesindustrien* (*Experience Industry*), Copenhagen: Books on demand.

Churchill, E., A. Girgensohn, L. Nelson and A. Lee (2004), 'Blending digital and physical spaces for ubiquitous community participation', *Communications of the ACM*, **47** (2), 38–44.

Csikszentmihalyi, M. (1997), *Creativity: Flow and the Psychology of Discovery and Invention*, London: Harper Perennial.

Csikszentmihalyi, M. (1998), *Finding Flow: The Psychology of Engagement with Everyday Life*, New York: Basic Books.

Csikszentmihalyi, M. and I.S. Csikszentmihalyi (1992), *Optimal Experience: Psychological Studies of Flow in Consciousness*, Cambridge: Cambridge University Press.

Deci, E.L. and R.M. Ryan (2000), 'The "what" and "why" of goal pursuits: human needs and the self-determination of behavior', *Psychological Inquiry*, **11** (4), 227–68.

Deci, E.L. and R.M. Ryan (2004), *Handbook of Self-determination Research*, Rochester, UK: University of Rochester Press.

Deci, E.L., R. Koestner and R.M. Ryan (1999), 'A meta-analytic review of experiments examining the effects of extrinsic rewards on intrinsic motivation', *Psychological Bulletin*, **125**, 627–68.

Deci, E.L., R.M. Ryan, M. Gagne, D.R. Leone, J. Usunov and B.P. Kornazheva (2001), 'Need satisfaction, motivation, and well-being in the work organizations of a former Eastern Bloc country', *Personality and Social Psychology Bulletin*, **27**, 930–42.

Dewey, J. (1934), *Art as Experience*, New York: Berkeley Publishing Group.

Dewey, J. (1938), *Experience and Education*, New York: Macmillan, reprinted in 1967, New York: Collier Books.

Dewey, J. (1998), *Experience and Education*, West Lafayette, IL: Kappa Delta Pi.

Dewey, J. (2005), *Art as Experience*, New York: Perigee.

Ehn, P. and R. Badham (2002), 'Participatory design and the collective designer', in T. Binder, J. Gregory and I. Wagner (eds), *PDC 2002 Proceedings of the Participatory Design Conference*, Malmö, Sweden, 23–25 June, pp. 1–10.

Gilmore, J.H. and B.J. Pine (2007), *Authenticity: What Consumers Really Want*, Boston, MA: Harvard Business School Press.

Google (2012), *Project Glass: One Day*, available at http://www.youtube.com/watch?v=9c6W4CCU9M4 (accessed 4 April 2013).

Greenbaum, J. and D. Loi (2012), 'Participation, the camel and the elephant of design: an introduction', *CoDesign*, **8** (2–3), 81–5.

Have, C. (2008), *Det store sceneskift. Fremtidens kommunikation (The Big Stage Shift)*, Aalborg: Aalborg University Press.

Herzberg, F. (1968), 'One more time: how do you motivate employees?', *Harvard Business Review*, **46** (1), 53–62.

Herzberg, F.I. (1969), *Work and the Nature of Man*, New York: Thomas Y. Crowell Co.

Herzberg, F., B. Mausner and B.B. Snyderman (1993), *The Motivation to Work*, Princeton, NJ: Transaction Publishers.

Jantzen, C., M. Vetner and J. Bouchet (2011), *Experience Design*, Copenhagen: Samfundslitteratur.

Jensen, R. (2005), *Fremtidsmagerne (Future Shapers)*, Copenhagen: Børsens forlag.

Jensen, R. and M. Dahl (1999), *The Dream Society*, London: McGraw-Hill.

Kim, A.J. (2000), *Community Building on the Web*, San Francisco, CA: Peachpit Press.

Kohn, A. (1996), 'By all available means: Cameron and Pierce's defense of extrinsic motivators', *Review of Educational Research*, Spring, **66** (1), 1–4.

Lund, J.M., A. Nielsen, L. Goldschmidt, H. Dahl and T. Martinsen (2005), *Følelsesfabrikken: Oplevelsesøkonomi på dansk (The Emotional Factory: Experience Economy in Danish)*, Copenhagen: Børsens forlag.

Maslow, A.H. (1943), 'A theory of human motivation', *Psychological Review*, **50** (4), 370–96.

Maslow, A.H. (1954), *Motivation and Personality*, New York: Harper and Row, reprinted in 1970.

Mintzberg, H. (1983), *Structures in Fives: Designing Effective Organizations*, Englewood Cliffs, NJ: Prentice-Hall.

Mintzberg, H. (1988), 'Opening up the definition of strategy', in J.B. Quinn, H. Mintzberg and R.M. James (eds), *The Strategy Process*, Englewood Cliffs, NJ: Prentice-Hall, pp. 13–20.

Mintzberg, H. (1989), *Mintzberg on Management*, New York: Free Press.

Mintzberg, H. (1993), *Structure in Fives: Designing Effective Organizations*, Englewood Cliffs, NJ: Prentice-Hall.

Mintzberg, H. (2009), 'Rebuilding companies as communities', *Harvard Business Review*, **87** (7–8), 140–3.

Newman, M.E.J. (2006), 'Modularity and community structure in networks', *Proceedings of the National Academy of Sciences USA*, **103** (23), 8577–82.

Nordic Innovation Center (2007), *User-driven Innovation. Localized*, available at http://www.nordicinnovation.net/prosjekt.cfm?id=1-4415-246 (accessed 28 July 2010).

Oldenburg, R. (1989), *The Great Good Place: Cafés, Coffee Shops, Community Centers, Beauty Parlors, General Stores, Bars, Hangouts, and How They Get You Through the Day*, New York: Paragon House.

Oldenburg, R. (2001), *Celebrating the Third Place*, New York: Marlowe and Co.

Pine II, B.J. and J.H. Gilmore (1999), *The Experience Economy: Work is Theatre and Every Business a Stage*, Cambridge, MA: Harvard Business School Press.

Pine II, B.J. and J.H. Gilmore (2011), *The Experience Economy*, Boston, MA: Harvard Business School Press.

Pink, D.H. (2010), *Drive: The Surprising Truth about What Motivates Us*, New York: Canongate.

Prahalad, C.K. and V. Ramaswamy (2004), 'Co-creating unique value with customers', *Strategy and Leadership*, **32** (3), 4–9.

Preece, J. (2000), *Online Communities: Designing Usability and Supporting Sociability*, Princeton, NJ: John Wiley and Sons.

Preece, J. and D. Maloney-Krichmar (2003), 'Online communities: focusing on sociability and usability', *Handbook of Human-Computer Interaction*, Thousand Oaks, CA: Sage, pp. 596–620.

Preece, J. and D. Maloney-Krichmar (2005), 'Online communities: design, theory, and practice', *Journal of Computer Mediated Communication*, **10** (4).

Preece, J., D. Maloney-Krichmar and C. Abras (2003), 'History of emergence of online communities', in K. Christensen and D. Levinson (eds), *Encyclopedia of Community*, Thousand Oaks, CA: Berkshire Publishing Group and Sage, pp. 1–11.

Rhee, Y. and J. Lee (2009), 'On modelling. A model of mobile community: designing user interfaces to support group interaction', *Interactions*, **16** (6), 46–51.

Robertson, T. and I. Wagner (2012), 'Ethics: engagement, representation and politics-in-action', *The Routledge International Handbook of Participatory Design*, London: Routledge, pp. 64–85.

Ryan, R.M. and E.L. Deci (2000a), 'Intrinsic and extrinsic motivations: classic definitions and new directions', *Contemporary Educational Psychology*, **25** (1), 54–67.

Ryan, R.M. and E.L. Deci (2000b), 'Self-determination theory and the facilitation of intrinsic motivation, social development, and well-being', *American Psychologist*, **55** (1), 68–78.

Toffler, A., W. Longul and H. Forbes (1981), *The Third Wave*, New York: Bantam Books.

Valler, R.J. (1997), 'Toward a hierarchical model of intrinsic and extrinsic motivation', *Advances in Experimental Social Psychology*, **29**, 271–360.

Valler, R.J. and R. Bissonnette (1992), 'Intrinsic, extrinsic, and amotivational styles as predictors of behavior: a prospective study', *Journal of Personality*, **60**, 599–620.

Valler, R.J. and G. Reid (1984), 'On the causal effects of perceived competence on intrinsic motivation: a test of cognitive evaluation theory', *Journal of Sport Psychology*, **6**, 94–102.

Wahba, A. and L. Bridwell (1976), 'Maslow reconsidered: a review of research on the need hierarchy theory', *Organizational Behavior and Human Performance*, **15**, 212–40.

Wellman, B. and K. Hampton (1999), 'Living networked on and offline', *Contemporary Sociology*, **28** (6), 648–54.

PART III

APPLICATION FIELDS

19. The social experience of cultural events: conceptual foundations and analytical strategies
Fabian Holt and Francesco Lapenta

19.1 INTRODUCTION

19.1.1 Chapter Objectives

This chapter presents a systematic review of conventional approaches to the experience of cultural events. The argument is that valuable approaches exist in various fields of study, but that the deeper conceptual foundations have yet to be clarified and examined. To this end, the chapter reviews existing approaches from an essentially sociological perspective on cultural experience as something that not only involves shared experience and interaction in a particular situation but also lifestyle aspects, social agendas and world views. One of the distinctive features of cultural events is their ability to engage participants in the experience of issues and agendas in both simple and complex forms. The bulk of the chapter is a theoretical outline that reviews and synthesizes complementary perspectives in the fields of sociology, communication studies and business studies for understanding the key dimensions in the evolution of cultural events over the course of the past couple of decades. More important than ever before is the media dimension, which has been overlooked because events have historically been defined by their difference from media experience, by the direct face-to-face interaction between bodies. This has led to the celebration of culture festivals and performances, for instance, as more authentic forms of social experience than disembodied media communications, separating the contexts of production and reproduction. This chapter argues that while important differences are real and existing, the romanticist narrative of the unmediated creates a false dichotomy, while in fact events and media, far from being mutually exclusive entities, have always evolved in a complex relation, even when this is not immediately obvious to organizers and participants. The recent development of social media has revolutionized the field, not only as the main communication platforms between events and participants but also in the more intense and more layered mediations along multiple communication channels and the more expressive information medium of video in media-sharing sites.

The main section of the chapter is a reflexive outline of three complementary approaches to the study of cultural events. The outline grounds these approaches in the conceptual foundations, drawing from diverse fields such as event management, media studies and marketing theory within a sociological discourse to account for important changes in the relation between cultural events and society. After this outline, the chapter further details two contemporary contexts for contemporary cultural events. The first is the postindustrial city and its cultural economy in which contemporary event culture emerged in the 1970s. The other perspective is how cultural events are transformed through new media practices.

After reading this chapter, you will be able to understand:

- unique aspects of experience and participation in cultural events;
- what it means for an event experience to be social;
- how cultural events and their management strategies are evolving within broader processes of social and technological change;
- how cultural events have evolved in the specific contexts of the postindustrial city and the expressive information channels of new media;
- how analytical approaches to events emerge from broader conceptual foundations;
- the three core analytical concepts of situations, spheres and leverage.

19.1.2   The Changing Role of Cultural Events in Contemporary Society

Cultural events have gained new and expanded functions in society since the 1980s when the term 'festivalization' appeared in the context of urban renewal and gentrification (Harvey, 1991; Holt with Wergin, 2013).[1] The field of cultural events includes commercial events organized for profit at one end and events organized by artists, public institutions and non-governmental organizations (NGOs) for more philanthropic purposes at the other. Overall, however, it is frequently difficult to distinguish between these interests. Many music and cultural festivals, for instance, illustrate the eroding boundaries in neoliberal societies between state, market and civil society (see, for example, Scammel, 2000). They involve all three sectors and engage participants as both citizens and consumers. The reason festivals attract interest across society is that they are increasingly recognized for their ability to mediate agendas of a complex world and not least for engaging people in these agendas through embodied, localized participation. Thus, cultural events increasingly become sites where civic utopian narratives of philanthropy, social movements and sustainability are intersecting with narratives of economic growth through consumption, tourism and place marketing.

Cultural events, moreover, have entered the mainstream of social life. In the process, they have lost some of their autonomy as utopian "third spaces" for sharing and imagining alternative futures in social movements and subcultures, for instance. The evolution in media practices has contributed to this development. Events have taken on new functions, not only a local, live, full sensory experience valued in discourse of authentic bodily presence and participation. They have also taken on new functions in the development of strategies for employing new media platforms in complex constellations to maximize the impact of events in a landscape of fragmented and fluid audiences. YouTube, for instance, is strategically positioning itself and indirectly also Google as the leading global platform for video broadcasts of important cultural events, with the implication that the platform not only gives access to but also creates a global mass public culture.

New media practices have intensified the communication dynamics of cultural events. Corporate brand events, for instance, have integrating techniques of installation art, interactive features and eventually social video for strategic circulation in global social media. Participatory media culture and its blurring of social spheres are also manifest among industry events that are increasingly taking advantage of organizing public festivities outside the closed halls of the trade fair to exploit the public attention in the media to influence policy makers and consumers. The changes in contemporary media culture have led to a point where the differences between live and mediated experience are used more strategically and constitute a powerful and necessary combination. The live event has become a fixture of corporate communications, even when events and media campaign activities are prioritized and combined differently. The media perspective is integrated in the conception of the event to optimize participation and the quality of media content. Thus, the media perspective no longer enters after the fact. The event has become a driver of media participation. It gains power from its localized experience in its context of origin and is consumed in a parallel array of mediated communications, interactions and representations.

19.2   APPROACHES AND CONCEPTS FOR THE STUDY OF CULTURAL EVENTS

The field of events management has been dominated by applied research approaches in the organizational nexus of city governments, commercial corporations, event production companies and communications agencies. These applied approaches have generally been slow to develop a theoretically grounded understanding of the historical, economic and social dynamics of cultural events. Also lacking are conceptual distinctions between different levels of analysis.

The events management literature is known outside academic circles for textbooks that are useful for the practical planning and organization of a variety of events (for example, Bowdin, 2006; Allen et al., 2008; Richards and Palmer, 2010). Many of these books are similar to guides for planning communication campaigns; they prescribe models of practice rather than analysing and conceptualizing those practices. In this discourse, events are organized not for the sake of the experience itself but for strategic and instrumental interests in branding organizations and places. In the 2000s, many city governments institutionalized and rebranded their events planning and permission departments into departments for events, culture and tourism. This was in many cases influenced by Florida's (2002) ideas about creative cities.

There is also a more specialized research literature that has appeared in journals such as *Festival Management and Event Tourism* and various journals of tourism, marketing and management. However, it is still largely applied research and often concentrates on the sports events industry. The sports industry has always had a bigger mass appeal, with broadcasts to mass media audiences, more sponsorship and advertising, and for these and other reasons not only sports events professionalization happened earlier then in the field of cultural events, but it also received greater attention in research and related literature. This chapter does not focus on sports events but rather on the current professionalization and evolution in cultural events. Although it does not exclude that some overlapping patterns characterize these different industries, it focuses on some key differences. One of the fundamental differences between sports event and culture events is the generally central role in cultural events of representations of self and social life, a particular cultural mimesis, to speak with Aristotle, including subtle distinctions and narratives around concepts of taste, age and class. In the more art-oriented events, reflexivity tends to play an important role and they sometimes presuppose familiarity with the canons and sophistication of "high" culture genres (Eyerman, 2006, p. 21). In comparison, sports emphasize bodily action and the rules of game. To narrow down the areas of interest of this chapter the following types of cultural events are included in its critical framework: (1) festivals for cities, communities, cultures, art forms; (2) art and book fairs; (3) expositions integrating culture with science and technology; (4) large public celebrations, ceremonies and commemorations; and (5) promotional events organized around cultural performance.

A common misunderstanding in the cultural events literature is that events can be organized more or less without specialist knowledge of content. Cultural events generally require most specialist knowledge of content as their core identity emerges from the particular combination of performances or installations that needs to be curated for this particular event and to give meaning to the particular time, place and audience. Thus, the DNA of a cultural event is often created through curatorial work of the core content, not just the visual design and storytelling or other more external components. This makes the curator or programmer a vital part of the event organization. The curation of cultural events requires analysis of talent, tastes and interests among specific consumer segments and the dynamics of fashions or trends. A superstar concert is fairly simple to curate because it is mainly about the market for one artist. But if the artist is performing as part of a special event, how do we know if it is the right artist for this particular event? In most cultural events such as music festivals, film festivals, urban cultural festivals and art biennials, the curatorial process involves the invention of a creative concept and a large group of artists, activities and locals with the goal of creating a coherent vision.

Professional curators of cultural events routinely testify to the importance of creating a program that is very contemporary, even visionary, because it is in the nature of events to constantly innovate and be ahead of the curve by exposing audiences to new cultural forms. This is partly because the event is an act of communication with a news value, but also because it requires more effort on the part of the consumer to participate in a festival, fair, exposition or public performance or ceremony, for instance, than watching a television show or reading a blog, and there are now more cultural events on offer than ever before.

The chapter builds on a conventional conception of expressive culture in the humanities to include both the arts and popular culture, but recognizes and examines issues pertaining to the expansion of culture outside the conventional boundaries of culture; what has been called "art worlds" (Becker, 1984) and "the field of cultural production" (Bourdieu, 1993) in the sociology of art. The evolving discourse of the experience economy in Northern European business studies is precisely linked with the aestheticization of everyday life and service environments, involving a higher design intensity, more events and within these contexts also the appropriation of expressive culture. In this context of consumer and corporate culture, culture and cultural experience are generally used as strategic entertainment. Culture becomes, in Yúdice's (2003) now famous phrase, "an expedient." Culture has increasingly become a tool in agendas of economic growth, mediating social conflicts and philanthropic causes.

The concept of event, whether it is a social, sports or cultural event, involves a break from the mundane everyday. The event is defined by a duality of exhibition and festivity, and it brings together communicative acts of curation, presentation, performance and consumer interaction. For participants, the recognition that many others are congregating in the same place creates energy and expectations for a special occasion. This is called "eventfulness." However, with culture, a special energy can emerge in the encounter with culture in its extraordinary context. For instance, the live music experience at a music festival or concert involves more than a musical experience, as music scholars have tended to think. But it is also more than a general feeling of festivity and eventfulness, as event management discourse would say. When any kind of art is effectively contextualized in an event, it comes alive as a social experience with meanings derived from its articulation in a special social domain outside of its everyday domain of art consumption.

Although the contemporary field of professional cultural events has been subject to little theorization, the broader conceptual foundations do not need to be invented from scratch. In the events management literature, authors commonly define events citing definitions in previous publications, complemented with common knowledge, without grounding it theoretically, and this limits the field and leaves it somewhat disconnected from research on events in other fields. It is not only the practitioners' discourse but also the early attempts at theorization in performance studies and media studies that lack a diverse but integrated disciplinary approach.

The dominant conceptions of performance in the field of performance studies evolved from the pioneering works of the 1960s by Schechner (1977 [2003]) and Turner (1969). They built on anthropological studies of traditional ritual events and integrated perspectives of behavioral sociology and theatrical performances. At the time, mass culture and media were marginal topics in the large areas of humanities, and they are still met with skepticism in performance studies (Auslander, 1999). In the 1970s, media and live events were still considered relatively separate empirical domains in academia. There was not really an academic discourse on cultural events. Only in the quiet recent post-ritual events literature have scholars taken an interest in analytical perspectives on the public and media in communication studies and sociology. This happened to some extent inside performance studies (Auslander, 1999), but the perspectives did not evolve there, but instead in media studies and sociology. It is indicative that the field grew from a conception of the media event[2] in linguistic categories of syntactics, semantics and pragmatics. "Syntactically, media events may be characterized, first, by our elements of interruption, monopoly, being broadcast live, and being remote," writes Dayan and Katz (1992, p. 10). This definition was underwritten by a neo-Durkheimian perspective of media events as occasions "where television makes possible an extraordinary shared experience of watching events at society's 'centre'" (Couldry and Hepp. 2011, p. 3).

Media events and liveness research has contributed to the understanding of important dimensions of performances and events in contemporary society, but is complementary because it does not primarily analyse participation in physical events. At the end of this chapter, we shall explore the role that new media are acquiring in the redefinition of the individual, collective, local and global discourse that cultural events propose to inspire.

For a more complete and systematic account of conceptual foundations for the study of cultural events, the following typology may be offered. The typology organizes strands of research on fundamental aspects of events. The strands have evolved within different disciplines, but to situate concepts and approaches in a broader interdisciplinary perspective, it is useful to understand these approaches in context. Moreover, they are complementary as they focus on different levels of analysis and are necessary for accounts of the notorious multitude of cultural events. This multitude may be difficult to account for in scholarly terms but it is easy to identify. When a big event is occurring, for instance, media reports frequently ask participants and experts about the nature of the event in the attempt to explain it to their media audiences. This produces numerous definitions that point out myriad aspects but does not create a coherent narrative. Questions about the nature of a major event are difficult to handle even for specialist scholars, and the nature of the event is often described as an enigma in journalism, providing statements by participants about their intense moments of experience. Scholarly writing about events is confronted with the same fundamental challenge of multitude. To constructively approach the problem in this chapter we offer an integrated typology that might provide useful insights to initiate a now necessary multimodal and interdisciplinary approach to the study of cultural events.

19.2.1   Situational Approaches to Performance in Anthropology, Performance Studies and Sociology

The first type of approaches are the situational approaches that grew out of an engagement with rituals and social behavior in pre-industrial and industrial societies without the same social fluidity and media complexity of contemporary advanced societies. The situational approaches tend to privilege an analytical focus on the immediate context of performance. They tend to stay within the temporal-spatial boundaries of the micro environment. The scholarly contribution lies in the capacity to not just describe individual experiences and situations but patterns of behavior and types of situations. This explains the centrality of concepts such as ritual and performance. Situational approaches are also characterized by an interest in how the situation relates to social life more broadly, for example, how it articulates and challenges everyday values and agendas in society. However, the prime site of inquiry was the situation itself, not its social or electronic mediations or the decision making in institutions, for instance. Meyrowitz (1985) offered a pioneer critique of situational approaches:

> In recent years, there has been a dramatic increase in the examination of social "episodes," "settings," and "contexts." Studies, theories, and critiques have suggested that personality measures are often poor predictors of everyday social behavior and that behaviors such as anxiety reactions are largely shaped by situational factors . . . As of now, the research on situations has supported the plausibility of situationism more than it has advanced toward a general theory of situations and behavior. Although there have been many empirical and analytical studies of situations, most of this work has focused on describing situation-specific behaviors as they exist at a particular time in a given culture. There has been relatively little work explaining the general process through which situations affect behavior, there have been few attempts at generating propositions for predicting why and how social situations change, and there have been virtually no analyses of how behavior will change when situations change. (Meyrowitz, 1985, pp. 27, 32)

This critique has paradigmatic implications. It puts conventional situational approaches into a completely new perspective by adopting a comparative methodological discourse of sociology and media studies. The critique highlights previously unrecognized boundaries of the situational approaches and points to the necessity of looking not just at more dimensions of the situation and the experience but the conceptual and disciplinary discourse. In other words, a situation can only be fully understood by considering the more complex structure of society and other forms of communication and experience. In particular, mediation and social change have been and are still to some extent ignored in studies with a situational approach. The epistemological risk is situationism: the isolation from the forces and contexts needed to explain the meanings and values of the situation. The concept of situational approaches is used in this chapter in a broad sense for a shared perspective in research within different traditions, but particularly anthropology, sociology and later performance studies. The founding figures in sociology such as Durkheim (1912) and Weber (1968) studied traditional rituals and ceremonies as part of large-scale theories of society, and it was this ritual perspective that was picked up in the research traditions that evolved with a more specialist focus, notably the folklorist van Gennep (1909 [1960]) and anthropologists such as Levi-Strauss and Turner. A different but clearly situational form of specialized inquiry is represented by Goffmann's (1959) study of social behavior. Situational approaches, moreover, dominate the field of performance studies that draws heavily on theater studies and has a strong interest in sited performances of extended theatricality (Kirschenblatt-Gimblett, 1999). Situational approaches continue to dominate in analyses centering on new performance spaces and experiences in those spaces.

19.2.2 Public Sphere and Social Movement Approaches in Communication Studies and Sociology

Meyrowitz convincingly argues that situational perspectives need to be complemented by knowledge of how media communications affects social behaviors in situations. Situations change over time, but not just through media. Changes in demographics, education, political culture and cultural policies are frequently playing into such social processes of change. But between social behavior and broader social change is a crucial level for the analysis of the event experience. This is the level that can be analysed from the concept of the event sphere. The event sphere is the microcosm that emerges within the time and place of the event. Rather than simply being a gated physical territory for a number of activities, the event is a social, aesthetic and historical space constructed through the curation of content, communications and designs that shape the core audience and the attitudes, ethics and atmosphere that emerge through participations. The event sphere should also not be confused with the identity of the event. Rather, it is a complex whole of interaction between different identities and images of the event among the diverse audiences of a mass event. The event sphere is also a fictional space, as illustrated by the fairy tales and themed areas of Disney World or the utopia counterculture of the Glastonbury rock festivals. The fiction takes on a performative dimension through liminal behavior, participant role-playing, installations and costumes. The event sphere, moreover, is an imaginary social order of a small society, usually modeled on mythical notions of a pre-modern village, even when fused with futuristic scenarios. In a festival area, for instance, a temporary micro society emerges with its own ecosystem of campsites, markets and subcultures with a daily rhythm over the course of a couple of days or more. Annual events gain a life-story dimension for participants and communities as a special occasion that puts past and present into perspective. The event sphere also involves specific elements such as emotional atmosphere, attitudes and ethical rules among participants, event architecture and spatial design, all of which helps create the sense of a coherent and recognizable event.

The event sphere is not an established concept, but recent research on cultural festivals has opened up a path of conceptualizations drawing on public sphere theory. Public sphere theory is historically linked to political culture, and a political public sphere is not the same as a festival or event public sphere. Above all, an event sphere is not necessarily political. Some events are conceived more within a service logic of the entertainment industry than within the cultural logic of difference to be found in cultural festivals in which ideology and social consciousness are defining aspects and motivating forces.

In his pioneering work on the public sphere concept, Habermas (1962 [1992]) described the emergence of urban cultural consumer spaces such as cafés, theaters and concert halls, but he also ascribed crucial importance to discourse and the ideological aspects of culture, which have later been developed in the theory of counterpublics; publics characterized by resistance, opposition and difference:

> The idea of a public is motivating, not simply instrumental. It is constitutive of a social imaginary . . . [W]hen people address publics, they engage in struggles . . . over the conditions that bring them together as a public. (Warner, 2002, p. 12)

The formation of counterpublics has been studied in various strands of cultural sociology, from social movement studies (Eyerman and Jamison, 1991) to urban collectivity studies (Maffesoli, 1988 [1996]), and beyond to the recent public sphere approach to cultural festivals (Delanty et al., 2011). The public sphere approach is particularly helpful for analysing how cultural festivals engage participants socially through the experience collectivity and difference.

Sennett emphasizes this aspect of diversity in his discussion of changing meanings of public culture in modernity. In his critique of contemporary culture, Sennett points out that

> [public once] meant not only a region of social life located apart from the realm of family and close friends . . . [it also meant that] this public realm of acquaintances and strangers included a relatively wide diversity of people. (Sennett, 1974, p. 17)

Sennett's study is relevant to a critical discussion of the development of cultural events as strategic entertainment in the postindustrial city. In particular, his skeptical description of vulgar intimacy, self-realization and withdrawal from societal commitment are echoed in contemporary cultural policy debates (Sennett, 1974, especially pp. 8–9). We are now seeing an increasing differentiation between cultural events in the conventional cultural sector and in the events industry emerging out of the service and tourisms industries.

19.2.3   Generalist and Specialist Approaches in Economics and Marketing Studies

Scholarship on events in economics and more applied disciplines such as marketing and management largely use the same general approaches developed from studies of more established and larger industries. Research on the role of events in the economy of tourism and cities, for instance, has adopted conventional models of input-output and cost-benefit analysis. Similarly, marketing research has operated from the fundamental idea of events as one of the media or avenues in the marketing mix, exploring its unique aspects of experience but still within a medium logic. These and other general approaches are useful for certain purposes, and they serve a particular role as tools of generalization and legitimization in impact studies. However, the generalist approaches do not capture what is unique about events. Moreover, theory developed from the analysis of events has continued to question the applicability of not just generalist models but also conventional principles of economics. This theory, moreover, suggests that the social experience is key to understanding economic activity in events. What follows is a discussion of these specialist approaches that account for aspects particular to events.

A fundamental aspect of approaches to event economics is their attempt at capturing the flows of economic activity following the particular social conditions and processes that constitute a cultural event for participants and business partners. The unique social value of the event to its various actors is to create different economic and organizational arrangements. The disruption of everyday routines in the experience of a festival, for instance, also applies to the extraordinary supply chain arrangements and the symbolic values for brands and local communities.

The first treatment of basic principles in event economics was conducted in Baumol and Bowens's influential study *Performing Arts: The Economic Dilemma* (1966) that used the performing arts as a model case for questioning conventional wisdom on the relation between labor productivity and inflation in classic economics. Baumol and Bowens argued that because there is little or no productivity gain in an opera or theater performance, the costs will rise faster than inflation and grow disproportionally compared with sectors with a productivity gain. Moreover, the wages have grown in opera houses because wages have grown in other labor markets where productivity has gone up. In the field of culture, productivity gain has happened especially in mass media distribution of entertainment. While this theory, known as 'Baumol's disease' remains true, the question about why the market value of performances and events have gone up in the age of digital media has caused scholars to think further. Frith argues on sociological grounds that the reason for the relatively prosperous economy of live music events such as concerts and festivals is the unique social values of the live experience. "The value of music (the reason why people are prepared to pay money for it) remains centered in its live experience" (Frith, 2007, p. 4).

The central role of social experience also forms the basis of the new marketing approach developed around the concept of social leverage by O'Brien and Chalip (2007). They were motivated by the recognition that sports events stakeholders have started to look beyond impact in a conventional sense to achieve longer-term sustainable outcomes. The authors also document a widespread scholarly critique of impact studies, not to mention the fact that rigorous impact studies have frequently arrived at disappointing results about the economic impact of events. O'Brien and Chalip developed an alternative to impact studies with potentially paradigmatic implications. Instead of focusing on outcomes, the effects, after the event, they focus on how events create value and work from the assumption that the main value comes from their ability to leverage processes beyond the event itself. For instance, an event might not generate profit within its immediate value chain but it can create social values, networks and business in other industries, and for this reason many events receive donations from sponsors and city governments.

In order to leverage the impacts, O'Brien and Chalip argue, a new analytical approach with a focus on strategic optimization is needed. They crucially introduce a turn away from measuring impacts to optimizing leverage (see also Chalip, 2004, 2006). Their research has produced a useful marketing model for systematically optimizing values for participants, sponsors, media and the community. The model is useful for big events with a complex structure but the principles are the same for small events. The model is concerned with physical participation and conventional approaches to broadcast media, so it can productively be complemented and developed with knowledge of new media spaces and practices.

The marketing optimization approach has the potential to integrate knowledge of new media dynamics, for instance, and its core elements can be further conceptualized to serve complex analyses of cultural events. If we look not only at the practical division into marketing units but also the processes in the event and its life cycle, new perspectives open up. An event serves particular needs in distinct sites of action, but it is also a combinational entity. From an economic and commercial perspective, the micro society of the event has other functions than its role as a world of experience for participants. These functions can be somewhat narrowed down to:

- a real-world consumer laboratory involving a multitude of social interaction in physical and virtual spheres;
- a marketing medium for promotion and sales;
- an innovation platform for products, services, new media and knowledge;
- a catalyst of social and economic action, elicited by extraordinary programming, mass audience formation and site-specific intensity.

The combination of these functions (laboratory, medium, platform and catalyst) accounts for an important part of the uniqueness and potentials of cultural events for society and business. The values of cultural events are not limited to the experience of a social situation, a cultural performance or a cultural public sphere.

Events also have limitations, however. Events have a short time-span, and it is an extraordinary situation from which experience and knowledge cannot automatically be transferred and implemented into everyday routines. Although it can be perceived as a real-world laboratory, the event is not an everyday laboratory, and this is both a strength and a weakness. The intense and overwhelming impressions from many activities and people create special energies that bring out certain desires and forms of human behavior that cannot be created in everyday life. Another problem is the complexity of influences that makes it difficult to distinguish the factors influencing buying decisions, for instance.

Methodically, the four functions proposed above suggest how the potential of the marketing leverage approach can be developed into a broader and more foundational conception of socio-economic approaches to understanding events. They also suggest that renewed attention should be paid to the new media practices that now embed all cultural productions and how they can be transformed into engines of economic growth and gain. It is clear that the economic action evolves around the particular social experience of the "cultural event" as an "extraordinary social experience" and how this experience is designed, organized, produced and consumed by local and global audiences. Thus, the event becomes a node among different social and economic practices, a source for understanding social change and the evolution of experience of cultural event, and the subject for the investigation of the new organizational and economic functions and structures that emerge from it.

To complement the analytical approaches and concepts discussed above, we would now like to offer two perspectives of particular relevance to contemporary cultural events. They are new media and the postindustrial city.

19.3   THE EVOLUTION OF CULTURAL EVENTS IN THE POSTINDUSTRIAL CITY

The above outline of analytical approaches needs to ground the event experience in its historical dimension and processes of social change. Situated performances, publics and socio-economic synergies are core concepts for understanding a cultural event. While cultural events relate very differently to history and society, the term "event" and the forms of design and participation have been fundamentally shaped by the conditions of culture in the postindustrial city.

The first mega events emerged in the late nineteenth century with the development of the Olympics and the World Expositions. They were both held in cities and played an active role in creating images of global culture. They created global publics in capital cities with the financial support of nation-states. Like all events, they were born in the image of their time, reflecting the world view of Western modernity with their grandiose format and claims to universalism. With the expositions, the exhibition of world cultures happened in the larger context of colonial imperialism (Roche, 2000). Clearly, a power relation between the mega event and the mega city was institutionalized.

In addition to the emergence of mega events with heavy involvement of the nation-state were cultural events in consumer culture and civic society. A market for public entertainment emerged with bars, clubs, dance halls, theaters and amusement parks in urban industrial centers (Nasaw, 1993). Since the 1970s, cultural events have become a fixture of urban public culture and city branding. Today more than half of the world's population live in cities, and the city and the event industry now constitute an indissoluble power relation. This originates in the postindustrial city when culture-led strategies of economic growth emerged and with them a new role of consumption. This is also the context of origin for the experience economy. Spaces of consumption were created in architecture, image and by increasing activities such as events. In other words, the city became a landscape of consumption for a broad population demographic (Zukin, 1991).

The crisis in the manufacturing industries in the 1960s contributed to a general crisis in urban economies. A city such as New York was close to bankruptcy in 1975, and many inner cities were not only poor but also left with empty and deteriorating buildings. The outside motivations for economic growth created a somewhat unstable ground for culture-led regeneration strategies, while they spread to smaller urban conglomerates or rural areas.

The consumption economy is most directly relevant to cultural events. Indeed, culture was for the first time employed by cities as an economic basis through its two main functions of consumption and marketing (Zukin, 1994, p. 11). This is the prime context of origin for many later policies and business discourses, including the experience economy, on emotions and aesthetics in shopping but also cultural forms such as architecture, museums and events. In these discourses of culture-led strategies of economic growth, traditional concepts of performance and ritual were replaced with cultural events. The landslide change in terminology reflects a shift from discourses of art worlds to discourses of outside agents of mega city developers, marketers and business entrepreneurs.

19.3.1   The Postindustrial Urban Economy

A long-term process since the 1960s, mega cities have experienced a combination of changes in real-estate development and demographic changes that have changed the conditions of cultural events. Commonly identified with the term gentrification, a growing population of professional middle classes forms the basis of a market for professional niche culture and more exclusive cultural events. In contrast, cultural events for a broader population demographic have been forced to move further away from the city center. Since the early 1999s, one of the most popular forms of mass events in cultural life has been rock and pop music festivals in rural areas where space is cheap and youths can party and have camping facilities. This kind of more unregulated cultural event and festivity has become rarer in the increasingly controlled and gentrified city. The early cultural festivals of European modernity created spaces for imagining different futures in a space outside the institutions of the market and the state. Their vision emphasized the celebration not of cities or holidays but art and civilization and the emergence of cultural festivals (Autissier, 2010, pp. 27, 30; BOP Consulting, 2011, p. 99). The cultural festivals were not concentrated in capital cities but in smaller cities, where they created new and alternative economies to the vanishing local industrial economies. The pioneering urban sociological work of Zukin (1991, 1994, 2010) and Grazian (2003, 2008) offer an insight into the socio-economic dynamics at work in these processes. In a discussion of the illustrative case of the Massachusetts Museum of Contemporary Art (MASS MoCA), Zukin writes:

> It is quite a wager that this museum will create a tourist industry and that tourism will save the town from economic decline. But when the last factories have closed their gates and neither business nor government offers a different scenario, ordinary men and women can be persuaded that their city is ready to enter the symbolic economy. (Zukin, 1994, p. 79)

Two general points can be drawn from this. First, culture-led growth strategies might not resonate with all population groups and involve conflicting interests between the cultural sector and other sectors. A shift from this old narrative of one-directional impact to one of synergies can be recommended. Second, the MASS MoCA is an illustrative example of two typical problems of culture-led strategies. A $1.8 million (by 1988 standards), state-financed feasibility staudy was conducted by outsiders for this small town community, even while a fiscal crisis started generating skepticism and there was no support for the project among the local arts community (Zukin, 1994, pp. 94–6). What is more, the project became an example of smaller city culture projects with content "imported" from the city. In this case, it was objects from the Guggenheim collection in New York.

The literature on the transformation of culture in the postindustrial city shows that the focus in the 1970s and 1980s was on conventional venues such as museums, parks and shopping. Later, as in the case of the MASS MoCA, more emphasis was on performances and events. There are a couple of reasons for this. One is the increasing fluidity in society that tends to be in favor of events with news value and intense dynamics of momentary encounters rather than the more stable structures of cultural institutions. The permanent exhibitions of museums, and the traditional programming of concert halls, have been challenged by a growing interest in public performances in new unconventional spaces. Big concerts used to be an urban experience but are now organized, pushed by gentrification, outside in smaller urban areas or at the borders of bigger cities. A core example is the DIY rock scene that emerged in Manhattan in the 1970s and has now moved to Brooklyn, New York with ad hoc rock shows in warehouses, lofts, basements and under bridges greatly contributing to the branding of the city's borough that now strongly competes with Manhattan itself.

19.4   THE TRANSFORMATION OF CULTURAL EVENTS IN NEW MEDIA PRACTICES

The intensification of electronic mediation in contemporary society is changing live events in complex ways. Key changes for cultural events include the communicative functions and meanings of the event itself. After detailing these aspects, we shall turn to changes in the relation with the city, with space.

Before the advent of electronic mediation in the late nineteenth century, performances and public gatherings more generally had a privileged role in communicating important messages and sanctioning dominant agendas in the form of ceremonies and parades, for instance. Carnivals and other folk rituals served to articulate community, social values and informal knowledge such as via song and dance. Electronic mass media meant that information could be distributed without embodied interaction and performance, and they became the infrastructure in the era of national media. Now everyone with a radio or television could hear a public speech by the president. Performances could be enjoyed independently of time and space. In this era, cultural festivals, for instance, could create a public sphere for minorities and otherwise dispersed specialist audiences whose interests were at the margins or even excluded from the institutions of power, including mass media. This has changed with the advent of networked media that in principle allow any media user to share information, and so cultural events are no longer a privileged site for articulating community and communicating the values of that community. But cultural events remain a privileged site for the embodied experience of cultural performance and community.

Second, media and particularly new networked and mobile media practices have created layered experiences. The event is mediated between private and public spheres, between the real and the virtual. This happens along multiple channels and through multiple forms of user mediation and participation. New media practices provide many ways of sharing and tracking information. For cultural events, this proposes a challenge to the private and intimate sphere that is central to building local communities with strong ties. But it is also an opportunity, as a single provocative act such as the Pussy Riot church performance in Moscow fired up the internet across the globe. The dimensions and meanings of events are now being defined in the contexts of social networking sites (Facebook), micro blogging platforms (Twitter) and media-sharing websites (YouTube,

Instagram and Pinterest). These platforms, communicative forms and social practices are redefining the very definition of eventfulness and the spatial and social boundaries of event genres. With more media practices embedded in events, the boundaries of the extraordinary shared experience that were once defined by elements of "interruption" (of daily life) and "monopoly" (in the case of the remote live broadcast of the extraordinary event) are now eroding. Well-known examples include the narratives of self that participants create through image sharing and production in their network among friends and their public marketing of event participation through the now leading user-driven event marketing in the events pages of Facebook. But more complex collective processes also occur when seemingly simple video essays of a festival, commonly produced from last year's event, go viral in network media and take on a powerful role in maintaining and shaping participant representations and experience of the event. A prominent example is the 2012 after video of the large electronic dance music festival in the Netherlands called Tomorrowland. The video had more than 30 million views on YouTube before the festival, and it follows the storytelling strategy that also penetrates the entire festival and its event architecture, drawing on models of adventure and fantasy universe from theme parks and Disney cinema.

Cultural events are being redefined by qualities that blend the power of collective mediated experiences with more intimate and personal experiences. New media practices in a way more closely resemble the personal and social dynamics once characteristic of the middlebrow art of family photography (Bourdieu, 1990). A ritualized use of media and media representations used to both separate the mundane from the exceptional and celebrate and consolidate individual histories, personal ties and social relations. Emerging social media representations are now overlaying all cultural events; at times enriching old forms of media coverage of collectively meaningful events; and at times, by means of their own substantial media coverage establishing an event as collectively meaningful and extraordinary (Ito, 2008; Ito et al., 2010; Lapenta, 2011; Papacharissi, 2011).

19.5   CONCLUSION

The motivating idea of this chapter was to complement the existing literature on the experience economy by examining the social dimensions of experience, specifically the experience of cultural events. The existing literature in Northern Europe has so far focused on the immediate situation, on the immersive experience of individuals, from the perspective of positive psychology and marketing communications. The core point in our conceptual framework of experience is that the focus on the immediate situation is strong not only in the aforementioned fields but also in ritual theory, performance studies and event management. By introducing the concept of public sphere, we have illustrated a distinctly different conception, recently developed as a post-ritual approach. To think of an event experience in the context of a public sphere involves other analytical levels and opens up other perspectives on the meanings and values of cultural events. The chapter further explored the complexity of spheres and embodied experience in relation to new media practices that have so far received little attention in the conception of cultural events and in the experience economy literature.

The methodical rationale of the chapter, then, has been to make clear that the concept of experience, in the context of cultural events, can productively be more grounded in mainstream social science traditions. We have sought to illustrate this by integrating and synthesizing approaches and highlighted complementary aspects to build a broader and stronger understanding of the topic.

The argument about taking the broader social dimension of experience more seriously and integrating approaches, however, also confronts barriers that should not be ignored. There are divisions between the traditions from which we have drawn. Not all of them claim expertise in the social dimension, and we are willing to view our argument as a sociological intervention, as we cannot represent all disciplines but ask questions and examine problems of relevance to them. More specifically, the approaches to experience in marketing studies and in public sphere theory not only present different analytical perspectives but also involve ideological contrasts. The concept of public spheres is closely linked with notions of critical social reflexivity, including a critical stance against capitalism and the market. The contrasting perspectives embedded in these traditions can highlight the complexity of the issue. Moreover, this also leads us to the conclusion that one cannot adopt unitary narratives in the account of contemporary cultural events and cultural experience. The way forward is to engage with explanations in different disciplines and their underlying ideologies, while also examining their relation with relatively separate but changing avenues of culture in more or less commercial forms. In contemporary society, conventional conceptions of culture still exist, for example, in urban micro scenes and arts festivals, but there are also a growing number of cultural events in the avenues of consumer culture and corporate culture. Furthermore, cultural events constitute spaces between civic society and consumer society, and they often also involve public institutions. The role of events as spaces in-between is fascinating, but also poses a challenge to scholars, practitioners and policy makers in the field as it becomes harder to clarify the interests and values. How, for instance, can the cultural department of a state or city government decide whether to support a cultural event that might serve cultural and civic values, but at the same time is corporately sponsored and draws people into a cultural sphere outside the political sphere? A festival, for instance, can advocate philanthropic causes but in the process de-politicizes those issues by reframing them as philanthropic and not political. And how are attitudes to politics changing when social issues are presented as part of the festival experience? These questions are not only of interest to social scientists and public institutions but also to event managers collaborating with public institutions and volunteers. They are relevant to everyone concerned with issues of citizenship.

The blurring of boundaries between spheres is central to our theorization of new media practices and how they are transforming cultural events. The deep transformations in media culture involve more hybrid social experiences that are produced in their local context of origin and consumed in a parallel array of mediated communications, interactions and representations. New media platforms and practices are redefining the very definition of eventfulness and the spatial and social boundaries of event genres. Media are no longer entering the event production and consumption after the event. Instead, they are integrated throughout the entire process, shaping the creative ideas and management of the event from the very beginning. This is illustrated by the fact that some events are produced to provide media content in global social media for branding purposes. With more media practices embedded in events, the boundaries of the extraordinary shared experience that were once defined by the interruption of daily life and the monopoly of broadcasting are now eroding. The event is now being redefined by qualities that blend the power of collective mediated experiences with more intimate and personal experiences. The social experience of cultural events is therefore also a mediated experience. This presents new challenges and opportunities for the study of cultural events and for professionals in the industry. We have pointed to key aspects and emphasized that the analytical mode can productively shift from investigating individual aspects of how events are ascribed meaning *in* the media to an investigation of how events are constructed *through* layered media practices that changes perceptions of space, mobility and cultural experience.

ACKNOWLEDGMENTS

The authors would like to express special gratitude to the editors of this volume. We would also to thank our colleagues in the research group 'Innovation in Service and Experience' at the University of Roskilde for inspiration. We are grateful for comments on an earlier draft of this chapter at a conference on experience economy in Roskilde in June 2012.

NOTES

1. The term refers to the increasing number of cultural events, but it also variously refers to cultural and spatial transformations such as (1) the increasing use of urban public spaces for cultural events; (2) the use of cultural events and particularly popular culture for promoting social and economic agendas; (3) the popularization of culture from arts scenes to reach broader, non-specialist audiences and media; (4) the growing power of public presence in a media-intense culture at the cost of attention to substance and long-term values; and (5) the carnivalization of cultural performances in the form of spectacular show effects, choreography and installations. The term festivalization has been used for such broad, complex developments that they might not be adequately represented by this term.
2. The influential book *Media Events* (Dayan and Katz, 1992) helped kickstart interest in media events and issues of liveness in media experience within media studies, with important contributions being a special issue on liveness in the *Journal of Communication Studies* (2004) and the edited volume *Media Events in a Global Age* (2010), both edited and with important contributions by Nick Couldry.

BIBLIOGRAPHY

Allen, J., W. O'Toole, R. Harris and I. McDonnell (2008), *Festival and Special Events Management*, 4th edn, Milton, Queensland: Wiley.
Auslander, P. (1999), *Liveness: Performance in a Mediatized Culture*, London: Routledge.
Autissier, A.-M. (ed.) (2010), *The Europe of Festivals: From Zagreb to Edinburgh, Intersecting Viewpoint*, Paris: Éditions de l'attribut Culture Europe International.
Baumol, W. and W. Bowen (1966), *Performing Arts: The Economic Dilemma*, New York: Twentieth Century Fund.
Becker, H. (1984), *Art Worlds*, Berkeley, CA: University of California Press.
Bourdieu, P. (1990), *Photography: A Middle-brow Art*, Stanford, CA: Stanford University Press.
Bourdieu, P. (1993), *The Field of Cultural Production: Essays on Art and Literature*, Cambridge: Polity Press.
Bowdin, G. (2006), *Events Management*, Oxford: Butterworth-Heinemann.

Chalip, L. (2004), 'Beyond impact: a general model for sport event leverage,' in B.Ritchie and D.A. Clevedon (eds) (2004), *Sport Tourism: Interrelationships, Impacts and Issues*, Clevedon, UK: Channel View Publications, pp. 226–52.

Chalip, L. (2006), 'Towards social leverage of sport events', *Journal of Sport and Tourism*, **11** (2), 109–27.

Couldry, N. and A. Hepp (2010), 'Introduction: media events in globalized media cultures', in N. Couldry, A. Hepp and F. Krotz (eds), *Media Events in a Global Age*, New York and London: Routledge, pp. 1–20.

Couldry, N., A. Hepp and F. Krotz (eds) (2011), *Media Events in a Global Age*, New York and London: Routledge.

Dayan, D. and E. Katz (1992), *Media Events: The Live Broadcasting of History*, Cambridge, MA: Harvard University Press.

Delanty, G., G. Giorgi and M. Sassatelli (2011), *Festivals and the Cultural Public Sphere*, London: Routledge.

Durkheim, E. (1912), *The Elementary Forms of Religious Life*, New York and Oxford: Oxford University Press.

Eyerman, R. (2006), 'Toward a meaningful sociology of the arts', in R. Eyerman and L. McCormick (eds), *Myth, Meaning, and Performance: Toward a New Sociology of the Arts*, Boulder, CO: Paradigm, pp. 13–35.

Eyerman, R. and A. Jamison (1991), *Social Movements: A Cognitive Approach*, Cambridge: Polity Press.

Florida, R. (2002), *The Rise of the Creative Class*, New York: Basic Books.

Frith, S. (2007), 'Live music matters', *Scottish Music Review*, **1** (1), 1–17.

Goffman, E. (1959), *The Presentation of Self in Everyday Life*, New York: Anchor.

Grazian, D. (2003), *Blue Chicago: The Search for Authenticity in Urban Blues Clubs*, Chicago, IL and London: University of Chicago Press.

Grazian, D. (2008), *On the Make: The Hustle of Urban Nightlife*, Chicago, IL and London: University of Chicago Press.

Habermas, J. (1962), *The Structural Transformation of the Public Sphere: An Inquiry into a Category of Bourgeois Society*, Neuwied, Germany: Luchterhand, reprinted in 1992, Cambridge: Polity.

Harvey, D. (1991), 'The urban face of capitalism,' in J.F. Hunt (ed.), *Our Changing Cities*, Baltimore, MD: Johns Hopkins University Press.

Holt, F. with C. Wergin (2013), 'Introduction', in *Musical Performance and the Changing City: Postindustrial Contexts in Europe and the United States*, New York and London: Routledge, pp. 1–24.

Ito, M. (2008), 'Introduction', in K. Varnelis (ed.), *Networked Publics*, Cambridge, MA: MIT Press, pp. 1–14.

Ito, M., S. Baumer, M. Bittanti et al. (2010), *Hanging Out, Messing Around, and Geeking Out: Kids Learning and Living with New Media*, Cambridge, MA: MIT Press.

Kirshenblatt-Gimblett, B. (1999), 'Performance studies', manuscript available at http://www.nyu.edu/classes/bkg/issues/rock2.htm (accessed 14 April 2013).

Lapenta, F. (2011), 'Guest editor's introduction: locative media and the digital visualisation of space, place, and information', *Visual Studies*, **26** (1), March, 1–3.

Lash, S. and C. Lury (2007), *Global Culture Industry*, Cambridge: Polity Press.

Maffesoli, M. (1996), *The Time of the Tribes: The Decline of Individualism in Mass Society*, London: Sage, original printed in French in 1988.

Masterman, G. and E. Wood (2006), *Innovative Marketing Communications: Strategies for the Events Industry*, Amsterdam: Elsevier.

Meyrowitz, J. (1985), *No Sense of Place: The Impact of Electronic Media on Social Behavior*, New York and Oxford: Oxford University Press.

Nasaw, D. (1993), *Going Out: The Rise and Fall of Public Amusement*, Cambridge, MA: Harvard University Press.

O'Brien, D. and L. Chalip (2007), 'Executive training exercise in sport event leverage', *International Journal of Culture, Tourism, and Hospitality Research*, **1** (4), 296–304.

Papacharissi, Z. (ed.) (2011), *A Networked Self: Identity, Community, and Culture on Social Networking Sites*, New York and London: Routledge.

Pine, B.J. and J.H. Gilmore (1999), *The Experience Economy: Work is Theatre and Every Business a Stage*, Boston, MA: Harvard Business School Press.

Richards, G. and R. Palmer (2010), *Eventful Cities: Cultural Management and Urban Revitalisation*, Amsterdam: Elsevier.

Roche, M. (2000), *Mega-events and Modernity: Olympics and Expos in the Growth of Global Culture*, London and New York: Routledge.

Scammel, M. (2000), 'The internet and civic engagement: the age of the citizen consumer', *Political Communication*, **17**, 351–5.

Schechner, R. (1977), *Performance Theory*, New York: Routledge, reprinted in 2003.

Sennett, R. (1974), *The Fall of Public Man*, New York: W.W. Norton and Company.

Turner, V. (1969), *The Ritual Process: Structure and Anti-Structure*, New York: Aldine De Gruyter.

Turner, V. (1982), *From Ritual to Theatre: The Human Seriousness of Play*, New York: PAJ.

Van Gennep, A. (1909), *The Rites of Passage*, London: Routledge, reprinted in 1960, New York: Kegan Paul.

Warner, M. (2002), *Publics and Counterpublics*, New York: Zone Books.
Weber, M. (1968), *Economy and Society: An Outline of Interpretative Sociology*, Berkeley, CA: University of California Press.
Yúdice, G. (2003), *The Expediency of Culture: Uses of Culture in the Global Era*, Durham, NC and London: Duke University Press.
Zukin, S. (1991), *Landscapes of Power: From Detroit to Disney World*, Berkeley and Los Angeles, CA: University of California Press.
Zukin, S. (1994), *The Cultures of Cities*, Malden, MA: Blackwell.
Zukin, S. (2010), *Naked City: The Death and Decline of Authentic Urban Places*, Oxford and New York: Oxford University Press.

20. From creative cluster to innovation platform: the rise of the *Doctor Who* experience in Creative City Cardiff
Philip Cooke

20.1 INTRODUCTION

In this contribution, an examination is presented of the complex ways in which an experience economy setting arose from origins in a traditional regional/national broadcasting context in a medium-sized cultural and political capital city, Cardiff in Wales. Home to the Welsh branches of the BBC and commercial TV channels, media deregulation in the 1980s gave birth to an explosion of media and new media start-up firms. These formed a powerful cluster that later exerted a locational influence on the broadcasters, bringing BBC facilities (*Porth Teigr* Drama Village) to the former harbour district whose low rent waterfront office-space attracted such firms, as elsewhere. Quality and cost decisions led BBC UK to decentralize drama production to this centre of excellence. Among the decentralized productions was *Doctor Who*. Such was the impact of the new and distinctive on-location scenery of the city that a supplementary film tourism industry developed. Experience economy investment in the *Doctor Who* Up-Close Exhibition on the waterfront followed, as did spin-off experiences related to *Torchwood*, now a cult series filmed in Los Angeles, and the BBC's *Casualty* and *Gavin and Stacey*, whose 'experience' can be visited in neighbouring South Wales harbour town Barry. An estimated €120 million per year is calculated to flow into the city-region's economy, a similar impact to that of the film tourism effect upon Ystad, where the *Wallander* series is set near Malmö, Sweden.

Today, adherents of the experience economy perspective believe that businesses must orchestrate memorable events for their customers, such that the memory itself becomes the product or the experience. Proficient businesses can begin charging for the value of the transformation that an experience offers. This, argue Pine and Gilmore (1999), is a natural progression in the value added by the business over and above its inputs. Slightly ahead of this formulation emerged a related one identifying the importance of creative industries to the economic as well as cultural welfare of societies (Landry, 1995). In what ways, if at all, are these concepts related? Creative industries are defined narrowly as concerned with the exchange of finance for rights in intellectual property (Lash and Urry, 1994) but broadly as displaying a core communal business model that originates ideas of expressive value, which they aspire to commercialize (Throsby, 2001). Clearly the narrow definition is almost completely different from the notion of an experience economy whereas the broad definition is much closer. Probably, it is Pine and Gilmore's explicit emphasis on takeaways in the sense of memories that differentiates them most, since this is implicit and seldom emphasized in creative industries discourse, which in truth is an equally economistic framing to that of the experience economy. And in its narrower definition, it is arguably slightly more economistic. In this chapter, the broader definition of creative industries is taken as a focus for the analysis of the emergence of an experience economy phenomenon. It thus contributes to that sub-set of both perspectives that has come to be known as 'film tourism'. The films in question can be cinematic or made for TV or even video, and nowadays, perhaps, sites of special social networking significance. Accordingly, the chapter begins by treating both activities as centrally concerned with innovation – here creative rather than scientific – which denotes a systemic approach in which institutional and individual impulses to be creative coalesce. Thus, for example, galleries, schools of design, broadcasters and creatives interacting, or more intimately involved, with these are engaged in recombining knowledge, expertise and skills to create novelty. As a path-dependent, evolutionary process this can lead to successive novelties, triggered by a catalytic one.

Since Landry's (1995) intervention, promotion of creative industries as catalysts of economic growth has been common but not everywhere equally successful. For years London's Millennium Dome seemed a great white elephant until rescued by Las Vegas entertainment investment. Sheffield's Rock Music Museum (National Centre for Popular Music) is just one of the many casualties of misplaced optimism towards the power of symbolic infrastructure. Ironically, independent movie mogul Harvey Weinstein saved the experience aspiration when he opened the British Music Experience in the former facility, renamed the O2 Arena since 2009 (Mugan, 2009). Indeed, it seems the creative industry contribution to economic development is hard to plan successfully. Nevertheless, the UK, as one of the countries pioneering the 'Creative City' (Landry, 1995) unquestionably takes the concept of creative industries contributing to economic welfare completely seriously, in the late 1990s establishing a ministry of state (Department of Culture, Media and Sport, DCMS) to oversee the broad field and give definition to the platform. In this case the notion of platform captures the diversity and sometimes 'related variety' (Frenken et al., 2007) of the many activities that recombine to make up the category of creative industries. These are more than a vertical sector or cluster; rather, they comprise networks of firms and organizations that cross-pollinate the distinctive creative elements that coalesce within. As such and in their complex and systemically adaptive forms, they are difficult to pin down and predict behaviourally or locationally. They constitute something like a self-organizing system (Mitleton-Kelly, 2006).

Thus it is that the UK government is conscious of the relative importance of the creative industries' share in the UK economy both in terms of value added and employment, but it does not have full control over their evolution. Nevertheless, the broad platform was, until the 2008–12 double-dip recession, growing and significantly contributing to UK exports (DCMS, 1998, 1999, 2001). This is testified to by DCMS-commissioned research in, for example, the annual DCMS' statistical bulletins on the UK creative economy (DCMS, 2009). Research on the direct impact of creative industries upon the UK economy has been coupled with a growing attention to the way these industries indirectly contribute to economic growth more widely through the diffusion of creative and innovative activities across sectors into related industries like industrial design (Tether, 2009) or related variety spillovers across the wider economy (DCMS, 2007).

Since the onset of actual experience economy wonders, which seemed to be very much associated with the boom period from the aftermath of the dot.com collapse in 2000 until that of the financial markets in 2008, scepticism has set in about the validity of Pine and Gilmore's (1999) original concept. Seen by some as an amplification of US marketing hype with something of a surreal twist signifying the last, excessive days of late capitalism, David Harvey referred to Dubai's 'snowdome in the desert', 'fantasy island' luxury apartments and seven star hotels as 'criminally absurd' (Harvey, 2008; Bennett, 2010). More recently, Freire-Gibb (2011), commenting on the special popularity amongst academics and policy-makers of experience economy thinking in Denmark, shows most to be disappointed with the results of their interpretations of the experience economy as an instrument of local economic development. It is probable that economic recession after 2008 has dealt a temporary, if not permanent, death-knell to experience economy initiatives in Denmark as well as elsewhere. As the author says, even Machiavelli advised city-state leaders 'to keep the people occupied with festivals and spectacles' (cited in Freire-Gibb, 2011) but 'when the party is over' perhaps the people have to prioritize other issues.

The conceptual dimension of this chapter considers the creative industries to be amenable to regional innovation system (RIS) analysis (Cooke and Schwartz, 2007). This is because its empirical focus is TV, film and digital media, a creative and innovative platform, it is more framed within the RIS paradigm, but where relevant reference is also made to the evolutionary related variety literature (Hoekman et al., 2009). Indeed the economic impact of creative industries can only be fully understood if evolutionary elements of both speciation and variety are considered. The chapter proceeds as follows. Section 20.2 summarizes the conceptual framework and reviews the current literature on innovation in creative industries. It furthers the succeeding discussion in the RIS and related variety frameworks. Section 20.3 presents initial findings on Creative City Cardiff's TV, film and digital media platform and Section 20.4 analyses the creative and experience innovations. Sections 20.5 and 20.6 discuss the findings and implications arising from the quantitative analyses including policy-related discussions that pervade the chapter. Section 20.7 contains brief conclusions.

20.2   SYSTEMS OF INNOVATION IN THE CREATIVE INDUSTRIES

In most advanced countries the service industry comprises most of the economy. However, most of the concepts and measures of innovation are derived from processes in the manufacturing sectors. Gradually, embryonic efforts have emerged that seek to correct this imbalance (Miles, 2007). Such efforts recognize that while manufactures are tangible, services are characterized by 'their intangibility, co-production with customers, simultaneity, heterogeneity and perishability' (Nijssen et al., 2006, p. 242). According to Miles (2007), understanding service innovation requires a better appreciation of organizational and market innovations, inter-organizational and client-facing innovations, as well as cultural and aesthetic innovations. Despite this, many service industries rely on manufactured inputs just as many manufactures rely upon service inputs. So the distinction between tangibles and intangibles may not be as important as some authors think (Dunning, 2000). TV, film and digital media are three of the more obvious elements of the creative industries platform or sub-platform, in this case, which are unthinkable without their associated hard technology. In line with this, Drejer (2004) argues that the boundaries between manufacturing and services are increasingly blurred especially around processes that lead to product and process innovation. Is there any case for ignoring the boundary completely? In fact not, because innovation is concerned with commercialization of new knowledge (Edquist, 1997). In manufacturing the market is for tangibles, while in services it is for intangibles. Hence, it is the market not the innovation or creation that determines distinctiveness. This is, of course, clear and by no means blurred or fuzzy conceptually-speaking.

Having said that, the understanding of innovation processes in cultural and creative industries is often said to remain unclear. Innovation here coincides with aesthetic, artistic, stylistic or in Stoneman's terms 'soft innovation' (Castañer and Campos, 2002; Handke, 2006; Stoneman, 2009). Stoneman (2009, p.33) defines soft innovation as 'innovation in goods and services that primarily impacts upon sensory perception and aesthetic appeal rather than functionality'. Accordingly, subjective judgement comes into play. This apparently creates difficulties in assessing novelty. A good example is Castañer and Campos (2002, p.31) who, in particular, highlight the following, from the Schumpeterian perspective: first, manufactures are compared only with competitor manufactures while artistic innovation is not. Second, creative destruction destroys or obsolesces instantly in manufacturing but not in artistic production. But this is clearly debatable. Even art, let alone creative industry output has a market. Just as apples, flowers and automotive products are presented in markets so auctions, performances or exhibitions occur in the arts and consumers buy or they do not. Creative destruction may obsolesce but many consumers do not buy the innovation. Rogue markets for Edison light bulbs exist after they were banned by statute in many countries in favour of novel light-emitting diode (LED) technology. Much value accrues from classic cars, trucks and even tractors and farm equipment. The aesthetic dimension of *Overhaulin'* is rather overlooked in this analysis.

This is well captured in Stoneman's (2008, pp.2–3) analysis. He distinguishes soft innovation as follows:

> The first type is innovation in products that are not generally considered functional in nature but instead offer aesthetic appeal, and/or appeal to the senses or the intellect. Examples are music, books, film, fashion, art, video games etc. Such products are found particularly in those industries that it has become recent practice to label the 'creative industries', encompassing culture, media and the Arts . . . The second type is aesthetic innovations in industries the output of which is not aesthetic per se but functional. In addition to their functionality, products in such industries may have many non-functional characteristics. These will encompass the basic senses of sight, touch, taste, smell and sound, for example: the appearance of furniture, the sound of a car exhaust, the taste of a meal, the smell of flowers in a garden design and the touch of a sheepskin rug . . . In addition many products will come with that distinctive but intangible quality encompassed by the concept of brand image . . .

One distinction worth making is that there is widespread evidence that innovation – commercialization of new knowledge – occurs with about twice the frequency in the creative platform as in manufacturing. Research shows that creative industries generate high spillovers in terms of products, knowledge and networks. Looking at the importance of these linkages for innovation processes, Bakshi et al. (2008) find that economic sectors that sell to and/or buy from creative industries are more innovative. In a recent study Sunley et al. (2008), focusing upon innovation dynamics specifically in the design industry in the UK, found that design innovation requires the combination of a wide range, or platform, of knowledge. Design emerges from the interaction between different network nodes that synthesize and recombine knowledge to produce emergent effects and new designs. They further found that relations with clients, as well as firms' routines and competences, are highly important to design innovation compared to inter-firm cooperation or the local cultural environment. These system effects in soft innovation make it amenable to normal systems of innovation analysis. Consider the Andy Warhol *Factory* that combined painting (silkscreens, lithographs, sculptures), photography (Billy Name), film (for example, *Chelsea Girls*), fashion (Edie Sedgwick), music (Velvet Underground) and so on. In this, key roles are played, first, by the platform of potentially, but not always realized, interlocking 'related variety' nodes of creative or commercial, market-facing business activity, and the inter-twining institutional knowledge-flows that may be sourced in many ways by actors. Training of skilled staff, consulting of design archives or pattern libraries, sampling retro tunes, consulting film libraries and photographic archives lead to soft innovation that saturates contemporary culture.

20.3 DESCRIPTION OF THE WALES CREATIVE CLUSTER

Wales has a creative economy that is mainly supported through the TV/film/new media production industry. In 2002, it was reported that Wales employed 4 per cent of the UK total in the audio-visual industry, which equated to 600 businesses and £350 million in turnover (Cardiff Council, 2006). Of these firms, the majority are related to TV and film or with a focus in one of those particular sectors based on a similar supply chain. This leaves only a small portion of the firms related to radio. Due to this, and the firms collected in the data set, the radio sector will not be analysed. Furthermore, to narrow down the location, within Wales, there are several areas that have concentrations of TV production firms, largely based on satellite BBC Wales production studios in the area; however, Cardiff is the most prevalent.

   Cardiff, as a local authority, has the highest saturation of creative industry employment in Wales at 4.6 per cent with Gwynedd, in Northwest Wales, having the second highest level at 4.1 per cent (Cardiff Council, 2009). Cardiff's hinterland, the industrial South Wales valleys, performs less well in terms of the creative industries as with other such old industrial belts; however, this may be lessened with the BBC Drama Village as a number of BBC employees reside in this area of 'authenticity' (Gilmore and Pine, 2007) and one of the long-term goals of the Drama Village is peripheral regeneration (Interview, BBC Wales, 2010). The TV industry employs 3800 people in Cardiff, of which BBC Wales directly employs 1226 (full and part time) (Cardiff Council, 2009; Interview, BBC Wales, 2010). Outside the large networks, Cardiff has a growing independent TV sector with some 200 firms, led by Boomerang, Green Bay Productions and Calon TV (Cardiff Council, 2006). The independent TV sector alone makes up almost 7 per cent of the creative businesses in Cardiff, while 28 per cent of those employed in the creative industries are employed in TV production. The relationship between employment and firms is characteristic of the larger British TV industry. A recent study concluded that

24 per cent of creative firms in Cardiff had only one full-time member of staff (Cardiff Council, 2009). This is supported by the survey findings for this study that had 64 per cent of firms surveyed with five or less employees and 22 per cent with one employee. Consequently, a large number of these firms use freelancers in order to remain competitive while retaining their intellectual property rights (IPR).

> Most of the people we work with in a creative sense, the lead creatives, tend to be freelancers. Some of them work with us on a returning basis, so at any one time there will be probably twice that number of people associated with the company. And then when we're in production with a documentary series or particularly with a large-scale drama numbers will go up way beyond that. (Interview, Green Bay Production, 2009)

The TV production cluster can be attributed to the presence of major broadcasters such as S4C, BBC Wales and ITV Wales as well as the city's status as the capital of Wales (Interview, Cardiff Council, 2006, 2009).

> I think Cardiff . . . first and foremost you've got the key, big TV production companies here. Obviously you've got the BBC, you've got ITV and you've got S4C and the whole Welsh language thing which is one of the main reasons why Cardiff has got that level of production companies and other infrastructure for TV and film production based around it; I think that is the key thing. (Interview, Cardiff Council, 2009)

> So I suppose TV is probably the largest of all the creative industries here that we have and Welsh language plays quite large part in that as well . . . So Cardiff specifically, obviously with the BBC being here and S4C etc, I would say is predominantly TV. I mean Cardiff seems to be, obviously because it's the capital city, it tends to attract the majority of companies and companies will tend to have an office here in Cardiff . . . (Interview, Creative Business Wales, 2009)

Cardiff is well connected to other locations within the UK; but it is also the home of the Welsh government, which supports the creative industries through funding opportunities and the availability of highly skilled labour due to the concentration of three major universities in the city (Cardiff Council, 2009).

> I was trying to find out why companies were located where they were in Cardiff. And a lot of it obviously linked with the creative industries in the, not the seedy areas, but the run down areas and a lot of it was down to the flexibility and the cheapness of places. (Interview, Cardiff Council, 2009)

As Wales is a bilingual nation with over 20 per cent of the population speaking Welsh, S4C is the Welsh equivalent of the UK's Channel 4, and receives £94 million to broadcast programmes through the medium of Welsh formerly from DCMS but since 2011 a reduced sum of £75 million through the BBC. In addition, other factors have been identified such as its central location, affordable rent and access. As demonstrated in Figure 20.1, these factors are supported by both this and other research. Cardiff Council has promoted its city-region using these factors in their Creative Industry Strategy since the late 1990s.

The number of firms in the same platform may be impressive given the relatively small size of Cardiff as a capital city (330 000); however, that does not necessarily mean there is an actual TV production cluster. In defining a cluster, the Cardiff TV produc-

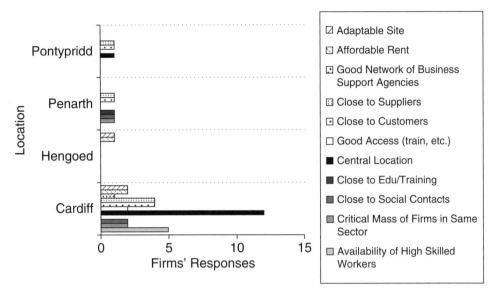

Figure 20.1   Reasons for locational choice in Cardiff

tion sector meets three of the four criteria: there is a geographic agglomeration of firms in the same sector; the firms are competitive; and the firms have links with other actors. However, the level of cooperation within the cluster is not as present as theory would suggest largely due to IPR protection. This is regularly alluded to by both firms and policy-makers who consider Cardiff to have a creative cluster that meets the aforementioned criteria, but not a TV production cluster. Based on this, and the data gathered in the surveys, the remainder of this contribution will consider the TV production firms and the digital media firms together. Of these, there is an agglomeration in Cardiff Bay, the city's reconverted harbour area, known as its (growing) media production cluster. This is based not only on the proximity of the firms but also on the descriptive data, the overlap between the industries and the existent but variable level of cooperation.

A further indicator of the impact of the location, outside of agency support, is the level of cooperation between government and firms in the cluster for innovation activity (see Figure 20.3). However, the industry (typically) perceives that more needs to be done by the Welsh government in terms of providing tangible objects to support the cluster and the region as opposed to paper strategies. This demand, being particularly city-specific, is not feasible at the governmental level; however, Cardiff Council is prepared to enhance the government's role.

we'll create some electronic interfaces both with the Council's own procurement systems, so when we go out to buy stuff the local companies, the local creative companies will be made aware of the potential. And we'll also link to things like the, you know, the Buy from Wales, Sell2Wales – these are procurement portals that traditional industries use, but the creative industries don't. And one of the most important things we've got to try to do, really, in that work is to try to make the relationships between the traditional industries and creative industries, so that they start to work in consortia . . . so they may not be the main aspect of responding to an electronic opportunity, but they've got a contribution to make and they can actually make some money off the back of that contribution, so it's how we facilitate the creation of consortia ... And then off the back of that then we'd be looking to encourage more businesses to business activity both between creative companies and the more traditional industries and all that kind of stuff. I think there's a lot of local economic gain to be had from that kind of stuff and I think it is important to know that traditionally creative industries just don't ... particularly the cultural side of creative industries, just don't engage in that kind of stuff. (Interview, Cardiff Council, 2009)

The growth and depth of the cluster have acted as a catalyst for local government in innovating client/supplier portals to have the cluster further engage with the traditional industries in the region. These include primarily the university sector, other clusters and venture capital.

20.3.1   University

The level of cooperation between the cluster and universities is reasonably high and can be attributed to the increasing importance of creative studies within academic institutions within the city-region. Within the Cardiff cluster area, there are three main universities. In addition, other universities are found in the broader city-region, most notably Newport University (which in 2013 merged with the University of Glamorgan to form the University of South Wales), which have well-developed art and design schools. Universities cooperate with firms in the region in the same way that the government does (Figure 20.2); however, the cooperation with universities occurs in higher numbers. To firms in the cluster, these institutions have become valuable sources of innovation, resulting in the universities increasing their initiatives to further develop talent for the

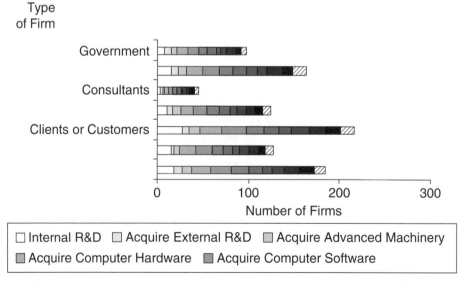

Figure 20.2   Cooperation in the Wales media production sector by innovation activity 2007–10

city-region in the future. An example would be the University of Glamorgan's satellite campus in Cardiff, the Atrium. The university's primary location is in Pontypridd, in the Cardiff periphery. To meet the demand and establish itself as a key factor in the Cardiff creative industry, the Cardiff School of the Creative and Cultural Industries at the Atrium opened in 2007. As part of the Creative Industries Development Initiative set forth by Cardiff Council, the Atrium's strategy was to construct a Media Lab (incubator), a support facility for animation, film/TV production and a Music Academy (established in 2008). Outwardly, this plan would enhance creativity in a non-creative transition-zone district of the Port of Cardiff, encourage entrepreneurship, retain a portion of the graduate population and increase the number of university spinoffs. However, critics argue that students are receiving creativity-based education without the business structure that would be essential in developing small and medium-sized enterprises (SMEs).

> My experience in my job is that the creative industries courses are not focused significantly enough on business. And they sometimes struggle, as everyone does, to understand the differences within creative industries and understand where business and culture are different and separate and have separate needs. And we are very focused in our universities on the creativity of creative industries and often lack the business dimension. (Interview, Creative Business Wales)

> What I tend to hear is that a lot of the creative industries courses teach a little bit of business, but they're not really equipping the students with enough knowledge . . . And some universities do it better than others, you know, some universities have a really strong enterprise department within the university and there are entrepreneurship champions based in all of the universities throughout Wales. And I know our enterprise department works very hard to try and encourage enterprise initiatives within those universities. But there's always that thing of you can lead the horse to water, but you can't make it drink, to use some terrible cliché, but you know what I mean. (Interview, Creative Business Wales, 2009)

This initiative is only one example that has yet to be developed. There are other initiatives, both public and private, outside of academic institutions to create incubators in this region to retain the talent in the area and enhance the economy.

20.3.2 Other Clusters

The media production cluster has an impact on the other clusters in the region, by elevating their level of support through collaboration and innovation. In the same way that the TV and digital media sectors grew towards being a cluster through an overlap in the sectors and collaboration, the other clusters benefit through collaboration. The media production cluster also benefits from successful initiatives used for other clusters. Through collaboration, particularly with the film cluster, the supply chain can be broken down and dispersed throughout the media production cluster. Furthermore, Figure 20.3 illustrates the relationship between the clients/suppliers for the media production cluster that enhances innovation across the region as whole, particularly in film. This further raises the profile of the region to an international scale.

Finally, these clusters enhance the overall creative knowledge platform of the city-region, mainly through knowledge spillovers. Innovations in the media production cluster in costume or set-design, for example, offer spillovers to more traditional

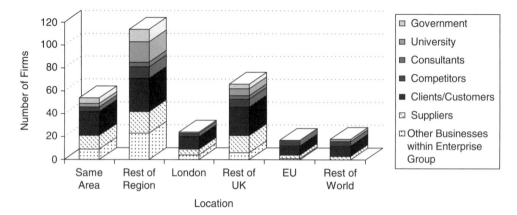

Figure 20.3   Location of firms that cooperate with the Wales media production sector on innovation activities

industries in the same way that innovations in the film industry can offer spillovers to the media production industry. These relationships are horizontal and based on related variety, which is why they are pertinent given the evolutionary character of the audio-visual field.

20.3.3   Venture Capital

Wales, in general, is lacking in venture funding support for new and existing businesses (Cardiff Council, 2006, 2009, Interview, Welsh Government).

> . . . I mean it's quite a sexy sector to get involved with, I suppose, so it always has that kind of attraction. We've got Terry Matthews who owns the Celtic Manor, for example, and he's got an interest now in the Institute for Advanced Broadcasting and things like that, so there is that kind of input. I mean there's a Business Angels network here called Xenos, which is part of Finance Wales, so we do have those kind of networks here as well. But the Wales Creative IP [Intellectual Property] Fund is the one that was kind of set up specifically for the sector. (Interview, Creative Business Wales, 2009)

According to the survey responses illustrated in Figure 20.5, such funding is one of many factors that can increase the level of innovation in the region. While there is not enough venture capital, there is one organization that focuses on funding ventures that also has a special interest in the creative industries: Finance Wales.

Finance Wales is an 'arms-length' subsidiary of the Welsh government that acts as an investment house providing equity and loan investments to companies based within Wales while managing the £10 million Creative IP Fund (since 2005). The Creative IP Fund is different to the other funds operated within Finance Wales, mainly because it does not operate as company investment but offers production finance with a sector-specific creative industries approach. Thus investment would not be into a company, it would be into a film, television series or a one-off television documentary as an example. The investment is into the project rather than into the company. This is not solely used by indigenous companies as Finance Wales also encourages inward investment if an external (non-Welsh or global, for example, US) company is interested in filming in the country or using Welsh-based resources.

> The fund is looking to develop the sustainable infrastructure and industry here and up-skill people, so people working in industry can benefit from working on these bigger productions that are coming in from outside and develop their skills so they can work on bigger productions or move from TV to film. So it's all about economic benefit for us. We always look for spend to be in the region. We don't necessarily look for Welsh content in film; it's all about spend in the region. (Interview, Finance Wales, 2009)

> . . . it basically will invest in music, film, television and new media projects. It acts as a gap fin-ancier, ultimately and is open to anybody in the world, as long as they spend pound for pound what they get. If they get £5,000 form the IP fund, they have to spend £5,000 here. And it's quite an aggressive fund, but it's been quite helpful in terms of film and television particularly. (Interview, Creative Business Wales, 2009)

For example, a Welsh-based independent TV firm could provide content that needed to be converted for use on an MP3 player and use the Creative IP Fund for the digital costs, as long as the latter firm is also in Wales. Looking at a more global example, Wild Dreams, a Welsh-based independent TV production firm, films all of their work outside the UK. They still receive funding from the IP Fund as the film crew are Welsh-based. In any case, Finance Wales does receive a return on their investment through IPR that could then be reinvested elsewhere.

While these examples demonstrate the creative methods implemented to ensure the spend is in Wales, in terms of TV production funding, the Creative IP fund is the only available source. The film industry has the Film Agency for Wales, as well as other Britain-wide funds. With competition on the global scale for this funding, other sources need to be made available, especially based on the innovation process needed in delivering content by small, independent TV firms.

Overall, the cluster has a unique position within the RIS, which is partially based on its prime location in the capital of Wales. This proximity to government not only enhances support for the cluster but the region as a whole due to the knowledge spillovers created by the cluster. Taking into account the wealth of talent and research and development (R&D) that can be supplied by the many academic institutions of the area, the innovative capacity of the city-region can only increase. Finally, the ability to 'source locally and think globally' in terms of clients/suppliers and output allows for maximum economic returns (Figure 20.4).

20.4 ANALYSIS OF THE INNOVATION PROCESS WITHIN THE CLUSTER

The media production cluster's innovative process lies in both content development and technology development. As mentioned above, the reason for this alliance, instead of a TV production cluster, revolves around IPR. The difference between the individual sectors (TV and digital), which is why they are collaborating, is both age-related and sector-related.

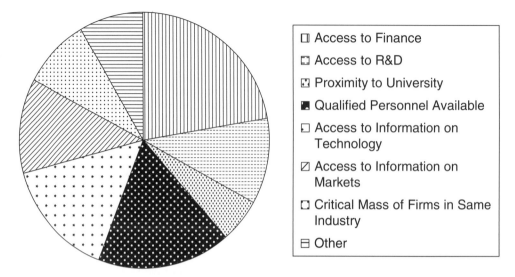

Figure 20.4   The success factors in promoting innovation in the media production sector

> The younger you are the more likely you are not to fuss about these sorts of things and collaborate anyway because you tend to see that any IP is essentially a fairly ephemeral beast. There's also the television sector in particular and to some extent most moving imagery as an industry is much more paranoid about IPR than software or pure design is. And I don't know why that is. (Interview, @Wales Incubator, 2009)

The innovation processes vary largely based on the firms that are being examined within the cluster. For example, a larger firm like BBC Wales would be responsible for in-house content and technology innovations all under the same roof. In addition, they would also be approached with innovative ideas for content from the independent production section to meet their external broadcasting quota (Interview, BBC Wales, 2010). Alternatively, the independent TV production firms would have in-house (including freelancers) content innovation processes as they are retaining their IPR while looking to digital media firms for their technological innovation.

An independent TV production firm that uses the in-house content innovation process is Green Bay Media, located in a mini-agglomeration of TV production firms in Pontcanna (a media-rich neighbourhood of Cardiff). In retaining their IPR, Green Bay has marketed a *Rivers and Life* series to S4C and, following from the idea and looking at rivers worldwide, later sold the content to *National Geographic* for international distribution. The innovation process is described putting emphasis on the decision of the broadcaster.

> And the reason we needed that [an equity investment from Finance Wales] was that our innovation process here is to do with development. Development is taking a raw idea; let's make a programme about chairs, and turning it into a marketable proposal. So in other words we will make a programme about chairs for a specific broadcaster in a specific style at a specific slot duration, aimed at a particular demographic, with these people being interviewed, this story being told, this structure for our programme, this narrative arc, these five parts, breaking up into a kind of hook at the end of every part before an ad break and so on and so forth.

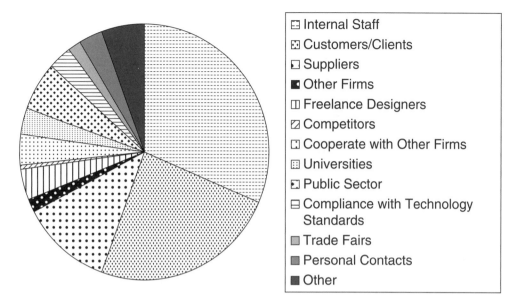

Legend:
- ⊟ Internal Staff
- ⊠ Customers/Clients
- ▭ Suppliers
- ◼ Other Firms
- ⊞ Freelance Designers
- ▨ Competitors
- ▢ Cooperate with Other Firms
- ⊞ Universities
- ⊡ Public Sector
- ⊟ Compliance with Technology Standards
- ▣ Trade Fairs
- ▤ Personal Contacts
- ◼ Other

Figure 20.5   Main sources of innovation in the media production sector 2007–10

> So we actually produce a very detailed programme specification or selling document for each and every idea that we are trying to market. And I suppose it's that process that takes the spend, because we will be developing twenty of those for every one that gets commissioned, so there's a very high attrition rate with them. But in order to get that right you really have to understand the broadcaster, you have to understand the nature of the market that they're operating in and their understanding of their own audience and their own schedule needs. So a lot of our work goes into taking that raw idea, the first moment of inspiration and tailoring it for the specific broadcaster. (Interview, Green Bay Production, 2009)

This explains the actual innovation process when creating content in terms of an idea for a broadcaster to review and potentially use. The creation of the physical programme requires pre- and post-production expertise as well as many of the suppliers outlined in Figure 20.6. For a larger company such as Green Bay Productions this may be completed in-house; however, the smaller independent companies increasingly seek support from either related firms or digital media firms. While the phases are explained, the people involved in the creative process are not highlighted. Project data for the TV production firms clearly demonstrate the use of internal R&D when innovating. This is largely based on retaining IPR.

Thus far, this section has explained the relationship between the firms and their need to innovate through technology. The innovation process is now highlighted using actual output for *Doctor Who* (Figure 20.6). This illustrates the type of firms needed to actually produce the programme as well as the technological innovations that allow the content to be further disseminated. All of this is after the initial innovation, which is the content itself. Digital media is actually located on both sides of the diagram in constructing the programme (input), or taking the content from an idea to a programme, as well as on the output side where the producers use technology to disseminate the content to a wider audience.

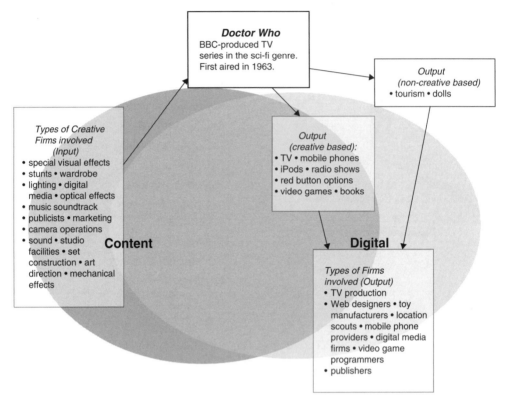

Figure 20.6   Innovation process for Doctor Who

So I think there's a lot of . . . and again taking a show like Dr Who, where it's got outlets on television, produced radio shows, podcasts, episodes specifically made for mobile phones, interactive red button options, interactive games and that sort of thing. I think if you look at the range of industries that would be involved in some of that production I think that's very broad. So I think, I guess there's just a general point that it ain't just about relationships and partnerships across traditional media. The way that audiences are consuming content is taking us into a lot of different directions and different businesses, different parts of the supply chain coming in to being there . . . Dr Who obviously being a sci-fi show there's a lot of computer generated images, special effects and that sort of thing, so quite specialist. (Interview, BBC Wales, 2010)

Other well-known examples for Cardiff TV include, but are not limited to, *Torchwood, Gavin and Stacey, The Sarah Jane Adventures, Merlin* and *Skellig*.

20.5   ANALYSIS OF THE EXPERIENCE IMPACT OF THE CLUSTER ON REGIONAL INNOVATION

The media production cluster has enhanced regional innovation and made Cardiff a national and international hub for the creative industries. Through raising the profile of the area the cluster has contributed to the success of other sectors within the creative industries, as well as sectors within the non-creative industries. This is not to say that one sector feeds off the other; rather, the relationship between the sectors is largely horizontal with innovation activities raising the profile of all. In addition, due to the presence of the cluster, the region contains a combination of firms that are both clients and suppliers, which, given the similar processes used in TV that are present in other sectors, benefits the whole of the region.

> And so because it's quite specialist to get the best suppliers we're looking across the UK, so we'd actually be procuring some of that expertise, say, from Soho, so although it's a Cardiff based business, a Cardiff based product, there's benefits elsewhere in the UK of that product. But increasingly what we're seeing is that supply is becoming more localised, you can see the benefits are becoming more localised as the expertise and the talent itself grows and becomes more localised. (Interview, BBC Wales, 2010)

While the cluster is contributing to innovation globally, the supply chain is becoming more localized, which could be attributed to the rising number of SMEs in the region that are meeting the demand for support roles for the cluster.

This can lead to agglomerations of freelancers and firms in other parts of the region. This growth can be seen in the rising number of firms found throughout Southwest Wales and Northwest Wales. Both areas can partially attribute their success in this sector to their actual locations, which are often classified as areas of 'outstanding natural beauty', providing the foundation for visual production. Either way, this solidifies the position that the creative firms are not located in the region due to its proximity to London but that this cluster is a viable source of creative innovation and part of the UK-wide contribution to the TV industry.

> And it's the same for television production and lawyers and where they all are and they can come to Cardiff and not go to London and the stronger the infrastructure we have here, the more that will become the case. (Interview, Welsh Government, 2009)

The cluster analysis has demonstrated that Cardiff, as a hub for the creative industries, can stand as an autonomous part of the industry supply chain, separate from London. However, from the firms surveyed, the level of cooperation within the region was activity-based and the first destination outside the region was not London but the wider UK. This could be due to the survey sampling, the known strengths and weaknesses of the cluster or the efforts of the BBC to enhance national innovation.

> . . . well the BBC has a strategy that it'll have I think it's seven key hubs through the UK. Let's see if I can remember them all, so there'll be Glasgow, Salford, Birmingham, Bristol, London, Cardiff and I've obviously missed out one, Belfast. So in those areas, Glasgow is already established. Pacific Quay is the new headquarters for BBC Scotland. And it has a certain amount of studio capacity as well as the headquarters building, if you like, a broadcast centre building. That's already sort of established and is evolving and developing. Salford is the newest, which essentially comes online 2012. Staff are in the process of beginning to be appointed to the roles there. The building is still in construction . . . And then London, obviously a very well established presence there, just developing Broadcasting House building in London and that's sort of nearing completion, so a continued strong presence in London. And I should say Birmingham as well, a lot of this is building related, Birmingham have got a new headquarters in The Mailbox, which is in the centre of Birmingham, so again, that's already established. And I think in terms of the other areas Belfast, Bristol, there are

discussions probably at a similar stage to what we are in terms of broadcast centre. (Interview, BBC Wales, 2010)

It's been often quoted as having . . .Wales has been quoted as having the largest broadcast sector outside of London. It's probably a lot different now due to Media City up in Manchester etc., but due to the content needs of channels like S4C, for example, things like that, we've always had a strong production sector here, television production companies here. (Interview, Creative Business Wales, 2009)

If their plans are successful, the BBC's efforts at UK-wide innovation in the TV and media industry will create more pockets of regional innovation on the periphery. To fully understand the extent of the cluster's impact on regional innovation, the following sectors are examined further:

● film;
● music;
● tourism.

20.5.1   Film

While the media production cluster is focused closer to Wales' broadcast centres, the film sector in Wales is located closer to the actual filming locations. Broadly, this would include the Southwest and Northwest of Wales, which are mentioned above in regards to freelancers and so on. This sector overlap is largely based on the film sector in the region as it is closely related to the media production sector based on the similar processes and shared experiences that are inherent in audio-visual production. This includes innovations in content and innovations in technology. To this extent, innovations that occur in the media production sector are relatively easily translated into the film sector and vice versa. This allows for many companies, particularly those in pre- and post-production to classify themselves as TV/film production companies, as well as digital media firms that exploit their IPR across both sectors.

When looking solely at innovation content, an example can be made drawing on *Doctor Who*, which was outlined in Figure 20.6. The original idea for the show was innovative, particularly compared to other sci-fi shows in the 1960s; however, the innovation did not stop with the original idea. In order for the series to span decades the content was a continuous innovative activity, to the point that, based on its success, the series was turned into a film. The film was then shot in Wales based on the locations used in the series.

Technological innovations are similarly related in the film industry. This can be based on Computer Graphic Interface (CGI), which has greatly transformed both the media production sector and the film sector. However, it can also be based on the means of dissemination in terms of digitized filming. While this innovation impacts both sectors, it also provides spillover into the Internet, adding it as another platform for audio-visual content. Finally, the tourism industry in West Wales thrives mainly due to its scenic beaches and holiday spots. This tourism industry now also doubles for film tourism that has spilled over from Cardiff-based TV tourism. This is discussed further below.

20.5.2 Music

The music sector in Cardiff is not as closely related to the media production sector as the aforementioned film sector. Nonetheless, innovation does occur between the music sector and the digital media side of the media production sector. In the same way that TV and film are starting to rely on the Internet as a platform for distribution, digital media has enabled music distribution via this method for over a decade. In addition, the other alternative platform only now available for TV and film broadcast, such as Apple's iPod, was originally designed as a music player. Given these examples, the music and media production sectors are more closely related than previously considered.

The innovation for the creative dissemination did not occur in the region; however, the success of Wales' biggest music company, Sain, can be attributed to collaboration between the music industry and the media production sector. Apart from this example, the growing music sector can be attributed to the success of the current creative industry's occupying Cardiff, as the media production sector has elevated Cardiff's image as a centre for creativity that was once only attributed to London. While this may not fall under innovation, it has enhanced the profile of the region.

> Music, obviously, is quite a large part of the creative industries in Wales, but what tends to happen with music industry here is that, whilst we've got the perception of having huge success in terms of artists who people know about, you know, the Stereophonics and Manic Street Preachers and Katherine Jenkins and, you know, Tom Jones and Shirley Bassey, generally what's happened is a lot of ... they don't create any economic impact for Wales, because they're all signed to labels or publishers or managers who are outside of Wales, so all the money kind of leaves Wales ... But that's changing now and now we've got one of the largest music label in Wales is a label called Sain who [provide a] Welsh language catalogue and that's all been digitized now pretty much and it's up on ITUNES, so it's available for the world. So those sorts of distribution channels have really opened up and created lots of opportunities for music. (Interview, Creative Business Wales, 2009)

Outside the creative industries, the tourism industry in the region has also benefited from the media production cluster.

20.5.3 Tourism

In 2006, Wales had 25.6 million overnight visitors and 54 million day visitors (STEAM, 2006). While the capital of Cardiff is a major attraction, according to Wales Tourism the number one place for visitors to Wales was the Northwest region. This is due to the mountainous terrain, scenic coastline, clean beaches and the relatively short distance from Ireland, England and Scotland. Augmenting holidaymakers, the film sector is growing in the Northwest region (Gwynedd), as well as the Southwest region (Dyfed) to meet the demand by filmmakers for local support firms, of which some are in media production. Recent films that have been shot in Wales are:

- *Harry Potter and the Deathly Hallows: Part I* – Pembrokeshire, Southwest Wales.
- The Ridley Scott-directed *Robin Hood Adventure* (starring Russell Crowe and Cate Blanchett) also used the same beach location as *Harry Potter*.

- *Clash of the Titans* (starring Liam Neeson, Ralph Fiennes and Sam Worthington) – Dinorwic Slate Quarry in Gwynedd, North Wales.
- *Dagenham Girls* (starring Bob Hoskins and Miranda Richardson) used the Hoover factory, Merthyr Tydfil.
- *Ironclad* at Dragon Studios (starring Oscar-nominated Paul Giamatti, James Purefoy, Brian Cox, Mackenzie Crook, Jason Flemyng, Derek Jacobi and Kate Mara).

In addition, numerous lower budget feature films have also been shot in Wales in the late 2000s including:

- *Patagonia* (starring Matthew Rhys and Nia Roberts).
- *Barafundle Bay, Mr Nice* (starring Rhys Ifans).
- *Submarine* (starring Paddy Considine) on location in Southwest Wales.
- *The Edge of Love* (starring Kiera Knightley, Matthew Rhys and Siena Miller).

All of these films have helped raise the profile of Wales, and have directly led to increases in tourism or 'film tourism', which equates to positive economic growth. According to Visit Wales, *The Edge of Love* production during 2007 brought increased tourism to Gwynedd (Misstear, 2009). As a more recent example, the *Harry Potter* filming in Wales in 2009 was expected to draw in visitors from around the world given the book's global market. The film previews, both in film and media, were made to showcase the Welsh scenery. In addition, it was anticipated that one of the characters in the *Harry Potter* film would be played by an actor made famous by the TV production *Gavin and Stacey*, another Welsh-based production (Misstear, 2009).

The close relationship between film and tourism is highly visible due to the global nature of film production; however, in the case of the Wales region, the media production sector was actually the first to achieve this spillover into the tourism sector. This is most visible with *Doctor Who*, as it is Wales's best-known TV series given its time on air and the *Doctor Who* Up-Close Exhibition in the waterside location of Cardiff Bay. To give an idea of the attractiveness of the exhibition, from July to November 2006 over 56 000 people visited the exhibit (BBC, 2007). In addition, local firms have benefited through offering *Doctor Who* tour packages. These TV tourism-related excursions have contributed to Cardiff's ranking as one of the top ten UK short breaks by travelsupermarket.com (BBC, 2007). Furthermore, this exhibit has further grounded the TV tourism industry in Cardiff, which was especially prominent with the *Doctor Who* spinoff series *Torchwood*.

So Doctor Who would be a good example (of TV production's impact on non-creative industries), as there is a Doctor Who exhibition in Cardiff Bay. I think it's still there, it's certainly been running for a number of years. So it is based within the Red Dragon Centre in Cardiff Bay, it's very visible in terms of attracting a customer base generally to that part of town and that particular complex. And that's obviously a benefit.

I think Torchwood was probably just such a gift for the Welsh tourism business, particularly Cardiff tourism business, because obviously the difference is Dr Who is made in Wales and a lot of the scenes are shot in Wales and some of them are portrayed as being in Wales, but Torchwood is Cardiff, that's where the hub is, or was before it got blown up. And there's a lot of scenic shots and that sort of thing, so the broader benefit of something like Torchwood and Dr Who is very significant. I'm not sure if there's been any studies done, but it's such high profile stuff. (Interview, BBC Wales, 2010)

Other than sci-fi series, the comedy *Gavin and Stacey* is a successful BBC UK-networked, Welsh-based TV series shot in Barry and the Vale of Glamorgan. Based on the high profile of the show, the success of TV tourism in Cardiff and the economic growth TV tourism now brings to the Vale of Glamorgan, th council's tourism strategy for 2010–15 added a *Gavin and Stacey* tourism experience to the local economy of Cardiff's smaller, neighbouring harbour town (Collins, 2010).

This list of examples of regional innovation due to the cluster is not exhaustive. Although Cardiff's creative sector has been critiqued for its lack of big publishing houses, the number of publishing SMEs is growing, particularly with magazine publication. The most well known is the print magazine *BUZZ*, which has a pulse on all things in Cardiff and the surrounding region with a special emphasis on the creative industries. In addition, a lesser-known online magazine called *Creative Boom Cardiff* (2010) is a regional magazine specifically focusing on the growing industry. While both of these examples are industry focused, this can still be attributed to the cluster due to the cluster composing the majority of the industry in the region.

20.6   DISCUSSION

We see that the creative industries are now a significant factor in several urban economies. Though we do not explore the rural receptivity to creative industries in this chapter, we hint that this also operates in Northwest Wales, in the Welsh-speaking heartland where a similar albeit smaller cluster to that in the Welsh capital, Cardiff, prevails. The industry thus clusters but does not necessarily reveal significant amounts of collaboration. However, it once may have, when firms were smaller and needed to cooperate to meet contract requirements from clients. Nowadays, the industry in Wales has enforced a hierarchical tier structure to the industry to streamline the commissioning process. Cardiff has become the centre of a major production cluster for TV, notable for digital media and increasingly for film. While the industry is relatively secure because of the continued existence of broadcaster clients with a Welsh agenda in Cardiff, it is clearly dependent as a creative cluster upon regulation and the regional and, to a lesser extent, UK broadcaster market with emergent global market relations in the offing. Accordingly, a number of discussion points, many of relevance to other creative clusters are implied.

Using the findings provided from this study, implications may be drawn not only for the media production cluster of Cardiff but for the wider creative industries and experience economy platform. More broadly, this clearly involves entrepreneurs and new businesses. However, key requirements arise from this research based on a combination of the criticisms of government officials and expressed problems encountered by firms at all levels of development:

• As always, there is the perceived commercial need for more (public) funding opportunities for businesses at all levels of development, especially new businesses.
• This includes a need for public initiatives and programmes to retain talent in

the region; in Cardiff this is met by an Arts Council for Wales-inspired Creative Industries Apprenticeship Programme.

- Sponsoring of more incubator space, particularly 'platform' incubation facilities that contain firms from a variety of sectors to foster knowledge and conceptual cross-pollination.
- Support for creative industry regional innovation by showcasing best practice products and services that may be applied to innovation in related creative industry areas.

With the BBC Drama Village opening in late 2011 as a joint venture between BBC Wales and the Welsh government, as we have seen some of these policy demands are being taken care of (Interview, BBC Wales, 2010). Nonetheless, more information on these individual points is needed.

Nevertheless, a few, more systemic problems remain. First, as indicated in Figure 20.4, financial support is a key factor in the innovation process for firms in the creative industries in Cardiff. For the wider canvas of Wales as a whole, apart from the film industry, most creative businesses have one line of financial support through the public-private venture capital fund Finance Wales, whose Creative Fund is publicly provided by the Welsh government. While these sources have played a leading investment role in the development of many creative businesses, it is simply not enough. The government is clearly supportive of the creative industries with this fund, the @Wales incubator and the many other support initiatives; however, for future success, further venture capital is needed:

> . . . no venture capital, so that's the big thing that's missing. (Interview, Cardiff Council, 2009)

> One of the great lost areas of equal opportunity is, I think, access to finance. If you come from a family that's got money and connections on the whole you're fine, if on the other hand you have a great idea, but feel really skint and have no connections, then you are rather less likely to become and succeed as an entrepreneur. (Interview, @Wales, 2009)

Accordingly, and again unsurprisingly, there is appetite from the creative industry community for more venture capital firms in Cardiff and Wales more broadly.

Second, the issue of retaining talent in Wales has been discussed at length over the past decade (not least in various Cardiff Council strategies). This issue largely lies with the number of universities in Wales. There are officially perceived by the Welsh Government Ministry of Education to be too many small ones competing with Cardiff as a prominent supplier of talent to the creative industries, which, however, lack the absorptive capacity to employ them all. Of course, a number of university graduates will seek creative industry elsewhere in the UK and overseas. It might then be expected that the remaining graduates could be absorbed into the surrounding economy. Unfortunately, this is not happening in Cardiff due to a combination of low mid-sector employment and, specific to the industry, either a few large businesses that require experienced candidates or many small businesses that can only maintain one or two employees.

> Wales is very good at developing talent and exploiting talent, but we are not so good at retaining what's needed in order to have some of the economic return of the talent we're good at creating and developing. (Interview, Welsh Government, 2009)

Addressing graduate positions in the creative industries is a prime area for policy support measures, particularly with the concentration of universities in the Cardiff area. The most recent addition is the University of Glamorgan's satellite campus, the Atrium, which specializes in the creative industries at its central Cardiff location, established in 2007.

The third issue relates to the question of incubation facilities. Until 2011 Wales had several national incubators, a constellation of Techniums, as they were branded, often sector specific and run with a varying degrees of success. In 2011 the Welsh government announced that it was selling most of them off to the private sector as many had remained largely empty. They were basically over-elaborately designed in architectural terms, relatively expensive in rental terms and under-provided with business intermediation services (Morgan, 2013). Cardiff was home to one of the less successful Techniums, as well as the more successful Welsh government-funded digital incubator called @Wales. As mentioned above, the incubator attempts to foster cooperation within the sector both internally and externally with a relatively high level of success, which is largely attributed to the age of the entrepreneurs. Unfortunately, this is only one success story.

The University of Glamorgan's Atrium had announced plans to open incubators relating directly to the creative industries but none were forthcoming, possibly because of budget cuts associated with the 2008–09 financial crisis and the negative spillovers of the crisis on the creative and experience economies. A model of the intended approach of integrating a teaching, research and commercialization platform could be the Workstation in Sheffield or Birmingham's Custard Factory, which allow the creative industries supply chain to be fulfilled through the varied businesses present there.

> So if you're a university graduate and you're a photographer, and you've just finished, you may end up in a building that's got a record label that needs a photographer and you may end up in a building with a journalist who needs a photographer. And the bringing together of the supply chain within the network is what's exciting. You know, universities, for me, have a habit of siloing themselves, siloing the businesses that have come out of college and the entrepreneurs in order to create incubators. And I don't think it's best for the companies. I don't think it's best for business. I don't think it's best for the students and I don't think it works for regeneration. (Interview, Welsh Government, 2009)

> If you look at something like the Custard Factory in Birmingham, for example, and you've got a very funky-looking brand new or funky-looking regenerated buildings and things like that and it's cheap, affordable, flexible leases for creative industries. It's all kitted out with broadband, very, very easy. And, I don't know, I think universities providing spin out space for students spinning out from that university, I think is great but maybe there needs to be more of a mixture in there though so that it's not purely just spin out companies from the same sector to encourage collaboration between new companies and the more established companies that will be more benefit, perhaps. (Interview, Creative Business Wales, 2009)

While this solution may seem like a quick fix, it is more pertinent in the context of creative industry training and recruitment issues discussed in the previous point concerning graduate retention. Such platform integration not only raises the profile of the location but also has economic returns through increased entrepreneurial activity.

Finally, there are successes to be highlighted from the evolution of what began as a regional or, from a Wales perspective, national, broadcast and print media industry established over the past century and, in the case of newsprint, even more. Deregulation of TV production in the 1980s gave Wales an extra broadcaster (S4C) that, like Channel 4 in the other parts of the UK, was regulated to commission programming only from independent production companies. This gave an enormous boost to creative start-ups, which as we have seen clustered in specific cheap rent locations. These clusters then became attractive for commissions from the other Cardiff broadcasters, BBC Wales and the commercial HTV (later ITV) channel. With some irony, the cluster's magnetic qualities, located like others in cities from Malmö to Toronto, in former harbour districts on the waterfront have now attracted the Drama Village facility where BBC UK and internationally use the local industry for commercial programming like *Doctor Who* and *Torchwood*. This in turn has evolved into a film tourism industry with 'experience economy' attractions like the '*Doctor Who* Experience' which attracts some 60,000 film tourists per year and contributes an estimated €120 million to Cardiff's economy (this is closely comparable to the Wallander-effect on film tourism in Malmö, Sweden as estimated by the Öresund Film Commission, 2009). Thus, the concept of a 'media production cluster' in Cardiff was based on the increasing number of links between the TV production sector and the digital media sector.

20.7   CONCLUSION

As shown, the media production cluster contributes innovative products and services to the wider industry. While not as structured, this type of overlap occurs in several sectors across the creative industries. An example would be TV production and film production based on the similar supply chain and related sectors. Given these successful examples, what once looked like a difficulty for regional innovation, particularly in the Welsh context, of having this same spillover into the non-creative industries has now been resolved. In the rarified world of an experience economy based on film tourism, government incentives would not have sufficed as the innovations needed to be showcased for their potential applications outside of their original purpose. This occurred through the powerful medium of worldwide media exposure of the product. A similar process operated in Switzerland after political conflict in Kashmir meant production of Bollywood films exploiting Himalayan scenery decamped to the Swiss Alps, causing a surge of 250 000 Indian tourists to visit the Interlaken area where the films were subsequently set (Lander, 2008). Wales has evolved a successful example of this as mentioned above in terms of *Doctor Who, Torchwood* and *Gavin and Stacey*. This has become a growing market for the BBC Drama Village but it is the global not local or regional reach that will fuel Cardiff's film tourism experience economy in the future.

A second main conclusion is that when research is conducted in an inclusive rather than an exclusive way, it may be possible to observe quite significant overlaps between apparently rivalrous concepts. Thus, TV drama may in itself have little to do with a memorable experience as denoted in the experience economy. But when it is recombined with the less ephemeral concept of place – meaning the real place in which a fictitious drama is set, a value associated with authenticity that is only sketched in to the drama but which, ironically comes alive in the dead space of the theatrical setting on location in the real world, turns it into an experience. The next step is the creation of a memory institution in the form of a theatrical exhibition or experience and a further round of potential value is created. This is in the nature of knowledge economy value-added, which creates novelty out of other novelties without much by way of any significant manufacturing process. There is, of course, always the need for content that can be creatively exploited in this business model. However, such is the entertainment experience of contemporary social networking that, to paraphrase McLuhan 'the customer has become the content'.

BIBLIOGRAPHY

Bakshi, H., E. McVittie and J. Simmie (2008), *Creating Innovation: Do the Creative Industries Support Innovation in the Wider Economy?* London: NESTA.

BBC News (2007), *Time Lord Tourism Boost for City*, available at http://news.bbc.co.uk/1/hi/wales/6450679.stm (accessed 17 February 2010).

Bennett, J. (2010), *Hello Dubai: Skiiing, Sand & Shopping in the World's Weirdest City*, London: Simon and Schuster.

Cardiff Council (2006), *Cardiff's Creative Industries Sector*, Cardiff: Policy and Economic Development Council.

Cardiff Council (2009), *Cardiff's Creative Industries: Final Report*, London: BOP Consulting.

Castañer, X. and L. Campos (2002), 'The determinants of artistic innovation: bringing in the role of organizations', *Journal of Cultural Economics*, **26** (1), 29–52.

Collins, P. (2010), 'Gavin and Stacey tourist trail for Barry', available at http://www.walesonline.co.uk/news/wales-news/2010/01/27/gavin-and-stacey-tourist-trail-plan-for-barry-91466-25691448/ (accessed 12 November 2010).

Cooke, P. and D. Schwartz (2007), 'Creative regions: an introduction', in P. Cooke and D. Schwartz (eds), *Creative Regions: Technology, Culture and Knowledge Entrepreneurship*, London: Routledge, pp. 197–214.

Creative Boom Cardiff (2010), *Introduction: About Us*, available at http://www.creativeboom.co.uk/cardiff/about/ (accessed 18 February 2010).

DCMS (1998), *Creative Industries Mapping Document*, London: Department for Culture, Media and Sport.

DCMS (1999), *Creative Industries Exports: Our Hidden Potential*, Prepared by the Creative Industries Export Promotion Advisory Group (CIEPAG), London: Department for Culture, Media and Sport.

DCMS (2000), *Creative Industries: The Regional Dimension*, Report of the Regional Issues Working Group, London: Department for Culture, Media and Sport.

DCMS (2001), *Creative Industries Mapping Document*, London: Department for Culture, Media and Sport.

DCMS (2007), *The Creative Economy Programme: A Summary of Projects Commissioned in 2006/7*, London: Department for Culture, Media and Sport.

DCMS (2009), 'Creative industries economic estimates' *Statistical Bulletin*, October, Department for Culture, Media and Sport, London.

De Propris, L., C. Chapain, P. Cooke, S. MacNeill and J. Mateos-Garcia (2009), *The Geography of Creativity*, London: NESTA.

Drejer, I. (2004), 'Identifying innovation in surveys of services: a Schumpeterian perspective', *Research Policy*, **33** (3), 551–62.

Dunning, J. (ed.) (2000), *Regions, Globalisation and the Knowledge-Based Economy*, Oxford: Oxford University Press.

Edquist, C. (ed.) (1997), *Systems of Innovation*, London: Pinter.

Freire-Gibb, C. (2011), 'The rise and fall of the concept of the experience economy in the local economic development of Denmark', *European Planning Studies*, **19** (10), 1839–54.

Frenken, K., F. van Oort and T. Verburg (2007), 'Related variety, unrelated variety and regional economic growth', *Regional Studies*, **41** (5), 685–97.

Gilmore, B.J. and J.H. Pine (2007), *Authenticity: What Customers Really Want*, Boston, MA: Harvard Business School Press.

Handke, C. (2006), *Measuring Innovation in Media Industries*, Berlin, Humboldt University.

Harvey, D. (2008), 'The right to the city', *New Left Review*, **53** (3), 23–40.

Hoekman, J., K. Frenken and F. van Oort (2009), 'The geography of collaborative knowledge production in Europe', *Annals of Regional Science*, **43** (3), 721–38.

Lander, R. (2008), 'Bollywood drives Indian tourists to Swiss Alps', *Times of India*, 5 August.

Landry, C. (1995), *The Creative City*, London: Comedia.

Lash, S. and J. Urry (1994), *Economies of Signs and Space*, Cambridge: Polity.

Miles, I. (2007), 'Research and development beyond manufacturing: the strange case of services R and D', *R&D Management*, **37** (3), 249–68.

Misstear, R. (2009), 'Pembrokeshire could star in the next Harry Potter film', available at http://www.walesonline.co.uk/news/wales-news/2009/03/17/pembrokeshire-could-star-in-last-harry-potter-film-91466-23162420/ (accessed 18 February 2010).

Mitleton-Kelly, E. (2006), 'A complexity approach to co-creating an innovative environment', *World Futures: The Journal of General Evolution*, **62** (3), 223–39.

Morgan, K. (2013), 'Path dependence and the state: the politics of novelty in old industrial regions', in P. Cooke (ed.), *Reframing Regional Development*, London: Routledge, pp. 318–40.

Mugan, C. (2009), 'The story of pop music', *Independent*, 10 March.

Nijssen, E., B. Hillebrand, P. Vermeulen and R. Kemp (2006), 'Exploring product and service innovation similarities and differences', *Research in Marketing*, **23** (3), 241–51.

ONS (Office of National Statistics) (2009), *Annual Business Inquiry*, London: Office of National Statistics.

Öresund Film Commission (2009), *Film Tourism in Skåne (presentation by Joakim Lind)*, available at http://www.scribd.com/doc/19743246/Speech-Script-Filminduced-Tourism-wallander-Mixed-Reality (accessed 4 November 2011).

Pine, B.J. and Gilmore, J.H. (1999), *The Experience Economy*, Boston, MA: Harvard Business School Press

STEAM (2006), *Scarborough Tourism Economic Activity Monitor, STEAM Report*, Scarborough: STEAM.

Stoneman, P. (2009), *Soft Innovation*, London: NESTA.

Sunley, P., S. Pinch, S. Reimer and J. Macmillan (2008), 'Innovation in a creative production system: the case of design', *Journal of Economic Geography*, **8** (3), 675–98.

Tether, B. (2009), *Design in Innovation, Coming out from the Shadow of R&D*, DIUS Research Report 09-12.

Tether, B., S. Metcalfe and A. Tajar (2006), 'Innovation in services: through the looking glass of innovation studies', DTI Occasional Paper, Department for Trade and Industry (DTI), London.

Throsby, D. (2001), *Economy and Culture*, Cambridge: Cambridge University Press.

21. Unpacking the spatial organization of the US videogames industry: lessons for research on experience industry clusters

Jan Vang and Ted Tschang

21.1 INTRODUCTION

The aim of this chapter is to analyse what shapes the spatial organization of the US videogames industry and identify implications for the to date dominant research on creative industry clusters. Development of creative industry clusters constitutes one of the most important ingredients in economic development policies for countries aiming to play a significant role in the new experience economy. There are numerous competing conceptualizations of what constitutes the experience economy, ranging from post-Marxist interpretations (Lash and Urry, 1994) over managerial definitions (for example, Pine and Gilmore, 1999) to more analytical attempts at understanding how the idea of the experience economy interacts with ideas about creative industries and/or cultural industries in different places (Cunningham, 2002; see Cooke, Chapter 20, this volume for an elaborate discussion of different perspectives on the experience economy). Across perspectives it is reasonably fair to say that the core of the experience economy is constituted by cultural or creative industries (but also covers reinventing traditional industries from focusing on their product to the total consumption experience). Seen in this perspective, this study is highly relevant as the US videogames industry revenue matches the US film industry's (or Hollywood's) box office returns. It is thereby one of the most important pillars of the experience economy. The industry also displays features not congruent with the finding commonly advanced in the currently dominant research on creative industries and can thereby help in pushing the theoretical frontier in respect not only of creative industries but the experience economy in general. Creative industries, being the core of the experience economy, consist of those sectors that serve consumer demands for amusement, ornamentation, social display, info-tainment and so forth (Scott, 1999; Caves, 2000; Power, 2010) where the aesthetic or symbolic value is higher than the use value. Ideally, the products contain, as argued by Pine and Gilmore (1999) in their seminal text, a designed experience in terms of an articulated theme, appeal to many senses, harmonization of supporting cues, elimination of negative cues and added merchandise. This is far from always the case but the gaming industry provides this in their successful games, where the player enters a fully designed universe. The creative industries include the production of theater, newspapers, film, dancing, music, toys and games, and similar industries (Scott, 1999, 2000; Caves, 2000; Pratt, 2004a; Aoyama, 2007; Power, 2010). According to some studies, the creative industries have been instrumental for growth and economic development in certain regions in the developed world. Studies estimate that those working in the creative industries constitute between 5 to 10 percent of the workforce in the developed world (Pratt, 2004b) and "represent some of the most dynamic growth industries in the world at the present time" (Scott, 2000, p.10). While one needs to be skeptical about the hype around experience economy (see Brambini et al., forthcoming; Maher et al., forthcoming) games are certainly interesting since the industry has displayed high growth rates during the current economic recession.

The perceived importance of the experience economy and creative industries has triggered extensive research on creative industries (and on redesigning content and business models in manufacturing). Contrary to studies of more traditional industries (that is, manufacturing) and other knowledge-intensive industries (for example, biotechnology), these studies' focus has not embraced explaining cluster formation and clustering processes by the "usual suspects"; being startups and spin-offs (Klepper, 2005), collaborations with universities (Feldman and Bercovitz, 2006) or entrepreneurship. Instead the bulk of studies have focused on understanding what the particularities of creative industries are that make them cluster in the largest urban cities (but see also Cooke, Chapter 20, this volume for a study on a mid-sized city, Cardiff's, evolution to become an experience hub).[1] Creative industries are characterized by a high degree of uncertainty in demand and volatile markets and hence rely on a one-off project-based organizational form (Pratt, 2002a, 2002b; Grabher, 2004; Scott, 2004; Vang and Chaminade, 2007). Project-based production, it is argued, helps in coping with the uncertainty and volatility stemming from new trends, fashions or simply the need for experimenting; doing so by flexible sourcing and allowing for the recombining of the competencies needed for making the new creative products (Christopherson and Storper, 1987). The underlying assumption is that cities provide the basis for the needed competence diversity. The experience economy is thus becoming equated with parts of the urban economy.

Yet, critical voices increasingly suggest that these "urban cluster" approaches need to be complemented with theories or approaches that more broadly explain the spatial organization of creative industries per se (Girard and Stark, 2002; Heydebrand and Miron, 2002; Johns, 2006; Vang, 2007); and not just the urban clustering part of their spatial organization. This perspective suggests that urban cluster approaches do not provide satisfactory explanations for the co-existence of multiple clusters, successful isolated firms and an uneven distribution of creative industries across countries. Thus, we maintain a weak understanding of the core industries in the experience economy. In this chapter we seek to contribute to the "new" stream of research theoretically by identifying existing explanatory gaps, and empirically by providing a grounded study of the spatial organization of the US videogames, which suggests how the gaps can be filled in. Thus, we aim to explain not just the clustering processes but the spatial organization of a creative industry, where spatial organization refers to the distribution of firms across space (in this case within a nation) and their interaction and thereby also push the research frontier of the experience economy.

The study purports two important findings with consequences for further theory building and policy recommendations. Firstly, that the spatial organization of the US videogames industry reflects the US videogames firms' use of specific governance modes not accounted for in the literature (that is, in-house capabilities or hierarchy, and distance networking), which allows them to function without being in dominant clusters. Secondly, our findings suggest that the uneven spatial distribution of videogame firms across the USA is explained by localized entrepreneurial traits, proximities to universities and spin-off effects. These are factors partly accounted for in the traditional Marshallian cluster literature and not derivable from the specificities of the largest urban settings.

The chapter is structured in the following way. We begin in the second section by reviewing agglomeration approaches focusing on creative industries, and by suggesting gaps in the research. The third section outlines our research methodology. In the fourth section, we lay out the empirical part of the chapter. The chapter concludes with a discussion of the research findings and implications for further studies.

21.2 APPROACHES TO STUDYING CREATIVE CLUSTERS: A REVIEW

This section introduces the dominant approaches and findings on the spatial organization of creative industries. We do not aim to provide a full account of the debate, and focus solely on the clustering aspects and its literature; thus, we do not include other recent approaches that relate to the spatial organization of the production chain (see Power and Hallencreutz, 2002; Pratt, 2002b, 2004a; Johns, 2006; also see Coe et al., 2004; Yeung, 2005 for general discussions). These papers seem to explicitly embrace the concept of experience as more focused on non-spatial aspects than on the spatial dimension of creative industries, hence we focus mainly on the papers dealing explicitly with the spatial organization of creative industries.

21.2.1 A Metropolitan View of Industries

The sheer diversity of literature explaining the clustering of creative industries makes a comprehensive review of it challenging. In Figure 21.1 we have provided a simplified model that summarizes the traditional explanation of clustering processes in creative industries. One can argue that this literature rests on variants of traditional Marshallian agglomeration factors and the so-called Jacobs factors (that is, urbanization factors). The importance of the urban factors to creative industries is emphasized by Scott (2001). Scott attempts to provide "a theoretical outline of how and why cities like these [Paris, New York, Los Angeles, Tokyo, Paris and Milan] come to operate as major poles of the cultural economy" (p.13). Hence, the analytical focus is mainly on why creative industries such as film and advertising tend to cluster in large(st) metropolitan areas, and not on patterns deviating from this pattern (that is, why they are located in smaller cities and how multiple clusters co-exist). Grabher (2001), for example, mainly analyses the London-based firms; not the advertising firms outside London. Scott (2002, 2004) looks mainly at Hollywood's and Paris' film production and Los Angeles' fashion industry, while Rantisi (2002) examines New York's fashion industry and Pratt (2002a) looks at the multimedia-oriented "Silicon Gulch" in San Francisco. An editorial in a special issue of the *Journal of Economic Geography* edited by one of the authors on creative industries underscores the same limitations in the literature (Lorenzen et al., 2008).

In line with the traditional studies of industrial districts and clusters, these studies link the locational choices of industry to knowledge externalities (that is, collective and

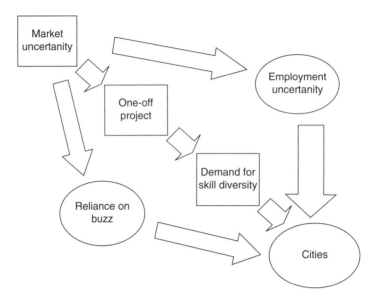

Source: Authors' own research.

Figure 21.1   Creative industries and why they cluster in cities: the dominant approach

interactive learning) in a broad sense; this being specialized or diversified labor markets, institutional specialization and recently an increased efficiency of "buzz" (Beccatini, 1990; Brusco, 1990; Amin, 1999; Asheim et al., 2007). These studies tend to differ from more traditional cluster or industrial districts studies on one significant dimension: by stressing the heterogeneous features of cities (Scott, 2001; Asheim and Vang, 2004; Asheim et al., 2005), that is, the wide diversity of skills, competences, age groups and ethnic communities. Traditionally, Marshallian-inspired studies of Prato in Italy emphasized the high degree of homogeneity in terms of shared values, visions and so on.

21.2.2   Face-to-face and Buzz

In recent works, it has been reasoned that we often find creative industries located in the biggest of cities because of the latter's high frequency of buzz, that is, the unplanned and haphazard aspect of face-to-face contacts (see Storper and Venables, 2004; also see Malmberg, 2003; Maskell et al., 2004; Asheim et al., 2007). Buzz is supposed to be superadditive in that it allows for the fast circulation of information (that is, the "matching problem" or who is available to collaborate and so on) and to some extent also knowledge circulation (that is, outcomes of experiments with collaboration techniques) (Storper and Venables, 2004).

21.2.3   Project Organization as Dominant Organizational Form in Creative Industries

Grabher (2001, 2002a, 2002b, 2002c, 2004) (see also Ekinsmyth, 2002 for a different perspective) links the need for buzz – "noise" in his vocabulary – to the "nature" of these industries and to the need for one-off projects, which rely on clustering in urban areas (see Lorenzen and Frederiksen, 2005 for documentation of this claim; see Vang, 2007 for an alternative view). The creative industries – as with several other industries – tend to rely increasingly on the "one-off" project form of work organization. Projects do not carry the burden of previous staff, conflicts and conventions; and allow for the sourcing of competencies from a vast possible combination of competencies. This provides a fluid organizational form adapted to innovations and flexibility. The mobility of the creative labor in the pool is made possible by a large geographically concentrated demand for their skills and their geographically concentrated network of weak and strong ties (Grabher, 2002a, 2002b, 2002c).

The ephemeral nature of creative industries is however exaggerated in this approach. By focusing on knowledge externalities it reproduces the Marshallian focus on the external dimensions (that is, collective and interactive learning and so on), while tending to ignore the importance of in-house mechanisms and other factors central to firms' location strategies. Hence, it provides at best a partial (yet valuable) explanation for the spatial organization of creative industries.

21.2.4   Summing Up and Suggesting Research Gaps

Creative industries cluster in large cities because of their need to source for diverse inputs, which are provided by the larger labor pool (Gibson and Kong, 2005). As opposed to the long-lasting types of collaborations typically found in industrial districts and clusters, project-based industries would appear suited to the one-off potential needs of creative industries (Whitley, 2005). At the same time, alternative explanations are emerging that suggest a need for moving beyond the dominant cluster approach (see Power and Hallencreutz, 2002; Aoyama and Izushi, 2003; Norcliffe and Rendace, 2003; Pratt, 2004a, 2004b; Aoyama, 2007; Vang, 2007). These studies starkly contrast with the urban bias of the earlier-mentioned literature, and suggest that the totality of a creative industries' spatial organization is determined in more complex ways. The reminder of the chapter sets out to conduct a grounded analysis of the spatial organization of the US videogames industry to fill this gap.

21.3   METHODS

The approach taken in this study was to begin to construct a multi-level view of a creative industry based on an embedded multiple case study (Yin, 2009). The choice of the case study approach reflect the nature of our research, being an exploratory study, inserted in a contemporary context, where we do not hold control over the phenomenon in question. We limited our study to the USA. This began with interviews of industry participants, specifically, developers, in 2003 and following through to 2008. The firms were purposefully selected. They represented firms located in different types of agglomerations. These initial interviews were conducted with designers and studio heads from 17 videogame companies (these were augmented in later stages during the ethnographic data collection stage through interviews with other designers and developers met in the studios and in developer conferences). The interviews were conducted as semi-structured interviews. Construct validity was assured though the dialog-based interviews. The qualitative interviews were supplemented with secondary information on the industry's production processes. This information was acquired from secondary and other sources, including the industry's periodical, *Game Developer*. The latter included more than 65 project postmortems highlighting various factors that inhibited or aided individual projects' development. These were used as a means for triangulation with different data sources. Finally, detailed case ethnographic studies were conducted on four studios – two each in the Boston area and the San Francisco Bay Area – consisting of several site visits – most of a week's length or more – to each studio over the course of five years. Apart from providing greater details in the mechanisms we are concerned with, we also used these findings as part of the method triangulation.

To further root our theories of firms' operation in the realities of the actual spatial organization, we obtained spatial data (by city of location) of the full set of studios listed on the main game development website (Gamasutra.com), and clustered and plotted these. For comparative purposes, we looked into the full list of products for selected clusters and firms by cross-referencing with other websites (that is, data triangulation). This helped determine the "quality" of the studios, and therefore the clusters. The locations of the publishers of their products were also been determined.

21.4   THE SPATIAL ORGANIZATION OF THE US VIDEOGAMES INDUSTRY

This section constitutes the empirical part of the chapter. We start with a general outline of the industry and its main production characteristics, and follow with an analysis of the influence of the various factors that affect the industry's spatial configuration – including those that are buzz-inspired, industry-specific and Marshallian in nature.

21.4.1   A Brief History of Videogames: Introducing the Context

The US videogames industry has only been around in its commercial form for over three decades, starting with just one or two person development teams and moving up to the current mixture of large in-house studios of publishers, and small to medium-sized independent studios. With the growth of household personal computers in the 1980s and 1990s, computer games have flourished and provided some stability to the market for videogames, primarily by way of providing an installed base of machines that could play those games, and that were constantly being upgraded (for example, through new microprocessors, and more recently, graphic cards).

The videogames industry at present consists of two types of actors: the studio, which develops the videogames, and the publisher (Johns, 2006), which funds the studios' development of the videogames, and acts as a bridge to the broader market of retailers and consumers by marketing and distributing the videogames. It is important to recognize that when we refer to firms, we are usually referring to the studio responsible for the creative work, and not the intermediary such as the publisher. The publisher is critical to the financial condition, and survival, of individual development studios.

By one count, in 2004, there were at least 430 studios, including internal studios owned by publishers.[2] By 2008, this had risen to 742, with 81 of the original 430 having dropped off the listings. In addition, in 2004, there were 1073 independent contractors who do outsourced work for other game studios or publishers on audio, design, production, programming, testing/quality assurance, video production and visual arts. There were about 116 publishers in the USA, but in 2002, the world's largest 20 publishers (including nine from Japan, three from Europe and eight from the USA) accounted for $15.5 billion in total revenue worldwide, which was highly significant as it is larger than the total videogames market in the USA of about $6.9 billion,[3] and represents a dominant share of the worldwide revenue, estimated at $20.7 billion.[4] These top 20 publishers published 687 titles worldwide, at an average cost of a couple to a few million dollars per title. Out of the US market of $6.9 billion in 2002, console videogames constituted $5.5 billion whereas computer games constituted $1.4 billion (IDSA, 2003).

21.4.2   The Spatial Organization of the US Videogames Industry

As Figure 21.2 shows, the US videogame industry is fairly well dispersed across the USA in a number of large concentrations (or clusters), as well as in many smaller concentrations and solitary studios. Concentrations of more than eight studios are few in number, namely New York with 16 studios, Austin with 14 studios, Los Angeles with 19 studios (including seven in Santa Monica) and Seattle with ten studios.

There are also some other secondary concentrations that do not show in the map, such as the smaller concentrations in the vicinity of the San Francisco Bay Area, including seven studios in San Raphael just north of the Golden Gate Bridge, five in Redwood City and four in San Jose. Thus, what appears to be metropolitan clusters can sometimes actually be mini-clusters or single firms spread out in the vicinity of a larger city. Another potentially interesting phenomenon is that smaller concentrations can be found all across the country. Concentrations of four or more studios can be found all over the country in cities like Redmond, Kirtland and Bellevue (all in Washington state), to Las Vegas, Atlanta, Chicago, San Diego, Portland (Oregon), Eugene (Oregon) and Houston. In this respect, the studios' locating behavior shows that at least some creative industries like videogames are not wholly concentrated in one or two cities or even co-existing in urban creative clusters. Our ethnography does not indicate that innovative firms will tend to locate in the biggest cities or their metropolitan areas. By innovative, we mean the risk-taking sense of breaking with established genres, narratives and type of interaction. Studios such as PopTop (St Louis), Oddworld (formerly in San Luis Obispo, California), Vicarious Visions (Troy, New York), Raven Software (Madison) and 2015 (Tulsa, Oklahoma) are examples of well-known firms not located in major videogame clusters.

The weak cluster size-innovation correlation is demonstrated by the second largest cluster in 2004 – New York City: by 2008, 11 of the original 16 studios listed in 2004 had remained, and of those that remained, one was a publisher (Take-Two), eight were producing smaller-scale or marginal products (for example, free, Flash-based or educational games) and only two had produced a larger-scale product (based on original research).

The stylized facts we observed on the spatial organization thus challenge the dominant cluster explanation in the following ways:

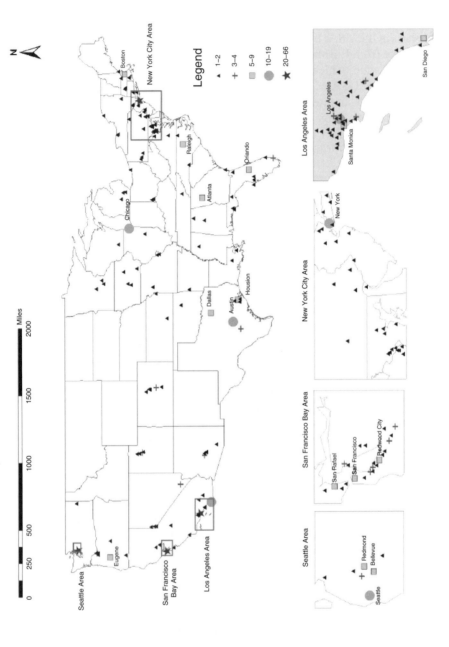

Legend

▲ 1–2
+ 3–4
■ 5–9
● 10–19
★ 20–66

Notes:
National map: For purposes of illustrating the concentrations on the national map more clearly, those studios that are located within a 50 mile radius of the largest metropolitan nearby area are added into that metropolitan area's total number of studios.
Regional maps: The four regional maps plot each studio in the region by its exact latitude and longitude.

Figure 21.2   Location of videogame development studios in the continental USA and the four largest concentrations

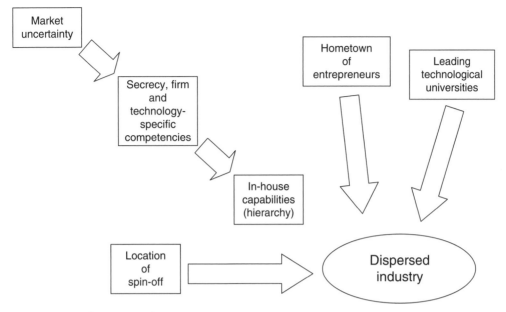

Source: Author's own research.

Figure 21.3   Creative industries and why they cluster in cities: a revised framework.

- The spatial organization of the videogames industry does not reflect the type of urban concentration one would expect based on the dominant literature on creative clusters.
- There is not much correlation between the size of a cluster and "industrial performance" (for example, the New York cluster).
- There are good examples of well-performing stand-alone studios or ones not embedded in clusters (firms are self-sufficient in terms of capability).

We now turn to explaining why the spatial pattern exists in the first place. Figure 21.3 gives a simplified graphic summary of the factors we identify as being this spatial pattern.

21.4.3   Persistence in the Spatial Organization of the US Videogames Industry

21.4.3.1   Why in-house capabilities and not externalities: the product development process

Our analysis suggests that the first factor that allows spatial distribution to occur is the nature of the production process. The US videogames industry is less reliant on externalities as it draws more on what is commonly referred to as hierarchy (Coase, 1937; Williamson, 2002) or in-house capabilities (Dosi et al., 2008). The link between the production process, in-house competences and firm locating behavior, and hence its contribution to understanding the spatial organization of the industry, will now be highlighted.

Videogame product development can be seen in terms of both individual work and team-based processes (with the latter being more production-oriented). Both creative and technical forms of work factor into these activities. The typical videogame development process consists of multiple stages (Baba and Tschang, 2001; Aoyama and Izushi, 2003). The lead conceptual designer may also lead the team from conceptualization through to the project's completion, or alternatively, another designer or creative director will take over from the conceptual designer and act as a keeper of the vision while managing the implementation of the design.

These processes are organized as projects, but with fairly different characteristics than identified in studies of other creative industries (hence, a different reliance on externalities). Firstly, videogame projects have a longer project cycle time. For example, in advertising, while the accounts themselves can last for longer terms of two to three years (Grabher, 2002b), the discrete advertising projects within each account tend to be much shorter. In contrast, videogames require a longer sustained period (for one and a half to four years) of constant interaction amongst team members on a single project. In addition, there is a focus on long-term in-house collaboration because of the nature of the game development process, and, therefore, a focus on permanent staff (based on interviews that we have conducted and all four game development studio sites that we visited for long-term observation). This time difference alone signifies a potentially different mode of work from short-term projects – in which the co-location of project partners becomes important (Grabher, 2002b) – and thus a different way of coping with a different type of market uncertainty. While advertising appears to cope with market uncertainty through location in places that allow for rapid recombination, videogame production focuses on deepening the firm's skill base rather than on rapid recombination of cognitively held knowledge. This intense onsite collaboration in the development of interactive products and the need for hierarchical control over creativity creates a closed system of production – unlike the networked labor pool seen in advertising and film production. In addition, this mode of production is aided by the fact that videogames are a virtual product constructed on computers with knowledge their developers gain from a variety of sources – both virtual (for example, the Internet) and traditional (for example, books). A second aspect of the production process is the need for secrecy. New projects are hardly ever discussed outside the studio, unless it is with publishers, or unless the publishers deem it necessary to provide the market with some news of upcoming titles. Secrecy it appears is taken seriously in a different way than that suggested by Saxenian (1996) in her seminal study on Silicon Valley; this has implications for the reliance on non-labor market-based localized externalities. One consequence of the longer project life cycle and the need for secrecy is that hanging out or idea sharing (as seen in the studies predicated on the buzz in a region) is not promoted.

21.4.3.2   The distant network dimension: the link to the publisher

The publisher is generally a critical actor in the system of a creative industry (Caves, 2000). The central external relationship in the videogames industry that all independent studios are preoccupied with is the relationship with their publisher. This suggests the potential convenience of co-locating videogame studios with their publishers, yet this is not the case. As shown later, the data bear out how much publishers rely on distant external studios, and seek to deal with the most capable of them. The studio's reliance on an in-house mode of product development is complemented by a reliance on a distanced network tie with a publisher. The publishers themselves face an unusual tradeoff. On the

Table 21.1   *Cities with the largest number of game development studios and major publishers*

City, state	No. of studios	Top 20 publishers (worldwide) with headquarters or regional headquarters in the city
New York, NY	16	Vivendi Universal, Take-Two
Austin, TX	14	
Los Angeles, CA	12	
Seattle, WA	10	
San Francisco, CA	9	
San Rafael, CA	7	
Santa Monica, CA	7	Activision
Chicago, IL	6	Midway Games
Eugene, OR	6	
Redmond, WA	6	Microsoft Game Studios
Redwood City, CA	5	Electronic Arts
San Diego, CA	5	
Atlanta, GA	5	
Bellevue, WA	5	
Irvine, CA	4	
San Jose, CA	4	
Las Vegas, NV	4	
Portland, OR	4	
Houston, TX	4	
Kirkland, WA	4	

one hand, the publisher has a strong need for control, over intellectual property (IP), over a game's particular implementation and so on. This suggests that publishers have good reasons for locating close to their contracted studios (or to pick game developing studios located in close proximity). And yet this is rarely the case. In our estimation, most of the studios that we studied (including all ten that we visited and certainly all four that we studied ethnographically) were located at a long distance from their publishers. Table 21.1 shows that while the major publishers happen to be located in or near concentrations of external studios, many publishers are also scattered across the country. The eight largest publishers, which earned a total of about US $6.5 billion in revenue in 2003, are scattered across different cities for the most part. Thus, these largest publishers appear to be scouring for the best (external) studios to work with or to acquire, regardless of where the studios are located. This observation is supported by evidence of the geographical separation between publishers and their internal studios. Many of the internal studios owned or acquired by the major publishers are not co-located with the publisher's main offices, and many are not even in the major concentrations. Of the top eight US publishers, only 17 of their 44 internal studios are in the same state as the headquarters. (In fact, the results are skewed by EA and Activision that have five of eight and six of seven in the same state, respectively.) Three other major publishers (Microsoft, Vivendi and Take-Two) have none in the same state. Some large publishers have tended to acquire studios (for their internal operations) that were operating in locations all over the world. For example, Take-Two Interactive, has studios and cities in the USA, including Boston, St Louis, the outskirts of Baltimore and all the subsidiary studios of Rock Star Games (publisher of the Grand Theft Auto series), including ones in Leeds, London Edinburgh, Vienna, Toronto and San Diego.

This pattern is visible in part because publishers simply have to work with the best (lead creative) talent wherever they are located. The how of this pattern of distance work is the familiar story of studios coordinating their work with publishers through electronic means and face-to-face meetings. Thus, while publishers do tend to be located in or near concentrations of videogame studios, the presence of strong studios outside those concentrations can be explained by these means of maintaining production relations at a distance.

21.4.4   Do the Traditional Clustering Processes Play an Important Role?

We next examine two central aspects of traditional cluster explanations – local suppliers and the labor market (that is, availability of skill sets) to determine whether these other factors also affect spatial organization in this industry.

21.4.4.1   Local suppliers
A traditionally important factor underpinning clustering, including clusters in high-tech areas and even Hollywood, is that of technology suppliers. The new media clusters are also said to benefit from localized suppliers because the clusters are network-based (Grabher, 2002a). While the videogame industry does not tend to have strong supplier networks, our interviews as well as the postmortem data suggest that the use of commercial tools and proven "middleware" or engine technology is becoming more commonplace. While tools are sourced from the few software companies that make them, wherever they may be, engine suppliers are another matter (where the engine is the core code displaying the graphics and making the game function). The sourcing is not well confined to the spatial boundaries of the cluster. Many studio licensees will have to use the best fitting engine regardless of where its developer (another studio) is located.[5]

21.4.4.2   Local labor markets
Studies of clusters also claim that labor supply is a critical factor attracting the firms to the cluster (Angel, 2000; Christopherson, 2002). Studies of project-based media firms have also observed that they can benefit when their networks can tap into surrounding labor pools (Ekinsmyth, 2002; Grabher, 2002b). Our ethnographies show that videogame studio heads consider both local and national labor markets to be important, but that the bulk of positions are often filled from the local labor markets. Many studio heads or recruiters still use local networks to filter for and to ensure the quality of potential employees, often from other videogame companies and other local industries. However, while labor markets are a factor, they are not necessarily the factor that causes firms to locate where they do. This observation is mirrored in studies of UK and Japanese clusters. The labor market can also be a factor for larger firms, such as publishers, in deciding where to locate their internal studios.

The different scale of production makes the videogame industry's requirements for human capital lower than industries such as the movie industry. As such, for certain types of games at least, it is still not very difficult to set up a studio in locations without an existing local videogame industry. Studios not located in any concentration need to fill their ranks from universities, from employees transferring from other local industries than videogames and the national videogames industry labor market.

21.4.5 On Dispersion, or How Multiple Clusters Came About

Thus far we have illustrated why the firms rely less on externalities and hence have greater degrees of freedom in choosing the location where to locate their firm. Yet, this does not fully explain the spatial organization of the videogames industry as the co-existence of multiple clusters (that is, dispersion) – particularly with no strong observable relation between the size of the cluster and the capability of its firms – and stand-alone firms. For this, we now address three additional motive factors that help us to more fully explain the dispersed locational pattern shown in Figure 21.2 (that is, variously sized concentrations all over the USA).

21.4.5.1 Entrepreneurial efforts
Entrepreneurial efforts can easily explain the phenomenon of lone or smaller numbers of companies locating in cities that seemingly have fewer videogame studios (from which a larger set could be spun off from), or the labor pool to sustain a concentration. Many cities have just one or two studios, and at least a few such studios are sufficiently well established to make their existence interesting. The lead creative as studio founder phenomenon shows up quite strongly in our data, as studios are located in cities often for no other reasons than convenience (that is, cities that are the founder's hometown or current residence), cost or personal reasons. One survey noted that "New studios are starting up everywhere, and so jobs are cropping up all over the country . . . Terrific programmers, sometimes whole teams, get disillusioned with the companies where they work and strike out to do it on their own." Furthermore, another powerful impetus is for studio founders to simply locate where they are currently at or where it is cheaper to live in than in the cities. It occurs, for example, when developers who "want to buy a house or raise a family are looking for jobs at videogame companies where the cost of living is lower and the pace is slower." These perspectives are reinforced in our interviews: Poptop Software was run by the founder in St Louis, Missouri – the city of his origin. It is a smaller studio with a number of titles to its credit, but still sustains itself without attachments to the major concentrations.

21.4.5.2 Spin-offs: locally comfortable but also footloose
This brings us to the question of how clusters arise. As observed by Klepper (1996, 2005; Klepper and Simons, 2000), in several studies of the automobile, laser and other industries, spin-offs from successful firms in the videogames case account for an important share of the clustering. That is, a cluster can form from a single firm or a few early firms. Paradoxically, this can underpin explanations of a spatially dispersed industrial organization. Successful spin-offs are usually either a function of learning based on earlier employment in successful firms or based on the ability to attract the best employees. In an industry such as the videogames industry, the low benefits from clustering allows spin-offs a higher degree of freedom to choose where to locate – often in the same

region but not necessarily near the parent firm. Often they will choose to locate closer to the parent firm for pragmatic reasons, for example, the employees already living near there and so on. The closure of a well-known studio in Boston – Looking Glass – led to the talent dispersing into several companies in the Boston area (for example, founders of Floodgate). A large proportion ended up in two local (Boston-based) startups that we interviewed – Irrational Games and Harmonics. A similar situation happened with Boston-based Impressions, a Sierra internal studio, when a group of ex-developers founded Tilted Mill (also near Boston), and other ex-developers seeded other studios around Boston, including Turbine Entertainment (this based on our interviews at Tilted Mill).

At the same time, the Looking Glass case also suggests a more footloose outcome, with key Looking Glass developers setting up studios or dispersing to studios as far away as Mind Control Games in San Rafael (near San Francisco), Ion Storm in Austin (Texas), the smaller Digital Eel in Seattle (being founders of it), Valve in Kirkland (Washington) and Canberra (Australia) (the last being Irrational Games' sister studio). Historical cases of well-known studios like id software and other cases from our data also support this relocation model, with founders of studios we interviewed migrating to Los Angeles, San Luis Obispo (California) and Boston, amongst other places, from elsewhere.

21.4.5.3 Universities as talent creators/incubators?

While the core team of new studios is usually comprised of experienced talent from existing studios (as was the case with all of the companies we interviewed at and visited for our ethnographic research), occasionally, local universities and other educational institutions also play a role as incubating grounds for talent or entrepreneurs. University engineering and other students tend to have a strong interest in playing and making videogames, and companies such as Raven and Vicarious Visions were founded by former students from the local high school and university, respectively. The Boston area was not known as a videogame studio concentration, but a concentration formed in part because of the large pool of university students. Looking Glass – one of the most well known companies in the 1990s – was formed by several former Massachusetts Institute of Technology (MIT) students who knew each other. Thus, the distribution of universities, especially world-class technical ones, may be a potentially important factor for explaining the spatial organization of the videogames industry.

In summary, we cannot claim that we have exhausted all explanatory variables behind the spatial organization of the US videogames industry. What we have been able to do is identify some central mechanisms affecting the spatial organization of the industry.

21.5   CONCLUSIONS

We have parsed out the mechanisms behind the spatial organization of the US videogames industry and contrasted it to the dominant research on creative clusters and thus provided new vital insights of relevance for the spatial organization of the experience economy. We have identified a spatial organization based on the co-existence of multiple clusters of firms (that is, studios) and stand-alone firms. Contrary to what would be assumed, we also find that the biggest clusters are not necessarily dominant (measured in terms of innovativeness), and firms in clusters of small or moderate sizes can persist and perform well. The above findings suggest that one dominant meta-explanation in economic geography's treatment of creative industries – that of agglomeration-induced buzz in combination with traded and untraded interdependencies – may not be sufficient for describing all creative industries' spatial organization. Our study contributes with our observations of the (creative) capabilities of the firm, and other industry-specific characteristics (that is, long project durations, lack of reason to connection to neighboring firms and smaller firm sizes) to help explain how it is that the videogames industry can both exhibit an independent (of the "cluster" of firms) nature and display a highly spatially dispersed organizational form. In addition, our case also suggests that entrepreneurship, the location of scarce talent and the distribution of world-class technical universities also need to be included in the framework.

We have illustrated how the spatial organization of the videogames industry can only be explained to some minor degree by conventional cluster factors. In other words, traditional agglomerative factors simply do not operate in a winner-takes-all fashion to benefit the firms located in the larger clusters or to lead to the emergence of dominant clusters. This runs counter to what the traditional cluster explanations would have predicted. Further research across regions, countries and creative industries will prove valuable for helping generalize our explanations, as indeed, other comparative research shows that national context even in a single industry can matter to processes such as skills transfer (Izushi and Aoyama, 2006). Our research on creative clusters also needs to be complemented with a less sectorial approach exploring synergies and convergences across spatially co-located cultural industries and spill-over effects and mutual dependency of manufacturing industries and creative or cultural industries. An unexplored aspect in this context is how manufacturing industries – increasingly conceptualized as moving toward a servitization paradigm – can learn from experience-based industries in respect to the design of their products and services and on how to reconfigure their business model (for example, following business models stemming from the games industry).

Nevertheless, the insight from our study suggests more freedom in locational choices and at least one candidate explanation for why firms are dispersed across regions and not concentrated in one or two regions, or at least not relying on Jacobs-type externalities, suggesting some caution for the current cluster-oriented policies. The study has empirical support in Cole's (2008) study on animation, Vang's (2007) study on news media, Brambini and Vang's forthcoming study on tourism and Cooke's study (Chapter 20, this volume) on Cardiff's evolution as an experience hub. This implies that the scope for constructing clusters based on experience-based industries is larger than the literature has acknowledged to date. However, as our study only consists of one country case, it is premature to draw strong policy conclusions. We do however wish to point out that: (1) focusing on building clusters based only on the connectivity of firms (as is often highlighted in the literature) is not likely to be the main effective means for building a local videogames industry and that (2) there is a larger scope for smaller clusters to become players in the industry than would be predicted based on the dominant creative cluster research. Further research especially in other business systems and countries will show if these factors are contingent on the specific US business system or features of the industry as such. Our study suggests that the spatial dimensions of the experience economy is a field in need of much more attention, including more attention paid to the link between creative industry clusters and the whole experience economy. Our study provides a first few hints, but much work lays ahead. Finally, there is a need to unpack the causes behind unrealized potentials of industries. Maher et al. (forthcoming) and Brambini and Vang (forthcoming) suggest that umbrella or place branding constitute important and overseen demand-oriented tools for partially overcoming problems linked to creating an experience-based cluster.

NOTES

1. For a discussion of the production and value chain-oriented studies, which are not included here, see Vang and Lucas (2006) and Pratt (2004b).
2. The top 20 publishers worldwide owned 65 such "internal studios."
3. 2002 US Entertainment Software Sales, Entertainment Software Association.
4. 2002 DFC Intelligence News Report
5. Of the seven companies in our data (that is, interviews and postmortem data) that discussed licensing engines, four used engines developed by other studios located in the same city.

BIBLIOGRAPHY

Amin, A. (1999), 'An institutionalist perspective on regional development', *International Journal of Urban and Regional Research*, **2**, 365–78.

Angel, D. (2000), 'High-technology agglomeration and the labor market: the case of Silicon Valley', in M. Kenney (ed.), *Understanding Silicon Valley: The Anatomy of an Entrepreneurial Region*, Palo Alto, CA: Stanford University Press, pp. 124–40.

Aoyama, Y. (2007), 'The role of consumption and globalization in a cultural industry: the case of flamenco', *Geoforum*, **38** (1) 103–13.

Aoyama, Y. and H. Izushi (2003), 'Hardware gimmick or cultural innovation? Technological, cultural, and social foundations of the Japanese video game industry', *Research Policy*, **32** (3), 423–44.

Asheim, B. and J. Vang (2004), 'What can RIS offer developing countries?', Paper presented at the Globelics Conference, Beijing, available at http:// www.globelics.org (accessed 15 December 2004).

Asheim, B., H. Hansen and J. Vang (2005), 'The creative class and regional growth: towards a knowledge based approach', Paper presented at the Regional Studies Conference, Aalborg, May.

Asheim, B.T, L. Coenen and J. Vang (2007), 'Face-to-face, buzz and knowledge bases: socio-spatial implications for learning, innovation and innovation policy', *Environment and Planning C*, **25** (5), 655–70.

Baba, Y. and M. Shibuya (2000), 'Tokyo game-soft cluster: analysis on formation process', *Journal of Science Policy and Research Management*, **15** (1), 33–47 (in Japanese).

Baba, Y. and F.T. Tschang (2001), 'Product development in Japanese TV game software: the case of an innovative game', *International Journal of Innovation Management*, **5** (4), 487–515.

Bathelt, H. (2005), 'Cluster relations in the media industry: exploring the "distanced neighbor" paradox in Leipzig', *Regional Studies*, **39** (1), 105–27.

Bathelt, H., A. Malmber and P. Maskell (2004), 'Clusters and knowledge: local buzz, global pipelines and the process of knowledge creation', *Progress in Human Geography*, **28** (1), 31–56.

Becattini, G. (1990), 'The Marshallian industrial district as a socio-economic notion', in F. Pyke, G. Beccatini and W. Sengenberger (eds), *Industrial Districts and Inter-firm Co-operation in Italy*, Geneva: International Institute for Labour Studies, pp. 37–51.

Brambini, A. and J. Vang (forthcoming), 'Policy measures for creating and integrated and brand-focused regional innovation system in a shadow destination: insights from Pisa's destination development', *International Journal of Business and Globalisation*.

Brusco, S. (1990), 'The idea of the industrial district: its genesis', in F. Pyke, G. Beccatini and W. Sengenberger (eds), *Industrial Districts and Inter-firm Co-operation in Italy*, Geneva: International Institute for Labour Studies, pp. 10–19.

Caves, R. (2000), *Creative Industries: Contracts between Art and Commerce*, Cambridge, MA: Harvard University Press.

Christopherson, S. (2002), 'Project work in context: regulatory change and the new geography of media', *Environment and Planning A*, **34** (11) 2003–15.

Christopherson, S. and M. Storper (1987), 'Flexible specialization and regional agglomerations: the case of the U.S. motion picture industry', *Annals of the Association of American Geographers*, **77** (1), 104–17.

Coase, R. (1937), 'The nature of the firm', *Economica*, **4** (16), 386–405.

Coe, N. (2001), 'A hybrid agglomeration? The development of a satellite-Marshallian industrial district in Vancouver's film industry', *Urban Studies*, **38** (10), 1753–75.

Coe, N.M. and J. Johns (2004), 'Beyond production clusters: towards a critical political economy of networks in the film and television industries', in A.J. Scott and D. Power (eds), *The Cultural Industries and the Production of Culture*, London: Routledge, pp. 188–204.

Coe, N., M. Hess, H. Yeung, P. Dicken and J. Henderson (2004), 'Globalizing regional development: a global production networks perspective', *Transactions of the Institute of British Geographers*, New Series, **29** (4), 468–84.

Cole, A. (2008), 'Distant neighbours: the new geography of animated film production in Europe', *Regional Studies*, **42** (6), 891–904.

Cornford, J. and R. Naylor (2001), 'Cutting edges in strange places: new media debates and the computer and video games industry in the UK', CURDS Discussion Paper 01/1, Centre for Urban and Regional Development Studies, University of Newcastle Upon Tyne, Newcastle.

Cunningham, S.D. (2002), 'From cultural to creative industries: theory, industry, and policy implications', *Media International Australia Incorporating Culture and Policy: Quarterly Journal of Media Research and Resources*, 54–65.

Dosi, G., M. Faillo and L. Marengo (2008), 'Organizational capabilities, patterns of knowledge accumulation and governance structures in business firms: an introduction', *Organization Studies*, **29** (8–9), 1133–53.

Ekinsmyth, C. (2002), 'Project organization, embeddedness and risk in magazine publishing', *Regional Studies*, **36** (3), 229–44.

Feldman, M.P. and J. Bercovitz (2006), 'Entrepreneurial universities and technology transfer: a conceptual framework for understanding knowledge-based economic development', *Journal of Technology Transfer*, **31** (1), 175–88.

Florida, R. (2002), *The Rise of the Creative Class: And How It's Transforming Work, Leisure, Community and Everyday Life*, New York: Basic Books.

Gibson, C. and L. Kong (2005), 'Cultural economies: a critical review, *Progress in Human Geography*, **29** (5), 541–61.

Girard, M. and D. Stark (2002), 'Distributing intelligence and organizing diversity in new-media projects', *Environment and Planning A*, **34** (11), 1927–49.

Grabher, G. (2001), 'Ecologies of creativity: the village, the group, and the heterarchic organisation of the British advertising industry', *Environment and Planning A*, **33** (2), 351–74.

Grabher, G. (2002a), 'Cool projects, boring institutions: temporary collaboration in social context', *Regional Studies*, **36** (3), 205–14.

Grabher, G. (2002b), 'The project ecology of advertising: tasks, talents and teams', *Regional Studies*, **36** (3), 245–62.

Grabher, G. (2002c), 'Fragile sector, robust practice: project ecologies in new media', *Environment and Planning A*, **34** (11), 1911–26.

Grabher, G. (2004), 'Learning in projects, remembering in networks? Community, sociality and connectivity in project ecologies', *European Urban and Regional Studies*, **11** (2), 103–23.

Grantham, A. and R. Kaplinsky (2005), 'Getting a measure of the games development business: developers and the management of innovation', *International Journal of Innovation Management*, **9** (2), 183–213.

Heydebrand, W. and A. Miron (2002), 'Constructing innovativeness in new-media start-up firms', *Environment and Planning A*, **34** (11), 1951–84.

IDSA (2003), *Essential Facts About the Computer and Video Game Industry*, Washington, DC: The Interactive Digital Software Association and the Entertainment Software Association.

Izushi, H. and Y. Aoyama (2006), 'Industry evolution and cross-sectoral skill transfers: a comparative analysis of the video game industry in Japan, the United States, and the United Kingdom', *Environment and Planning A*, **38** (10), 1843–61.

Johns, J. (2006), 'Video games production networks: value capture, power relations and embeddedness', *Journal of Economic Geography*, **6** (2), 151–80.

Klepper, S. (1996), 'Entry, exit, growth, and innovation over the product life cycle', *American Economic Review*, **86** (3) 562–83.

Klepper, S. (2005), 'Entry by spinoffs', *Management Science*, **51** (8), 1291–306.

Klepper, S. and K. Simons (2000), 'The making of an oligopoly: firm survival and technological change in the evolution of the U.S. tire industry', *Journal of Political Economy*, **108** (4), 728–60.

Lash, S. and J. Urry (1994), *Economies of Signs and Space*, London: Sage.

Lorenzen, M. and L. Frederiksen (2005), 'The management of projects and product experimentation: examples from the music industry', *European Management Review*, **2** (3), 198–211.

Lorenzen, M., A.J. Scott and J. Vang (2008), 'Editorial: Geography and the cultural economy', *Journal of Economic Geography*, **8** (5), 589–92.

Maher, S., A. Brambini and J. Vang (forthcoming), 'Policy measures for creating an integrated and brand-focused innovation system for film industries in shadow nations: an application to Australia's national film industry', *International Journal of Business and Globalisation*.

Malmberg, A. (2003), 'Beyond the cluster: local milieus and global connections', in J. Peck and H. Yeung (eds), *Remaking the Global Economy*, London: Sage, pp. 145–62.

Maskell, P., H. Bathelt and A. Malmberg (2004), 'Temporary clusters and knowledge creation: the effects of international trade fairs, conventions and other professional gatherings', Working Paper, Spatial Aspects Concerning Economic Structures (SPACES) 4, Faculty of Geography, Philipps-University of Marburg, Marburg.

Norcliffe, G.B. and O. Rendace (2003), 'New geographies of comic book production in North America: the new artisan, distancing, and the periodic social economy', *Economic Geography*, **79** (3), 241–63.

Pine, B.J. and J.H. Gilmore (1999), *The Experience Economy*, Boston, MA: Harvard Business School Press.

Power, D. (2010), 'The difference principle? Shaping competitive advantage in the cultural product industries', *Geografiska Annaler: Series B, Human Geography*, **92** (2), 1–14.

Power, D. and D. Hallencreutz (2002), 'Profiting from creativity? The music industry in Stockholm, Sweden and Kingston, Jamaica', *Environment and Planning A*, **34** (10), 1833–54.

Pratt, A. (2002a), 'Hot jobs in cool places. The material cultures of new media product spaces; the case of the South of the Market, San Francisco', *Information, Communication and Society*, **5** (1), 27–50.

Pratt, A. (2002b), 'Managing Cceativity in the cultural industries', *Creativity and Innovation Management*, **11** (4), 225–33.

Pratt, A. (2004a), 'The cultural economy: a call for spatialized production of culture perspectives', *International Journal of Cultural Studies*, **7** (1), 117–28.

Pratt, A. (2004b), 'Creative clusters: towards the governance of the creative industries production system, Unpublished manuscript, available at http://www.lse.ac.uk/collections/geographyAndEnvironment/whos Who/profiles/pratt/a.c.pratt@lse.ac.ukPublications.htm (accessed 10 December 2004).

Pratt, A. (2006), 'Imagination can be a damned curse in this country: material geographies of filmmaking and the rural', in R. Fish (ed.), *Cinematic Countrysides*, Manchester: Manchester University Press, pp. 127–46.

Rantisi, N.M. (2002), 'The competitive foundations of localized learning and innovation: the case of women's garment production in New York City', *Economic Geography*, **78** (4), 441–62.

Saxenian, A. (1996), *Regional Advantage: Culture and Competition in Silicon Valley and Route 128*, Cambridge, MA: Harvard University Press.

Scott, A.J. (1999), 'The cultural economy: geography and the creative field', *Culture, Media and Society*, **21** (6), 807–17.

Scott, A.J. (2000), *The Cultural Economy of Cities*, London: Sage.

Scott, A.J. (2001), 'Capitalism, cities, and the production of symbolic forms', *Transactions of British Geographers*, **26** (1), 11–23.

Scott, A.J. (2002), 'A new map of Hollywood and the world', *Regional Studies*, **39** (9), 957–75.

Scott, A.J. (2004), *On Hollywood: The Place, The Industry*, Princeton, NJ: Princeton University Press.

Storper, M. and A.J. Venables (2004), 'Buzz: face-to-face contact and the urban economy', *Journal of Economic Geography*, **4** (4), 351–70.

Taylor, M. and B.T. Asheim (2001), 'The concept of the firm in economic geography. Editorial', *Economic Geography*, **77** (3), 315–28.

Tschang, F.T. (2007), 'Balancing the tensions between rationalization and creativity in the video games industry', *Organization Science*, **18** (6), 989–1005.

Vang, J. (2007), 'The spatial organization of the news industry: questioning assumptions about knowledge externalities for clustering of creative industries', *Innovation: Management, Policy and Practice*, **9** (1), 14–27.

Vang, J. and C. Chaminade (2007), 'Cultural clusters, global–local linkages and spillovers: theoretical and empirical insights from an exploratory study of Toronto's film cluster', *Industry and Innovation*, **14** (4), 401–20.

Vang, J. and M. Lucas (2006), 'Review of Scott and Power's cultural industries and the production of culture', *European Planning Studies*, **14** (2), 285–7.

Whitley, R. (2005), 'Project-based firms: new organisational form or variations on a theme?', *Industrial and Corporate Change*, **15**, 77–99.

Williamson, O. (2002), 'The theory of the firm as governance structure: from choice to contract', *Journal of Economic Perspectives*, **16** (3), 171–95.

Yeung, H. (2005), 'Rethinking relational economic geography', *Transactions of the Institute of British Geographers, New Series*, **30** (1), 37–51.

Yin, R. (2009), *Case Study Research: Design and Methods*, 4th edn, Thousand Oaks, CA: Sage.

22. Concept experiences and their diffusion: the example of the New Nordic Cuisine
Jon Sundbo, Donna Sundbo and Jan K. Jacobsen

22.1 AIM OF THE CHAPTER

One type of experience that involves all senses is food and eating. This chapter deals with an innovation, the New Nordic Cuisine, which is a new attempt to rethink food production and global food consumption. It may be considered an innovation movement – the self-proclaimed Nordic Cuisine Movement. The rethinking is based on material factors such as methods of cultivation and new food products, and on new experiences of food and meals. The aspect of experience, what we shall term meaning-creating experience, is crucial since this is what distinguishes this food consumption approach from more quotidian approaches. Meaning-creation (which will be explained later) is when experiences give meaning to peoples' lives (cf. what Pine and Gilmore, 1999 term a transformation economy). The experience is not only individual but those behind it also attempt to make it collective as part of a kind of social movement.

The aim of this chapter is to explain the New Nordic Cuisine in terms of a conceptual innovation and the diffusion of this innovation in society. The notion of concept will be explained later. A concept is, however, more than a product. It may include, for example, methods and principles, aesthetics and ethics. This will not only explain the food movement that the innovation has resulted in, but also provide a general understanding of development of social movements based on experiences. The chapter thus also contributes with a theoretical presentation and an empirical illustration of concept innovation as a general phenomenon in the experience economy.

This topic of food and meal experience is important for two reasons. First, there are only a few scientific investigations of food and meals based on an experience perspective (however, see Mossberg, 2003; Mossberg and Johansen, 2006; Svejonova et al., 2007; Jacobsen, 2008a, 2008b). Historical studies of food consumption and meal habits are numerous (for example, Black, 1996; Grew, 2000; Kiple and Kriemhild, 2000), but they do not examine them as innovations. Second, the transformation of elitist food and meal approaches to social movements has not been studied, particularly not in an economic innovation perspective (with a few exceptions such as Jacobsen, 2008b and Mayer and Knox, 2010). Thus we do not know the conditions on which such a transformation – if it will happen – depends. Therefore, this chapter examines such a transformation. The examination is based on Rogers's (2003) model of new innovative elements' diffusion and adoption in the society through social groups. The model, which is based on Tarde's (1903 [2000]) theory, emphasizes how late adopters imitate early ones and how the adoption of new innovative elements or concepts such as New Nordic Cuisine becomes a social movement – if the concept is successively imitated by a larger part of a population. We look at the elitist beginnings of the new food concept (created by restaurant chefs and food magazine journalists) and then investigate how the concept may be the basis for a social movement. The latter requires certain social conditions for the transformation into a social movement (meaning other parts of society take up the concept) and how it may create industrial and economic development. A social movement also creates economic demand because people want certain products, services and experiences related to the movement.

The chapter starts by presenting a suggestion for a theoretical understanding of such a transformation process. Since experience is a core part of the New Nordic Cuisine concept, we discuss, in theoretical terms, the role experience has in this development and transformation process and how this particular aspect can be understood. This includes the suggestion of a typology of experiences that can help us to understand and explain the development and diffusion of a food concept. Thereafter empirical case studies are presented and discussed to further deepen the understanding of the concrete process of development and transformation of what has been termed the New Nordic Cuisine in Denmark. This leads further to a final discussion of the possibilities of industrial development of the New Nordic Cuisine.

Although the concept is quickly developing into a global elitist movement, it has not yet become a global social movement. However, both the elitist movement and a possible social movement challenge industrial production and delivery systems since the New Nordic Cuisine concept is geographical in nature and food products may not be readily exported from one country to another. We might see completely new economic global exchange systems in which experience plays an important role. Two challenges to industrial policy are discussed: how to create economic benefits based on a concept and how to secure the ownership of food concepts and avoid imitation of it.

In the conclusion we also discuss the perspective of using a typology of experiences and a diffusion model in analysing concept innovation diffusion.

22.2   THE CONCEPT: THE NEW NORDIC CUISINE

New Nordic Cuisine is an idea about how food should be sourced, prepared and served. It emphasizes the purity and freshness of raw products, uses raw materials that are special to the region (Denmark or the Nordic countries), combines the best traditional way of cooking with innovative modern preparation methods and attempts to produce healthy meals. The food should be in harmony with nature, that is, it should be organic, animal welfare should be taken into consideration and the raw materials should be those that are natural for the season (Jacobsen, 2008b).

New Nordic Cuisine has become a trend in Danish and other top Nordic restaurants and the trend has diffused to other countries (Nickelsen and Scheuer, 2009). New Nordic Cuisine has become a cooking paradigm (to apply Kuhn's concept of scientific knowledge; see Kuhn, 1962 to culinary art). Among top chefs there have, in modern times, been several paradigms replacing each other over the last 50 years. This started with the development of the new French Haut Cuisine in the 1950s and 1960s of which Fernand Point from Vienne is seen as the father. The Haut Cuisine was the fine cooking of heavy meals emphasizing fat, meat and thick sauces. The experience was very much the form of the meal: how the food was organized on the plate and, mainly, how it was served. In the 1970s this development led to the French Nouvelle Cuisine, introduced by French chefs such as Michel Guérard and the brothers Troisgros. This paradigm emphasized health, low fat and small portions. The experience aspect of the Nouvelle Cuisine was the variation and innovation in taste and the focus on health. In the 1990s and the 2000s a new paradigm, molecular gastronomy, was developed by chefs outside France, primarily in Spain led by Ferran Adria, but also, for example, Heston Blumenthal from England (Svejonova et al., 2007). This paradigm used scientific methods from chemistry and physics to deconstruct the raw materials and reconstruct them in a new way. The form became important; foam and jelly became popular. Food on the plate is not what it seems to be. The experience is the surprise.

The New Nordic Cuisine was invented in the Nordic countries, particularly in Denmark by the chef René Redzepi and the food entrepreneur Claus Meyer. How it was invented is described later in the chapter. The New Nordic Cuisine is to some degree a paradigmatic confrontation with molecular gastronomy and its emphasis on chemical and physical preparation methods. The concept has been diffused, first in Denmark, later in the Nordic countries and then globally and its diffusion has been rapid within the global food elite (chefs and gastronomy journalists) and has become a new paradigm and discourse within this elite. One of the most remarkable manifestations of this has been that the Danish restaurant Noma, which in 2010, 2011 and 2012 was elected the world's best restaurant by international chefs and food journalists in a contest organized by the *British Restaurant Magazine*. Noma's chef, René Redzepi, has become one of the new top stars of international cuisine – succeeding Ferran Adria from the famous El Bulli in Spain (see Svejonova et al., 2007).

The New Nordic Cuisine emphasizes locally grown raw material. It might be characterized as the cuisine of uncooked plants and flowers and reintroduction of old methods of preservation. However, the New Nordic Cuisine has adopted elements from molecular gastronomy, thus traditional dishes are prepared in completely new ways. This is why it is called the NEW Nordic Cuisine; it is not just a reintroduction of dishes from days gone by. The experience of this paradigm is that many plants, fish and animals that one thought inedible are delicious when served in New Nordic Cuisine's restaurants.

The concept of New Nordic Cuisine has started to influence people in the Nordic societies. However, until now, mostly as something people enjoy in the top restaurants and experience via exposure in the media where Nordic chefs such as René Redzepi and Claus Meyer have become international stars. The influence on peoples' daily home cooking is, until now, limited as we shall come back to later.

22.3 BACKGROUND FOR A RESEARCH INTEREST IN THE NEW NORDIC CUISINE CONCEPT AS A TYPE-EXAMPLE OF THE EXPERIENCE ECONOMY

Agriculture and food production are currently reaching the mature level of the product life cycle (Vernon, 1966). This is particularly the case with the very industrialized agricultural sector, such as the Danish one, which is highly specialized and primarily concentrates on the production of pork meat and milk products. The Danish agricultural sector is concerned with mass production and competes on quantity and price. Productivity increases, competition from countries with lower wages, land prices and a relatively low innovation rate have pressed the sector, thus making profitability difficult. Farms have started closing down their pig factories, the large food industries have realized that they need to be much more innovative in the future and farming is outsourced to low-wage countries. The whole Danish food sector is facing either a meltdown (as was the case 50 years ago with the – then – proud Danish shipyard industry) or a radical innovation movement that can change the whole food system.

This situation has attracted political awareness about the food sector. The New Nordic Food Movement has been seen by some politicians in Denmark as one concept that can turn this development around. The political goal is to extend the concept to open up new profitable production and export possibilities, but how this should be done has not yet become clear. The most concrete idea is to include the concept in tourism promotion of Denmark. Politicians also see the exports of new Danish products and a new branding possibility.

The development problems of the agricultural system in Denmark also threaten the peripheral regions, which traditionally have based a large part of their economy on farming and food industries. Thus, the political interest for the New Nordic Food concept is also based on regional policy. The government and regional authorities in Denmark have launched several large food development and innovation research programmes. Experience is a core element in most of them and the New Nordic Food concept is included in many.

Further, a social movement towards more organic and healthier food has developed in all countries including Denmark over the last decades. As mentioned above, the New Nordic Food concept includes organic and health aspects. The potential for making this a broad social movement therefore exists, particularly as the New Nordic Cuisine concept includes an element of experience: eating organic food does not involve suffering; it is even gastronomic and fun. The concept thus offers people a better life.

22.4 THEORY

We aim to explain New Nordic Cuisine as a concept innovation that places great emphasis on experience and the diffusion of this innovation in society. This requires a theoretical framework that can explain the diffusion of conceptual innovations. Thus, we start this section by defining what we mean by experience and discuss what the idea of experience diffusion means. We present a typology of experiences that are used in the following empirical analysis. Then we define the notion of 'concept' that has been used several times. Finally, we present a theoretical framework based on two models designed to explain the diffusion of an innovation dependent on the concept of experience and how this diffusion process may result in a social movement and industrial development.

22.4.1 Experience

Generally, we could define experience as a mental phenomenon that happens to a person when he or she is hit by certain external stimuli such as sight, a smell, a sound, a tactile feeling or a taste (Jantzen and Vetner, 2007; Darmer and Sundbo, 2008; Jantzen et al.,

2011; see also Jantzen (Chapter 8, this volume). These stimuli can be provided by experience products such as film, art or the design of a car. To produce experiences thus demands external stimuli, which could, for example, be food.

The concept of experience employed here attempts to explain a diffusion process seen in an integrated framework. Experience related to food and meals is not seen as an isolated phenomenon and the only decision factor for peoples' attitude towards food (a pure 'experiencing man' view), but is related to the physical consumption of food, service elements as found in distribution and serving meals at restaurants, canteens and so on and social elements such as family and friendship group interaction, ideology and others. Other factors that influence peoples' decision and thus the diffusion process may be:

- Materiality (technology) (which also has been emphasized by Latour's 1987 analyses of social and technological change).
- Social norms (in different social strata or developed in interactions on social information technology (IT) media) and systems of 'fastidiousness' (what tastes good and what does not).
- Economy (which price people are willing to pay for goods, services and experiences).
- Media (puts pressure on people by communicating messages).

The aspect of experience cannot be separated from these other elements. The element of experience in food consumption and meals may have several functions in this multidimensional practice and be of different types. The analysis offered here will show empirically which functions and types. By the type of experience we mean how the experience is based in different parts of peoples' behavioural alertness. This concept is grounded in a sociological assumption about how people have a set daily routine, however, they are open to some changes based on the experiences they gain from the surrounding environment. Different types of experience trigger different aspects of daily routine behaviour in the people who experience (respondents), and thus create different memories and future experience awareness.

In theoretical terms we could suggest that the different elements of experience influence peoples' food and meal attitudes and behaviour and thus determine the concept diffusion process. This suggests a typology of experiences varying from the most biologically basic experiences (sensorial ones) to the most socially constrained and acquired ones (meaning-creating and learning) (Figure 22.1). This typology is a theoretical construction that might be useful in analyses of experiences in general.

The empirical analysis in this chapter intends to illuminate which types of experiences influence the diffusion of the concept of the New Nordic Cuisine. This will give us a deeper understanding of which types of experience determine the development and diffusion of food and other concepts.

22.4.2   Concept

The notion of concept has been used in describing service innovation (Scheuing and Johnson, 1989; Lenfle and Midler, 2010) and experience innovation (Sundbo and Hagedorn-Rasmussen, 2008). A concept characterizes a wider service idea, for example, a discount airline (started by Ryan Air), which is based on a combination of a low level

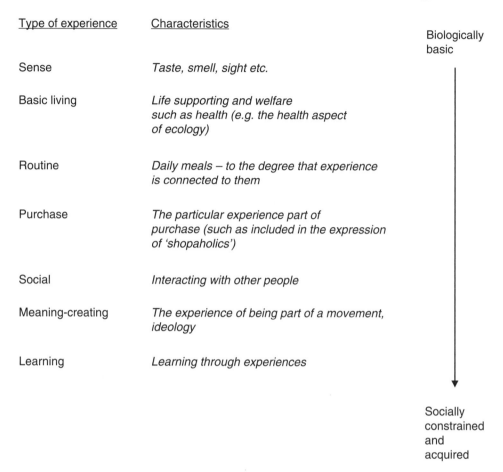

Figure 22.1   Typology of experiences

of peripheral extra services and payment for them, flight at times and to places with many passengers, using cheap airports far away from city centres and so forth. The notion of concept may also be applied to innovations that imply a large degree of experience such as the New Nordic Cuisine.

A concept may include new products – goods and service products, new processes and procedures, new market behaviour and new consumption patterns. The notion may be compared to that of a paradigm (Kuhn, 1962), which characterizes a particular way of providing scientific knowledge including fundamental, improvable axioms, rules of method and agreement in a scientific community on what are the most relevant and important issues. A concept is not a characteristic of scientific knowledge, it is an idea about a business, but it resembles a paradigm in that a fundamental idea is the basis for certain outputs, methods and norms in the operating community.

In an innovation framework a concept characterizes a radical innovation (Abernathy and Utterback, 1978) that is structural or architectural (Gallouj, 2002). It combines new products, new methods, new organization, new market behaviour and so forth. Services are not characterized by radical product innovation as is the case in manufacturing (Miles, 2004) where an innovative product (for example, the personal computer) can revolutionize a global market. However, a radical concept innovation in services comes close to this (if we take the discount airline example).

22.4.3   Concept Innovation and Experience

By innovation we mean the business implementation of an idea; it may be a new product (whether goods, service or experience), a new method of production or delivery, or new market behaviour. Experience providing firms and institutions are innovative just as other business sectors are (Sundbo, 2009; Fuglsang et al., 2011) and entrepreneurs start innovative businesses in experience industries just as in other industries (Andersson and Andersson, 2006; Sundbo, 2011). Innovation, including concept innovation, thus is relevant when studying experience industries. Food experience innovation and diffusion in particular has not received much attention in the literature (however, see Mossberg, 2003; Franck, 2005; Svejonova et al., 2007; Fisker and Olsen, 2008; Jacobsen, 2008b).

A concept may be purely experiential, that is, it is a basic idea of how people get an experience. Rock festivals (starting with the Woodstock festival in 1969) are an example of this (Sundbo, 2004). A concept may also be a mixture of technological goods innovation, service innovation, even innovation about how material is extracted from the soil (farming, fishery and so on) and experience innovation. This may be termed a concept. A concept may include elements from all the economic spheres that the industrial system provides and that Pine and Gilmore (1999, p. 6) have included in their model of products: commodities (agrarian extraction from soil), goods (produced by manufacturers), services and experiences.

The New Nordic Cuisine is such a concept. It includes a basic idea (of being in contact with nature and the use of organic and healthy local raw materials), new farming methods and raw materials, new products, new services such as new ways of preparing and serving food at restaurants and new distribution systems (markets and e-business), and finally, new elements of experience. These are also multi-faceted; they include a new way of experiencing meals in restaurants, and new engaging ways of providing food (for example, via food markets, e-business, collecting food from nature and establishing one's own kitchen garden). The experience field covers leisure, tourism and daily routines such as cooking daily meals. The experience aspect of New Nordic Cuisine may be argued to be the most important for the consumers. The physical, raw material part of the concept is a necessity; however, the experience of making, eating and discussing New Nordic Food and the reinvention of old techniques and raw materials distinguish this concept from other food concepts such as traditional day to day food or Haut Cuisine food.

A concept includes material and behaviour, and it may include aesthetic elements if it includes experiences; further, it may include ethical considerations (such as ecological norms and ethics).

The concept of the New Nordic Cuisine thus covers all industrial sectors from the primary one (farming, gardening and fishery) over manufacturing and services to experience (including tourism) and even social life outside industries in the formal economy (since making and consuming meals based on this concept is a common social activity for many friendship groups and families, who – in principle – could use raw material merely from outside the formal economy, that is, from their own cuisine garden and even fish and hunt themselves).

Another example of a food concept that has developed into a social movement (whose diffusion is not yet complete) is the Italian Slow Food Movement (Mayer and Knox, 2010).

22.4.4   Diffusion of Concept Innovation

Here we study the diffusion process and need a framework that can explain this including phases in the process. A theoretical framework can be taken from the social change tradition in American sociology of the 1950s and 1960s (for example, LaPierre, 1965; Moore, 1967). The framework is taken from the innovation diffusion theories within this tradition. These not only see diffusion as a technical market penetration of certain technologies or services or experience products; they also attempt to explain how such diffusion processes may imply social changes (in peoples' behaviour, norms, values and interaction patterns).

The often ascribed father of the social change diffusion theories, the classic French sociologist Gabriel Tarde (Clark, 1969), has a general theory of social change. He sees social and economic change processes as a series of innovation diffusion processes (Tarde, 1903 [2000]). Each process can be described as times when entrepreneurs invent or discover something new (it might by a new technology, a new behaviour, new norms and so on). The knowledge about this innovation is communicated throughout society and some early adopters take up the innovation (for example, use the technology or carry out the new behaviour). The innovation is further diffused by later adopters who imitate the early ones and finally when – or if – it is adopted by the rest of society (termed laggards by Rogers, 2003), the innovation is fully diffused and the society has been changed socially. How deep this change is depends on how central and important the innovation is to the society.

The American sociologist Everet Rogers (2003) has applied Tarde's theories on a specific study of diffusion of new technology in agriculture. He has made an operational model of Tarde's theory that sees the diffusion of a technological innovation as being divided up into different phases.

Tarde (1903) like Rogers saw the diffusion process as an economic development process because it included economic behaviour including purchase and production. Far from all innovative ideas or inventions become fully diffused. Many fail at different stages of the diffusion process for different reasons. Theory and empirical research may provide further understanding of which ideas fail, when and for what reasons.

Tarde's social and economic change theory included an understanding of social systems. Innovators and early adopters are understood as people who have, or will get, a high social status. Laggards are understood as people with a low social position. The theory claims that new elements are diffused by people of lower social status who imitate those higher up in the rank. Tarde (1897), however, also pointed out that innovation diffusion may easily raise resistance. The resistance may be passive, the potential later adopters find the innovation unpractical or not in accordance with their value system, or in rare situations be more revolutionary – the lower status group reacts against those of higher status by not adopting their behaviour.

Tarde assumed that the diffusion processes generally proceed and they have a progressive impact on the economy, for example, by diffusing innovations relevant to business, the processes provide new goods and services to solve peoples' problems, create economic growth and jobs and give people a better life. We could also add that they diffuse experience business elements and give people a more interesting and entertaining life.

22.4.5   Model of Concept Diffusion

The aim of this analysis is to get a better understanding of how a concept of food can create social change in the form of a social movement and economic development in the form of new and innovative production and distribution systems, new meals and tourism behaviour and new export patterns. We need a theoretical framework that can explain the social change and economic development processes that the invention of the New Nordic Cuisine concept may result in. We shall suggest a model for stages in the specific food production and consumption diffusion process that the New Nordic Cuisine concept is assumed to follow. The concept of the New Nordic Cuisine is used as the example in the presentation of the model.

Experience is a core factor in the example in this model; however, experience is not the only important factor in the New Nordic Cuisine concept. As mentioned, other material factors such as agricultural raw material, fish and so on are also important as are behavioural factors such as peoples' norms and values and service factors, for example, restaurants, travel agencies, distribution and retail.

The model is based on Rogers's (2003) model of diffusion of innovations. We suggest a theoretical standpoint that claims that experience is a core element of the concept but does not make the diffusion process different from other diffusion processes where, for example, goods or services are the core elements. Experience is a social and economic element as are material things (such as goods) and service behaviour (such as advice from a lawyer or cleaning). Experience may, at least according to Pine and Gilmore's (1999) theory, add more value to the concept than other elements and thus have a greater economic value. But fundamentally, it is an element in what people buy and consume in line with goods and services.

Diffusion of a concept may theoretically be assumed to be a more complex and slow process than the diffusion of a single new element (such as, for example, a new app to a mobile phone or a new material for machine equipment). A concept implies fundamental changes of peoples' norms, values and daily behaviour and new production and economic structures.

The model for the diffusion process of concepts is represented in Figure 22.2. The diffusion process is assumed to lead to social change (phase 4) and economic development (phase 5). In the example of the New Nordic Cuisine experience is a core factor. One may theoretically state a hypothesis that experience drives the diffusion of this food concept, which means that the next phase of the process will only be implemented if the actors in the foregoing phase have had an important experience when relating themselves to the concept. By relating we mean that the concept gives them one or more particularly memorable experiences (for example, when visiting a restaurant or a festival), that it becomes important to their everyday life (for example, as a meal or food preparing culture) or

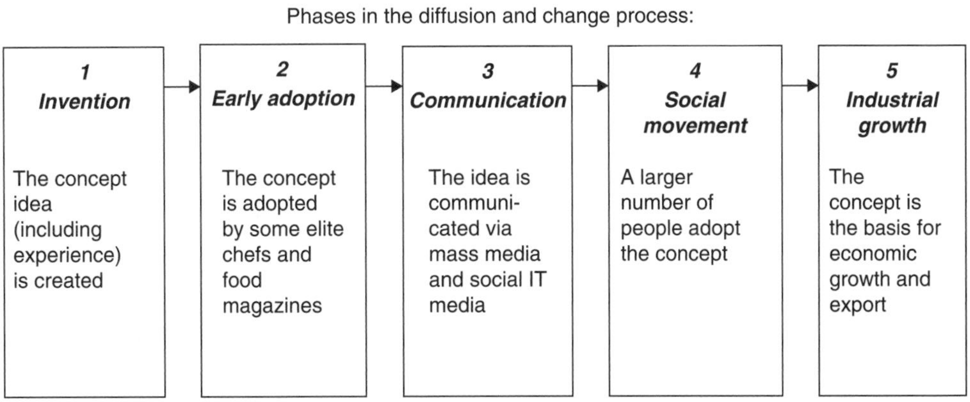

Phases in the diffusion and change process:

1 *Invention*	2 *Early adoption*	3 *Communication*	4 *Social movement*	5 *Industrial growth*
The concept idea (including experience) is created	The concept is adopted by some elite chefs and food magazines	The idea is communi-cated via mass media and social IT media	A larger number of people adopt the concept	The concept is the basis for economic growth and export

Figure 22.2   Social and economic change: model of diffusion of concepts applied on New Nordic Cuisine as example

that it becomes an important part of a distribution system (for example, via articles in magazines and newspapers or in shops, supermarkets and food markets).

22.5   EMPIRICAL INVESTIGATION

22.5.1   Analytical Approach

Empirical investigation of the New Nordic Cuisine concept should follow the above theoretical model of diffusion (Figure 22.2) to investigate whether the diffusion follows the model and thus leads to social change (phase 4) and economic development (phase 5).

The diffusion process has actually (by year 2012) come to a stage in which phase 3 is developing and has started to move into phase 4. However, phase 4 is only rudimentary and there is always a possibility that the diffusion process stops before phase 4 is fully developed.

This section presents the results of the investigation of the phases for which we have empirical data. These phases and the investigation are the following:

1. invention;
2. early adoption;
3. mass media communication;
4. social movement (wide social acceptance);
5. industrial growth; this phase is hardly reached yet, thus it is only empirically inves-tigated sporadically. Instead we discuss the challenges that the New Nordic Cuisine concept presents to industrial development and policy.

The empirical investigation particularly looks at the experience factor – how much it determines the development process and which type of experience (see Figure 22.1) we observe.

22.5.2   Methods and Data

The investigation of the phases of the diffusion of the New Nordic Cuisine concept is based on different methods and different types of data. An operationalization of the characteristic of each phase pointed out which method and empirical material could be used to investigate the phase. A total investigation of the development of the social movement and the economic consequences would be very resource demanding and difficult to carry out methodologically. As the diffusion of the New Nordic Cuisine concept is still in its first phases, a general investigation of its diffusion in the Danish – not to mention the global – population would require a huge survey with the prospects of only few results. Likewise an analysis of the concept's economic impacts would run into huge statistical problems of isolating the effects of this concept from other economic factors. Therefore it was decided to operationalize the investigation of the diffusion of the New Nordic Cuisine concept by studying and analysing selected cases of each theoretically defined phase. The material thus includes:

1. Invention: the birth of the concept. This can be dated to a seminar in 2004 (Jacobsen, 2008b); however, the birth of the concept was the result of a preceding process. The empirical material is based on interviews with the two of the organizers of the seminar and documentary material.
2. Early adoption: how the gastronomic elite adopts the concept. Empirical material is based on one event, MAD Food Camp in Copenhagen in August 2011. The material is based on observations made by seven research-observers, qualitative interviews (20 interviews with chefs, journalists and other experts participating in a symposium and with producers who sold food at the festival), a small semi-structured survey (92 visitors), photos and a collection of other objects.
3. Mass media communication: how the concept is communicated and discussed in the global mass media. The material consists of selected articles from Danish and international gastronomic magazines and newspapers. Further, it is about interaction on the social IT media Twitter and Facebook in September 2011 about MAD Food Camp. Randomly selected sites with contributions have been read and the content categorized.
4. Social movement: how the concept – perhaps – is becoming the basis for a social movement in Denmark. The material consists of the semi-structured survey. This material is supplemented by a structured survey of 137 visitors at another food event, a two-hour ferry trip from Copenhagen in August 2011 in which food products from the island of Bornholm were promoted. Both events promote New Nordic Cuisine, the MAD Food Camp as a core element of the festival and the ferry trip promoting food from Bornholm as an example of New Nordic Cuisine. The structured survey materials were in both events supplemented with less structured qualitative interviews with selected participants and researchers' observation. These interviews and observations make it possible to assess the participants' social position, motivation for coming and identification with New Nordic Cuisine as a social movement and which types of experience (see Figure 22.1) they had.
5. Industrial growth. This phase is only empirically investigated through participant observation of attempts to establish publically funded projects and centres. The

participant observations have been based on the authors' participation in two such projects and the encounter with other projects and centres.

22.5.3   Research Questions

The empirical investigation particularly looks at the experience factor – how much it determines the development process (see Figure 22.2) and which type of experience (see Figure 22.1) we observe. In the following section we analyse the empirical material with the aim of answering two questions:

1.   What happens in each phase of the diffusion process and how does it lead to – or not lead to – the next phase. This will provide knowledge about conditions for social change and economic development via diffusion of concepts.
2.   What is the content of the concept New Nordic Cuisine? This is not clear from the above theoretical approach and practice may show that it is not clear to the actors involved either. We will thus come to know more about the concrete concept, but we will also know more about what a concept is – for example, that it might lead to multi-interpretation of the actors and different identification.

Throughout the analysis we emphasize the importance of the experience element of the concept and which types of experience the actors have.

The idea of experience as the core driver of the diffusion process presented above is critically discussed. The empirical analysis of the experience factor shall be the basis for a final discussion of what we have learned about the theoretical aspects of the experience concept, particularly about the types of experience.

22.6   RESULTS OF THE EMPIRICAL INVESTIGATION

22.6.1   Invention: The Birth of the Concept

The concept of New Nordic Cuisine was invented at a seminar with Nordic chefs in autumn 2004 (Jacobsen, 2008b). According to the interviews, the driver was the Danish food entrepreneur, Claus Meyer, who owns several restaurants, catering firms and other food enterprises (Nickelsen and Scheuer, 2009). He has always been occupied by promoting good, natural raw material and regional cooking traditions. He has also been a TV star and has produced a TV series on regional Nordic food. He organized the seminar together with other experts and it concerned how to promote regional, healthy and natural food. The seminar ended with the formulation of a manifesto, the New Nordic Cuisine Manifesto, that stated a series of principles (Appendix 22.A).

The Manifesto mostly concerns the chefs' relation to nature, low fat and states that they should only use pure, fresh, seasonal raw material that reflects the Nordic nature and cultivating culture. The Manifesto does not emphasize the experience of the users (for example, restaurant guests) much and the founders were not focused on the consumption experience – the concept of experience employed here was unknown to them at that time. The chefs' implementation of the principles and journalists' writing about these principles and the Nordic food may create experiences to people. This, however, requires that the Manifesto is implemented in practice in the restaurants – that it is staged (as Pine and Gilmore, 1999 express it). The seminar in 2004 was a learning experience for the participating chefs because it created a completely new food concept.

The staging of the New Nordic Cuisine principles took place after the seminar by Nordic restaurants having developed a special style of the food and international gastronomy journalists having written about it. Chefs outside the Nordic countries have also been inspired by the concept. Restaurant guests and readers of the gastronomy articles have gained a special experience – not particularly of the Manifests principles, but of the new food style. This has mostly been a sensorial experience.

22.6.2   Early Adoption: How the Gastronomic Elite Adopts the Concept

The MAD Food Camp in August 2011 represents an event where people from the global gastronomic elite had a common experience that confirmed the New Nordic Cuisine as an international concept.

The MAD Food Camp took place over a weekend on a field in an old shipyard area. The festival was organized by Claus Meyer, René Redzepi from Noma and others. Many volunteers participated. The theme of the festival was vegetables and herbs. The festival was divided into two parts, a symposium for professionals (chefs, journalists and others) and a market where producers of raw food materials and prepared food products presented their products. The weather was extremely rainy and the field was transformed into mud. The symposium took place in a circus tent. The symposium was led by René Redzepi and was a series of talks with a few demonstrations of cooking. The theme was the environmental state of the world and how we should follow nature in our food consumption and not work against it. Environmental scientists and chefs presented the talks and demonstrations. The symposium was very creative. For example, René Redzepi served living red ants. This was based on two talks, one by a scientist that argued that the weight of ants in the world equals the weight of people and to eat ants is ecologically sound and another one by a chef from South America who told about how he had presented some innovative dishes for Indians and they replied 'It tastes good – something like ants.' Some speakers argued for families having their own kitchen gardens and that food plants should be planted in city parks. Other speakers emphasized old farming methods and local food and food traditions from all over the world, but also how traditional meals could be created in new, innovative ways in restaurants, for example, in Japan and Sweden.

The message of the presentations, as we observed, was to follow nature and use local raw materials. This may be Nordic, or Danish, or Zealandish to people in Copenhagen, but, as food journalists explained in interviews, it would be Provencal to people in Provence, Portuguese to people in Portugal and so on. The interviews with chefs, journalists and other professionals showed that they were very enthusiastic about the message of local food and living with nature. However, this did not particularly emphasize Nordic food products.

As we could observe, the atmosphere was very enthusiastic. A journalist declared in the interview: 'I have never been to anything similar. Food festivals use to be in elegant hotels with lots of demonstrations of cooking. Here we are in a hole of mud with many local food producers, families visiting the food market and the symposium is full of talks about the environment made by scientists.' The festival seems to potentially be an epoch-making event. The chefs and journalists were not coming because of the 2004 Manifesto but because they expected to get an experience because René Redzepi was one of the organizers and his reputation had already become worldwide. The interviewees were generally not fully aware of what experience they should expect. What they, according to the interviews, experienced was a mixture of ecology, nature philosophy and regional proximity. What they did not experience was a national manifestation of Danish or Nordic food products. The raw materials from Zealand, Denmark and the rest of the Nordic countries are outstanding and can be found in the Zealand, Danish, Swedish, Greenland and so on nature or grown ecologically by everyone. However, every region in the world has the same possibilities. The message from most interviewees was that people should experience the special nature in advanced cooking in every region in the world. However, a few journalists were critical and asked whether or not this was just a revival of the old ecological movement.

Of the participants that were interviewed using the semi-structure questionnaire, 28 persons were professional chefs, producers or journalists. They were asked what 'Nordic food' means to them. Only two interviewees said it did not mean anything. Table 22.1 shows that 'Nordic food' has a different meaning to the professionals. First, it means local raw material and second, it means that food should be in harmony with nature and the seasons. Only 14 per cent of the interviewees saw 'Nordic food' as being related to Danish or Nordic food culture. Only 11 per cent saw it as related to particular ways of preparing the food (which was the essence of the former gastronomic movements, particularly the molecular one). The experience element of 'Nordic food' seems to be mostly meaning-creating: to experience a connection to nature, seasons and local food growing traditions.

Table 22.1   What does Nordic food mean to you? Participants at MAD Food Camp symposium. Answers from professional chefs, producers and journalists in percentages

	Yes	No
Does Nordic food mean something to you	93	7
If yes: What does it mean? (several answers possible for each interviewee)		
Healthy, organic food	11	
Food in harmony with nature and seasons	18	
Local raw materials	39	
A gastronomic movement	11	
Vegetables	7	
Innovative preparation of meals	11	
Cultural roots in Denmark/Nordic countries	14	

Note: *N* = 28.

Source: Material from a survey to participants in the MAD Food Camp in Copenhagen, August 2011.

22.6.3   Communication

The New Nordic Cuisine has been mentioned in food magazines and newspapers in Denmark in the years following 2004 and later in the Nordic countries. The restaurant Noma, in which René Redzepi is the chef, and which is jointly owned by him and the entrepreneur Claus Meyer, has played a particular role in spreading the concept. Internationally, food journalists started a communication process around 2008 when restaurant Noma, for the first time, entered the top of the list of world's best restaurants in *Restaurant Magazine* and also had a star in the *Michelin Guide* (in 2012 it had two stars). Since 2010 when Noma, for the first time, was voted the world's best restaurant, the number of articles in the international press has increased tremendously.

A total quantitative counting of publicity of the New Nordic Cuisine is not possible since very many local media have mentioned New Nordic Cuisine. A qualitative investigation of the content of a sample of media (magazines, TV broadcasting, books, newspapers) shows that two aspects are most prominent: recipes (how to cook specific dishes) and stories about the most famous Nordic chefs. These aspects emphasize the more basic living and purchase part of the experience and only little the meaning-creating and learning part. The theme of New Nordic Cuisine as a social movement, that is, how it is connected to peoples' daily life such as purchasing food, health aspects, its economic implications, is not touched upon much. If such aspects are mentioned, they are mostly connected to ecological and environmental issues. There are only a few examples of specific Nordic food products mentioned. However, analyses of social media such as Twitter that we have made show that New Nordic Cuisine increasingly is discussed there as a social movement.

22.6.4   Social Movement

By studying the MAD Food Camp we can investigate New Nordic Cuisine as a social movement. The festival was open to everybody who paid the entrance fee. The audience could visit the many stalls, listen to talks, cook with children and experience and participate in food laboratories and other forms of activities. The guests could buy food from the stalls, but mostly the stalls were pedagogical exhibitions that told about the food. People could also buy food to eat on the spot. We observed that this part of the festival was separated from the symposium. There were elements of the new food ideology in some talks and some stalls, but in many ways it could have been a food market to be found anywhere; however, it had an emphasis on ecology, fresh vegetables and local producers. The visitors obviously gained an experience and were very engaged. This could be seen from the relatively many visitors on the most rainy day, where they did not seem to bother about the bad weather.

We observed that the participants were frontrunners in a food and gastronomic movement. They were mostly food enthusiasts, so-called foodies: 34 per cent of the interviewees said that gastronomy is their hobby and only 3 per cent were not interested in food. Only 8 per cent came just to get free food. Many families visited the festival, particularly on the non-rainy day. They also seemed to be enthusiasts who wanted to teach their children good food habits; this was confirmed by the survey. The visitors' experiences were primarily learning and meaning-creating; however, the observers were in doubt

Table 22.2   Why do you come to the festival? Visitors at MAD Food Camp. Answers from non-professional visitors in percentages (several answers possible for each interviewee)

Heard about it, curiosity	28
To socially experience the event	36
Inspiration, interested in gastronomy	47
Interested in the New Nordic Cuisine Movement	15
Interested in ecology	11
To see and buy the food products	9
To learn about Nordic food culture	3
To get free food	8

Note: $N = 64$.

Source: Material from a survey to participants in the MAD Food Camp in Copenhagen, August 2011.

about whether there was some special New Nordic Cuisine element in the experience or whether it was mostly a confirmation of an existing environmental meaning-creating experience.

It is therefore interesting to see what the interviewees answered about their engagement in gastronomy and New Nordic Food. In Table 22.2 we can see why they attended the festival and in Table 22.4 what Nordic food means to them.

Almost half of the visitors (47 per cent) came because they are interested in food and sought inspiration. However, 36 per cent also came because they wanted to experience the social event; 28 per cent had no prior opinion, they just came because of curiosity. The majority of visitors can, based on these results, be seen as early adopters who came to get an experience that could confirm their prior engagement in the movement. Others were later adopters, who learned about the movement at the festival. However, they were open to the movement since only 3 per cent were not interested in food and gastronomy.

These results can be compared to another experience-based event, a ferry trip in which food products from the island of Bornholm were promoted. The theme was not New Nordic Cuisine, but food products from Bornholm. The audience of this event were later adopters rather than the frontrunners of the New Nordic Cuisine Movement that visited the MAD Food Camp. The audience on the ferry boat trip were not attracted by meaning-creating experience elements: a debate panel that was organized only attracted 4 per cent of the audience and only 3 per cent said that the panel debate impressed them mostly. This audience was primarily attracted by a non-food experience (the boat trip in itself) and then by sensory and purchase experiences (a cheap meal at sea), which can be seen in Table 22.3. Of the participants, 45 per cent came because of the food, which also impressed them mostly followed by the exhibition and encountering local food producers. The locality, Bornholm, also meant much to the participants (48 per cent said so), thus the regional origin was part of the purchase experience.

The MAD Food Camp festival thus seems to be a particular meaning-creating and identity-making experience. In Table 22.4 we can see what meaning the visitors ascribed the movement. We can see that the identity of a New Nordic Cuisine Movement is not completely clear or uni-dimensional. We can see that particular Nordic products are not

Table 22.3   Reasons for participating in the event and most impressive experience. Ferry boat trip promoting food products from Bornholm. Answers from visitors in percentages (several answers possible for each interviewee)

Questions and answers	
Reasons for coming:	
The food	45
The boat trip	61
The panel debate	4
Knowledge of food products from Bornholm	48
Most impressive experience:	
The food	53
The exhibition	45
Meeting the producers	26
The debate	3

Note: N = 137.

Source: Material from a survey to participants in a ferry boat trip presenting food products from Bornholm, August 2011.

Table 22.4   What does Nordic food mean to you? Visitors at MAD Food Camp. Answers from non-professional visitors in percentages

	Yes	No
Does Nordic food mean something to you?	79	21
If yes: What does it mean? (several answers possible for each interviewee)		
Healthy, organic food	13	
Food in harmony with nature and seasons	11	
Local raw materials	24	
A gastronomic movement	6	
Vegetables	13	
Good raw materials	13	
Restaurant Noma	10	
Cultural roots in Denmark/Nordic countries	24	
Traditional daily fare	6	

Note: N = 64.

Source: Material from a survey to participants in the MAD Food Camp in Copenhagen, August 2011.

a core of the movement. Local raw materials are mentioned by 24 per cent, and recovery of Nordic or Danish food culture also by 24 per cent. This emphasizes local or regional food and food culture but not Nordic or Danish standard products that can be exported. Harmony with nature and seasons means something (11 per cent answered that it does) as does the health and environmental aspects (however, only 13 per cent mentioned this). The latter result tells us that the New Nordic Cuisine Movement is not just a recovery of the old environmental movement. Neither is it a recovery of old local daily fare (which only 6 per cent mentioned); the innovative element is included in the movement.

The experience that professional and non-professional people have had at the MAD Food Camp festival has subsequently been discussed internationally in the social IT media, particularly Twitter. The discussion also refers to articles in newspapers and magazines. An analysis shows that the main message in the discussion is enthusiasm about being part of the movement and those who participated in the MAD Food Camp were particularly lucky. The discussion emphasizes the aspects of local food, being in harmony with nature and contributing to a greener world. The messages include environmental issues, however, most of them are discussed within a framework that can be characterized as learning and meaning-creating experience such as 'great chefs can help us live in an environmentally responsible manner and give us great food experiences'. The discussion is not a purely environmental discussion, but includes the element of experience, both aesthetic and as a learning and meaning-creating experience. The discussion does not emphasize particular Nordic food products very much, thus this aspect does not seem to be a core part of the emerging social movement. The message is generally 'local food', not 'Nordic food', and local food means local wherever in the world.

22.6.5 Industrial Growth

The New Nordic Cuisine Movement has had an economic effect in Denmark as it has attracted gastronomic tourists to the country, particularly to eat at the restaurants (of which others than Noma carry out the New Nordic Cuisine). This effect is documented by the Danish tourist authority. VisitDenmark estimates that one third of foreign tourists come to Denmark with the purpose to visit Danish restaurants and foreign tourists' restaurant expenditure increased from 600 000 billion € in 2011 to 800 000 billion € in 2012.

From participant observation it can be concluded that several projects and centres about food business development have been established in Denmark and the Nordic countries since 2007. A few of them are called Nordic food centres, but most of them are defined within a wider scope to renew the Danish agriculture and food sector – without having any particular predefined conceptual solution to the development problems of the sector. The experience element is emphasized in most of them. The special New Nordic Food ideology is not included in all of them, but is emphasized in some. It is still too early to conclude anything about the effect of these projects and centres.

Basing food industrial development on a concept with a strong emphasis on experience such as the New Nordic Cuisine meets new challenges, which call for innovative solutions. Theoretically we can argue that at least two challenges are faced.

1. *It is a challenge to create economic benefits based on a concept (whether called 'Nordic' or 'Danish').*

Traditionally, a country such as Denmark has been able to create national income and industrial development by exporting raw or manufactured food products. This is not obvious in an experience-based concept such as the New Nordic Cuisine, which is based on principles of relationship to nature, local food and particular cooking and serving methods and aesthetics. The concept of New Nordic Cuisine is seen from the user side not the producer side. The importance is what the chef or any family does not that they should use raw or manufactured material from any particular country. Since using local products is a core value of the New Nordic Cuisine concept, this is anti-import oriented.

If an economic benefit must be created, the concept must first be communicated and diffused. Next, a system for back-remittance of money to the country of origin (in this case Denmark) that cannot be based on the purchase of a good but on experience-based concepts should be developed. This requires innovative thinking of industrial development and business models, which cannot be based on the traditional industrial export way of thinking. Innovative business development could, for example, be to sell knowledge about the New Nordic Cuisine concept as a knowledge business service or establishing restaurants and enterprise canteen chain companies based on the concept and local food (anti-McDonaldization; see Ritzer, 2004). Another possibility is to export special raw or elaborated Danish products to countries or regions where there is a lack of these raw materials. However, these products must be seen as supplementary products to the local raw material. This is part of the concept. Even the great chefs use some products in addition to the local ones. Which supplementary product areas are saleable must be investigated. Probably this will require both user-oriented investigation and laboratory and cuisine experiments.

The results from the ferry trip with food products from Bornholm show that it may be possible to brand and sell regional non-mass produced food products, at least within the same country. Further research is needed to investigate whether this is possible on the world market and whether this would be in harmony with, or against, the concept of New Nordic Cuisine.

2.   *It is a challenge to secure the ownership of food concepts and avoid imitation.*

Only a vague system of rights to conceptual innovation (that implies peoples' behaviour) exists. The patent system cannot be used. If, in this case, people in other countries redefine New Nordic Cuisine as 'local cuisine', there is no connection to Nordic or Danish food industries or other types of business. The attraction of people to Denmark to experience the 'roots of the New Nordic Cuisine' – the tourism aspect – can be ensured if the country is branded in the right way. To ensure the export of the supplementary products mentioned above requires development of a new branding and distribution system. The existing Danish mega-food companies (Danish Crown producing meat and Arla producing dairy products) may either not be able to do it because they are too connected to an old-fashioned food concept or they need to redefine their business radically, for example, by system exports to large firm canteens and public meal systems (for example, in schools).

22.7   CONCLUSION

In this section we conclude, based on the empirical analysis (particularly of the MAD Food Camp), on which types of experience determine the diffusion process of the New Nordic Cuisine concept and the consequences to industrial food policy. This will be a combination of answers to both research questions raised: What happens at each phase of the diffusion process and what is the content of the New Nordic Cuisine? Thereafter we shall conclude on the concept diffusion models and the experience typology as general theoretical tools to understand social change and economic development via diffusion of concept innovations.

To the chefs, journalists and other professionals, the most important experience types were the sensory (since the symposium emphasized the presentation of the food) and the meaning-creating ones (New Nordic Cuisine as a professional movement) and to some degree purchase experience (since the chefs and food producers discussed how to provide local food). The learning experience may also be said to be important as the professionals in the interviews said that they came to the festival to get inspiration; however there were not many demonstrations of food preparation, but much talk about nature and environment, thus the meaning-creating experience was much more important than learning. Basic living was an element, but not as an experience for the professionals themselves; they saw the New Nordic Cuisine chefs as the saviours of other peoples' health and welfare and this element was thus more a part of the meaning-creating experience (to improve other peoples' helath and welfare create a meaning for the chefs' work). Routine experiences were not part of the professionals' benefit (since the New Nordic Cuisine emphasizes innovation in food preparation and the concept does not emphasize cooking methods nearly as much as, for example, the molecular gastronomy paradigm does).

To the ordinary visitors – those who are early adopters and the followers of these – the most important experience types were the basic living ones and the meaning-creating and learning ones. The sensorial and purchase types were to some degree important since the visitors could taste and buy food products; however, this fact was not the most emphasized in the interviews. Social experiences were not emphasized at the MAD Food Camp, but are obviously a factor in the succeeding interaction at the social IT media. Routine experiences were not obvious since many respondents in the interviews said that they miss a translation of New Nordic Cuisine in day to day situations in the family (they do not know what to do in these situations since they cannot cook Noma food).

We can conclude that the most important type of experience for both professionals and non-professionals was that of meaning-creating. This states that New Nordic Cuisine is really a social movement – in fact an ideology, both among professionals and among ordinary people. The movement has primarily to do with basic living, but also to some degree with sensory experiences. This meaning-creating experience progresses in the first phases of the diffusion process because it engages people. However, the emphasis on meaning-creating experiences also calls attention to the difficulties in coming to the next phases where the movement really becomes a mass movement and where industrial growth, however in a new form (for example, small, differentiated food product series), is created. This demands an emphasis on purchasing and routine experiences, thus many people in the world use the principle of the concept in their daily behaviour and habits and buy specific products that gives them a purchasing experience of New Nordic Food – or local food since that seems to be the essence of the concept.

This difficulty, because of lack of routine and purchase experience elements in the New Nordic Cuisine, in reaching the next diffusion phase is not in favour of a new national industrial growth policy in Denmark or other Nordic countries. The 'Nordic' aspect of the concept and the movement are not connected to Danish or Nordic raw materials, but seems to be a characteristic of where the movement emerged. This conclusion suggests that New Nordic Cuisine will not be a saviour of Danish or Nordic food exports. However, it may create a new food consumption and distribution system based on local food products, which may result in a revival to small local food producers (farmers, fishermen, manufacturers, distributors) everywhere in the world. Economically, the challenge to, for example, Danish industrial policy is to get economic growth out of the social movement. There might be possibilities to brand and sell non-mass produced regional food products globally, but the conditions have not yet been researched.

This analysis of development of a food movement illustrates that a typology of different experiences may be a useful instrument in understanding a social and economic development. The experience concept thus not only remains a description of actual behaviour and sensing, but can be an analytical concept that can contribute to explain fundamental and dynamic social and economic phenomena. The change and diffusion model has also worked as a tool to understand diffusion of concepts and their impact on social and industrial movements. This model may be an analytical tool for understanding the emergence and diffusion of experiential concepts in general and a tool for understanding the development of the experience economy.

REFERENCES

Abernathy, W.J. and J.M. Utterback (1978), 'Patterns of industrial innovations', *Technological Review*, **80** (7), 2–29.
Andersson, A. and D. Anderssson (2006), *The Economics of Experiences, the Arts and Entertainment*, Cheltenham, UK and Northampton, MA, USA: Edward Elgar.
Black, M. (1996), *The Medieval Cookbook*, London: British Museum Press.
Clark, T.N. (1969), *Gabriel Tarde on Communication and Social Influence, Selected Papers. Selected and with an Introduction by Terry N. Clark*, Chicago, IL: University of Chicago Press.
Darmer, P. and J. Sundbo (2008), 'Introduction to experience creation', in J. Sundbo and P. Darmer (eds), *Creating Experiences in the Experience Economy*, Cheltenham, UK and Northampton, MA, USA: Edward Elgar, pp. 1–12.
Fisker, A.M. and T.D. Olsen (2008), 'Food, architecture and experience design', *Nordic Journal of Architectural Research*, **20** (1), 63–74.
Franck, K.A. (2005), *Food and the City*, London: Wiley.
Fuglsang, L., J. Sundbo and F. Sørensen (2011), 'Dynamics of experience service innovation: innovation as a guided activity – results from a Danish survey', *The Service Industries Journal*, **31** (5), 661–77.
Gallouj, F. (2002), *Innovation in the Service Economy*, Cheltenham, UK and Northampton, MA, USA: Edward Elgar.
Grew, R. (2000), *Food in Global History*, Boulder, CO: Westview Press.
Jacobsen, J.K. (2008a), 'Under the surface – looking into springtime. A gastro-theatrical experience in Madelaines Madteater', in O. Harsløf and D. Hannah (eds), *Performance Design*, Copenhagen: Tusculanum, pp. 281–97.
Jacobsen, J.K. (2008b), 'The food and eating experience', in J. Sundbo and P. Darmer (eds), *Creating Experiences in the Experience Economy*, Cheltenham, UK and Northampton, MA, USA: Edward Elgar, pp. 13–32.
Jantzen, C. and M. Vetner (2007), 'Oplevelsens psykologiske struktur' ('The psychological nature of experience'), in J.O. Bærenholdt and J. Sundbo (eds), *Oplevelsesøkonomi. Produktion, forbrug, kultur* (*Experience Economy. Production, Consumption, Culture*), Copenhagen: Samfundslitteratur, pp. 27–49.
Jantzen, C., M. Vetner and J. Bouchet (2011), *Oplevelsesdesign: tilrettelæggelse af unikke oplevelseskoncepter* (*Experience Design: The Planning of Unique Experiences*), Copenhagen: Samfundslitteratur.
Kiple, K.F. and C.O. Kriemhild (eds) (2000), *The Cambridge World History of Food*, Cambridge: Cambridge University Press.
Kuhn, T.S. (1962), *The Structure of Scientific Revolutions*, Chicago, IL: Chicago University Press.
LaPierre, R.T. (1965), *Social Change*, New York: McGraw-Hill.

Latour, B. (1987), *Science in Action: How to Follow Scientists and Engineers through Society*, Cambridge, MA: Harvard University Press.

Lenfle, S. and C. Midler (2010), 'Innovation in product-related services: the contribution of design theory', in F. Gallouj and F. Djellal (eds), *The Handbook of Innovation and Services*, Cheltenham, UK and Northampton, MA, USA: Edward Elgar, pp. 722–42.

Mayer, H. and P. Knox (2010), 'Small-town sustainability: prospects in second modernity', *European Planning Studies*, **18** (10), 1545–65.

Miles, I. (2004), 'Innovation in services', in J. Fagerberg, D. Mowery and R. Nelson (eds), *The Oxford Handbook of Innovation*, Oxford: Oxford University Press, pp. 433–58.

Moore, W.E. (1967), *Order and Change*, New York: Wiley.

Mossberg, L. (2003), *Att skapa upplevelser* (*To Create Experiences*), Lund: Studentlitteratur.

Mossberg, L. and E.N. Johansen (2006), *Storytelling: Marknadsföring i upplevelsesindustrin* (*Storytelling: Marketing in the Experience Industry*), Lund: Studentlitteratur.

Nickelsen, N.C. and J.D. Scheuer (2009), 'Tilblivelsen af det nordiske køkken – Claus Meyer som institutionel entreprenør' ('Emergence of the Nordic Kitchen – Claus Meyer as institutional entrepreneur'), *Psyke og logos*, **30** (2), 672–94.

Pine, B.J. and J.H. Gilmore (1999), *The Experience Economy*, Boston, MA: Harvard Business School Press.

Ritzer, G. (2004), *The McDonaldization of Society*, Thousand Oaks, CA: Pine Forge Press.

Rogers, E.M. (2003), *Diffusion of Innovation*, 4th edn, New York: Free Press.

Scheuing, E. and E. Johnson (1989), 'A proposed model for new service development', *Journal of Service Marketing*, **3** (2), 25–34.

Sundbo, J. (2004), 'The management of rock festivals as a basis for business dynamics: an example of the growing experience economy', *International Journal of Entrepreneurship and Innovation Management*, **4** (6), 587–611.

Sundbo, J. (2009), 'Innovation in the experience economy. A taxonomy of innovation organisations', *The Service Industries Journal*, **29** (4), 431–55.

Sundbo, J. (2011), 'Creative artists and entrepreneurship', in K. Hindle and K. Klyver (eds), *Handbook of Research into New Venture Creation*, Cheltenham, UK and Northampton, MA, USA: Edward Elgar, pp. 328–43.

Sundbo, J. and P. Hagedorn-Rasmussen (2008), 'The backstaging of experience production', in J. Sundbo and P. Darmer (eds), *Creating Experiences in the Experience Economy*, Cheltenham, UK and Northampton, MA, USA: Edward Elgar, pp. 83–110.

Svejonova, S., C. Mazza and M. Planellas (2007), 'Cooking up change in Haute Cuisine: Ferran Adria as an institutional entrepreneur', *Journal of Organizational Behavior*, **28** (5), 539–61.

Tarde, G. (1897), *L'Opposition Universelle*, Paris: Le Plessis.

Tarde, G. (2000), *Social Laws*, New York: Batoche Books.

Tarde, G. (1903), *The Laws of Imitation*, New York: H. Holt and Co.

Vernon, R. (1966), 'International investment and international trade in the product cycle', *Quarterly Journal of Economics*, **80** (2), 190–207.

APPENDIX 22.A   THE NEW NORDIC CUISINE MANIFESTO

As Nordic chefs we find that the time has now come for us to create a New Nordic Cuisine, which in virtue of its good taste and special character compares favourably with the standard of the greatest cuisines of the world. The purposes of the New Nordic Cuisine are as follows:

1.   To express the purity, freshness, simplicity and ethics that we would like to associate with our region.
2.   To reflect the different seasons in the meals.
3.   To base cooking on raw materials whose characteristics are especially excellent in our climate, landscape and waters.
4.   To combine the demand for good taste with modern knowledge about health and well-being.
5.   To promote the Nordic products and the variety of Nordic producers and to disseminate the knowledge of the cultures behind them.
6.   To promote the welfare of the animals and a sound production in the sea and in the cultivated as well as wild landscapes.
7.   To develop new possible applications of traditional Nordic food products.
8.   To combine the best Nordic cooking procedures and culinary traditions with impulses from outside.
9.   To combine local self-sufficiency with regional exchange of high-quality goods.
10.   To cooperate with representatives of consumers, other cooking craftsmen, agriculture, the fishing industry, the food industry, the retail and wholesale industry, researchers, teachers, politicians and authorities on this joint project to the benefit and advantage of all in the Nordic countries.

Source: Jacobsen (2008b).

23. Experiencing everyday life anew: applied theatrical and performative strategies
Gry Worre Hallberg and Olav Harsløf

23.1 INTRODUCTION

In this chapter we examine and discuss the concept of the experience economy as an indicator of the need for spaces (in-between) that allow for an aesthetic, sensuous and poetic mode of being in the midst of everyday life. This approach is rooted in critical theory and a phenomenological understanding of experience.

The production of surplus value is viewed as the continuous dominating principle of current Western society. This principle leads, as emphasized by Weber and the early Frankfurt School, to a fundamental de-enchantment of the life-world of modern man and to the dominance of the premises of the economic rationality.

However, the French sociologist and phenomenologist Maffesoli supplements this viewpoint when he argues that we are currently witnessing a re-enchantment of the world where the aesthetic mode of being is activated in everyday life (2007). In our opinion the experience spaces amplified by the experience economy can be seen to encourage such re-enchantment, and it is the unfolding of the aesthetic dimension (Baumgarten, 1750–58 [1986]; Guillet de Monthoux, 2004; Kirkeby, 2007) within these spaces that can be understood to contribute to the deep and full quality of the spaces.

Additionally, our theoretical and methodological outset is theatre and performance studies. Firstly, we shall map out the theatre as an economic concept, that is, 'the business theatre'. As Pine and Gilmore (1999) point out, every business is a stage, and companies are now designing memorable events for which they charge admission. The theatre has always provided what is hoped to be memorable events and has always had three functions: one on the stage, one in front of the stage and one behind the stage. Behind the stage theatre is also a business that stages experiences that involve customers in an intrinsically personal way. The value that the experience holds determines the submissions worth – also behind the stage.

We shall extrapolate the relationship between theatre production and theatre experience within the currently prevailing economies of the theatre. Secondly, we shall examine how the application of theatrical and performative strategies applied in contexts outside the art institution can potentially open enchanting and liminoid experience spaces such as the ones indicated above.

The experience economy is about holding the key to the experience. Furthermore, we have noticed that a new type of utterly attractive experience space has grown forth from the world of theatre and performance. Thus, more specifically, we shall look at a new tendency within the performance art world that we term live and relational fictional parallel universes: fictional frame stories are acted out live in certain framed spaces between performers and audiences (or relational co-participators) resulting in tasense of being in a parallel, yet real, universe. SIGNA (Denmark), Punchdrunk (UK), Post restante (Sweden), Collective Unconscious (UK), Fiction Pimps (Denmark) and Sisters Hope (DK) who were all constituted in the third millennium and were all bred as a hybrid between performing and visual arts are examples of this phenomenon.

These fictionally framed spaces have grown in popularity throughout the last decade as the attraction towards them indicates, and participants talk of addiction to fiction as discussed in 'I need my shot of fiction!' (Hallberg, 2009), but also see reviews of, for example, Punchdrunk and SIGNA, their Facebook fan pages and the growing popularity of other fictional framed spaces such as The Borderland (Sweden), The Poetry Brothel (USA) and the general growing popularity of pervasive games, live action roleplay, computer gaming and virtual realities.

The experiences within these spaces are claimed to be full and deep and even addictive because they differ so much from everyday life events and open the aesthetic, sensuous and poetic mode of being in the world. We argue that a thickened theatricality frames the space and thus the unique and other-worldly experience and that the theatrical frame is strengthened by six artistic strategies (Fischer-Lichte, 2005; Hallberg, 2009): the installation strategy, the performance strategy, the strategy of style, the strategy of site specificity, the strategy of narrativity and the strategy of interaction. Collectively, they thicken the theatricality and thus the performativity, which frame the space and can be regarded as a method or even a toolbox to design a universe – a full and deep experience space.

Unfolding these experience spaces outside art institutional contexts is potentially to support a poetic revolution. The term was born out of the movement using fictional strategies to frame experience spaces, such as the ones mentioned above. Accordingly, a cause is at the centre of the universe design. Furthermore, the cause is to evoke the sensuous, aesthetic and poetic experience of everyday life within a societal frame where the economic dimension is still dominating and arts have become autonomous and exclusive – even though profound disruptions within both systems are currently happening. Within the art world interactive, relational and dialogical approaches attempt to explode the autonomy from within, to dissolve the gap between stage and floor and suspend the exclusivity. Within the world of economics,tendencies such as arts in business, green bottom line, corporate social responsibility and not at least the experience economy soften the premises of the economic rationality.

Will these disruptions ultimately create a new status quo? For example, a society where the sensuous mode of being is at the centre of experience – a sensuous society?

23.2   THE ECONOMIC STRUCTURE OF THEATRE

If you have but once arranged a theatre night in The New Theater in Copenhagen for a large group (more than 20), you will understand what the modern business theatre has to offer and how the performances are presented, realized, priced and calculated. You call the theatre and get connected with 'ticket ordering – groups' and immediately there is a friendly voice on the phone who provides you with several alternative suggestions for how a group of this size can be placed in the house – together in a long row or perhaps preferably in a block on four rows. There are also several balcony options. A special solution is to place a few people in a box and the rest on the floor – this provides for an amusing communication in the group and creates life in the theatre room before the curtain.

When placement is in order, the voice tells you that now he or she will attempt to find a decent price – or more likely, the exactly right price, and after a minute or so, where it can be presumed that internal discount systems are consulted or hardcore percentage calculations are carried out, the price offer is presented. To the best of your abilities, you divide the number of participants with the price and end up with a number in the area of 200 or 300 Danish kroner, which you usually choose to accept based on the information you received during the preliminary conversation that some of the seats are quite expensive.

This model corresponds to the wine cases of supermarkets that are marketed as '4 + 2' – meaning six bottles of wine where one is of a finer 'reserva' and the other is a little less fancy while the four are ordinary *vino tavola*. On frequent occasions there is money to save by taking the bottles one by one yourself from the shelves.

Then the voice asks if you are interested to learn what the restaurant has to offer before the show. If you are, you will be presented with both the facilities and the gastronomic options. The latter are few, but they are easy to decide upon on the phone. If the group is not interested in eating at the theatre, the voice can offer to have drinks ready during intermission. It is cheaper to order by phone now than upon arrival or in the bar during intermission, where there is also crowded and an amount of waiting time is expected of course.

The price for the tickets, the potential dinner and drinks are added together and you disclose the number on your credit card, which is immediately subtracted from the summed up amount. Furthermore, you provide your phone numbers and your email address (for the sake of a receipt) and also, if you want your tickets sent to you, your postal address.

The amount subtracted from your account can easily end up in the area of 10 000 to 15 000 kroner. Even though the voice clearly has plenty of time, the conversation rarely takes more than ten minutes in which a product has now been sold – a theatre experience for 20 people.

After hanging up the phone, you have a pleasant feeling that you were in contact with a competent member of the theatre's staff, and before your inner eye you picture a grand, illuminated office in the administrative department behind or next to the stage, where the rooms of the direction, the economical supervisor, the production manager and their secretariat are situated. That the person has most likely serviced you from his or her home computer in the kitchen or the dining room in a small rural village or suburb does not occur to you (and you would rather not want to know!). The phone number is in any case from the Copenhagen area or at least it is a number that in no way indicates the province. In the same way as several English theatres put desired costumes on sale on the theatre's website, so that housewives, home seamstresses and hobby tailors can bid on them, the booking is also outsourced from the theatre house for good economical reasons.

If you, in closing, had asked the voice what he or she thought about the show by the way, there would probably also have been a pleasant and comprehensive standard answer for this.

The institution of theatre has always had three areas of function: one on the stage, one in front of the stage and one behind the stage. These functions have throughout history been more or less separated. Looked upon as economies, they have appeared in these forms:

- The high-profile art or experimental theatre in which stage and backstage closely interact.
- The performance theatre, the pedagogical-social theatre and the referential theatre in which stage, backstage and audience interact.
- The business theatre that is exclusively staged and administered backstage.

The business theatre is a developed backstage theatre. With the above-mentioned The New Theatre as an example, some might erroneously think there is a connection between the artistic quality of the product being sold and the business concept. This is wrong. The New Theatre does sell shows whose literary and musical quality lie within the expressional forms of popular culture and thus outside the domain of art criticism. But it does not need to be this way. It would be easy to imagine that the art theatres sought to sell their products by the concept of the business theatre if they had the need for it – for instance, The Betty Nansen Theatre or Odin Theatre. But this does not seem to be the case. It appears, however, that The Royal Theatre is trying to approach this concept.

This does, however, demand a uniform product. In other words, a package that consists of expectations, possible dining, show with drinks and an ending, which could be an afterlude in the bar, the café at the theatre or in the neighborhood of the theatre. In this package the show itself must not impose. Here the modern musical has shown the way with its light and sound show, its filmic design, genre-less music (Wagner- or Ellington-light) and technological climaxes (helicopter in Miss Saigon, barricade in Les Miserable, the heavenly ladder in Cats). This uniform concept, which in the musical theatre ensures success, could very well be transferred to the art theatre and thus ensure quality.

In some way, this was what the Italian theatre genius Giorgio Strehler did at the Piccolo Teatro in Milan in the early 1990s. He worked with Dr Faust by Goethe during a number of years with thorough conceptual studies and through his seminars for invited scientists. After that, he could put on the performance as a trilogy over the course of three nights and sell it for several years. However, he did not need to create a package with introduction, dinner, drinks and ending.

A more thorough model for a theatre could be to set up all of Beckett's plays over a number of years, for instance. From the start, a general Beckett concept would have to be developed and to it would be added a row of expectation paradigms. A philosophical-literary introduction tied to bookstores, book cafés and galleries is a necessity, as is an existential-philosophical (absolutely free of theatre) media strategy. A gastronomical programme (far from the dinner and drinks menu of the musical) could also be developed, just as the outro in particular would be very important here. As opposed to the more or less anonymous singing and acting cast of the musical, a high-profile and regular team could be of significant importance (in the same way as The Royal Theatre used it for many years).

In a model such as this the theatre would not have to stick to a single dramatist. Like the Tjekhov Theatre in Moscow and the Brecht Theatre in Berlin it would be quite possible to maintain a high-profile core product and at the same time make room for the plays of other dramatists within the same concept. Furthermore, it seems to be a business-wise asset that these theatres can market such shows as 'Tjekhov Theatre plays Moliére' and 'Brecht Theatre plays Miller'.

The English Shakespeare scene The Globe is probably the world's most developed theatre business. Here there are a museum, tours, merchandise/bookstore, restaurant, café, bar and theatre all under the same roof (actually, the scene itself isan important aspect of the reconstructed authenticity, without a roof. It is thus an important part of the concept that there are no plays in the winter and during rainy weather). Here as well, they perform other plays than Shakespeare. Young dramatists are encouraged to write for the stage (meaning the concept of the theatre) and directors, set designers and producers are welcome with their ideas. But the physical frames and the concept must be adhered to. A play sent in which calls for a covering of the theatre's room would most likely not be taken on.

Today the experience of theatre has to be produced. The actor and revue theatre director Preben Kaas said in the 1970s that he read all the sent-in manuscripts. Even though only one in a hundred sent-in texts was any good, this one good text made all the other readings worth it. The theatres might still receive a manuscript through the mail every once in a while, but when directly asked about this (in the 1990s) none of the theatre directors could remember when they last had been send a manuscript.

Today the dramatic material is developed, selected or sought out by the dramatic director and sometimes the other dramaturges of the theatre with the intent to create an experience for the audience, which can fill up the theatre in a given period of time, as calculated according to economical and repertoire demands. If a given theatre has four different shows in one theatre season, they start up the process some years in advance for four experience economical projects. Some theatres carry out this work from a theatre economical and dramaturgic judgement and without any real experience of economical expertise. The result is a variable audience attendance (for example, Gasværket, formerly Østre Gasværk Theatre). Others, however, use this expertise as a foundation for dramaturgy as well as choice of repertoire, set design and performance in practice. Furthermore, some others practise an entirely new way to relate to experience spaces and create immersive theatre experiences or what we term live and relational fictional parallel universes. These strategies are applied in contexts outside the theatre and art institution, which allow for different modes of experience in the midst of everyday life.

This points to how we understand experience as such and the intensified need to experience. This approach is rooted in critical theory and a phenomenological understanding of experience, which we shall discuss in the following section.

23.3 THE NEED TO EXPERIENCE

As indicated by Pine and Gilmore (1999) and specified by Sundbo and Sørensen in the Introduction of this Handbook, the experience economy can be understood as a business movement that has emerged after the agriculture, manufacturing and service economies. The reason for the occurrence at this point in time is explained through Maslow's (1954) theory of a pyramid of needs. The lower layers have been fulfilled and we now seek to fulfil the needs in the upper layers of the need pyramid – these being sensational and emotional. Experiences can satisfy these and we are even willing to pay a high price for them.

Another different, yet related, way to understand the attraction is a phenomenological (Merleau-Ponty, 1945) way of looking at available modes of being or states of becoming through times. Critical theory argues that Western society has been dominated by the premises of the (manufacturing) economic dimension such as efficiency, duty, reason and discipline since industrialization (Marx, 1867 [1978]; Adorno and Horkheimer, 1947 [2001]; Marcuse, 1955 [1970]; McKenzie, 2001; Hardt and Negri, 2003; Lazzarato, 2004; Boltanski and Chiapello, 2005). Furthermore, these premises oppose the premises of the aesthetic dimension understood as the sensory and emotional-oriented (Baumgarten, 1750–58 [1986]; Drotner, 2001; de Monthoux, 2004). Additionally, the aesthetic mode of being is isolated from work and everyday life with the establishment of the modern art system, due to the concentration of the aesthetic dimension in art and its location in an inaccessible system (Drotner, 2001). Thus, the modern art system has established itself from a series of positions since the mid 1700s, for example, the autonomy of the art and the art genius. Consequently, only special people – that is, artists as opposed to 'ordinary people' – have permission to base their living on the aesthetic mode of being within the exclusive and autonomous system. Another consequence is that the aesthetic dimension has been perceived as inferior to the economic on a societal level, meaning that the economic premises are dominant in our Western society. As a result of this exclusiveness, 'ordinary man' is imposed to live his or her work and everyday life within the premises of the economic dimension.

Yet philosophers like Dewey (1934) did rather early define the essence of experience as aesthetic and Cassirer (1931 [1967]) focused on the symbolic character of existence. Thus, there exist alternatives to the exclusive conception of aesthetic, lately also put forth by French sociologist and phenomenologist Michel Maffesoli. Like the Frankfurt School he believes that the industrial economic paradigm has been dominant since the mid 1700s. But in opposition to this school he argues that this paradigm was saturated in the 1950s to 1960s even though we did not realize that until now, which the financial crisis among other symptoms indicates. With his concept of the re-enchantment of the world (Maffesoli, 2007), which relates directly to the sociologist Max Weber's concept of the disenchantment (*entzauberung*) of the world (1918–19), Maffesoli argues that the values of creation (creativity), the emotional sense, aisthesis (an aesthetic mode of being in the world in the original sense of the word) and focus on the moment are now being (re)bred as key modes of being. These are opposing the modes of the former paradigm – as listed above: duty, discipline, rationality, efficiency and utilitarianism (as a goal in itself) and focus on the future. Hence both the Frankfurt School and Maffesoli stress the potential of the aesthetic dimension, but Maffesoli (1982 [1993]) argues that the aesthetic dimension, or Dionysus as he likes to call it, is evident in many situations of everyday life (the nightclub, the techno party and other modern day rituals) and not only within the art system. Moreover Maffesoli (2007) argues that change manifests itself more rapidly in everyday life than in the institutions that are out of kilter with everyday life. That is also why they build on former paradigms – like a star that is dead but still shines even though it has lost its ability to attract.

Lately there have also been signs of convulsions, displacements and disruptions within both the art and economical institution as the experience economy demonstrates. Within contemporary art practice and research we see a growing interest in artwork that focuses on provoking the positions of 'the modern art system' (Bourriaud, 1998; Bishop. 2004; Thompson and Sholette, 2004; Bolt, 2009). By using interactive, relational and interventionist strategies that break with the conception of the art genius and the autonomy of the arts, certain contemporary artists wish to make art more accessible and democratic (such as the ones working with the concept of live and relational fictional parallel universes mentioned above, but also see Ajemian, Superflex, Hamou, Ha-Ha, Schlingenschief, Tiravanija, Trampolinhuset to mention a few). Just as the experience economy is a sign of change within economics from manufacturing to service to experience as pointed out by Pine and Gilmore (1999). In this light we are slowly approaching a societal structure where the aesthetic and economic dimensions come closer to each other and at its centre – the experience of the world and the need for more sensuous and poetic modes of being.

23.3.1   Spaces In-between – Democratization of the Aesthetic Mode of Being

The experience (economy) is often manifested as framed spaces that allow for alternative and intensified involvement in situations. These spaces can be understood as areas where the aesthetic and economic dimensions are not only disrupted, but have already been fused. They provide a sort of in-between where the premises of everyday life are put on hold and a sensuous and emotional experience is accentuated. They are spaces in-between.

The term 'spaces in-between' is based on ritual theory and the idea of the liminal phase (Van Gennep. 1909 [1960]) – a between and betwixt (Turner, 1969 [1995]) mode of being where the premises of everyday life are put on hold and a sensuous experience is accentuated. This state is often used as a reference to describe the artistic experience, thus Bourriaud borrows Marx's term 'interstice' (gap) when applied to (relational) artworks, and theatre studies label it transitional, transformative (Féral, 2002; Fischer-Lichte, 2005) and liminoid, which is understood by performance researcher Richard Schechner (1985) to be more temporary than liminality. Hence, we define spaces in-between as spaces where the premises of everyday life are put on hold and an aesthetic, liminal and potentially transformative experience is activated. As indicated, the research on spaces in-between extends to different fields of study, among others to theatre and performance studies.

23.3.2   Theatricality and Performativity

The traits of theatricality and performativity are studied in this subsection as tools or strategies for the creation of experience spaces that manifest themselves in a state of in-between: in-between everyday life, which we argue is rooted in the economic dimension and that sensuous experience inspired by the aesthetic dimension. Thus, these are spaces such as the ones Maffesoli points out – where the merging of the new is already happening – outside the institutional contexts.

Within the art world the 1990s was amongst other things recognized as 'the performative turn', indicating the growing popularity of a relatively new art form, performance art, and the use of its methods. Thus, a number of theorists occupied themselves with distinguishing theatre from performance art. Not least by looking at what it does to the register of theatrical codes such as narrative discourse, mimesis and characterization. Where theatre is often an enactment of the playwright, performance art is a creation of the artist performing her/him/themselves. Furthermore, the principle of 'as if' is fundamental in theatre, whereas performance art conflates presence and simulacra, image and dissembling (Davis and Postlewait, 2003). However, it has been argued how they both share the trait of theatricality and how performativity is actually one of the fundamental modalities of theatricality.

Based on the studies of the theatre researchers Josette Féral (2002), Erika Fischer-Lichte (2002, 2005), Willmar Sauter (2000) and Solveig Gade (2008,) we define theatricality as: A frame within which a parallel reality that is staged in a specific manner becomes the operational reality – and following this premise – which effects the being and interaction of and between people that take place within the frame (Hallberg, 2009). It is argued that the participants can liberate themselves from the constraints of everyday life by being (bodily) present and interacting under different circumstances than in everyday life within the theatrical space and the parallel reality it creates (Féral, 2002; Fischer-Lichte, 2002; Schechner, 2002). Creating an alternative space, call it virtual or utopian (Kirkeby, 2007), such as experience spaces manifested outside the art institutions, can be understood as a theatrical space.

However, there is a tendency within the performance studies tradition (Davis and Postlewait, 2003; Butler, 2007) to perceive theatricality negatively – as a conception maintaining subjects within the constraints constructed by the societal institutions and the conducts of behaviour following these. Society is thus viewed as a stage controlled by a pre-written script. Butler (2007) argues that the potential of liberation from the script – our agency – lies in the possibility of individual interpretation of the given. Thus, the focus is on the repressive aspect of theatricality, understood as the non-reflected and repetitive pattern of discourses imposed on the subjects by the 'grand script of society'. Illustrated by the drag-parade, the performance, on the other hand, is perceived as a releasing opportunity of liberation.

Yet the contemporary experience spaces tend to operate within a theatrical frame wherein performative freedom is liberated as also suggested by the Canadian theatre researcher Josette Féral. In the preface of the journal *Substance* (2002) she identifies the relationship between theatricality and performativity. Her argument is that performativity and theatricality are not divergent to each other, but rather that performativity is an element of theatricality. It is the network of impulses and uniqueness that is always present within the theatrical frame:

> In integrating performativity within itself, theatricality sees it, as one of its fundamental modalities . . . (Féral, 2002, p. 5)

This allows us to understand every space of experience as an interaction of theatricality and performativity. Like Butler, Féral defines theatricality as the structure or 'pre-written' script, within which performativity is released as a network of impulses and 'free play'. However, Féral understands theatricality as the precondition of performativity and not as something to overrule.

Performativity can then be understood as a strategy amongst others that intensifies the theatrical frame and thus the experience within it.

23.4 LIVE AND RELATIONAL FICTIONAL PARALLEL UNIVERSES

As mentioned in the introduction to this chapter the experience economy can be considered as a trait where the one holding the key to the experience wins. Accordingly, a new type of utterly attractive experience space has grown forth from the world of theatre and performance – what we term live and relational fictional parallel universes: fictional frame stories are acted out live in certain framed spaces between performers and audiences (or relational co-participators) resulting in the sense of being in a parallel, yet real, universe. Imagine a setting like this:

> In the middle of the room a woman is standing, wine flowing from her wrists and down her hands – or is it blood? Her face is beautiful, sad, and serious; her make-up is heavy and delicate at the same time. Her lips are marked out with red lipstick, her cheeks are flushed, and the black mascara is running a bit. She wears a tight skirt of checked tweed, which stops below her knees and her legs are covered by skin-coloured pantyhose which are running. Her shirt is in off-white lace from an indefinable time. Who is she? Around her is a semicircle of people, behind her is a woman dressed in the same clothes – is it her sister? In her hand she carries a bottle filled with a strong red fluid – it has to be wine? And on the floor there are apples, some of which are half-eaten. Without raising her voice, but rather as if dictated by an insisting gaze, the woman in the back invites the young people in the circle to approach her. They each take a swig from the bottle and empty it on the woman's wrists. Some of them stand as petrified, others are hesitant, and others still have great sensitivity. The mood is oppressed, exhilarated, and solemn all at the same time. Tears break out from the woman in the middle, but they are not tears that command the stopping of events, quite the contrary actually. A liberation and a pleasure from the aesthetic intensity.

This scene is from the fertility ritual performed by the artistic duo Sisters Hope in a live and relational fictional parallel universe.

The performance group SIGNA describe these universes as 'enigmatic timeless environments for the audience to explore and live in' (signa.dk, 2012). This relatively new tendency evidently places itself within different artistic traditions and in particular it draws on performance, installation and interaction strategies. This hybrid genre breaks with the known categories and it was considered if SIGNA could even be categorized as theatre art when the group was nominated for the distinguished theatre award Theatreffen 2008. Die Erscheinungen der Martha Rubin nonetheless received its nomination, to which this text accompanied it:

> This is about immersing yourself in a new world, not only intellectually and spiritually, but also with your whole body. The audience moves around in a derelict city made of freight containers. They take part in life in this no-man's land, drinking and dancing with the inhabitants, getting a massage or visiting a peepshow. Soldiers go on patrol, arrest visitors and interrogate them. The underlying themes are power, proximity and deception, a strange young woman who sleeps for days and weeks on end in a shrine above the container city and then suddenly awakes. Her name is Martha Rubin. You can visit her, make sacrifices to her, and hope that she opens her eyes for a few moments. 'Die Erscheinungen der Martha Rubin' is a highly unusual form of theatre. The performers improvise for up to 84 hours, yet most of them are not professional actors. The audience can influence and decide what they experience. They research the background and are like ethnologists – or just observers and tourists, if they prefer. The Danish-Austrian performance duo SIGNA reproduces the fascination of computer games in real life and brings remarkable immediacy and warmth to the theatre, as well as a strong element of unsettling energy.[1]

Source: Photo by Julie Johansen.

Figure 23.1   Sisters Hope performing The Cleansing

In these universes there is no stage or room for the audience, no manuscript, the actors are not professional, the performances often play out as long improvisations, stretching across several days, in which the performers live as their fictional characters in an other-worldly universe.

This immersion into another realm of reality with other universal laws demands that the sensing viewer trains his or her ability to navigate within this room. It brings with it a new set of social rules, which provides both performers and audience with a special opportunity to try out other self-images and forms of fellowship than the ones they participate in on a daily basis. Because of the interactivity the audience helps to define the work and in this way it is unresolved from the start and thus open to the impulses that happen.

The impenetrable, fictional frame is thus the cornerstone in the creation of the parallel universes. This means that anything is allowed – except for breaking the fiction! In other words, as a performer and an interactive quest one might love, fight, make slander, create intrigue, become deaf, dumb and blind, be in a state of ecstasy, play a puzzle for four days and so on, all within the fictional frame, but never break it.

The experience within these spaces are claimed to be full and deep and even addictive because they differ so much from everyday life events and open the aesthetic, sensuous and poetic mode of being in the world (Fischer-Lichte, 2005) and the theatricality that frames the space is strengthened by six artistic strategies (Hallberg, 2009).

23.5 SIX ARTISTIC STRATEGIES THAT STRENGTHEN THE THEATRICAL FRAMING[2]

The six artistic strategies are: the installation strategy; the performance strategy; the strategy of style; the strategy of site specificity; the strategy of narrativity; and the strategy of interaction. Below the qualities of each strategy that contribute to the theatricality of the space are extracted. For people interested in creating full and deep experience spaces inspired by the tendency of live and relational fictional parallel universes, they can be regarded as a sort of toolbox where each strategy is a parameter that the facilitator can focus more or less on depending on the desired outcome.

Installation art strategy refers to installation art as spacious visual art and, thus, not rooted in the world of performing arts. However, architect and art theorist Nicolas De Oliveira (2003) investigates the genre and circles in five installation categories, one being the immersive escape category, which 'lowers' the participant into a parallel realm of reality: 'a room which radically separates itself from the reality of the ordinary day, narratively, conceptually, aesthetically etc . . .' (De Oliveira, 2003, p. 6). Thus, the immersion in the escape category contributes significantly to the construction of the theatrical in that the theatrical is precisely understood as a parallel reality, which is staged, or framed, in a particular way. The installation strategy contributes to this frame in an entirely physical way – it is not just a virtual or narrative parallel reality but rather one of manifest material. In the live and relational fictional parallel universes performers inhabit the installation, and thus expand what we normally understand about installation through the application of humans. This is the contribution of the performance strategy. The strategy of style secures that the installation in which the performers and co-participating audience is immersed is other-worldly and enchanted. The installation strategy is inextricably connected to the strategy of style, but it is still characterized as an independent strategy because it is also implemented on the other strategies, that is, the strategy of site specificity, the performance strategy, the strategy of narrativity and the strategy of interaction. The style often has many '*unheimliche*' (Freud, 1919 [1982]) elements and is both a demand of the place in which the performance takes place, of the interior and every objects – from the underwear of the performers and their toothbrushes to tiles and power cables, performers – their appearance, tone of voice, voice register, language use, the sound – music, songs, scent, food, taste, the level of interaction with the audience – everything. The strategy of style refers to the frame of mind that is present in the universe and that penetrates all the elements, from scent, sound and taste, and the attitude, appearance and language of the performers. With the strategy of style a room is constructed that is radically different from what we experience in our normal life, and thus the sensation of being on an expedition to 'a different place' and being in a parallel universe is augmented. The strategy of style is thus a strategy for staging the universe within the frame in a special way. This special way encourages nostalgia for several of the people present. The journey into an otherness also becomes a journey inside oneself, and the (lost) past, which the strategy of style refers to, and awakens intimate feelings. The strategy of style concept thus 'thickens' the reality of the installation and contributes to the construction of theatricality by setting a frame in which the people present are removed from their usual surroundings by being placed in a room that physically and atmospherically separates itself in a radical and consistent way from everyday life, thus drawing the people towards the other type of perception that this involves. As mentioned, the strategy of style plugs into all the other strategies, including the strategy of site specificity, which indicates that that the installation and narrative always begin in the physical space where the universe will be manifested (very seldom at an actual theatre). The negotiation with the surrounding environment makes us relate to and incorporate this environment into the fiction. To use the possibilities that the place already offers thus provides a sensation of greater authenticity. A merging occurs between the authentic and the staged when the physical conditions are the same. The place, like the surrounding room, is an inevitable part of the installation; the four walls of the installation, including windows and doors, ceiling and floor thus thicken the 'reality value' of the installation. The temporary aspect that the place also has, because it is only for a brief time that it is possible to be here (as long as the universe is manifested), further intensifies the experience value within this pocket of time. The fleeting nature of the place points towards the transience that all rooms and modes of being we inhabit includes – again a potential intensifying factor – as the critic, Janus Kodal, from the Danish newspaper *Politiken* pointed out after having participated in the live and relational fictional parallel universe, Nika is Dead (SIGNA, 2002): 'It is as if it tells us that if we don't immerse ourselves in life, it disappears. Immersion is a must, both in life and in the intense quarter of life which is art.'

As mentioned, the strategy of narrativity begins in the physical space and it is the narrative logic above anything else that is adhered to the live and relational fictional parallel universes. The integration of this in the performance of the performers is the most crucial part of the rehearsal time. It is critically important that the narrative logic of the parallel universe is followed. Thus, the performers are raised to be 'naturally' present in this narrative and the audience to take it seriously. Ultimately, nothing from the outside or from the inside must be capable of breaking the narrative frame. The strategy of narrativity thus strengthens the parallel reality and thus the theatrical by constructing an alternative mental, or reflective, logic, which is imbedded in the participants of the performance installation as the 'natural' mental navigational point. This logic is furthermore constructed around discursive narrations that separate themselves radically from the ones we participate in in everyday life, and thus the feeling of being in a parallel universe is intensified. All the while, one could argue that the more the narrativity is turned on, the more we risk compromising the interactivity, meaning that a dominating narrative will disturb the interactive, and a dominating interactivity will disturb the narrative – the more narrativity there is in a room, the more it must be controlled by a dominant, narrative factor (the artist) and thus the intervening interaction of the participants (the amateurs) is scaled down (for more on the relationship between narrativity and interactivity see Skjoldager-Nielsen's theory on the double performativity, which takes place between performer and audience (Skjoldager-Nielsen, 2008, pp. 53–65). With this in mind we now turn our attention to the last strategy: the strategy of interaction. The strategy of interaction contributes amongst other things to the construction of the theatrical by incorporating the presence of the audience in the parallel reality. Thus, the frame around the staged parallel reality is strengthened because the presence of the audience does not challenge it. If there were objects or subjects that could not be explained or that we would have to ignore in the parallel reality, it would lose its function as a believable parallel universe and thus diminishes the possibility for immersion. Thus, as we can talk about installed

Source: Photo by Stine Skøtt Olesen.

Figure 23.2   *Fiction Pimps performing poetic street politics: an ode to the fifth culture emerging in 100 years from now. The street actions of Fiction Pimps are part of the poetic revolution*

performers, we can also talk about 'installed audiences'. This means that the state of meeting is intensified, which is distinguished by its atmospheric and immersive character, by which it stands as an even larger contrast to the temporal action-orientation that so many other experience offer, such as role-playing.

These six strategies collectively thicken the theatricality, and thus the performativity, which frames the space and can be regarded as a method or even a toolbox to design a universe – a full and deep experience space. Unfolding these experience spaces outside art institutional contexts is also to support a 'poetic revolution'. With more and more people becoming inspired to act on their poetic selves in everyday contexts, will the poetic disruptions then ultimately create a new status quo? A society where the sensuous experience is at the centre – a sensuous society?

23.6   MOVING TOWARDS A SENSUOUS SOCIETY

Since the financial crisis in 2008, the time we have been living in has been known as 'The Crisis'. But we could examine the crisis, not just as a slump in the output of industrial capitalism or manufacturing economy, but rather as a sign that the economic paradigm is nearing its end as the dominant logic of society.

Western society has been based on economical imperatives such as optimization and rationality, which leaves no space for more sensuous, inspired and gentle modes of being. But these values could very well form an emerging paradigm that we could call the sensuous society.

In the sensuous society the general mode of being is defined by the aesthetic dimension, which has exactly the sensuous experience at is core, as described above. This means that the current economic rationality that dominates all spheres of societies today will be replaced. So, it is a very radical idea. But the basic principles of societies have changed several times.

The notion of a sensuous society furthermore reshapes the role of art and artistic practice. The exclusive autonomous art system is also a result of the dominance of the economic dimension. Within this autonomous zone the art genius is a celebrated figure, who is conceived as someone with a very special (transcending) intelligence. In a sensuous society, however, we believe that this will be a more common intelligence as, for example, artist Joseph Beuys points out – simply because we all have this creative potential within us, and if our mode of being in the world is the sensuous, then this potential could be released.

As we see it, the movement towards a sensuous society is already happening. Within the corporate world Theatre-in-Business agents are staging transitions. Sisters Hope specifically intervene in the educational system, Fiction Pimps and Club de la Faye roam the streets and the new urban forum Theatrum Mundi (initiated by sociologist Richard Sennett) asks how different artistic practices can inspire the design of the city to make it vibrant and vital.

23.7   CONCLUSION

In this chapter we have examined and discussed the concept of the experience economy as an indicator of the need for spaces (in-between), which allow for an aesthetic, sensuous and poetic mode of being in the midst of everyday life.

The experience economy is about holding the key to the experience. We have looked at the business of theatre and, accordingly, we have interpreted a new type of experience space; live and relational fictional parallel universes that have grown forth from the world of theatre and performance and hold a very attracting effect on its participants who become larger and larger in number.

Rooted in critical theory and a phenomenological approach, we have discussed how the attraction might be due to the liminal and sensuous experience it opens in the midst of everyday life – an everyday life that is, to a large degree, dominated by economic premises. The experience economy could ultimately become a player in changing this status quo and thus undermine the economic system as such, and thus the dominating premises might become inspired by the arts as they would in a sensuous society.

However, the experience economy could also guide the world in another direction, and it is possible to critically discuss how the experience economy might also affect experience spaces. At the heart of the experience is the event (Kirkeby, 2007). The event is a moment in time and space in which life itself unfolds between us. There has

Source: Photo by Stine Skøtt Olesen.

Figure 23.3   Acorn falls: what is the final blow that makes an acorn fall?

been a shift from sender-dominated experience spaces to ones that occur in interactive meetings between the sender, who to a greater extent establishes a framework for the event, and those who step in as co-participants in the situation. It is a journey for the co-participants to open up to and contribute to the event. The relatively new attractive experience spaces discussed in this chapter, live and relational fictional parallel universes, never serve – they only exist as physical rooms or spaces of opportunities. Participants or co-creators must want and have the courage to step into the space and live out the new logics of this particular universe. Trust that you will be able to navigate just as if you are a traveller in a remote foreign country. How do you react or respond in such a situation? What do you think and feel? What moves inside you and why? You and the event are in a relationship based on the give and take principle. This might create a much more powerful impact than an event planned and manifested in every detail. That is the risk of the accumulation of events designed in a time of the experience economy, which perhaps might have too much focus on easily digestible consumption and acceleration of capital. As with the poetic revolution, a way to go about this is to place a cause at the centre of the event. When you have a cause and create a vibration centred in a universe and manifested in events that inspire others, the world will start moving in a certain direction. The live and relational fictional parallel universes offer landscapes where new dreams can be projected and transformed into actual manifestations of a desired future.

NOTES

1. See berlinerfestspiele.de/en/archiv/festivals2008/03_theatertreffen08/tt_08_programm/tt_08_programm_gastspiele/.
2. Developed by Hallberg on the basis of analysis and practice in relation to a row of cases of live and relational fictional parallel universes (Hallberg, 2009, 2011, 2012).

BIBLIOGRAPHY

Adorno, T.W. and M. Horkheimer (1947), *Oplysningens dialektik* (*Dialectics of Enlightment*), Amsterdam: Querido Verlag, reprinted in 2001, Copenhagen: Gyldendal.
Baumgarten, A.G. (1750–58), *Aesthetica*, reprinted in 1986, Olms.
Bishop, C. (2004), 'Antagonism and relational aesthetics', *October Magazine*, **110**, 51–79.
Bogh, M. and F. Tygstrup (2011), 'Working the interface: new encounters between art and academia', in J. Quaresma (ed.), *Investigaçao em Arte e Design: Fendasno Método e na Criaçao*, Lisboa: Ediçao Cieba, pp. 102–14.
Bolt, M. (2009), *Suicide of the Avantgarde*, Copenhagen: Eks-skolens trykkeri.
Boltanski, L. and E. Chiapello (2005), *The New Spirit of Capitalism*, London: Verso.
Bourriaud, N. (1998), *Relational Aesthetics*, Dijon: Les presses du rée.
Butler, J. (2007), 'Performative acts and gender constitution: an essay in phenomenonology and feminist theory', in H. Bial (ed.), *The Performance Studies Reader*, London and New York: Routledge, pp. 519–31.
Carlson, M. (1996), *Performance: A Critical Introduction*, London and New York: Routledge.
Cassirer, E. (1931), *Kant and the Problems of Metaphysics*, reprinted in 1967, Chicago, IL: Quadrangle.
Davis, T.C. and T. Postlewait (eds) (2003), 'Theatricality: an introduction', in T.C. Davis and T. Postlewait (eds), *Theatricality*, Cambridge: Cambridge University Press, pp. 11–19.
De Monthoux, P.G. (2004), *The Art Firm*, Stanford, CA: Stanford University Press.
De Oliveira, N. (2003), 'Introduction', in N. De Oliveira, N. Oxley and M. Petry (eds), *Installation Art in the New Millennium – the Empire of the Senses*, London: Thames and Hudson.
Dewey, J. (1934), *Art as Experience*, New York: Penguin Group.
Drotner, K. (2001), 'Æstetik: Pædagogik eller kunst?' ('Aesthetics: pedagogy or art?'), in K. Drotner (ed.), (*eAt skabe sig – selv* (*To Create Oneself*), København: Gyldendal.
Féral, J. (2002), 'Introduction' and 'Theatricality and the body', *Substance*, **31** (2–3), 3–16 and 110–67.
Fischer-Lichte, E. (2002), 'Grenzgänge und Tauschhandel' ('Border crossings and barter'), in U. Wirth (ed.), *Performanz*, Frankfurt am Main: Suhrkamp, pp. 277–300.
Fischer-Lichte, E. (2005), *Theatre, Sacrifice,Rritual*, London and New York: Routledge.
Frayling, C. (1993), 'Research in art and design', *Royal College of Art Research Papers*, **1** (1).
Freud, S. (1919), 'Das Unheimliche' ('The uncanny'), in *GesammelteWerke. Chronologischgeordnet*, Hrsg. v. Anna Freud u.a. Bd. XII, reprinted in 1999, Frankfurt am Main: Fischer Taschenbuch-Verlag.
Gade, S. (2008), 'Rammenomværketiverden – Relationelleogintervenerendestrategierisamtidskunsten' ('Framing the work – relational and interventionist strategies in contemporary art'), PhD thesis, Theatre and Performance Studies, Department of Arts and Cultural Studies, University of Copenhagen.
Guillet de Monthoux, P. (2004), *The Art Firm, Aesthetic Management and Metaphysical Marketing*, Stanford, CA: Stanford University Press.
Hallberg, G.W. (2009), 'I need my shot of fiction!', Master's thesis, Theater and Performance Studies, Department of Arts and Cultural Studies, University of Copenhagen.
Hallberg, G.W. (2011), 'Crack my world', in L. Korsemann (ed.), *Dansk Gadekunst* (*Danish Street Art*), København: Dansk gadekunst, pp. 372–87.
Hallberg, G.W. (2012), 'Transformative impact of future mind tours', *ISSUES Magazine*, **2**, Copenhagen.
Hallberg, G.W. and A. Lawaetz (2011), 'Protected by the fiction', in I. Ntalla (ed.), *Critical Contents Contemporary Culture*, Goldsmiths, Vol. 1 Novelty, available at http://www.criticalcontemporaryculture.org/gry-worre-hallberg-anna-lawaetz-%E2%80%93-sisters-hope-E2%80%93-protected-by-the-fiction-%E2%80%93-between-art-and-pedagogy/.
Hardt, A. and M. Negri (2003), *Imperiet* (*The Empire*), Copenhagen: Informations Forlag.
Harsløf, O. (2011), 'Den producere de teateroplevelse' ('The produced theatre experience'), in B.L. Røge, M.T. Jensen, L. Lowy and G.W. Hallberg (eds), *Theatre-in-Business: udfordringer og potentialer*, Copenhagen: Department of Arts and Cultural Studies, University of Copenhagen.

Kirkeby, O.F. (2005), *Eventum Tantum: Begivenhedens ethos* (*Eventum Tantim: The Ethos of the Event*), Frederiksberg: Samfundslitteratur.

Kirkeby, O.F. (2007), *Skønheden Sker: Begivenhedens æstetik* (*Beauty Happens: The Aesthetic of the Event*), Frederiksberg: Samfundslitteratur.

Lazzarato, M. (2004), 'From capital-labour to capital-life', *Ephemera*, **4** (3), 187–208.

Lehmann, N.O. (2002), 'Pragmatiskdualisme: dannelse mellem rationalitet og rationalitetskritik' ('Pragmatic dualism: learning through rationality and rational criticism'), in M.B. Johansen (ed.), *Dannelse* (*Learning*), Århus: Århus Universitetsforlag.

Madison, D.S. and J. Hamera (eds) (2006), 'Introduction', in D.S. Madison and J. Hameras (eds), *The Sage Handbook of Performance Studies*, Thousand Oaks, CA: Sage.

Maffesoli, M. (1982), *The Shadow of Dionysus: A Contribution to the Sociology of the Orgy*, Albany, NY: State University of New York Press, reprinted in 1993.

Maffesoli, M. (2007), *Le réenchantement du monde – Morales, éthiques, déontologies* (*The Reenchantment of the World*), Paris: Table Ronde Editions.

Marcuse, H. (1955), *Eros and Civilisation*, Boston, MA: Beacon Press, reprinted in 1970, London: Sphere Books.

Marcuse, H. (1964), *Detén-dimensionalemenneske* (*One Dimensional Man*), Boston, MA: Beacon Press, reprinted in 1980, Copenhagen: Gyldendals Uglebøger.

Marx, K. (1867), *Das Kapital*, Moscow: Progress, reprinted in 1978, Copenhagen: Rhodos.

Maslow, A. (1954), *Motivation and Personality*, New York: Harper.

McKenzie, J. (2001), *Perform or Else: From Discipline to Performance*, London and New York: Routledge.

McNiff, J. (2007), 'Realising the potentials of educational action research for renewable cultural transformation', Paper presented at the American Educational Research Association Annual Meeting, Chicago, available at http://www.jeanmcniff.com (accessed January 2011).

Merleau-Ponty, M.V. (1945), *Kroppensfænomenologi* (*Phenomenology of Perception*), reprinted in 2009, Helsingør: DetlilleForlag.

Nielsen, T.R. (2011), 'Interaktive dramaturgier i et systemteoretiskperspektiv' ('Interactive dramaturgy in a system-oriented perspective'), PhD thesis, Department of Dramaturgy, Aarhus University.

Pine, B.J. and J.H. Gilmore (1999), *The Experience Economy*, Boston, MA: Harvard Business School Press.

Sauter, W. (2000), *The Theatrical Event – Dynamics of Performance and Perception*, Iowa: Iowa University Press.

Schechner, R. (1985), *Between Theater and Anthropology*, Philadelphia, PA: University of Pennsylvania Press.

Schechner, R. (1988), *Performance Theory*, New York: Routledge.

Schechner, R. (2002), *Performance Studies: An Introduction*, New York: Routledge.

SIGNA (2002), http://signa.dk/politiken (accessed April 2013).

Skjoldager-Nielsen, K. (2008), 'Interaktivitet' ('Interactivity'), Master's thesis, Theater and Performance Studies, Department of Arts and Cultural Studies, University of Copenhagen.

Thompson, N. and G. Sholette (2004), *The Interventionist*, Cambridge, MA: MIT Press.

Turner, V. (1969), *The Ritual Process: Structure and Anti-structure*, New York: Aldine de Gruyter, reprinted in 1995, New Tork: Aldine Transaction.

Van Gennep, A. (1909), *The Rites of Passage*, Paris: Nourry, reprinted in 1960, Chicago, IL: University of Chicago Press.

24. Radical change in health care to achieve superior patient experience
Albert Boswijk

24.1 INTRODUCTION

Those who work in health care environments are continuously engaged in improving the safety and professionalism of primary medical processes. Many attempts and projects have also been undertaken to improve the patient experience, especially from a hospitality point of view. Hospital projects in which we have been involved all started with the best of intentions: the medical institutions often had a highly hospitality-driven reception area and a properly functioning front office, but all too often they were hindered as soon as the medical processes started and the medical staff took over. From having a patient-centric focus, the process switched to a medical-centric process and patients were emotionally lost. Possible causes could be the complexity of integrating the personal needs of patients with doctors' needs and medical requirements. Or it may simply be the case that the institution's hospitality manager had his processes in order up until the moment that the patient entered the operation room. We describe in this study how the Henry Ford West Bloomfield Hospital reconciled the dilemmas of a patient experience-driven organization versus a medical process-driven organization. This is an example of a radical systematic approach of a chief executive officer (CEO) and his executive board in order to achieve a healing environment beyond imagination. The study is described on the basis of the competing values framework of experience value creation (Quinn, 1988; Boswijk et al., 2012), as described in the earlier theory chapter of this Handbook (Chapter 9).

In short, organizations can be analysed and assessed along two dimensions: internal versus external orientation and flexibility versus predictability or control. Through these two dimensions, four orientations can be differentiated: (1) market focus; (2) process and quality focus; (3) people and culture focus; and (4) creative and innovation focus. We have added a fifth focus: revenue and cost structures. These five different orientations and the values behind them are in apparent conflict with one another, hence the name competing values framework. In this case study, the following perspectives may be differentiated within the context of patient experience creation:

1. Formulating a vision and a higher purpose of the patient experience and the organizational ambition.
2. Defining community experience and patient experience propositions.
3. Defining and organizing the processes that are expected to improve the patient experiences.
4. High-performance, culture- and talent-based selection in order to be able to deliver the improved patient experience.

5. Revenue model and the way to capture the created value of the value-added services that make up the experience.

24.2   THE CASE

The Henry Ford West Bloomfield Hospital is a privately owned hospital with 300 beds that was founded in 2006.The proprietor and investor is the Henry Ford Health System founded in 1915 by Henry Ford. He formulated a vision for an, ideal, hospital concept whereby the hospital would be like a hotel. The foundation was looking for a true hospitality professional from outside the health industry who could execute Henry Ford's vision The foundation found one of the most respected hospitality professionals in the world, Mr Van Grinsven (background: Ritz Carlton, extensive experience in the East and a hospitality education at the Hotel School of Maastricht). The new CEO was commissioned to develop a hospital beyond imagination and he started the project by forming a committed top team. Together with his team, he worked out in detail the vision and defined the ambition of this new hospital.

24.3   BUILDING A GUEST-CENTRED HEALTH COMMUNITY

How to build a consistent approach to a guest-centred health community where guests, patients and the community can enjoy spending time involved in such activities as wellness, massage, listening to concerts and dining, which will all support the healing process? The process took place along the steps explained in the following subsections.

24.3.1   Formulating the Vision

The first step is formulating the vision in terms of a higher purpose and ambition, thinking beyond the boundaries of our imagination, sincerely placing patients and the community at the centre of attention.

In order to become a hospital beyond imagination and a rule-breaking initiative in the health care industry, the CEO opted for a blue ocean strategy (Chan Kim and Mauborgne, 2005) in order to distinguish his approach from the crowded market of grey hospitals that all compete on the same issues.

The CEO saw the Cirque du Soleil as a guiding principle for the health care industry, that is, to create – and provide his guests with – exceptional experience value, with manageable cost structures by reducing waste.

The vision of the patient experience was formulated as follows: Transforming lives and communities through health and wellness – one person at a time. And the mission: To improve people's lives through excellence in the science and art of health care and healing.

24.3.2   Formulating the Guest Experience Value Propositions

To explore his market, the CEO decided not to choose the traditional route of market research and focus groups. Instead he visited the local communities in his role as president and discussed life issues with them to discover the habits and customs of the various communities in the area. He learned about his potential clients and got to know them by visiting families at home in their private environment in order to discover their hidden needs and unexpressed wishes. The patient experience value propositions were designed based on the input of the different communities.

It was discovered that the leading power in health care decisions were for 99 per cent of the communities the decisions of women. They decide where their children, grandparents and spouses will be treated and they influence their community members. Women are no longer satisfied with traditional health care services and are looking for additional programmes and activities for their physical and mental wellbeing. This is why the complete concept and focus of this new health community was developed around health services and wellness concepts for women, in the knowledge that, once the women were visiting the centre, the men would follow. The key approach was and is to become a community centre for physical and mental wellbeing. A place where healthy people would like to come. The main entrance is designed to experience a first impression of wellness, vitality and health care versus sick care.

The value propositions were formulated on the basis of guiding principles based on core values that were also to become the backbone of the high-level culture and performance structure. These working principles consist of the following values:

- each patient comes first;
- respect for people;
- high performance;
- learning and continuous improvement;
- a social conscience.

Based on our own research in a Dutch regional hospital, GHZ (Boswijk and Peelen, 2007; Loot et al., 2010), we know that during treatment, patients predominantly experience the down-side of the emotional spectrum, which involves such feelings as insecurity, fear, anxiety and anger (Hill, 2007). Each phase of a patient's journey involves specific feelings, emotions and needs. In addition to the patient's needs and feelings, the emotions and needs of the patient's spouse, partner, family and friends also play an important role. They are sometimes even more likely to incur negative experiences. A patient's journey begins long before his treatment in a hospital and does not end until long after his discharge. On the basis of our research, we arrived at a patient journey (Table 24.1) as described in our recent publication (Boswijk et al., 2012).

The patient's experience (and by the way the experience of the partners and family members) – starts at home, not in the hospital – is an emotional process and it also ends at home. This journey deviates from the medical treatment process. A challenge that every hospital is facing is to fulfil and integrate its patients' needs with the medical process. The Henry Ford West Bloomfield Hospital has taken the patients' journey as the guiding principle.

Table 24.1 The patient's journey

Patient-relevant moments	Emotions	Needs	Family needs	Strategic options	Ideas
awareness of physical complaint, orientation phase	uncertain, worried, concerned	information about symptoms, illustrations	information about symptoms, illustrations		presence on disease, communities
diagnosis and GP referral	surprised, shocked, concerned, relieved, at least I know . . .	reassurance, information about course of disease and prospects, what can I expect?	the right information, what did the doctor say?, expectations regarding course of disease	reverse process, hospital approaches patient	hospital initiates patient contact
awaiting treatment processing result, limitations in lifestyle	tense, uncertain, afraid of the end results?	information on course of disease and perspective, what can I expect? . . .	how can we help you?	reverse the process, hospital approaches patient	proactive, preparation to treatment
orientation, consult, unplanned consulting hours	dependent, tense, worried, uncertain	information about the treatment, asking questions, discussion with doctor	accompany and listen and ask questions, provide support	personal invitation from the doctor	personalize, personal invitation per patient, coach
admission, consult, start of treatment	dependent, no longer in control, tense, worried, feeling small	detailed information about the treatment, asking questions, dialogue with nursing staff	accompany, listen and ask any remaining questions	patient feels recognized	being informed about the guest, knowing his file

Apart from all standard medical treatments, the Henry Ford West Bloomfield Hospital offers the following wellness treatments:

- Vita Wellness Centre, integrative therapies and services, for example, massage, acupuncture, reflexology, yoga and chiropractic care.
- Sleep-well products to promote restful sleep.
- Patient support for smooth transitions from hospital to home.
- Pharmacy with room delivery before discharge and a free home delivery service.
- Gourmet and healthy dining, 24-hour room service on the basis of freshly cooked, treatment-matched ingredients.
- Educational cooking courses for professional chefs of (health) institutions.
- Educational cooking course for patients and their family members, the community and for school kids.
- Earth-friendly merchandise.
- Community events, for example, music concerts.

In this way, a new experience value curve was created with attractive, increased value propositions for the (health of the) community and lower cost structures for operations. One of these value propositions is food and restaurants. All food is freshly cooked and chefs are trained and inspired by top chefs from all over the world. Menus are created in order to serve patients the best possible nutrition for their treatment. The Henry Ford Community Centre for wellbeing recently opened a greenhouse, which is the first hydroponic (the concept of soil-less gardening) greenhouse in the state of Michigan) where vegetables and herbs are grown in an extremely efficient and sustainable manner.

24.3.3   Designing the Processes and Organization to Make Them Work

In order to support these experience value propositions, the management needed to formulate, install and execute additional blue ocean strategic questions. The core of the strategy was to increase the value of the experience for both patients and visitors, while reducing the cost structure for the hospital in the following ways (Chan Kim and Mauborgne, 2005). These questions were formulated as follows:

1. Which of the factors that are taken for granted by the health industry should be eliminated?
2. Which factors should be reduced well below the health industry's standard?
3. Which factors should be raised well above the health industry's standard?
4. Which factors should be created that the health industry has never offered?

Regards the first point, research indicated that 60 per cent of the activities of nurses had nothing to do with the patient. Bureaucracy and maintenance tasks were pulling the nurses away from their core activities. If you really want to become a guest- or patient-centred organization you have to eliminate the root causes. Which processes create and support value and which don't.

Regards the second point, structural investment and focus on waste reduction and efficiency but only in the context of patient-centredness.

Regards the third point, the differentiating factor here is personalization of service. This is a unique selling point and puts the patient first.

What the industry has never offered is the value of eating fresh food and offering education concerning healthy life and eating styles.

The Henry Ford West Bloomfield Health Centre offers cooking classes and a cooking auditorium for professionals and patients. It even teaches schoolchildren all about fresh food and supports the mission against children's obesities

All decisions are consistent with the strategy. Every decision was tested against the following key parameters; the organization calls this their moral compass:

- safety and quality;
- compassionate care;
- memorable experiences;
- efficiency.

Note the order of these criteria. These criteria anchor the patient journey and experience with the high-quality medical processes and therefore create efficiency end financial results.

The CEO struggled during the first years to get these principles adopted by his team and staff. Finally, the results convinced the medical staff that his vision was the right one to follow. In July 2010 the Henry Ford West Bloomfield Hospital achieved ISO 9001:2008 certification for the first time. Since opening, the Henry Ford West Bloomfield Hospital has consistently been in the 99th percentile for likelihood to recommend in comparison with the other hospitals in Southeast Michigan.

24.3.4   Human Capital and Culture

One of the key success factors of the Henry Ford Hospital is its human resources strategy. This strategy is based on the following four mainstays:

- a talent-based organization;
- a high-performance culture;
- advocating customer value;
- sustained excellence.

The key to its success is that all staff, including the doctors and nurses, must have a talent for relating to other people. Every staff member is assessed, with no exceptions, against the desired competence profile. The basic principles are to select on Talent, train on Functionality (creating a fit) and professionalism, and Invest in your people.

The organization has a high-performance culture with empowerment to the staff. They are the people who are executing tasks every day and making sure that the unexpected needs are fulfilled.

24.3.5   Revenue Streams and Cost Structures

What are the revenue streams and the costs structures? How is money made in the Henri Ford West Bloomfield Hospital? The Vita Wellness Centre, Earth-friendly merchandise, cooking classes for professional chefs of health institutions, educational classes for kids create new revenue streams besides the traditional medical revenues.

It is already clear that by 2012 the new hospital has succeeded in achieving black figures. They believe their wellness services have helped them to establish an environment where patients truly experience they are being cared for from a holistic point of view, with a superior quality of medical treatment.

The hospital became cash-flow positive one year ahead of schedule. It has outperformed its net income budget every year since opening in March 2009. It has increased its intake volume every month since opening and increased its market share each year in an economy that was in a downward spiral and in a market with a shrinking population.

The decision to become a talent-based organization has had a significant impact on reducing personnel turnover due to excellent employee engagement and on reducing harm, and it has resulted in outstanding customer engagement scores and – subsequently – positive financial results.

24.4   CONCLUSION

We consider the early success of this new hospital concept is due to the following factors:

- The vision in terms of a higher purpose formulated by the CEO, and the way this vision was consistently executed and led the way.
- The synergy between a hospitality professional outside the medical field with his medical team (and other teams) and the belief of the Henry Ford Health Foundation in his vision.
- The choice for a blue ocean experience value strategy, the conscious choice to make a difference with experience-based, patient-centric and community-centric value propositions in order to create exceptional value with manageable cost structures. And to stay consistent to the strategy, testing every decision against the strategy along the way.
- The link with the local community and their norms, beliefs and attitudes, thereby focusing on hidden needs and unexpressed wishes.
- Focusing on women's behaviour as the leading power to take health decisions in order to increase the experience value of patients and visitors in order to capture experience value.
- The choice for a talent-based, high-performance culture (only medical specialists with social skills and specialist medical skills).
- Increasing revenue structure with wellness services and decreasing cost structures for non-strategic elements.

Further study is required to determine which experience value propositions create the best experienced value for the patient and the hospital organization.

REFERENCES

Boswijk, A. and E. Peelen (2007), *A New Look at the Experience Economy*, Amsterdam: Pearson Education.

Boswijk, A., E. Peelen and S. Olthof (2012), *The Economy of Experiences*, Bilthoven, the Netherlands: European Centre for the Experience and Transformation Economy.

Chan Kim, W. and R.A. Mauborgne (2005), *Blue Ocean Strategy: How to Create Uncontested Market Space and Make the Competition Irrelevant*, Cambridge, MA: Harvard Business School Press.

Hill, D. (2007), *Emotionomics, Leveraging Emotions for Business Success*, London: Pearson Education.

Kim, W.C. and R. Mauborgne (2005), *Blue Ocean Strategy*, Boston, MA: Harvard Business School Press.

Loot, M.S., A. Boswijk and E. Peelen (2010), *Patient Experience at GHZ*, Gouda, The Netherlands: GHZ Hospital, Gouda.

Ostenwalder, A. and Y. Pigneur (2009), *Business Model Generation*, Toronto: Self-published and co-created.

Quinn, R.E. (1988), *Beyond Rational Management: Mastering the Paradoxes and Competing Demands of High Performance*, San Francisco, CA: Jossey-Bass.

Index